"The Maiden of the Barren Rime" by Sweet

Published by Sweet Discords LLC

www.storiesbysweet.com

ISBN-13: 979-8-218-37229-3

Cover design by: Sweet
Character Portraits by: Arlowa R
Printed in the United States of America

The Maiden of the Barren Rime

SWEET

For Content Warnings, please scan the QR below or visit:

www.storiesbysweet.com/content-warnings

MOVEMENTS

Lanholde
N
W
E
S
Fort Kowleth
Recet's Den
The Marquian Ocean
The Lithe
Lac Rizzo
Rabbet's Pass
Harlowe's Gate
The Fallow Peaks
Harlowe's Gate Passage
Mapped By:
Wera Alrust
Windenhofer Procurements
The Harrowed Woods
Sandere

Dramatis

Personae

Sebastian

To all those who were made to think they were monstrous
for simply being human.

Thank you to Liam O'brien for sparking the flame,
and to Hozier for fueling it.

Winter Wind blows through the valley, pushes us into our homes.

Pleading she knocks at our windows, scorned she continues to roam.

I

The Brambled Beauty

Mina quieted at the sound of unfamiliar voices on the wind.

"Are you sure this is the right cabin?" It was a feminine voice, on the younger side, with a slight Tinian accent, most likely from the North Coast judging from the way they dragged the "er" in "sure."

"Of course this is the right cabin! It's the only cabin in this damned forest!" A masculine voice spat back. Staunchly Lanholdian, Mina could almost feel the thick tension in their tongue behind her own teeth. The gravel of age and annoyance ground up from the back of their throat.

Mina picked up her pace, leaping up into the treetops, crossing miles in minutes towards the voices with no more sound than the rustle of wind through pine needles.

She stilled. The branch beneath her feet barely creaked.

They were outside her cabin. A young woman with thick glasses and even thicker curly hair checked the compass in her hand as the short, sturdy man beside her impatiently tapped his foot and picked at the split ends of his long, braided beard.

Mina placed a hand on the hilt of her sword as she watched them through the canopy. The man's leather armor bore a crest depicting a mountain top and three diamonds, with glinting, well-polished stripes on his pauldron pronouncing his rank. Seven; a general of lauded stature. Why he traveled with the young woman was unclear.

She was clearly not a noble. The slight roll forward of her shoulders, the patterned bandanna holding her hair out of her eyes too weathered or wrinkled for even a disguised royal to wear, and a decent soldier would never keep their guard down as much as hers was in an unfamiliar place. Perhaps she had hired the knight as security on her journey.

A journey Mina would take no part in.

She shifted to sit easily and silently, making sure not to catch the beaver skins hanging from her pack beneath her. A few more minutes and they would leave, then she could prep the skins and start to smoke the meat in her satchel as planned.

"Well," the woman stuffed her compass into her jacket pocket. "At least it's a nice day out to wait. Sun's still warm enough to cut the edge off the autumn chill."

Annoyingly, she made her way to the porch of Mina's cabin and took a seat on its rough wooden steps. Mina ground her teeth slightly. Maybe a splinter or two would poke her through her patchwork skirt and urge her away.

The man huffed and kicked at a tuft of crabgrass. "You think this chill has an edge? Just wait until you're on the Peaks." The tuft came loose, sending dirt and now homeless pill bugs scattering. "If we ever get to the fucking Peaks."

Dammit, Mina thought. They were here for an expedition.

"Ya know, we could always go with another alpinist," the woman offered. "Beto Lamar's homestead is about a day's ride west from here."

"A day's ride but three weeks past our deadline," the man said. "This girl can bring us back to Lanholde in under a month." He stomped over and stood on the steps, too proud to sit, but not proud enough to not lean on the railing for support. "She *will* get us there in a month."

"Even if she's already off on an expedition?"

"She's not," the man gestured over his shoulder. "The windows are open. And this cabin is too well maintained for its owner to just head off for two months with the windows left open."

Mina thudded her head against the tree trunk. *Of course. An observant and stubborn knight.*

She inhaled deeply, held it, then exhaled, taking her frustration down a little, unclenching her jaw just a touch. She'd piss them off enough that they'd rather stand Lamar's extra three weeks in the cold than put up with her, and if that didn't work, ask for a ridiculous amount of gold to scare them off.

Three more weeks in the cold. Three more weeks to die. The unwilling thought made her teeth ache.

She climbed down from the pine she had perched in and moved soundlessly towards the drying rack staked beside her cabin. She removed one of the rungs filled with beaver skins from her pack. A loud and forceful snap echoed through the woods as she dropped it into place.

The trespassing pair jumped. The knight drew his sword as the woman bladed her feet into a wide stance, arms lifted, ready to perform some sort of cast.

So they were a *magic wielder* and a knight.

"Get off the porch," Mina stated bluntly as she hung another rack.

Out of the corner of her eye, she watched the knight's jaw fall agape while the woman's disposition relaxed. She straightened up out of her fighting stance, and Mina caught the faint sound of a cork squeaking back into a bottle on the wind.

"My apologies, miss. We're looking for the alpinist that lives here," she said. "Would that be you?"

"No," Mina lied. "I'm a hunter. The alpinist lives to the west."

The woman arched an eyebrow and looked to the knight. He flared his nostrils, puffed out his chest, and stomped over towards her.

"I am Sir Murmir Gargic, general-rank knight of the Lanholde Royal Army, proud servant to King Fritz Reinhardt."

"Never heard of him," she lied again.

The knight sputtered, whatever bullshit speech he had prepared dying on his tongue. "You never—"

"Sir Gargic," the woman whispered behind him, calling his attention and allowing him a moment to regain his composure.

Annoying.

"Well, he's heard of you, and has specifically recommended that we seek you out to lead us up the Fallow Peaks. We're in a bit of a time crunch, so if you don't mind talking terms so we can start the expedition today—"

"If that's the case, then I guess your king expects you both to die," Mina droned, mono-toned and matter-of-factly. "I'm a hunter, not an alpinist."

The knight's breathing shallowed as her jab at his ruler crawled under his skin. He inhaled deeply, a tirade building, when the woman placed a hand on his shoulder.

"How much would it cost for you to be an alpinist?" she asked.

Mina drifted her dull gaze over towards the woman, finding her with a smirk on her lips and a knowing glint in her eye.

"Seven thousand gilt one way," she answered. "The real alpinist to the west charges half that."

"I'm sure." The woman shrugged. "But the alpinist we're looking for fits your description exactly. Female alpinist. Rough around the edges. Lives alone in a cabin deep in the Sandere Woods, five hundred paces off of the last bend in Woodgullet Road, heading northeast." She rattled off the details as if she were reading them off a sheet of paper.

Mina blinked slowly, then repeated. "Seven thousand gilt one way."

"Deal."

Gods fucking dammit. An unfortunately familiar tug pulled at her spine.

Sir Gargic fished out a scroll from one of the pouches on his belt, while the woman brandished a quill and a bottle of ink. He scrawled something down on it, then turned the parchment in her direction: a contract of duty.

His thick, stubby finger pointed at the **7,000g** written next to the terms of payment. "Seven-thousand gilt to be delivered direct from the Capitol's treasury upon our safe arrival." His finger traveled down the page to a long signature line. "All you need to do is sign here."

She did, reluctantly. Her arm dragged by that damned tug.

"Mina," the woman read her name aloud, standing on the tips of her toes to watch as she wrote it. "I'm Wera Alrust."

Mina snapped the quill once she finished, dropped it to the ground, and headed into her cabin.

"Where are you going?" Sir Gargic barked behind her. "You're under contract to—"

"Packing," Mina answered. "Can't climb a ten-thousand-foot cliff face with just a bow, a sword, and a can-do attitude." She paused in the doorway. "Just two going up?"

"Five," Wera answered. "Six if you count yourself."

"I don't."

Last-minute trips up the Fallow Peaks were nothing new to Mina, as much as she loathed them. They were always inconvenient and pressing, which meant the travelers were stressed and distracted — which meant the death count was usually higher than the average one or two losses. Expeditions such as this were few and far between, at least. Most travelers knew to prepare well in advance for the perilous journey, contracting her months ahead of time instead of minutes.

She closed all the windows and locked the shutters, made sure her books and sheet music were lifted off the ground in case the fall rains caused the lake to flood, and tucked the more expensive of her instruments away as she filled the pack she kept by the door.

"Flint, whytewing leathers, tarp, rations, climbing axes..." she muttered to herself as she rifled through it — taking stock to make sure she had everything she needed — then picked up a fiddle and bow leaning against a hard wooden chair. She loosened up the strings a bit and unstrung the bow to keep the horse hairs from snapping, then shoved it in with the rest of her gear.

"Where are the other three?" she asked as she stepped back outside and locked the door.

"Back on the road, waiting with the wagon," Wera replied.

"You can't take a wagon up a mountain."

"We don't plan to." She was, frustratingly, smiling at Mina when she turned around. "Ready to go?"

"Lead the way."

Sir Gargic headed off, impatience and frustration bringing out the ill-manner child in him. With such thin skin, it wouldn't be long before he broke their contract, or he died. Rabbet's Pass most likely, which would be convenient. She could leave his corpse in the caves there, and they wouldn't have too far of a walk back to Sandere afterwards.

After only a few wrong turns through the thick wood, the seldom-used road emerged. A simple covered wagon pulled off to the side let the four horses that drove it graze lazily, while two more members of their party hung around it: an old woman with her hair up in a tight bun, sitting on the ground making daisy chains out of dandelions, and a young man with a sharp haircut and a well-coiffed mustache scrawling in a notebook as he sat in the driver's seat.

Sir Gargic's spine straightened and chest puffed out as he put on a bit of bravado. "We've returned!" he cried, waving grandly.

The old woman and mustached man looked up from their work. The woman abandoned her dandelions and stood to meet them, while the young man looked them over and flipped to another page in his book; quill taking off in a fury.

"Ah! Are you the young lady who will be guiding us?" The old woman smiled sweetly. "My name's Tanir and the boy on the cart is Enoch." She turned over her shoulder and hollered, "Wave hello, Enoch!"

Enoch raised his hand partially, too engrossed in whatever he was writing to look away.

"Mina." Mina met Tanir's gaze, and the old woman's brow furrowed. She was looking for the appropriate response, a sign of expression to source Mina's first impression of her. Mina watched her bottom lip shift subtly, a minuscule pucker as her teeth bit behind it uneased to find nothing.

Annoy the knight. Unnerve the old woman. Now she just had to find the others' weaknesses.

"You'll have to leave the wagon and loose the horses an hour or so up the road. They'll slow us down and will be hunted by the beasts of the Harrow."

"Oh, uh—" Tanir swallowed. "That sounds like something you should discuss with Master Windenhofer. I'll go get him for you." She flashed another smile, this one fueled by nerves, and hurried off into the back of the wagon.

Enoch snapped his notebook shut and leaned over the side of the driver's seat. He rested his chin on his hand dramatically, abandoning the fierce focus he held when writing to gaze at Mina with puppy dog eyes. "Did you know you are extremely beautiful for an alpinist?"

Sir Gargic sputtered with embarrassment. Wera shot Enoch a disgusted look.

Mina stared at him blankly.

"I know," she said after a moment.

Enoch choked on his spit at her response. Wera burst out into a fit of laughter, drawing Mina's attention.

Laughter wasn't a response she was used to receiving.

"Don't forget to write that one down," Wera wheezed through her giggles. "'My attempts at flirtation failed tremendously as usual.' A good archivist doesn't leave out any details!"

"Enough of that, Enoch!" Sir Gargic snipped, hitting him on the arm. "She comes highly recommended by The Crown of Lanholde, and you will address her with the respect that such a recommendation warrants!"

"S-sorry, M-mina," Enoch stammered, still caught off guard by her curtness as he leaned back away from her, rubbing his injured arm.

"I hear we have a new face joining our motley crew!" a warm, deep voice cheered from inside the wagon. The cart bounced as a tall, lean man, with a wide smile and a thick shag haircut, stepped out of it, Tanir following behind.

"Hello, I am Sebastian Windenhofer. It is wonderful to meet you!" the man extended his hand out in greeting.

A soft breeze blew between them as Mina considered his outstretched hand. His fingers were long, as to be expected of someone of his height, and his palms were oddly covered with an even layer of callous.

She did not shake it.

"Mina," she said to the hand, in the same bland manner that she had introduced herself to everyone else.

Sebastian seemed unbothered by his spurned handshake, and instead clasped his hands together and nodded his head softly, "Mina." There was a slight hum to the 'M' as he said it. "Tanir mentioned that you wished to speak to me about something regarding the horses?"

Mina's distant stare met his attentive gaze. Sebastian didn't flinch. "You'll have to leave the wagon and loose the horses an hour or so up the road."

"Why's that?" he asked.

"The woods are too thick for a wagon to fit through, and the mountains are too steep," she answered. "The Harrowed Woods that border Sandere and the Peaks are filled with hungry monsters who will be lured by the thought of a four-course horse meal, too."

"I see." Sebastian brought his hand up and tapped his fingertips lightly against his lips as he thought. "Would it be better for the horses if we left the wagon and let them loose now as opposed to when we get closer?"

Mina paused, and tilted her head to the side, caught off guard by his question.

"Have I spoken out of turn?" his voice wavered.

"No, it's just that I've never had someone ask to let the horses out early," she replied, much more candidly than she intended. She straightened her head, collecting herself. "There'd be less chance of them being attacked. Not many monsters here in these woods."

"That settles it, then." Sebastian addressed his crew, "Gather your belongings, we will be continuing on foot from here. Wera and Sir Gargic, unhitch the horses and send them back down the road, please."

"Ugh, my penmanship gets so poor when we're walking," Enoch groaned as he slid down from the driver's seat.

"Guess you'll have to save your sonnets for when we're in Lanholde," Wera remarked as she started unbuckling one of the horse's bridles. "We've got nothing but walking ahead of us now."

Sebastian returned his attention to Mina. "It should only take us a few minutes to get packed up. Would you like a cup of tea while you wait?" He reached inside his overcoat and pulled out a tea kettle and mug. Twirling the mug around his finger by its handle, he juggled the kettle with one hand and caught it by its base. Steam rose from its spout.

Not *just* a magic user. He was a wizard, capable enough to demonstrate his talents so casually.

Or cocky enough to make a big show over the few skills he did have.

"No," Mina replied, tapping the canteen attached to her belt. "I have a canteen."

She could have just left it at 'no'.

"Of course." He threw the tea set into the air as if he were throwing away a piece of paper over his shoulder and with a snap of his fingers they vanished.

Definitely a show-off.

"I have a few things to pack myself if you'll excuse me," he continued, smiling again, still wide as it shifted to a slightly different shape, then headed back into the covered wagon.

Mina watched him walk away.

If he wasn't just a show-off, then maybe they'd make it a mile past Rabbet's Pass.

🜁

"So, Mina, would you care to tell us a little about yourself?" Sebastian asked as they walked up the rest of the road. Considering how chatty they were while getting their shit together, Mina didn't have any hope of a quiet walk to the Harrow's beginning. "I'm sure there's much more to you than living in these woods and leading expeditions through the Fallow Peaks."

"That's all there is to know," she replied.

Sebastian chuckled, a rumble out from his chest that buzzed in Mina's ears. "I'm sure that's not true. What about 'how you got started leading expeditions'? Doesn't seem like a job someone just falls into."

"It's not."

"Then how'd it happen for you?"

"Someone had to do it. So I did it."

"And what did that entail?"

"Doing it."

"Sebastian," Tanir interjected, "perhaps it'd be best if we shared a little bit about ourselves first." She smiled at Mina. Mina kept her gaze forward, praying that the treeline would take mercy on her and move closer on its own. "I'm the company medic, been working with Sebastian since he had a particularly rough encounter collecting basilisk venom a few summers back. Poor thing hobbled to my home half turned to stone, and insisted I travel with him on his adventures ever since."

"You faced off against a basilisk?" Enoch piped up from the back of the pack. "When we rest for the evening, you'll have to sit down with me and give me the full story. You too, Tanir. It should definitely be added to my records."

"Are you volunteering to go next then, Enoch?" Sebastian asked.

"I— uh—" Enoch jogged up in front of them and turned to walk backwards as he spoke, "Well I met—"

"Don't walk like that," Mina interrupted. "If you fall and break something, we'll have to leave you behind, or I'll have to kill you."

His steps slowed as his eyes widened. "Wh-what?"

"It's quicker than the duskwolves tearing into your flesh and snapping your neck." It was brutal imagery, but not entirely false.

"She's kidding, Enoch," Sebastian said.

Enoch's voice hollowed. "H-how can you tell?"

"Because if you did break something, Tanir would gladly patch you up," he reasoned.

"Though I'd give you a scolding while I did it for not listening to the expert," Tanir added, drawing out the title expert to appease Mina's non-existent good side. "So turn around and continue your story."

"Right." Enoch turned around quickly at her instruction, gathered his composure with a shudder of his shoulders, and turned his head slightly to the side to speak, "I met Sebastian on a truly fate-defining day. Wandering the Coast of Carvons, I was lost, looking for inspiration to strike."

Wera groaned.

"And it did! As I sat on the beach, begging the great and powerful ocean to lend me some of its majesty, a geyser of sand erupted from underneath of me, sending me skyrocketing through the air. Whilst I fell from the heavens, I looked down at the ground below me. What once was a beach was now a golden temple! And upon the roof of this temple stood the great Sebastian Windenhofer, my new muse! Since that day, I have traveled alongside him, cataloging his adventures to tell the world of his greatness."

"You know that the rest of us were on top of that temple too, right?" Wera chided before addressing Mina. "Please take his tales with a grain of salt. For an archivist, he seems to have a selective memory. I'm the cartographer. Sebastian was the first person to hire me out of school, and I've been traveling with him ever since."

She looked back at Enoch and snickered, "See? Short, sweet, and to the point. Your turn, Sir Gargic."

"Indeed." Somehow, the knight puffed his swollen chest even bigger. "Unlike the rest of my compatriots, I am not under the employ of Master Windenhofer, but rather a liaison of The Crown of Lanholde. They've tasked the two of us with uncovering and collecting a few precious artifacts that The Crown has a vested interest in. We are on the last leg of this journey now."

Everyone's attention landed on Mina, heavy with expectation, a burdensome weight. They had offered their stories without her agreement. There was no need for her to respond. Responding would only embolden them to keep prying.

Sebastian broke the thick silence and turned to Tanir, "Did you really have to tell the basilisk story, Tani?"

"It's one of my first and favorite memories of you," she replied.

"You should've waited for winter," Mina commented, against her better judgment. "Basilisks get sluggish and less alert in the cold. You can sneak up behind them and slice off their heads in one strike if your blade is sharp enough. Just make sure to cut about a foot below their jaw so that you don't pierce the venom gland."

Her unexpected advice, matter-of-fact and brutal, garnered shocked and confused expressions from everyone but the wizard. Maybe it was the right call, then. The more alien she seemed, the better off they all would be.

"Aha! You're a hunter too!" Sebastian — frustratingly — cheered. "I knew there was more to you!"

If Mina could meaningfully scowl, she would have. The sight of his smile stabbed at the corner of her eye as she kept her gaze forward. Wizards were known to be fascinated by curiously temperamental creatures, of course it would be harder to break him.

"Now, do you have any other comments, questions, concerns for our happy little troop? Perhaps some tips on how to deal with those duskwolves you—"

"You're all loud," she stated. "It'll draw things to us, and cause trouble on the Peaks."

"Why's that?" Tanir asked.

"Avalanches."

"Wait," Enoch said. "There's going to be snow on these mountains?"

"What did you think we bought all those cold weather clothes for?" Wera scoffed.

"Lanholde has a cooler climate. I just thought winter wear was the fashion there."

Wera sent a pleading look Sebastian's way. "Did you really have to hire him, 'Bastian? We could have just left him stranded on that beach."

"True," Sebastian shrugged, "but we need entertainment on this journey, and watching the two of you bicker could rival some of the best traveling shows."

As those around Mina talked, and laughed, and teased each other, the surrounding trees grew in number. Their trunks twisted, more gnarled and oddly shaped, their canopy so thick it shifted the shade of the lower leaves lighter from the lack of sunlight. The group came to a halt as the road ended at a wall of forest: the start of the Harrowed Wood.

"Right. Which of you can fight?" Mina asked as she headed to the front of the pack.

All of them raised their hands.

Wera and Sir Gargic she understood but the others... "This isn't the time for jokes."

"We wouldn't have gotten this far if we couldn't hold our own, lass," Sir Gargic said. "Trust me, I was wary myself when I first met them, but even Enoch is worthwhile in a scrap."

"Hey!" Enoch whined.

"Cartographer, you're with me at the front," she instructed before they wasted more time chatting. "Medic and Archivist in the center. Wizard and Knight in the back. Listen more than you talk. Keep an eye out for anything moving that shouldn't be. If you see something, say something. And if something does attack us, no matter what happens, stay behind me."

Mina didn't wait for them to finish pairing off before weaving her way through the trees. She didn't even acknowledge Wera as she hustled to fall in place beside her.

"So," Wera drawled after a few minutes of silence between them, "why'd you pick me for the front?"

"You're a mapmaker," Mina replied. She didn't look at Wera as she spoke, her stare focused on surveying the forest in front of them. "If you make a map of the Harrow and the Peaks and take down the trail I use, I may never have to lead people through here again."

If she had to suffer through another expedition, at least she could make this one of use.

"You seem a little young to retire," Wera remarked. "And you need income to upkeep that cabin of yours, right? Though with seven thousand gilt an expedition, I'm surprised you haven't gotten yourself something a little sturdier to live in."

She could feel the pressure of Wera studying her face, looking for something she'd never find.

"There are other ways to make money that don't involve being bothered." She changed the subject, "People think that there are just wolves, bears, various small-time magical beasts here. The Harrow is untouched. Nature and magic are uncontrolled and unforgiving."

"Probably because of the runoff from the Peaks or some past geological event. I'll make a note to have Enoch look into it." Wera took out a small notepad and jotted something down. "If that's the case then I'd bet there are many ways to cross over into parts of Elphyne here too, probably a bunch of fae circles, areas where the veil is thin. Would you be able to point them out when we pass them?"

"Just write down the trail taken and there's no need to worry about any of that."

She heard Wera's pen skip on the page and a heavy exhale out of her nose.

There it was. She hated being talked down to.

Wera abandoned the topic and turned to basic questions about the flora and landmarks, easy enough that Mina could answer with little thought as she tuned one ear to the forest as best she could through the whispers of those walking a little too far behind her.

"Would you look at that," Sir Gargic remarked, voice slightly muffled and strained. He talked out of the corner of his mouth in a bad attempt to be quiet. "She's actually talking to Wera."

"People do often talk to each other," Sebastian said coolly, not feeding the knight's judgment.

"Yes, but she's so—"

"Are we talking about the Brambled Beauty?" Enoch whispered.

"The what?" Sebastian deadpanned.

"You don't like it, sir? I'm trying to figure out the perfect way to describe such a terrifying and alluring creature."

"Alluring?" Sir Gargic guffawed, "She's so cold!"

"Yes! She's cold!" Tanir added, voice peaking with a burst of realization.

Mina ground her teeth to keep from chewing them out. It was better that they didn't know how well she could hear, and she had bore much harsher digs than their rude observations anyways.

"Just because she's different than us doesn't make her less of a person," Sebastian chided. "And Tanir it's unlike you to make assumptions about someone you've just met."

"Oh no, I wasn't trying to be cruel. I was just—"

A low gurgle deep within the ground, quiet and out of place in the harmony of forest sounds, environmental interrogation, and gossiping whispers, stilled Mina's stride. She barred her arm across Wera's chest, stopping the preoccupied cartographer, and held her other hand up to halt those behind them.

Their footfalls and chitchat ceased abruptly. Mina turned her head to the side, putting a finger to her lips to signal them to stay silent and wait.

She drew forth the sword that rested on her hip and crept forward, listening, eyes fixated on the forest floor. The gurgle reached her ears once more, louder and more guttural; hungry. Mina stopped, bladed her feet, and whistled a line of bird song.

"A meadowlark?" Sebastian whispered.

For a fleeting moment, she noted how keen his ear was, then a massive maw erupted out of the earth, lunging at her. Wind at her heels, Mina leaped at it, rocketing towards the toothy mouth at incredible speed, and drove her blade down through its top lip. The beast let out a terrible, gargling roar, shaking off the actual dirt and plants from its mimicking hide to reveal an ornery terramawg.

With the momentum of her jump and the leverage of her impaled sword, Mina vaulted over the bulbous amphibian's earthen hide. She snapped her hips around, pivoting midair to face the beast's back, and drew forth her bow in the same fluid motion.

The air stilled as Mina ran her fingers from the grip of her bow to its string. The water in the air collected, crystallized under the brush of her fingertips, forming an arrow of pure ice. She aimed for the creature's third, slitted eye, a weak point that rested on the nape of its neck, and fired. A roaring gust of wind shook the trees, following in her arrow's wake as it soared through the air, embedding itself deep into the terramawg's brain.

Mina kept her focus on the beast as she descended, landing on a nearby tree bough without a glance back. The terramawg seized, the frost from her arrow glaciating its mind, and collapsed into a blubbery heap, returning to the mass of earth and withering foliage it disguised itself as.

Mina secured her bow on her back and slid down the tree's trunk.

"Keep moving," she said to the group as she retrieved her sword from the terramawg's corpse.

It was as if they too had been immobilized by her ice. Sir Gargic's hand rested on the hilt of his broadsword. Tanir had pulled out a handaxe from somewhere. Three thin daggers were laced between Enoch's fingers like claws. A swirl of inky liquid hovered over Wera's palm, while her other hand rested on her chest. Sebastian's hands were coated in flame.

All of their mouths hung agape.

A dull pang pushed against Mina's chest at the sight.

"Great Gods. Save some for the rest of us next time, will ya?" Sir Gargic shuddered.

"It was quicker if I handled it," she stated. "Now come on. There's more ground to cover before nightfall." Mina turned on her heels and walked away, stepping across the terramawg's body and taking care to drive her heels in a little harder as she did so.

"Hey, wait up!" Wera ran after her, manipulating the ink back in its vial and pulling out her notebook once again."How were you able to tell where it was?"

Tanir pulled a stupefied Enoch along, “Come on. You should be jumping with joy. Action like that is sure to make your book even more exciting.”

“Well,” Sir Gargic remarked to Sebastian with a heavy exhale, “I guess we know why she’s so cold now.”

Sebastian hummed in acknowledgment, nothing more. Nothing until moments later, when under his breath a murmured thought slipped out.

“The wind even changed direction.”

The reverence in his tone, unheard by everyone else, bristled against the back of Mina’s neck.

II
A Misanthrope's Misery

Mina stopped in a small clearing of trees and took off her pack. "Are you all capable of making camp on your own while I track something down for dinner?"

"Oh, that won't be necessary," Sebastian said, reaching into his outer coat pocket.

"Save your rations for the mountain," she insisted. "Have a hot meal while you can."

"And we will." He pulled out what looked to be a playing card, pressed his lips against it, threw it on the ground, and snapped his fingers. The card grew in size; unfolding on its own into a medium-sized boulder.

"What a trick," Mina stated, as dry as her droll manner of speaking could muster. "Don't see how that makes dinner."

"Mina, you are in for a real treat!" Tanir went to place a hand on her shoulder. Mina shifted subtly out of the way, letting her hand hit air.

Sebastian peeled open a portion of the rock, holding it open for the others to enter, one by one, squeezing, somehow, into the compact space. He gestured for Mina to follow suit with a smile and wave of his hand.

She squinted her eyes to try and soothe the sting.

"So it's a magic tent," she said.

"Yes," he replied.

"Is it warded?"

"Yes."

Mina paused, looking back between the tent and Sebastian's bright smile, which was starting to make her head hurt.

"If this is a trap, it will be your end," she warned.

"Understood," he nodded his head towards the entrance, "after you."

Mina picked her pack off the ground and slung it over her shoulder, keeping a distrusting eye on the wizard as she entered.

Well-trained wizards were capable of fantastical magics; magics that could hurt, could conjure, could manipulate the mind. Mina's dealings with them had been minimal, precisely how she preferred it to be with such unpredictable individuals.

She stepped through the tent flap, hackles raised and knuckles white around the hilt of her sword, steeled for anything. Anything, but an average-sized foyer.

Sporting a coat rack and shoe bin, two hallways split by a staircase, and a plethora of picture frames hung on the wall, it was reminiscent of a well-kept townhouse. An odd choice. Wizards often kept lavish palaces, or hovels infested with nature, to flaunt their magical talents. This space felt like a home.

And it made Mina's skin crawl.

The sound of the door locking behind had her pulling her blade out of its sheath and pointing its tip at Sebastian's throat.

"Don't worry," the humming resonance of his voice didn't waver at her threat. "You can leave as you like. The lock just keeps people out."

Mina held her blade steady.

"I understand that you may be a bit on edge right now," he continued, his tone much too lighthearted for his circumstance. "This must be your first time in a place like this."

"It's not," she sneered.

He raised an eyebrow. "You've been in a commorancy before?"

"Is that a fancy word for a townhouse?"

That smile, that wide, blinding smile of his, somehow grew even bigger and brighter. So bright, in fact, it forced Mina to look away and keep it from burning her corneas.

"In a way," he replied cheekily. "Would you mind sheathing your sword so I can take off my coat without having to worry about being stabbed?"

Mina lowered it instead, knowing better than to sheath it. The sting of his smile subsided as he turned away from her.

"So you've been in a townhouse before?" he asked as he unbuttoned. "Does that mean you've been to a city?"

"I have," she answered, though she didn't know why. She was certain he hadn't cast anything on her. She would have felt a spell forcing her to speak to him — drawing the words up from her throat, manipulating her jaw — if that were the case.

"Interesting," he slipped his arms out of his sleeves. They were sturdier than the thick wool of his coat let on. No prized fighter or gladiator, but definitely stronger than magic users typically were. "So, the luthier you go to for your fiddle lives in a townhouse similar to this."

The statement raised the hairs on the back of her neck. She lifted her sword.

How did he know that? How could he possibly know that unless—

His breath puffed out in a cloud of vapor as he hung his coat on the rack, startling him. He turned slowly towards her, pupils dilating with a hint of fear, as he found the edge of her blade much closer than before.

"I'm sorry. I didn't mean to alarm you. I am unfortunately very clever and very observant and noticed the scroll of your fiddle peeking out from beneath the flap of your pack," he kept his speech measured and calm, as if he were trying to soothe a raving beast.

She looked for the lie. A nervous shift in his gaze, a lick of the lips, a swallow. Or if he was a practiced liar, a too-focused stare, a held breath, a flexed jawline.

He just looked back at her. A cautious look — she did have a very sharp blade a little over an inch from piercing his jugular — but nothing that denoted dishonesty.

She held him there just a moment longer, letting the tension linger to see if some expert mask he wore to hide his true motives could withstand the pressure, but instead of breaking he softened. Caution turning into a glimmer of curiosity.

Irritating.

Mina soothed her unease with a long-drawn exhale and slowly sheathed her sword. His breath returned to being unseen. She never felt the change herself, but from the reactions of others, the sudden drop in temperature seemed shocking. If it bothered Sebastian, however, he didn't let on.

He didn't even shiver.

"Right, enough pestering your guests, 'Bastian," he said to himself before treating her to a soft, close-lipped smile that drilled into her molars. "Let me give you a brief tour."

Seeing no other choice, Mina followed his lead, if only to avoid any more pains caused by his expressions.

"There are three floors to the commorancy. The first has the common areas, the second, the assigned and guest bedrooms, and the third has the study rooms. We'll work our way up."

He headed down the hall to the left of the staircase. "This place isn't a home in the traditional sense, but a magical construction housed in its own pocket-realm nestled somewhere in the leylines of magical energy that course through the Realm of Mortals, and all realms parallel to it. Here's the restroom." He gestured to the first door they passed. "We all have private ones in our sleeping quarters, but it's always good to have one close to the entrance, just in case."

Mina focused her attention on the seemingly endless collection of picture frames hung on the walls. Photos and drawn portraits of Sebastian and his employees posed and unposed in various settings. Newspaper clippings detailing their adventures. Awards celebrating their accomplishments. Pieces of art and random hangings of pressed plants scattered among them.

"This is the dining room." Mina barely kept herself from bumping into Sebastian as he stopped to open the next door.

Stupid. She knew better than to let herself get distracted by something so trivial.

"It wasn't originally this big, but one time we had to shelter the crew of a missing Pivya Armada ship after we found them stranded on a desert island in the middle of the Sennian Sea." He sighed heavily, his gaze becoming distant as he recalled the memory. "A hundred sweaty, stinking sailors crowded around a tiny dining table will definitely teach you the value of space."

Sebastian's focus returned to the now, turning to Mina expectantly. She glanced into the room quickly, realizing that he wouldn't move on until she did.

Long and wide, it held a behemoth of a table wreathed by dozens of chairs.

"It's too much for our small troop so we tend to take our meals in the kitchen," he shut the door and walked just a few steps down the hall, "which is conveniently placed next to the dining room!"

Sebastian threw open the door grandly, and the cookware jumped to attention.

"At ease," he instructed, and they returned to their inanimate form. He turned to Mina with that searing smile. "I love a home-cooked meal, but I hate doing the dishes. So I thought, why not enchant them to clean themselves?"

Mina walked away, sparing herself further injury, while urging him to keep on track.

"Right. Moving on." Sebastian jogged to catch up with her.

"This room?" She pointed to the next door.

"The Junk Room," he answered.

"What makes it magic?" she asked.

"You stick your hand in, think about what you want, and it will come to you."

Mina walked past it. There was no reason to stop, she'd never be able to use it anyway.

"The next room you'll want to peer into," Sebastian advised from behind her. "It's just around the corner, through the double doors."

She ground her teeth and picked up her pace. She wasn't running away from the wizard. Mina didn't run away from anything, no matter how much pain it caused her. She simply wanted to get this showboating masked as hospitality over with.

And if the pounding headache and itchy skin subsided as a result, then that was just a bonus.

After a sharp turn, she came upon the double doors, made of opaque glass and covered with metal vines of ivy. She gripped the handles tightly and flung them open, determined to take just a brief glance before continuing on, only to be stuck in place by waving wildflowers and low-hanging trees.

A wild garden filled the room with well-cultivated flora and sunlight. Butterflies and their dragon counterparts flitted through the air. The distant bubbling of a stream rode on the false breeze that brushed against her cheek.

Sebastian's chuckle was closer than expected. *He* was closer than expected. His laughter hummed in her ear from where he stood over her shoulder. "Do you like it?"

Her skull pounded, like a rubber band had been snapped around it.

Fuck.

"It's unexpected," she stated and slammed the doors closed.

She caught Sebastian's jolt out of the corner of her eye.

He cleared his throat and walked away.

"Come along," he said, his words stiff, disappointment palpable. The pounding stopped, the tightening rubber band slacking. It was easier to breathe in the chill of his cold shoulder.

Safer.

Sebastian breezed down the hall, giving brief explanations of the rooms they passed: a hot spring, a training room, a containment room for hazardous objects, and finally, the infirmary. The foyer taunted Mina at the end of the hall. If Sebastian kept his offended pace up for the rest of his tour, she'd be back out that front door and into the forest that didn't make her skin itch and eyes sting in no time.

"I'm telling you it had to be her," Wera's voice seeped from the other side of the infirmary door, anchoring Sebastian in place and stalling their progression.

"Perhaps we should have Sebastian take a look at it then," Tanir's muffled voice responded prompting, much to Mina's chagrin, Sebastian to open the door and step into the room.

"What's the issue?"

His question was met with a pair of short screams. Wera clutched her open shirt closed, while Tanir nearly jumped three feet in the air.

"Sebastian Windenhofer!" Tanir scolded, "How many times have I told you to knock?"

"I-I-" he stammered. His broad shoulders tensed up in embarrassment. He gestured back towards Mina standing outside the door. "Sorry, Wera, I was giving Mina a tour and I overheard you and—"

"You!" Wera pointed a finger Mina's way. "What the hell did you do to me?" The cartographer's bashfulness must have been momentary, as without hesitation she opened her shirt back up again to reveal a long splotch against her chest, roughly in the shape of Mina's forearm.

It wasn't how she thought she'd get out of her contract — offending, disturbing, those were the smarter ways out — but Mina knew what was to follow now. Questions she couldn't answer, arguments heated only by one side, an escalation to violence even. So she did the reasonable thing.

She left.

She let her steps carry her faster than the wind, tapping into the nature thrust upon her, and arrived at the foyer door in an instant. She reached for the handle and found her arm held back by an unseen force. *A bind.*

She tried again, gritting her teeth as she attempted to push past her body's stalwart resistance to move. Harried footsteps behind her grew louder.

The wizard said she'd be able to leave!

The bind pulled back tighter, accompanied by a familiar tug at the base of her neck.

The contract.

"Mina."

It was as if an arrow pierced through her. Mina yipped in pain and whipped around to face her assailant, drawing her sword with a hiss.

Sebastian pulled the hand he had placed on her shoulder back, and stared at the mist rolling off of it. "Huh."

Mina watched him carefully as he turned his hand over, her body tense and ready to strike at any moment, her shoulder still throbbing from the pain of his touch.

His eyes met hers.

She held her breath.

"Give me a moment to handle Wera, and we'll continue our tour." He smiled, swiveled on his heels, and headed back down the hall.

Mina's sword clattered to the ground as the breath she held ripped from her chest. She clutched a hand over her heart as an agonizing sting, a hundred piercing needles, seized it. She fought to breathe through the pain, to keep herself standing, to keep herself conscious.

Years had passed since she last suffered like this, and a singular, terrifying thought echoed in her mind.

This expedition could be the death of her.

△

The rest of the tour passed quickly. Mina couldn't tell if Sebastian knew how uncomfortable she was, but she was as grateful as she could be when he briefly glossed over the third floor's various study chambers before showing her to the guest room.

"And this is where you'll be staying," he gestured towards a plain door, uncustomized, unlike the other bedroom doors they had passed.

Mina made sure to keep her eyes down as she stepped past him and entered. It was well-furnished but not ostentatiously so, with a sizable bed and small closet, a desk, and a bathroom adjoining it.

"Supper will be served in about two hours." He pointed to the wall clock above the desk. "But a bell will ring throughout the commorancy as a reminder."

Mina grunted, unwilling to risk turning around to address him.

She collapsed onto the floor as the door thudded closed behind her. Her body ached, every muscle throbbing from the stress of being bombarded by Sebastian's hospitality. She looked up at the bed she couldn't lay in, the chair she couldn't sit on, and turned her attention towards the bathroom. The corner of a deep porcelain tub peered back at her.

A bath would help. Decent hygiene was necessary for survival.

Mina got to her feet, ignoring her body as it screamed at her, and turned on the tap. Steam swirled in the air as she slowly undressed, beading back to water as it brushed against her skin. Peeling off the last of her dark leather armor, Mina caught a glimpse of herself in the mirror.

It had been years since she last saw her reflection so clearly. Her hair was still roughly shorn and short, dark and thick, though much more knotted and matted than expected. It had been a while since she last brushed it. She was more toned, the muscle from years of hiking and hunting on her own adding definition to her pale limbs. She turned and caught the shimmer of her scars in the light.

Her fingers trailed over the ellipses that crossed her chest. The faint markings wrapped around her entirely, only visible if the light shone just right, or someone looked too closely. She learned long, long ago, that if she turned the right way, she could pretend her skin was flawless. But they were there.

They would always be there.

As would the wrought iron band she wore around her neck.

The tub filled, and she stepped in gingerly, taking her time as steam billowed from it, clouding her vision. Mina exhaled as the water rendered her aching muscles weightless. She would never feel the heat of it, but its buoyancy she could claim. The tub was long enough for her to stretch out and bob atop the surface, releasing tension in her body that had lived there longer than it should have; pains from long before the suffering of the past few hours.

The stings of smiles and kind gestures were ailments she knew well enough to avoid, but pain that strong, that worrying? Years had gone by since that. She was so young and panicked, feral from struggling to survive in the forest for months, when Mrs. Harlowe found her raiding their chicken coop. The image of a savage child tearing out a hen's throat with her teeth would have terrified a lesser person, but Mrs. Harlowe invited terror in for a hot meal instead.

It was like eating glass, but Mina had been too hungry, and too ignorant to care. When they had washed her, and clothed her, and hugged her, and wrote off every wince and whimper as a symptom of her hypothermia - Mina had thought it was just the lingering wounds from her journey — until they put her down to bed. One ruined cabin and a night from hell later, the Harlowes learned their lesson. And Mina learned just how wounded she was.

The remembrances filled her heart with a deep and dull ache that hurt her more than Sebastian's smile ever could.

So, Mina brought soap to her scalp and ran her fingers through her hair to wash them all away before the cooling water turned to ice.

🜃

I am too weak to hunt. I must eat their food to survive. Mina repeated the mantra in her mind, hoping her body would believe it and spare her from any more pain this evening. She couldn't risk passing out.

From outside the kitchen door, she heard them talking. Talking about their interests, the journey to come, the journey that had passed. As the squeak of the door announced her entrance, their conversation halted.

They all turned to stare at her. Mina did not stare back. She kept her focus on the table itself. The safe, expressionless table.

"Take a seat wherever you like," Sebastian instructed.

She made her way to the far end of the table next to Tanir, making sure to keep well out of Sebastian's sight line. Tanir, in turn, rolled down the sleeves of her sweater and shimmed down the bench closer to Sir Gargic, keeping ample space away from Mina as she sat.

"Now, Mina, it's tradition here that whenever we break bread with someone new to our little troop, we conjure up their favorite meal." Sebastian's gaze stung her cheek. "What should I have the kitchen whip up for you?"

The cookware on the stoves and counters jumped to attention.

"I don't have a favorite meal," she answered.

The utensils wilted at her response.

"Come on, dear," Tanir encouraged. "Surely, there must be something you like?"

Mina ignored her question and locked eyes with Wera. A safe move considering she'd been staring daggers at her since she entered.

"Pick," she said.

Wera's eyes narrowed. "Why?"

Annoying.

Mina inhaled deeply and dug her nails into her palm to keep her temper from rising.

"Just pick."

She kept Wera's gaze, letting her look into her eyes, and watched as confusion mixed into her indignation.

"Shepherd's pie with mushy peas and parsnips," she answered slowly, cautiously, watching Mina intently as she spoke. "Baked beans and Eddenshire pudding."

Mina broke her stare to address the kitchen. "That'll work."

The cookware sprung to action, cooking at an enchanted pace. In just the time it took for Mina to lower her gaze back to the table, settings appeared before her, as did two tankards filled with some sort of liquid. Two kinds of water, perhaps. It wasn't any cultural table setting she knew of.

"So," Sir Gargic cleared his throat, "as I was saying. There I was at the mouth of the siren's den...."

Mina's heart raced as the food slid across the table in front of them.

I am too weak to hunt. I must eat their food to survive.

She picked up a spoon and scooped up a bit of one of the piles of mush on her plate. Pins and needles didn't shoot up her arm at the action. Her muscles didn't convulse, threatening to break the bones in her fingers.

She took a bite.

It was rare that she was relieved to taste nothing.

She ate quickly, lifting the plate and shoveling the meal into her mouth, worried that whatever deity decided to spare her from pain would take back their gift before she finished. She paused for a moment to catch her breath and wash it all down, picking up the tankard to her left and chugging it.

"Holy shit," Enoch murmured. Mina looked up at him briefly and caught him wincing from the elbow Wera jabbed into his side.

"Well, enough of my tales," Sir Gargic sighed as he finished his ramblings. "What about you, Ms. Mina? You have any yarns to spin about what we're to expect on the mountain?"

"Death," she snapped between bites. "Winds so cold they turn the air in your lungs to ice."

Unease. Dread.

If she made this journey sound as treacherous as possible, perhaps they would give up, void her contract, and she could go back to an isolated cabin, a stiff cot, and a time when she didn't have to worry about being wounded by the kindness in a wizard's eyes.

The left tankard she emptied refilled on its own, and she cleared its contents once more before continuing, "The snow is white and endless, so blinding in the sunlight and so all-consuming in the pitch of night that men are driven mad. The creatures that are cursed to live there are as lethal as they are starving. Desperate in their constant search for food, their famine has sharpened their hunting skills to be greater than any other predator on this continent. Frostlyon kits can kill a man as soon as their eyes open.

"Behemoths beyond comprehension, older than the Realm of Mortals itself, call the Peaks their home. The chill eases the ache of their ancient bones. They will hear your breath from deep below the ice, and rupture the earth around them just to get a sweet taste of your flesh. The beasts, behemoths, could be survivable if it weren't for the battering blizzards that leave even the strongest of folk mere husks of themselves. Having your body hammered by hailstones the size of an ogre's fist for days on end tends to take its toll."

The metallic scrape of Mina's fork against her plate echoed in the newly fallen silence, making for an ominous button to her speech.

"She's kidding again, right?" Enoch whispered to Sebastian.

"I'm not," Mina answered before Sebastian could. She locked eyes with Enoch. He trembled under her vacant stare. "And I wasn't kidding about the duskwolves either."

"Not to worry, Enoch." Sebastian placed a hand on the archivist's shoulder. He jumped at the sudden contact, but didn't look away from her. "That's exactly why King Fritz requested Mina to be our guide."

"And King Fritz is never wrong," Sir Gargic confirmed.

"How are you liking the food, Mina? Not to doubt your skills as a hunter, but I'm sure it must be a treat to have your food cooked for you," Sebastian remarked innocently, kindly, mannerly.

Stupidly.

The mash in her mouth turned to spikes mid-chew, piercing her tongue, the roof of her mouth, in between her gums. She inhaled deeply, bracing herself as she swallowed, bearing the pain of a dozen razors sliding down her throat without a sound. It wasn't enough to render her unconscious, but it was a more than unpleasant end to her meal.

It was enraging.

How dare they.

Enoch's eyes finally left hers, widening at the sight of something just to her right. Mina followed his gaze and found the fork she was using crumpled into a twisted ball in her hand.

She dropped the metallic lump on her plate with a clatter.

"I'm full."

Everyone tensed as she stood, shivering as their breath began to plume, watching her cautiously as she walked out of the room.

Behind her, their fearful, racing hearts beat in time with the anger thudding in her ears.

🜁

Mina waited in the guest room until everyone fell asleep, then made her way back to the foyer. She couldn't break her contract, but she couldn't sleep in the commorancy either. She held her breath as she reached for the door handle, and didn't exhale until the door opened and she stepped out into the dark forest.

The tent flap closed behind her, falling back seamlessly into the boulder illusion. The itch left her skin. The tension in her body subsided, blown away by the night breeze through her hair. The nocturnal chitters of wildlife welcomed her home. She had no need for light even on this moonless night, and made her way through the darkness uninhibited, finding a tall pine nearby to roost in.

Sitting high up in its boughs, angled so that the commorancy rested as a small, gray blemish in the corner of her eye, she looked out over waves of swaying leaves among a sea of stars. The bark scratched against her neck, the trunk pressed hard against her hips, but Mina didn't care. Comfort wasn't something she missed. It was something she hardly knew in the first place.

Against the shushing rustle of the swaying trees, Mina's mind couldn't quiet. The anger she'd been holding back from dinner, from long before dinner, chewed at her thoughts.

She should have walked away. Should have taken the loss of her beaver skins and a few days camping out in the woods over another expedition. It served no purpose. Now that the folks in town finally tolerated her, she made more than enough gilt from selling soaps and pelts and foraged goods to keep herself and the cabin.

A heavy crosswind shook her tree bough, catching the long plane of her sword sheath and tapping it against her calf. The memories it carried were a thousand times heavier than the iron itself. She could almost hear Mr. Harlowe telling stories to the adventurers they lead below.

He and the wizard would have talked each other's ears off.

The first pounds of a headache started up as her traitorous mind recalled Sebastian's smile.

Mina's temper surged, and she only had herself to blame.

She pulled her fiddle from her pack and played, furiously at first, her fingers flying across the strings as her bow bounced against them. Irritation, aggravation, vexation. The wood of its neck started to squeak from how tightly she gripped the fingerboard. Hairs snapped off of her bow.

She pulled herself back, caging the fury howling inside her. If she broke her fiddle now, there was no fixing it. She would not find a horse tail to pluck from on the Peaks, nor have the time to source wood fine enough to replace a splintered scroll.

Her song shifted from murderous to mourning at the thought; at a hundred thoughts. Some new. Most old, and deep, and half-felt.

Mina allowed the music to consume her, closing her eyes in the futile hope that it would grant her the release she ached for. She didn't need to hear her thoughts, the forest or its creatures...

...or the subtle rustle of a tent flap, as her melancholy tune poured over the skyline of the Harrow and trickled down into the clearing below.

III

Hospitable Hostility

Once they began their climb in earnest, there would be no turning back. Rabbet's Pass. Three days.

Three days to convince them that dealing with the frozen horrors of the Peaks alone was far better than having her around. Or that traversing the Peaks at all was a terrible idea and that they should just turn around and find another path. One less frigid, more forgiving, and that did not end with her finding them stiff and lifeless with their soft parts torn out by hungry jaws.

Mina's hunting knife missed the sharpened end of the arrow she was shaping and nicked the tip of her finger, slicing a sizable sliver of flesh clean off. The injury pulsed slightly, dark blood trickled down her hand, but with a swipe of her thumb across it, the blood froze over, and the flesh returned, whole again.

The tent flap rustled behind her.

"See! I told you all she'd be here." Sebastian cheered as he and his troop filed out of the commorancy. "Good morning, Mina!"

Mina scored the edge of the arrow one last time and stood, stuck it in her quiver, and sheathed her knife. She did not turn to address them, keeping her eyes on the trail ahead instead.

"We'll continue north without stopping until we reach where the Harrow thins," she pointed up at the white mountain tops swallowing half the sky through the cloud cover in the distance. "Cartographer. Stay beside me and take note of the path. Everyone else stay vigilant, and behind me."

"Would it kill you to say please?" Wera scoffed behind her.

Mina started the day's hike without answering.

It didn't take long for Wera to trudge up beside her, notebook in hand and quill scribbling harshly. The others had caught up quickly as well, judging by the distinct quartet of footsteps following behind them. Collapsing the commorancy must have been just as easy as setting it up.

"You could at the very least call me by my name," Wera snipped.

"The ground will get harder the closer we get, so it'll be easier to make out the path," Mina stated, attempting to change the subject.

"You really can't muster up an apology at the very least? A curt 'sorry' would do."

"No."

"No?!" Wera squawked, voice bouncing off the gnarled tree trunks.

Mina snapped her head to the side and glared daggers her way. "Keep your voice down."

"You are unbelievable!" she hissed, frustration and ire still present as she lowered her volume. "We invite you into our home, feed you, offer you comfort, try to get to know you, and you have the nerve to continue to look at us like *that*." Wera waved her ink-stained hand in front of Mina's face.

"That?"

"Like we're nothing. Like you might as well be looking at a wall!"

Her words cut deeper than Mina expected. The goal was to upset them, wasn't it? She knew what to expect when people were upset.

"I never asked for your comforts." Mina turned her head back forward, back to the path ahead, to the Peaks. Unless Wera's next words involved ending the contract, whatever she said didn't matter. She hated being dismissed, her lashing out was just a side effect of Mina's eventual freedom.

"Proper hospitality is granting comfort even when it isn't asked for! You should be grateful!"

Anger froze over sense.

"And how do you know what comforts me?" Mina snapped at her. "When have any of you asked? You speak of hospitality like it's something that everyone searches for." The frozen muscles in her face found movement in her temper, curling her lips into a snarl. "You may map the world, but you'd be naive to believe you know the needs of every being in it."

Fear softened the anger in Wera's face, widening her eyes, hitching her breath—yet she did not back away.

"Well, maybe if you just told us—"

"I am telling you! You just won't listen!" Mina roared. Plumes of breath tumbled out of Wera's lips and she jolted back. Frost began to form on the tips of her eyelashes. "And now you take grievance with me because of your own ignorance! Is it because I hurt you? One slight brush of frostbite, and now I'm your greatest enemy?! Would you rather I had let the terramawg eat you fucking whole?! I'm certain being swallowed alive and dissolved slowly in its stomach would have been much less painful."

Mina's hands ached with the need to grab Wera by the throat, to squeeze until she conceded, apologized, begged.

"Huh. Who knew someone so cold-blooded could have such a hot temper?" Wera remarked as if her life weren't in imminent danger. "It's a good thing, too. I was getting worried you couldn't feel anything at all." She turned her cheek and went back to her note-taking. "You're correct. We don't know you, but Sebastian would like us to. Especially considering we will be traveling together for quite some time."

Mina gripped the pommel of her sword instead of Wera's neck and faced forward, confusion taking the air out of her anger.

"Caring for the wizard's fancies is not in my contract," she said, trying to wrap her head around Wera's reaction. "I am to lead you to Lanholde. That is all."

"Fine then. I will make sure he is aware," Wera replied. "Now, you said that the ground will get harder the closer we get to the mountain range, are there any other defining landmarks on the way?"

There was no screaming match or insults hurled her way. No one cowered in fear or burst out into tears. Had the others even noticed their dispute? Where were the threats or blades being drawn?

Something else lingered beneath Mina's confusion, unidentifiable and uneasy. Not because of distrust or worry that there was some other scheme afoot, but because this unknown feeling pulled along with it the meager wisps of relief.

"Mina?"

"There's a large ash tree coming up. Thousands of years old. Cross to the left of it, not the right."

Mina kept an ear out for any whispers behind her, any bitter words or complaints about her behavior, and instead heard yet another regaling of Sir Gargic's past adventures and Tanir and Enoch discussing Lanholdian fashion trends.

"Why not the right?" Wera asked.

"A myrevole colony nests underneath the roots, making the ground soft for them to hunt."

If her lashing out was not enough to deter them, then her goal would be much harder to obtain. Odd emotions and misplaced relief be damned, she needed to get out.

"Though with your big feet and heavy footsteps, they'll probably come after us anyway," Mina added to the answer she shouldn't have given.

A tight chuckle came out the corner of Wera's mouth. "You're one to talk. Telling us to worry about being quiet on the Peaks, when those goddamn boots of yours could wake the dead."

"How about instead of worrying about my boots, you worry about keeping those lines of yours straight?" Mina side-eyed her journal. "Is that supposed to be a tree or?"

Wera snapped the journal shut.

There it was.

"You know what? I forgot to ask Sebastian something. Excuse me." Wera walked off, muttering insults under her breath.

The uncomfortable feeling left, and nothing replaced it.

Not even relief.

🜁

It was a little after noon when the rumblings of stomachs and whispers of lunch reached Mina's ears.

"Do you think we'll stop soon?" Enoch whispered to Tanir. "My stomach's starting to growl."

"Perhaps we should have Sebastian ask her," she whispered back. "If we ask her, she probably won't listen." Tanir turned back over her shoulder. "Sebastian? We should stop for lunch, don't you think?"

No, you shouldn't, Mina thought.

She heard Sebastian fish something out of his pocket. "It's about time for it," he said. "How does some soup and grilled cheese sandwiches in the commorancy sound?"

Awful.

Mina grit her teeth. The thought of trying to trick her mind to sit through another meal with them turned her stomach. There was no way it'd work, not after the wizard's "treat" comment. She scanned the forest for a solution. She couldn't give them her rations, and even if she could, she wouldn't, unless she was looking to starve. Hunting would take too long.

The approaching canopy of oblong leaves and branches bowed by dark fruit ahead, however...

"Mina—" Sebastian called to her just as she neared the first plum tree's trunk.

"Cover your heads!" she barked as she drove her heel into it, taking care not to stop walking.

The others yelped in surprise as fruit rained down upon them. Mina held out the bottom of her shirt and caught a half dozen for herself.

"Grab what you can and keep moving," she instructed. "This is whistfly territory."

"Whistfly?" Sir Gargic squawked.

"Terrible little creatures that attack anything still and warm-blooded." A half-truth. Whistfly season in this neck of the Harrow had ended months ago, but she highly doubted that any of them knew that. None of the other expeditions had. "They'll slip in any space they can, into your ears, up your nose, underneath your eyelids to burrow behind your eyes and feast on the tender, wrinkled flesh of your brain. But only if you stay still. Their wings have trouble keeping up otherwise."

"Good Gods," Tanir lamented. "It's like this whole place was made by devils."

"Not devils," Mina took a bite out of one of the plums, "but close."

"Well, if we set up the commorancy—" Sebastian started.

"You mean stop to set up the commorancy?" Mina countered. "Wouldn't be wise. You're seasoned adventurers. A few hours of walking on barely elevated terrain shouldn't have you stopping already."

"The girl's right, Sebastian. We could stand to walk some more, plus these plums are fantastic," Sir Gargic praised through a wet mouthful. "Do you know what variety it is? This would make a fine gift for His Majesty."

"They'll rot before they reach him," she said.

"Not with how cold the Peaks are! Freezing food preserves them—"

"Or shatters them. One wrong shuffle and it's plum dust."

Sir Gargic ran a tongue along the inside of his cheek and spit a pit out into his hand. "Then I'll keep the seeds. Our court herbologists are some of the best in the continent, I'm sure they can figure it out."

"And if it's the soil?" Mina asked.

"The soil?"

"If it's the soil that can grow the plums. Only this soil."

"Well then," he laughed. "I guess you'll have another seven-thousand gilt in your pocket."

"Your king would send his herbologists on a quest through one of the most dangerous places in this realm... for some dirt?" Mina threw the plums up in the air and started to juggle them in taunt. "A half-dozen dead herbologists all because His Majesty sought to fill his gullet with plums."

She heard him take a deep breath, a grumble of discontent preceding what she assumed would lead to a long tirade chewing her out for even implying his king was cruel. The thud of a hand on the pauldron of his leather armor stopped it.

"Mina!" Sebastian cheered. "I didn't know you could juggle!"

She let a plum slip out of her grasp, aiming it conspicuously to hit Sebastian in the chest.

It splattered against his coat.

"Guess I can't."

🜁

Their footsteps were faltering, breath catching whenever they hit a blister or patch of raw rubbed skin.

"Mina," Sebastian called, the hum of his voice reedier with exhaustion. "We should look to make camp."

"Not here," she replied. She had to push them further, ruin their feet a bit more so that each step they took in the morning would remind them how horrible she was, and have them cursing her name and tearing up her contract by the afternoon.

"There's a clearing up ahead that looks promising," he argued.

"I think you mean compromising."

"Then find us somewhere uncompromising,"

"That's two miles ahead."

Enoch whined. "Two more miles?"

Sebastian sighed with more exasperation than Mina thought him capable of. "There has to be somewhere within the next five hundred feet for us to make camp. I respect your expertise, but we've been walking without a break for the past eight hours."

"Let's just stop walking now, 'Bastian," Wera snipped. "The commorancy's got wards. Whatever danger Mina can concoct won't be able to get through."

Concoct.

Mina took the phrasing as a personal challenge. She cast her eyes down subtly, checking to see if the hoof prints she'd caught scattered here and there on the path were still fresh, and closed her hand into a fist at her side. Her nails sunk into her palm with little resistance, breaking the skin and drawing blood.

"Wera, I'm sure Mina will find us a stopping point soon," Sebastian assured her, "Right, Mi—"

A chorus of bloodcurdling squeals rose out of the surrounding forest, growing louder, hoof beats creating a heart-racing percussion. Mina unsheathed her sword and glanced over her shoulder.

"Bristle boars. Run."

Horrified recognition crossed Sebastian, Tanir, and Sir Gargic's faces.

"Fucking hell," Sir Gargic drew his blade and shoved Enoch in the shoulder. "The woman said run. Fucking run!"

Mina could have easily outpaced them, one windswept step, and she'd be a mile away, but then the boars would stop chasing them. They only hunted when they smelled fresh blood in the air. So she jogged at the front, freezing her injured palm when she could hear the boars' ragged breathing closing in, unfreezing it when the squeals faded, until they reached the final row of snow-topped pines that marked the Harrow's end.

They were panting like dogs in Summer's heat, feet shuffling through the frost-crusted grass as Sebastian set up the commorancy. They entered their tent wordlessly, too fatigued and bitter to care whether or not Mina came with them. Except Sebastian.

Because clearly the man couldn't take a hint if it hit him upside of the head.

"Well, that was thrilling," he huffed, his voice lilting and somehow joyful. "Once everyone gets cleaned up, we'll have dinner."

Mina ignored him as she dug through her pack, looking for the wire and sticks she'd brought to set up some snares.

"Do you need to freshen up or—"

"I have to scout the perimeter," she cut him off.

"Is there something specific we should be worried about? I can adjust the commorancy's wards a bit to—"

"It's prep for tomorrow's journey."

"Anything I can help with? If it's the two of us, the work will go faster."

"If it's the two of us, then that's one more person I have to keep from dying," she said, the sting of his offer itching her ears. "Eat your dinner. Stay out of my way."

Mina felt his gaze on the back of her neck and for a fleeting moment wondered if the kindness finally left his eyes.

"Alright then," he said after a minute. "I'll leave you to it."

The tent flap closed, leaving Mina alone with nothing but the hollow whistle of the wind shaking the trees to keep her company. She looked back, expecting the illusion to ripple as the wind blew hard against it, for the flap to be thrown open by the breeze. But the boulder was stalwart, sturdy. No need for stakes or weights to hold it down, which the wind seemed to almost take offense to.

Mina grabbed her snares and ran, as far as she could until the forces that bound her to her contract stilled her feet: farther than she expected but still closer than she cared for. At least she didn't have to worry about them watching her hunt.

She set the snares up around the perimeter and went to work. There was a lot of meat she had to gather and little time to do so. She unsheathed her bow and listened, to the wind, to the forest. Less prey lived out here, an inconvenience, another annoyance. She should have hunted the night before rather than thrown that pity party for herself.

The knock of antlers against a tree, a beat out of rhythm from the sounds of the woods, caught her attention,

and Mina disappeared into the wind.

🜁

Night had long settled in by the time she made it back to the campsite with a stag and some hares on her back. She had dressed them a ways away from the camp, leaving their organs and bones to keep any predators off her trail, and carried the meat in their skins.

She built a fire with fresh wood, a small one for smoking, and used the skins to tent the meat above it. By the time she woke in the morning, she'd have enough jerky to last her most of the trip, but she'd need to butcher some of the beasts they'd encounter in Rabbet's Pass to make up the rest. The idea of having to eat raw frostlyon wasn't well-received, but it was better than bones or nothing.

Mina changed into her whytewing leathers and set up her bedroll a few yards away, opting to take shelter on the ground rather than having to combat the high winds that rolled down the mountains and shook the canopy. She finished off the last of the plums she collected with a rabbit leg she roasted.

No pain, no panic, only a peaceful evening. Mina went to pull out her fiddle, inspired by the whistling winds to find a song that would compliment it, when a shimmer of magic surrounded her.

"Have I done something to offend you?"

She drew her blade and swung towards the intruder's throat without a second thought.

Sebastian, unfazed by the sheer speed of her strike, stopped it with a glowing hand, holding it in the crook between his neck and shoulder.

"I didn't mean to startle you, but if I didn't silence my steps, you would have just walked away."

A smart idea. Mina moved to stand, to walk away as he suggested, but slammed her head against an unseen barrier instead.

She fell back on her ass.

"I am also sorry for using a Dome of Encasement. But we've got to clear the air before we start our ascent," he sighed, "and like I said. I knew you would walk away."

"I could kill you right now," Mina snarled, keeping her focus on the ground. It wasn't worth the risk to stare him down. Not in this close of quarters.

"I get that. Now." Sebastian took a deep breath. "Have I done something to offend you?"

"You haven't done anything to offend me. I have no use for your apologies. Go back to your tent and leave me be," she turned her back to him, hoping he would get the hint.

"Then why were you so..." he considered his wording, "...*gruff* today?"

"That's just how I am."

"Is lying part of who you are as well?"

Mina grit her teeth. "I don't know what you mean."

"Whistflies are a seasonal insect, and considering it's the beginning of Autumn now and not Spring, I very much doubt they would have burrowed behind our eyes to feast on the tender, wrinkled flesh of our brains while they're hibernating."

Mina scoffed, "We had to keep moving."

Sebastian sighed. "Do I want to know how you managed the boars?"

"The less time we spend in this forest, the more time we have on the mountains."

He hummed in frustration. "Fine then. Why can't you look me in the eye?"

Goosebumps rose up her arms, her heartbeat quickened. "I don't know what—"

"You were able to stare down Wera without a problem during your... disagreement, yet with me, it seems that since last night you can't bear to look at me," he explained thoroughly and quickly. "And while I'm fine with your scorn, I can't allow you to take your hatred of me out on my friends. So. I apologize wholeheartedly for any slight or slander I have mistakenly caused you. If you let me know how I've hurt you, I will do whatever it takes to stop—"

Needles drove into Mina's lungs as his heartfelt sorries fell upon her. Her skull threatened to cave in. In defense, she whipped around and smacked her hand over his mouth. If his lips froze shut, it didn't matter. A bit of frostbite was much better than her mauling him to death.

"Shut up!" she hissed, anger boiling over. She locked eyes with him. His gaze went wide in surprise, crossing a bit as he glanced down at her hand, but did not pain her. The sudden steam pluming from her palm, however, did.

She pulled away with a yelp and held her hand to her chest. It stung and throbbed in time with her heartbeat. A new kind of pain.

"What the hell is wrong with your face?" she asked, studying her palm as the steam subsided, and the pain pulsed away into an entirely different feeling. A sensation Mina hesitated to name.

"It's not my face," he answered with a light laugh. "I was born under a Salamander Moon."

Mina ran two fingers over her palm, sending a shiver up her spine from the difference in sensation. "A Salamander Moon?"

"It means I've got a natural affinity for fire magics, so I tend to run warmer than most folks. Making someone steam from touching me is new, though." He looked at her hand. "Were you born under a Boreal Moon? It would explain the frostbite."

Mina looked up at him then, her face stoic as usual. "I didn't know what a Salamander Moon was. What would make you think I'd know the Boreal version? Let alone what moon I was born under."

His gentle curiosity morphed into something blinding and skull-splitting as Sebastian laughed.

"You're right," he chuckled. "That was a dumb thing to ask."

She winced and turned away from him.

"Look," she said as his laughter petered out. "You have not offended me." The words stung her throat as she spoke them, but she pushed through the pain in the hopes that they would coax him to leave.

"I know isolation. I know space," she continued, trying to ask without asking, betting that he could understand her. "I am distant. I survive."

A rush of the wind through the treetops filled the silence between them.

"Okay." There was a certainty, a slow knowing that carried with it a promise that he'd follow her instruction.

Yet, he still sat in front of her, long, folded legs mere inches from hitting her knees.

"Leave then," she said.

Sebastian inhaled deeply. "About that..."

Mina's stomach dropped.

"What do you mean 'about that'?" she drawled out.

"So." He popped his lips. His fingers drummed on his kneecap in triplets. "You ever do this thing where you act before thinking?"

"No."

He inhaled again, sharply, and hissed through his teeth. "Well, I did." He exhaled. "Unfortunately, a Dome of Encasement lasts about eight hours." He raised his arm and knocked against the invisible ceiling overhead. "And I can't dispel it."

Mina sunk her fingers into the earth below her rather than his eye sockets. "And how big is this dome? It's about a yard tall, considering I cracked my head against it just trying to stand."

"And a diameter of about a yard and a half wide," Sebastian added.

Mina exhaled as much of the building rage inside her as she could. There wasn't much she could do about her predicament, but she could keep herself from sleeping next to a corpse at the very least. "You are. By far. The *stupidest* and *most obnoxious* man I have ever met in my entire life."

"Honestly," his fingers stopped drumming, "I'm just glad to be the most *something* in anybody's life."

The shift in his voice was subtle, but carried a great weight behind it. An accent she hadn't caught before. A tinnier 'in' in 'something'. A bassier, more rounded 'oh' to his 'most'. It lured her to glance back at him, to see if her guess was right. That if he spoke one more sentence, the curve of his lips would betray his heritage.

Unfortunately, it only served to summon her frustration at full force.

"You don't have a bedroll."

His fingers resumed their drumming on his knee. He shrugged his shoulders and huffed a meager, nervous laugh. "See. That's the thing about acting before thinking—ah!"

Mina couldn't kill him, but she sure could make him suffer.

She ripped the bedroll out from underneath her and smacked him with it over and over again. Not hard enough to break his neck or anything, but with enough gusto to let out a decent chunk of her aggravation.

"Idiotfuckingwizarddumbassdopeysmilingshit—" The insults flew from her lips with every hit of the mat against his raised arms until she threw the bedroll over his head with one final blow, bouncing off the force field behind him to smack squarely against his back. She turned away and moved as far as their cramped quarters would permit, pushing her nose up against the invisible barrier when she laid down.

"Stay to your side," she commanded.

"Do you—" he hesitated, shifting as he grabbed the bedroll and dragged it onto his lap. "Do you want your bedroll back?"

"No." The word climbed out of her throat against her will.

As she knew it would.

"But—"

"No."

Sebastian fell quiet for a moment. Mina held her breath, waiting for him to do something stupidly chivalrous like drape the bedroll over her or attempt to cover her with his coat.

The grass crunched softly underneath him and the thwap of the bedroll hit the ground as he chose sense over chivalry.

Yet still, her breath held, waiting until his breathing evened out, and the slight rumble of sleep from his chest brushed against the back of her neck.

🜁

Dreams were a rarity for Mina. But they were never true dreams, only memories.

Memories of ice and snow, of crystalline walls and frosted floors, of an endless chill that she had long grown numb to. Cruel laughter, the bite of chains against her back, spindled fingers holding her gently as their nails sank into her cheeks. Nightmares that — no matter how terrified she was — fear alone could not wake her from.

On this night, however. This incredibly infuriating and taxing night. Mina dreamt of something different. A memory of somewhere else.

There were no chains, no laughter, no ice. Only light.

Light in a color she didn't know the name of, that she could not recall ever seeing, coupled with that nameless feeling that had lingered on her palm. They surrounded her, covering her skin, binding her arms and legs together snugly. It even seeped into her chest, thrumming along with her heartbeat.

Though swaddled, she felt no fear in being bound, and took long sought out comfort in a feeling she had long forgotten:

Warmth.

IV

A Day of Discoveries

First, came the murmuring.

Next, a pressure against her chest, over her arms.

Then, the burning.

Mina woke up with a jolt — throwing the weight that bound and burned her off — and hopped to her feet, sword drawn and ready to strike.

"Don't kill us!" Enoch shrieked.

Her sleep-addled mind caught up with her well-trained body, stilling her blade. The blinding light of early morning faded to something much more tolerable, revealing the wide-eyed and frightened stares of Sebastian's troop as they stood around her. Steam rolled off her body in waves as the pulsing partial pain she had experienced from touching Sebastian's face the night before rippled across her skin.

"What have you done to me?" she hissed as she checked over herself.

"Talk about one hell of a wake-up call," Sebastian grumbled behind her. "Next time, would one of you just ring a bell or something? Murder-scream 'rise and shine'? I'd like that a lot more than being thrown ten feet."

"Your cuddle-buddy here is the one to blame for that," Wera snickered, looking at Mina smugly.

The pain subsiding into the eerily 'comforting' feeling she recalled in her dream — *warmth* — combined with Wera's insinuation gave her pause. Her adrenaline subsided, leaving her aching and tired as she sheathed her sword.

That pressure.

The burning.

How long had Sebastian been holding on to her? And how was he still alive to tell the tale?

"Don't tease her now, it was all my fault." Sebastian's footsteps crunched closer across the thin blanket of snow that had fallen. "I trapped us both in a Dome of Encasement last night."

"Sebastian," Tanir tutted, shaking her head.

"Well, that's one way to do it," Sir Gargic muttered under his breath.

"Not like that," he groaned. "I did it to clear the air before we start climbing. Which brings me to my next point." Mina's throat went dry as he stepped closer.

Closer.

"Everyone, leave Mina alone. Listen to her, of course, when it comes to surviving our journey, but otherwise give her plenty of space. I'm afraid our outgoing nature may have been too much for her."

"His outgoing nature must have been just right last night," Enoch whispered to Wera, but Sebastian clearly didn't catch it.

"Understood?" his voice rippled across Mina's shoulder.

"Understood," they replied.

"Good. Here is your bedroll back, Mina."

She went to grab it from him, barely turning his way, barely glancing at him to try and cut some of the pain taking it from his hands would cause, and found herself paralyzed.

In another life, perhaps she would have gasped. Perhaps her jaw would have dropped in awe. Perhaps even tears would have streamed down her face as she saw Sebastian's hair; brilliant and blazing with color.

What color, she did not know, but it was the same as the warm light in her memory.

The little emotion she could feel sent soft tingles through her. So minuscule that those unplagued wouldn't have noticed.

To Mina, she may as well have been struck by lightning.

Her hands ached to touch it. Her mind screamed at her to run from it. So she settled for staring; wondering quietly in the back of her mind why the sight of it — so clearly a gift — didn't cause her any pain at all.

"Mina?" Sebastian called, voice lilting in concern. "Your bedroll?"

She made the mistake of pulling her gaze from his hair to look him in the eye. Her retinas stung as she found him once again looking at her kindly, despite his evident confusion.

"Pack up your tent, put on your winter gear, and let's move." She snatched the bedroll out of his hand and stalked off, fighting the undeniable urge to spend the rest of her day leering at him, pain be damned.

Color. The wizard's fucking hair had turned a color.

A distracting, devious, delightful—

A taut rubber band snapped around her skull.

—color.

After holding her all night.

It snapped again.

Years. *Years* had gone by in black and white. And while she was thankful the first color she saw wasn't blue, she cursed whatever fates relished in tormenting her by having it bloom from the top of an arcane idiot's skull.

Mina tore a piece of jerky between her teeth as she dismantled her makeshift smoker. What a fucking inconvenience this all was.

She snuck a glance Sebastian's way and watched his hair dance in the breeze. Vibrant strands lilting, shifting as the wind blew through it, tempted her. She followed it as it dipped down with its master to pick up a tent turned playing card, tracing one wily strand in particular that made its way to brush against his cheek.

A slight smile lifted that cheek, and her jerky tried to stab through her throat mid-swallow.

Gods fucking dammit.

There had to be a way to study this color phenomenon without torturing herself.

"Will the walking order be the same this leg, lass?" Sir Gargic asked her.

And let that hair out of my sight? Absolutely fucking not.

"No." She shoved the jerky into her pack. "You all will take the front, and I'll be in the back. If something attacks, I'll take point. Try to stay behind me if that is the case."

"You'll take the back?" Distrust dipped in every syllable. Mina glanced Sir Gargic's way and found him standing with his arms crossed behind her, eyes narrowed, and beard drooped under the pull of a frown. "How do we know you're not going to abandon us?"

It took all the effort in the world to keep her eyes on Sir Gargic and not the brilliant beacon bobbing closer. "I've signed a contract that states I must escort you to Lanholde. That word is binding."

"People break contracts all the time."

"Not me."

"Sir Gargic," Sebastian placed a hand on the knight's shoulder and Mina's focus immediately flew to his hair. "Mina has had multiple opportunities to abandon us and she hasn't. I don't believe she will now. Right, Mina?"

"Like I said. That word is binding." She let herself linger on his hair for another moment, then forced herself to turn her back to it. "After you all, then. The trail is clear enough for the next few miles. Keep your voices down, and I'll tell you if you need to look out for anything."

"The same pairs as before?" Tanir asked.

"Same pairs as before just," she gestured towards the path ahead, "in front of me."

"Sounds like a plan!" Sebastian used his grip on Sir Gargic's shoulder to steer him towards the front of the group. Mina's gaze slowly followed, tracking his brilliant locks, as Tanir and Enoch trailed after them.

"So this trail," Wera asked as she sidled up to her. "What's it called?"

"Zanok's Lure," Mina answered, her eyes remaining on the back of Sebastian's head as they walked. She'd have to look at other things eventually, listen for the rumblings of avalanches or wild beasts, but there was time before their path turned treacherous.

"Why's it called that?"

"Zanok was a mountain man who used to promise uneducated travelers an easy journey through the range. He'd take them down this path."

"Was he the one who taught you how to navigate the Peaks?"

"No. He was a cannibal who used the daily snowfall around here to hide death traps. Turned his expeditions into edibles."

"O-oh," Wera stammered, the tip of her quill scratched across the page. "S-so I should make note for future travelers to be cautious of traps?"

"No. I disarmed all of them. Killed Zanok too."

Her pen stilled. "You killed—"

"He ate people. He was a monster. I kill monsters," she explained. "Plus, this is an easy path to start the ascent."

She stared at Mina, perhaps trying to tell whether she was lying or not.

"Alright," she said with a deep inhale, collecting herself. "Why keep the name then?"

"Keeps people away. Keeps it clear for me, and those who contract me to use," Mina said. "Rename it something else on that map of yours. Then people can use that and leave me the fuck alone."

"Right," Wera paused for a moment, brushing the feathered end of her quill across her cheek in thought. "What's your last name?"

"I don't have one," she answered without thinking, distracted by the way Sebastian's hair illuminated in the sunlight as he crested over the hill ahead.

Wera scoffed. "Come on. Even orphans have last names."

"Well, I don't," Mina snipped. "I don't see how last names are important for map making."

"I was going to name it after you, considering you were the one to fix it up and kill that monster of a man. But if you're going to be a bitch about it—"

"Harlowe." The name stabbed her tongue as she said, but it was worth the pain. It was better for her to name it after something that mattered rather than some bullshit like 'Smooth Snow Valley'.

"Harlowe? Is that your—"

"It's not. But if you are asking me for a name, there's one to use."

The feather of Wera's quill flicked with a flourish in the corner of her eye. "Harlowe's Gate. Has a nice ring to it, don't you think?"

She could almost hear the old man grunt in agreement.

"So," Wera's voice turned light and playful, putting her on edge immediately, "what happened last night?"

"I slept."

"That's all?" Wera teased. "Must have been some sleep to leave you so distracted."

Mina bristled. "I'm not distracted."

"Please." She rolled her eyes. "Did you forget I've been walking next to you for the last two days? Your eyes are normally shifting all over the place, scanning for threats, hazards, something you can use as an excuse to keep us moving. But right now, they are fixed on one point."

Wera dipped her quill forward slowly, dramatically, to point at Sebastian.

"Don't pretend to know me," Mina said with a bitter edge, though if she could sweat, she would have been dripping. Her heartbeat kicked up to a concerning speed. "My eyes are focused on the front of the pack. Which means I can keep track of the turns up ahead while keeping the building slopes of the mountains around us in my peripherals."

"Couldn't you do that from the front?"

"It's common for the creatures that hide on this path to wait until a group passes and pick off the people in the back. Stick the strongest on the end and that's not a problem." Mina wasn't often grateful for her dry voice, but it definitely gave her an advantage when it came to lying under pressure.

Wera stared at her for a long while. Mina kept looking forward, refusing to cave to her silent challenge.

"Sure," Wera drawled out after a doubtful snort and returned to her sketchbook.

Annoying.

🜁

Mina let them stop for lunch. They had to eat a warm meal to fend off the cold, especially as the rising elevation turned brisk into bone-chilling...

...and it would give her the opportunity to focus on anything but Sebastian's hair.

They were shocked when she told them. Even more shocked when she insisted that she make their meal. Sebastian, painfully, supported her in the effort, saying it was important for them to experience new environments. Whether it was a lie or not, Mina couldn't tell, but the others accepted his reasoning with little complaint, granting her the space to do what she needed.

Though the trees had thinned dramatically, there were still enough standing to house some wildlife. In a cluster of pines not far from where they'd rested their packs, she found a pair of snowcocks nestled in the lower branches, too heavy to escape the speed of her arrows. A small pile of firewood awaited her when she returned, assembled in a pyramid, the snow beneath it tamped down to offer a level resting spot.

Mina set the bloodied birds in the snow and kicked the wood in on itself. She pulled out the dry brush they had placed in its center and rearranged the sticks into a small pallet stack, weaving the brush throughout to give her flint the best chance to catch. She struck it and rained down a miserable amount of sparks that snuffed out as soon as they landed. Again, more sparks but no catch. Again and again, to no avail.

Of course, they fucking got me wet wood.

She threw her flint back in her pack, moving to stand and gather branches from one of the dead trees around, when the tinder erupted in a blaze before her.

The fire knocked her back on her ass with its raging, brilliant hue; the same shade as the hair of the wizard hurrying towards her.

"Sorry! Sorry!" Sebastian called. "I was trying to be sneaky, but I went overboard with the heat! I didn't mean to scare you, I—"

Mina held her hand up to silence him, eyes fixated on the fire in front of her. She couldn't feel its heat, but what used to be just swirls and flickers of gray and white flame now glowed in a shade so beautiful and so warm that bitter bile burned the back of her throat. She fought against the gnawing urge to touch it, knowing that while she would not feel its heat, she would still blister and burn.

She turned her back to them both, the fire and its maker, and set to work butchering the birds. Sebastian's footsteps crunched away in the snow shortly after.

Anger, *scorn*, rose within her.

Her hands, normally steadfast and methodical while they butchered, shook. The fire's glow taunted and teased her from behind, making her reckless in her attempts to hurry. She took off too much meat removing their skins, stabbed herself as she picked out the pin bones that normally came free with ease when she plucked, but none of her mistakes lingered. She felt no pride nor shame in her work to begin with.

She skewered the birds on her blade and turned back around to face the fire, and found the others gathered around it, basking close to its warmth. Their footsteps must have been muffled by the thousand bitter thoughts bubbling in her brain, silenced by the memory of warmth haunting her hands. How many fires had she sat in front of ignorant? What had she done to deserve to be denied this?

And why did *this* wizard have to be one to grant her it?

The dancing color of the flame enthralled her, vexed her as she lifted her sword to roast the birds above it.

"Is that sanitary?" Enoch asked.

"If it's cooked enough," Mina replied.

"What sort of bird is it?" asked Tanir.

"Snowcock."

Wera snorted, drawing Mina's attention away from the flame, a scathing glare ready to be delivered. Instead of the cartographer's thick glasses, Mina's glare landed on the trees behind her, no longer bearing snow on their needles.

Fuck.

She stood abruptly, causing the others to step back. There was no icy crunch to their stumble. Their steps sunk deep. The snow beneath them, covered just minutes before in a thin layer of ice, had turned back to powder.

She pulled her bird-burdened blade off the fire and readied it to strike.

"Ready yourselves. There's a—"

The snow erupted beneath her feet before she could finish.

A large claw snapped around her chest as a dozen crysteceans burst from the ground, mandibles gesticulating wildly as they cried out in hunger. Mina struggled against the ice crab's iron grip, trying to recover her bearings as the creature's maw snapped at the snowcocks pierced on her sword.

"Hungry, huh?" Mina snarled. "Fine then. Open wide!" She drove the point of her sword down its open throat, burying it in its soft palate for a moment to free her hands.

The crystecean thrashed in pain, swinging Mina through the air wildly. She gritted her teeth and wrenched her hands between the claw and her body. The beast had crushed a few of her ribs already. She wasn't going to let it cleave her in half as it tried to writhe away from death.

The shelled claw cracked as she pried it apart, tearing sinew and spilling its blood with little effort. Her feet touched the ground for barely a second before she ran back up its large plated body. Its meaty, cumbersome claws reached aimlessly for the blade lodged in its throat. Mina grabbed the hilt herself, the gouges in her sides painless and unhindering, as she vaulted over the creature gracefully and ripped her sword through its skull and down its back.

Mina scanned the chaos, the billows of powdered snow kicked up from the crysteceans' arrival, for Sebastian. Flashing blurs of flying claws and death cries from the creatures as the others fought back drowned into the background as she waited with bated breath to catch a glimpse of his blazing locks among the whiteout.

Instead of a glimpse, a brilliant burst of flame rendering a crystecean to ash lit her way.

Rushing there directly would be foolish. The pain would be unbearable. If the path towards him was the most effective way of routing the enemy, however...

The wind carried Mina's steps as she leaped through the air, bouncing from crab to crab at impressive speed, severing their heads from their thick-plated necks with a singular swipe of her sword. Each strike sent a shooting pain through her chest, adding to the growing discomfort from her side wounds, but she pressed on until she reached her destination — and split the crystecean in front of the wizard in two with a downward strike.

The flame building in Sebastian's palm snuffed out, his jaw falling slack at the sight of her. "Well done."

Mina bit the inside of her cheek to bear the sting of his praise. Her head was pounding, spinning. Her joints a little looser than they should be. It was a risk to take any more injury, but only a few of the beasts remained. With the wizard behind her, she could lure them towards her and slay them without harming herself; ending the battle quickly and—

A claw, four times the size of the others, rushed out from the clouds of snow behind Sebastian. Without a second thought — without a moment of hesitation or rational excuse to try and protect herself, she grabbed his collar — sending fire through her veins, and pulled him behind her. With a surge of stubbornness, determination, she fought against the searing pain and cleaved the massive claw in two.

A bone-shaking roar cleared the snow from the air as a crystecean queen reared back in agony.

Mina's knees folded underneath her, giving out against the roaring waves of agony that hammered her every muscle. She drove her sword into the ground and hung onto the cross-guard to hold herself upright, clinging onto it as much as she clung onto consciousness.

"Mina!" Sebastian's shout sounded muffled and miles away.

Her body attacked itself, punishing her for acting so selflessly, so stupid. The corners of her vision darkened as her broken ribs buried deeper into her chest. Her blood felt acidic, eating away at her as her racing heart forced it through.

"Stay— behind— me—" she grunted. Even her own voice sounded leagues underwater.

She needed to hold on for just a little longer. If she avoided getting hit for just a few minutes, or doing foolish things for no good reason, her body would heal, and she could take the queen down without fear of losing herself.

"Mina," Sebastian's voice singed the side of her cheek, deafeningly loud despite its whispered worry. She went to shout at him to stay away, working up the strength to move her mouth, but his hand was on her shoulder before her lips could even part.

Her world went dark.

🜁

Endless hunger.

Ceaseless cold.

She opened her eyes to find a behemoth charging at her, warm mouth opened wide to consume her, and dove in.

Her icy claws tore its throat apart as she dug her way through to the creature's heart. With how lovely the heat of its innards coating her leathery skin was, she could only imagine how wonderful the still-beating organ would feel in her stomach.

The beast writhed around her, muscles flexing in an attempt to expel her invasion. It was all for naught as she followed its throbbing arteries to her target, and sunk her teeth into the pulsing flesh.

One, two bites, and she swallowed its heart whole.

Yet her hunger did not subside, the heart's warmth vanished before it could reach her stomach, and the flesh around her followed suit as the crystecean queen stilled.

Endless hunger.

Ceaseless cold.

Relentless rage.

She burst from its chest, shrieking in fury.

More. Yes. More warm flesh to line her bottomless stomach would soothe her starvation, erase the aching chill from her limbs.

She landed on the queen's massive corpse and followed the pulsing trails of heat that swirled around her sight, salivating as their spasms grew larger. Her stomach cramped, making room for her next meal as she found their source.

A pathetically small creature compared to the behemoth she stood upon, but the warmth it radiated was immense. Surely, it would ease her hunger; and if it didn't the creatures that stood trembling next to it would make a lovely snack.

Her wings unfurled, and she raced through the air, faster than mountain winds, claws extended and jaw unhinged.

One of the creatures beside it shrieked as she approached, and her wings grew heavy; fatigue overpowering her hunger and forcing her eyes shut.

🜁

Mina woke up to a stabbing pain through her skull.

"Tanir!" Sir Gargic shouted.

A flash of metal swung through the blur in Mina's eyes, and she wrenched her head back, slamming into something hard as she strained against the ropes that bound her.

"What have you done to her, you monster?!" The knight held his sword to her throat.

Her eyes adjusted as much as they could, clearing her vision despite the sting behind them. She was still outside, still in the clearing though the snow had shifted dramatically. They must have tied her to a tree. Sir Gargic stood in front of her, seething with rage. An expected reaction, much like the wide-eyed stares of Wera and Enoch standing off behind him.

"Answer me!"

"Gargic! Leave her alone!" Tanir commanded, her voice breaking as she shouted. Mina turned to find the medic with tears in her eyes, looking back at her as Sebastian held her hands in his. A soft glow, the color of flame, emanated from his palms.

He was the only one not looking at her.

"Did you heal me?" Mina croaked out, her vocal cords always struggled to remember how to work after a transformation.

Tanir nodded, and Mina's stomach threatened to turn under her pitying gaze.

"A poor choice," she remarked.

"How dare you!" Sir Gargic pressed his blade into her skin. It quivered as he trembled with anger. "You owe that woman your pathetic life! Apologize!"

Mina looked down. Her body was so weak, even if she did break free from her bindings, they could kill her with little effort. She couldn't choose much in her life, at least she could choose to die without a fight.

Things would certainly be easier if she died.

"Apologize!" His grip tightened around the hilt, preparing to strike.

"She can't!"

Mina stiffened. Her heart resumed racing as she locked eyes with Tanir.

How does she—

"What do you mean she can't?" Sir Gargic spat.

"She's cursed."

Mina's throat went dry as her jaw locked up, tight and unmoving.

"Cursed?" Sir Gargic backed away, but kept his blade raised and at the ready.

"I saw it when I healed you," Tanir pulled her hands from Sebastian's and approached her. "I touched you, a small healing spell to help ease your injuries and rouse you, and I saw you; bound by barbed chains of ice. They blackened your limbs with frostbite, threatened to cave your chest in and snap your neck. And your face—" She reached up to brush her hand across her jaw. Mina pulled away as much as she could, letting Tanir stroke the air. "Who did this to you?"

The pressure in her jaw turned unbearable, the curse making damn sure it kept shut.

"A cursed maiden. A Cursed One," Enoch breathed. The look in his eyes turned from fearful to astonishment. Mina hated that look. "The beauty and the beast all in one."

Wera rubbed her chest. "Damn. I got off easy then, huh? Does the curse make you freeze everything you touch?"

The hinge of her jaw made an audible pop. Mina's throat flexed, trying to cry out in pain, but her vocal cords were rendered immobile.

"She can't answer you," Sebastian spoke up, his focus still on Tanir. "You said there were chains on her face?"

"Binding her jaw, piercing her nose and mouth, and gouging out her eyes," she replied.

Enoch snapped his fingers as a revolting spark of inspiration twinkled in his eye. "That's why you swallowed that vodka the other night like it was water!" he exclaimed. "You can't taste or smell!"

He stepped closer, Wera following suit, studying her.

"And you're not blind, so—" A knowing smile crept up Wera's face. "What color is my coat?"

The muscles in her jaw relaxed.

"Gray," Mina answered to stretch it out.

"Enoch's scarf?"

"Dark gray."

"Sebastian's hair?"

Mina paused, gazing at his blazing locks. They were the reason she was in this mess, the reason she had lost all sense of self-preservation. Yet she harbored no hatred at the sight of them.

"Also gray. Wizard," she called out to him.

He finally looked at her, expression achingly unreadable.

"Continue straight up this path until sunset, if you're quick, you'll reach a natural arch that bridges across two mountains. Make camp before it, not after. It's the marker to Rabbet's Pass— "

"We're not leaving you," Sebastian interrupted.

Mina flinched as a sharp pain shot through her chest.

"Are you insane, Windenhofer?!" Sir Gargic protested. "You saw the monster she turns into!"

"Yes, a heatseeker, but her transformation was my fault." Sebastian's gaze never left hers, and though she feared its sting — afraid of the pain it could bring sending her back into that insatiable abyss — she could not look away.

"Isolation. Space. Distance." He scrunched his nose in disappointment. "Even now, we aren't heeding your warnings."

He gestured to the others surrounding her. They all took a few steps back.

Sebastian continued, "You survive, correct? Sleep in the cold, hunt and forage for your food—"

"But wouldn't staying in the commorancy be surviving as well?" Wera interjected. "Especially with all the dangers in these mountains?"

"Not for her," he answered. "We've grown used to it, depend on it, but it's still a luxury. Even more so for someone who could stand for hours in these freezing winds and never once feel the cold. Isn't that right, Mina?"

She stayed silent. Watching. Unsure where Sebastian's speech was leading.

"Sir Gargic," he addressed the knight, his tone shifting to something formal and snipping. The hum behind it now commanding instead of charming. "Considering how much back and forth I had with the Courts of Lanholde over my own contract for this expedition, I assume that Mina's contract has a flexibility clause built into it, allowing The Crown and their appointed liaisons to amend it without renegotiation?"

Sir Gargic reached into his pack, pulled out her contract, and scanned it quickly. "Yes, it does."

"Enoch, lend Sir Gargic your quill. I need him to add a clause to her contract."

"What are you doing?" Mina's question fell on deaf ears as Sir Gargic prepared to take Sebastian's notation. Her fear accelerated her healing. In just a minute more she'd be strong enough to break these binds and seize that contract from their hands. The ropes creaked as she strained against them.

"Break free from those binds, Mina, and I'll render you to ash."

She stilled immediately. There was no bluff behind his threat — delivered without looking at her — only promise.

"What would you like me to add?" Sir Gargic asked.

"In addition to the clauses and conditions of employment, the alpinist shall follow the expedition leader, Master Sebastian Windenhofer's, commands until the completion of her contract, or the removal of the curse placed upon her — whichever comes first — to the best of her ability."

Beneath the ropes, threads slithered. Invisible. Tangible only to her. The Fae's Folly wrapped over her arms, her legs, across her chest, around her neck, spreading as Sir Gargic wrote.

Sebastian locked eyes with her, "People break contracts all the time. But not you."

Mina inhaled sharply as the threads tightened, secured by the final dot of punctuation.

"That word is binding."

Either he was extremely clever, or he knew exactly what she was. Though the pressure of the binding faded quickly, sinking deep into her skin to root itself to her nerves, her bones, her psyche, Mina scolded herself for underestimating him, for getting distracted by the promise of color and change.

The wizard was far more dangerous than she thought.

Cruel To Be Kind

Sebastian's first command was to lead them to a safe spot along the path where they could set up the commorancy.

His second was to patch herself up inside of it.

The third, to eat lunch with them.

Innocuous things. Easy things.

Trying to lure her into a false sense of security.

Disappointment, resentment, self-loathing pestered Mina's thoughts. She ran through Sebastian's addendum over and over again, looking for a loophole, but without the contract as a whole in her hands, she couldn't know the full scope of how screwed she was.

Isolation. Space. Distance. They were given to her as she led them to safer ground and was coerced into the commorancy, along with eyes following her every move as if she were a sideshow act... or a monster.

The latter was more accurate.

Mina walked straight into the infirmary, determined to finish Sebastian's stupid to-do list quickly and regain some sliver of freedom.

"The antiseptics are labeled in the glass door cabinet to the left of the—"

She let the door slam in Tanir's face and stalked over to the cabinet she'd pointed out. The antiseptics were numerous, labeled with fine script handwriting, most of their names foreign to her. Mina grabbed the strongest one she recognized and removed her breastplate carefully. The twin gouges that framed her rib cage were slow to heal after the curse's damage, the flesh still flayed open, edges of her skin raw and ridged from the crystecean's claw.

A cluster of small gasps followed the drawn-out squeak of the door opening. The others entered to address their injuries, minor sprains and cuts, from what Mina gathered.

She uncorked the antiseptic with her teeth, spit the cork onto the counter, and poured the thin liquid on her open wounds. Mina felt nothing. Wera and Enoch hissed out the sting instead. The cuts bubbled and fizzed as Mina set the bottle down and riffled through a drawer labeled "sutures" for a hooked needle and some thread.

"Dear *Gods*," Enoch warbled under his breath as she pinched the edges of her wound together and sunk the needle into her flesh.

"Enoch," Tanir chastised quietly. "You're turning gray. Look away."

"She's just... sewing herself. No pain meds, or numbing cream, or—" Enoch's ramblings dipped off into a gag.

"Look away, dumbass!" Wera scolded. "We've still got a shit ton of hiking to do today, and the last thing we need is to carry your passed-out pansy ass the rest of the way up."

We? The wizard would command me to carry him. Or carry all of you as if I'm your goddamn draft horse.

She felt the tug of his command with every stitch, tension tightening and loosening, guiding her hand like marionette strings. The puppet master himself left the room quickly, Sir Gargic in tow. Perhaps he could hear the string of curses she threw his way in her mind.

"Have you had medical training?" Tanir asked as Mina tied off the final stitch. "Your sutures are impeccably neat."

She didn't reply. Instead, she turned her attention to her breastplate and ran her fingers over the large holes the wings of her monstrous form had torn through the back.

"Check that cedar chest in the corner. There should be white thread in there," Tanir offered as she tied off the bandage wrapped around Enoch's bicep. "A thicker needle, too."

Mina kicked open the chest, holding her strength back from shattering it, but still hit hard enough to vent some frustration before she set to work patching up the torn leather.

Five years this breastplate went with not a scratch on it, then less than three days in on this cursed expedition and the wizard had her almost tear it in two. Mina could chastise herself up and down — was chastising herself up and down — for not reading that contract, but she had signed dozens of contracts like it before. The real issue was that damned *Sebastian*.

Her needle grazed the edge of her pointer finger.

Why didn't he just burn her alive when she turned? Or void the contract and tackle the Peaks on his own? Their commorancy negated most of the need for her expertise anyways, and her familiarity with the summits was definitely not worth the risk of her transforming again.

And with the amount of pain she'd undergone so far, that risk was high.

Perhaps he'd been waiting for an opportunity like this? That smile he gave after finding her struggling to leave the commorancy. The way he spat back her own words. He knew that the contract bound her to their expedition by more than legal means, but the vacant look in his eyes as he made the amendment... Shouldn't there have been some sick glimmer of joy if he'd gotten what he was after?

"He means you no harm," Tanir spoke, pulling Mina out of her thoughts. She looked up from her sewing to find that only she and the medic remained in the infirmary. "Back in the day, Sebastian wound up being poisoned by those basilisks because he didn't want to kill them to get their venom. In fact, he was hoping to domesticate them."

"So, he's looking to make me his pet?" Mina tied off her stitch and snapped the thread between her teeth.

Tanir knocked over a few of the medicine jars she was needlessly reorganizing. "No! That wasn't what I was—"

"The patching is done." Mina slipped on her breastplate. "Now, lunch." She walked out of the infirmary without another word, leaving Tanir sputtering.

The medic scrambled out the door to follow behind her, hurried footsteps creaking across the hardwood floor of the hall as they headed into the kitchen. Wera and Enoch were already at the table, eating stew and talking lightly. They jumped as Mina slammed the door open.

"H-hey, Mina!" Enoch squeaked out. "Tanir! Sebastian and Sir Gargic seemed to be running a bit behind, so we went and placed an order with the kitchen. Rabbit stew with mushrooms and carrots."

Mina slammed her ass down on the bench and the enchanted cookware slid a bowlful down to her. She grabbed it, brought it to her lips, and guzzled the stew, barely chewing the meat and vegetables before swallowing. Tasteless as always, but it went down easy much to Mina's subdued surprise.

Being able to eat without pain wasn't worth the price of becoming a wizard's dog, however.

"So, Mina, when your beast form—"

Mina washed down the last of the stew with whatever liquid filled her tankard and smacked the empty cup onto the table, cutting Enoch off.

The command released; the gentle pull of the threads vanishing, an all-over itch taking its place. Mina stood and stomped out of the kitchen, following the curse's insistence to leave the commorancy and return to the frigid mountain landscape.

Without the wizard and his hair of flames distracting her, she'd at least be able to properly scout the area before they set off; be able to pretend she had some freedom running up the mountainside, feeling the wind against her face. Maybe she'd find a reason as to why crysteceans were hunting this far south to take her mind off things.

"Mina," Sebastian called out behind her. The hairs on the back of her neck raised, but she kept on walking.

"Mina, stop."

The invisible threads returned, wrapping around her legs and rooting her to the floor.

"I patched up. I ate," she spoke loud enough for him to hear. She wouldn't turn to address him even if she could. Even if his vibrant hair tempted her in the corner of her eye. "I'm leaving now."

"Good," Sir Gargic spat as he walked around Sebastian and into the kitchen.

Sebastian remained silent.

He had to be studying her. She could almost feel his eyes darting over her back. Mina kept looking ahead, even though some idiotic little thought in the back of her brain urged her to see if his gaze was just as vacant as before, or if it was back to its stinging kindness.

Why should she care how he looked at her?

Why was a part of her *searching* for the sting?

"Be back in twenty minutes," he said with no affliction, and the tension binding her legs released.

🜁

Mina disappeared into the wind. Let the mountain gales guide her steps, become her limbs, fill her lungs. Her mind was still her own, still ruminating, rebuking herself as it searched the snowscape for answers to questions it was too afraid to ask. As she ran along a mountain ridge she got a bird's-eye view of their path ahead and found the snow puckered, rippled from the crysteceans' burrows.

She stopped before the trail did, tugged back by threads, signaling that time was up all too soon.

She held firm for a moment, waiting for the misty clouds ahead to clear so she could take one final glimpse, get one final guess at how far the damage had spread. The threads tightened, applying more force, digging into her flesh with invisible strands to the point where she was sure she'd find herself riddled with thin cuts.

The cloud cover parted for the briefest moment, showing Rabbet's Pass and the snow surrounding it just as disturbed. The threads whipped her around and sent her legs running. Lifting her knees, guiding her footsteps, robbing her of choice. Enraged, Mina took control of her own facilities, running faster than such shallow bindings could manage.

She arrived back at the campsite just as Sebastian was condensing the commorancy, and the others gathered round a squawking Sir Gargic. Mina slipped into the boughs of the pine they all stood under unnoticed. She returned in twenty minutes, technically. The wizard never clarified that he needed to see her return.

"Everyone says 'the enemy of my enemy is my friend', but real soldiers know that it doesn't fucking matter how nasty the guy is you're both against, if someone hates you that much they'll stab you in the back," Sir Gargic pontificated below her.

"Mina doesn't hate us that much," Wera, of all people, replied. "She definitely doesn't like us, but I wouldn't go so far as to say hate."

"She looks at us like we're flies on shit," he scoffed.

"Yeah, but she saved our asses, didn't she? Got herself all fucked up keeping Sebastian from becoming The Headless Spellcaster."

"And landed herself as the wizard's errand girl for her troubles." He looked at Sebastian. "Speaking of. Looks like this plan of yours to keep that monster under control didn't work there, Windenhofer."

Mina hated the idea of complying with Sebastian's commands without a fight, but she hated cocky condescension even more.

Sebastian stuffed the pocket watch he'd been staring at back in his pants pocket, and looked up just in time to catch her dropping silently behind Sir Gargic; unbeknownst to any of the others. She kept her focus on Sebastian's hair instead of his eyes, but she still felt the sting from his pleased expression pricking at her corneas.

"What plan?" she asked.

The others shrieked, drew their weapons, and attacked on instinct. Mina tilted her head to the right to avoid Enoch's daggers, then to the left for Wera's ink, and caught the axe Tanir threw just in time to swing it back around and block Sir Gargic's blade.

"Is the path clear for us to head out, Mina?" Sebastian asked as calmly as if he were inquiring about the weather.

The others, finally processing their failed attacks — and who they were attacking — glanced between the two of them, slack-jawed and terrified. A sizzle behind Mina as Wera's splattered more-than-just-ink ate away at the wood, preluded the squeak of the tree's trunk collapsing. Mina held her free hand up, catching the falling pine as they all jumped back.

It was thankfully a young one, just under a ton in weight. Any heavier and her arm would be visibly shaking, which wouldn't help much when it came to intimidation.

"The crysteceans shook up the snow all the way to Rabbet's Pass. There are pitfalls hidden everywhere and about of foot of powder we'll have to hike against while navigating around them."

"Would it help if I melted the snow as we went?"

"Not unless you're looking to take an ice slide down into a bottomless pit."

"Refreezes that quickly, huh?" His eyebrows lifted in slight surprise. "Good to know." He hooked a thumb towards the trail. "Lead the way."

His command tugged at her limbs. Mina placed the tree down and threw Tanir's axe in front of its owner's feet before the threads could force her to.

"Cartographer," she called for Wera to join her as she started off up the path.

"Actually, Mina," Sebastian interjected. "I need to speak with Wera about handling her more acidic paints carefully. Stay next to Sir Gargic until we make camp for the night."

"What?" Mina stopped, the threads of his command holding her in wait until the knight took his place by her side.

"I'm keeping a close eye on you, beastie," Sir Gargic growled into her ear.

How dare he.

Mina glared at Sebastian and bit her tongue to still her rage. Biting back at the pompous knight wouldn't be nearly as satisfying as conveniently forgetting where one of the pitfalls was and letting him drown in frost.

Sebastian averted his eyes and quickly pulled Wera to the back of the group.

Coward.

"Come on, beastie, let's get to walking," Sir Gargic said, bumping her shoulder purposefully as he passed her. "You've already wasted enough of our time today."

They sunk into the soft snow slowly, pushing up the rising elevation against pounds and pounds of extra weight. Their bodies already tired from the fight, their breathing quickly turned heavy; the effort of their slow shuffle exacerbated by the winding trail around the pitfalls.

For her past expeditions, the rise to Rabbet's Pass provided a good assessment of their endurance, tested the quality of their footwear, the strength of their resolve. In these conditions, the path could be considered torture. Even Mina could feel her legs starting to tire.

Then again, her legs had also been forced to shift from plantigrade to digitigrade and back again in a matter of minutes.

Still, Sebastian's merry band kept pace, marching through the snow to a dragging beat. Like ants carrying meal scraps back to their colony.

"I'm getting sick of this, beastie." Sir Gargic huffed as Mina took a sharp turn to the right instead of continuing forward.

"Sick of what?" she asked. "The climb? Then you should head back to the Harrow and find another path."

He growled in disgust. "I'm sick of you trying to trick us."

"Trick you? How have I *tricked* you?"

"How have you—" he barked out a laugh, "How haven't you tricked us?! Here we are thinking that you're just some ill-mannered hermit, when this entire time you've been a monster waiting for the chance to kill us. You've even managed to convince The Crown— *My King*— that you're nothing more than a sheltered maiden!"

How dare he.

"Is that why the wizard put you here?" Mina seethed. "To keep an eye out for my tricks?"

"I insisted." Sir Gargic huffed and puffed, his anger exasperating his breathing even further. "You might have him fooled, but it'll be a cold day in Hell before I let a monster make a mockery of me."

"I haven't fooled *anyone.*" Her fingers ached to sink into his eyes and pluck them from their sockets. "The wizard's a fool all on his own."

"Save your excuses, beastie. I ain't buying," he chuckled cruelly. "Just like I'm not buying this little ruse of yours."

"Ruses, tricks, fools. Spit your accusation out already, shit beard."

Sir Gargic smiled. "Those 'pitfalls'. Surely, they would leave a pucker in the ground." He stuck his craggy-nailed finger in her face. "You're having us walk in these nonsensical patterns to tire us out." He stepped away from her, striding off her path to walk straight up the summit.

Mina dug her heels into the ground to brace herself against the invisible threads urging her towards him.

"Knight," Mina warned.

He waved to her condescendingly, twiddling his fingers like a princess saying goodbye to her courtiers, and continued walking.

"Sir Gargic?" Sebastian called, "What's going on?"

"That *thing* is a liar, is what's going on!"

How dare he.

The wind blew through her empty fingers. Before he could even blink, she could tear off his lips and silence that hideous mouth of his forever.

"I told you, Sebastian, *it's* playing us."

How dare he.

All she had to do was let the threads pull her towards him. If she was clever enough, she could make it look like an accident. See, Wizard? See how the knight's neck is twisted, back of his skull caved in, brains and blood staining the snow and rock? It's all because of you. Because you—

I can't think like that.

Sir Gargic kept hissing, "*It's*—"

The pulse of her building bloodlust was interrupted by an echoing crunch — hollow, haunting — followed by the dull roar of hundreds of pounds of snow falling; punctuated by Sir Gargic's scream as the ground bottomed out beneath him.

The binding pulled taut around her waist, and Mina flew forward after him, hurdling down into the collapsing cavern.

"You arrogant fucking asshole!" Mina shouted over his screams. "Still think this is a fucking trick, you worthless sack of shit?!"

The knight gave no response. His screams stopped as his panicked scrambling turned into boneless flailing against the whipping winds.

"And now you're fucking unconscious?!" Mina twisted into a dive, aiding gravity and the pull of Sebastian's command to bridge the distance between them. The ground closing in, sharp, icy stalagmites waited to embrace them. The hole spread too wide for her to reach the walls, and with the binds demanding that she stay next to Sir Gargic, there was only one solution to keep herself from becoming skewered meat.

Mina grabbed Sir Gargic by his collar and tossed him, straining against the rushing winds, back towards the top. The threads yanked her up, negating the physics of her falling, to follow him. At the apex of her rise, where the contrasting forces balanced out, Mina used her momentum to kick him in the chest: hard.

There was no relief in volleying his limp, useless mass, only more anger. The constant kicking and pivoting of her body to strike him over and over again dizzied her, and deepened the lingering ache in her muscles. She let out a guttural scream as they reached the precipice, launching him one final time into the wide, cloudy sky. Mina flipped herself over him, drove her heel down into his chest, and landed them both back on the path, right in the middle of Sebastian's troop.

"Mina!" they gasped.

She caught her breath in heaving gulps as she loomed over Sir Gargic's unconscious body.

Tanir took a step forward. "Is he—"

"He's fine," she growled as she grabbed him and slung him over her shoulder. She turned her back to them and moved to retake her place at the front. "Let's go."

"Mina," Sebastian called after her.

She kept walking.

"Thank you for jumping in after him."

Mina should have kept on moving. It was getting close to sunset. She was tired, aching, and her thoughts were sinking into a murderous mire of muck that would be hard to pull herself out of. But the shot of pain his apology sent through her jaw—

How dare he.

—was just too much.

She whipped around and locked eyes with him. "I. Did. Not. Jump." She stalked towards him while the others parted in fear of her ire. "I was *pulled.*"

Sebastian swallowed, but stood his ground. "Pulled?"

Mina threw Sir Gargic at him, let the threads pull her along with him, and caught the unconscious knight over Sebastian's shoulder, just as he ducked.

"'Stay next to Sir Gargic until we make camp for the night,'" she snarled in his face. His breath billowed tenfold. Ice formed on his jacket from where her arm rested heavily against it. Fear, confusion, quickly gave way to realization. Sobering sadness clouded his gaze.

Good. Let him feel the guilt of his carelessness.

Mina swung Sir Gargic around, slung him over her shoulder, and resumed their hike.

It took a minute for the soft crunch of their footsteps to follow behind her.

🜁

There was no anger, relief, sadness — just familiar numbness at the sight of the massive arch marking the start of Rabbet's Pass.

Mina dropped Sir Gargic onto the ground for Tanir to fuss over while Sebastian set up the commorancy. She'd definitely broken a few of his ribs, and unless the medic was near master level, he'd have more bruises than clear flesh for a while. Disappointingly, his breath was too even for one of his ribs to have punctured his lung. If one had he'd remember her wrath with every miserable breath.

She stood off to the side, watching them in her peripheral as the light shifted; the sun sinking towards the horizon. It was slow at first, then the color of the world changed all at once. Mina rubbed her eyes as the snow, the mountains, everything tinted in the alluring warm glow that colored Sebastian's hair and burst forth from flames.

She looked around for the source, expecting a massive wave of fire heading towards them, and as she glanced up at the sky, she lost herself.

The sky burned. A glorious blaze more beautiful than anything she'd ever seen. Did it always turn this color? Was it an ill omen, or something that only she was able to see? She ached with the urge to scale the nearest mountain top, to climb as high as she could to touch the brilliant hue and bathe in it.

Why today was she given this gift? Why couldn't it have been on a day not marred by her suffering? Something stirred inside her chest, and an unfamiliar pressure pushed against her eyes.

Why did her body want to cry? She wasn't in any pain.

"Mina."

She kept gazing into the molten clouds, ignoring the wizard.

"Come inside and eat dinner with us," he said.

His command pulled her towards the tent, tore her focus from the heavens, but left her with just a tent flap to lash out at as Sebastian left her behind.

Interlude

The Unwilling Puppet Master

Amber light coated Sebastian's palm as he held the spigot, heating the water flowing from it just below boiling. It stung as he splashed his face, rinsing away the sweat, the grime, but not the guilt. He rubbed the cleanser in circles, focusing on the repeated rhythmic motion, and rinsed once his skin felt raw. He grimaced at his reflection as he toweled off.

He still felt dirty.

"It'll be alright, 'Bastian." He ran a hand through his hair, fixing the errant copper strands as he spoke to himself. "Now we know how powerful her bond to the contract is and that we have to be thoughtful when giving commands. It's alright to make mistakes. This is an experiment." He let his forehead fall against the mirror and exhaled. "A really, really, shitty experiment."

He closed his eyes and saw storm clouds. Mina's gray eyes dark, with rage, bore through him. The chill of her arm on his shoulder sent a shiver down his spine even in its memory. He couldn't remember the last time he felt the cold. Even surrounded by the ice and snow as they climbed, the air felt as temperate as a spring day.

His breath fogged up the mirror. Perhaps he should dress more warmly for the rest of the journey. At this rate, he'd have his first case of frostbite well before he'd have any real breakthroughs on what to do about her curse.

"She was able to eat lunch painlessly," he reminded himself. "And can look me in the eye when she wants to tear out my throat so—" He straightened up, inhaling deeply as he did, and nodded at his reflection. "It's a start."

He grabbed a thicker cardigan out of the back of his closet, not knowing just how cold Mina's aura could get, and headed down to the kitchen, determination restored.

The door handle was cooler than normal, the kitchen itself even colder, as if the chill of oncoming Fall had slipped in through some unknown crack in the commorancy's construct.

Even though everyone, save for Sir Gargic, sat around the kitchen table, the room was unpleasantly silent. Wera, Enoch, and Tanir still wore their coats as they worked; Enoch scribbling in his journal, Tanir sewing what looked to be a new pair of gloves, Wera inking the details on one of her maps. His stomach knotted up.

They never worked in the kitchen.

Mina, the source of the chill and his crew's detachment, sat unmoving, still in her blood-spattered armor. If it weren't for the occasional blink, Sebastian would have thought her a porcelain mannequin: face truly expressionless, eyes dull, nearly lacking that telltale spark of life.

So vastly differently from the raging storm that threatened to descend upon him just hours ago.

"You're all busy this evening," Sebastian remarked as he shut the kitchen door behind him. The others looked up from their tasks like children caught playing with matches. "Work couldn't wait until after we ate?"

"I figured it best not to waste time while we waited for you to join us. Enoch and Tanir agreed." Wera smiled apologetically as she capped her inkwell. "Plus, after a day like today, I'm sure Mina appreciated the quiet. Right, Meens?"

Mina stared at her blankly. "Meens?"

"What? Don't like the nickname?"

Mina ignored her question and turned towards him as he took his seat at the head of the table, looking at him without making eye contact. A new habit. One that only deepened the freshly carved pit in his stomach.

"Dinner?" she asked.

"Right." He gave her a small smile to try and soothe her ire, a nervous habit since childhood he'd never been quite able to shake, before addressing the cookware, "Kitchen, the drawing straws, please. Just five of them."

Five wooden sticks appeared on his place mat, the middle of each painted with a different colored band. He scooped them up, hiding the colors in his palm, and shifted them around before holding his fist out towards the center of the table.

"Alright, everyone. Three... two... one. Draw!"

Wera, Enoch, and Tanir raced to grab a straw. Mina did not.

"Erm," Sebastian cleared his throat. "You're supposed to grab a straw when I say draw, Mina."

"For what?" she asked.

"It's how we decide who chooses what for dinner." He tilted the straws towards her. It made sense that she'd be confused, it wasn't as if she'd have anything to draw straws for alone in the woods. "Go on. Take one."

A small grimace barely crinkled her face as she reached out and grabbed a straw.

Sebastian pulled his arm back and looked at the green-banded straw in his hand.

"Now what did everyone get?"

Wera held hers up proudly. "Green!"

"I got blue," Enoch pouted.

Tanir shimmed in her seat joyfully, giggling, "Red for me."

They all looked at Mina. She begrudgingly held up her purple-banded stick. "Dark gray."

"Right. Sorry." Sebastian considered setting himself on fire, but plastered on his brightest smile instead. "You got purple, which means you get to pick dessert!"

Mina looked away with a sneer.

His expression fell into a tight-lipped grin. Nothing good would come from showing her his disappointment. He turned to Wera and held up his straw. "Looks like I'm picking a side dish with you."

Wera gave him a sympathetic frown back, shooting Mina a sidelong glare.

"Let's go with honey-glazed ginger boar as our entrée," Tanir said.

"An excellent choice." Sebastian pointed his straw at Wera. "You pick first."

"Hmmm." She wrapped one of her curls around her finger in thought. "How about cabbage, chive, and beansprout gyoza?"

"I'll go with roasted pumpkin and potatoes then. Enoch?"

"Cider and water," he answered.

"Really?" Wera teased. "Only cider?"

"Oh, I'm sorry. I don't enjoy drinking glorified paint-thinner recreationally," he teased back, rolling his eyes so dramatically Sebastian couldn't help but laugh.

"And Mina?" he asked. "What would you like for dessert?"

She kept her attention on the straw in her hand, twirling it back and forth through her fingers. "Nothing."

"I'd still like for you to pick something."

The straw stopped between her middle and ring fingers. Mina looked up at him.

"Pick a dessert, Mina," he instructed, keeping his tone jovial, encouraging. Not demanding or controlling. Just a gentle nudge against the curse. There was no real harm in ordering dessert, even if it wasn't necessary to survive.

An audible crack rang out as her jaw fell open. Her brow furrowed slightly as she spoke, "Mulberry pie."

Tanir shivered and scooted away from Mina, towards him. Wera pulled her shawl tighter.

"Mulberry pie it is," Sebastian said lightheartedly, even though his skin crawled with regret.

The cookware sprung to life, and Mina returned to staring off into the distance.

"So," he turned his attention to Tanir, "how is Sir Gargic?"

"Four broken ribs, a shattered collarbone, whiplash, patches of frostbite, and his chest is painted bright red with bruises," Tanir sighed. "I used a healing incantation to set the bones back in place and put him to bed. The poultice I spread over his torso should accelerate the healing process of the rest while he sleeps."

"Serves him right for being an ass," Wera remarked. "I can't believe he thought she was lying about those snow pockets."

"You can't?" Mina drolled.

"Mhmm. You're a pretty direct person. If you wanted to kill us, you'd just kill us."

"What makes you believe that?"

"The fact that you haven't already tried to does." Wera sipped her cider. "Heatseeker Mina doesn't count as a try, by the way."

"It doesn't?"

"No, it doesn't," Sebastian agreed.

Mina didn't bother to look at him. "Huh."

All he had to do was grin and bear her scorn for a while. He deserved it. Once he could show her that she could trust him and that he only wanted to help her, they'd be back to the beginnings of banter and camaraderie.

They'd be back to last night.

A different chill passed over his arms. Like cool water on a hot summer day. The sensation that lingered longer than the pain after he'd been thrown awake.

He shouldn't be thinking about *that* now.

"Plus, you could have easily killed Sir Gargic while kicking him out of the pitfall," Tanir added, bringing Sebastian's thoughts back to the present. "I saw the placement of your strikes from the boot print bruises you left. You aimed for his upper chest to minimize the damage, didn't you?"

"No. It was the best place to strike to build momentum."

Sebastian held his tongue.

Targeting his core would have been better. Would have leveraged his center of gravity to her benefit.

Why are you lying?

Was it another tactic to keep people away from her? To keep them from getting too close? A calculating, feigned indifference built up from years of hurting others or—

The scream of pain that ripped from her throat at his touch echoed through his memory. The sting of the gale-force wind that blew him back as she transformed, a phantom pulsing on his skin.

—or from years of others hurting her.

The arrival of their meal pulled him from the ice and snow and sound of crystecean claws. His stomach was far too empty and growling after all the exertion of the day to ruminate. He could save it for later when he poured through book after book to try and figure out just what the hell she was.

The boar was beautifully glazed, and the gyoza balanced between crispy and soft. He hummed happily as the roasted pumpkin melted on his tongue. Nearly losing every limb and definitely losing hours of sleep to get the materials to construct the kitchen had been well worth it.

Mina's frantic scraping and hurried chewing, however, brought him right out of his culinary bliss.

The food had been out for five minutes, and her plate was a little over halfway cleared. She crushed the remaining gyoza and vegetables into a mash — massacring them as if they had murdered her entire family — and lifted the plate, pouring the mixture into her mouth and clearing the last of her meal in one large gulp.

"Mina?" Sebastian called as she stood.

She stilled, back to him. Her hands balled up into fists at her sides. "I ate dinner."

"I can see that," he huffed a laugh. If that was how she ate dinner, she could make a killing competing in a tavern's eating contest. "At least stay for dessert."

Mina sat back down immediately and a slice of mulberry pie slid in front of her.

"I'm not hungry," she said.

"Take a few bites for my sake."

They all shivered as the temperature in the room dipped lower. Mina locked eyes with him, the swirling storm clouds back in the gray of her irises, and picked up a forkful without looking. She took a bite and chewed, slowly. The muscles in her face tensed.

He held his breath.

She swallowed roughly and took another bite, opening her mouth wide enough to flaunt red-stained teeth as she placed the pie piece on her tongue. Juice started to seep out of the corners of her mouth, painting her pale lips scarlet and dripping down her chin in two fine lines like those that framed a puppet's jaw. Too much juice for such a small piece of pie.

Sebastian's stomach lurched as a pool of blood trickled out when she went in for more.

"T-that's enough," he rasped.

Mina dropped her fork on the table.

"I'm sorry. I didn't—"

She held up a hand to silence him as she took a drink, washing the blood down with water and a sickening gulp.

"There's a tonic in the infirmary you can gargle," Tanir said, a slight shiver in her voice. "It's in the ice box in a squat glass bottle with a spring of neem embossed on the bottle."

"I have to stay for dessert," Mina replied, her monotone voice hoarse.

"No, you don't," Sebastian said, hopefully reversing his command.

She stood to exit.

"But you will stay in the commorancy tonight!" he spat out more desperate than intended, but quickly collected himself. "And spend some time with us in the third-floor library."

He had wanted to wait until after dinner was finished to issue the command, when her stomach was full and her mind a little more open to their arrangement after another painless meal, but—

The temperature plummeted, turning their breath into white puffs and snuffing out the ribbons of steam from their dinner.

"What?" Mina hissed.

"We need to discuss the details for tomorrow's leg of the journey," Sebastian replied. He breathed deeply, steadying his voice, bolstering false confidence in the face of her fury.

"Then discuss it now."

"I'd rather do it in the library."

He focused on keeping his teeth from chattering as he held Mina's gaze, baring the fierce focus that wished to tear him apart. There was that spark of life, there was the emotion — humanity — that was missing from her face. Why was only anger allowed to show?

His friends and his cookware trembled as they played unwilling spectators to their frigid staring contest. Sebastian could feel frost forming on the tips of his eyelashes.

He smiled, sadly, sympathetically. She had to know he didn't want it to be like this. That he was only trying to help.

Mina scowled at it, turned on her heels, and left, slamming the door behind her.

"S-s-sebastian?" Enoch stammered.

"Yes, Enoch?"

"If-f-f you're t-t-trying t-to freeze to d-d-death, could you do it when we're n-not in the room?"

"A-and when we're n-not e-eating?" Wera added.

He looked down to find the top of his water frozen and his dinner cold as ice.

"Sorry." He conjured three small warming domes and sat them over their plates with a flick of his wrist.

"Don't forget to heat up yours," Tanir said as she warmed her hands over it.

Sebastian sighed and looked down at his plate. The boar had lost its sheen, the pumpkin looked like bland mush. "I'm not hungry right now."

"Sebastian—"

"Don't worry. I'll eat something a little later, Tani." He stood, needing to be anywhere else but the kitchen; needing to do something to ease the shame and guilt bubbling in his stomach. "Finish your meals, and make sure to have some pie. I'll be in my study."

△

The chill in the air spread throughout the commorancy, as did the destruction of furniture and screams of rage echoing from Mina's room. Sebastian made a mental note to cast a restoration spell on it tomorrow before they left for the next leg.

He flipped through the piles of books and scrolls he pulled from this personal collection, searching for information on heatseekers, fae, chains made of ice— anything that would help shed some light on her curse, what she was, why it happened...

...how he could break it and end this awful, awful contract amendment his stupid, stressed brain came up with.

Every wail and crunch of wood had him fighting to stay seated. To ignore her tantrum in the hopes that she would calm down on her own. Getting up and going to her would ease his conscience for a moment, until she tore his throat out with her bare hands and he felt even guiltier having made her into a murderer.

A knock at his study door interrupted this third rereading of a paragraph on baobhan sith.

"Enter," he called.

Tanir opened the door, bundled up in her winter gear, with a mug in hand.

"I brought some tea to help soothe your stomach," she said.

Sebastian straightened up, rolling out his long too hunched over shoulders, and gave her a small smile as he took the mug from her. "Thank you."

He took a sip and grimaced. The tea had gone cold.

Tanir sighed. "It was piping hot when I left the infirmary."

He coated the palms of his hand with a low flame to warm it back up. "I know it was."

The walls shook as a loud bang rang out, followed by yet another primal scream.

"You know I normally don't doubt your decisions, but this—" Tanir gestured towards the door as she mulled over her words. "What is your intention?"

"To break her curse," he said, voice coming out much more exhausted than he expected.

"Alright. Considering the traditional 'true love's kiss' route seems a bit far-fetched, how does having her bound to follow your every command help with that? Taking away her freedom like this is—"

"Cruel?" he offered. "Horrible? Manipulative?"

Tanir shrugged her shoulders uncomfortably. "Your words, not mine."

"It's an experiment," he said, reiterating the same explanation he'd been repeating like a mantra in his mind. "She can't tell us about her curse, so I'm using the commands to find out more about it. Test its structure to try and find a weakness."

Tanir scrunched her nose in scrutiny. "Is it really worth all this anguish?"

Sebastian's brow furrowed. Her unexpected disapproval stung.

"What?"

"I understand using the contract to keep her heatseeker form in check. I'm not sure if that's how it works, but I trust you," she explained. "However to go this far when she was living just fine with her curse for so long seems... unkind."

Sebastian's chest grew tight, palms warmer than he cared for as he clenched his fists. "And letting her live alone, isolated, because she's afraid of hurting others, isn't?"

Tanir was the understanding one. Surely she—

"If it means causing her pain and you to hate yourself, then yes." She nodded. "It is much kinder to leave her be."

The notion didn't sit well on his skin, in his bones, deeper than he expected.

"I can't."

"Why?"

Because my chest feels like it's going to cave in at the thought.

"Because."

"The woman tore the inside of her mouth and throat to shreds because you forced her to eat dessert," Tanir snipped. "You better have a better reason than 'because'."

"I didn't know!" Sebastian set his mug down with a clatter. "If I had known, I never would have told her to do it! I never would have listened to Gargic and forced her to hike beside him! I—" He placed his head in his hands and pulled at his hair. "I hate this."

Tanir let out a heavy sigh and rested a hand on his head, fingertips soothingly scratching his scalp. "Then why not let her go? She has a point. If she sits down with Wera and Enoch and tells them the way forward, what to look out for, we should be quite capable of making it up the mountains on our own."

It would be easier. *Gods*, would it be easier. He could let her go back to her woods, think up some other clever way to help her out, maybe send a more experienced member of his guild her way to assist. All actionable items.

All of them a type of failure.

Why did he care if he failed her? He barely knew her.

The strike of a violin answered where words couldn't. A fierce allegro replaced the sounds of rage and destruction, conveying a fury deeper and more complex than Mina's screams could.

Tanir's hand stilled on his head. She stared at the door to his study, confused.

"That's why," Sebastian answered. His chest loosened a bit, Mina's playing making it easier to breathe somehow. "When you saw her — the manifestation of her curse — you mentioned her eyes, nose, and mouth were covered, but not her ears. Were they uncovered when you saw her?"

She thought back. "Yes, I believe they were."

"I don't think whoever cursed her would have been so careless. Why alter all of her other senses but let her hear without some sort of impairment?" he questioned, drumming his fingers on his desktop as the current results of his subconscious ruminations spilled out. "And if she is so unfeeling, so withdrawn, how would she be able to play something with so much depth?"

He shrugged. "Sure, you can hear her anger, but there's worry and fear and sadness in that melody as well." He pulled his distant focus from the door to Tanir. "You can hear it, can't you?"

Tanir closed her eyes and listened for a moment.

"I can," she said, voice a bit dryer, eyes watery when she reopened them. "How did you know she played?"

"I noticed the scroll of her violin in her pack the first day," he explained. "When she left the commorancy late that evening, I went to go check on her, and overheard her playing."

The song still filled his thoughts whenever his mind sat idle. Not the frustrated toccata at the start — the same punching mixture of fury and frustration that billowed through the halls of the commorancy now — but the mournful requiem that followed. Her silhouette high up in the trees lit only by the moon, the loneliness and longing that hung on every note. His drumming fingertips stilled as he fell into the memory again.

A deep, familiar ache stirred from scars he hoped had long faded. Of dark bedrooms and closed doors. Of waiting for hours, days, years for the light to come. To stay.

His study door flew open, pulling him out of his trance as Wera and Enoch rushed in, bundled up in coats and scarves.

"First the screaming, now the violin?" Wera asked. "The hell is going on?"

Enoch half raised a trembling hand. "Also, could we maybe turn up the heat in here? It's hard for me to catalog when my fingers are frozen."

"Sebastian." Tanir looked at him sternly, and Sebastian braced himself for a scolding.

"If you're going to attempt this, you need to involve us as well." She gestured between the three of them, leaving Enoch and Wera more confused. "I'm honestly offended that Sir Gargic knew of your intentions with Mina before we did."

"It wasn't my choice. He cornered me as soon as I came in for lunch," Sebastian pouted, crossing his arms over his chest.

"Wait. What *intentions* do you have with Mina?" Wera's expression morphed from miffed to amused with a smirk and cocked eyebrow. "You were asking me a lot of questions about her on the hike. Reeeaaaally curious about what she and I were talking about."

Her implication left Sebastian flummoxed, stalling in sudden panic, face flushing.

No— it's — I mean I can see how— but it's not— with the contract that would—

"He intends to break Mina's curse by using his commands to test the limits of it," Tanir answered for him, "Right?"

"R-right." Sebastian cleared his throat. "Right. Yes. There's definitely some fae magic involved, considering a heatseeker is a fae creature and all. Fae magic... fae are magically bound to hold the deals they make... I figured it was worth a shot. That it could be used to override some of the aspects of her curse. Which has been an accurate guess so far."

"So Mina's a fae?" Enoch asked.

"Maybe," he gestured to the mess of academia in front of him. "I'm still looking into it."

"I'll dig through the Guild library and reach out to some personal contacts as well," Enoch offered.

Sebastian nodded, ever grateful to have someone as passionate about research as he was as a companion. "Thank you. I'd greatly appreciate it."

"So, is the violin a fae thing?" Wera asked, swirling a finger above her head. "Does the surging strings of a sonata soothe her inner heatseeker's wild temper?"

He shrugged, "I don't know. You'll have to ask Mina."

She narrowed her eyes. "What do you mean I have to ask Mina?"

Sebastian couldn't help his smile. "She's the one playing."

In perfect unison, her and Enoch's jaws dropped.

"*That's* Mina?!"

Sebastian nodded. "It is. And you may be on to something with the music soothing her. It's gotten warmer since she started playing, hasn't it?"

Enoch looked down the bridge of his nose and exhaled. "I can't see my breath anymore."

Perhaps some hope still lingered that she wouldn't hate them forever.

△

Sebastian would have bet good money on Mina trudging into the library, demanding that they all spit out whatever they wanted to know about Rabbet's Pass, before stomping back to her room.

He did not expect her to quietly enter, slip past the others without drawing their attention, and take a seat on the floor in front of the fireplace beside him.

"What do you want to know about the Pass?"

Sebastian jumped at her monotone, barely stopping himself from throwing the bestiary he was reading at her.

"Mina!" he squawked. Sebastian cleared his throat to bring his voice back down to its normal octave. "How long have you been there?"

"Just a few minutes," she answered, keeping her attention on the fire. "You need to work on your passive listening. Just because this place has a lock doesn't mean you're safe."

"True," he chuckled lightly and sat his book to the side. "But I've got a lock *and* wards, remember? Gods help any intruder who tries to get past those."

"And if it were one of your own?"

He could sense the question behind her question: *"And if I were to turn?"*

Sebastian shrugged. "I'm a decent judge of character." A heatseeker in the commorancy wouldn't be ideal, but it was nothing they couldn't handle.

He watched the amber glow from the flames flicker across her face. In its light, her porcelain complexion was painted human.

"Does the fire help with the cold?" he asked.

"No."

"Then why sit so close?"

"Rabbet's Pass is a series of ice caverns," she changed the subject, "a pitch-black labyrinth that a lot of monsters call home."

Did fire have something to do with her curse? Did she just not want to talk about it? It was a simple question. Maybe it was a rude thing to ask? I'll have to ask Enoch if he knows of any fae etiquette books, but— It was such a simple question! It had to be the curse. Something with fire. Gods, please don't make me have to set her on fire to break this fucking thing. I can't—

"So we'll need torches," he replied as his mind ran in circles.

"If you're looking to be swarmed," she countered. "The beasts'll be tracking our scents once we enter. The torches would serve as nothing more than a beacon to guide their way to their meal."

"If you can't see, how have you led others through it in the past?"

"I can see," she clarified. "Others can't. I tie a rope 'round my waist and have them hold on while I lead them through. It is a slow pace, but two weeks faster than going around. Prepare for three days in total darkness."

"Question," Wera called, looking up from the paints and parchment scattered across the table she worked at. "How am I supposed to draw a map of a place I can't see?"

"I'm sure Mina will describe it to you as we walk," Sebastian answered. "Won't you, Mina?"

"No," she replied. "Noise draws the beasts too."

"Speaking of drawing," Enoch interjected, standing from the couch he was sprawled across to walk Wera's way. "What do you think?"

She squinted at the journal he held open in front of her. "Is that supposed to be a... terramawg?"

Enoch's mustache twitched in displeasure. "It's not *supposed* to be a terramawg. It is a terramawg."

"Like an abstract interpretation of a terramawg or—"

Enoch huffed, stomped over to Mina, and — in a very brave move for a notoriously cowardly man — dangled his journal in front of her face.

"Mina, you killed the damn thing. Is this a terramawg or not?"

She stared at it for just a second.

"I've never seen a terramawg that shape."

Enoch bristled and pulled his journal away. "What do you know?"

"How a terramawg actually looks," she stated, earning a laugh out of everyone except the archivist.

"Yeah, well, I'd like to see you try! You can't even see color!" he fussed.

Mina stood and snatched the journal out of Enoch's hand, much to Sebastian's surprise.

"What the hell?" Enoch balked.

She grabbed a piece of charcoal from Wera's supplies, retook her spot by the fire, and flipped to a clean page of the journal. The scratching sound of charcoal on paper filled the room as she knelt over it, covering her work from Sebastian's view no matter how he shifted in his seat.

As quickly as she started, she finished, jumping to her feet and shoving the journal in Enoch's face; the cartilage of his nose giving a pop from the force.

"A terramawg," she stated, and sat on the floor once again.

Enoch's breathless "holy shit" was all that it took to get everyone to abandon their seats and crowd behind him. Sebastian reached around him and ran his thumb over the edge of the image. If it weren't for the charcoal that stained it, he would have thought he was looking at a photograph.

"Mina!" Wera shrieked in his ear. "You can draw?!"

Mina turned over her shoulder and looked at her. "Clearly."

"How?!"

"Practice."

Wera ripped the journal out of Enoch's hands and stomped over to her.

"You're being a little shit, aren't you? 'Practice'," she mocked. "I've been drawing for years, and my photo-realism isn't even close to being this good!" She smacked the drawing with her knuckles. "What did you do? Capture one of these things back at that cabin of yours and draw it over and over again?"

"No. That's the first terramawg I've drawn."

Wera sputtered. "Then how did you get so good?!"

"I told you," Mina said. "Practice."

There she was again, being vague for some unknown reason over something so trivial. If there was any time to force her to let them in a little, it was now. He just had to be cautious not to hurt her.

"Explain," Sebastian said. An open enough command, nothing too specific that she couldn't find a workaround if it caused her harm.

Still, he braced for the temperature to drop again, for her rage-filled gaze to pierce through him once more. Instead, Mina closed her eyes for a moment, took a deep breath, then turned around to face them.

"I practiced by drawing plants. I drew plants so I could learn and remember what they looked like and their various properties. Lily of the Valley berries and wild blueberries look similar to me but capturing the subtle differences: the specific shade of gray of the berry, the size, how much space there is between the clusters, and the tapering of the leaves: taught me how to distinguish the two. I used this same practice to catalog various creatures and their tracks as well."

"How did you know which plants were poisonous in the first place?" Enoch asked. He paled a bit. "You didn't eat them to find out, did you?"

"No," Mina answered. "Mr. Harlowe taught me."

"Aha!" Wera thrust her arms in the air in triumph. "I knew Harlowe was more than just a name! He was your teacher!"

"You could say that."

"Was he the one who taught you violin?" Tanir asked.

"No."

Sebastian followed up, "Who taught you then?"

"A tutor."

"A tutor?" They all echoed.

"A tutor," Mina repeated.

They looked at each other for a moment, processing through shared confusion.

"What else did the tutor teach you?" he asked, cautiously. He was already pressing his luck.

"Piano and flute."

"How old were you?"

"I don't know."

The simple statement stopped his train of thought completely. The laundry list of questions he'd lined up shredded.

"You—" Sebastian's chest hurt, her dull gaze carried a new emptiness, and a harrowing thought emerged. "Do you know how old you are now?"

The emptiness spread, opening an old hole in his heart.

Mina looked at him without looking at him. "No."

A spark of anger — sudden, surging — left Sebastian warmer than he liked. He swallowed it.

Getting upset wouldn't uncurse her any faster.

"Where's Mr. Harlowe now?" Wera asked. She placed a hand on Enoch's shoulder as she tried to change the subject. "I'd love to send him a copy of the map once I've finished."

"He's dead."

The friendly smile she wore wilted. "Well, that attempt to lighten the mood backfired."

Mina shrugged her shoulders. "That's what happens when you ask too many questions."

Wera scoffed. "Can you blame us? You've never talked this much!"

"I'm only talking because the wizard commanded me to."

"You don't need to explain anymore," Sebastian replied, dirty guilt crawling up his spine.

She kept looking at him, studying, watching, waiting — her empty expression made it hard to tell.

"I'm sorry," he added.

Emptiness turned into yet another sneer. She turned her back to him, clearly favoring the fire over his sad attempt to apologize.

Sebastian couldn't blame her, he'd be disgusted with him too if he were in her shoes.

"Would you play the violin for us sometime, Mina?" Tanir asked out of the blue.

Her question hung in the air, long enough that Wera returned to her maps, Enoch to his attempts at drawing. Sebastian patted Tanir on the back and gave her a sympathetic smile — the attempt was definitely appreciated — and headed back to his seat.

Mina turned her head, barely over her shoulder, as he picked up his bestiary.

"If I'm told to," she answered, catching Tanir just as she resumed her sewing, glancing at Sebastian briefly as she returned to watching the flames.

He barely had a moment to dissect what her answer meant when the library door flew open.

"Tanir you are a miracle worker!" Sir Gargic announced with a joyous laugh. "I feel like I'm a teenager again!"

"Glad to hear it," Tanir replied, halfheartedly, without glancing up from her sewing. "Do be careful, though, the pain-relieving qualities of the poultice are temporary, and the bones you broke aren't healed completely."

"Understood." He saluted and sauntered over to the chair across from Sebastian, taking a seat with a broad swing of his leg. "Windenhofer! Glad to see you and the rest of the troop are unharmed."

Sebastian raised an eyebrow. "Why would we be harmed?"

Gargic's eyes were locked onto the back of Mina's head. "You never know," he drawled, lighthearted tone hardening. "There are a lot of dangers on mountains like these."

"Like walking into pitfalls on purpose?" Sebastian quipped.

Months of traveling together and Sir Gargic never gave a hint that he could be so antagonistic. Pompous and prejudiced on occasion, as was expected from someone of his age and station, but this? Gods, one would have thought Mina had killed his entire family.

Sir Gargic smiled tightly at his comment but wisely changed the subject. "Any luck on cracking open the lock on The Dorminian Jewelry Box?"

Sebastian sighed. "No, unfortunately. Wearing gloves helps with the poison thistles, but makes it difficult to move the intricate puzzle pieces locking it."

"Well, at least it's just poison and not a curse." Gargic's eyes drifted towards Mina again, a snide smirk curling the corner of his mustache. "Usually things like that are cursed for good reason."

A burst of arctic air snuffed out the fire and froze the breath in Sebastian's lungs before he could rebuke. He couldn't move, the cold was so severe and sudden, his inner flame could not steel against it. Couldn't keep his muscles from seizing, or a frosty film from forming over his open eyes.

Sir Gargic trembled before him, his body spasming as it tried in vain to fight off the cold. Icicles grew from his beard, binding the wiry hairs together as Mina's footsteps crunched across the frozen carpet.

Sebastian could only see her arm as she reached into his blurry field of vision. The black of frostbitten fingers bled up her forearm into blue. A blue spreading darker, darker, revealing an unseen pattern of white chains wrapping around her flesh. She loomed beside the knight for a moment, her breathing ragged — *restrained* — then closed her hand around his beard; one finger at a time. With a quick twist of her wrist, the hair broke off in her palm.

Mina lifted the fistful of beard to Sir Gargic's eye level.

"I have spent some time in the third-floor library," she said, her level voice shaking with a building fury — like the rustle of leaves before a storm. She opened her hand and let the icicles fall one by one onto the floor. "Now, I spend the night in the commorancy."

Her arm left Sebastian's sight as she walked away, slamming the library door behind her on her way out.

The arctic air seeped out of the room with her. Just enough for the inner flame that swirled within Sebastian to reignite. He hopped to his feet, re-lighting the fire and conjuring a large warming dome to fill the room and thaw the others out.

"I-is everyone al-alright?" Tanir asked, teeth still chattering, as her muscles loosened. She turned her shaking hands over. "I d-don't see any s-signs of frostbite."

"Some of my paint is lumpy, but otherwise I'm f-fine," Wera answered, grimacing as she shook her bottles. "Enoch's mustache is a little w-wilted, though."

"No!" Enoch tapped his fingers over his drooping mustache. "I just rewaxed it."

"Tanir and Wera, go help Enoch with that," Sebastian said evenly, his breath thick with heat as his eyes bore into the back of Sir Gargic's head.

The knight kept quiet.

"Uh..." Enoch stalled, "I don't need—"

"Of course." Wera looped her arm underneath Enoch's and dragged him towards the door. "Come along, Tani. We've got a mustache to rewax."

"Following right behind you."

Sebastian waited until the door clicked shut to speak.

"What are you doing?"

"Being the voice of reason for your bright-eyed troop," Sir Gargic replied as he bent over to collect his hair off the floor.

"The voice of reason?!" Sebastian balked, "Since when is insulting a woman and almost killing yourself just to spite her, reason?"

"When it brings results." Sir Gargic turned to face him and held up the broken strands of beard. "Now we know exactly how dangerous she can be."

Sebastian inhaled deeply, clenching his fists, letting the heat pool in his palms. Then exhaled slowly, unfurling his fingers to release it gradually. Level-headed salamanders were a rarity. He wouldn't lose his hard-earned reputation over some old-fashioned knight with a superiority complex.

"I told you I would make sure that Mina was no danger to us," he said evenly, still making his disappointment known.

"You were just as frozen as I was during her little deep-freeze temper tantrum, weren't you?" he taunted. "That thing is a ticking time bomb that can go off at any moment."

"*She* only did that because of *you!*" The heat was a little harder to let go of. It clung to his fingertips as thrust his hand towards the door. "The woman's had one hell of a day, let alone one hell of a life with a curse like that! She doesn't need you making her feel worse about it!"

Sir Gargic gave a belittling tsk. "You're making a lot of assumptions there, Windenhofer."

"Just like you keep assuming she's going to kill us? Which — considering she didn't kill you just now, *and* saved you from becoming jelly at the bottom of an icy pit only hours ago — I would say is an assumption that has soundly been proven wrong."

Sir Gargic crossed his arms and scowled. "Even the most well-behaved hound can still bite."

Sebastian took another deep breath and clasped his hands together. If he touched anything else in the room, he was sure it would singe. A problematic notion. Sure, he had been through a lot today, but it was no excuse for his magic to be so reactive.

"Sir Gargic." Frustration would only fuel the fire, and would rile Sir Gargic up. Composure and control were key. "You have been a wonderful travel companion thus far in our journey. You have helped us complete our quest, as well as protected me and my comrades on multiple occasions. I am quite grateful for that."

Composed, controlled, but assertive. "While I understand your concerns with Mina, the actions you have taken are in stark contrast to the values that my team and I hold. I ask that, on your honor as a knight, you respect the way I run my expeditions and professional affairs in the same way I would respect you commanding a militia."

The aging knight studied him for a moment, pursing his lips, narrowing his eyes, making a big show out of his consideration.

"On my honor as a knight, I shall." He uncrossed his arms to stroke his shortened beard, the wiry bristles resembling an ill-assembled push broom without the extra weight. "On one condition."

"What condition?" he asked instead of rolling his eyes.

"We all fight against her." Sir Gargic replied. "Just once."

Sebastian blinked a few times as he processed his request. "What?"

"I want to see how well we could stand up against her if it came down to it."

He wanted them to fight against Mina.

Mina, who could lift a thousand-pound pine tree without a grunt. Mina, who could move so fast, she became invisible to the naked eye. Mina, who cut through the half-foot thick plating of a crystecean claw with a single swipe of her sword.

"Someone could get seriously hurt."

He huffed a laugh. "Not if we use that training room of yours."

That... was doable. As much as Sebastian hated to admit it, the notion sent the wheels in his head turning. There could be a lot to learn fighting someone of Mina's prowess, and it could provide yet another opportunity to test the limitations of her curse.

"Fine," he acquiesced. "But give us a day or two. We don't know exactly what will happen on this next leg of the journey, and the last thing I want is for us all to be exhausted in the face of another crystecean attack."

"Of course." With a stilted nod, Sir Gargic walked past him. "Now, if you excuse me, I'm going grab some food and some ale and mourn the loss of years worth of growth."

He shook his beard as he left the room, revealing the "mustache waxing" trio eavesdropping just outside the door.

"You heard the man, folks," Sir Gargic proclaimed at the sight of them. "Better gird your loins. We've got one hell of a fight ahead of us."

△

Everyone else had gone to sleep hours before Sebastian put down his books and shuffled to the kitchen to assemble himself a turkey sandwich, making up for the meal he skipped earlier.

The only information the bestiaries gave him on heatseekers was how to kill them, not one word on how to calm them, or any record of curses involving the fae beasts. He considered going on a goodwill mission to expand the Northern Practitioners' Guild's book collection after receiving their payout from Lanholde out of frustration. Surely, there was some manner of dealing with fae creatures that didn't involve slaughtering them on sight.

His sandwich tasted duller than usual, dampened by his disappointment at coming up empty, and his lingering worries about Sir Gargic's behavior. Being in such a dower mood wouldn't solve things, and it wasn't as if he didn't learn anything about Mina's case today. He had learned quite a lot, even if it was by less-than-desirable means... but it all only served to confuse him even more.

Mysteries enamored him. There was no job too difficult or too intricate, so long as there was a bit of a puzzle to it. Mina's past tutor puzzled him, even more so than her not knowing her age.

Each answer sprouted more questions, spreading through his mind like ivy as he finished his meal and made his way up to bed. When he got like this, root-bound by thought on his search for answers, it was nearly impossible to untangle his attention until he came to a conclusion.

The soft song trickling out of Mina's room as he walked past, however, uprooted him immediately.

"When the skies grow dark at night, and the moon has gone in hidin'
Do not fear, have no fright, for the sun will soon be risin'
Though the flowers have gone gray, and the birds have all fall'n hush
Know that soon it shall be day, paint the world with golden brush."

But mother, you may say, what if the sun has gone?
Do stay near the firelight.
And keep sleeping 'til the dawn."

Sebastian didn't dare wipe the tears that trickled down his face, lest she heard him outside her door. He stood there, listening, as she sang round after round of the lullaby.

Sadness. Regret. Loneliness. And worst of all, hope. Not hope for something better but the hope to survive, for suffering to end, colored every note. A shade of hope he knew all too well. Every new family. Every nun's sad smile.

He wondered just how many times she had sung that song to herself until her voice faded away mid-phrase.

He'd do whatever it took to make sure she never sang it again.

VII
Empty Slate

After such a shit day, Mina considered herself lucky to have a memory-less sleep.

The knock at her door, however, promptly reminded her that her luck was always fleeting.

She sprung off the ground, out of her bedroll, and threw open the door, hand on her hilt ready to strike.

"What's the matter?" she asked before Sebastian's brilliant hair blinded her sleep-blurred eyes.

"Good morning, Mina," he greeted. "How long have you been up?"

Mina took her hand off her hilt and sighed. His words alone were already giving her a headache.

"How long ago did you knock?" she said as she rubbed her eyes.

"Oh, but you're—" Sebastian started. "Never mind. I'm sorry for waking you."

"Oh, but you're?" she repeated. It was incredibly annoying whenever people swallowed what they wanted to say. "Spit it out."

"You're already dressed, was what I was going to say. But then I realized that you probably sleep in your armor out of habit. That way you're ready in case something were to attack in the middle of the night."

Mina studied his face for a moment. His brows drew together slightly as his eyes darted across her face, searching for a non-existent reaction.

"That's a lot of thought in a short amount of time," she remarked.

He closed his eyes and sighed. "Yes, it is. It's a common occurrence, unfortunately." A small, soft smile crooked his lips. Mina could only witness it for a moment before its appearance drove a spike through her skull.

She looked back over her shoulder at her bedroll to spare herself. "What did you wake me for? Come to scold me for last night?"

A dull chill ran up her spine. It had been a long, long while since she lost control of her temper to that degree. Years since the cold rage constantly roiling inside her consumed her.

Changed her.

The knight was lucky she was able to maintain some semblance of control over herself, had it been another time and another place, she would have frozen his lungs solid and torn them from his chest with her bare hands.

Which is exactly what She would have wanted.

"No. Last night was Sir Gargic's fault," Sebastian assured. "I'm here because I need your help in my study. I think I've come up with a solution to help us see as we travel through the caverns."

"The problem is already solved."

He shook his head. "Having us follow you single file like school children is hardly a solution. Will you help?"

"If I'm told to."

She was banking on his cleverness. She hated how her will could be taken away by him at any moment — had screamed and destroyed to vent the depth of her irritation — but she was not so clouded by disappointment that she didn't notice the small benefits of her situation.

For one, having two meals relatively pain-free did not go unnoticed, and judging by the horrified look on Sebastian's face as the dessert he made her eat cut open her mouth, she was fairly certain he'd never make that mistake again. Her skin hadn't itched since he told her to stay in the commorancy, even sitting in the library and speaking to the others had been tolerable. She barely felt a sting from their astonishment over her drawing ability, much to her surprise, and while being forced to answer their questions was incredibly intrusive, she couldn't recall a time when anybody showed that much honest interest in her.

The true intent of that interest was still suspect, and she wasn't quite sure how she felt about it, but she knew she didn't hate it.

Nor did she hate Tanir asking her to play for them, despite the toothache the hopefulness in her asking gave. She never played for anyone. The Harlowes had passed before she picked up the violin.

She could never be able to willingly play for his little troop, or assist him in his study — that would be too kind — but if a certain flame-haired wizard told her to...

"Mina, come assist me in my study."

...she'd be unable to refuse.

"Packing first," she said as she moved to roll up her bed. "I'll be quick."

"I've told you, you can leave your things in here. Dawn is a bit a ways," he said. "Even after we finish up, we should still have plenty of time to eat and pack before we have to set off."

"I'd rather be safe than sorry." She slung her pack over her shoulder. "Lead the way."

"Right." Sebastian started down the hall towards the stairwell. Then stopped suddenly, spinning around to face her. "What other instruments do you play?"

"I told you last night." Mina stopped as well. "Violin, piano, and flute."

"Those were the ones you were tutored in." Of course he'd be pedantic. "Are there any others?"

"What does this have to do with your solution?"

"Nothing." He shrugged. "I was just wondering."

Mina stared at him, searching for the intent behind his questioning, but the thoughts running through his mind were too numerous to pin down.

"All of them?" she asked.

"Is there quite a lot?"

"Bodhrán, daf, bongos, bugle, soprano clarinet, cornet, hulusi, harmonica, ocarina, piccolo, bandura, lyre, lute, guitar, mandolin, and vihuela," Mina counted on her fingers. "Any instrument that could be classified as woodwind, strings, or percussion I can learn how to play."

Sebastian nodded slowly, "That is a lot more than I expected," and continued up the stairs.

If Mina could crack open Sebastian's head and view the inner workings of his mind, she would expect to find his study there. Cluttered workbenches, shelves bowing under the weight of cauldrons and spell books, and cabinets with drawers and doors ajar as various herbs and components sprung from them crowded the floor space and lined the walls. Dozens of machines whirred, ticked, trilled, popped, and hummed in the background — each arrhythmic on their own — but together formed a lively pattern. Sebastian moved through the room effortlessly, stepping over the trunks and piles of parchment that littered the floor without a single glance down.

Mina let her curiosity get the better of her, following not the wizard, but the glint of what looked like sunset glistening out of one of the half-opened cabinet drawers. A cluster of rocks, polished and semi-translucent, shone in the low light of his study. Perhaps the wizard had found a way to capture firelight and turn them into gemstones.

"Mina?" he called.

"What?" she replied, slowly tilting her head side to side to watch the light dance over them and bring the flames trapped inside back to life.

"Over here, please."

Mina pulled herself away reluctantly and joined him at his desk. He pointed to the wooden chair in front of him. "Have a seat."

She did.

"I'm going to snuff out the lights, and I need you to describe what you see," he said.

"Go ahead."

Sebastian snapped his fingers and the room darkened a bit.

"Well?"

"I see a wizard sitting at his cluttered desk in his cluttered study, only it's darker than it was a moment ago."

"What do you mean by darker?"

Mina considered his question. "Like how some fabrics turn darker when they're wet."

"Interesting." He tapped his fingers across his lips. "And is it still without color?"

The warmth of his hair only deepened in the dark. "Still without color."

"I'm going to light a small flame on my fingertip for a moment. You don't need to do anything. I just want to test something." A small flame ignited on the tip of his index finger as if it were a candlewick, and he waved it back and forth across her field of vision.

It took more self-control than she liked to keep herself from following its warm glow.

"Fascinating," he mumbled, his voice rumbling deeper in the back of his throat from the unconscious utterance. The flame disappeared and with another snap, the room lightened again.

"You have an eyeshine in the dark," he remarked before scribbling something down on a piece of parchment.

"An eyeshine."

"Yes. A lot of animals have them. It's where their eyes shine back light in the dark. Kind of like a mirror. Deer are an excellent example. Have you noticed it during your night hunts?"

"On occasion. Usually, if I'm hunting at night it's just me, so there's no need to carry any light that would make them shine." Mina's shoulders tensed, uncomfortable with the information.

Yet another thing that made her inhuman outside of her control.

He stopped writing. "Did you know you had it?"

"No."

A moment of silence hung in the air before the scratch of Sebastian's pencil picked up again. "Well now that we do know, it's pointing me in the right direction for creating these noxulars."

"Noxulars?"

Sebastian slid the parchment in front of her. It was a crude sketch of a pair of goggles, broken down into layers, with slanted chicken-scratch handwriting denoting the purpose and function of each part. "Night Sights could be another name for it. What do you think?"

Mina looked over the drawing. She was smart, but she was no inventor, so—

"I think your handwriting looks like shit."

Sebastian wrinkled his nose. "You and the Guild. I'm glad I found Enoch when I did. Otherwise, they were going to make me attend a penmanship class." He took the drawing back. "Luckily for you, you don't need to read this in order to assist me with assembling it."

"I am not a tinkerer," she said.

"I don't need a tinkerer, I need a stitcher. Tanir mentioned you're quite skilled with a needle and thread." Sebastian pointed to his sketch, "I can make the lenses and imbue them with magic, but I know nothing about how to fit them to a face. I figured perhaps a leather band would work."

She took a more detailed look at the drawing. There were worse assignments he could give besides sewing. "A leather band with a strap and buckle in the back to adjust the size."

He smiled. "I knew you'd be the right person for the job."

Mina turned away from him and his stinging grin, and began to rummage around the room for materials.

She quickly found the method to his madness. The scraps of leather were located near clumps of sheep's wool and beeswax. The needles with shards of glass and dried rose thorns. Spools of thread nestled between balls of twine and live vines of ivy, and the buckles were tossed into a broken drawer filled with coins and keys.

Mina expected the wizard to try and talk her ear off as they worked, but as she sat down on the floor, nestled in the corner between a cedar chest and the wall, she looked up to see him testing materials intently, back turned to her as if she were just another clutter filled cabinet.

She took the razor blade she found near the needles and cut the leather to shape, leaving slits to curve the frames as necessary. The rhythm of her needle threading in and out matched the tempo of the whirring machines, quieting her mind in the same way prepping pelts and chopping firewood at her cabin often did.

A hand holding two thick lenses broke her trance.

"Here," Sebastian said. "Make sure they fit."

She placed her needle between her teeth and grabbed the lenses out of Sebastian's hand without looking, brushing her fingertips against his palm carelessly.

She stilled.

True warmth. Not the burning pain she'd felt when she covered his mouth with her palm. Something stronger than the fading warmth that had followed. Warmth like the dreamt memory she'd almost forgotten in the wake of flaming hair and cursed transformations.

She would have left her hand in his without any thought, but the invisible threads of his command pulled it away to slip the lenses into the lipped eyeholes she created.

"Fits," she said. "Needs glue though."

"I've got a couple of options. You'll find them near where you got the leather," he said. "Hand them back to me? I'm going to use them as a template for the others."

Mina removed the lenses and held them out to him. He wrapped his hand around hers and held it for a moment.

"Huh. No steam this time," he remarked, then took the lenses.

Mina returned to her sewing, trying to ignore the slight spike in her heart rate and the urge to reach out and grab his hand again, but could not stop herself from noting, "Would have made it hard to hold the needle."

"Why's that?"

"Burns."

"Ah," he cocked his head to the side and drummed his fingers across his lips. "Wonder what was different this time. Maybe it's because I commanded you to do it?"

"Don't know. Those lenses won't make themselves, though," she said. She needed him to get back to his corner and leave her alone, or else her stupid, disobeying body might do something that they'd both regret. "Not in time for breakfast at this rate."

"Psh. Now that I've done it once, it'll fly by. I bet I'll even finish before you," he taunted.

Mina scoffed. "Bold words, Wizard."

"Just watch me, Alpinist."

Sebastian playfully kicked at her ankle, knocking her leg out from under her and causing her to mess up her stitch. Mina glared at him as he scampered away and had the equivalent of a sledgehammer driven through her skull as he snuck a peek back at her, and winked.

Dumbass.

🜁

"Alright everyone," Sebastian said as he passed out the noxulars, the arched entrance to Rabbet's Pass looming behind him. "These'll allow you to see in the dark as if you were seeing a black and white photo. We haven't tested the range of view yet, but as long as you keep Mina in your sights you should be just fine."

"No talking, no noise of any kind unless it is a life or death necessity," Mina added. "Tap once on the person in front of you's shoulder if something is wrong and we have to slow down. Tap twice if something is wrong and we have to stop. These taps should be a chain reaction that leads up to me."

"Question." Enoch raised his hand. "Is it safe for us to tap you, or are you gonna go all psycho monster on us?"

Wera chimed in, "Follow-up question. Are we gonna get frostbite if we tap you? I kind of need fingers to do my job."

"You have gloves on?" Mina asked.

"Yes?"

"Keep wearing them."

"And the monster part?" Enoch asked.

"Heatseeker," Sebastian corrected.

"And the heatseeker part?"

Mina walked over and reached towards him. Enoch shut his eyes tight in fear, flinching as she grabbed his arm and placed his hand on her shoulder. After a few seconds of nothing more than a bit of frost forming on the wool of his gloves, he peaked one eye open.

"Boo." Mina swatted his hand off her and stomped towards the archway. Sebastian's quiet chuckle ticked her eardrums, like a cello's vibrato. "Order is as follows: Cartographer, Medic, Archivist, Knight, and Wizard. Let's go."

They fell in line with little complaint — not one muttered insult from Sir Gargic much to her surprise — and began their ascent into the caves.

The shifting elevations and uneven tunnels made Rabbet's Pass difficult. The random patches of slick snow and ice through twisting passages made it dangerous. The beasts that prowled its labyrinth made it deadly. The darkness made it impossible.

If Sebastian's invention worked, however — coupled with the map Wera was making — she may never have to lead an expedition again. It wouldn't be just some snide comment to dissuade people from hiring her services, anymore. It'd be an actuality.

The thought sat uncomfortably in the back of her mind, setting her more on edge as they were fully immersed in the cavern's pitch. It was as if she were naked without the familiar weight of a rope tethered around her waist. The five pairs of footsteps she'd grown used to's rhythm still pattered on, at least.

But their footsteps were the only thing she heard.

No distant mewls of frostlyon cubs, no skittering of txia claws as they darted in between cracks, nor the telltale drips of whytewing saliva as they stalked their prey hungrily from the cavern's roof. Just the patter of their feet, the wheeze in their lungs as the changing inclines and freezing temperatures tested their endurance, and the echo of them both bouncing off the cavern walls.

An hour went by, then two. The nagging in her gut was undeniable now, raising her hackles that something was wrong.

There was always quiet before a storm.

The tunnel they ascended leveled out into a wide plateau. Mina held up her hand, signaling them to stop. She pulled out her bow from its sheath and waited for the subtle squeak of Wera uncorking her vials before firing an icy arrow towards the ceiling above.

The ice shattered on the stalactites, tinkling like the strike of wind chimes as its splinters bounced above, before clattering to the ground.

"What the hell is she doing?" Sir Gargic hissed.

"Shhh!" Mina listened for any signs of life stirring. The crack of ice would send a swarm of txia scrambling for a meal any other day, but still, there was nothing.

Maybe it wasn't enough. Icicles fell all the time, maybe the beasts thought it was that.

"Mina—" Sebastian whispered.

I need to go bigger.

"Oh, the salt and sun might bleach my hair, and turn my skin to rubber!" Mina sang, "But damned I'll be if they'll keep me from my mermaid lover!"

She paused, listening as the sailing song bounded around the cavern, poured into the hidden nooks and passages creatures loved to nest in.

Nothing.

"She's trying to get us killed!" Sir Gargic spat.

"Mina," Tanir called, "are you feeling alright?"

"Talk!" she demanded as she switched her bow out for her sword. She banged its flat side against a stalagmite. "With hair of silk and eyes of green, breasts bigger than no other, I'll drown just to suck her tits and die a happy fucker."

Wera cackled in the background while Sir Gargic bickered with Sebastian and Tanir about stopping her.

"Oh ho! What a way to go! The taste of fish upon my lips is all I want to know!"

Enoch's reedy tenor voice joined her, "Oh hey! What else can I say? The reaper wears a tail of scales and goes by Moira Maeve."

Nothing. Nothing. Nothing. No signs of movement, no sounds of life besides their voices— even as she closed her eyes to focus solely on how the sound bounced, all she could sense was the sharp vibrations bounding off stone: no fur, no bodies, just stone and ice and bones from climbers or meals long passed.

Mina screamed a piercing, terror-inducing scream — rivaling a banshee's war cry — as her fear, as it most often did, turned to anger.

The others fell silent.

"Mina," Sebastian said after a moment, "tell us what's wrong."

She paced back and forth as her worries tumbled from her lips, loosened by his command.

"There's no chuffing, or scratching, or shuffling. I know for a fact that we passed a frostlyon den an hour ago and that the arrow I shot should have sent a swarm of txia our way! The echoes are too sharp, too fast, they're only bouncing off stone." She stopped and looked Sebastian in the eye, unafraid of the sting behind the dark glass of his noxulars. "It's just us in here, and it shouldn't be."

"Isn't that kind of a good thing, though?" Enoch asked. "Considering all those things could probably kill us?"

Mina glared at him. "Would it be a 'good thing' if all the fish disappeared from the sea?"

"N-no?"

"Also, you were flat."

"What?"

"You were flat. Sing through here," she tapped the bridge of her nose, "not here," she tapped her teeth, "next time."

"Alright, so we're the only ones in here," Sebastian interjected. "Now, what?"

"We keep moving. Keep an eye out for anything strange."

"Can we talk?" Tanir asked.

"Clearly."

"Can we sing?" Wera snickered.

"I don't care." Mina turned around and started walking. "This plateau goes on for a bit, with some slight inclines. We'll break when we're nearing the end of it, then in the second half we'll have to do some scaling."

"See I told you Sir Gargic," Wera continued. "That was her singing in the woods, not a mockingbird."

"Hah. Still could be a mockingbird," he scoffed. "That song was respectable."

"You've heard Mina sing before?" Sebastian asked.

"Yeah, when we grabbed her from her cabin. We weren't sure if it was her because, well— no offense Meens, but ya don't seem like the singing type."

"Shocking," Mina grumbled.

"What I want to know is where the hell you learned 'Moira Maeve'," Enoch marveled.

"I'm sure she could ask you the same thing," Tanir remarked.

"I grew up on the Coast of Carvons! Raunchy shanties are lullabies there! I can't help it," he defended. "Now why a hermit who lived her entire life alone deep in landlocked woods—"

"I go into Sorin to sell furs," Mina interrupted. "Heard some sailors singing it as I walked past one of the pubs."

"And you picked *that* song?" Sir Gargic scoffed.

"She probably picked it because of the rhythm and pitch," Sebastian theorized. "The even pacing probably kept the sound waves consistent enough for echolocation."

"Nope. It was just the first song I could remember," she replied.

"Ya know, Sebastian," Wera said, "I believe there are a feeewww more stanzas to that song."

"Are there?"

Enoch gave a low whistle. "Oh, yes, there are."

"There are thousands of creatures missing," Mina barked. "Focus on that instead of the damned song!"

"Somebody's shy!" Wera sang.

"Somebody needs to get their ass up here and take some notes on these caves," she seethed.

Wera cackled, triumphant at pushing her buttons, and ran up alongside her.

🜁

They stood in awe, necks craned back and faces pale in the shadow of the thirty-foot wall of rock and ice.

"A little bit of scaling," Sebastian muttered.

Mina looped the rope through the back of his harness and secured it with a knot. "A bit. There will be a whole four days of it soon. You'll need to use your pitons then." She walked back to Wera and tied the other end of the rope to her own harness, tethering them all together in one long chain. "I'll climb. When you feel the pull, lean back and walk up the wall."

"You're going to carry all our weight?" Tanir asked. "What if you fall?"

"What if she drops us?" Sir Gargic grumbled.

"There's a reason the wizard's in the back," she said.

"Yeah, I— erm— have a levitation spell that'll cushion the fall," Sebastian said. "How did you know that?"

"It made sense. You know things," the words stung her tongue as she said them, though they really shouldn't have. It was a fact. Not a compliment.

Mina's thin fingers slotted into the shallow cracks, and she drove the toe of her boot into the rock, carving out a foothold with one swift kick.

"D-did you just—" Enoch sputtered.

"Quiet," she warned. "I need to listen for fractures."

The creak of the rope and repeated impacts of her boots were the underscore to their ascent, bouncing all around the hollow cavern and still finding no purchase on life.

There were no signs of a mass exodus or death. The little snow that covered the cavern floors was untouched, no paw prints or tail drags. It was as if the creatures she'd seen tear people apart and come charging at her from the darkness had never existed at all. As if they were just a nightmare of hers, a boogeyman under the bed.

It had been some time since her last expedition, two seasons at least. Perhaps nature had run its course in the cavern. Food had gone scarce, some new predator or disease had made its way through, plenty of things could have happened in that time.

Her worry subsided a bit. There was still a lot of cavern left to go, perhaps they'd find a clue later on.

"So, Mina," Sebastian huffed, halfway through the climb. "Considering how... uneventful the current leg of our journey has been, I was wondering if my troop could train with you tonight."

"Train?" she asked.

"I want to see how you fight," Sir Gargic stated.

"You're crazy!" Wera balked. "You saw how she massacred those crabs, didn't you?"

"Crabs are one thing," he replied. "Man versus man reveals true character."

"'Bastian, you can't be serious."

"After talking it over with Sir Gargic last night, and thinking over it some more this morning, I figured since Mina is such a skilled fighter that perhaps we all could stand to learn something from dueling her." Mina could tell his teeth were clenched from his tone. "It'll be perfectly safe, of course, Mina. We have these collars in the training facility that'll allow us to fight full force without risking serious injury, and I'm sure Tanir will provide plenty of potions and aid if needed—"

Mina's stomach lurched.

"Not for me," she said.

"What do you mean, 'not for you'?" Tanir asked. "I'd be glad to offer you potions—"

"Not. For. Me." she repeated.

I'd rather swallow actual fucking knives.

"Oh," she breathed. "Right. Uh— what would work?"

"Raw herbs."

"Right. I'll bring some of those as well."

"No collars for me, either." With her luck, her body would try to break its own bones if she had to wear something enchanted to protect her. "Others will need it."

Sir Gargic snorted a haughty laugh. "I knew you wouldn't back down from a challenge."

If she could roll her eyes, she would have.

"You should pay a visit to the library. You've forgotten the definition of a challenge. Brace yourselves," Mina grunted out a warning as she sprung off her footholds and up over the edge of the wall. She landed on her feet, digging her heels into the ground to steady herself as the others' momentum threatened to tug her back down.

They let out a trickle of fearful grunts and whimpers from the sudden rise and drop.

"Start walking," she called as she trekked forward, pulling them up with each step.

"Holy shit," Wera groaned as she crested over the edge, struggling as the weight of the others shifted onto her harness.

She would send them all plummeting if she didn't catch her footing.

"Stop walking," Mina called. She looped around, grabbed Wera by the harness, and pulled her forward. "Start walking."

One by one they crested over the edge and without her asking — not that she could ask — turned to help her pull the weight of the others over. A first, as far as her other expeditions went.

She allowed them a moment to catch their breath and shake off their fear.

"We have to do that for four days?" Sebastian panted.

"That's what I said."

He ran a hand down his face wearily. "I'm gonna have to make a batch of levitation potions."

"Won't help. Had an expedition try that once," Mina interjected. "The wind blew half of them away."

"Fuck." He drummed his fingers against his lips. "What about something to help us stick to it, so we're all carrying our own weight a bit more?"

"So long as you're flat. There's no walking like that up The Lithe." Mina untied herself from them. "Come on, we have more ground to cover before we call it a day and

I get to kick your asses."

🜁

A myriad of equipment lined the high walls of the training room. Sparring dummies, cork targets, moving pells, she even spotted a whetstone tucked away in the corner. Sebastian's hand dropped in front of her face, holding a thick leather collar studded with metal sigils.

"Here. The sigils will ricochet any blow they sense has enough force to sever a limb and will keep your vitals stable if you sustain enough damage to be lethal."

Mina walked away. "I told you no."

"But you could get seriously hurt!"

"Then I get seriously hurt. I survive, Wizard." Mina took her spot at the far end of the sparring mat. "Whoever gets knocked out or subdued loses?" she asked the group.

"Sounds fair to me," Sir Gargic answered.

"Who's first?"

"I'll go!" Tanir volunteered, placing the last of her herbs at the far edge of the sideline bench. She wielded her large, duel-bladed battleaxe as if it were lighter than a feather as she crossed the room and assumed a battle stance. The older woman had guts, and a whole lot of strength hidden underneath her proper speech and soft touch. The force behind the axe she hurled at her head the day before was evidence of that.

"Act or react?" Mina called.

"React."

Wrong choice.

"Wizard," Mina drew her sword. "Countdown."

"Alright." Sebastian cleared his throat. "Three. Two. One. Fight!"

With the wind's speed beneath every step, Mina ran across the length of the gym in a second. She lifted her sword to swipe at her throat.

Tanir spoke a single word and all but coated Mina's body in lead.

Her speed quartered by the spell of indolence, Tanir's axe blocked Mina's blade with little effort.

Well, shit.

It had been years since her strikes moved at such a human pace. Each swing of Tanir's axe tested the merit of her form more than her strength. Bittersweetly, her muscles still held the memory of years of drills, matching each of Tanir's blows, whispers of metal and young shouts across vast fields of ice behind each strike. Speed meant nothing if she didn't have the technique to back it up. And if she didn't learn that technique fast enough, then—

Tanir's axe blade got a little too close for comfort as the phantom sting of icy chains lashed across Mina's back. Panic heightened her senses. Long buried memories crawled across her skin.

She needed to end this spell.

Mina switched her grip, taking her sword in her left hand, and swung a sloppy strike towards Tanir's stomach. The medic dipped her axe to block the blow, falling for the goading attack and exposing her neck.

Mina punched her square in the throat.

The lead melted away as Tanir lurched back. Her speed returned, Mina grabbed her by the collar and drove her forehead into the bridge of her nose. A force field bounced Mina's head back as it cushioned the blow and stabilized Tanir's neck. She slumped in Mina's grasp, earning a chorus of ooo's and sharp gasps from the onlookers.

Mina took the sharp aching in her joints as she lowered Tanir down onto the ground and walked back towards her end of the mat.

"Cartographer," Mina called as Sebastian roused Tanir and helped her to the sideline.

"Alright," Wera sighed and took her place across the room.

"Act or React?"

Wera looked over at the others and brushed the back of her hand over her nose. "Act."

Mina sheathed her sword as Sebastian counted down.

"Three. Two. One. Fight!"

A fine mist filled the air, obscuring Mina's vision entirely. She readied her bow and closed her eyes, waiting for the telltale squeak of a cork coming loose from a bottle. A slosh followed the squeak, then a whistle as Mina opened her eyes to find a barrage of acidic droplets bolting towards her. She let them splash across her and felt no sting, only a mottled tightening of her skin, and conjured an arrow of ice from the mist that surrounded her to fire back through the fog.

The power built up from her draw — causing a gust of wind to follow in its wake — cleared the air as it flew, granting Mina the perfect view of her arrow smacking Wera in the chest. The force field flashed across her body as she fell to the ground, a whiny wheeze bursting from her throat as the wind was knocked out of her. Wera turned over on her side and ripped off the headscarf she dropped over her face as she struggled to catch her breath.

"I thought that would work," she heaved. "How are you still standing?"

Mina looked over the light splatter of burns that dotted her armor and skin. "You thought a light mist and some acid rain would stop me?"

"That wasn't just a mist. That was poison."

Mina watched the others remove the cloth masks and face coverings they'd slipped on.

"What type?"

"Curopulm."

"Ah." Mina conjured another arrow and drew it back. "Should have used that on someone else."

Wera slapped her hand on the mat. "I'm tapping out!"

Mina lifted her bow at the last second and hit a bullseye on one of the targets hung on the back wall.

Wera struggled to her feet and hobbled off to the side. "Tani, is it possible for a lung to be knocked loose?"

"No, dear," Tanir replied. "That sounds like a collapsed lung."

"Fantastic."

"Alright, who's next?" Mina called.

Enoch looked at Sir Gargic, who was studying the edge of his sword intently, then Sebastian, who patted him on the back and said, "You're up!"

He let out a heavy sigh and trudged over with a nervous shake in his knees.

"Act or react?" Mina asked.

"Act." He grumbled, "Obviously."

Mina sheathed her bow and stood unarmed.

"Really?" he whined. "Not even the sword?"

"I'm not gonna need it."

"Well then," Sebastian cut in. "Three. Two. One. Fight!"

Enoch reached into his vest pockets and threw six thin daggers, no bigger than pencils, at her. Mina wove through them and raced towards him, planning to knock the archivist out in one punch when a growing whoosh caught her attention. The daggers circled back, flying through the air to attack her side. She dived out of the way, but barely had time to rush Enoch again as the daggers pivoted their trajectory to intercept her attacks.

Mina kept her eyes on him, searching for an opening as she dodged. He wasn't a magic wielder, so there had to be some type of focus on him that he was using to direct the daggers...

...like the ring he kept fiddling with.

With how fast the daggers were maneuvering to protect him, it would take a very lucky break to get close enough to break his finger. She had to sever the connection. Maybe if she used an arrow to freeze the metal, or—

She caught a faint, high-pitched humming as she attempted to sweep under Enoch's legs. Rolling out of the way of the daggers, she stood to attack again, and the hum dipped in pitch: perfectly timed with the daggers turning direction.

Mina jumped back to her starting position and waited. The daggers hovered around Enoch, eager for her next advance.

He had the balls to smile. "You gonna draw that sword now?"

Mina locked eyes with him, her stare cold and vacant, and watched a cold sweat bead on his brow.

"What are you staring at?"

She walked towards him, eyes never leaving his, and stood just in front of the wall of quivering daggers between them.

Enoch chuckled nervously. "I-I know what you're doing. You're trying to intimidate me, trying to psyche me out. W-well, guess what! You haven't been able to land one hit on me for the past minute. I-I'm not afraid of you, sweet—"

Mina pursed her lips and whistled.

The daggers clattered onto the ground.

"—heart," Enoch squeaked out just before Mina broke his jaw.

He fell so hard on the ground, he bounced.

One cocky motherfucker down. Another one to go.

"Knight," Mina spat.

"Really?" Sir Gargic taunted. "You sure you don't want to save the best for last?"

"I am," she admitted, her hatred of Sir Gargic soothing the burn her words left on her tongue. "Act or react?"

Whatever he chose it didn't matter, she would take her time with the fight, make sure he felt every blow, but hold back enough to keep him standing so that stupid force field wouldn't cut her off.

"React," he hissed.

Mina unsheathed her sword and glared daggers into his beady little eyes.

"Oh boy," she heard Sebastian whisper under his breath before calling, "Three. Two. One. Fight!"

She took off, the wind carrying her strides as she ricocheted across the walls, making sure her blade connected with Sir Gargic every time she passed by. Sparks flew from his armor as she ripped her sword across, pulling out groans and seethes of pain. They were the only notion that he'd been struck in the first place, as the wind — enraged by her resentment — drove her faster and faster. The knight tried his best to figure out her attack patterns, getting a parry off here and there, but his blade struggled to find real purchase.

Mina let him have his shallow wins, let a leg drag a little so he could nick at her ankle, bounced back a little more dramatically after a half-assed block. It made his frustration so much more rewarding when she changed her approach mid-strike and threw him off his rhythm yet again.

His counterattacks slowed, the dozens of strikes he endured catching up with him. His head lulled forward. If Mina could have smiled, she would have as she raced towards him, ready to deliver the final blow now that his spirit was broken.

Or so she thought.

There were moments in a fight when time seemed to slow. Usually, a sign of her intense focus, that the enemy she was facing was particularly tricky and that she needed to center herself to overcome them. Other times, it was something life-threatening and unexpected rushing towards her: her first avalanche, a crystecean ambushing her as she fought off a pack of frostlyons, the stomach-dropping crack of a rock loosening beneath her a hundred feet above the ground; threats to her and her alone.

Not threats to others.

Never.

Yet time slowed as a throwing knife, hidden, then hurled by Sir Gargic, flew towards Sebastian. His focus on Mina, the wizard was blissfully unaware of the blade, expertly aimed to pierce his throat. Sir Gargic's head lifted to face her with a knowing smirk, and he shifted his stance. He had planned for this.

The only way for her to stop the knife was to drop her sword and draw her bow, twisting her body to where she'd land prone to his attack, and earn a sword to the stomach.

The pounding in her ears grew louder and louder. The pain would be unimaginable if she did it, but she could withstand it.

She wanted to withstand it.

And she wanted to tear that smug smirk from Sir Gargic's face with her bare hands.

Mina let her sword clatter to the ground and pulled back her arms instead of reaching for her bow. She mimed a draw, conjured forth an arrow, and threw it like a spear at the throwing knife. A thousand thorns pierced through her, driving deep into her flesh as the invisible chains that housed them constricted. She screamed against the pain and forced her body to twist one more time, her need to survive and rage bracing her for the sting of Sir Gargic's sword as she landed.

His gauntleted hand grasped her throat and squeezed.

"What the hell was that?!" Wera shouted.

Time moved once again.

"Well, well, beastie. Guess that heart of yours isn't as cold as I thought," he rasped in her ear, wet breath coating her skin. "The collar would have blocked it, you know, but now your rash tendencies have earned you a sword in the gut. Speed and strength can get you far, but cunning gets you farther."

How dare he.

"Does it now?" Mina lifted her slowly darkening hand to show his sword pierced through her palm. She grabbed the hand wrapped around her throat and crushed it. The growing freeze radiating from her brittled his blade until it broke off in her palm. His knee snapped in half with a sickening crunch as she drove her heel into it, tearing a bloodcurdling scream from him that only grew louder as she flipped him around by his broken hand, dislocated his shoulder, and buckled him down to a kneel. She held the shard of sword embedded in her hand to his throat.

The force field thrummed between them, trying in vain to push Mina off.

How dare he.

Pain pulsed through every inch of her body, but her rage kept her from fading, from letting the blood darkening her vision pull her under. A voice screamed at her to kill him, slit his throat and use his skull as a wine glass, or fine jewelry.

The horrid ones' bones always glisten whiter.

Mina let go of him, dropping him face first on the mat, and stepped on his back as she hobbled towards the herbs.

She learned to ignore that voice long ago.

"Mina," Sebastian's worry pierced her nearly shattered eardrums, and the dark ring around her vision closed in.

"Fuck off," she hissed.

"Mina!" Her steps fumbled as her knees buckled for a moment and all sound was muffled by static.

"Fuck off!" she roared. She finally reached the bench and shoved a handful of herbs into her mouth. The world spun, and she dropped her head between her knees and chewed, focusing on the sound of her breathing rather than the howling rage needling at her to feed it; to let it take over and tear Sir Gargic apart. The room stopped spinning as she swallowed, and the herbs' healing properties spread throughout her body.

Mina unfolded herself and studied the sword tip sticking through her palm. Shoving another handful of herbs in her mouth, she unbuckled her leather breastplate and tore off the bottom hem of her hemp shirt underneath. She draped the fabric strip over the bench, steadied her arm across it, and drove her fist down on the broken blade. It sliced through the rest of her hand with ease, and clattered onto the floor.

The pain was minimal, nothing more than a slight pinch, but the amount of blood pouring out was concerning. Mina spit the mashed-up herb into the gushing wound and rubbed it in before covering it with a thin coat of ice. Round and round she wrapped her makeshift bandage, the pain fading and strength returning throughout her body with each pass.

She wiggled her fingers, making sure that despite the stiffness, things were starting to heal properly, and, satisfied that each finger moved when she willed it to, grabbed another bunch of herbs as she stood.

"Wizard," she called as she chewed them. "Let's finish this."

"You can't be serious," Sebastian said. "You're in no condition to fight."

Mina refastened her breastplate with both hands in plain view of him, fingers deftly maneuvering the buckles as she walked to reclaim her sword.

"I heal fast," she replied. "Act or react?"

"Mina."

She walked back to her side of the mat. "Act or react, Wizard."

Sebastian huffed as he stomped over to the opposite side. "Are you always this stubborn?"

"Act or react?"

He rolled up his sleeves, frustration and disapproval furrowing his brow. "You asked for this."

"I know." Mina stood firm. "Act or react?"

"React," he spat.

"Countdown?"

Sebastian's gaze was hardened, perturbed. The sparks swirling in his irises raised goosebumps up her arms. Sir Gargic satisfied revenge.

This—

Mina cracked her knuckles

—was for dominance.

"Uh—" Wera uttered, ending the tense silence. "Fight?"

Mina drew her bow and ran up the walls, firing a barrage of icy arrows at him.

Sebastian summoned a brilliant inferno, burning as it swirled around him and turned her attacks to steam, the heat intense enough to create a whirlwind.

Just as she had planned.

She kept firing, creating more and more steam as her arrows evaporated against his defenses, until the room turned into a foggy moor, obscuring her movements. Wera's strategy had its merits, it just needed better execution.

Mina tracked Sebastian by his breathing — now ragged from the humidity — as she stopped her assault and moved silently through the fog. She had to get close to him, had to catch him off guard.

She untied the bandage from around her hand — the bleeding stopped though the cut was still raw — smoothed a layer of ice over it, and tied it across her face. All the planning in the world would be worthless if he burnt her eyes out of their sockets.

She resumed circling, bouncing off the walls as his panting guided her aim. Instead of a constant barrage, she plotted her shots to focus his flames, conditioning him to strike straight on without thinking.

"I'm just going to keep melting them!" he shouted.

Mina fired another onslaught of arrows and leaped after them.

A cone of brilliant fire swallowed the ice,

"I thought you wanted a—"

and she dove right into it.

"—fight!"

The damp bandage incinerated, clearing her sight just in time to see Sebastian's face, slack-jawed and horrified, as she grabbed his smoldering, outstretched palms.

A rush of wind billowed from them, the chill of her touch trying to suffocate the roar of his flames. Mina pinned him on the ground, fingers interlocking between his as she held his hands above his head and sat on his stomach.

The flicker of the force field, protecting his head as it slammed on the mat, petered out. He stared up at her, terrified.

"Out fighting you wouldn't work," she said, ignoring the growing tightness across her body as her skin and armor sizzled. "I had to outsmart you."

"I could have incinerated you." His voice shook as he spoke. The amber fire in his palms snuffed out.

"Not with the steam. It condensed on my skin as I moved through the space and took the brunt of the fire when I jumped through."

"And why are you holding my hands? It would have been safer to—"

"They're your casting point," she interjected. "You might have some vocal spells, but as long as I'm holding on to these, you're unable to cast." Her own breathing had grown ragged, her chest tighter than before as her heart hammered against it. "I win."

Sebastian's fear melted away. A different spark flickered in his eyes, coupled with an impressed smile that gave her a sudden migraine. She closed her eyes, flinching for just a moment.

He bucked his hips, flipping them over and pinning her beneath him.

"What were you saying about winning?" he mocked. Mina glared at him for a moment before turning her head away as much as she could, his expression too much for her to bear.

His grip tightened around her hands. "Tell me why you can't look me in the eye."

"It hurts," she hissed, his command pulling the admission out of her.

Sebastian lifted off her slightly. "It hurts?"

Mina used his weight shift to her advantage, thrusting her hips just like he had and knocking him off balance. She brought her legs up and hooked them around his neck before twisting them both over.

He gasped for air as she squeezed her thighs on either side of his throat, and choked out, "Alright. Alright. You win."

Mina untangled herself and hoisted him up as she stood.

The metallic splash of water drew Mina's attention to the sideline bench as Wera wrung out her hair. "When I suggested we add a sauna to the commorancy I was thinking in the hot springs."

"It's bad enough you beat the hell out of us," Enoch added, his speech stilted as he held an ice pack to his slowly healing jaw. "Now you're trying to give us heatstroke?"

"Warning an ally of your attack could lead to your death," Mina replied. "I caught that nose swipe earlier, Cartographer. If I wasn't honoring the rules of the match, I would have subdued you the minute I saw that.

"Archivist, Wizard, Cartographer, you all suck ass at close-range combat. Cartographer, you lack a solid defense. Poison is too particular. Archivist, that ring is fucking obvious. Knight—"

Sir Gargic twisted his head from where he lay on the bench as his bones reset.

There were so many things she wanted to say to him. It was a dirty fucking trick he pulled, but it was her own hubris that allowed her to be tricked.

She'd do the same thing in his shoes. Dirty tricks turned the tide when fighting life or death.

She hated him.

She hated herself.

"You could have killed me," Sir Gargic stated.

"Could have," Mina replied. "Didn't."

"Why not?"

"I kill monsters."

"I've been acting pretty monstrous," he countered. "Almost murdered Sebastian."

"Wait, what?" Enoch grumbled.

"Almost. Monstrous," she replied. "Not a monster."

They stared at each other, not in malice as before, but in bitter respect.

"Understood," he said.

"Duels are over," Mina announced and headed towards the door.

"A-are there no notes for me?" Tanir called after her.

"No."

"Mina, wait for a moment," Sebastian commanded.

She stopped.

"I command you to eat meals with us, to eat when you are hungry from the kitchen, to spend your time not scouting or continuing our journey to Lanholde in the commorancy, and to sleep in your bed when you feel tired or need rest."

Mina's heart dropped into her stomach, the memories of a thousand knives grazing across her skin and waking up to find the Harlowe's cabin destroyed, shoving it down.

"The locks and wards," she replied. She couldn't warn him outright. "Are there any set outside the guest room door?"

"W-why?"

Mina looked back over her shoulder and found his face blinding with worried kindness.

She turned away and left.

⚝

They parted ways after dinner, some going off to their studies, others going back to train some more. Mina made her way to the library.

Back at her cabin, when her chores were done, and she had her fill of music, Mina would read. Poetry, textbooks, fiction, memoirs, they lined her walls, bowed the shelves, only breaking in pattern to frame the instruments she'd hung up.

She never read fairy tales. They left a bitter taste in her mouth.

The library's collection was vast, and ever-changing, covers in a dozen different languages flickering in and out as she scoured the shelves, looking for a title to pique her interest.

Arctic Creatures and Their Habits, shimmered as she walked past. She grabbed it before it flickered out of sight and flipped through its pages. It had been a while since she read anything in Tangerish, but perhaps it could provide an answer as to where the creatures of Rabbet's Pass had gone.

She sat on the floor in front of the fire, admiring how its sunset colors painted the pages as she read. The book was thick, going into remarkable detail about hundreds of animals and insects — some of which she'd never seen — that roamed the snow banks and glaciers of tundras far away from the Fallow Peaks. The diagrams of the creatures she did know were decently accurate, missing a few minor details here and there or having a slightly misshapen anatomy.

As for answers as to why the cavern was empty, there were too many and none at all at the same time.

The pull of Sebastian's command grew stronger as she neared the end of the book. She needed to sleep. Healing over and over again from the day's injuries left her eyelids heavy and joints aching, but the certain pain of laying on that mattress made her push on as long as possible.

She read the last page and was yanked up against her will, dropping the book on the floor as her legs dragged her out of the library. When she got to Lanholde she'd cut the strings off of every marionette she saw out of solidarity.

The invisible threads lifted her wrist and wrapped her hand around the handle of the guest room door, but a band of leather tied around the knob kept her from turning it. Mina ran her fingers beneath it and pulled up a drop of firelight. Glancing around the hall, she found no one.

She quickly unraveled it from the handle and stepped inside the room.

Mina held it in her hand as if it were made of the most delicate glass, shifting it slightly to admire its color. It was one of the stones from Sebastian's study, intricately wrapped in wire to form a pendant. The strip of leather it hung on would be too weak to sustain the constant cold of the mountains, or the force of a well-placed attack.

Her iron collar weighed heavy around her neck.

Carefully — *incredibly carefully* — she unclasped its chain, keeping the band pressed firm against her throat with her other hand as it slightly stung her fingertips. She slid the pendant onto it, holding her breath until the clasp was locked again. Tracing a finger along the scale patterned setting, she admired how it sat between her collarbones; the light pouring through it painting her skin in much the same way the sunset did.

Mina tucked it away beneath her breastplate and fell into bed.

He must have seen me looking at the stones. Why didn't he say anything? Why did he make this? Didn't he have better things to do? Puzzle boxes to solve, a mountain to scale.

Her eyes fell shut.

She could picture him, hunched over his desk, tongue pinched between his teeth, just like it had when he assembled the noxulars. He'd have to use that big magnifying glass of his to weave the wires, taking tiny pliers to shape them into scales. Whytewing scales, to be exact. The same sort of pattern as her armor.

What a waste of time.

Mina placed her hand above the pendant. She could have sworn she felt the warmth of his touch still lingering on it. But that was more likely delirium as she slipped to sleep.

Painlessly.

VIII

All Good Things Must

"When the skies grow dark at night, and the moon has gone in hidin'."

Mina was small again, surrounded by warmth, blurred flickers of firelight dancing above her.

"Do not fear, have no fright, for the sun will soon be risin'."

A woman sang gently, her voice low and familiar.

"Though the flowers have gone gray, and the birds have all fall'n hush."

Her footsteps creaked across a wooden floor Mina could not see.

"Know that soon it shall be day, paint the world with golden brush."

The bright chime of a mortar and pestle underscored her lullaby. Mina grew impatient.

"But mother, you may say, what if the sun has gone?"

I want to see you. Let me see you. Mina went to speak, but all that came out was a cry.

"Do stay near the firelight."

The scraping stopped and the woman's footsteps grew closer.

"And keep sleeping 'til the dawn."

A shadow eclipsed the firelight.

"Now, now, darling," the woman cooed, "there's no need to fuss."

A hand descended from the shadows, one fingertip covered with a shining paste of herbs. The woman ran her finger across Mina's forehead and down her tiny nose. The scented oil filled it with a cool tingle, pleasant and comforting. Her crying stopped as her eyes grew heavier with every inhale.

"There we go." The hand disappeared. "Sleep well, my dear Mina."

That wasn't what she called her.

"Mina."

She tried to cry again, but found her muscles too relaxed to make a sound in protest.

"Mina."

🜁

"Mina!" Wera shouted.

Mina jolted awake, reached for her sword, and crashed to the ground, ensnared by a tangle of bedsheets.

"Oh dear," Tanir fretted.

Mina tore the sheets and stood, fists held up at the ready. "What's wrong?"

Wera doubled over in a fit of laughter. Tanir held a hand over her mouth to conceal her own.

"Nothing's wrong, dear. You're just late to breakfast," she said. "Sebastian sent us to make sure you were alright. It's not like you to sleep in."

"Sleep in?" Mina looked at the clock. She'd woken up at dawn since she was a child. How the fuck could she have overslept by an entire hour?

She patted the back of her breastplate. The stitches marking where her monstrous wings burst forth before were still intact. There were no signs of destruction in the room, save for the sheets she just shredded.

Had she really slept through the night, in a bed, unscathed?

"You went from sleeping angel to feral warrior so quickly," Wera wheezed, "only to fall flat on your ass!"

Tanir snorted, but quickly collected herself. "Wera, don't tease. We'll tell the others you're alright, Mina, just make sure you head down soon so you can get something in your stomach before we set out."

She shoved the still cackling Wera out of the room, leaving Mina alone, staring at the mattress.

🜁

She stood in the cavern, eyes closed, listening, waiting. There was their shifting feet, clatters of metal and glass, and whispers behind her as the commorancy was emptied and packed up, but still no skittering or mewling or growls.

"Well?" Sebastian's question tickled her eardrums.

"Nothing." She opened her eyes and found him standing just over her shoulder.

"That's... concerning. I assume you still want us to keep an eye out for any explanations for their disappearance?"

"I don't care what you do."

"Then you won't care if I walk next to you today?"

The pendant hidden beneath her armor weighed heavy against her collar.

"Nope."

"Alright then," Sebastian said. She could hear the smile in his voice. He turned to the others, "We're trying a new order today, folks. Let's go... Mina, me, Wera, Gargic, Enoch, and Tanir."

"Medic, then Archivist," Mina amended.

"Sorry. Tanir then Enoch to keep the back." He leaned forward and whispered to Mina as she started their hike. "Why that order?"

"Archivist's daggers can target many opponents, close range or far. Could stop an ambush."

"Is that why you assigned me to the back so often?"

"Are you going to pester me with questions this entire leg?"

"I'll let you pester me back."

"I've tried that, but you seem to be more of an entomologist than an exterminator."

"Is it question time with Mina again?" Wera butted in. "'Cuz I've got a million things I'm dying to know."

"I'll leave your ass behind when you trip and fall because you're too busy talking," Mina replied.

"That doesn't sound like a 'no' to me," she said, looking up at Sebastian. "Does it sound like a 'no' to you?"

"Sounds like as long as we watch our steps, we can ask as many questions as we like," he replied.

Mina sighed. Even if she did say "no" the questions would happen, now or later.

"Let's see..." Wera hummed. "Were you born in the cabin you live in?"

"No."

"Where were you born then?" Sebastian asked.

"Kirava."

Wera's turn. "Is that where you grew up?"

"No."

"Where did you grow up then?"

Mina's mouth snapped shut.

"Uh... Mina?" Wera pressed. "You gonna answer that or?"

Her throat tightened up.

"I don't think she can answer that one," Sebastian said.

"Damn. Okay. Next question. What's your favorite song?"

The tension on her vocal cords dissipated. "I don't have one."

"Favorite instrument?" Sebastian offered.

"Don't have one."

"Favorite sword technique?"

"Don't have one."

"Favorite gemstone?"

"I don't have a favorite fucking anything!" Mina snapped, tired of repeating herself; of having her shortcomings rubbed in. It was a half lie. She had a favorite color, though she didn't know the name of it, but it wasn't like she'd be able to say it either way.

"Sorry," Sebastian and Wera apologized in tandem. Mina rubbed her ears to try and ease the sting it left behind.

"Are you two long-lost siblings or something?"

"Maybe," Sebastian said. "Did any of your parents have a torrid love affair near Josiski City before they found each other?"

Josiski City. That explained the bit of accent she'd caught every now and again. The wizard was from Yosorik.

"Nope. They've been happily married for thirty years," Wera answered. "And considering my parents are barely over five-foot-six and me and all five of my sisters are just as short, I highly doubt a six-foot-seven bean pole like you could have sprouted from those seeds."

"I see. Maybe the kids at the orphanage did have a point. Maybe I am half-giant and my mother really did tip my cradle and throw me out of the sky."

"Oh, that's a question!" Wera said. "Mina, you're an orphan too, right?"

"The people who bore me are dead," she replied, taking a moment to chip away at a thick patch of ice that would have sent the others sliding.

"Did you grow up in an orphanage?" Sebastian asked.

Mina paused, recalling sitting in her classroom of ice as the others ran drills around a frozen lake.

"No?"

"No?" Sebastian and Wera repeated.

"You know, I'm only getting bits and pieces of this conversation back here," Enoch shouted, "but I can see where you're coming from, Mina. They do sound like siblings."

"Well, we are like a family," Tanir laughed.

Enoch hummed in thought. "You're the wise eldest sister, Sebastian and Wera are the rambunctious middle siblings. I'm the precocious youngest sibling, and Sir Gargic is our taciturn uncle."

"What does that make Mina?" Sir Gargic grumbled.

"The alpinist the family hired," Mina stated.

"You said 'no' like it was a question," Sebastian said, refocusing the conversation. "So you grew up in a sort of orphanage?"

"It's complicated."

"It has to do with your curse, then. Where you grew up."

His words crawled across her skin. She couldn't let him press anymore. She didn't want him to.

"Cartographer. We're moving faster than normal," she explained. "We should hit the last portion of this main tunnel structure by the end of the day. After that is a segment called the Vice. Then we'll be back out in the elements."

"So just one more day until we see the sun again?" Tanir asked.

"One more day until you see the sun," Mina repeated.

"Thank The Gods."

"Hey, maybe we should have the kitchen make us a picnic so we can eat lunch in the gardens today!" Enoch suggested excitedly. "It won't be the real sun, but the skytiles in there will feel close to it."

"That sounds like a fine idea to me," Sir Gargic said. "What do you think, Windenhofer?"

"I think that can be arranged."

"No turkey sandwiches in the basket, though," Wera said.

"I conjured the kitchen, I'll have it make as many turkey sandwiches as I want," Sebastian protested.

"And if you do that, we'll all be tired and cranky for the rest of the hike."

"We'll have coffee with the sandwiches."

"Hot coffee with cold cuts?!" Wera recoiled. "And here I thought you had taste."

Their childish bickering effectively ended the question session as they argued back and forth about what to eat. There was a familiarity to it. Memories of the Harlowes' Harvest Hail gatherings. The other homesteaders near their woods laughing, chattering through the night while Mina tried to get some sleep in one of the oaks. Their children pulling each other's pigtails and yammering on and on about the newts they found under rocks by the lake.

"Family" didn't sit right. "Family" carried expectation, examples that needed to be set, competitions that had to be won. Their laughter was much kinder than a family's. Her stomach didn't sink at the sound of it.

🜁

Beyond the double doors of frosted glass and metal vines she'd shunned during Sebastian's tour sat a room filled with eternal springtime.

A worn dirt path wove between the trees and brush, across small hills of lush clover and wildflower beds. Mina strolled down towards the garden's creek, waving grasses turning to silt and rock, and stopped to tear a handful of the tiny, five-petaled flowers that grew like moss between the cracks of one of the boulders.

She crushed them between her palms.

Sap oozed through her fingers. Her boots sunk into the muddy sand of the creek bed as she reached the water's edge. The sap turned to suds as she dipped her hands in.

It was soapwort. It was real.

Mina glanced around the impossible pocket of nature stuffed within a single room. It was real. Not just some wizardly illusion.

Which meant the cool, tingling scent from her dream that tickled her nose every time a gentle breeze brushed against her cheek was real too.

She inhaled deeply and followed. Down the creek, back up the rocks to where the soil was dryer but still sandy, and a dozen bushes of lavender sat swaying in the breeze.

Her heart hammered in her chest like it did before a fight she knew she could win.

Lavender.

She collapsed onto them, burying her face in their flowers and inhaling deeply. For years, she had harvested them for Mrs. Harlowe, watched her hang bushels of it from the rafters of the cabin, making soaps and lotions, candles and tinctures. Was this what it smelled like then? Their little wooden hovel bursting at the seams with the delightful scent as spring turned to summer? No wonder it sold like crazy in town.

Mina's eyes grew heavy as she snuggled into the crop, forgetting her hunger in favor of a lavender-induced nap. She could grab something from the kitchen to eat during the next leg. The cavern was clearly abandoned, there was no reason for her to worry about the food attracting unwanted attention.

"Mina?" Sebastian called. "Come have lunch!"

"Fucking needy ass wizard," she hissed as the pull of his command lifted her to stand. She broke off a couple of stalks and stuck them into her bindings, safely under her clothes, and stomped up towards the sound of the others setting up their picnic.

"Good Gods, woman," Sir Gargic coughed out as she walked past him. She took a seat at the far end of the blanket, next to the embroidered belt bag Wera carried. "Did you buy out a perfumery?"

"What the hell is a perfumery?"

"It's a shop that sells colognes, scented lotions, potpourri, incense, anything and everything that could make a person smell good," Tanir explained, looking up from her sewing project. "You smell like you just rolled around in lavender, dear." Her expression turned to confused bemusement as she studied her. "Look like it, too."

"I tripped on my way to the creek and fell into some grass," she lied. "Must have been lavender."

"You?" Sir Gargic huffed in disbelief. "Tripped and fell?"

"Tripped and fell."

"You're more agile than a cat."

"Cats can trip."

"That's true," Enoch said as he piled some sort of salad onto his plate. "My Aunt Clarice had a cat called Stumbles. He was so cute, black and white with long fur and gold eyes, but was always bumping into corners, tumbling down the halls when chasing after a toy... She actually had to put cushions around all the counters and dressers because if he jumped down from them, he'd land on his face."

"Poor kitty. Did he get hurt a lot?" Tanir asked.

"That's the funny thing. Stumbles never broke a bone in his life, and he's still kicking."

"Doesn't matter how often you fall, so long as you fall right," Mina remarked. She grabbed a roll from the scarce amount of food at the center of the blanket. "Where's the wizard and the cartographer?"

"Right here," Sebastian grunted behind them. He trudged towards the blanket with a comically large picnic basket cradled in his arms. Wera followed behind, carrying two pitchers filled close to the brim.

"Sebastian," Tanir scolded. "It's just the six of us!"

"I know." He dropped the basket in the middle of the blanket. "It's my fault for asking the kitchen to make a traditional picnic basket. I stopped the conjuration when I saw the cutlery getting ready to spatchcock a duck."

"Good." Wera handed a pitcher to Tanir then took her seat next to Mina. "You're sitting next to me. That'll make this easy."

"It'll make what easy?" Mina mumbled with her mouth full. She went to reach for the pitcher when a flat wooden case was tossed at her.

"Open it," Wera said.

"No."

"Open it," Sebastian repeated.

Mina unlatched the lid and lifted it. Two dozen little chalk-looking things, wrapped in waxed paper, sat in two neat rows in various shades of white, black, and gray — save for three that shone brightly: one in the softer tones of sunset, one the blinding shade of firelight, and one the deep warmth of Sebastian's hair.

"They're oil pastels," Wera explained. "They work kind of similar to charcoal, so you should be able to draw with them easily."

Mina picked up the deepest one and twirled it around her fingers to read the label:

Amber.

Sebastian's hair was amber.

"What do I need these for?" she asked.

"You need them to learn your colors since you can't see them. You drew that terramawg near perfectly, using just charcoal and blending to mimic the different shades of his hide. I figured having labeled pastels could help you match the shades of gray to the actual names, like—" Wera held up her glass. "What color is this lemonade?"

"Cloudy light gray."

"Okay, now pick the pastel that matches the cloudy light gray the closest."

Mina looked back at the box and picked out two. "It's between these. This one is too dark, the other is too warm."

Wera smiled. Mina turned her head away slightly to avoid the headache. "See, I knew it would work. What are the names?"

"Blonde and Yellow."

"Lemonade is yellow, not specifically the shade you had in your hands but—" Wera grabbed the small sketchbook attached underneath the lid of the pastel case and opened it to the first page, "—if you blend the yellow with the white—" she took the pastel out from her hand and mixed it with the splotch of white she scribbled on the page. She held the splotch up next to the glass. "—you should get close to it."

Mina took the sketchbook from her and looked between the glass and the shade Wera created.

"Now it won't be perfect all the time. Value doesn't necessarily translate from color to black and white perfectly so there will be some similar shades, but it's a start." Wera gestured between the case and the sketchbook. "They're all yours. Enjoy."

Mina's fingers cramped up and she dropped it.

"Hey! If you didn't like it, you could have just—"

"Mina. I command you to use those pastels and sketchbook as you see fit," Sebastian said as he finished pulling out all the food from the basket and took a seat on the other side of her.

She picked up the sketchbook and smoothed out the pages that had creased from the fall before returning it to the case.

"Oh," Wera said. "Really? Over something as small as a sketchbook? How did Mr. Harlowe give you the book you used to catalog plants?"

"He didn't. I made the paper and bound it myself."

"Okay, but how did he teach you how to do it?" Sir Gargic asked, "Because if you ask any scholar, education is a—"

"Mina!" Sebastian cut Sir Gargic off, perhaps sensing another derogatory rant brewing. "Why do you have bits of lavender in your hair?"

"I tripped and fell into a patch of them."

"You... tripped?"

Enoch scoffed, "We went over this already. Mina had a Stumbles moment."

Sebastian looked even more confused. "Stumbles?"

"What I really want to know is why there's no ice in this lemonade," Enoch pouted.

Wera and Tanir groaned.

"Because the tap water is already cold, and ice would just water it down," Sebastian defended, a little bit of cattiness in his tone, much to Mina's surprise.

"Just because the ice melts when you hold the glass and waters your drink down doesn't mean everyone else should suffer!" Enoch argued.

"Well, then you should just get up and head to the kitchen and get some ice for yourself."

"Or Mina could make him some ice," Sir Gargic said.

"Yeah, Mina!" Sebastian agreed, caught up in the spat. "Make Enoch some ice!"

She lifted her arms as if she were drawing her bow, formed an ice arrow, and stuck the tip of the arrow in Enoch's glass.

"Oh, come on!" Enoch whined while the others laughed. It did look rather stupid sticking out of his cup.

"Alright, Mina," Sebastian wheezed as he caught his breath, "make him some ice for real this time."

Again, she lifted her arms as if she were drawing her bow, formed an ice arrow, and stuck the tip of the arrow in Enoch's glass, right next to the other one.

Nobody laughed this time.

"Um. I was thinking more ice cubes instead of ice arrows?" Enoch said after a moment.

"And?"

"And... could you make them?"

"I can go outside and carve some from the cavern if I'm told to," she replied.

Sir Gargic scoffed, "Don't be ridiculous. You're the personification of frigid. Just make a couple of cubes the same way you do your arrows!"

A long-forgotten but easy-to-slip-on shame crawled up her spine.

"I can't." Mina wanted to shrink into herself.

"Can't or won't?"

She picked at the last bits of roll in her hands, wondering how quickly she could bury herself under the dirt.

"Can't," she admitted.

"Why can't you?" Tanir asked.

"I don't know how," she mumbled.

More silence.

Motherfuckers can talk for hours about imaginary family dynamics, but they can't move the fuck on from me being a shit—

"Hey, there's no need to be embarrassed about it!" Wera consoled. "Enoch can get his ass up and head to the kitchen. You may be frosty, but you're not an ice machine."

"Hurry up and eat," Mina snipped. "We can be out of the caves by sunset if we push. Save a day of travel."

"That's good," Sebastian said. "You're changing the subject, though."

"What subject?" Mina palmed a fistful of finger sandwiches and stuffed her face with their bland mush. "I can't make ice cubes. End of story." She reached for an apple, and Sebastian grabbed it out of her hands.

"Wrong," he mumbled through his mouthful as he took a bite out of it. "Beginning of story."

"Are you trying to piss me off?" Mina snatched the apple out of his hand and took a bite out of it herself.

"A little. You give honest answers when you're angry."

"Now, I'm gonna lie just to spite you."

Sebastian arched an eyebrow, almost amused by her defiance.

"Mina. Tell me the truth. Why can't you make ice cubes?"

She tried her damnedest to keep her mouth shut, but the pull of his command forced the words out. "I left before they could teach me." She glared at him. "Jackass."

"Sticks and stones." Sebastian grabbed another apple out of the basket. "Now. Are you gonna play along for a bit, or am I gonna have to use our little contract hat trick every time I ask you something?"

"Do that and I'll kill you."

"No, you won't. I'm not a monster."

"Then I'll make your life a living hell."

"Wrong again." He shrugged with a cheeky smirk. "One command and I could have you treating me like a prince for all eternity."

"Then I'll hate you. I'll hate every fiber of your being for all eternity."

"So you don't hate me now?"

No.

A spike of pain tore through her skull, down her spine, and buried into her heart. She turned the apple in her hand to sauce and looked away from him. "Gods, you make my head fucking hurt," she spat. "Just ask your stupid questions."

"Who's 'they'?" Enoch asked through a mouthful of lettuce.

"Tutors," she grumbled.

"These tutors got names?" Sir Gargic asked.

Her mouth snapped shut just as she went to eat another sandwich, causing her to smash it against her lips.

"Too close to the curse that one is," Tanir remarked.

"I've got one," Wera said, dusting off the crumbs on her skirt. "Were you born with ice magic?"

Mina's jaw unlocked. "No."

"What?" She caught Sebastian's whisper.

"Aha! So you're a trained mage like me and Enoch!" Wera smiled.

"Nope."

"Exactly," Sebastian said. "Trained mages can't control purely elemental magics."

"Then how did she get her ice magic?"

"Perhaps it's part of the curse?" Tanir offered.

"But it helps her," Enoch said. "Curses are supposed to hurt."

"Not if you're Queen Farica," Sir Gargic said.

"She was asleep for seventy years!" Enoch balked. "Not only did all of her friends and family die, the entire world changed around her!"

A knot in Mina's stomach joined her lingering headache. She didn't want to bury herself anymore, she wanted to run.

Seventy years.

"Sure, but she married a king and hasn't seemed to age more than a day since she woke ten years ago."

"And I'm willing to bet she'd give all of that up to hug her parents again," Sebastian countered bitterly. "And a youthful complexion isn't exactly the same as being able to patch up nearly mortal wounds with ice!"

Mina got up and left. She didn't have to hear them discuss her like she wasn't there, like she was some riddle to be solved instead of a person.

"Mina?" Sebastian called.

"I ate," she spat. "Finish up in fifteen, or I'll drag you up this mountain by your throats."

🜂

They came out of the commorancy like dogs with their tails between their legs.

"So, uh," Sebastian stammered as he slinked up behind her. "Same order or?"

"Whatever," Mina said. "I don't give a shit."

She walked away, diving into the weaving maze of caverns that signaled the end of Rabbet's Pass. The closer they got, the tighter it would get. Hopefully none of them were claustrophobic.

"This is... a very intricate cave structure," Sebastian remarked.

"I guess."

"D-did you get lost your first time here?"

"Nope."

"Really?"

"Really," she lied.

The sound of their footsteps was deafening as it bounced around the vacuous ice walls. Even the others fell quiet under their booming, their ragged breathing almost offending. Mina could hear Sebastian chewing at the inside of his cheek, his heartbeat racing in double-time compared to the others, his stomach gurgling with unease.

"I don't know what I did exactly, but I'm sorry," he said, breaking the silence and unleashing a flood of unwelcome noise. "We're all sorry."

"An apology means nothing if you don't know what you're apologizing for," she said. "You might as well be selling bottled air."

"How about you tell us what we did wrong instead of just walking away then," Wera snipped.

"You know what you did," Mina grunted.

"It ain't our fault that you can't talk about how freaky you are," Sir Gargic barked. "So don't rake us over the coals for trying to piece together what we can!"

"What is there to piece together?! I'm Mina. An alpinist who lives alone and leads people through the Fallow Peaks. That's it!"

"You're more than just that," Sebastian said.

"Well, that's all that matters."

"Mina, we're just trying to—"

"I know what you're trying to do," she interrupted. "I know. It just— I just—" The words kept catching in her throat. "A beat dog runs from the sight of a fist."

Sebastian sighed. "You don't want to talk about it or hear people talk about it. Mina, I—"

You're sorry.

Even the thought stung.

"I know."

"Gods," Sir Gargic scoffed. "Can't you just let the man say it?"

"No."

"Can't take a compliment, can't take an apology," Wera tutted. "What can you take, Meens?"

"A beating."

"*Okay.*" Sebastian clapped. "I'm all good. Thank you all for your... input. Mina—"

She braced herself for another attempt to apologize.

"—I may need your assistance on a project again. What poisons are you immune to?"

Mina unclenched her jaw, her shoulders eased a little.

"All naturally occurring poisons and most conjured poisons."

"All naturally occurring poisons?"

"That's what I said."

"What conjured poisons do affect you?" Sir Gargic asked.

"You know I'm not stupid enough to answer that."

"Tanir," Sebastian called, "did you ever get the test results back on that swab you did of the jewelry box?"

"Yes, sir," she replied.

The medic's speech was too airy, as if she were talking in her sleep.

"What did you find?"

"Hmm. I don't remember."

The hairs stood on the back of Mina's neck. Where was the high-pitched whine of Enoch's ring?

"Did you write it down in your journal? I thought we—"

Mina stopped. Her breath caught, mind numbed, as she finally noticed the slight vibration of her sword sheath against her thigh.

Sebastian bumped into her. "Mina? Why did you—"

"Enoch."

"What?"

She brushed past him. Tanir stood, staring off into the darkness at the end of the line, her goggles pushed up on her forehead. Enoch was nowhere to be found.

"Tanir," Mina grabbed her shoulders. "Where's Enoch?"

Flecks of white swirled in her unfocused gaze.

"Hmm." Tanir gave a sleepy smile. "I don't remember."

Sebastian approached. "Tanir, what do you mean—"

Mina pulled him in front of her, bearing the pain of touching him as she wrapped her arms around him and grabbed his hands. Steam billowed between them as she puppeted his palms to cup Tanir's face.

"Mina!"

"Eyes."

Her hands trembled against his as he tilted Tanir's head back and held open her eyelids.

Ice flowers bloomed across her irises.

Dear one, humans are much more pleasant when they see pretty things. Like freshly fallen snow, or swirling frost on their window panes. Her voice oozed out of her memories. *Don't you want to give them pretty things?*

"She's charmed," Sebastian murmured.

Mina's grip tightened as anger and fear screamed at her. How did she miss it? How did a *fae* slip in under her nose and steal Enoch away?

How dare it take one of her friends.

"What's going on?" Sir Gargic asked.

"Where's Enoch?" Wera followed.

"He's gone," Mina spat at Sebastian's back. "We have to keep moving."

"Like hell we are!" Sebastian argued. "He's part of our family! We can't leave him behind."

"*I* have to leave him behind," she said. It didn't matter how much she wanted to hunt down the fae and tear its throat out with her bare hands, she couldn't. The last thing they needed to deal with on top of a missing party member and a prowling fae was a famished heatseeker.

"Mina, you know these caves better than anyone!" Wera said. "Put this aloof 'I don't care about anybody' bullshit aside and find him, will you?"

She clenched her jaw to stand the blistering pain as she squeezed Sebastian's hands.

"If I'm told to," she hissed.

Sebastian pulled his hands from Tanir's face and turned them over to squeeze Mina's back.

"Save Enoch."

She released him and rushed towards Wera.

"Do any of your inks have iron?"

"Y-yes? The paints—"

"Do any of them glow?"

"Yes."

"Which one?"

Wera pointed to one of the vials on her belt bag. "This one, but only when exposed to air."

Mina drew her sword and smashed the hilt against it, breaking the glass. The paint immediately illuminated as it oozed down the side of the satchel onto the ground.

"Hey—" Wera's protest choked off as Mina took the tail end of her own scarf and shoved it in her mouth.

"Don't scream," she demanded as she threw Wera over her shoulder and took off.

Whether it was the makeshift gag or true strength of will, the cartographer kept her terror reined in as Mina ran through the tunnels at a gale-force pace; sword drawn, retracing their steps as the vibrations in her blade grew stronger.

"F-fuck—"

"Shhh," a bell-like voice giggled on the wind, silencing Enoch's hissed expletive.

Mina stopped. Her sword felt electric in her palm. She sloughed Wera off her shoulder, setting her down wobbling and pale.

"Listen to me," Mina whispered in her ear. "Enoch's in one of these caverns. I'm going to grab him and throw him to you. Swirl whatever iron paint you have around the two of you like a shield until the wizard gets here, or I cut this bitch's head off. Nod if you understand."

Wera nodded.

A wanton moan poured out from a large crack in the wall beside them.

Wera's eyes widened in disbelief. Mina took a deep breath to prepare herself.

The whimpers and moans grew louder as they stepped through the crack and crept down the pathway that lay beyond it. One sharp bend and the tunnel opened up.

Naked and trembling, Enoch leaned against a stalagmite in the center of the frozen alcove, blissfully smiling as a young woman with snow-white skin and blanched hair stroked his cock.

"Oh, you naughty boy. Your sniveling brought us some unwelcome guests," the rimefae turned towards them and smiled. "Hello there, cousin. I see you brought a plaything of your own. Have you come to join us?"

Mina readied her sword. "Rot in Hell, you frigid bitch."

"Aww. You're no fun." Enoch's shaft darkened in her grip. "Take one more step, and I'll break it off."

"Oh?" With a flick of her wrist, Mina's sword flew through the air and severed the fae's hand from her arm. Mina chased after her blade, grabbing Enoch as she flew past him, and tossing him to Wera at the alcove's opening.

The fae shrieked and unfurled her white leather wings to take to the air.

"What?" Mina taunted as she unwedged her sword from the wall. "I didn't take a step."

"How can you even hold that blade?!" the rimefae cried as the flesh around her severed wrist blackened.

"Like this." With the wind at her heels, Mina leaped towards her with breakneck speed—

—and embedded her sword into a patch of ice.

Before she could process what happened, a glimmer of white flashed in the ice's reflection and the fae's fist burst out of it.

Mina flew across the cavern as the punch connected with her jaw, but instead of smashing against hard stone, a freshly amputated arm hooked around her throat and held her to the wall.

"You know they warned me that you liked to play rough," the rimefae's breath brushed against her ear as her head emerged from the ice, "but that sword is just unfair!"

Mina lifted her knees, building momentum, and slammed her feet against the wall; ripping the fae out of the ice and over her shoulder onto the ground. She sprung after her, both hands on the grip of her sword held above her head to bury the blade in the rimefae's chest, when the fae touched a small sliver of frost on the ground and disappeared into it.

Her goading giggle bounced around the alcove.

"Wow, cousin!" Mina dodged out of the way as the rimefae swooped down at her from another patch of ice. "You're still so strong!"

She was fast, but Mina was faster. She wove around every strike the young fae tried to land, avoiding any frozen sections on the ground while keeping an eye out for the growing speck of white that signaled her emergence.

Up and down, side to side, the fae dove in and out of every patch without a sense of pattern, except for one: the first patch she dove through, sporting a large, iron-tinged gash from where Mina's sword had torn through it after being knocked back by her punch, remained untouched.

Mina's tactics pivoted from avoiding the rimefae's attacks to marring her escape routes. She'd have to repair her blade, but the damage would be worth it once she severed the fae's head from her shoulders.

She watched the blur of white like a hawk, sullying the ice before she could come through it, until there were only two options left. Mina allowed her to pass through the first and smashed her blade across the second frozen surface as she left it. The fae flew towards the final swatch of ice, but Mina, as always, was faster.

Tap. The gentle clang of Mina's sword against the ice echoed through the cavern.

The fae hovered in the air, the playful smile on her face warped into a puckered sneer of frustration.

Mina tapped the tip of her blade on the ice once more, but not enough to mar it. "I'm done playing hide and seek." She raised her sword.

The rimefae smiled, a toothy, thin grin cut all the way up to her cheekbones as her eyes looked off to the side. "That's alright. I've found some new friends to play with."

"Save Enoch."

The invisible threads of Sebastian's command tightened around Mina's body, stopping her tapping as the rimefae turned her gaze towards the alcove's entrance. The bright amber glow of Sebastian's fire flickered behind Wera's swirling shield of paint.

With a sweep of her hand, the air around the rimefae crystallized and a barrage of frozen spikes flew their way.

Mina leapt off the wall, the unseen binds aiding her speed for her to get close, but not close enough. The wind left her back and curled up her arm, hearing her unspoken plea as she raked her sword through the air in a sweeping backswing.

A squall tore through the alcove, dislocating her shoulder as it shattered the spikes on impact. Mina bit through her bottom lip to keep herself from screaming as her nerves turned to razors in retaliation. Fuck giving the bitch the pleasure of hearing her scream.

Mina landed in front of them, standing as tall as she could, and glared at the fae through blood-blurred eyes.

"Oh!" The fae cocked her head to the side. "How fun!" Another batch of spikes crystallized in the air around her. "Bet you can't do it again."

Mina's sword trembled as she lifted it.

The rimefae backed up, eyes widening with fear.

A rush of roaring flame engulfed the alcove.

Mina tilted her head to find Sebastian standing behind her, eyes burning from the glow of his inferno as it melted every last inch of ice. He closed his fist, cutting off the stream of fire from his palms, and turned to her. "Are you alright?"

"Do I look alright?"

The fae was gone, but the threads of his command kept pulling at her.

"Windenhofer we need your hands again!" Sir Gargic called behind them. "Tanir's still out of it!"

"Set up the commorancy in here," Mina said, sheathing her sword.

"What? But—"

"You said to save Enoch." Mina lifted her dislocated arm with her good hand and slammed her shoulder into the wall to pop it back into place. "I'm saving Enoch."

Wera and Sir Gargic stood just outside the alcove, huddled around a shivering but still lust-drunk Enoch, while Tanir stared glassy-eyed at the ceiling, sticking a frost-coated tongue out with a smile.

"We don't need you!" Sir Gargic spat. "Sebastian's heat—"

"Will do jackshit as long as that hand is still wrapped around his cock," Mina cut him off. "Cartographer. Where's that iron paint?"

"In the vial next to the one you shattered."

Mina uncorked the bottle and held her breath as she poured a dollop onto her palm. Usually tolerable, she felt every second of the paint slowly eating through her flesh. Her body was pushed well past her built-up resistance to the metal, punishing her for protecting them.

"Hold him steady," she demanded as she rubbed her hands together, spreading the paint before slapping Enoch in the face.

"Gah!" Enoch hollered as he came to his senses. "W-w-why am I-I n-n-naked?" he chattered. His eyes widened as he looked down at himself. "I-i-s-s t-t-tha—"

He fainted.

"Hey. Tanir," Mina called her attention as she walked up to her.

"Yes?" she asked dreamily.

Mina slapped her with her other hand. "The snow's not real."

Tanir shook her head and touched the handprint on her cheek. "What? Where? Oh my Gods, Enoch!" Mina stopped her as she moved to rush over to him.

"Get into the infirmary and get ready, I'll bring him in," she said, shoving Tanir towards the alcove. She wedged her way between Wera and Sir Gargic and scooped Enoch up in her arms. "Cartographer, take that iron paint and draw a thick ring around the commorancy. Gargic, summon a lidded jar of iron filings and thirteen iron pitons from the Junk Room. Drop the jar off to me in the infirmary, then drive the pitons into the rock following the painted ring."

Sebastian held the door to the commorancy open for her. "What do you need me to do?"

"Assist Tanir until I tell you otherwise," she said. "You have to stave off the frostbite from spreading any further until we can get that hand off of him."

"Put him on the table here," Tanir instructed as they entered the infirmary. "I've put a warming blanket down to slow down the freezing in his spine."

Mina set him down, then hobbled over to the sink to wash off the paint still corroding her hands. Blackened layers of skin sloughed off as she scrubbed, leaving her palms raw and slightly bloodied, pits forming in the spots where the paint had clumped.

"Alright, beastie, here ya go," Sir Gargic said. He stood in the doorway lidded jar of iron filings in one hand, iron pitons in the other, his gaze honed on Enoch as he lifted his noxulars. "Good Gods, it looks even worse in color."

Mina took the jar from his hands, shaking slightly as she forced her stiffening fingers to curl around it. "Pitons. In a ring. Now."

Sir Gargic grimaced as he looked her up and down. "You look pretty shit in color, too."

"Gargic! Just do what she fucking says!" Sebastian snapped.

The knight flinched in shock before trudging off.

"Are those for Enoch?" Sweat beaded over Sebastian's brow as he stood above him, the palms of his hands glowing like coals, warping the air with their heat. The mild playfulness that seemed to linger behind all his expressions was gone, his jaw set like cement as his distant stare threatened to burn a hole through Enoch's chest.

"How's your aim?" she asked as she unlatched the lid with her teeth.

"Excellent."

"Can you fire off something hot enough to incinerate?"

"I can."

"Here's what's going to happen. I'm gonna tap that hand with my sword, and it's gonna run."

"It's gonna run?!" Tanir gasped.

"It'll run," Mina shut the infirmary door. "It'll try to scurry out of the room, back to the bitch it came from. Once it hits the floor, turn it to ash, and I'll mix it in with the shavings to make sure it stays like that."

Sebastian nodded. "Got it."

"Get ready. One— fuck!" Mina yanked her hand back from her sword hilt as the slightest brush against it scalded her.

"Mina, your hand—" Tanir moved to examine it.

"Focus on him!" she barked as she grabbed a nearby pile of gauze. "Again. One," Mina drew her sword, clumsily wrapping the cotton padding around it. "Two." She held her blade over Enoch's crotch, just beside where the severed hand gripped him. Sebastian dispelled the heat from his hands. "Three." She pressed the point against its wrist and the hand sprung alive.

Its spindly fingers released Enoch's shaft and skittered down his body, off the table, like a rat running from an exterminator.

With a snap and a point, a spark flew from Sebastian's index finger and latched onto it. Molten embers spread across its pale flesh, consuming it as it writhed into a pile of ash. Mina dropped her sword on the ground and rushed to dump the filings onto it.

"Come on," she urged through gritted teeth as she swirled her hand above it and conjured a pitiful whirlwind to funnel the pile into the jar. She snapped the lid shut and collapsed to the ground.

"Thank The Gods, he's warming up," Tanir sighed in relief. "You did it, Mina."

"I know," she groaned. The subtle tension puppeting her movements, supporting her from the moment she blocked the rimefae's attack, released. An invisible titan sat on top of her, driving twin spears through either side of her skull. She closed her eyes to keep the light from stabbing through her corneas, and tried to focus on her breathing as the room spun around her.

"They warned me you liked to play rough." The fae's bright voice taunted over and over again as the room spun faster and faster— until something lifted her up to sit, forcing her to purge the contents of her stomach.

"That's it." Tanir patted her back. "Get it all out."

Another set of hands held back her hair. "Shit. Is that blood?" Wera asked.

When did she enter the room?

"Looks like it. Sir Gargic, you ready?"

"Yes, ma'am."

Mina's heaves subsided, and Wera wrenched her head back as a gloved hand squeezed the sides of her jaw. Pulpy liquid filled her mouth, choking her as the hand moved to hold her jaw shut.

"Mina," Sebastian's voice rang out from farther in the room, "Swallow."

She forced the concoction down her aching throat and the room stopped spinning. The titan left to torment someone else.

"There ya go, your color's coming back," Tanir said.

"I didn't think you could get any paler, but boy was I wrong," Wera smoothed her hand on top of Mina's head, sending a hundred needles into her scalp. She smacked her hand away.

"Ow!" Wera yelled.

"Fuck!" Mina shouted as a shooting pain ran through her hand.

Tanir sighed. "Well, I guess we know that the gloves work now."

"Gloves?"

Tanir grabbed Mina's hands and studied them. The medic wore a pair of gloves made of thin leather, the fingertips of which hung loose, too long for her short fingers.

They were the same pale shade as the sewing project she'd been working on. Mina watched cautiously, perplexed that she wasn't screaming in pain as Tanir touched her. There was only a slight ache.

"They're made of seal leather. Severe burn victims wear them in the winter to protect their sensitive skin while maintaining most of their mobility. Helps keep their appendages warm, just in case the nerves are too damaged to feel the cold." Mina hissed as Tanir ran her thumb over one of the deeper sores. "You told Wera you were immune to poison during your fight."

"And?"

"This looks like chemically induced necrosis... and you're not healing as quickly here compared to the rest of you. Did the fae do this?"

"No."

"Do you know what did?"

"The paint."

"The— paint?" Tanir sent an accusatory glare Wera's way.

"I-it's just gouache!" Wera stammered. "It's acacia, water, and iron oxide! There's no reason it should do that!"

"It's the iron, Tani," Sebastian interjected. "Iron is incredibly toxic to faefolk. Do you need something to draw it out, Mina, or did you get all of it off when you washed your hands?"

"It's gone. These kinds of wounds are just slow to heal." She flexed her fingers, their movement slow and stiff. "The callouses will take forever to get back."

"Good Gods, your hands look like you held hot coals, and you're upset your calluses are gone?" Sir Gargic scoffed.

Mina looked up at him. "Remember how fucking wrecked your hands got when you first started sword training? Imagine that, but your sword is slowly eating through you." She looked back down at her hands.

"Fuck," Wera said. "And it's gonna be hard to play violin without them, too."

Mina wished she could cry.

"Where are you going?" Tanir asked as she stood. Mina ignored her and went to pick her sword off the ground. "Wait! Don't pick that up! It'll only make your hands worse!" The medic shoved the pair of gloves. "Here."

"I'm not taking your gloves."

"I made them for you. You won't have to worry about touching us or grabbing us if you need to."

"Then I'm definitely not taking your gloves."

"Mina, put the gloves on," Sebastian commanded.

She ripped the gloves out of Tanir's hands and put them on, picked up her sword, and stomped out of the room.

"Come on, Meens! Did I say something wrong?" Wera shouted after her.

"Leave her be, Wera," Sebastian said.

"I shouldn't have mentioned the violin."

"It's not just that," he said, their voices slowly fading as she walked away.

"Then what is it?" Tanir asked.

Sebastian's voice was barely louder than a whisper. "I think she's scared."

🜂

"Wow, cousin! You're still so strong!"

Who was she? Mina didn't remember any of the other kids looking like her.

The smell of lavender, though faint, hit her immediately as she entered the garden. She made her way towards it, pausing by the creek for a moment to look at her reflection. Dark trails of blood — poured from her eyes, her nose, the corners of her mouth — laid frozen on her face. She brushed her thumb over her cheek, breaking a piece of the trail off.

Then again, she didn't look the same as she did back then either.

She rinsed her face in the water, dispersing her horrifying visage with ripples, and made her way to lay in the lavender patch.

Their perfume washed over her, strong but not as jarring as before. The way it tingled in her nose less foreign and more comforting, yet her muscles still tensed — jaw clenched, spine rigid — unwilling to release to the flowers' will as easily as they did before.

"I think she's scared."

Fifteen years. Fifteen years without seeing a single one of them. There was once a time when she wished to, when she was young and learned what life should have been for her, angry and bitter, but she never sought them out. Going after them would only bring trouble. It was safer to hide away, keep her nose down, prepare to face them if they did come.

She would have killed her. She still wanted to kill her, but not out of rage or hatred or revenge. Killing her was the only way to know she'd never come back.

The lavender wore Mina down, seeping into her system, making her eyelids heavy.

He'd be scared too if he knew what they were capable of.

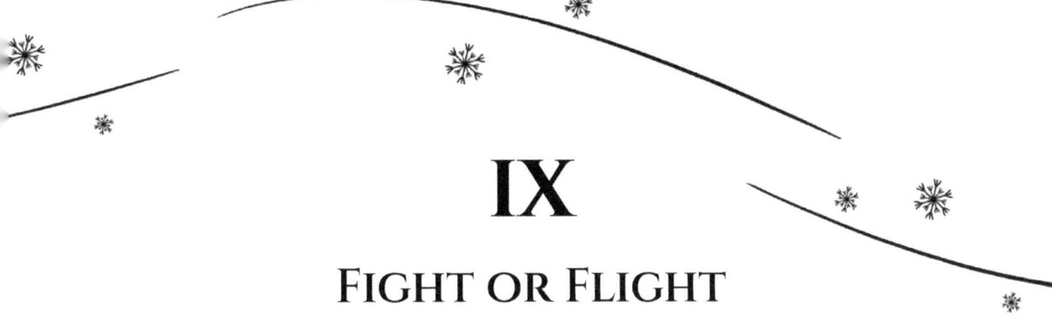

IX

Fight or Flight

"Now, Mina, it's tradition here that whenever we break bread with someone new to our little troop, we conjure up their favorite meal." Sebastian smiled at her. "So, what can I have the staff whip up for you?"

The cookware on the stoves and counters jumped to attention.

"I don't have a favorite meal," she answered.

The utensils wilted at her response.

"Oh dear," Tanir cooed beside her, "surely there must be something you like?"

Mina looked across the room to Enoch. "What's your favorite?"

His eyebrows shot up in surprise. "My favorite?"

Mina nodded.

"Oh, um, asado de tira with verdurajo," he answered, "paired with a nice malbec."

Mina smiled and looked at the utensils. "That sounds good to me."

The utensils hopped to work, cooking at an enchanted pace.

"Why did you pick Enoch?" Sebastian asked her.

"I don't know." She shrugged. "He just looked like he needed a good meal."

His smile brightened and Mina's chest tightened. "Well, that's awfully kind of you. Hopefully, you'll be able to find your favorite food soon so we can treat you just as kindly."

"That would be really nice."

"I bet I know what it is, Meens," Wera teased.

"Really?"

"Yup!"

The food and drink slid across the table in front of them: a beautiful rack of ribs surrounded by a bounty of grilled vegetables.

"Let's have a toast," Sebastian said, prompting them all to raise their cups. His mouth moved as if he were speaking, but no sound came out.

"Cheers!" Tanir cut him off. They thrust their cups together, laughing, and Mina struggled to keep the smile off her face as she took a sip.

🜁

The chime of the dinner bell woke her, eyes simply snapping open rather than her jumping to her feet, ready to attack. Mina touched her lips, trying to remember what it felt like to smile, but her expression remained unmoving. She pulled out the sprigs of lavender from underneath her breastplate and tossed them to the ground as she stood. She didn't know the flower could alter memories, but then again, she'd never slept on a bed of the stuff.

Mina stopped by the guest room first, changing out of her blood-stained white leathers back into the patchwork ones she wore back at her cabin.

"Oh," Sebastian said as she stepped out into the hall, nearly knocking into him. "It's been a while since I've seen you in those."

"It's been five days," she replied.

He ran a hand down his face. "Gods, it has been, hasn't it?" He sighed. "Feels longer."

"You looking for me or something?"

"No. I was just heading down to the kitchen. Right place, right time."

Mina said nothing as she continued to make her way down the hall. Sebastian fell into step alongside her.

She braced herself for a comment, be it a criticism or condolence, but nothing came. Their footsteps, a steady, unison rhythm, felt more and more like a ticking clock as they headed down the stairwell, approaching the first floor.

The worst thing about a ticking clock was never knowing when it would ring.

Mina stopped as they reached the bottom step. "You haven't asked me about today."

Sebastian stopped one step ahead of her and turned around. "I figured it'd be best if we all discussed it over dinner. That way everyone is present, and you don't have to repeat yourself." His gaze darted across her face, studying her. "Is that alright? Or is there something you wish to tell me away from the others?"

"No," the word forced itself again.

"Alright." He nodded gently. "There is one thing I want to ask you, though." He took a step back up to her level. "Earlier you insisted that you had to keep moving but stayed in place. Bruised my hands a bit, you were squeezing them so tightly." He paused for a moment and glanced towards the ceiling, tapping his lips as he worked out the right words to say.

A light bruise had blossomed on his thumb.

"Is assuming that, when your actions contradict your words, I should issue you a command relevant to the situation, the right course of action?"

Mina's first thought was to tease him about how wordy his question was, fueled by a sudden tightness in her chest, almost identical to the sensation his compliment gave her in her altered memory.

An out-of-place sensation among the turmoil turning, twisting her deeper thoughts.

"Clearly." Mina stepped around him. Chest still tight, nagging at her to say something more, "Mrs. Harlowe used to draw a bath with salt in it for Mr. Harlowe when he returned from the Peaks. Eased the bruises he got on the journey."

Sebastian lingered a moment before following after her. "That was kind of her. Did she ever draw a bath for you?"

"No," she replied, walking out into the first floor's hall. "Frozen tubs tend to shatter."

Mina quickly made her way to sit next to Tanir as they entered the kitchen. Sebastian took his seat at the head of the table.

"Will Enoch be fit to join us, Tani?" he asked.

"Yes. I left him just a few minutes ago with a change of clothes," she answered. "It'll take the poor man a bit to put them on, but he insisted on doing so himself."

"You're one hell of a healer to have him up and about already," Sir Gargic remarked. "An injury to a man's pride like that is no laughing matter."

"Well," Wera said, "That really depends on the type of injury and how much time has passed."

Mina gritted her teeth at the memory of Enoch quivering in enchanted ecstasy.

"And how much time has to pass before I can beat his ass for falling for a rimefae's tricks?" she snipped.

Tanir bristled. "Will you be beating my ass as well, then?"

"I'm considering it. What the fuck happened back there?"

"Mina, what part of when everybody—"

"When everybody is here, you all are asking me questions," she cut Sebastian off. "I have some of my own."

Mina turned her attention back to Tanir. "It couldn't have been a song, I would have heard it. Was it the smell of maple sap or the sight of snowfall?"

Tanir pulled back a bit. "Snowfall."

"But you were wearing the noxulars."

"What do the noxulars have to do with her being charmed?" Sebastian asked.

"You enchanted them. Things that alter the senses make it hard for the fae to charm someone, especially if that thing is enchanted."

"That would have been good to know beforehand," Tanir grumbled.

"You know now," Mina replied. The medic deflated, defenses lowering. "You took them off, didn't you?"

"We both did," she admitted. "We saw the snowflakes and weren't sure if something was off with the goggles, considering the rest of you didn't seem to notice it."

Mina turned away from her. "If you see something strange, say something, same goes for if you hear something or smell something."

Silence lingered for a moment; anticipation for some reason.

"Is that... all you have to say?" Tanir asked.

"Obviously."

Wera laughed.

Mina sent a scowl her way. "What?"

"That really was quite the ass-beating, Meens."

She crossed her arms, doubling down on her decision. Tanir's dismay was enough punishment for her mistake. The real focus of her ire was probably laughing it up in the Barren Rime as they spoke. "There's no point in kicking someone when they're down. Especially when there are other things to worry about."

"There's nothing to worry about," Sebastian dismissed.

"Really?" Mina sneered at him. "How about the fact that the frozen cunt only took Enoch instead of both of them."

"Perhaps she only enjoys the company of gentlemen," Sir Gargic snickered.

"They don't give a shit about gender. Most of them barely care about species."

"And what about you then?" he pressed.

"What about me?"

"Do you have a preference?"

"No?"

"Really?" asked Wera, head tilting to the side like a curious dog. "You don't even care about species?"

Her nails sunk into the wood of the kitchen table. So much shit they don't know, and who the fae fucked around with was their first concern?

"I don't—"

The kitchen door creaked open.

"Enoch!" Sebastian cheered, a little too enthusiastically. "Look at you! Up and walking!"

Enoch waddled in, his steps careful and wide. Instead of heading to his usual seat, he toddled over to Mina and dropped to her feet in a prostrate bow.

"My life is yours," he said.

"Not interested."

"I will do anything you ask of me for the end of time. You ask me to take a bolt for you, I will. You ask to give up writing and I will never pick up a pen again. Even my firstborn, I—"

Mina picked him off the floor by his collar and carried him like a kitten in its mother's jaws to his seat.

"Not. Interested." She dropped him onto the bench, and he yipped, doubling over and grabbing at his still-sore groin.

Her hand seized as she let go of him, recoiling from having too much strain on the healing tendons.

Sebastian grimaced at the sight. "Mina. Have Tanir look at your hands before dinner is served."

"W-what's wrong with her hands?" Enoch fretted.

"She'll be fine." He patted his shoulder reassuringly. "Now, we all decided that tonight you get to pick the entire meal."

"Thank you. That's quite kind." Enoch smiled softly and called over his shoulder to the kitchen: "Asado de tira with verdurajo, paired with a nice malbec, please."

"Take off your gloves and hand them to me," Tanir instructed as Mina returned to her seat.

The bleeding had stopped, congealing into the deeper pits the paint had corroded away. The skin was still mottled, peeling in places and shining in others as the raw skin tried to toughen itself. Tanir placed the gloves on her own hands as she inspected the wounds.

"You weren't kidding when you said these wounds would be slow to heal," Tanir noted. "But they are healing. Can you make a fist for me?"

Her fingers curled in disjointedly, spasming and shaking as she forced them down.

"Alright, that's enough." Tanir stopped her as her hands trembled in their half-closed position. "If you force them too much, you'll only do more damage." She handed the gloves back to her. "Keep these on until the larger sores heal over."

"You know, Meens, drawing with those new pastels might help the healing process along," Wera offered.

"Practicing the violin once you regain some of your mobility might help build your calluses back up as well," Sebastian added. His expression soured slightly. "Though it'll be uncomfortable at first."

"I'm used to uncomfortable," Mina replied.

The clatter and sizzle of the kitchen's cooking blossomed in the silence.

"Speaking of uncomfortable," Sir Gargic said as he cleared his throat. "That creature back there was your cousin?"

"No," Mina replied.

"But she called you cousin."

"We're not related if that's what you're getting at."

"Well, did you know her?" Wera asked. "She seemed to know you."

"I don't know." Mina looked down at the table, mind churning. "She's too old."

"Too... old?" Enoch swallowed. "Don't tell me she was some type of ancient fae disguising herself as a young woman."

Sebastian's brow furrowed. "Hypothetically, Mina, if you did know that fae, how old should she be?"

"Thirteen or fourteen at the most," she replied, causing Enoch to pale, "but most likely younger."

"I-I'm n-not," he stammered, "Sh-she—"

"Like I said. She is too old. Not a teen," she locked eyes with Enoch, "and it wasn't because of some glamour."

"R-right. Okay, that's comforting... I guess. All things considered." He looked back at the kitchen. "Is the meal almost done? I could really use that glass of wine."

"How long ago would it have been since you last saw her?" Sebastian asked.

Mina's teeth cemented against each other.

"Mina?"

She looked away from him, remaining silent.

"Okay." He drummed his fingers over his lips. "I've got it. How long ago did you first meet Mr. and Mrs. Harlowe?"

Her jaw unlocked. "About fifteen years ago."

Sebastian leaned forward, his thoughts running a mile a minute behind his eyes. "And had you run into any fae before her during those fifteen years?"

"No."

"That doesn't make any sense," Sir Gargic scoffed. "What, you met her as a child then? You've got to be in your late twenties now. How the hell is she supposed to be younger than fourteen?"

"You're right, Sir Gargic," Sebastian drawled, "it doesn't make sense."

Their meal, now finished, slid in front of them, but Mina could not take her eyes off Sebastian and the excited smirk he wore — no matter how much it stung her eyes.

"You're assuming that Mina has spent all the years of her life in the Realm of Mortals, when I'm willing to bet good money she has not. The 'sort of orphanage' she stayed at might have been in the Realm of the Fae, where time is rather tricky. Mortal years could fly by in fae minutes. Fifteen mortal years could be one or two, or even just a week in Elphyne depending on which region you're in and the will of its ruler, which is why she believes that the fae should be much younger than what we saw."

He paused for a moment, the puzzle pieces slotting in his mind stalling as he got closer to the full picture. His zeal petered out, the smile left his face as the sparks of excitement in his eyes dulled in pity. "And why you don't know how old you are."

Mina's racing heart beat against her chest, threatening to squeeze the air out of her lungs with every thump. Not painful, but his words were close enough to the truth to cause discomfort. An eagerness for him to solve it fought against a voice that whispered for her to run. She turned away from him and picked up the wine that had just appeared to soothe the sudden dryness in her throat...

... only for it to dry out more.

Mina spat the drink back into her glass, choking as the burning coating it left on her tongue brought tears to her eyes.

"Mina!" Tanir fretted bedside her as she coughed violently, trying to clear the sting at the back of her throat.

"I'm sorry! I'm so sorry!" Sebastian panicked. "I didn't mean—"

"Stop apologizing, Sebastian! You're only making it worse!" Wera scolded.

Mina grabbed the other glass in front of her, hoping it was water, and chugged it. The burn subsided, leaving behind a thin film on her tongue much different than anything she'd felt before, and an unexpected warmth.

She caught her breath and pointed at the wine. "What the fuck is that?"

"Malbec," Enoch replied. "It's a type of red wine."

"It's awful!"

"No, it's not! It's a very fine wine! It's got deep notes of black cherry and— and— turmeric—" He shook his head. "Why am I explaining this to you? You can't even taste—"

A spark of realization zipped around the table. Mina's stomach dropped.

Sebastian jumped up from his seat, his smile so big and brimming with joy, she had to look away. "You can taste it, can't you?!" he exclaimed. "Can't you?!"

Mina took another sip of the wine, more prepared to bear its sting, but her face still puckered. There was no use hiding. "Unfortunately."

"Try some of the vegetables and tell me how they taste."

Mina palmed a handful of the vegetables and shoved it in her mouth, following his unintentional command. "Nothing," she mumbled through it as she chewed.

"And the lavender!" Her stomach sank even deeper as he continued. "You can smell lavender now too, can't you?"

Mina lowered her head. There was nothing wrong with them knowing, was there? Why did it feel wrong? Why did it feel like an axe was going to drop on the back of her neck?

Not an axe. Barbed chains of ice.

"Why didn't you tell us? How did it happen? Is it just the lavender and the wine, or is there more too?" Questions rushed out of Sebastian like river rapids. "When did this start to happen? Was there some type of sign? Do you have any idea of what could have caused—"

"Sebastian," Tanir interjected. "How about we take our time with the questions and enjoy our meal before it gets cold?"

"I know but—" Sebastian stammered as he sat back down in his seat, "—but this is huge! It's wonderful news!"

"True. At least something good came out of my suffering," Enoch said as he chewed, puffing his chest out. "My favorite wine is the first thing Mina's ever tasted."

"Your name was also the first of ours she spoke," Wera added.

Mina pulled her gaze up from the table, "What?"

"Really?" Enoch lit up. "My name was the first?"

Wera nodded. "Followed by Tanir's and then Sir Gargic's."

"I didn't say their names," she refuted.

"Yes, you did," Sir Gargic said.

"Sir Gargic's name I understand," his name, as hideous as it was, rolled off her tongue effortlessly. "but Enoch—" Mina stalled, mind trying to catch up with how easily she spoke. "And... Tanir..." she said slowly.

"See! I told you, you said them!" Wera gloated.

A dull yet still giddy rush overcame her. "I did, didn't I, Wer—" her name caught in Mina's throat as if she were coughing up a lump of needles. Mina's mouth hung open as she struggled to breathe, tears gathering in her eyes.

"Is something wrong?" Sebastian asked.

"N-no," the word forced itself out of her in the form of a bloody cough she barely managed to cover with her napkin.

"You just coughed up blood, and that's a 'no'?" Wera asked.

Mina said nothing, folded up her napkin to conceal the blood a bit, and washed the remainder of it down with a drink of water. There was no reason for her to feel as disappointed as she was.

"Well, three names, smelling lavender, and tasting wine are some pretty great things to come out of this hard day," Sebastian broke the heavy silence. "Let's enjoy our meal, as Tanir said. We can discuss more about this in the study tonight, if Mina's up to it."

They all dug into their meals, and while the warmth the wine left on her tongue was a welcomed change, the experience was dulled by a dissatisfied hunch that bowed Sebastian's shoulders.

Great. I've disappointed him, too.

🜁

Mina couldn't shake Sebastian's disappointment from her mind. It lurked behind her thoughts, taking the spotlight when her attention fell idle. Laughter and smiles returned to him as the night carried on, but she couldn't help but see its stain behind them. With it brought this unknown feeling, close to shame, but calling it such would do it injustice. It stiffened her joints and tensed her jaw, a deep ache in her body begging for relief, yet sitting — idleness at all — felt wrong.

The memory was clearly the cause. The image of his downtrodden expression, an infection desperately needing treatment. Her hands, despite their injured state, were restless, yearning for the fiddle they were not fit to play.

So she drew.

In the confines of her room, she drew what she wanted to see from the wizard. Her amber pastel glided across the page in shaky strokes, the lines thicker than she'd like in some places, until the feeling went away... until Sebastian smiled up at her from the parchment.

Mina stared back at him, something akin to the warmth of the malbec faintly blooming in her chest, until her eyes closed under the weight of sleep.

🜁

"Don't take your noxulars off. Shout if you see, hear, smell, taste, sense anything weird," Mina addressed the group the next morning. "Things are gonna get tight at the end of this. Keep your breathing even, and your focus on the person in front of you. Wizard, there may be some parts that are frozen over that you'll have to melt."

Wera raised her hand. "When you say tight, can you give specifics?"

"The narrowest point is two and a half feet wide and about a foot and a half tall."

"Two and a half feet?!" Sir Gargic gawked. "How the hell do you expect me to fit through there? Or Sebastian?"

"Or Enoch?" Enoch added.

Tanir patted him on the back. "You're not as broad-shouldered as you think, dear."

Mina glared at Enoch, wearily. "Wizard, there may be some parts that are frozen over that you'll have to melt," she repeated slowly.

"And what if it's rocks, genius?" Sir Gargic mocked.

She held up a gloved fist. "I'll clear them."

"Mina, you can't do that!" Tanir scolded.

"I can and I will if necessary."

"Mina. Listen to—"

"Wizard," she cut Sebastian off. "I'm leading. And if the one leading gets stuck and can't get the others out, then you shall face a death of starvation while they get the lucky hypothermic end. The paint marred my palms, not my knuckles."

He scowled. "That hardly makes it better."

"Rather hardly than nothing." She opened the front door. "Come on, we've got to make up for lost ground."

She froze mid-step, barely saving herself from being burned by the iron ring outside.

Mina looked over her shoulder to glare at Wera and Sir Gargic. "Did you have to put it so close?"

"I got it," Sebastian brushed alongside her and broke the circle by kicking out one of the pitons, taking a chunk of the iron paint out as well. "There you go," he said. He tilted his head towards the cavern outside. "After you."

Mina shoved him aside lightly as she stepped out of the commorancy.

"Do you hear her?" Enoch asked Mina as they waited for Sebastian to pack up.

"No," Mina said, closing her eyes for good measure to hone her focus. She could hear their heartbeats, the different patterns of breathing, the assortment of subtle scratches, squeaks, and clangs from their clothing, but nothing more than that. "I didn't hear her yesterday, though, so my hearing shouldn't be solely relied upon."

"Great," Enoch exhaled, his voice shaking with nerves.

"I've adjusted my sword belt to make up for it."

"What does—"

Mina walked away as Sebastian's footsteps approached her, taking the lead and resuming the same order as the day prior.

"Come on, Mina. What does your—"

"Just because I can't hear her, doesn't mean she can't hear us," she announced as she made her way out of the alcove and into the tunnel. "Or see us for that matter. The bitch can travel through ice."

"So, keep the conversation superficial?" Sebastian asked as he caught up to her.

"Or we could not talk at all," Mina replied. "I know silence is a novel concept to you all."

Sebastian leaned over her shoulder, cupping his hand over his mouth as he whispered in her ear, "Yes, but if we talk and feed her misinformation, it could benefit us next time we face her."

She gave him a sidelong look. It wasn't a terrible idea.

"Ugh. What did you eat straight out of the fireplace this morning, Wizard? The charcoal on your breath is obnoxious!" Mina growled, shoving him back.

"Wait, Mina, you can sm— "

"Just as rude as always!" Sebastian scolded, cutting Wera off. "And after I saved you yesterday!"

"Oh what, that little wind trick you pulled? You almost tore my fucking arm off!"

"Sebastian! Mina! Are you—"

"Don't get me started on you, ya old broad!" Mina hollered at Tanir. "Some medic you are! I went above and beyond to keep Sonnet Sam from turning to Sally, and you go ahead and botch the job!"

"Hey! He may be dickless, but at least he can still piss!" Wera added, catching on quickly to their game. "It takes some talent to make that happen."

"Talent?" Mina scoffed. "I piss dickless every fucking day!"

"Can we stop yelling about dicks, please?!" Enoch squeaked. "It's a very sensitive subject right now!"

"Gods! If it wasn't for the money, I would have left you all to rot."

"You hear that, Gargic?" Sebastian said, turning over his shoulder to shout back to the knight as they walked. "I told you we should have contracted Vilkas."

"Vilkas? Vilkas?!" Mina roared. "The 'gentleman mountaineer' who charges you an arm and a leg to kill two-thirds of your expedition?!"

"At least the conversation would be nice," Sir Gargic scoffed. "Wouldn't have to be yelled and grunted at by some uneducated, backwoods hermit every day."

"Uneducated, huh?" Now she didn't have to pretend to be angry. "Porit woon dunbradt, woon tuutit nara a bohm. Ne orror dunsheen sama woon, hon'um va duntin wenna shiksi ahn m'woono hahnnah dundahn lowle m'ohhonnah bohmumnd cluh sheer dunni bohme, umnd dun brah hah ti thwat hannasim ban'ni." Mina cleared her throat, "None of you speak Tubazi? Tei roti Yosik, fizeer?"

"Meaumu Yosik?" Sebastian's eyes widened, a shocked smile curving up the corners of his mouth despite his best bitter acting.

"Cristi. Traspimu dis par das ultmeaumi ilburn. Irmo zapeer min't oviis pinnor fixon blumon cad roush sisin min't roral't ashgapil vasmoor. Tonmini das imol shameau tor di halmeau ahrmnor irm phisseer chazmeau anidin pos talas ultrorroriz moorcak Lanholde soosoomir mir't roramir rassh."

"What the hell is she saying?!" Sir Gargic snarled.

"She— uh—" Sebastian stammered.

"Gonnor puli hira pis. Spimu omin unpact min't luh roush disdas Roral Gunfachi't ash cushon o—" Mina placed a hand on her sword as it vibrated against her side, "—asa hik id gunin meaupal —" a flicker of white flitted between patches of ice scattered around the tunnel's walls, closer and closer, "— par unsz!"

She drew her sword and buried it in the ice patch beside her, casting the rimefae away. They all stood in silence for a moment.

Her blade stilled.

"So that's how it works," she remarked.

"Was that her?" Sebastian asked.

"It was her." Mina sheathed her sword and continued hiking. "I'll be able to tell when she's coming, so if I start up an argument, keep an eye out for a glowing white spot in any of the patches of ice you can see. You all have pitons on you?"

"Yes," they answered in various ways.

"Are they iron?"

"They are," Sebastian answered.

"Then keep a piton in reach and stab it through the ice if her white spot is near you."

"Can you warn us next time you two decide to hold a spontaneous stage show?" Tanir asked, a bitter edge to her tone. "I thought I was going to have to perform an exorcism or something."

"Sorry, Tani," Sebastian apologized. "Warning you all would have tipped the fae off if she were watching. Great job catching on, Wera."

"Thank you, thank you." She bowed. "As a reward, please tell me what glorious insults you just hurled, Mina. 'I piss dickless every fucking day' nearly broke me."

Sebastian chuckled. "Yeah, that— that was a good one."

"I told you to translate, wizard. Did I not?" Mina said. "Go on. Tell Wera what I said."

"Oh-ho no. We're finally sailing smoothly as a group. A good captain knows not to rock the boat."

"Bravnor," she scoffed.

"Lospimu mon reti o forspimo mu hanat at bravmi't Lanholde culi chazes."

Mina looked back at him and sneered, "You wouldn't dare."

"Wouldn't dare what?" Wera asked.

"Nothing," he snickered. "So long as Mina behaves."

Her heart rate skyrocketed, a slight burn like the warmth of wine flared inside her cheeks. She flipped him off, turned around quickly, and walked a little faster than before.

🜁

The maze-like twists and turns, sudden drops and elevations, converged into one tunnel that closed in with every step. Once the ceiling brushed the top of Sebastian's head, they paused for a moment to collect themselves before progressing, with Mina telling a tall tale about one of her past patrons being squeezed so tight they shat themselves and their companions had to be pulled through it.

A slight bow of their head quickly turned to crawling, clambering up the small inclines like primates, until they had no choice but to lie on their stomachs and wriggle their way through.

"How the hell did you lead expeditions through this?" Sir Gargic grunted. "Weren't they all blind?"

"I wish I were blind," Wera whispered low enough that only Mina could have heard.

"I pulled them," Mina answered. "Simple as that."

"You pulled them through this stone sausage casing?" Sir Gargic questioned.

"Usually, it's coated in iceslyth slime. Reduces the friction and glides them through."

"B-but there's n-n-no s-s-slime n-n-now," Wera stammered. The shake in her voice raised the hairs on the back of Mina's neck. Her breathing quickened, turning quickly to hyperventilation. "S-s-so w-w-we-"

"Wera, calm down," Sebastian tried his best hand at soothing.

"Calm down?!" she shrieked, "I can't breathe! Let me out!" She tried to move back, scratching frantically at the rock and ice enclosing them. "Let me out!"

"Shit. Tani, do you have any anxiolytics?"

"I do, but the side effects are quite diuretic, and her muscular control would—"

Mina's breathing quickened as Wera's panicked thoughts spread through her head. It *was* too tight in here. The walls *were* closer than before. Without the iceslythes how did she expect to make it out of here?

Her rational mind fought against it, scrambling for control. What could she do to calm her? She couldn't give kind words, couldn't reach her either, and even if she could, the pain— a heatseeker in this tight space would surely slaughter them all. When she came to, she'd be left alone with their corpses. What would be the point in carrying on if that were the case?

For her to survive, they all needed to survive.

Sebastian's rationalizations, Sir Gargic's grunts as Wera fought against him, Enoch's whimpers, and Tanir's fussing grew louder and louder, clouding her mind until she screamed, "Enough!"

Her shout cut through the cavern and bounced back, bringing a memory with its echo.

"It works much like the hypnotism mortals use," her tutor said with a sick smile. "Only much stronger and harder to resist." She watched the poor prisoner dance in his cell, a smile on his face despite his bare feet blackening with frostbite.

"Hypnotism?" she asked.

"It's a method of mind control at its best, and a way to focus the mortal mind at its worst. One of the Seelie court members taught it to them years ago, wanting to ensue a little bit of chaos by using it for amusement. Of course, the mortals had to bungle the gift, using it as treatment."

"It's medicine?"

"To them. The repeating patterns of sight or sound can help still the mortal mind, apparently."

"You're the reason I'm in this mess!" Wera shrieked at her, bringing her back to their current predicament. "Don't you dare—"

"I know! But I've gotten dozens of people through this, so just shut up and listen to the sound of my voice!" Mina inhaled deeply and sang an elongated, alto "ooo". Her voice bounced back, a mesmeric underscore as she spoke rhythmically. "Listen, to my voice, pay attention to the pattern. As I sing, focus, breathe, and move forward. It'll lead you to salvation."

She repeated her "ooo" as the echo layered her spoken word over top. Wera's breathing slowed and her struggling subsided. "Say aye, if you'll follow as I lead."

"Aye," Wera and Sir Gargic said in unison. An unexpected effect, but one she wasn't opposed to.

"By the light, by the light, by the light, of the lantern," she sang, the song she often overheard the children sing at the market making for a great round. "We must go, we must go, we must go, to the stream. To collect, to collect, to collect, the bark of willows. For the witch, for the witch, for the witch, who swallows dreams."

They resumed crawling, all of them moving behind her at a steady pace, the even shuffling of their clothing adding to the hypnotic quality of the song.

"By the light, by the light, by the light, of the lantern. It'll lead, it'll lead, it'll lead, us to her home. Close your eyes, close your eyes, close your eyes, when you approach it. See her birds, see her birds, see her birds, you'll be a crow."

"By the light, by the light, by the light, of the lantern. May it's warmth, may it's warmth, may it's warmth, lead us home. To our beds, to our beds, to our beds, of cotton linen. And to sleep, and to sleep, and to sleep, dreams free to roam."

Mina's voice consumed them, its vibrations soothing as she repeated the round over and over again.

And it hurt. Her throat grew dry as her jaw ached, but she kept singing. Her tone gained a subtle hoarseness, her pitch slightly off-key by the end of the first hour.

Mina took a deep breath at the end of the last verse to prepare for the next, when something patted her boot and a full, baritone voice picked up in her place.

"By the light, by the light, by the light of the lantern," Sebastian's voice formed a stunning harmony when paired with the echoes of her melody. Part of her sought to sing along with him, but the respite of him taking over was more than welcome. She listened to their shuffling. Wera moved along, her breathing still even, but another sound crept beneath it, a slight buzz in the walls: the sound of high winds.

The buzzing grew louder as they progressed, a distant whistle adding to it, as a breeze brushed against her face.

"Do you feel that, Wera?" Sebastian asked, his voice a bit raspy as well. "That breeze means we're near the exit, right, Mina? There seems to be a little more light in the tunnel, too."

"It means there's a hell of a windstorm out there," Mina answered. "It's unusual at this part of the range, but not unheard of. We won't be able to cover much ground until it passes. So it would be wise to head to one of the nearby outcroppings quickly and make camp."

"Oh, come on now, beastie. It's just a breeze. I'm sure—" Sir Gargic's ill-informed correction cut off as the breeze turned into a tear-inducing gust. A pinpoint of light seared their eyes as the tunnel curved into its final stretch.

"You were saying?!" Mina shouted over the wind's screams.

"I can summon a brief Shield of Deflection when we get out there," Sebastian said. "We'll need to move quickly, though. It'll only last for a few minutes."

"Oh, so the spell we need to last longer you can only hold for a few measly minutes, but your completely useless Dome of Encasement lasts for eight hours," she scoffed.

"Useless?! It's not useless! It's the perfect arcane summon for an emergency shelter!"

Mina reared her foot back and kicked him in the shoulder.

"Ow! What was that for?!"

"What about that night was an emergency then?!"

"It— It was a communication emergency! I had to talk to you for the good of the expedition!"

"And you couldn't have picked a shorter summon for that?!"

"I told you I wasn't thinking!"

"Can we save the needless bickering for when we're out of the tunnel?!" Wera snapped, anxiety returning as her hypnosis broke.

They fought against the wind to reach the tunnel's end, only to be met by a whiteout blizzard. The others stumbled out behind her as she tried to see through the snow, brooding over how much easier it would be if the wind just calmed down.

Then it did.

As soon as Tanir stepped out into the sun, the wind stilled... but the view didn't clear. Snow hung in the air like fog, flakes shifting gently to and fro, hovering in the air without a breeze keeping them aloft. Her sword kept shaking too.

Violently.

"Thankfully the wind died down," Sebastian remarked, unknowing.

The snow chuckled. "I was just thinking the same thing."

"It's a fae," Mina called. They brandished their weapons.

"*Just* a fae?" Part of the snowfall shifted, forming long limbs and a svelte chest hovering in the distant sky; wide, batlike wings beating slowly. "I know I've grown up quite a bit since I last saw you, but am I truly that unrecognizable?"

The fae disappeared in a flash, then reappeared inches from her face. Mina jumped back, pinning herself against the mountainside. Her heart dropped into her stomach.

His face was older but his sharp, shark-fin nose and bright, deep-set eyes were just the same as they were when they were children.

"Bormir," she gasped.

He smiled, thin and menacing as it silt up the sides of his sunken cheeks. "Hello, sister."

Fear.

Fight.

Mina went to draw her sword and grabbed at air.

"Have you lost something?" His eyes drifted to look high above her head.

She followed his gaze and found a crystalline hand dragging her sword belt up a thick vein of ice.

"You bitch!" Mina shrieked and leapt after the rimefae, scaling the rock face as fast as she could.

Bormir's snowy form condensed above her, grabbed the belt, and pulled the rimefae out with it. The pair smiled down at her and disappeared with just a single beat of their wings.

"Too slow," they taunted, reappearing a half a mile behind her. Two figures high in the sky, shaded by the snowfall.

"Mina!" Sebastian shouted.

"Mina?!" Bormir cackled. For as far away as he was his voice was heard without strain. "Is that what you call yourself?!"

"Mina," the rimefae forced her name out of her throat like a hairball. "How disgusting."

"Hey! Don't be rude! Mina's a fine name!" Wera shouted. "If you want to fight, then let's fight! Keep insults out of it!"

Bormir clicked his tongue in disapproval. "How... peculiar. They're so willing to fight for you, and yet they don't even know your real name." He twirled her sword belt around his wrist, waving her sword in taunting circles. "Right, Riktanya?"

Mina's stomach turned. The name carried Her debauched laughter and the scrape of chains behind it.

She'd tear his throat out with her teeth so he could never speak it again.

"Rot in Hell!" Mina shrieked, enraged. The wind swirled at her heels as she leapt off the wall towards the whiteout. She wouldn't be able to reach them on her own without wings, but with the gust from her arrow, she'd get close. She drew her bow, twisting her body to fire behind her just in time to notice the long, serrated jaws of a dingin emerging out of the snowy fog.

Mina fired at the beast, abandoning her advance, and tumbled through the air from the blow-back.

"Oh dear, Eirlys," Bormir tutted as Mina landed all the way back by Sebastian's feet. "She's gone and ruined our little surprise." With a flourish of his hand, the snowfall shifted. Its flurries cleared from the air to fully solidify his form.

Mina's stomach became an abyss, goosebumps crawled up her spine as a sea of shadows emerged not a hundred feet from them. Grunting, growling, panting, snarling, all the sounds of life she missed in the caves grew louder as Bormir's shroud of snow retreated, leaving a thousand pairs of wild eyes staring back at them.

Eager to strike.

"Fuck," Sebastian swore under his breath.

Sir Gargic chuckled nervously. "Guess we found your missing monsters, beastie."

"My, you're so stoic, sister!" Bormir's brilliant leather wings, twice the size of Eirlys' beside him, billowed back and forth, taunting her as much as his words. "Perturbed as always, of course, but where's the shock? Don't you want to know why? Why we've taken all these disgusting creatures under our command? Why me and your sweet, baby cousin are here after so much time apart? Go on! Ask away!"

Her anger was dangerous, yearning to feel his flesh slip through her fingers. To hear his screams and revel in the horror on his face as she made him watch his death. He knew she could not ask those questions. How he knew it, she didn't care. Mina wrangled her temper, shut out the dark voice that begged to be released, to punish them. All that mattered was getting her sword and getting away from them to fight another day.

"Well then," he sighed. "I guess we'll be taking this and our leave." He tossed the sword belt in the air and caught it. "It's only fair since you took Eir's hand, right?"

"Mina—" Sebastian's cry fell on deaf ears as Mina rose to her feet and crossed the gap in a single step, surging forward into the horde.

Height. That's what she needed. The whytewings would grant it.

Mina wove through the beasts deftly, dodging out of the way of their claws and fangs, provoking them to attack each other. A swarm of txia snaked towards her, glistening scales raised along their spines, quilled tails poised to strike. She greeted them, barely feeling the sting of their quills sinking into her arm as she scooped a dozen up and snapped their necks in the crook of her elbow.

A flock of whytewings, the deformed runts of ice wyrms, circled above her at the smell of txia blood. Mina springboarded off of the matted fur back of a charging frostlyon into the air and scattered half of the lifeless txia into the sky. The whytewings swooped down, the rimefaes' control bowing to their natural instinct to feed, and Mina grabbed one by the tail as she fell through the air, hoisting herself to stand on its back. She threw the remaining carrion as hard as she could, angling the flock's pattern into the perfect runway to reach her targets.

The world blurred around her as she ran across the whytewing's smile, the wind at her back, and hurled herself through the air towards Bormir.

"Cousin." He tossed the sword belt at Eirlys. His speed rival to Mina's, Bormir deflected her enraged tackle with an arching kick to the ribs, flinging her farther up in the air. She ignored the dull stabbing that dammed the breath in her lungs to right herself as she volleyed higher, and drove her heel into the top of Eirlys' head. Bormir flew past them, stealing the sword belt from Eirlys' grasp.

"You had us worried, Riktanya. It's good to see how selfishly you threw those mortals to the wolves just to get this little letter opener of yours."

Wind beneath her step, Mina launched off Eirlys' skull after him.

"After what Eirlys saw the other day—"

He hovered above her, unbothered by how fast she approached.

Cocky prick.

"—it looked like you were protecting them."

Her body seized with pain just as her fist was about to connect to his jaw. Her stomach flipped as her momentum stalled. She barely managed to grab hold of the base of her sword sheath just before she fell.

Or rather, Bormir allowed her to grab it.

"It seems as though you're being torn in two, sister." He pouted, a mocking pity. "Might there be some truth to what I said?"

It should have been the wind from his beating wings stinging her skin, not his words. She lifted her legs and kicked at him aimlessly. "Fuck off!"

He tilted his body back, billowing his wings, pulling further out of her reach. "Does the great Riktanya, mother's favorite, actually care for a bunch of mortals?"

"No," Mina lied. Pressure built around her skull. The ghosts of cold, thorned chains squeezed blood into her vision.

A curtain fell over Bormir's face. The bemused sadism slipped away. His pout fell. Eyes dulled. Deep beneath her rib cage, something uneasy crawled in response.

"You're boring me," he stated, distant and disappointed. "I came to see my sister Riktanya. Not this weak, malformed mortal wannabe." He loosened his grip on her sword belt, flattening his palm. "Perhaps a heatseeker would be more fun to play with. I wonder if the damage you take now translates to that form."

Mina stilled as the belt slowly slipped down towards his fingertips. She glanced below.

The horde of beasts looked more like a swarm of cockroaches than monsters.

He had goaded her this high.

"Well, there's only one way to find out," Bormir smiled. "You want your sword so badly? Have it."

He let go.

Everything went quiet as Mina plummeted, spinning in an endless void of white. Her body screamed at her to take action to save it, but her mind was clueless as to how. Flattening herself would only delay the inevitable, but perhaps make it easier for her spine to snap on impact. The bestial malady that possessed her would be hard-pressed to make a recovery before she shifted back, leaving her alone in the cold, hard snow, writhing in pain and begging for death, with a hundred hungry beasts eager to tear her flesh apart.

And then, amongst the frigid vortex, a streak of warmth. Brilliant, burning, beautiful, sparking an idea like it would kindling.

Mina flattened herself, turning her back to the fast-approaching earth, and unsheathed her sword. With its point to her left side, just beneath the last rib, she screamed out all the pain, all her fear, all her anger — and drove the blade through until her consciousness ran out.

🜁

Endless hunger.

Ceaseless cold.

Pain.

She roared at the discomfort, and tried to fly from it, her wings unfurling and leaving waves of snowfall in the wake of her swoop. But the pain followed, growing as she flew closer to the mass of writhing, warm bodies and the brilliant feast of heat that lay just beyond it.

There it was again, that puny creature that had escaped her jaws, burning hotter than before. The radiation of its heat blossomed in her wave-formed vision. Drool poured from her maw as she cut through the horde, the blood of the unfortunate creatures blocking her path only an appetizer; an insult compared to the warmth her quarry promised.

Endless hunger.

Ceaseless cold.

Bathe in its blood, consume its heart and it'd all go away. She was so close now. The creature dared to stand its ground against her, its heat pouring over her skin. Her jaws parted in a hungry smile.

Then everything went black.

🜁

The searing pain in her stomach woke her as she crashed into Sebastian, her sword driving deeper as he caught her.

"Tanir!" he shouted.

"I'm here." Mina watched Tanir approach her through blurry eyes. She grabbed her jaw, forced it open, and shoved a handful of herbs inside. Mina swallowed them whole. "We're going to need to—"

"Pull it out," Mina rasped, voice broken and hoarse, hardly able to stand even with the ground solidly beneath her feet.

"Absolutely not." Tanir took her axe and carefully cut open her breastplate. "If I do that, you'll—" The words died on her lips as she tore open Mina's undershirt and got a good look at the wound. "Holy shit."

Sebastian's grip around Mina tightened, its sting barely noticeable against the searing of the sword in her stomach.

"You have to pull it out," he insisted.

"She'll bleed out if I do that. The iron slows her healing, and it's not like I can perform surgery on her right now, even with the others holding the beasts back."

The world spun around Mina. "Cauterize it."

"What?" Sebastian asked.

His voice muffled, she hadn't been able to hear the mob of beasts raging behind them since she landed. Darkness encroached on her vision, buckling her knees until she had no choice but to cling to his coat. "Cauterize it."

She could barely make out his face as he looked down at her, but the sudden hitch of his breath gave away his fear.

"Sebastian." Tanir cleared the tatters of her breastplate and shirt from her back, bearing the exit wound. "I'm going to pull out her sword. You need to heat your fingers as warm as red-hot metal, nothing higher than that. Three fingers in the wound on her back all the way to the knuckle, three fingers in the wound on her stomach, hold it for thirty seconds. Ready?"

Sebastian swallowed. "Mina. Hold on to me."

She dug her fingers into his coat and pressed her head against his shoulder as he pulled his hands away.

"Ready?" Tanir warned.

Mina shook as she dragged the sword out, and was all the more grateful for the herbs the medic forced down her throat. She didn't know if she would transform if she passed out again, nor did she want to find out. The iron slowly poisoning her was worry enough.

"Now."

Mina jolted as Sebastian coaxed his fingers inside, and sunk her teeth into his thick wool collar to muffle her scream. Tears welled in the corner of her eyes, her vision going white despite them being closed. The burn of his touch was sharper than any blade, fiercer than any chain whip. It seared beyond her flesh into her bone, her nerves, her blood, her mind, threatening to turn her into his flame.

And as its rampage ended, both too quickly and not quick enough, a deep pulsing ache was left behind; her body desperately trying to hold on to the fleeting warmth.

Gentle hands pulled the wool away and put herbs in its place.

"Swallow," Sebastian said. He smoothed the back of her hair and pulled her closer to his chest. "It's done." The sting of his touch was nothing more than a tickle compared to his fire, or the iron wreaking havoc on her cells.

Or the shrill of Bormir's whistle.

The roars of the beasts and sounds of battle returned.

"Son of bitch." Sebastian's frustration rumbled in his chest.

"I'd ask if you charmed them, sister, but we all know how lacking you are!" Bormir taunted from above.

"Big cousin Riktanya couldn't even kill me!" Eirlys added. "That handsome wizard of hers had to step in to save the day!"

"Ah! What an astute observation, cousin! In fact, all of her little collection of mortals have more promise than she does."

"I know! Once the beasts injure them enough, let's take them with us! They'd make such wonderful pets!"

"It'll be a cold day in Hell before I let you take any of them!" Sebastian shouted.

"It's already cold in Hell, kid, but I like your pluck," Bormir hollered back, voice booming and all-consuming in their ears. "I can't wait to break you and make you mine."

Mine?

Mine.

The pain dulled as rage flooded Mina's veins, sending dark thoughts and buried memories swirling. How dare they take her sword. How dare these vermin follow their commands. How dare they try to take them away from her.

She could not stop them from swallowing her whole.

How dare they take what's mine.

"They are beneath you, dear one. Nothing more than beasts," the memory of Her voice cooed in her ears. *"And what are beasts meant to do?"*

"Gileathen."

Mina shoved Sebastian away as her fury overtook her. She turned around slowly to face the horde, finding the creatures sitting on their haunches like good little pests.

The wind stilled, waiting for her orders.

"There she is! Finally!" Bormir cheered, mocked. "All hail the Winter Wind's Chosen, Riktanya the Chained!"

"Wow! Your true nature's so pretty, cousin!" Eirlys gushed. "Why would you ever suppress it?"

Mina stood tall, despite her singed innards, despite her screaming psyche, despite the corrosive iron seeping through her bloodstream.

Despots do not show weakness. They do not hobble or lower themselves around those beneath them, especially when those beneath them have the gall to disobey.

Bormir and Eirlys' goading praises felt like the squealing gnats in her ears. She walked into the mass of sniveling beasts, bound by nature to bow to her apex, wanting to get a closer look at the pair who dared to float above her as she rent them from the sky — when a frostlyon, a young, handsome, headstrong male, decided to defy her will.

His scruff rippled, pupils expanded in fear, mid-lunge: a split second of primeval awareness that this action would not only lead to his death, but to the eradication of his pride. The downbursts were swift, the wind plummeting from high above in an invisible meteor storm, and eviscerated the frostlyon and his kin. Their bones shattered together, the sickening unison like lightning splitting an ancient oak, and became shrapnel that tore the flesh apart; their capillaries bursting from the shift in pressure.

The base of her skull pulsed, a ripple of some unwanted feeling crawled across her skin: a weakness. ***An example had to be made***, the silken voice of her wrath consoled. One death was nothing; paltry, compared to a hundred deaths in an instant. The whimpers and stillness of the surviving beasts, shocked by the display, was testament to its effectiveness.

The fae shrieked like dying rabbits.

"That's it! That's the cruelty I know, and Mother—" Bormir's words were swallowed by the snapping of his spine. Their praise made the unwanted feeling spread, raked its claws across her mind. They needed to be silenced, punished. How dare they mock her, hurt her, take what's hers, speak Her name. ***How dare they. How dare they. How dare they.***

How dare they make her do this.

The ferocity of the downburst was tenfold, shredding their wings as they were ripped from the sky and slammed into the snow. The ground shook from the impact as a shock wave of wind and snowy fallout surged forth, scattering the beasts into a frenzied flee. Mina bore it: the roar of the gale, the sting of its tendrils cutting flesh and bruising muscle— urging it to wash away her turmoil.

When instead, it snuffed out her fury.

The mountain fell silent, giving plenty of room for the heartbeat pounding in her ears, the stiffness in her lungs, the throbbing of her joints, to grow. She fell to the ground, her knees shaking out from underneath her, into the blood-soaked snow. Fragments of pale white fur floated in the blackened powder like stars among the void.

Mina picked up a clump and stroked it, her trembling hands staining it further. How dare she do this. How dare she allow them to goad her. How dare she ruin such a beautiful thing. It was frightened, manipulated, angry; of course it lashed out. How many times had she lashed out for the same reasons?

And how many times had she been forgiven for it?

How dare she.

How dare she.

She was no better than Them. She was no better than Her.

"Mina."

She stilled.

"Mina," Sebastian repeated. The concern in his tone, more painful than the poison coursing through her veins.

"Go, Wizard," she croaked. Her voice sounded as if it came from another body.

"M-mina, we have to—"

"Tanir," he cut her off, and dropped into a hushed whisper. "Set up the commorancy. Press your lips against the card and whisper 'Clementine' before you throw it and snap. Prepare the infirmary, have Enoch grab the magnets we discussed last night. I'll let Wera and Gargic know when it's time to set up the wards."

Crunching footsteps faded away to join the others, but only one set.

"Just leave," Mina whispered. She gazed down at the handmade gloves, shredded and barely clinging to her hands. The last of the blackened tissue faded from her fingertips, concealing her chain link scars.

"Whether it's to the Realm of the Fae or to death, I said I wouldn't let them take anyone them. That includes you."

"Wizard—"

"Mina, I command you to come with me into the commorancy and have your wounds treated by Tanir."

The strings of his command pulled against her. She struggled to stand, her muscles tensing up from the iron's continued assault. A warm set of arms scooped her up. Mina hissed in pain as the warmth turned to scalding.

"I also command that you must be carried by me for however long it takes to get you to the infirmary."

The pain vanished, much to her disappointment. She deserved to suffer.

She kept her focus on his coat, not wanting to look up and see the pity in his kind gaze, as he carried her across the frozen plain to the outcropping she'd pointed out earlier, into the familiar halls of a home a monster like her shouldn't be in. Should never have been welcomed into.

Sebastian laid her on the examination table carefully. Tanir appeared next to her immediately and held a vial to her lips.

"Drink this," she said.

Mina kept her mouth closed and distant gaze trained on the ceiling.

"Open your mouth, Mina," Sebastian said, and her lips parted. "Just pour it down her throat, Tani."

Tanir tilted Mina's head back and dumped the concoction down her gullet with experienced precision. She removed the scraps of breastplate and shirt that hung loosely around Mina's shoulders, and inhaled sharply at the sight. "You were right, Sebastian.

The veins surrounding her wound have turned black, and are slowly spreading. I'll need to cut away some of the cauterized tissue before we use the magnet to draw it out."

"Enoch, can you bring me over a scalpel, some alcohol, and the magnet?" Tanir leaned over her face. "Mina, do you want me to sedate you for this? It's going to be painful."

"No," she said, both against her will and with it.

"Alright then." She turned to address Enoch elsewhere in the room, "Grab that padded, wooden dowel for her to bite down on as well."

"No."

"N-no?"

Mina locked eyes with her. "No."

"Mina, put—"

Tanir held up a hand to quiet Sebastian. "Don't force her. I'm sure she has her reasons. Just make sure to stay as still as possible for me, Mina."

Mina sucked her cheeks between her teeth as Tanir prodded open the wound and began to cut. Each nick, each pull of flesh, had her nerves writhing, but she held firm, welcoming the pain as penance. She deserved to feel every jab, every hurt she could.

"Enoch. Magnet." The shuffle of metal between hands was her only warning before Tanir attempted deveining her through her stomach.

Mina sunk her nails into her palms and her teeth into her cheek, piercing both as the magnet siphoned the iron out of her. She whimpered just a bit, but still held firm despite the blood pooling on her tongue, and the muscle spasms ignited by her taxed nerves.

The pain subsided as Tanir put the magnet down for a moment, and Mina found herself disappointed.

"Sebastian, could you hand me a tissue?"

Tanir took the cloth and rubbed it up Mina's chin, cleaning up the blood, and gently pried her lips apart to assess the damage.

"Hmm," Tanir hummed. Their eyes met and the medic smiled in pity. "Alva."

All the pain, all the feelings, all the thoughts, stopped; consumed by the vastness of sleep.

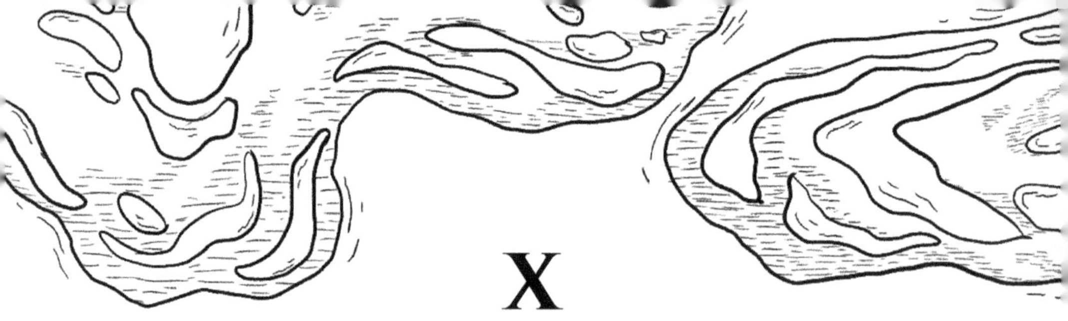

X

Tenderness and Tactics

Mina awoke in her room. The lavender perfume that lingered on the bedsheets was bittersweet, tainted by the loathing numbness that had settled in her bones. Her joints, her muscles, her head, everything was unbearably stiff, and she wondered why her body even bothered to wake to begin with.

She turned on her side, following her limbs' incessant need to move, and found a folded note on her bedside table, next to a glass of water and a bundle of herbs. Mina knew better than to pick up the note, knew that she should just close her eyes and let fatigue pull her back under, yet her traitorous arm still reached forward to grab it.

Mina,

Eat these herbs when you wake. Tanir says they'll treat your soreness and assist with your kidney's healing process.

Your leathers are in the laundry and will be returned to you by the end of the day. I cleaned your sword. It's lying on top of your wardrobe. The clothes Wera picked out for you are there as well. Wear them.

Once you're dressed, head down to the kitchen and eat something. Tanir suggests something not too hard to chew, with lean protein and high fiber. I say a big bowl of mac and cheese, but feel free to order whatever, just make sure you eat.

Fair warning, one of us will be waiting outside your door when you leave. It's just in case something happens to you medically, or you need our help, nothing more than that. You have my word.

- Sebastian

It was difficult to chew the herbs at first, but soon her joints loosened and the ache in her muscles eased. Moving, however, would be near impossible if not for the pull of Sebastian's commands lifting her to stand against reality's crushing weight.

She untied the loose cotton frock Tanir must have changed her into and ran a hand over the bandages neatly warped around her midsection. They were smoother than she expected, coated with a thin layer of wax to keep them from getting damp, but still had some give to them as she pressed her fingers into her wound.

It hurt. But not as badly as she wanted it to.

The clothes Wera left her must have been from her own wardrobe, intricately patterned and billowing, but much too short in the sleeves and hemline for Mina's height. She didn't care to look in a mirror. All that mattered was eating something to satisfy her contract, and after that—

After that—

Enoch all but flew out of his chair when Mina opened her door.

"T-that was fast," he sputtered. "Sebastian dropped his note off less than an—"

Mina walked past him. All that mattered was eating, and after that—

After that—

After that—

The kitchenware jumped to attention when she entered.

"Mac and cheese," she muttered and took a seat at the empty table. She stared at the wood grain until the dishes slid in front of her. The bowl of sauced pasta, trailing ribbons of cheese as she scooped into it, turned to yet another tasteless mush in her mouth.

Part of her thought that her suffering would have led to some reward.

The other part knew that her suffering was overdue punishment for being rewarded too much.

She swirled her spoon around the bottom of the bowl once she emptied it, drawing lines in the remaining sauce.

She ate.

And now it was after.

"It's good to know that notes work." Mina froze at the sound of Sebastian's voice. She hadn't heard him enter. "I am sorry it only gave you an hour of rest, though. You can go back to sleep if you need it."

She watched the trails she left slowly fill as the sauce slipped down the sides of the bowl and settled.

"What would sleep do?"

"Help you heal?"

"And then?"

He was silent for a moment.

"Are you done eating?" he asked.

Mina pushed her empty bowl forward.

"Come with me then."

She stood and followed Sebastian out of the kitchen, keeping her head down and eyes cast to the floor.

"No shoes?" he remarked as they walked. "I left your boots by the door, didn't I?"

"Oh," Mina muttered, glancing at her feet. "I'm not wearing shoes."

"It's alright. It's not like you really need them in here anyways."

Mina stopped as the hardwood shifted to stone and the air turned damp. She looked up to find her vision clouded. Steam swirled around a bubbling hot spring, where the others soaked causally.

Wera perked up at the sight of her. "You're gonna join us, Meens?"

"Yes, she is," Sebastian took off his shirt and stored it on one of the shelves along the wall before moving to his trousers. "She's fine to get in the springs with her injury, right, Tanir?"

"She is. The water might help it heal, even."

"Thought so." Sebastian turned to Mina and shrugged. "Come on then. Take off the clothes Wera gave you and get in the spring."

"Really, Windenhofer," Sir Gargic huffed.

"Really, what?" he asked as he walked around the edge and climbed in.

"You have to tell the girl to take her clothes off?"

"If I didn't she'd just walk into the water, skirts and all," he replied. "And I don't think Wera would appreciate that."

"You're right. I wouldn't. Salt stains can be a bitch to get out," Wera added. "That color does look good on you, though, Meens, even if everything is a bit flooded. I know you're a bit taller than me, but you've got much longer limbs than I thought."

Mina didn't acknowledge her as she undressed and placed the clothes on the shelf beside Sebastian's.

"Have you ever been to a hot spring before, Mina?" Tanir asked as she approached the pool. "Wera was telling us on the ride up to your cabin that there are a few located in the mountain basin south of there."

"No," she mumbled.

"Why not?" Enoch asked, and was answered as Mina stepped in, clearing the steam out of the room. All except Sebastian hopped out of the water on instinct, gasping, yipping, shivering as the water chilled.

"I got it," Sebastian squeaked, igniting his palms and dipping them into the spring. Billows of steam filled the air once more. They slowly climbed back in, testing the waters with fingers and toes before taking the plunge. Their seating arrangement much closer to their leader than before.

Sebastian cleared his throat. "So Wera, Enoch, I heard word back from the Guild. They really like your annotated atlas proposal, but want to see an example of one of the passages before committing to publishing it. Do you think you could have something finished for me to send over this week?"

"This week?" Wera mulled it over. "Well, the maps of the Naymia just need a few embellishments. I don't want to include all of them, but maybe the Lunar Rainforest? What do you think, Enoch?"

"Have you figured out that overlay effect? I've got some of the expedition notes and local folklore from the area collected and ready to go. I just need you to show me how you want it applied."

"Overlay effect?" Sebastian asked.

"We thought it'd be cool if we could showcase how the layout of the rainforest changes at night by having the lunar map hidden beneath the solar map. For the book I'm thinking of using thermochromic inks, but for the handheld map I've been playing around with the wax Tanir coats her bandages with."

"I'm mixing it a bit thinner than I like for the bandages," Tanir explained, "but the parchment's so absorbent that the thinned wax can lock into the fibers rather easily."

Mina sank further into the water as they prattled on, growing uneasy with every second. There was a pattern to this, and they were not following it.

"You're not asking questions," she stated, interrupting Sir Gargic as he asked about translations for some ancient scrolls. "You always ask questions."

"That's true," Sebastian said after taking a moment to process her meaning. "But considering the severity of the situation, we thought it best to give you some time instead of bombarding you like we tend to do."

"And yesterday wasn't severe?"

"Yesterday you volunteered. Just like you are now, I assume?"

Mina looked down at her blurred reflection in the opaque, swirling water. "I don't know what I'm doing now."

"Well, judging by your behavior, I'd say you're in a state of emotional shock," Tanir said.

"Shock?"

"You're here without your sword," she noted.

"I stood in front of you in the kitchen for five minutes before I spoke," Sebastian added.

"Honestly, when I saw you exit your room, I was convinced you were sleepwalking," Enoch said.

"Even as we're talking to you, it's like you're wearing a porcelain mask." Wera sighed. "I'm used to you being stoic, but this... this is heartbreaking."

Mina stared at Wera for a moment, trying to read her expression to understand what "heartbreaking" meant to her.

"You're still the same to me, beastie," Sir Gargic commented. "A little more quiet, sure, but I always knew something like *this* would happen to ya."

The irksome smirk behind his push-broom beard washed away as a splash of water smacked him in the face.

"What the hell was that for?" he sputtered.

"To remind you of your honor as a knight." The fierceness behind Sebastian's even tone and pointed stare tightened Mina's chest. She rubbed her hand against it, trying to ease the muscles.

"Is something wrong with your chest?" Tanir asked.

"No," the word tumbled out of her mouth.

"Tell her the truth, Mina."

"It's tight," she replied at Sebastian's behest.

"That's not an uncommon symptom of emotional shock. Is your heart racing as well? Are you lightheaded or dizzy?"

Mina placed two fingers against her neck to check her pulse. "No to both."

"Alright. As we talk more, physical symptoms like that may come up, so try to keep aware of your body. It may help you feel a little more present as well."

Present.

Mina pulled her hand away from her neck and glanced at it a moment. The palm shined with scar tissue, still pitted in places but healing, and there were some dark stains under her nails.

Blood.

She sunk it underneath the water and out of sight before the memory of frostlyon fur floating in the dark remains of its owner could consume her thoughts.

"*Questions,*" Mina reminded.

"Right, how about we start with what we know before we start with questions?" Sebastian laid back against the stone ledge. "Eirlys calls you cousin. That cheeky son of a bitch, Bormir, called you sister."

"They're both dead now," Sir Gargic offered.

"No," corrected Mina.

"No? But you snapped their spines and threw them faster than a counterweight trebuchet!"

"Into snow," Sebastian clarified. "From Bormir's little display when we first saw him, it seems as though he has the ability to manipulate and travel through snowfall, much like Eirlys has the same control of ice. If their heal time is anything like Mina's, their bodies probably started repairing themselves mid-fall, and they teleported as soon as they touched powder."

Sir Gargic grumbled. "Fine then, we know that her true name is—"

"Mina," she cut him off before he conjured the memory of Her laugh. "My name is Mina."

Sir Gargic scoffed. "*Mina*," snark oozed between his teeth, "the Chained. Which is more complete than whatever you were when you froze us all in the library."

"You don't have control over that form, do you?" Wera asked her.

Mina's jaw glued shut.

"What makes you ask that, Wera?" Sebastian asked.

"She turns into a heatseeker when she's on death's door, hence the stabbing herself while falling. If she had control over this... *Chained* Mina or knew what triggered it, wouldn't she have just turned into that instead? Unlock that wind magic it gives her to guide herself down to the ground safely rather than turn into an angry, hungry monster?"

Sebastian pursed his lips and shifted them back and forth in thought. "That's a smart thought. Though it's not just her 'Chained' form that had wind magic. Mina has wind magic normally."

"No, I don't."

Sebastian furrowed his brow in confusion. "Yes, you do."

"No, I don't. I have ice magic," Mina insisted. "I summon ice arrows, and create ice patches over wounds. Ice magic."

"And the gusts that surge from your bow, and the small cyclone that you summoned to block Eirlys' ice spikes? What do you call that?"

"Weird."

Sebastian blinked.

"Weird," he repeated. "I—"

"Sebastian," Tanir interrupted. "I can tell that you're about to launch into a big explanation. Can it wait for when we're done with our answers and questions?"

He pouted and exhaled deeply through his nose. "Yes. Questions and answers first. What else do we know?"

"We know that she's betrothed."

Their heads all snapped to face Enoch.

"No, I'm not," Mina refuted.

"That's a bold statement to make, Enoch," Wera said.

"No, it's not," he whined as he shrunk against the wall behind him. "Tanir, you said that her necklace looked like it was made of iron while you were operating on her. I thought I saw something like it before in a pawn shop, so I did some research while she was resting. That's a Grinbac betrothal collar. They were popular during Queen Pikan's reign."

"Queen Pikan?" Tanir said. "But that was what? Thirty, forty years ago now?"

"Must be a family heirloom or something," he replied. "It is, isn't it, Mina?"

Mina touched the iron band around her neck, not caring for how it stung her healing fingertips. "No, it's not."

"Well, did your betrothed pick it up from a vintage shop or something? It's wild that they'd get you something iron when it hurts you, but maybe they liked the 'bond as strong as iron' symbolism behind it."

"I'm not betrothed," she repeated.

"Then did you buy it yourself?"

"No."

"Did the Harlowes give it to you?" asked Wera.

"No."

There was a slight, almost nervous chuckle beneath Sebastian's voice, "Enoch, I don't want to question your expertise. History and culture are definitely your subjects, but are you absolutely sure that it's a betrothal necklace?"

"Do you mind if I take a closer look, Mina?" he asked.

"No," her body responded for her.

Sebastian nodded at Enoch to proceed.

He swam towards her, and peered closely at her neck. Her heartbeat picked up its pace as goosebumps prickled up her back.

"Just what I thought," he reached his hand out to point at it and Mina jerked back.

"Enoch," Tanir warned.

"Sorry!" he squeaked. "I'm not gonna touch it or anything, I swear. It's just got the telltale initials joined by a knot engraved into it. M.I. knot N.A."

"M.I., N.A.," Sebastian spelled out. "That's how you got your name, isn't it?"

Mina eased back down into the water as Enoch backed away and returned to his seat. "They read it when they found me. Thought it said Mina."

"They?" Wera asked.

"The Harlowes."

"Interesting. So it was given to you before you met the Harlowes, when you were just a kid." Sebastian glanced at Enoch. "Much too young for it to be a betrothal necklace, then."

"Why wear it then?" Sir Gargic asked.

"Is it enchanted?" Wera asked.

"No," Mina answered

"Then what is it?"

Mina fiddled with the amber pendant around it for a moment. They had to know not to take it off of her. If something happened, another injury or the like, and they removed it —

Cold phantom chains slithered across her skin.

"My sword," she said. "When that bitch took it, she didn't pull it into the ice. What kept her from doing that?"

"I thought we were supposed to be asking you questions," Sir Gargic grumbled.

"The iron," Sebastian answered. "She couldn't pull the iron in with her because she was using fae magic."

"When the streetlamps come on at night, what do guardians do to their children?" she asked.

Sebastian's jaw slackened. "Uhhh..."

"They call them home?" Wera offered.

Mina stared at Sebastian, willing that fast mind of his to solve her simple puzzle. His eyes lit up in recognition.

"If you take it off, you get called back to the Elphyne."

Sir Gargic rolled his eyes. "Well, that's stupid. Just ignore it."

"It's not really something she can ignore," Enoch said. "Fae magic is some of the most powerful magic there is. It's primordial. If something's calling her back to it, it'll drag her there by force."

"And a measly band of iron will stop that from happening?"

"The universe has an odd system of checks and balances," Sebastian said. "But I suspect there might be more to her necklace than just the iron." He sighed and slumped deeper into the water. "However, seeing that it was given to her prior to meeting the Harlowes, I have a feeling that she can't tell us more about it."

"Maybe that amber pendant has something to do with it," Enoch noted, and Sebastian tensed. "Grinbac collars don't bear pendants."

"The pendant is just something I found," Mina interjected. "Nothing more."

"Sounds good to me," Wera sighed as she leaned her head back into the water, "I'm just glad to hear that Mina's not engaged."

"Oh, really?" Tanir asked, "Why's that?"

Wera smiled and winked at Mina, stinging her slightly. "No reason."

Sebastian cleared his throat. "How about we discuss our plan going forward?"

"You're going to go on without me," Mina said.

Sebastian ignored her. "Knowing what we know now, it's likely that they'll attack again, and perhaps bring reinforcements. Let's start carrying some iron on our persons to help bolster our defenses. I'm thinking some iron rings from the Junk Room might be a suitable option."

"Or you can just go on without me," Mina repeated.

"Do I have to remind you that you have a contract to uphold?" Sebastian snipped.

"Is your crew being abused for decades by sick fae fucks really worth upholding a stupid fucking contract?"

"That's not going to happen, and I don't break contracts because of things that aren't going to happen." He smiled tightly. It didn't hurt to see it. "Plus, I have the notion that those two are going to come after us whether or not you're with us."

"Okay, so," Sir Gargic continued on. "Iron rings. I suppose you want us to keep putting the iron barrier up around the commorancy every time we set up camp, correct?"

"Correct. I'll look into making some earplugs to prevent them from charming us, and I'll retrofit the noxulars to work as sunglasses as well. Our scarves should deter any scent-based enchantments as long as we keep them over our noses." He nodded at his own idea. "Mina, I'll ask you to assist me with that later. Are there any places in particular we should be extra vigilant?"

"I don't—" Mina's stomach knotted. They should be cursing her name. Packing up her things and throwing her out into the snow. "I don't know."

"We'll just assume everywhere then."

"We need to fit Mina with a non-iron dagger, or something she can hide on her person," Wera offered. "I have a feeling she'll need it again. What with them being airborne and Mina being... not..."

Sebastian nodded solemnly, his face falling a bit. The knots in her stomach twisted tighter.

"Alright," he sighed. "Alright. We've faced worst foes before, we'll face these ones and make it out fine as well."

Mina focused on the swirling spring water. Her heart raced. Her body threatened to collapse into itself. It was her fault they were dealing with this. Her fault that they were going to get hurt for no reason. She couldn't protect them, not for long, not without having to unleash the part of herself that seemed to eat away at her humanity like it was nothing more than a light snack.

"What purpose does it serve to keep me around?" she asked the water. The words tumbled out in a fast, shaky crescendo. "The mountain is treacherous, but you all are capable. You have magic tricks that eclipse my skill set. I'm clearly their target. With the iron rings they won't be able to touch you all, and half the fun for them is touching. You can just go! And don't say a damn word about that contract because you and I both know that it's just some bullshit excuse!"

Her shout echoed off the stone, bouncing around the room until it slipped into silence.

"Man, this water sure is hot," Wera said, "And would you look at that, my hands are all pruned."

"My hands are getting pruned too," Tanir added, "Come on Enoch, Sir Gargic. I'm sure you're turning to prunes too. I think it's time we head out."

"My hands are just fine," Sir Gargic harrumphed.

"Mine are too." Enoch glanced around the room and shifted his tune. "B-but I do need your help with some writing I'm doing about King Fritz's history, Sir Gargic. Your first-hand knowledge of His Majesty would be invaluable."

"And you need it now?"

"Mhmm. Right now."

Mina didn't look up. Their ripples sparkled across the water's surface as they got out and quickly left the room.

Silence hovered in the air, thicker than the steam that swirled with it. So heavy, and all-consuming, that at the trickle of Sebastian moving through the water, Mina jumped.

"Stay put," he said, rooting her to the spot while her body itched with the need to run. The pale of his arms waded through the smoky water, the warm glow of his hands bringing color to its depths as he placed his palms on either side of the stone ledge she sat on, caging her in.

"Look at me."

Mina kept her head down as she lifted her gaze. He wore the same expression as when he amended that stupid contract. Gaze fierce, focused, yet unreadable. As close as he was to her, all she could tell was that both the possibility of a million emotions and no emotion at all racing through him were an equal sum.

She wasn't sure which terrified her more.

The tightness in her chest, her racing heart, the buzzing waves that made her skin aware of every movement: she'd call it terror, but fear made her want to fight, made her want to run. This feeling had her frozen.

Or perhaps that was just his command.

"Maybe I wasn't clear the other times I've said this, so let me fix that." His tempered, measured tone dripped into her ears and trickled down her spine. "We are not leaving you."

"It has only been a week and I have brought nothing but suffering to this expedition," she protested. "It would be foolish to keep me around."

He clenched his jaw. "It would be more foolish to travel through these peaks without a guide."

"A written one would suffice. I can sit down with the archivist—"

"Enoch!" He snapped. "You can say his name! Don't backslide now just because you're scared!"

Mina's breathing hitched. It was a million emotions then, and coming to the surface now was anger.

"That's what it boils down to, right? You're scared of them. Scared of yourself. Scared of hurting us."

"And you're not?"

"Of course I am!" he shouted. "I'm fucking terrified of the people I care about getting hurt, and that includes you!"

Mina winced as his admission threatened to split her skull in two. "Then just—"

"Then just leave you behind, right? And what does that solve? You still get hurt in the long run, you're still left suffering because of this stupid fucking curse, and I can't leave you to those fucking rimefae dogs."

"And what—"

"Why? That's what you're wondering, isn't it? You can't ask the question outright, so you're trying to dance around it, aren't you? Why don't we just leave you alone? Why put up with your attitude? Why don't we just cast you to the side? Because that's what everyone else has done to you, and look at what that has accomplished! But in just six days with us, your condition has changed more than it has in the fifteen years you've been in this realm, hasn't it?"

He wasn't listening to her. Wasn't he supposed to be smarter than this? None of her improvements mattered over their own lives. Why couldn't he just make the right choice? Why did she have to push him towards it?

Mina lifted her head up to face him and taunted, "So you're solving a puzzle, and you don't want it to go away before you crack it."

Sebastian's eyebrows shot up and the water between them started to bubble. "No," he hissed.

Then what's making you be such a stubborn idiot?

"Then what is it?"

His gaze darted over her face, studying her as he searched for the answer.

"I can't tell you because I don't want to hurt you," he seethed. "I've already had to watch you suffer enough today, had to watch you plummet from the sky screaming, and writhe in pain at my touch because you were too rash, too headstrong, and too self-reliant to wait just a moment." His eyes turned glassy. The anger less forceful, more swallowed, as his voice went raspy. "If you had waited, I could have done something. I could have cast a spell that would—"

"I don't hesitate."

"It's not hesitating, Mina. It's—" he closed his eyes for a moment, taking a deep breath before exhaling shakily, "—it's strategy."

"Is it?"

"Among other things." It was a weary, strained confession. "I'm sorry for getting so upset. It's just that you're—" Sebastian opened his eyes and his fretful expression went slack, "—pink."

"What?"

"Your lips. They're pink." His gaze lingered on her mouth.

Her heartbeat, already pounding, throbbed in every muscle, every joint. She had no idea what he meant and found herself looking at his lips, slightly parted as he breathed through the heavy fog of steam that billowed around them, for an answer. They had a slight fullness to them, not as plump when compared to hers, but still well shaped; the top curved like an artisan's bow, and the bottom—

Her hand lifted out of the water to touch it when the air stung against her skin, allowing the searing pain her lingering numbness from the day's events dulled to surge forth.

"I'm burning," she said.

The words dispelled the enchantment seemingly cast on him. "What?" Sebastian panicked, his gaze darting over her quickly, trailing down her body before landing on the water bubbling around them. He jumped away from her, ripping his still-smoldering palms out of the water.

"Good Gods, Mina! Why didn't you tell me sooner?!"

"I just noticed."

"Can you stand?! Are— are you blistered?!"

She lifted her arms out of the water. They were a shade of gray, splotchy and slightly darker than their usual pallor, but that would fade over time. "Not blistered."

The wafting steam cleared from the air once more as the water cooled.

"O-okay," he warbled, and settled back into the spring, retaking his seat on the other side. "Okay. Maybe that's why your lips turned pink. I was slowly boiling you alive."

Her heartbeat slowed to a more manageable tempo with the distance between them restored.

"You didn't notice either," she remarked.

"It takes a lot to burn me. High heat tolerance... and cold tolerance." He shrugged. "The slow chill settling into the water now that I'm not casting is rather pleasant, actually."

"The chill caused by my ice magic." She glared at him, there'd be no negotiating with him tonight, but she could still sow the seeds and show him just how greatly he was underestimating their situation.

Starting with how dangerous she was to them.

"No," he sighed. "It's because you're a rimefae."

"You're too confident about that." Mina slouched back against the wall, crossing her arms over her chest. The tightness had faded as her heartbeat steadied and, overall, despite the aches that lingered in her healing body, she felt lighter. Less clouded. She could actually feel the chunks of ice shifting around her as she moved, could actually see the well-worn stones that made the room feel as though they were in the middle of a cave.

Sebastian studied her for a moment and smirked. Mina shifted her gaze to look over his shoulder, easing some of the sting from his grin. She caught the flash of one of his hands igniting again and slipping into the water. "For good reason. When you summon your arrows, how would you describe it?"

"Describe it?"

"Like when I heat my palms, it feels like they're buzzing. That my cells are rubbing together rapidly, drawing energy from the sparks of magic in my DNA."

"I freeze the water vapor in the air as I draw my bow to form it."

"Okay, and how are you freezing the water vapor?"

"I touch it."

Sebastian pulled his hand out of the water, and the pool around her began to ice over. "Kind of like how the water is touching you now, and turning to ice?"

"Clearly."

He put his hand back in. "Can you make an arrow right now, and hold it for a moment for me to see?"

Mina sat up straight and mimed drawing her bow to conjure one forth. She held it in her hands as it dripped into the spring.

"When you made this, were you thinking 'freeze this water'? Was there some cold part inside of you, you were tapping into to shape it?"

"No. I just drew an arrow."

He chuckled. "In both senses of the word."

She dropped the arrow into the water. "Is there a point to this?"

"If it were ice magic you were using, you would be pulling the water vapor out of the air and willing it to freeze. The shape of your arrow would be much more tailored, and while it's definitely cold, it wouldn't have started to melt as you held it," he explained. "What you did instead was still the movement of air as you drew, which allowed the water vapor to freeze as you touched it. Normally, the potential energy of the stilled air is dispersed when you fire, which is why that giant gust follows your arrow. But because you didn't fire, it trickled out gradually, clearing some of the steam from the air above us."

She looked up. The steam above the spring was much thinner than the thick clouds along the walls.

"So?" she sunk into the water until it lapped against her chin.

"So... when you summon the wind, like when you run or when you did that little tornado trick with the ashes yesterday, was it something that you willed, or was it instinctual?"

"It's instinctual, sometimes, I think. Other times it's willed. And other times I'm..." A slight breeze, soft and cool, breathed against her forehead, "asking."

"Was—" Sebastian hesitated. "Was what happened today 'asking'?"

"No." A slight layer of ice crystallized around her at the memory of her crueler self seizing her despite the warmth Sebastian's touch imbued. "That was commanding."

He slipped his other palm into the spring, though Mina wasn't quite sure if it was his conjuration or his laughter that thawed the water around her.

"What?" she growled.

"S-sorry," his voice wavered as he tried to wrangle his laughter in. "I know it's rather serious but— it's funny how much you sound like me when my sparks started to burn. Life really is a circle, huh?"

Mina scowled and sunk lower until her nose blew tiny ripples against the surface.

"It's a good thing. It means I can teach you how to control it better..." He pursed his lips for a moment. The bridge of his nose furrowed. "... I think."

She blew bubbles in the water to convey her agitation.

"I've never heard of anyone using wind magic, now that I think about it. There's a couple of creatures that have something close to it, but a person? Perhaps it's a rare birth trait like light magic. I'll have to do some more research, query the Northern Practitioners to see if they know of any individuals that wield it as well." Sebastian sank deeper into the water and mindlessly tapped his fingers against his lips. "I'll ask Enoch to take a look too, after he and Wera finish up their sample. He knows a lot more history and folklore than me, really knows where to look as well."

He pulled out of himself to address Mina's sliver of a floating head. "But wind and fire go hand in hand. There might be a few hiccups in the beginning, but we'll get a handle on it."

Sebastian stared at her.

Mina stared back.

They blinked.

"Well?"

"Well, what?"

"What do you think?"

"Think of what?"

"Me teaching you."

Mina mulled his ramblings over. The feeling of total dominance over the winds she had while consumed by wrath, though its memory left her nauseous, was... empowering. The idea of having that without having to sacrifice her sense of self, or tear her arm out of her socket—

"If I'm told to, I don't suppose I have a choice."

Sebastian frowned. "You have a choice. If you don't—"

How is he still so dense?

"If I'm told to," Mina repeated louder, glaring at him. "I don't suppose I have a choice." She lowered her voice and rolled her eyes. "I hate repeating myself, Wizard."

He sighed. "Alright then." He dipped into the water, down to Mina's level. "Duly noted."

Silence settled, a softer, more comfortable blanket this time. Mina closed her eyes and let the water hold her weight, hoping to lighten the heavy weariness settling in. She never was able to stay in a bath for this long, even keeping the tap running in the guest room tub couldn't stave off the ice.

She didn't hate it. Perhaps if she could feel its warmth, she may have even called it nice.

"Mina."

"Hm?"

"As you see fit, you can leave."

Mina inhaled deeply as the threads holding her there slipped away. Exhaled. "Five more minutes then."

"Alright." She bobbed in the water as Sebastian shifted to float beside her. "Five more minutes."

🜁

"It's not hesitating, Mina. It's—" he closed his eyes for a moment, taking a deep breath before exhaling shakily, "—it's strategy."

He knelt in front of her, arms caging her in. Drops of water glistened on his bare skin like the dew that dusted the forest by her cabin with stars in the sun's rising light.

"Is it?" she asked, again.

"Among other things." It was a weary, strained confession. "I'm sorry for getting so upset. It's just that you're—" Sebastian opened his eyes and his fretful expression went slack, "—pink."

"What?"

"Your lips, they're pink." His gaze lingered on her mouth.

Her heart still threatened to bruise her ribs, electricity still hummed across her skin, but she wasn't scared by it. Not with the warmth of the water, the warmth of his hands resting just beneath its surface, barely brushing against her thighs. His hair, slightly frizzed, painted deep amber. His strong, expressive brow smoothed in awe. His eyes, darkened by his wide pupils. The sharp slope of his nose, the fullness of his cheeks molded by the lingering lines of his smile, his stubble brushed chin; in this seemingly endless pocket of time, she took in every detail, toured his face's gallery before settling on his lips yet again.

If mortals were made by gods, as so many often claimed, then a fine goddess of the hunt carved his lips in the shape of her favorite bow. A tool lovingly crafted for a master to wield.

Mina was an accomplished hunter.

She lifted her hand out of the water.

Perhaps she was worthy to wield it.

Sebastian stilled, just as transfixed as she was, as her hand cupped his jaw. She brushed her thumb over his bottom lip and his breath tickled against it, a gentle warm wind that pulled her forward, pressing her lips against his to capture it.

🜁

Mina jolted awake, gasping for air. She scrambled out of her bed in panic and stumbled as quick as she could to the bathroom. Her throat, lungs, mouth, lips, burned with a fury that rivaled the sear of Sebastian's cauterizing touch. She collapsed into the bathtub, clawed her way up to the faucet, and opened her mouth under the rush of cold water.

Coughing, choking, she drank as much as she could, until the flames fell away, and she was left sore and soaking. She turned the water off and laid there, panting, staring up into the darkness.

That was a kiss.

That was what a million lifetimes' worth of songs were written about, enough poems and stories to fill the seas twice over. That was what newspapers proclaimed soldiers fought for, what children in the street so freely gave away to each other in fits of giggles followed by taunting nursery rhymes. What sealed lifelong bonds, and ended lives.

But that's not what really happened.

All that happened was a conversation, a moment of peaceful silence, then a command for her to head to her room and rest. Why would she dream—

Mina touched her lips, still haunted by his warmth. Her chest ached. Her healing wound throbbed. Her stiff hands creaked. Her throat threatened to shred apart. And yet, all she could think about was that soft breath. About how good it felt against her skin. About how perfectly her lips seemed to fit against his.

She never thought of kissing. It was just another useless, social act she was banned from; no different from a handshake or saying hello. When Mr. Harlowe kissed his wife before every expedition, or when Mrs. Harlowe placed one against her husband's cheek when he brought her a cup of tea before bed, she never felt a sense of longing. Even reading those books that had people swooning over grand, romantic kisses that preluded long-awaited acts of carnal desires was never more than an exercise to understand how those unafflicted lived so she could hide among them.

Now the imprint of his lips lingered, leaving her imbalanced, uncomfortable. As if she'd cut her hair a bit too short, or as if her sword had suddenly lost its weight. She pressed the back of her hand against her lips, hoping to push the feeling aside, to no avail. All it served to do was disappoint her with how rough and lifeless it was by comparison.

Would he still look at her like that as she was now? Look at her as if she were made of pure magic, as if she were the key to some ancient, unanswered riddle, while she was lying in a half-filled bathtub, snot-nosed, drenched, and wheezing?

Why did she care if he did?

Could his face even look like that? Or did her unconscious skew his expression just as badly as it did the truth of that memory? He was a fine-looking man, handsome in the dictionary sense, but in that moment... he embodied sunset.

Mina lifted herself out of the tub and trudged over to her desk, unbothered by the trail of water running down the back of her linen shift. She turned on the lamp, pulled out her sketchbook, tore the portrait she drew the other night, and tacked it to the wall.

Sebastian's smiling face stared back at her as she sat down in her chair and studied him.

"Dammit," she swore, picking up her pastels. She couldn't compare her dream to that drawing. Not just from memory, at least. His expression was wholly different in it, more exuberant than awestruck.

She had to draw him again. Twice in fact: once as she recalled him looking in her dream and again from a different, untainted memory. Back when they first met, when she shot the terramawg. That would do.

They all seemed captivated by her then.

Mina awoke at the desk and grimaced at the puddle of drool staining the last drawing she worked on before sleep dragged her into its depths. She wiped off as much as she could and tucked her sketchbook away. Stepping back, she admired her handwork: a sea of amber locks, different angles, dozens of expressions.

Now she could study him properly, truly understand if the Sebastian in her dreams — that made her yearn for things she had no business yearning for — was an accurate depiction of the quick-minded mage. She had to assess every detail with the utmost scrutiny: the sharp angle of his jaw, the length of his eyelashes, the light flair of his nostrils when he was exasperated, the wrinkles that formed at the corner of his eyes when he smiled that made them sparkle.

Mina jumped when the breakfast bell chimed, rubbed her dry eyes, and turned her attention from her wall of wizards to dress. She grimaced at the new sets of stitches scattered across her breastplate. The leather wouldn't be able to take much more damage. The grim thought that perhaps there were a few slain whytewings she could skin outside crossed her mind for a moment, but it had been too long since they had passed; their hides would shred as soon as she started to cut.

As she opened it up to slide it on, her gloves fell out of it, digging the pit in her stomach deeper with the new, tiny patches holding them together. Tanir had worked so hard on them, and she ruined them in less than a day.

The halls were clear as she headed down to the kitchen. The others' voices hummed behind the door. They'd probably make some remark about her tardiness, saying that she must have had a good sleep or some nonsense, ask how her wound was healing or if her hands were less stiff. All of it an unnecessary prologue to what they really needed to talk about, getting their asses to Lanholde on time while two powerful fae sadists waited for their chance to strike.

She entered and found breakfast well underway, but Sebastian was noticeably absent.

"M—" Tanir choked on her food. "Mina! You're up!"

"Clearly," she grumbled and took her seat beside her. A fresh plate of bacon and eggs appeared on her placemat.

"How are your stitches?" she asked. The lilt in her voice was higher than usual, her tempo stilted, but Mina was too hungry to invest any true interest in it. Odd behavior with this group was often explained shortly after it occurred.

"I see you got your gloves. Do they fit alright? I wasn't sure with the patches if it made them too loose."

Mina put her fork down and wiggled her fingers in the air. "Fits."

Wera stared at her through the cracks between her outstretched digits.

"What are you staring at?"

"Are—" Her eyes narrowed and lips pursed. "Are you wearing lipstick?"

"What?"

"Lipstick," Enoch explained. "It's a type of tinted balm that a person puts on their lips to color them."

She'd read about that before.

"I know what lipstick is," she snapped at him, then sneered at Wera. "First of all, where would I get lipstick from?"

"Your pack, the Junk Room..."

"Secondly, what would I even wear it for?"

"To look nice? Make yourself feel good?"

"And smearing a paste on my mouth to make them a different shade of gray would do that?"

The corner of Wera's mouth quirked up, threatening to break into a migraine-inducing smile. "So, you're not wearing lipstick?"

"Fucking clearly!"

"Good morn—" Sebastian's boisterous cheer, a clear attempt to defuse the tension he heard outside the door, cut off mid-step. "—ing," he finished the phrase in a wheeze.

"Morning, Sebastian," Wera turned around in her seat. "Mina's lips are pink."

Interlude

Clear Commands. Cluttered Compulsions

Sebastian didn't care for complex emotions, he'd had quite enough of those growing up. Complexity was best saved for puzzles and mysteries. He tried his best to keep his feelings simple. If he was happy, he was happy. If he was sad, he was sad. If he was angry, he was angry, though he tried not to be for long.

Nothing, however, was simple about his current situation.

There was relief and pride and joy stepping out of the tunnel, quickly followed by anxiousness, annoyance, and worry that only deepened with a peppering of sadness and anger as he watched Mina scramble for her sword.

Fold in fear as Mina rushed into the mist.

A dash of dread from the snarling horde.

Disappointment as she abandoned them.

Anxiousness, annoyance, worry, sadness, anger, fear, dread, disappointment, frustration, exasperation.

Hopelessness,

At the sound of a far-off scream,

And the sight of a body, limp when it was usually so strong,

The wind rushing past it instead of from it,

Falling out of the sky.

Terror at a familiar roar.

Hope.

Determination.

Doubt.

Relief, panic, worry, sadness, anger, fear, dread, disappointment, frustration, exasperation, rage, disgust, self-loathing, guilt, hatred.

Confusion, terror, resentment, sadness.

Compassion. Dejection. Hope. Hopeless. Disappointed. Proud.

Sebastian was sure he didn't breathe until he tucked her into bed.

"She'll be fine," Tanir said, rubbing his shoulder gently as he knelt beside her mattress.

"You think?"

"She heals fast, and I'm sure drawing out the iron will help. She stabbed herself in the kidney on purpose, you know."

"That's—" not what he was worried about, "—good."

Tanir inhaled sharply. "Good in the grand scheme of things." She paused a moment. "I've never seen anything like it. That was horrible." The waver in her voice was more than enough to pull him out of himself. The perfect excuse to put a lid on the boiling pot, and hope it sorted itself out into stew.

He patted her hand. "Let's talk this all out together, shall we? The past few hours have been a lot, to say the least. How long does this sleep spell last?"

"It'll be about an hour at most, but after all that, I wouldn't be surprised if she was out for longer."

"Right." Hopefully, she would rest a bit longer. She needed it.

Sebastian made sure to lock her door as they left. He had already violated her privacy enough by using his skeleton phrase to open it, he didn't want to strain the thin layer of trust he'd built up with her any more than he already had.

He had the kitchen whip up a few pots of tea: breakfast blend for Sir Gargic, matcha for Wera and Enoch, elderflower for Tanir, a bergamot black for himself, and a batch of shortbread cookies before ringing them down.

There were no smiling faces, just light nods in greeting as they all joined him at the table, their bodies moving out of habit while their thoughts were far off, buried in what they'd just witnessed. Sebastian wanted to say something, anything, to fill the silence, but even he couldn't help but ruminate. Tanir had already finished her third cup of tea and a plate of cookies by the time everyone settled, and Mina's scream still rang in his ears.

"She could have killed us," Enoch, finally, spoke. "That time in the library when Sir Gargic kept pushing her. She could have killed us without even lifting a finger."

"Forget just killing us," Sir Gargic said through stuffed cheeks, coating his beard in crumbs. "She could slaughter an entire army if she wanted. Take over a whole kingdom, even."

"But she didn't," Wera added.

"I know." Enoch ran his finger round and round the lip of his teacup. "That's the thing I keep reminding myself of. She didn't kill us because we're not monsters."

"Neither were those beasts," Sir Gargic countered. "Sure, that frostlyon had it coming, but his kinfolk? That was more than defending herself. That brother of hers said it best, Riktanya is cruel."

"No," Tanir interjected, thankfully quicker than the string of insults that raced to the tip of Sebastian's tongue. "She was scared and hurt, just like all of those poor animals were. You can't blame her for lashing out."

"Tell me, what do you think would have happened if one of us tried to stop her? I know I would have been turned to blood sausage." He had the gall to turn to Sebastian. "What about you, Windenhofer?"

He took a sip of his tea, letting its sugar sweeten his tongue. "I think I'd be fine."

"Think? You don't know?"

Sebastian took another sip and kept his eyes locked with Sir Gargic's. No. He didn't know. The woman he saw change in a blink, stride into the battlefield as if she were a vengeful goddess so absorbed in her own divinity that the world seemed to turn around her, was not the Mina he knew.

Or maybe she was. She'd only existed in his world for a week now, and today was a humbling reminder of that.

Sir Gargic smiled and looked away. "Well. It's good to know you have a healthy fear of the girl."

"I know she wouldn't hurt us," Wera proclaimed.

"Really?" Sir Gargic doubted.

"Not only did she have full control when she lost herself in the library, but she even shoved Sebastian away from her before she turned out there." Wera leveled Sir Gargic with such a definite and disapproving glare, even Sebastian felt the need to apologize. "She was in pain, fully leaning on him for support, and yet she still chose to protect him."

She wagged her finger in Sir Gargic's face. "And so far, it's only been something emotional that's triggered that sort of change in her, unlike her heatseeker form."

"An emotional trigger?" he scoffed. "What kind of holistic, psycho-bullshit is that? All I did in that library was poke the bear a little."

"You said 'things like that deserved to be cursed for good reason' quite pointedly at her." Sebastian hung his hands down beside him to keep his palms from setting fire to the table. "One would suspect that being told that this horrible curse placed upon them, that robbed them of nearly all of life's joys, was earned, would be more than enough to infuriate them."

"Not me, it wouldn't."

"Perhaps." The sugar from his tea left his taste buds. "By the way. How is King Fritz holding up without you there to lick the shit off his asshole?"

Sir Gargic jumped to his feet, Sebastian's insult turning him red-faced and fuming instantly. "How dare you insult my king!"

"Now, now, Sir Gargic," he tutted. "Don't let my silly little words trigger such an *emotional response* out of you."

The knight bristled, his nostrils flared with a deep frown, and he sat down out of embarrassment. Sebastian hated himself for taking satisfaction in seeing him truckle.

"Alright," Tanir called their focus, easing some of the tension in the room. "Mina's wounds will heal. There may be some stiffness, the healing might be a little slow, but she'll be up and moving by morning, if not sooner." She passed her stern yet reassuring gaze around the table. "If anybody's gonna know about this power that she has and how to handle it, it's her. Speculating will only lead to hard-to-change assumptions."

Her attention stopped on Sebastian. "We've all got a mountain of work to do. Let's busy ourselves with that until she wakes up."

It was not a suggestion.

"Agreed." He was glad for Tanir to take the lead. "You're all dismissed."

Sir Gargic rose and left, shaking the table with the force of his footsteps. Wera and Enoch stood, but lingered.

"Should someone keep watch outside of her door in case she does wake up?" Wera asked.

Sebastian inhaled deeply. "Yes, I'll—"

"Enoch, if you'd please," Tanir interjected.

Enoch glanced between the two of them, unsure.

Sebastian's stomach hurt, Tanir's edge tying knots in his gut.

"We'll do it in shifts, Enoch," he assured, smiling despite his nerves. He gave a short nod to dismiss them and they left without protest.

"What's really wrong with Mina?" Sebastian asked quietly, knowing they would most likely be listening outside the door.

Tanir turned to him, gaze studying and sympathetic. He braced himself for the worst.

"Are you alright?" she asked.

His hands balled into fists beneath the table. Mina was going to die, wasn't she? Go insane and tear herself apart.

"I'm fine," he rushed out. "Just tell me what's—"

"She's fine, Sebastian. I've told you this a dozen times now," Tanir insisted. "What I'm worried about is you. You're tamping things down."

"I'm not 'tamping things down'. I'm—"

The bruise Mina's teeth left on his shoulder ached.

"—staying calm. I need a clear head to handle things."

Tanir's sympathy worsened, now tinged with doubt. She stood and placed her hand in his hair. Her fingernails soothingly scratched at his scalp. "Be gentle with her, Sebastian." She gave his head a final pat then pulled, heading towards the door. "And yourself, too."

He struggled to find a response as she left.

Be gentle with her.

Be gentle with her.

There he lay, floating as the ripples Mina left in her wake faded.

Not only did he almost boil her alive, but he almost kissed her.

Fuck.

Why would he do something so stupid?

Why would he go and complicate things further?

She flinched when he told her he cared about her. How bad did he hurt her then? Was it a pinch, a stab, another burn? Maybe it wasn't even pain. Maybe she didn't want to hear it from him. Maybe she was repulsed by the thought of him caring for her. She should be.

But she reached for him then, didn't she? In that moment, her eyes were on his lips just as much as his were on hers, and she started to reach for him.

Or she was just getting her hand out of the boiling water slowly cooking her.

Regardless, Mina was back after that moment. Not fully, but the wry wit he'd grown to adore returned. Her gray eyes focused, Autumn skies instead of a far-off fog. While he floated, a drift in conflict — guilty to be proud of seeing how his partial confession changed her both mentally and...

His thoughts drifted to the pink plush of her lips.

...physically.

"Well, well, well." Sebastian jumped and opened his eyes to find Wera smirking down at him from the edge of the hot spring. "Don't you look relaxed. I take it your little tête-à-tête with Mina went well?"

"I scolded her and scalded her."

"Kinky."

He ran a hand down his face in exasperation. "Wera."

"I know. I know." She hiked up her skirts and sat down at the edge to dangle her feet in the water. "I'm just teasing ya. Though if anybody could get a little kinky without turning into an ice sculpture, it would probably be you, salamander. I bet the poor thing's never even—"

"Wera, if you finish that sentence, I'm going to make it so hot and humid in this room your hair will look like a turkey tail for days."

"So you yelled at her, huh?"

"A bit. Yeah."

"And how'd she react?"

"She made a snarky comment about how her ice magic was the reason she wasn't sous vide."

"That's good. I guess letting out whatever was bothering you helped the both of you out."

"It's not all out. I'm still bothered."

"Hot and bothered?"

Sebastian super-heated his palms against the water's surface, sending massive plumes of steam in the air.

Wera held her hair down to protect it. "I'm sorry! I couldn't help myself!"

He stopped.

"You know you can't give me a perfect setup like that. Your mind really must be muddled."

He sighed. "This isn't good."

"The rimefaes that are stalking us, the increasingly difficult mountain terrain, our cursed alpinist? Honestly, it's pretty par for the course for us. I can count the 'cakewalk' contracts we've had on one hand."

"There's too many..." his heart throbbed in his chest, his head threatened to burst if he dared to think another thought, "...feelings involved with this one. I can't keep as level of a head as I normally do."

"Well yeah. That tends to happen when you like someone. That's why they call it 'having feelings'."

"I've liked people before. I like you all quite a bit," he noted. "And I've been upset over things involved with you all. I bawled like a baby when I almost lost Tanir to those slave traders in Kisquet, but I was able to hold myself together enough to come up with a plan and get her back."

"Isn't that what you're doing now? You have a plan to figure out Mina's curse. You're trying your best to be careful with your commands, asking us for help—"

"If she didn't transform, if she fell out of the sky and that was it, I don't think I could have controlled myself." Sebastian rubbed his eyes to keep them from tearing. "Gods, I haven't been afraid of that since I was an apprentice."

"Huh."

Sebastian lifted his head out of the water. "Huh?"

Wera crossed her arms and pouted. "So you'll roast an entire battlefield of monsters for her, but what about us? You wouldn't raise a little hell if one of us died?"

"I don't want to think about that."

"It's a fair question to ask."

Sebastian pursed his lips in contemplation. "Maybe."

"Maybe," she repeated, deadpan and moody.

"I mean, I've definitely gotten a little caught up the few times one of you has been severely hurt or in trouble, but to that level?"

He looked down at his hands. "It's gonna be hard, but I've got to put a damper on these feelings. Plus, it's not like they'd lead to anything anyways."

"Well. If that's what you think is best."

Sebastian snapped his gaze up from his hands to her. Wera was busy looking at the ceiling.

"Wera."

"Yes, sir?"

"Oh, don't you 'sir' me right now. You agreed with me way too quickly. You never agree with me that quickly unless you're up to something."

"I'm not up to anything," she said, not even trying to be convincing. "I'm just glad to hear I won't have any competition."

"C-competition?"

"Mhmm." Wera gave him a knowing smile. "I mean Mina's smart, beautiful, more clever than she lets on, and can lift me like I'm a feather. She and I are already pretty close now, so I'll just make sure we get to know each other better. Then when you eventually break her curse — which I know you will — I'll make my move."

Sebastian frowned, nostrils flaring slightly. She was just teasing him. There was no reason to feel any sort of way over it.

"Because, you know, once you're able to break the curse, there should be no reason I couldn't be with her, right?"

"You seem very confident about that."

"I mean — she did pick me to go save Enoch with her," she said. "And she lets me call her a cute nickname, and she even sang me that really sweet song to help me calm down in the tunnels today."

Sebastian fought back the urge to list every special, kind thing that Mina had done for him so far. "Then I wish you both the utmost happiness."

"Man. You're really sticking to your laurels on this, huh?"

"Of course I am! I can't pursue her! Especially now! With the curse and the contract and the— the—" In his moment of crisis, the thought of introducing Mina to his mentor shook loose. "'Oh, Sebastian, how did you and your wife meet?' Well, you see, Mina here was under a rather nasty curse, so I decided to amend our existing contract so that she was bound by magical means to follow my every command without question."

"Wife?"

Wera's comment went unheard. "Gods, it's no wonder she can't even bear to look at me! She probably thinks I'm doing all of this to manipulate her! She obviously knows I'm attracted to her now after I stared at her mouth like a punch drunk school boy for ten fucking minutes just because her lips turned pink—"

Wera stuck her fingers in her mouth and whistled. "Woah, Sebastian! Easy boy! What do you mean, her lips turned pink?"

"Well, uh." He scratched at his chin nervously. "I got a little heated while I was venting my frustrations and basically turned the hot spring into a Mina soup pot. Hot enough, apparently, to splotch some of her extremities and turn her lips from their pale, blue-tinted shade to a warm, blush pink."

"You think it'll last?"

"What?"

"Her lips. You think they'll stay like that?"

"Gods, I hope not," he said without thinking — the vision of her just inches away from him, her breathing heavy as she waited for him to make a move haunting him — then quickly corrected himself. "Fuck, no, I mean, I don't know if it will. It's probably just because of the water." He leaned back into the spring, fingers drumming against the stone nervously, conjuring quickly snuffed out sparks. "I'm the worst. I can't believe I said that."

"Typical man," Wera sighed. "A woman gets a little color on her lips and suddenly, you wanna wipe it off of her, so you don't get distracted."

"Like I said. I'm the worst," he groaned.

"You're not the worst. And if it's any consolation, it's been harder for her to look me in the eye, too."

"Really?"

"I smiled at her earlier and she winced before looking somewhere else." Wera stood and headed towards the door. "Don't make any decisions tonight. A crazy ass day can lead to people doing crazy ass stuff. Get some sleep and see how you feel in the morning."

Sebastian pouted. "I hate it when you serve me with my own advice."

Wera smiled. "No, you don't. You love it because it shows I listen to you."

He was grateful for a night of dreamless sleep after everything, and treated himself to an early morning of gathering iron rings and testing out modifications for the noxulars. His study seemed... emptier despite its abundance of clutter, and he found himself looking over his shoulder at the corner of the floor by the cedar chest he kept his spare blanket and pillow in. Mina had only been in his study once before, why did he still expect her to be there? He was the one who decided to let her sleep a little longer this morning, after all.

A little chemistry to sort out the glasses, some tracking and flexibility enchantments on the rings, and Sebastian's sense of duty was satisfied. His stomach's complaints could finally be heard.

He headed down to the kitchen, creations in hand, debating in his head what enchantment would work best for the earplugs he'd ask Tanir for, when he caught the telltale, animated and boisterous rumblings of a Mina-lead argument through the kitchen door.

He couldn't help but smile at the sound. Mina's combative nature, though more a symptom of her circumstances than a want to stir the pot from what he could deduce, had greatly concerned him before. After seeing her stripped of that brashness, however, he'd gladly weather whatever storm she was stirring up now.

He took a deep breath and swung open the door.

"Good morn—"

Pink.

Short, choppy raven hair, gray eyes, porcelain skin, and full lips still stained the same dusty rose as the night before took his breath away.

When had he started looking for her when he entered a room?

"Morning, Sebastian," Wera turned around in her seat, completely out of focus as all his attention was locked on the stoic face staring back at him. "Mina's lips are pink."

A subtle flex of her eyebrows, her eyelids raising slightly: Mina's subdued version of surprised disbelief, flashed on her face for a moment before she picked up the back of her spoon and started studying her appearance.

She touched her fingers to her lips, an action his own fingers twitched with jealous longing for. "They look the same."

Wera's head snapped back to face her. "What do you mean, they look the same?"

"They look the same. What more is there to explain?"

"You see the world in grayscale with almost outstanding color accuracy. How can you not tell the difference when—" She stopped, realization course-correcting her thoughts. "You're not seeing things in grayscale. You're seeing things completely desaturated. You're desaturated."

"Do you know what could've caused this, Sebastian?" Enoch asked, breaking Sebastian out of his trance.

With his well-documented quick wit and vast intelligence, he replied with an elegant, "Huh?"

"Are you feeling alright?" Tanir asked. "You look a little flushed and seem a little—"

"Gobsmacked," Wera offered.

"Oh no, it's just that uh— that I was up rather early working, so I'm a little fuzzy. No tea, no breakfast, running on fumes," he fumbled to form coherent sentences. "But pink! Pink is good. It looks—" He stopped himself before he could ruin such a good thing by hurting her with compliments. "And desaturation that's—" He paused another moment as the logical part of his brain finally recovered. "That makes perfect sense."

"Windenhofer," Sir Gargic called.

"Yes?"

"The hell are you still standing at the door like a startled deer for if you're starving?"

"Right." Sebastian took his seat at the end of the table. "Anybody want anything in particular?"

Wera laughed.

"What?" Sebastian looked at her, bewildered.

"We've already started without you 'Bastian," Tanir gestured to the table cluttered with half-eaten breakfast.

"Ah. Then I'll have the usual, kitchen."

The cutlery set to work and Sebastian set to sipping his tea, hoping it would help level out his many, muddled thoughts. But there he was again, staring at Mina's lips, appreciating them from a different angle.

"Sebastian," Wera snipped.

He tore his eyes away and found Wera glaring at him. "Wera?"

She rolled her eyes and exhaled in exasperation. "Why does desaturation make 'perfect sense'?"

He blinked at her a few times, processing her question, and finally found his derailed train of thought. "Desaturation is the process of adjusting the intensity of light from something when it comes to color theory, correct?"

"For the most part."

"Well, if we think about the symptoms that we know about, it's as if everything has been removed from her, desaturated and dulled in some way or another. In fact, because of the partial senses she has gained, I would say that it's not that she never had those senses to begin with. She's always had them. They're just suppressed by her curse."

"But I can't see it," Mina said. She didn't face him as she spoke. "I tasted the wine. I smelt the lavender."

Sebastian's heart ached at the slouch of her shoulders, the downward cast of her gaze. They were minuscule things, and would have gone unnoticed by most, but from the minute she snarled in his face after saving Sir Gargic he knew if he was ever going to truly help her — truly know her — he'd have to be better than most.

"No worries. I'm sure you'll be able to see it soon," he said and gave her a smile she'd ignore.

"Is there something that you think may have caused it, Mina?" Tanir asked the one question he didn't need an answer to.

Me.

"Bathwater always freezes," Mina answered.

The warm feeling in his chest cooled immediately. Was that really what she thought it was? The water?

"Interesting. So, because Sebastian was able to keep the water warm consistently, it thawed you a little?"

Well, yes, it was the water in that sense. But if it wasn't for him, it wouldn't have been that warm in the first place, certainly not to the point of almost boiling.

"How about we just stick a flame or something under her bathtub, then?" Sir Gargic offered. "You're all about experiments there, Windenhofer. Wouldn't that be a decent theory to test out?"

It would, and he hated that.

Enoch perked up as he carefully dabbed his breakfast out of his mustache. "Oh! Those soup stones would probably work!"

"Soup stones?" Mina asked.

"They're these enchanted rocks you can use instead of coals or a fire to heat up your soup. When you put them in water, they heat up and in just a minute or two your soup's boiling! You'd need to pull a couple from the Junk Room, I think, to combat your freeze factor, though." Enoch turned to him. "What do you think, Sebastian?"

"Yeah, Sebastian," Wera repeated unnecessarily. "What do you think?"

His breakfast slid onto the table, distracting everyone else enough that he could shoot a sneer in her direction. He was starting to miss the days when she was fresh out of art school and overly professional with him.

"I think it's worth a shot," he replied. "What do you think, Mina?"

Please say no. Please say it's a stupid idea and that you should just have me heat the hot springs for you instead.

"Building a fire to cook with isn't that hard," she replied.

Sebastian took a bitter bite of his omelet.

"It can be if you're inside and don't have a fireplace or a big stove," Enoch argued.

"Then just go outside and build one."

"Some people don't know how."

"There are plenty of books on it."

"Some people can't get books or don't know how to read."

"Then you and the cartographer make a picture book and hand it out as you travel."

"I don't know how to make a fire."

"I do."

"Are you offering to teach us how to make a fire, so we can make a picture book?" Wera asked.

Although she was about to take a bite, something paused her, and she said, "No."

A small chill ran up Sebastian's spine, the way it always did since he noticed how often her 'no's' were forced out against her will.

Sir Gargic scoffed. "Then why even bring it up?"

"Mina," he interjected, "*could* you teach Wera and Enoch how to build a fire?"

She glanced at him out of the corner of her eye. "If I'm told to."

That phrase was one of the few times she willingly made eye contact with him, and he relished every second of it. It was her way of telling him what she wanted, a little peek into the full person she was beneath the weight of her curse. Mina wanted to help people, even if she could never say it.

A sinking realization pulled under, into the memory of her hands shaking against his in the cavern. Of blood pouring from her eyes, her nose, injuries that shouldn't have been caused by an overexertion of wind magic. Of her, wounded but holding strong, pulling him out of the way of the queen's claw then collapsing on the ground in agony without the beast scratching her.

"And if something does attack us, no matter what happens, stay behind me."

Mina wanted to help people, even if it might kill her.

In fact.

"What purpose does it serve to keep me around?"

She didn't care if it did.

"You're crying," Mina noted, pulling him out of his head.

"What?" His throat was tight as he spoke, and finally, he noticed the stinging in his eyes.

"Sebastian, are you alright?" Tanir fretted.

He blinked rapidly, sending the remaining tears rolling down his cheeks.

"Oh wow," he sniffled and laughed to sell his lie. "Sorry, the hot peppers in my omelet are actually quite spicy today. Well done, kitchen."

The cookware rattled in appreciation.

Sir Gargic laughed along with him. "Then it's a shock that it hasn't burnt a hole through the table if it's strong enough to make you sweat!"

"It definitely is." He wiped his dripping nose off on his napkin and scrambled for anything to take his mind off its current downward spiral. "Oh! I have some gifts for you all!"

Sebastian picked up the small crate containing their noxulars and rings and passed them out.

"I applied a coating to the lens that's reactive to sunlight and modified the existing light reflection enchantment so that once the light threshold reaches a certain number of lumens it automatically transitions to shade. The rings should readjust to your finger size as you put them on, and I've imbued them with a tracking spell. If you tap it three times with your thumb—" He demonstrated on his own hand. Four red beams of light appeared out of his ring and pointed at them. "It'll show you where the others are."

"Very impressive, Sebastian."

"Thank you, Tani. By the way, do you have any extra pairs of those earplugs you wear for harvesting mandrakes?"

"I do."

"Enough for all of us? I'm thinking of using the Ear of The Dog spell on them, so we can still hear while wearing them, and have the added protection the enchantment provides."

"No need. The plugs are already enchanted."

"Really?"

"Yeah." Tanir giggled. "They're called The Colic Cure and are made for new mothers with babies who won't stop fussing. It can tell when a baby's crying and cancels out the noise."

"Man. I could have used them when my little sister was born. The minute my poor mother put her down, she wouldn't stop screaming," Wera remarked.

"There's not gonna be a weird screaming baby monster we have to look out for on this next leg of the journey, is there, beastie?"

"No," Mina replied. "If there was, I wouldn't be going this way. The path forward has a lot of steep elevation changes, narrow pathways, sudden snow squalls, and avalanches coming off of the surrounding peaks."

"So no talking?" Wera asked.

"Some talking. No shouting. The sound alone won't cause one, but if you happen to scare a pika or a mountain goat, and they take off running, that'll definitely do it."

"Things actually live up here?" Enoch asked.

"We're not that high up. Only about eight thousand feet. We'll ascend another seven thousand over the next four days if there's no..." she paused for a moment, her hand gripped her fork tightly, then released as she sighed, "interruptions. Then it's the big climb."

"That's the four days of straight rock climbing?" Sir Gargic asked.

"The Lithe. Ten thousand feet."

△

Maybe it was because they were in the heat of battle, maybe it was because his mind was too fixated on the lingering smell of Mina's burnt flesh on his coat, but he hadn't realized just how red the beasts' blood was against the snow, or how much carnage had truly been left in their wake. They all stood, studying the crimson-mottled landscape. A gentle yet frigid breeze wove around them.

Sir Gargic cleared his throat and stepped forward to pull out one of the iron pitons and break the ring around their campsite. "Let's get going. We've got a lot of ground to cover, right, beastie?"

Sebastian's stomach turned. Mina wore the same expression she did when he found her scrapping listlessly at the bottom of her empty bowl.

"Mina. Lead the way," he commanded.

Her body turned for her, feet, then torso, then head.

"What order?" she asked as she walked past him.

He wanted to walk alongside her, he really did. Wanted to be right there to protect her if anything were to happen, but he'd be too busy fighting with himself about how to talk to her, how to let her know how important she was to all of them, to him. Too busy trying to cheer her up to keep an eye out for any potential dangers.

He knew himself. When a problem took root, he had to solve it. Especially when the problem involved someone he cared for. That's why he formed his little troop, to keep himself out of trouble when the problems consumed him.

"Wera, Sir Gargic, Enoch, Tanir, then me in the back."

Mina stopped for just a moment, a very brief moment that he wouldn't have caught if he hadn't been watching her so intently, then let his command tug her along.

"Come on, Cartographer," she called for Wera, who raised an eyebrow at him.

Sebastian tapped the corner of his noxulars lightly, then pointed at Mina

Watch her for me.

Wera gave a wicked smile and fanned herself dramatically, teasing him one last time before jogging ahead to catch up with her.

Enoch and Tanir moved to fall in line with Sir Gargic, but Sebastian grabbed their shoulders to hold them back a moment.

"I need your advice on something meadowlark related." He didn't speak in a whisper, that would draw Mina's attention immediately.

"Alright then. Let's discuss as we hike," Tanir said, and urged them all forward.

Sebastian waited a bit to speak, watching to make sure Mina seemed decently distracted by Wera.

“I’ve realized, recently, that meadowlarks get injured when they protect people. Not by weapons or attacks but by an unnatural part of their anatomy.”

“Protect willingly or unwillingly?” Enoch asked.

“Willingly. Which is why I believe they prefer to lead the flock into battle. That way, protecting others is just a happenstance.”

“But they’ve been doing it outside of happenstance. The caves, the training room—”

Sebastian’s throat went dry at the memory of Mina on the training room floor, trembling in pain as she waited for the healing herbs to work. She’d gone through all that for him, hadn’t she?

“Because I think that at some point in their life, they’ve decided that saving others is worth more than saving themselves. Even if it means death or something worse.”

“Something worse?” Tanir asked.

“An unwilling homecoming,” Enoch explained.

“That’s what I realized over breakfast today,” he admitted.

“Oh, Sebastian,” Tanir cooed.

“Did you really think he was crying over peppers?” Enoch asked. “We’ve seen him do shots of king cobra chili hot sauce!”

“When did I do that?”

“When we were at Taj’s Tavern to celebrate escaping Dormina’s Temple. Sir Gargic challenged you to a drinking contest. You won, but were completely blacked out by the end of it and pestering people for more dares. Wera came up with the hot sauce shots.”

“Of course she did.” He pouted, then frowned even deeper as he watched Mina field Wera’s questions with shrugs and curt answers rather than the somewhat animated banter they had grown into. He sighed to try and lessen the weight on his chest. “How can you tell someone they’re important to you, without actually telling them? When any of you lot doubt your worth, I can make one hell of an argument against that nonsense, but with Mi—the meadowlark... I’m at a loss.”

“Yeah, a slideshow of all the great things about meadowlarks is pretty ineffective if the meadowlarks are writhing in pain watching it,” Tanir noted.

“Then it’ll have to be actions if words can’t do it,” Enoch offered. “Actions can easily be passed off as things that just happened. The meadowlark seems to think this is an us versus them situation. You need to make them realize there’s only an us, and they’re included in it.”

“And the meals, the hot spring, and the library conversations haven’t done that?” Sebastian groused.

Enoch and Tanir glared at him. “Obviously not.”

“That’s just basic hospitality. You know that,” Tanir said. “It just feels like it’s more than that because it takes more effort with them.”

“If the meadowlark was the same as any other new member of our team, what would you do to make them feel welcome?”

“Well, normally, I give them the grand tour, treat them to their favorite meal, talk to them to learn more about their history, their interests, and craft one of the study rooms to suit those interests,” he prattled. “A lot of it just comes naturally, you know? Points of connection happen on our mission, or in our downtimes. Like it wasn’t until you saved me from being hauled to jail in Tussleberg that the walls between you and me started to come down, Enoch."

"Interesting." Enoch cast a sidelong look at Tanir. "Can you tell me what meadowlarks are interested in?"

"Easily. It's music," Sebastian answered. "They were telling me the other day about their personal collection." His head almost came loose and spun around completely when Mina had listed them. "It sounds as though they're able to play almost any instrument by ear. I'd love to tell them how amazing that is and that their violin playing is one of the most beautiful things I've ever heard right next to their voice, but—"

"But you haven't crafted a music room for them?"

Enoch's rightful question caught Sebastian off guard. "I— uh—"

"You gave them a tour, shared many meals with them, spoke with them about their interests, next on the list is crafting a study room, right?" he shrugged. "I mean, I know mine was pretty obvious given my line of work, but you had still had it made up less than three days after you hired me. That poor meadowlark. It's been over a week and nothing. Well, not nothing. They did get a rather nice pastel kit—"

"Alright, alright, I get it." Sebastian bristled. He hadn't given her nothing. He made her that amber pendant, but they didn't need to know that. If he told them, they'd tell Wera, and he'd never hear the end of it. Even worse, Mina might actually hear.

His pride surged seeing it hang on her necklace, *the* necklace that kept her tethered to this realm. He didn't want to know what it would feel like to see her without it.

"You have to treat the meadowlark a little differently. Have to take more control than you're used to, be more careful with your boundless positivity, but that doesn't mean you have to change everything," Tanir said. "You've just got to be clever, remember?"

"I remember," he stated like a scolded child.

"I have another idea as well."

"I'm all ears."

"Though I find myself disagreeing with him more and more these days, Sir Gargic had a point with his sad excuse to try and prove that he was stronger than them," Tanir said. "Instead of fighting each other, though, how about we start training to fight together? I don't think the meadowlarks have ever truly fought as part of a team, and after yesterday and with more battles to come, it might be good to hone that skill. It'll show them that they don't have to protect us. We all protect each other, that's just what happens naturally when fighting as a unit."

Brilliant.

"This is why you all are the best." Sebastian pulled Tanir and Enoch into a hug, overjoyed as the tangled web of "what to do" started to unravel. "Three heads are definitely better than one."

"Windenhofer," Sir Gargic called their attention. "Beastie says to keep up. She ain't coming after ya if you all get lost."

△

Despite the ache in his knees, the stiffness in his shoulders, and the overall strain on his body from the first half of the day's journey, Sebastian was buzzing. He took his lunch in his study, barely chewing as he drafted the schematics for Mina's music room. She couldn't see color, but her apparent fascination with amber set the theme. Maybe it was the particular shade of gray that she liked, or, judging by how she tilted her head back and forth while looking at them, perhaps it was the way the gemstones caught the light. That was something he could work with.

Getting the instruments would be tricky to conjure by traditional means, but if Sebastian lied a bit and said she was his apprentice — a claim his own former teacher would validate without question — he could ask the Guild to grant her access to the Northern Practitioner's Music Club's instrument collection. They would require proof of musical ability, however.

Which is how Sebastian found himself outside of Mina's door, just in time to hear:

"Say another word and I'll kill you."

"Mina?!" he shouted. "Is everything alright?!"

A muffled, "son of a bitch," slipped through the door, followed by the telltale sound of Wera's cackle.

"Everything's fine, Sebastian," Wera hollered back. "Mina's just a little flustered."

"I'm not flustered!" Mina protested. "Y-you're the one who—"

"Oh, she's so shy! If you could blush, you would right now, wouldn't you?" Wera teased. "Aww, our sweet little virgin Mina!"

"W-what the h-hell?" Mina stammered. "I wouldn't— You— I'm not a virgin!"

Whether or not she was blushing was yet to be confirmed, but Sebastian sure was.

"I'll come back another time!" he announced, voice significantly higher than before. "Sorry to intrude!"

XII

Promises, Pacts...

Sebastian's frantic footsteps fading down the hallway were barely noticeable over the sound of blood pumping in Mina's ears.

"What was that about?" she hissed through her teeth, barely keeping calm as she drowned in frustration, fear, and embarrassment.

"You said not to tell him, right?" Wera looked at the mural of Sebastians behind her. "He probably heard that empty threat of yours through the door, and would have burst in here if I didn't scare him away."

"It wasn't an empty threat," she warned. "Whatever you were about to imply about my thoughts regarding the wizard. Don't."

She arched an eyebrow. "Why not?"

Mina's heart was about to break through her rib cage.

"Because I'm still trying to figure it out. And any outside influence might skew my efforts to research the source of this plague."

"A plague? Thinking about Sebastian is a plague?"

Mina gestured to the drawings. "What else would explain this?!"

"About a dozen things you don't want me to say. But for conversation's sake, let's say it's not at all an emotionally fueled obsession with the color orange."

"Amber."

"That explains the necklace, then," Wera remarked. "So, let me take a wild guess. You first saw 'amber' back when we found you two sleeping in the snow, right?"

Mina's skin crawled. The one thing she had to herself lost so easily. All because, in her harried need to understand what the fuck was going on with the wizard today, she had left the guest room door open just a crack.

"What gives you that idea?"

"When he went to give you your bedroll, you froze as soon as you saw him. Add in the fact that you had us follow behind with the lamest excuse I've ever heard and could barely take your eyes off him until we stopped for lunch, and it makes a compelling case." Wera stepped towards her. "The first thing you saw in color was Sebastian's hair. Why didn't you tell us?"

Mina stepped back, sat down in her chair to disguise the growing weakness in her knees. She couldn't hide it any longer. If she were being honest with herself, the idea of telling someone — although she didn't understand why —granted her more relief than she expected. "I will answer you, but you must make me a promise first."

She just needed to take precaution.

"It depends on the promise."

She looked Wera dead in the eye and extended her hand. "Promise me that you will never tell the wizard about this conversation."

Shock passed briefly over Wera's face. She collected herself and took Mina's hand. "I promise you."

A phantom thread wrapped around them as they shook, ghosting across the skin of their hands before vanishing. A feeling Mina was all too familiar with as of late, but unnoticeable to the cartographer.

"I didn't know what was happening at first. You all didn't know about my eyes to begin with. You didn't know until I turned. It's unwise to trust strangers," she rattled off all the unspoken justifications she'd given herself since she first saw Sebastian's hair color.

"We're not strangers anymore," Wera argued.

Mina considered her next words carefully. "By definition, we are not."

Wera scowled, not caring for her aloof reply. "You could have told us after the wine."

"And you wouldn't have jumped to conclusions? Or asked me a thousand questions I couldn't answer? Or say something that might have taken it away?" She looked away from her, the notion of the latter weighing heavier than she cared it to on her chest. "Sometimes people keep things to themselves. Sometimes there is a reason for privacy."

"And I waltzed in here without knocking," Wera said with a heavy sigh, "and ruined that."

Wera rubbed her eyes, smudging her glasses slightly, and gave Mina a sad smile that stung deep. "You called this a plague. Plagues are something people have to survive, and often experts are brought in to consult leaders on the best plan of action to keep their people safe." Wera extended her hand out once more. "Consider me your Sebastian Windenhofer expert."

Mina stared at her blankly. "You? An expert?"

"You thought him and I were siblings, didn't you?"

Not really, that was just to change the subject, but she wasn't blind to the fact that the two of them were close. Her offering to leverage their friendship so easily, however...

"And what do you get out of this?"

"Who said I have to get something out of this?"

"No one. But no person or thing in this realm or any of the others does shit for free."

"Well," Wera smiled wider, fueling Mina's growing headache. "I don't think I can tell you exactly what I get out of it, so I'll just say it's conversation. I've been traveling with our merry band for a while now, and things can get pretty boring from time to time."

There seemed to be no malice behind Wera's searing smile as far as she could tell, so Mina retook her hand and shook it. Invisible threads sealed their pact as she said, "Then you shall be my expert."

"Great!" The word screeched in Mina's ear as Wera rushed towards her bed and jumped on it, turning from dignitary to childlike with little hesitation. She patted the empty spot beside her. "Come on then. Tell me what exactly is plaguing you about him."

Mina stayed in her chair.

"We've only got a few minutes left before we have to start the second leg of today's hike." She sang, teasing, urging. "You don't want to talk about it while we're out there, do you? He might hear."

Mina groaned as she stomped over.

"It's his stupid face," she said as she dropped on the bed. "The way it moves. The way it looks."

Wera stared at her wizard wall. "His expressions?"

"Those too." Mina crossed her arms. "He keeps making new ones I don't understand, and I can't trust myself that I'm remembering them right. My mind keeps playing them over and over again, so they've got to be distorted, but—" She looked at the two pictures she drew of him in the hot springs sitting side by side together. One from her dream, the other from her memory, but somehow still near-perfect copies of each other. "I'm not certain."

"So you're drawing him to study his expressions, so you can learn how to read them?"

"And so I can tell the difference between what's perceived versus what's reality."

Wera hummed in contemplation. "Do you do this with the rest of us?"

"No."

"Why not?"

"Because you all don't plague me. You're not always on my mind." Mina pointed to the drawings and scowled. "That bastard is, and it's *so* fucking distracting."

Wera snorted, and re-situated herself on the bed: stomach on the mattress, chin resting on her hands, and legs swaying in the air. "So what about his expression today was bothering you? You seemed to be pretty engrossed in your drawing when I came in."

"After breakfast today, he's been avoiding me." Mina stood and picked up the half-finished drawing. "He looked like this then." She showed Wera the picture and tapped on the tears running down his cheeks. "He said it was because of the hot peppers, but there's no sweat on his brow or upper lip. That's what happened when we had that spicy curry for dinner after the battle royale."

"Ah," Wera frowned and sat up, tucking her knees beneath her. "You noticed that too, huh? I'm not sure what was happening there, but, I know he was definitely upset."

"Upset? Looking at me upset him?" Her chest grew tight, painfully so. The hole that had been forming in her stomach ever since she saw his tears became vacuous, pulling her body into it. Though to Wera, she was sure, she looked just as emotionless as she always did.

"I don't think it was you that upset him!" she consoled. "Maybe he was just tired from getting up early to work!"

"He said he'd have me work with him on the noxulars yesterday." Mina turned the picture back around and looked at him. "Yet he did it all by himself this morning."

Eyes wide, tears streaming down his cheeks.

Upset.

She slammed the picture back on her desk, face down.

"He'd probably tell you why if you ask him." Wera shrugged. "He tends to bottle up his emotions, so just one good nudge should have him spilling his guts all over the place."

"Then he'd be too sick to hike."

Wera laughed. "No, not literally. I mean, if you push him to explain what he's feeling, he will."

Mina mulled the suggestion over. Going to the wizard directly was a thought that made her muscles squirm, but it could be a much quicker and more effective way to put an end to the ceaseless Sebastian-centered questions running through her mind.

"Break's over," Mina announced, grabbing her pack and slinging it over her shoulder. "Your expertise has been noted."

"Wonderful," Wera stretched and stood. "More hiking." She stopped before she headed out the door. "Oh, and don't worry, Meens." She winked again and pierced Mina's brain for a brief second. "Your secret's safe with me."

🜁

Sebastian seemed lighter after their break, less upset.

Probably because he's kept away from me.

Wera, out of some sense of duty Mina couldn't quite grasp, tried her best to keep Mina's mind occupied. She kept asking questions about the range they were hiking, about the flora and fauna in the area, about the possible weather conditions, any events of historical significance: questions that went beyond her role as cartographer.

Perhaps she was trying to gather details for their atlas project to spare Enoch the displeasure of talking to her about it.

When they reached their resting point for the evening, Mina supposed she should have felt relieved that the hike had gone rather smoothly; that there were no signs or interferences from her false relatives. Instead, the pit in her stomach hollowed even further. They were biding their time, waiting for the right opportunity to strike.

Just like they were trained to do.

Just like *she* had been trained to do.

But that look in Bormir's eyes, just before he let go. That wasn't a part of it. It was distant, almost... sad. She never would have tolerated any display of—

"Hold on a minute, Meens," Wera called, stopping her from heading into the commorancy as she painted the iron circle around it. "I have another question for you."

"Then ask the question," Mina deadpanned.

"If you watch the sky over there for a little bit, could you tell me what direction the clouds are moving?"

Mina looked up at the patch of sky she pointed to and was greeted with the seeping orange hues of the gently setting sun.

"Well?" Wera pressed. Mina could hear the light smile inching up the corner of her mouth.

There was a flutter in her chest, nothing painful, just a tickle of some emotion she couldn't place.

"It'll take me more than a second," Mina snapped, more out of habit than out of ire. "Practice patience."

She stood there a moment, taking in the sky burning brighter and brighter, as Wera took her sweet time painting their protection despite Sir Gargic's grumbles of discontent.

Mina took off a glove and lifted her hand, pretending to check the direction of the wind, while she admired how warm her skin looked in the amber light. No matter how she turned it, her chain link scars could not be seen, until a thick cloud cover rolled over the sun, filling in their faint outlines with its shadows.

"They're moving southeast," she announced, and headed into the commorancy for yet another meal she couldn't taste.

Except for the wine, which, with the drink straw drawn by Enoch, was a malbec once again.

Sebastian hardly spoke as they ate, his mind clearly elsewhere, working out a hundred invisible problems, thinking a thousand invisible thoughts. Mina tried to decipher what she could without watching him too obviously. He'd stop in the middle of bites to suddenly look up at the ceiling for a moment, drum his fingertips across his lips, then, either with a furrow of his brows or brief lift of a smile, return to his meal.

The furrows were clearly a bad conclusion, the smiles a viable solution of some sort. The problem, however, was yet to be seen.

It probably involved her. She was the source of most of his problems.

His silent mutterings and brief revelations continued into the library, raining down over the large pile of papers and books in front of him.

But where his revelations were silent, Enoch's were not.

"I found her!" he exclaimed, nearly dropping the journal in his hands.

"Come on, Enoch!" Wera scolded as she wiped the blot of ink his sudden shout made her spill on her map.

"Sorry but—" his voice shook, and he pointed to the page. "I found her! I found Eirlys!"

Sebastian gave him his full attention.

"I've been reading any published journals or biographies that mention traveling through the Fallow Peaks, and I found her. She did what she did to me, or what she was going to do, to this merchant, Rodney Oakenbrau."

And now, he had Mina's full attention. The name itself sounded like a stag spewing up its lunch, and her memory of the man behind it was not much better.

"Oh, Oakenbrau," Sir Gargic lamented, shaking his head. "That poor bastard."

Of course.

"You knew him?!" Enoch squawked.

"I know him. Poor man was tricked by that awful snow siren."

"Was he now?" Mina asked.

Sir Gargic narrowed her eyes in warning as she drew his focus. "What are you going on about, beastie? You think I'd lie about him losing his manhood to one of your kind?"

"No," Mina replied. "But that doesn't mean *he* didn't." She set the book of herbs she'd been pretending to read down. "Go on, Enoch. Tell us what happened to the man in his own words."

Enoch lingered on her a moment, uncomfortable under her full focus, then cleared his throat.

"And now, dear reader, we discuss the reason you have truly decided to pick up this book."

Mina could picture the bastard at some desk, the thin, waxed whiskers of his mustache wobbling as he narrated his writing just to hear the sound of his own voice.

"I am not so ignorant of a man to think that you, dear reader, would have spent your hard-earned money just to read a humble merchant's many exploits. No, I know full well that you're here to learn the truth of that well-spread rumor that tickled the ears of my rivals and shocked the late Queen Regent to the point of fainting. The truth behind how I lost my cock.

"You may remember a time a few years back when the newly-wed Prince Dries Filart and his Prince Consort Atlan of Hobblebrooke visited The Court of Lanholde on their wedding tour. The Prince Consort's sense of fashion charmed and delighted many of the nobility, but none were quite as smitten as The Queen Regent was with the spotted chilla fur he sported. And thus word was sent out to all the kingdom's knights and nobility that she wished to purchase as many pelts as possible, as quickly as possible.

"The tricky thing about spotted chillas though, is that they only live in the rainforests of Varn, which just so happens to be on the wrong side of those blasted Fallow Peaks. The Hobblebrooke princes did the smart thing, took their wedding tour counterclockwise 'round the continent to avoid that frozen hellscape. The rest of us enterprising individuals, however, did not have the luxury to take a year to fulfill Her Majesty's request. So off I set towards the icy ascent with enchanted satchels filled with enough fur to outfit five giants and a few brave knights looking to win their queen's good graces.

"Now, very few know this, but there is a path up the Peaks that will turn a two-month journey into one if one is brave enough. And dear reader, we were more than brave enough, more than capable enough, even. I survived Zanok's Lure, named for that dreaded cannibal. Lived three days in darkness among the ravenous beasts of Rabbet's Pass. Survived blizzards and frostbite, and a ten-thousand-foot climb straight up a monolith of ice. With nothing but the slow descent down to Lanholde in front of us, how was I to know that the true frigid horror was waiting—"

Enoch stopped. His eyes grew wide as a slight tremble took over his hands. He swallowed his nerves and finished the sentence, "—in the form of a raven-haired woman taking shelter from the cold."

Mina could feel everyone else's eyes resting on her shoulders, but she kept hers trained on Enoch, masochistically eager to see just how prideful the cockless Oakenbrau was.

"Now, I did not have my wits about me when I found her in my tent — libations celebrating the near end of our journey coursing through my veins — otherwise I surely would have thought twice about approaching her. She was a beautiful thing; hair as dark as the cold, night sky, eyes as gray as winter's clouds, and skin as pale and pure as snowfall, how could I say no when she lured me into my cot, whispering—"

Enoch slammed the journal shut, either unwilling or unable to continue.

Sir Gargic jumped up from his chair and barreled towards her. "I knew you were—"

"He's lying," Wera stood, and cut Sir Gargic off. "Enoch, did he say when this happened?"

"Y-yes. It was seven years ago."

"Right. And as we all know, Mina's the only one who can lead people up this trail, she wouldn't just appear—"

"Oh, she very well could have," Sir Gargic snarled. "We saw those fae tricks for ourselves! She—"

"She *what?*" Mina hissed. "Had her first solo expedition with a bunch of entitled men when she was just barely a woman?"

"What the fuck does age matter when you fae fuck with time anyway?"

"What does a cockless conman's word matter when he is clearly trying to maintain his pride?"

"Oh what, like your word is better than his?" Sir Gargic pushed past Wera to stick his stubby nose in Mina's face. "You've lied about smaller shit. Of course, you'd fucking hide that you froze an innocent man's cock off for fun!"

"Oh, it was so much fun having a drunk, grown-ass man wander into my tent in the middle of the night." Her hands ached to tear his bulbous snout off his face and throw it into the fireplace. "A real treat hearing him mutter about all the things he would do to me on his way there after weeks of unwanted advances and mockery."

"And you let him?" Wera asked, voice warbling. Mina broke her glaring contest and glanced over the knight's shoulder to find her eyes wide and beginning to water. "You didn't kill him. You should have killed him for that."

The old fear, the pit in her stomach as she heard his footsteps crunching in the snow, the culmination of the inevitable, she remembered it well.

Made the decision right then and there, she'd never feel a fear like that again.

"I got it over with," she ground out, spite slipping through her gritted teeth. "Taught him and all the other men like him a lesson. Word must have spread that the coldhearted alpinist of the Sandere Woods was not to be touched. I never had another problem after that."

"Or you chose some poor man at random to get your point across." Sir Gargic stuck his finger in her face. "Secured your solitude with a sacrifice."

Vengeance consumed her. She needed to see the shock of horrific revelation wash down his face. Needed him to know, needed them all to know that her isolation, her cruel and callous nature, was justified.

"Wizard," she called. "It seems Sir Gargic is incapable of understanding truth from fiction."

Silence.

"Wizard!" she snapped.

Before she could turn to glare daggers at him, a blur of amber rushed past her. The slam of the library door echoed in the hollowness it left behind.

Sebastian had left the room.

And new emotions took root.

Anger, as it always was, as it always would be, chief among them.

But that was not what made her chase after him, abandoning all need for vengeance, validation.

"Don't leave!" Mina shouted down the hall, stopping him just before he could enter his study. With the wind at her heels, she caught up to him in two strides but continued walking past. "I am the one who upset you," she said over her shoulder. "I should be the one to go."

"You—" Sebastian grabbed her by the wrist as she passed by. "Hold on!"

The burn of his touch faded instantly as her hand grasped his wrist back.

"You haven't upset me."

"Then what reason did you have to leave like that?"

"Because I—" Yet again a million emotions, in a shade similar to the ones that confused her in the hot spring, rippled across his face. "How could I not be upset, hearing that someone hurt you?"

"It didn't hurt."

"Really?" His grip around her wrist tightened, his eyes — severe, determined — searching hers. "Tell the truth."

"It is the truth!" The forced words came out freely. "It didn't hurt. There was nothing. No burn, no sting, no headache, or tightening chest."

"And what about your feelings? Your emotions? Your mind? Those things he said to you, about you, the things he *did.* Weeks upon weeks of it! How much torment did he put you through for you to accept that what happened that night was the best resolution?" His palm glowed, heat building. "Don't you try and tell me it didn't bother you."

Mina loosened her hold on his wrist slightly.

"I have been through far worse."

From the way all the emotions but one drained from his face, Sebastian didn't need his command to know that she spoke the truth.

He inhaled deeply. "That doesn't make it okay."

Something stirred.

"What?" Mina asked.

His hand still held strong around her wrist, an anchor now instead of a cage. "If I cut you once. Would that make it okay for me to cut you a dozen times after that?"

Her mind turned over his question, looking for the trick behind it. "No."

"Then by that logic, just because you suffered once — just because you've been through worse — does not mean you have to suffer any more after that."

"I can—"

"Just because you can take it doesn't mean you should."

The something stirred again. A phantom that glided ever so slightly across her skin, around her spine, over her mind.

"That is what has upset you? That I've been hurt?" she asked.

"Yes."

"And that is why you didn't wake me today and command me to assist you in your study?"

Sebastian, for what felt like the first time, blinked; rapid and bewildered, as if he'd just been slapped.

"What? No, I—"

"Then I must leave. I am only going to upset you more." If such a small instance of her suffering had caused him such turmoil, truly knowing her — knowing all that made up her horrific existence — would drive him mad.

She didn't wish to turn such a bright man to madness.

"Mina!"

She tried to pull away, but her traitorous hand still clung to his wrist.

"Release your command."

"No."

"Then I'll make you." With a sharp tug, Mina knocked Sebastian off his feet and dragged him down the hall.

"Really?!" Sebastian shouted as he struggled to get his legs beneath him.

"Really. Keep holding on and I'll start running. The cartographer had a hard time withstanding it from over my shoulder. I wonder how long your arm will last before it's torn from its socket."

"Well, if that's the case, then." He grunted. "Mina. Sit."

Like lassoing a raging beast, a hundred threads wrapped around her and forced her to the ground.

"Fuck you!" she spat as her knees slammed against the hardwood. "Don't you have any fucking sense of self-preservation?!"

"No more than you do!" he snapped right back.

"If I upset you so goddamn much—"

He flicked her in the middle of her forehead.

"You don't upset me! Your circumstances upset me! And if anything, you leaving would only upset me more!"

Mina, with all her cleverness, cunning, and callousness, found herself at a loss for words. The combination of his flick and his declaration knocked most of the wind out of her aggravated defensiveness, so she crossed her arms over her chest, unwillingly pulling Sebastian closer to her, and folded herself up in defiance. She stared at a corner, feeling a million things she didn't want to feel or hadn't felt before. The plague of confoundment he'd infected her with was spreading quickly, inflaming her cells and destroying her synapses.

"If you push him to explain what he's feeling, he will."

"Explain," she demanded.

"Explain what?"

"Your statement," she replied, turning her cheek away from him even more out of... shame? Something close to shame. "I don't understand it."

"O-oh," Sebastian stammered. "Well um—"

He shifted beside her, folding his long legs up in a more comfortable position, causing his knees to press up against her side as they had nowhere else to go with her still holding on to him. Whatever force determined the execution of his commands must have favored this one. There was no pain at his touch, only a slight warmth where his hand wrapped around her bare wrist.

"It's difficult to explain. Part of it because I have to choose my words carefully, and leave a lot of the context out to keep from... causing harm. And then most of the reason I'm not completely sure of myself. But—" He drummed his fingers on his knee, the same ascending triplet rhythm he usually trailed across his lips. "The way that I grew up, people never stayed for very long. Either they sent me away or they left. I promised myself that I would never send anyone away without very good reason."

Mina moved to speak, but Sebastian squeezed her wrist.

"Like stealing thousands of gilt from a poor beggar, or slaughtering innocents for sport. Truly extreme, horrible, and unjust things."

"I slaughtered those frostlyons," she protested half-heartedly.

"But you were provoked, your magic was powered more by your emotions than your will, and you did not revel in their death. And as for people leaving, I only allow it if we are parting on amicable terms, and if I know that someday I will see them again." His palm traveled up her wrist and slipped into her hand. "If you were to leave now, not only would it not be amicable, but given our current circumstances, I fear that I would never see you again."

The warmth of his hand in hers, Mina swore, stirred a swarm of moths, determined to eat her heart for how much it ached.

Yet, she made no effort to pull away.

"I've told you, your troop is more than capable of surviving the rest of the journey a—"

"It is not my survival I'm worried about."

The moths tickled at the base of her brain, still hungry.

"You shouldn't." It was a weak argument, delivered too quietly to make an impact, but she had to do something to convince him of how worthless she was.

Sebastian chuckled, the first half of a low, f-major arpeggio. "And you shouldn't stare directly into the fireplace. But I know I'm not going to stop you from doing so."

She unfolded her arms and held up their joined hands. "Clearly you could."

His hand shifted once again, drawing her attention away from the corner to it as he threaded his fingers between hers.

He spoke softly. "I could. But I won't. That's a promise."

Unseen ribbon, silken and smooth, raised goosebumps up her arm as it wrapped around their joined hands, bolstering the warmth of his touch lost to her gloves with its own brief heat. The something shifted once again, and despite the moths dancing on her lungs, Mina could have sworn she was breathing deeper than before. That something had moved, less than an inch perhaps, but enough to lessen a pressure she didn't know was compressing her chest.

Sebastian subtly jolted beside her and gulped. Mina faced him fully and found him staring, eyes wide in surprise, at their hands. He felt it. The Fae's Folly. The universe's solution to keep those born so close to its own creation, who could harness nature's power and shape it to their will, in check. Mortals rarely noticed it until it was too late, until a fae twisted its words against them, masters of turning shackles to jewelry that they were. The elemental magic burning in his veins must have made him keenly aware of such things.

He released her hand, and with it his command. His knees against her arms turned into a branding iron for a brief second before he shifted away.

"So," he cleared his throat, "all that being said. Considering that you'll be continuing to travel with us, the group thinks it would be beneficial for all of us to start training together. Practice fighting as a team. A lot of our mistakes last time were because we've never truly fought as a cohesive unit."

"You mean a lot of *my* mistakes," she corrected.

"Our. It was my mistake as a leader to not suggest this sooner." He stretched his legs along the floor, nearly reaching the other side of the hall. "Additionally, we'll need to start on your magic lessons and, once your hands are healed, start on unlocking that Dorminian Jewelry Box."

Mina removed one of her gloves and showed him her hand. The last remains of the deeper wounds, nothing more than a few layers of scar tissue now, glistened in the light as she curled her fingers to showcase their restored deftness.

"My hands are close to healed. It's just the matter of calluses now."

"Good. Have you been drawing like Wera suggested? I'd be honored if you—"

"That's an awful lot to do in a short amount of time. Training, lessons, locksmithing," she changed the subject. "We are navigating one of the most dangerous terrains in the Realm of Mortals, ya know. While being hunted by a bunch of assholes."

Sebastian sighed and leaned his head back against the wall.

"I know. That's what I've been trying to figure out all day. On top of some of the other day-to-day projects I've got going on."

So he hadn't been ignoring her. He'd been thinking of ways to help her. Because he was upset by her circumstances and wanted to fix it.

"Other projects?"

"Another time," Sebastian stood and stretched, avoiding the subject instead of changing it. "Let's head back to the library and I can go over what I've got so far with you. See if it properly accounts for the difficulties of our journey. And check in with the others, of course." He paused a moment, considering something. "Now that I think about it, it's odd that they haven't tried to check in on us."

Mina closed her eyes and listened. Sebastian's heartbeat, unusually fast, and his breathing, deep and measured to possibly combat it, were the loudest sounds. But just beyond that, through the disjointed ticking of clocks and whirs of the various magics and machinery each room held, she heard the mutter of voices.

"I swear to The Gods, woman, if you don't let me out of this room!" Sir Gargic's distant bellow bounced off the books and three bodies in the library. "She could be slaughtering him as we speak!"

"If she were slaughtering him, the defense system would have gone off by now," Wera replied. "Give them some time to work things out!"

"Sir Gargic thinks I'm going to kill you," Mina opened her eyes and replied. "Wera's trying to calm him down."

"Then we best be going then," Sebastian said as he headed down the hall. "Otherwise we'll have to add handling an irate, acid-washed knight to our already full to-do list."

XIII

...And Partnerships

Name long forgotten, face unforgettable, her governor circled around her, a gesture meant to be threatening, but instead, it gave away his annoyance.

"Here we find ourselves yet again, Riktanya," he said. "I'm beginning to think you like being adjusted."

She didn't. He knew she didn't. But she wouldn't let him see it. Not anymore.

She slowly inhaled as she heard him stop behind her: to the left, near the first winch. She held her breath as he slid the holding pin out and cranked.

One. Two. Three. Four. Five.

The chains that crossed over her right side threatened to tear her limbs out of their sockets, partially dislocate her neck. He slid the pin back in place and held her there for a moment, lopsided in the air, testing her tenacity as much as her ligaments.

"Nothing like a good stretch, right? That's what you were thinking when you purposefully ignored your dance tutor's instructions, wasn't it?"

It wasn't. Her feet were too blistered from running ten miles the day before to do the steps.

Her lungs were burning, head aching with the need to breathe, but she couldn't let go yet, not until he tightened the other side.

"But then again, a fumbled quadrille is hardly enough to warrant this. I'm not that cruel." His footsteps echoed across the frozen floor as he moved to the second winch. "Betraying Mother's trust, however? Comprising the most important duty She has given you? Now that is more than worthy."

One. Two. Three. Four. Five.

Six.

Just enough to be off-kilter, uncomfortable, but not enough to disturb her as the more severe tilt. She exhaled slowly, so slowly, and let herself resume breathing in the little space she managed to carve out between the chains and her bare chest.

"You gave that mortal water," he tutted, shaking his head as walked back in front of her. "You know how the Matron likes to keep Her pets on a schedule. And to top it off, you loosened your siblings' chains! You know how important proper alignment is to your growth!"

She kept her gaze forward, locked on the wall of ice in front of her. The walls glistened in the same hue as Her eyes, cold and sharp but lacking any depth, and watched her just the same. She learned her screams were useless before she could walk. Tears were dried with slaps. Fighting back with tenfold retaliation. Silence was the only form of defiance she could take, and even that was swiftly robbed from her.

"Yes," Her voice needled up her spine. "Proper alignment is very important."

The governor bowed. "Dearest Matron."

Every cell in her body screamed at her to run.

The left pin slid out of place, the winch cranked.

One.

The little room she made was stolen.

"And yet, you skew My dear one."

The governor kept his head down. "She gave one of Your mortal pets water off schedule, loosened her siblings' chains during her duties as Life Bearer, and was slacking during her dance lessons."

"I see," She said. "My dear one is quite cunning. The water surely has earned a morsel of that mortal's trust, which is highly coveted by many. The loosening — while I'm not thrilled at the idea that My children's refinements have been delayed — I am delighted to hear how cutthroat My dear one is. Taking advantage to keep herself at the head of the pack. The dancing, however—"

She trembled at the rattle of chains unfurling behind her.

"What kind of Mother would I be if such carelessness was tolerated?"

She willed her muscles to relax as the chain whistled through the air and struck against the back of her knees.

🜁

Mina fell onto the floor, knees throbbing in pain, body shaking, mind screaming at her to run.

Where was she? Her eyes were too blurred to get a clear picture, but the floor beneath her was wood, not ice. It wasn't the wood of her cabin, though. A trick? Was She coming?

She caught a familiar glisten beside her: the polished curve of her fiddle's scroll peeking out from her pack. Trembling, she crawled towards it, her legs too cramped to move, and pulled it into her arms. If she could hear it, this was real.

She propped herself up against a wall, jammed the lower bout into the crook of her neck, and raked her quivering bow over the stings.

Her fingertips stung more than they should have — her nerves adding an unexpected vibrato to her strokes — but a wave of relief washed over her as the familiar notes filled her ears, grounding her as she softly sang along.

"When the skies grow dark at night, and the moon has gone in hidin'

Do not fear, have no fright, for the sun will soon be risin'

Though the flowers have gone gray, and the birds have all fall'n hush

Know that soon it shall be day, paint the world with golden brush."

But mother, you may say, what if the sun has gone?

Do stay near the firelight.

And keep sleeping 'til the dawn."

When she closed her eyes, she could picture Mrs. Harlowe standing outside her door singing the lullaby. Back then it was toneless. Its intention was well-meant, but most of all it was familiar. A song she somehow heard before, despite never learning it. Its memory lingering, tangible. It was the first song she taught herself after her hearing had improved. A reminder of when things were easier.

She opened her eyes. The commorancy's guest room, that's where she was. She must have fallen asleep at her desk again, judging by the chair knocked on its side. Her fingertips hurt because her callouses had been stripped by iron paint.

Mina's bow slowed, her singing trickling off, and she leaned her head against the wall. A memory. A nightmare. It had been a while since she had one of those, especially one unmanipulated by some unseen force. Mina shuddered as she recalled the eighty lashes she got that day. Nine for her siblings, twenty-three for the mortal, and forty-eight for the dancing.

If she lingered on the thought, she'd be back, recalling every torment she survived with terrible, all-consuming clarity. So she thought of other things.

This morning they'd have breakfast, then begin their hike. Sebastian would walk beside her this time and, so long as everything seemed on an even keel, they'd start her magic lessons as they climbed. She had her reservations, not wanting to be distracted by the wizard in case Bormir or Eirlys showed up, but Sebastian was adamant about practicing outside. That understanding her wind magic in places with no wind was like trying to understand how a fish swims by putting it on land.

Lunch, he wanted her to have Tanir check out her hands before she picked up her fiddle. Whoops. Then more hiking, then dinner, then group training. Sir Gargic seemed excited about it which disturbed her, but then again, he was a knight. One didn't go into that profession unless they enjoyed a bit of bloodshed. Maybe if they finished up quickly, she could get some reading in.

Mina looked warily at her desk, at the papers and pastels looming over the edge.

Yes, reading might be best for a bit.

She wiggled her feet as the cramps in her legs released and stared longingly at the bed. Her body was sore, tired from sleeping so poorly for the past three days. But the rattling of chains and Her voice, unnaturally smooth like a stilled ocean, off of those endless tinted walls of ice kept her from crawling beneath the covers.

The clock on the wall ticked on, and she picked up her violin again. In an hour or so, the others would start to stir, she could at least use the time to try and rebuild her callouses. Sebastian and Tanir were sure to scold her anyways for playing so mindlessly in the first place, might as well make it worthwhile.

A piano adagio, long-held notes to build her endurance while keeping things quiet to not wake the others. She started with a piece she knew well, "A Crown of Columbines", but as she closed her eyes she found her notes drifting, adding in triplets and ascending arpeggios where there shouldn't be. Had she done so back then, back when her hands were barely big enough to wrap around the neck, her knuckles would have been bleeding mid-sequence. Her instructor's switch moving faster than the eye could see.

Mina added more in defiance.

Eventually, the rhythm of her gentle strumming was interrupted by off-tempo footsteps making their way down the hall. One set rolled, even, barely thudding against the ground: Sebastian. The other set sharper, one foot brushing across the ground before every third step: Wera. Mina waited a minute for their steps to fade and, when met with silence, decided that now was as good a time as any to eat breakfast.

Being with people in the present made it easier to avoid the memories of the past.

She listened in before entering, finding the bubble of a slowly heating tea kettle and the rustle of papers. She wondered how often the pair got up early to work together, and why she was grinding her teeth at the thought of it being often. Her hand turned the doorknob and opened it much quicker than she had planned—

—before snapping it off its spindle.

"Morning, Mina," Sebastian greeted her without looking up from his paperwork.

"Wera," Mina ground her name out in warning, finger pointed at the cartographer's headscarf. Wera shivered and turned towards her, eyes wide in confusion as her body trembled from the cold sent her way. "What color is it?"

"B-blue?"

Blue walls. Blue eyes. Always watching.

The doorknob crumpled like tinfoil in her fist. "Take it off."

"Uh—" Wera thought twice and swallowed whatever comeback she had. "O-okay." She slowly pulled her headscarf off, letting loose a bushel of curls, and tucked it away out of sight.

Mina inhaled deeply to calm her nerves. Wera didn't know. Wera didn't deserve her anger.

She stomped into the kitchen and took her seat at the table, dropping the mangled doorknob on it. A teacup slid in front of her, filled with dark tea. The same as Sebastian's, she noticed, a gesture that soothed her ire a little more. At least that was some semblance of normal.

Sebastian cleared his throat. "So, you can see the color blue now."

"Unfortunately," Mina grumbled.

"Any other colors?"

She exchanged a quick glance with Wera. "No."

"That explains the big reaction then. I can't imagine what it would be like to just have one color suddenly appear out of nowhere. Before we head out, we can take a walk around the gardens, slowly introduce you to the shade, so you're not so overwhelmed when—"

"I'm not overwhelmed," she interjected. She stared daggers at her reflection in the teacup. "I just fucking hate it."

"How can you hate a color you've never seen before?" Wera asked.

Mina gripped her cup tightly, but kept careful not to shatter it. "I didn't know it was a part of this realm."

Sebastian shifted in his seat and scribbled something down. "Well, that just about confirms our desaturation theory, Wera. It's not a total removal, but a block or filter."

"So you've never seen blue the entire time you've been here?"

"Define here," Mina replied.

"Since you met Mr. Harlowe."

"Never."

Wera turned to Sebastian. The two shared a wordless conversation of expressions. Sebastian furrowed his brow and pursed his lips. Wera tilted her head in Mina's direction. He glanced at her a moment before his eyebrows shot up in recognition, and he scribbled another something down.

Mina crossed her arms and slouched onto the tabletop.

"It's a rare color, right?" she asked.

Wera grimaced and shook her head.

"How bad is it?"

"The sky is blue."

Dread set in as Mina pictured those beautiful amber sunsets she watched tainted with the shade.

"Oh."

"I hate to tell you this, but blue's my favorite color," Wera admitted.

"Change it."

"Nope," she popped the 'p' playfully. "Even if you can call me by my name now, I ain't changing it."

"It's a bad color." Mina looked at her reflection in the tea again, stoic expression hiding her distress. "Tanir said my lips were blue," she muttered.

"And now they're pink," Sebastian noted, forcefulness of speech drawing her attention to him. "There are plenty of good things that are blue in this realm. Hydrangeas can come in a rather pretty shade of it. I have a very nice robin's egg linen shirt."

"You have a shirt made of eggshells?"

Sebastian and Wera both broke out in a fit of laughter that both eased the tension in Mina's jaw and gave her a headache.

"Well, aren't we all in a good mood," Tanir remarked as she walked into the kitchen, casting a quick glance of concern at the missing door knob. "Good morning all."

Mina stiffened as Tanir's icy eyes met hers. The medic knitted her brows and cocked her head.

"Is there something wrong, Mina?"

Mina rested her hand on the hilt of her sword.

"Mina can see the color blue now, Tani," Sebastian answered for her, "and it seems that there may be some bad memories associated with it that she's unable to discuss. I have a feeling she's a bit unnerved by your eyes."

"Oh. Well—" Tanir thought a moment, then walked over to Wera and held out her hand. "Mind placing a drop or two of that yellow paint you've been using to ward the commorancy here?"

Wera nodded as poured a small splash of paint onto her waiting palm. Tanir rubbed her hands together and held them over the table for Mina to inspect.

"No burning, no poison, no blackened veins. Does that ease ya a bit?"

Mina studied Tanir's hands, palms lathered in a different shade of gray, skin freckled and slightly wrinkled, and removed her hand from her blade.

"You'll get paint on your mug," she said, still avoiding eye contact.

Tanir smiled. "I'll make sure to wash my hands."

🜁

Mina fought the urge to run back into the commorancy at the sight of the massive expanse of blue sky looming above her. The shade was slightly different from the palace's icy walls, but still too close for comfort. She took off up the trail the second the iron circle was broken. The faster they hiked, the faster she could get away from its all-seeing azure.

Hurried footsteps, in long-legged gallops, crunched in the snow after her.

"You're not trying to skip out on your first lesson, are you?" Sebastian teased. "If anything, it should take your mind off of the big, blue elephant in the sky."

"Then by lesson, you mean lobotomy?"

"I'm sure Tani could give you one. I'd miss your wit, though."

Mina cringed as his compliment stung her ears and sparked another flutter in her chest.

"Have me speak into a recorder before the procedure then to capture it," she replied. "Clearly. I know. Fuck you. Bravnor."

Mina snuck a glance at him out of the corner of her eye and found him staring back at her, brows furrowed and mouth puckered in an exaggerated, displeased pout. There was a slight tickle in her diaphragm, and a small trickle of something close to pride that made her want to poke around and see what other cartoonish expressions she could draw out of him.

"Ib das fachi halult po di chaz, meaupaler? Y?"

She couldn't see his eyes behind his noxulars, but she could picture them widening in some sort of fleeting shock that coupled with how quickly his eyebrows disappeared into his bangs and his pout pulled back into a tight line.

He flared his nostrils and inhaled deeply.

"No. It's not," he ground out before exhaling. "The first part of today's lesson is an assessment quiz."

"A quiz," she repeated, exaggerating her monotone as much as she could to express her displeasure.

"We already know how conjuring your arrows works, but I suspect more of your capabilities utilize your wind magic than you think." Just like a proper professor, he ignored her lack of enthusiasm. "So, first, a question. Could you navigate the next few hundred feet of this hike with your eyes closed?"

"If I'm told to."

"Great! Close your eyes."

She did.

"Now, tell me what you can hear in as much detail as possible."

Mina trusted her muscle memory to guide her steps as she focused her attention on the sounds surrounding her, down to the smallest squeak.

"Farthest away there is snow, shifting from the light breeze running across it, and the soft bleats of about three mountain goats. A mother and two kids. It's an echo, and I can't hear their hoof beats, so they're most likely on the other side of the rock formation to my right.

"Closer are footsteps, six sets including my own. Sir Gargic is telling Tanir and Enoch about how he stopped an assassination attempt on King Fritz's life the day before his coronation; all thanks to a stomach bug. Enoch is fiddling with his dagger ring which keeps changing pitch, shaking the daggers in his belt holster. Tanir keeps making half-hearted hums, pretending that she is listening. Wera is scribbling in her notebook, drawing instead of taking notes by the sound of her quill strokes. You just conjured a flame in your left palm. Now you're making it spiral. You've turned it counterclockwise."

"Alright, that's enough," Sebastian said. She could hear the smile tuning his voice.

She opened her eyes.

"Describe what it's like to listen so focused like that."

Mina tilted her head in confusion. "It's... similar to learning a song by ear. I hear all of it at once, then choose certain patterns to focus on. There were some details I skipped because there's so much."

"What did you skip?"

"Everyone's heartbeats, their breathing, the gurgle of their stomachs."

"You can hear our heartbeats?"

"Only if they're loud enough. The climb has Sir Gargic's heart pumping hard right now. If I were in a closed space, it'd be more clear, though."

"Which makes sense because when you're listening like that, you're listening to the wind."

Mina sighed heavily. Of course he'd say that.

"Explain."

"Even with the most powerful potion to increase your hearing, you shouldn't have been able to hear me light a flame. With no kindling of any kind, my fire is silent." He lit his palm once again to prove his point. There was no sound, but Mina might have been too fixated on the flickering amber ribbons to notice.

"And even if there was sound, you certainly wouldn't have been able to hear this." The flame twisted into a small vortex in silence. "To create a spiral like this, I'm focusing on raising the heat at different parts of the base flame in order to form a small, spinning wind system. That's why you could hear the change. When you focus like that, you're listening to the vibrations on the wind rather than the sound itself."

He snuffed out the flame, much to her dismay.

"You say it gets better in an enclosed area. That's probably because there's less movement in the air to interfere." He snapped, then pointed a finger in her face. "I knew you were using echolocation in the caves."

"Be quiet!" Mina smacked his hand away, swatting it as much as she wanted to swat the cluster of invisible moths that fluttered up her spine and across her skin the more he analyzed her. She shuddered at the thought of how attentive he would be when they started working on that jewelry box he kept going on about.

"Is this just gonna be a lecture or are you gonna fucking teach me something?" she grumbled.

"I mean, I did teach you something." He shrugged sarcastically. "I just taught you how your selective super hearing works."

"Wizard."

"What happened to 'professor'?"

"Snarky asshole it is, then."

"Oh. So you can't handle being poked back then, huh, lila doar?"

She glared at him. "Little bear?"

Sebastian snickered and changed the subject. "So, first lesson." He conjured the flame again. "You're going to change the flame's shape with your wind."

Incensed by his cockiness, Mina blew at his palm, making the fire flatten for a moment. "There. I changed it."

He tutted. "Did you test all of your tutors like this?"

"Here we find ourselves yet again, Riktanya."

She turned away from him, glancing at the unnerving blue sky watching her before reining in her focus to the steep, snowy incline ahead of them.

"Shape it with the wind," she stated. "Any other instructions?"

"Mina—"

"Any other instructions?" she insisted.

He exhaled, a quiet one, but still heavy with weary. "I'm going to drop behind you. Close your eyes and listen for it like you did before. That should give you a good starting point."

Mina closed her eyes, and listened. Listened to shifting, crunching snow under their feet, changing its tone as the angle of their path shifted upwards. Listened to Sebastian's footsteps slow and fade slightly as he pulled away from her. Listened to the low hum of his flame, volume and shape unchanging.

She couldn't hear it when she was looking at it, in fact, she couldn't hear it now. She could feel it, buzzing against her eardrums, just as clearly as she could feel the wind brushing up against her face and lapping, somehow, at her heels despite the thick leather boots she wore.

When she succumbed to her darker nature, she had control of it. Whatever she asked for the wind would deliver to the best of its ability. Yet in the caves she had to plead for its help. Running with the wind at her back, using it to conjure her arrows came naturally. So why not this?

She thought of the shape of the fire, the swirl Sebastian had shown her before. Pictured a tiny cyclone of flame spinning from the force of the wind around it... but nothing changed. She continued honing in on that image, growing more and more frustrated with no results, tripping, even, as her extreme focus made her footing slip. Eyes still closed, she caught herself.

"If you need to take a break to focus on the climb—"

"No. I—" Mina tried to stand but couldn't as the curious wind at her heels pulled against her gently.

"How about we just get to the top—" Sebastian's words faded behind the shift in pitch as his flames started to dwindle. The wind raced up her legs, leaving goosebumps in its wake, to tickle her earlobes. Listen. She had to listen.

"Wait," she snapped, just before he could snuff the fire out completely.

"Windenhofer," Sir Gargic's voice threatened to break her concentration. "What's wrong with her?"

"Quiet," Sebastian demanded, just as strong as the restored flame in his palm.

It wasn't what she saw that would change it. It was what she heard, what she felt. The subtle change in pitch — in *vibration* — from before. It needed to be slightly higher. If only she could slide it down somehow, like fingers down frets.

The wind changed from a lap at her ear to a flutter — no, a buzz — that thrummed back down her legs; the exact same frequency as his fire. Mina rose to her feet carefully so as to not break the connection, and once standing, followed her instinct and shifted her right heel just a centimeter to the right. The vibrations shifted, tighter, faster, higher; both in her body and in her ear.

Sebastian's half-arpeggio laugh harmonized perfectly with it.

"That's my girl."

The pitch spiked, blasting in her eardrum as the vibrations turned into a lightning strike. Mina opened her eyes and covered her ears to try and block out the searing ringing the pop left in its wake. Beneath it, she caught another half-arpeggio muffled, as if she were a hundred feet underwater, followed by a baritone melody; wordless but still identifiable by its rhythm as Sebastian's voice.

She turned around to face him and saw his mouth flapping away, lips and teeth more precise in movement than the sounds coming out.

"What?" she asked, and Sebastian jolted back a bit. Sir Gargic's mouth moved behind him, stout arms flailing in the air at some small annoyance, involving her, judging by how often he pointed in her direction.

Sebastian said something to Sir Gargic and waved Tanir forward. Mina uncovered her ears to see if it would help, but the ringing was still the only clear sound. Panic seeped in, and she frantically stuck her fingers in her ears to try and clear them.

This was worse than before. She'd rather hear the world one note than not at all.

Tanir waved her hands frantically to try and stop her, and Mina pulled her hands away to find them covered in blood.

Blood was good. Blood could be fixed.

She reached into her pack and pinched a few springs out of the herbs she'd begun to keep in its side pouch. With shaking hands, she shoved them into her mouth and chewed as she watched and waited for the cluttered chorus of muffled sounds to match the animated debate the entire group seemed to be having.

"I was being careful! I can't even wrap my head around how—"

"Wizard," Mina called. "Stop shouting. Avalanches."

Sebastian's body relaxed like a marionette cut from its strings. Her own racing heart echoed the sentiment.

Tanir patted between his shoulders. "I told you it'd be alright."

"Thank The Gods it was!" Sir Gargic groused.

Enoch nodded frantically. "Yeah. How about we save the magic lessons for when—"

"No," Mina interjected.

Enoch squawked out a nervous laugh. "No? But you practically went deaf just now!"

"Beastie, this trail is getting narrower and narrower. Need I remind you that you are contracted to get us to Lanholde in one piece?"

"Damn. And here I thought I could just dismember you to make the travel lighter." Mina turned around and started back up the mountain, showing her fear would do her no favors. "I could get you there blind, deaf, and missing an arm if I had to."

"I believe that's Mina-speak for, 'she's fine, let's keep moving forward'," Wera said.

She placed a hand on Sebastian's back and shoved him forward to start their train up again.

"So, um," Sebastian caught up to her in just a few strides, "whatever you did worked."

"I know. I made a spiral."

"Uh-huh. And then you snuffed me out."

"Oh," Mina said, stomach knotting. So the 'pop' affected more than just her. "That wasn't intentional."

"Okay." There was a slight sigh of relief behind the word. "So, what I observed or what you experienced. Who should go first?"

"I'm still finding the words for mine." And hearing his voice, clear and warm, helped to ease her lingering panic.

"Your feet are your casting point. When you stood, you shifted your heel just a smidge, and all of a sudden, the smallest gust of cold wind turned my flame into a tiny twister. It tickled, actually." He chuckled lightly in reflection. "It makes even more sense considering it looked less like you tripped and more like your foot was swept out from underneath you when you fell. Which could make it a difficult casting point to work with..." He drummed his fingers on his lips in contemplation.

"It won't be difficult," Mina insisted.

"Oh, really?"

She frowned. "I run with it, jump with it, climb with it, fight with it. If I can master that, I can master some juvenile summoning."

"You—" Sebastian paused to gather his thoughts. "You use your wind magic for all that? But you insisted you had ice magic!"

"I never really paid attention to it before! It was just a *thing* that would happen."

"Then has the eardrum bursting happened before? You didn't seem worried about it, but then again—"

"No. That's new."

"Then I guess it's your turn now," he grumbled in a different shade of frustration than the ones she knew. A friendly frustration, almost. "Tell me what happened."

The words tumbled out of her mouth, forced by his unintentional command.

"I was trying to picture the fire spinning as you showed me, kept trying to see the wind blowing against my face twisting around the flame humming in your hand. Which is when the wind around my feet knocked me down. As soon as you started to extinguish your fire, it crawled up my legs to lap around my ears."

"Crawled?"

"It happened back in the caves too. From the heel, up my side, through my arm. Here it reminded me that you said to listen," she continued. "So I listened. But I'm not listening, it's vibrations. With my violin, vibrations create the pitch. I thought about sliding my fingers down the fret and the wind made me the fret. I twisted my foot — same as twisting a peg to tune a stringed instrument now that I think about it — to make the pitch match how your spiral sounded, and it worked. Then the pitch surged like a tea kettle."

The urge to purge herself of an explanation faded and let her fall back into silence as Sebastian hummed in contemplation beside her. A b-flat, two below middle-c.

"Could be fallout from building up too much kinetic energy," he mused. "We'll need to figure out a way to test this safely, though."

"There are herbs to take, and lessons are learned through mistakes," Mina replied.

"Not my lessons. Especially not if they hurt you."

"I never said—"

"You said you were able to summon it in the cave, right?" He ignored her protest. "We'll work on replicating that. Try to see if you can have the wind pool in your hand. Alright?"

He glanced down at her, jaw tight and eyebrows drawn back. An irritating expression, a false one plastered on to hide some other thought. Mina memorized it as best as she could to try and parse it later; though the noxulars covering half of it would barely make it worth the effort.

She scoffed and turned her cheek to him.

"Whatever you say, *professor.*"

🜁

Wera took Sebastian's place in line for the latter half of the day at his behest. He said it might be better for her to stick close to Mina as the rocky, snow and ice covered path up this part of the range got narrower. Especially with her nose buried in her journal, making rough sketches for her next map.

But Mina knew it was because he doubted her ability to practice casting while they climbed.

The exercises he made her do after her eardrums burst were paltry. Tricks for children. Which made it all the more frustrating when she couldn't so much as summon a wisp of wind into her hand. He wouldn't say it, he was unnecessarily polite in that way, but Mina could tell he was disappointed in her. That she wasn't meeting his expectations. That he doubted her.

And she was determined to show him just how wrong he was.

"Okay!" Sebastian shook one of the burlap bags full of something he called projection stones. "Sir Gargic and Tanir. You two draw first."

The knight and the medic stuck their hands into the bag and pulled out a marble each.

"Vix pack," Tanir read.

"Learbix," Sir Gargic followed.

Sebastian nodded and switched out bags.

"Enoch."

Enoch grabbed a marble. "Mid-Morning."

Then Wera. "Three."

Mina. "Hemlock forest."

And lastly, Sebastian, who pouted as he read, "Rain."

He stomped over to a terminal in the back corner of the training room and placed the stones on its dais.

"Everyone put their collars on," he instructed. "Anybody got a suggestion for the safe word this time?"

"Kazoo?" Enoch offered.

Sebastian chuckled as he turned the terminal's rotary to enter the phrase. "Kaa... zooo."

Satisfied that all the details had been properly entered, he clapped his hands together and walked over to grab a collar.

Mina jumped as the landscape of the training room changed completely. A thick and ancient forest bloomed around her, moss and brush rippled in a wave to replace the mats and wooden floors. The benches shifted into a fallen tree trunk, covered in lichen and fungi, yet the supplies and equipment resting on them stayed in place. The ceiling above her dimmed as dark clouds rolled over it, blocking out the light and bringing a light trickle of rain.

Mina reached out a hand and watched the raindrops shatter into ice crystals as they bounced off her palm. Her hair was already freezing solid.

"Rain must be miserable for you too, huh?" Sebastian remarked as he returned, shield collar securely fashioned to his neck.

Mina shook her head like a dog in response, knocking a coat of icy sludge to the ground with a wet thud.

Wera snickered behind them. "You two look like a pair of drowned cats." She'd retied her blue scarf over her head, wrangling in her curls and protecting herself from the rain a bit more than the others. The color was still unnerving, but the urge to snatch it off her head and tear it to shreds had subsided.

"You're lying if you're saying you're thrilled about it raining," Sebastian said.

"I didn't say I'm thrilled. But it'll be a good test of how much stronger my blood manipulation is getting."

"Blood manipulation?" Mina asked. "You move paint."

"Paint mixed in with a drop of my blood," Wera clarified. "I don't have any elemental or psychokinetic magic, but I can move my own blood around."

"And it's disgusting," Enoch commented.

"You're just jealous that you have to rely on that little ring of yours."

"Or you're jealous that my daggers don't lose steam because of a little drizzle."

Wera stuck her tongue out at Enoch, and he gave a smug chuckle in satisfaction.

"Yup," Sir Gargic groaned as he stretched his arms over his head. "Looks like it'll be us three carrying the team this go-about."

Mina crossed her arms over her chest, sending ice crystals bouncing onto the forest floor. "We'll see about that."

"Right then. Mina, since this is your first time training in a projection field, let's have a little refresh as to how this works," Sebastian said. "At my command, the assault will begin. We'll have three waves of vix packs and one learbix attacking us at random intervals. The creatures' attack patterns are based on their real-life counterparts, but the attacks themselves have been altered to only deal force damage. No stabbing or slicing or anything like that."

Mina grimaced. Not as effective as a training tool as it could be then.

"Each of these projections has a damage threshold. Once you meet or exceed it, the projection disappears. We need to clear all of them in order for the training to be a success. If all of us get knocked out or pushed out of the projection field's range, then it's a failure. If things get hairy, just shout the safe word that Enoch suggested and the projection will end."

"Kazoo?" Mina checked and as quickly as it came, the forest retreated. Ending the rain and returning the room to its former state.

Sebastian chuckled. "That's the one. Everyone ready?"

"Vix packs take a swarm-like approach to hunting," Enoch informed the group as they moved into their starting formation. "Keep an eye on your blind spots. One will try and hit you there, then the others will pile on."

"And the learbix?" Tanir asked.

"Imagine a dairy bull, only twenty feet tall and an abomination," he replied. "And horns. Fourteen sets of horns running down its spine in addition to the four on its head."

"Good to know." Sebastian stepped a bit away from Mina and readied his stance. Mina drew her sword. "Alright then. Toffee."

The forest returned, bringing rain and clouded skies once again. The group fell quiet, waiting and watching the forest for movement. Save for Mina, who, after just a moment of closing her eyes, took off into the forest in a blur towards the sound of shifting brush.

"Kazoo!"

Just as Mina found the first vix, an ugly little inbred of a hyena and a lemur, the creature and the brush it hid in vanished, driving Mina's blade into the training mats instead of its skull.

"I had it!" she shouted, turning back to sneer at Sebastian on the other side of the room.

"That's great." He shrugged. "Not the point of this exercise, though. This is a group training session. Not a 'Mina takes out all the monsters on her own' session."

Mina stomped back over towards the group like a scolded child.

"Start it again," she snapped.

"Toffee."

The projection restarted.

Mina waited, much to her annoyance, for the pack to approach. The others heard their movement in the surrounding trees much too late, adjusting their position while the first vix was already soaring through the air towards Tanir. The creature's natural instinct to attack the oldest among them first was ill-formed, as the medic drove her axe through its skull with ease.

Mina raced off, honing in on the other pack members trying to regroup in the forest behind them.

"Kazoo."

The vix she managed to skewer as she dove into the bushes disappeared off her blade.

"Mina," Sebastian stated.

"She killed one!" Mina shouted and pointed to Tanir. "I'm not taking them all out!"

"You're right. I wasn't clear enough. We're supposed to face these attacks together, Mina. Work *together* to beat the monsters to succeed, alright?" He inhaled deeply.

"Alright. Let's start again!"

And so they did. Over and over and over again.

Mina waited for the pack to descend on the group and took the first wave out with her arrows.

"Kazoo."

She waited for each one of them to land an attack before slaughtering the remaining vermin.

"Kazoo."

She stood back and let them fend for themselves.

"Kazoo."

Keeping to herself, goading some of the vix towards her by imitating their calls once they attacked seemed to satisfy the wizard, allowing them to get far enough into the projection that the deep roar of the learbix shook the trees.

The beast, surprisingly quick for its size, burst through the treeline. Its four wild eyes, swirling with bloodlust, locked onto the meager flames Sebastian hurled at a vix nipping at his heels. Mina cleared the ankle-biters surrounding her with a single swipe and met the bull's charge.

The closer she got, the more her body fought back, threatening to tear her skin apart if she took one more step, to implode her skull if she moved one more inch. Yet still, she moved, leaping through the air with her blade drawn and aimed between the bull's horns as best she could as the corners of her vision darkened.

"Kazoo!" Sebastian shouted just before she connected.

She tumbled onto the training mat and only gave herself a second to catch her breath before rising to her feet.

"I had him," she panted and spat out the blood draining down the back of her throat.

"Yeah, and at what fucking cost?!" Sebastian yelled. "Look at you! You would have taken out that fucking learbix only to leave us with down an ally and up a heatseeker!"

"Tanir would have—"

"That's not the fucking point!" His anger echoed off the training room walls. Steam rolled off Sebastian as he approached, bearing the same expression as he had in the hot spring, only darker. His frustration and anger taking the lead and fueling Mina's own irritations.

"Then tell me the fucking point!" she roared back.

"You're supposed to work with us!"

"What do you fucking mean? I am working with you! I'm staying with the group! I'm not killing all the monsters! What else do I have to do?!"

"Fight alongside us, not *for* us! Be my *partner*, not my protector!"

Sebastian's ranting faded into the background, dwindling her anger along with it, as his unwilling commands took hold.

And Mina finally recognized it. The something.

The same something that shifted the night before, that moved and let her breathe a little easier.

Both known and unknown. Wanted and unwanted.

Yearned for, hoped for, pleaded for.

Powerful enough to withstand ~~minutes~~, ~~hours~~, days.

The promise of ending the unending.

The loosening of chains.

"Start it again," Mina said, the last of her ire leaving her in a rush as a sense of freedom, a weightlessness, washed over her.

"Are you even listening to me?!" Sebastian balked.

"I heard you," she repeated. "Start it again."

She turned and walked back to the group, ignoring their cautious and somewhat intrigued stares.

"Fine," Sebastian hissed, retaking his place among the group. "Toffee."

The forest blossomed around them, the rain fell, and Mina felt freer than she had in a long time.

"The main pack is moving closer, from northwest down to west of us," she whispered the thoughts she could never voice before aloud. "They sent two scouts ahead to move to the south to try and ambush us from behind, planning to draw our attention from the main attack. They're going after Tanir again."

True to her word, two vix launched from the tree line behind them. Mina ran to greet them, snatching them out of the air by their tails to hurl them towards Sebastian and Wera.

"Heads up!" Mina didn't pause for a second, running to take point next to Tanir right as the pack descended upon them. Soaring daggers and hearty grunts joined their fight as Enoch took care of the vix descending from above them and Sir Gargic handled the ones trying to skirt around their blind sides.

The low, metallic bong of the next wave of projections conjuring buzzed in Mina's ears.

"Next pack is coming!" she announced as she pinned a vix beneath her boot and pried its spine out of its hunched back. "Enoch, sweep your daggers through the eastern canopy."

The wounded yips of skewered vix rang out as he sent his daggers through the trees, thinning out the next herd that descended upon them by half. Wera and Sebastian fielded the rest easily, the smaller crowd size allowing them to get the most out of their rain-suppressed magics. Enoch continued to rake his blades counterclockwise through the surrounding forest, driving out the final pack before they could organize their hunting strategy.

Their scrambled structure made for an easy slaughter, allowing each of them to handle a couple of vix themselves. Which meant that this time, Sebastian was ready when the learbix's roar shook through the room.

Just like before, the learbix was enraged by the flicker of his flames and set its sights on the wizard. And just like before, Mina felt the undeniable urge to step between them, to stop the abominable bull dead in its tracks.

She watched carefully as Sebastian switched stances, blading his feet as he lifted one arm, palm facing towards the beast, and pulled back the other. The flames would harm the creature for sure, break its charge, and allow the others to finish it off after a few rounds of attacks. But what if it could be better?

The wind carried Mina's steps towards him.

What if his flames could swallow the bull, just like they had done to Eirlys back in Rabbet's Pass?

A partner, not a protector. Maybe it was the choice of words, or his stance triggering some long-forgotten muscle memory that had her spin into him; slipping his crooked arm over her shoulder and taking his outstretched one by the wrist. Startled, his spell sparked early, but still hot enough to catch as the wind swirled up from her heels, across her body, and down her own arm to fuel it.

The roar was deafening as a raging wildfire surged from their combined casting, consuming the learbix in brilliant amber light and incinerating it instantaneously. Sebastian closed his palm and the flames extinguished, leaving nothing but a flash of charred earth before the projection vanished.

A bright victory chime rang throughout the training room.

Mina turned her head to face a Sebastian already staring at her, eyes wide in disbelief.

There was that tickle in her diaphragm again.

"Well. That worked," she said.

Sebastian's eyebrows shot up as his mouth fell agape. He pulled his arms away, and in a move that not even an oracle could have predicted, cupped his hands on either side of Mina's face.

The pain was immediate, blinding. Mina knocked his hands away and jumped back.

"Watch your hands, Wizard!" she snapped.

"I'm sorry but— you smiled," he marveled as he broke into a brilliant smile of his own, Yosik accent breaking through in his excitement. "You actually smiled."

Mina touched her mouth and found it set into a thin, slight frown.

"I—" she stopped as she felt it: the corners of her lips raising slightly. Not nearly as big and bold as Sebastian's, but definitely reminiscent of its embers.

"Holy shit, that's an actual smile!" Wera exclaimed, inciting a chorus of compliments and utterances of celebration from them all.

She could feel her lips hitting some unseen barrier, preventing them from growing wider at the swell of tingles, tickles, and flutters that coursed throughout her body. But that barrier wouldn't last forever.

Mina, for the first time that she could remember, felt happy.

The chains were not as binding. Their icy barbs not buried so deep that she could not be spared.

For the first time since she left the Barren Rime, Mina had hope.

XIV

Old Habits, New Perspective

Mina's face hurt.

Not hurt in the bruised or battered sense. Hurt like the lingering ache she was sarcastically looking forward to after she scaled The Lithe.

Who knew smiling was such a workout?

Sebastian's training plan had been quickly cast aside in favor of testing and theorizing what exactly led to such a breakthrough, and what the limitations of the change were. Could she laugh? (No.) Could she add more inflection to her speech? (A little.) How big could she smile? (Barely anything more than a thin, closed-lip grin.) Had anything else changed?

She sent Sebastian off on a ramble when she told him they'd have to wait until after she slept to know for sure. Ranting about how she should have told him sooner that sleep factored into her changes in sensory perceptions, as if it were some key element to cracking her whole curse wide open.

Whether it was or wasn't, seeing him so excited made her excited. Which was an odd sensation, not exactly foreign, but to be able to identify it so clearly was definitely new. Scary, even, to see how easily her own diminished emotions were swayed by his. An unwanted side effect of the contract, perhaps.

Sleep came easy after a long evening of experiments and eager chatter, and though her sleep was dreamless, Mina awoke to find that yes, many things had changed.

The first, and most obvious, was that her bedroom walls had color to them. Madder red, from what the pastels said, and russet brown for the trim. The furniture, the floor, even the case her pastels sat in bore variations of the same russet shade, some darker, some lighter. It must be a popular color, something to tie a room together by fading into the background.

A small smile crawled on Mina's face as she looked into the mirror and touched her lips. They weren't fully pink, those pastels still sat gray in the box, but there was definitely a different hue to them, a little red among the gray to warm them up. Warm like the steaming water that rushed from the sink tap.

Mina ran her hands back and forth under the water in a trance, basking in the light warmth rolling over them. The spigot must have been close to boiling, but Mina couldn't care, the subdued — but much more prevalent than the day before's — heat was well worth the stiffness of a mild burn. She considered calling for them to take a break today instead of climbing, so she could draw herself a bath and revel in the warmth. Maybe even feel something close to human because of it.

Even her body seemed lighter as she walked downstairs to the kitchen, or maybe it was the sensation of feeling her linen shirt, soft and well-worn, brushing against her skin for the first time. She opened the door in a wide, loose swing, and found Tanir,

Wera, and Sebastian already halfway through their first cup of tea.

"Well?" Sebastian asked, placing his mug down just before he could take another sip.

It stung to look straight into his eyes, especially when they were sparkling with hopeful anticipation, but Mina couldn't look away.

"Your eyes are brown," she said, and was forced to look away as a blinding smile split his face, bigger and more joyous than she'd ever seen from him before.

"Anything else?!"

Mina held a hand up to block her view of him as she walked over to her seat.

"The walls of the guest room are red," she stated. "The hottest tap setting has warmth to it. Linen is soft, and lightweight."

Wera waved at her discreetly, keeping her hand close to the table as she signaled that it was clear for Mina to lower her hand.

"That's excellent, Mina. Truly excellent." Sebastian's tone was reverent and warm. "Would you like a cup of tea?"

Mina's jaw tightened up, teeth cemented against themselves and held tight by unseen chains. She cast a tired look at Wera and shook her head.

Wera turned to Sebastian. "That's still a no."

He sighed in disappointment, deepening Mina's frown. "Alright then. Still plenty of work to be done."

"But! A lot of progress!" Tanir cheered. "Perhaps we'll be able to crack this thing by using commands alone."

"Yes, perhaps." Sebastian tapped his fingers on his lips, gaze distant as he retreated into his head a bit. "Have to be careful, though. We don't want another mulberry pie situation."

He came back to the present, picked up his teacup to take a sip, and cast a glance at the kitchen. He nodded at the utensils and pointed at Mina.

With some rattling and the whistle of a kettle, a cup of tea appeared before her: brown, warm, and *fragrant*. Mina fought to keep her soft smile off her lips as she lifted the cup, steam twirling off of it dissipating as her cold touch cooled it, and drank. The last whispers of heat warmed her mouth briefly, as the fragrance coated her tongue just as much as it stained the air around it. It swirled around her mouth like fog on a fall morning, heavy, firm but not unpleasant. A strong hand against her back, steadying her. Or a wizard's command to 'hold on'.

"What's in this cup?" Mina asked.

"Black tea with bergamot," Sebastian answered.

"Bergamot?"

"It's a type of fruit. Kind of like an orange. It tends to grow in tropical climates. I like its oil in my tea, it adds a light burst of citrus and smells wonderful."

Mina looked to Wera as she held the mug up to cover her smile and let the bergamot tickle her nose. "Is there bergamot in the garden?"

"No, unfortunately," he replied. "The garden's climate is too cool for it."

"Damn." She snuck a glimpse at Sebastian out of the corner of her eye and lowered her cup a bit.

"Damn?" He looked at her intently for a moment, before his eyes widened and his brows raised in bemused realization. "Oh. Damn."

Tanir and Wera burst out into a fit of laughter, and Mina felt that flutter tugging at her diaphragm hard enough to hitch her breath.

🜁

Lunch came quickly between the ease of the trail's incline and the group's continued chattering about how much had changed for Mina in such a small amount of time. They talked more about her than to her, which, while well-meant, still soured her mood, and she'd be lying if she said it didn't make her eat her lunch faster than usual.

With her sketchbook and pastels in hand, Mina snuck away into the garden, taking refuge behind a willow's curtain of leaves downwind from the lavender patch. The swipe of her palm across the paper, the sticky snap of the pastels, added a calming beat beneath the burbling creek's melody. A much-needed respite, quiet and self-contained enough to allow her to focus totally on trying to capture the smiting smile she barely managed to catch a glimpse of that morning.

Estimating Sebastian's expressions proved much harder than capturing them from memory. There were too many tiny details to choose from. Would the crinkles around his eyes be deep or shallow? Would they curve up, down, somewhere in between? Would one eye be more closed than the other? How high would the tip of his nose rise? Would his hair fall forward to cover his forehead as it often did towards the end of a hiking day, or would he have pushed it back just as he smiled in order to get a clearer view of the source of his joy?

"What are you doing?" Sebastian's voice tumbled softly down her spine. Mina snapped the sketchbook shut and whipped around to face him.

"Practicing the new drawing technique Wera taught me the other day," she lied.

"And I can't see?" he studied her face, eyebrow arched quizzically.

"I'm still practicing." The sketchbook creaked under her white-knuckled grip. "I'll show you once I get a little more refined."

He nodded slightly and bowed his head to avoid getting smacked by the willow's branches as he sat down in front of her, "I want to ask you something."

"Then ask me something," she said, and slipped her sketchbook back into her pastel case.

He knit his bow as he looked at her, scanning across her face as if he were searching for a specific piece in a jigsaw puzzle.

"Can you dance?"

She tilted her head in confusion. "If I'm told to?"

"No, not like that. Let me rephrase." Sebastian drummed against his lips. "Were you taught to dance like you were taught to play violin?"

Mina gave a curt nod. "You noticed during the training?"

"How could I not? It's not often that you get swept up into the starting position of a tango promenade while staring down a charging learbix."

"So you were trained to dance too."

"One of the couples that adopted me thought dance classes would teach me discipline and help with my attitude problem." Sebastian chuckled, more discordant than his usual laugh. Flatter, leaning close to a minor key. "Didn't do much to keep me from setting the kitchen table on fire while they yelled at me for not eating all my herring, but it did teach me to be light on my feet. Which, in a roundabout way, brings me to why I'm bothering you when you clearly wish to be alone."

"It's just quieter," Mina explained to lift some of the weight that suddenly settled in her stomach at his statement. "There was a lot of chatter today."

Sebastian frowned. "We'll try to cut back on the theorizing in this second half. There were a lot of breakthroughs today, you know."

"I know." Mina looked away from him, finding that instead of a sting, the kind worry in his eyes had begun to make her nauseous. "Now, back to the bothering."

"Right." Sebastian dropped his hands against his knees with a clap and squared up his shoulders. "I think dancing might be the key to helping harness your wind magic."

"Explain."

"I'm going to." She caught the soft smile he gave out of the corner of her eye. "If we think about the times you've successfully used your wind magic, without injuring yourself, it's all been channeled through learned, physical movement. Things that have been ingrained in your muscle memory for the most part. Running, jumping, climbing, drawing and firing your bow, for example. Considering how seamlessly that combination attack occurred yesterday, I would say that it was because your dance training kicked in unconsciously, making it easier for you to focus your casting through your movement."

"As opposed to the tuning fork method where the movement and sensation are mostly foreign," Mina noted.

"Precisely. The more familiar the movement, the less chance of error," Sebastian agreed. "The tuning fork method is a clever name," he started to slip into a state of introspection, mumbling, "Could provide a great physicality for you to ground yourself with. Back when I was first training with my master, I had something like it as well, maybe there's other musical motifs we could explore as a means to—"

"Let's get started then." Mina stood and stepped out from under the willow's curtain, taking care to keep her pastel case close to her side.

"Now?" Sebastian squeaked, 'oh' Yosik round, as he stumbled after her.

"We still have a half an hour before we continue our ascent. No reason to waste time."

"Right— uh— Let me go and grab Enoch." Sebastian rushed up the hill towards the door.

"Enoch?"

"I have a thirteen-year-old's bitter, bare-bones understanding of dancing at best," he explained with a nervous chuckle. "Enoch's the one with all the culture know-how!"

The slam of the garden door behind him battered her eardrums, leaving her in a brief stupor that was quickly overcome by anger.

Mina raced out the door after him, ready to chew the wizard's ear out for overthinking things again, when his frantic voice stopped her just outside the training room's door.

"Look, I know it's last minute — and I'm very sorry to ask you this without running it by you first — but could you please help me give Mina dance lessons?"

"Dance lessons?" Enoch squawked.

"To help her channel her magic."

"Sebastian, I'm sure you're more than capable of showing her a couple of moves. I've seen you sweep a few barmaids off their feet every now and again."

"This is not the same thing! You know I can't just do that with her!"

"What? Because of the 'no touching' rule? I'm sure if you command her—"

"I can't do that either!"

"Why not?"

"Because I don't like forcing her to do things she doesn't want to do!"

"She was the one who insisted on starting lessons right now, right?"

"Yes."

"Then it sounds like she wants to, to me."

"M-maybe. But if I command her to dance with me, it could mess up the whole experiment, and add a forced, artificial layer that could block her from channeling her magic properly," Sebastian stammered. "A-and besides, I don't know what types of moves I should suggest to her. I-it'd be awkward just sort of watching her dance for me alone—"

"Stop. I've heard enough," Enoch sighed. "If I watch you stumble anymore it's going to be very hard to wax poetic about how calm and collected you are under pressure. Let me collect my things and I'll help you. You got any—"

Mina took off before she could hear the rest of his sentence, rattling some of the picture frames down the halls as she ran with the wind to hide her pastel case back in her room. She returned to the garden, with minutes to spare, before Enoch and Sebastian entered, the latter awkwardly carrying a large, wind-up gramophone.

"Alright. We're back," Sebastian panted, "and we brought music."

"I could have grabbed my violin," she said.

"Oh no no no. Don't want to taint the experiment," Enoch tutted, earning a glare from Sebastian. "Now, Mina. What dances do you know?"

"Tango, quadrille, waltz, a few reels, ballet, flamenco, and various ceremonial dances."

"Any modern social dances?"

"Such as?"

"Swing dancing, line dances, tap?"

"Never heard of them."

"Then you definitely had a very traditional tutor." Enoch turned to Sebastian, who was struggling to find a level patch of grass to sit the gramophone on. "What's the goal here? Having her futz around with her wind magic is all well and good, but what should it look like?"

"Uh, well... how about we start with creating a constant gust around her? A simple ring of wind."

"Ballet then. How about some non-traveling chaînés?"

"I can do fouettés," Mina offered.

"How many?"

"Many."

He rolled his hand in the air, urging her to explain further.

"Five hundred was the most."

Enoch stared at her, eyes blinking rapidly as he processed her claim.

"I take it that's a lot?" Sebastian asked.

"It is," Mina answered.

"It… is. Put on something in 4/4 time. Instrumental, repetitive, but not annoyingly so."

"Concerto for Alvaneya," Mina suggested.

"That is just—" Enoch shook his head in disbelief. "Yeah. Put on what she said if you've got it."

Sebastian rustled through his coat and pulled out a record. "Yup. Got it."

"Just?"

Enoch tilted his head in confusion. "Just?"

"That is just—" Mina repeated, taking her turn to wave her hand in the air for him to continue.

"You have good taste."

Mina winced as the compliment rang harshly in her ears.

"So, that one hurt, but calling you beautiful before didn't?"

"Calling her what?" The record scratched a bit as Sebastian fumbled dropping the needle.

"Nope," Mina popped the 'p' pointedly, then cocked her head to the side. "Fouettés?"

"Fouettés," Enoch nodded, taking a few steps back as the starting notes of the concerto poured out of the gramophone. "Take a break every one hundred, though, alright? Making you do the full five hundred just seems cruel."

Mina inhaled deep, picking a spot on the horizon — the knob of the garden door — and spun.

It had been years since she'd danced, but her body retained the memory perfectly, almost as if she'd finished a dance lesson just the day before. A chill ran down Mina's spine at the phantom sense of her dance instructor's cane lashing under her arms.

"Alright, Mina," Sebastian called over the music. "I want you to try and summon a ring of wind around you that follows the direction of your extended leg."

"Your working leg," Enoch corrected.

"Your *working* leg," he repeated.

There was that tickle in her diaphragm again.

Mina could already feel the wind pooling at her ankles, favoring more the ankle of her supporting foot than her working one. She recalled the sensation of it racing up her leg like it had after it tripped her, and the recollection became reality. The wind twirled up her leg, brushing dirt and leaves against it, and she shifted her attention to the air rushing past her working knee as she cut through it, picturing the wind and dirt and leaves spinning in a trail behind.

"Whatever you're doing right now is working, Mina!" Sebastian said. "Now, see if you can get the ring to spin alongside you without touching you."

She barely thought of it for a moment before the wind pulled away and formed a ring around her, spinning in perfect sync with her own turns.

"There you go! Now! Here comes the tricky part. Try and keep the ring spinning while you stop."

"Gradually slowing the speed of your turns might be your best bet," Enoch offered.

"Yes! Great idea, Enoch!" Sebastian clapped him on the back. "Try what he suggested!"

Mina hesitated, kept on spinning, as doubt tinged with the fear of disappointment made it difficult to breathe. What if she couldn't do it? What would happen then?

Would they be mad?

"It's alright if you can't. You've already made great progress in a short amount of time," Sebastian said. "You should be proud!"

"Hell, magic aside, you should be proud of doing eighty flawless turns!" Enoch added.

Proud.

She should be proud.

Then Mina felt it. The undeniable knowing that if she wanted the wind to keep spinning, it would. Without begging, without question, for she sensed deep in her soul that it was proud of her.

So she stopped, as scared and as unsure as she was, and let herself be proud too.

"She's doing it!" Sebastian hollered, grabbing onto Enoch, shaking him as he jumped in excitement. "Mina, you're doing it!"

"I can see that!" Mina called back as she watched the swirling stream of the garden's debris dance in a ballet of their own around her. She dipped her hand into it and let the breeze run through her fingers like water through a stream. The dirt and small rocks scratched against her knuckles. The leaves and blades of grass tumbled across clumsily. And little blue flowers wove in between, twirling, pirouetting, wild and free.

She pinched one between her fingers before it could rush past.

Winter's speedwell.

"No tears, dear one. Take pride in what you've done."

Mina crushed the flower between her fingers and the wind died.

Sebastian stopped the music. "Hey, what happened?"

"I don't know."

Mina headed towards the garden door as Sebastian walked to meet her.

"Your expression went absolutely blank for a second before the spell broke, did something cross your mind or—"

She walked past him.

"Where are you going?"

"I have to get ready to head out."

"But we still have ten minutes left!"

"Then we'll leave early. Gain an extra five minutes of travel."

"Mina. Stop," he commanded.

The threads of his command pulled her to a standstill.

"Enoch, do you mind returning the gramophone to the Junk Room for me?"

"Gladly."

The squeak of sweaty palms across its lacquered wooden base, the grunt of effort as he lifted it, and the slap of his awkward steps led to Enoch racing across her field of vision and exiting out of the garden door instead of her.

Even footsteps rolling across the grass followed, growing louder until Sebastian's brilliant bushel of amber hair and brown eyes, warm and patient, stepped in front of her.

"To understand how your magic works, and to improve your control over it, you have to tell me what you're experiencing," he spoke gently, kindly, a dull but not unwanted ache at the back of her ear. "You couldn't understand why I was upset. I can't understand why you lost your concentration. So I'm going to ask you to do what you always ask of me. Explain."

"It was a memory."

"Tell me more."

"It was a..." the words struggled out of her throat, "...bad one."

"About?"

Chains tightened around her neck while threads fought to pull out an explanation.

"Pride," Mina croaked.

"Pride?" Sebastian furrowed his brow. "What about pride?"

"It's bad."

"Well, that's not true."

Mina stared at him.

"It's not," he emphasized. "Pride in excess can be, but that's called hubris. You weren't thinking you were some all-powerful being more important than any other life on earth and untouchable by death, were you?"

"No."

Sebastian gave a soft, burning smile. "Then there's nothing to feel bad about, lila doar."

"But it could lead to that," Mina countered.

"It could, or it couldn't." He shrugged. "But I'd be willing to bet a lot of money on the latter. Now, before you try and argue with me, tell me the things that did work. What did you feel?"

The thread snapped as the chains pulled taut.

"Mina?"

Her jaw tightened, bottom teeth threatening to punch through the roof of her mouth. She put her hand over her mouth, attempting to signal him that her silence was forced.

"Oh." Sebastian cocked his head to the side. "But you were able to tell me what happened before."

The chains loosened.

"The wording," Mina coughed out.

"The wording?"

"The wording."

His brow furrowed even deeper in confusion. "How did I ask it last time?"

"Tell me what happened."

"So a command, not a question?" he clarified.

"Clearly."

Sebastian's expression eased back into its normal state. "Well then. Tell me what—"

"Windenhofer?" Sir Gargic opened the garden door in a wide, hurried swing. "There you two are! We've been waiting for you!"

"Waiting for us? We still have—" Sebastian pulled his pocket watch out of his back pocket. "We're five minutes behind."

Sir Gargic clicked his tongue in disapproval, not at Sebastian, but at Mina.

"What? Ya get a little more color in your life, and you forget how to tell time, beastie?" he teased. "Don't get too distracted now. You still have a contract to fulfill, ya know."

Mina stepped around Sebastian and stomped towards the door. "How could I forget?"

🜁

Wera and Enoch were hard at work on their atlas, barely bothering to look up when Mina entered the library.

She'd tried to finish her drawing, but found herself unnerved at the imagined smile. She switched to playing her violin, but found her fingers drifting to Concerto for Alvaneya's opening chords and her legs carrying herself around the room, mapping out the steps for a tango to it when they should have been practicing a pas seul.

She was too in her head, her subconscious too unruly, and she needed to get out of it. A decent book would be able to do just that.

Mina watched the flickering library shelves carefully, reading each spine as they popped in and out of existence, until a familiar title caught her eye: **Butcher, Baker: Candlestick Maker.** She pulled the novel off the shelf, her new-found smile creeping up her lips seeing that the next volume of the series had been published.

"I don't know if you'll like that one," Enoch commented from behind her.

Mina looked over at him. "What?"

"Well, that's the third book in this—"

"I know that."

Enoch's eyes shot wide as the corners of his brows flicked upward in surprise. "You know that?"

"I read the first two."

He smacked Wera on the shoulder, jolting the brush in her hand mid-stroke.

"Hey! Watch where you're smacking!" she snapped.

"Mina's read the *Butcher, Baker* series," he said, ignoring the death glare Wera shot his way.

She traded her death glare for disbelief.

"Sh—" Wera looked over at Mina. "You—"

Now it was Mina's turn to glare. "I can read, you know."

"I know. But I didn't think you'd read romance novels."

She glanced down at the book in her hands. "It has adventure, and action."

"And sex," Enoch added. "The sex is a big part of it."

"So?"

"Do you skip the sex scenes then, or?" Wera asked.

"No. I read them," Mina said, and cocked her head, amused with confusion as their expressions grew in shock. "That surprises you both."

"I mean," Enoch gave a broken chuckle, "given everything we know about you. Everything that's happened to you. You don't seem like the type to be into that sort of thing."

"Well, I don't read them for the sex."

"Then what do you read them for?"

"To be someone else for a bit. To go somewhere I've never been before," she explained, an unexpected defensiveness rising. "I live alone, in the middle of nowhere. Even with all the hunting, gathering, and bringing things to market, there is still a lot of time left in the day to fill. Music makes the hours pass, so does reading. And I'll read just about anything."

She grabbed a chair, turned it so that the back faced them, and took a seat. "Regardless of if it has sex or not."

"Guess that's that then," Wera sighed, the rustle of papers following after as she returned to work.

"You should check out *Ophelia and the Mirror Passage* once you're finished," Enoch offered. "It was originally written in Ortrian, but the Plainspeech translation is pretty on par."

"Noted," Mina grunted, opening the book and shutting out everything beyond its pages.

Where their story had last left off, the titular "Butcher", a young hit woman by the name of Cassandra, and Thomas, a former baker who was once her target, now accomplice, had finally realized who the true head of Cassandra's assassins guild was and were on the run from them.

Mina could picture the storm that the book opened up with, roiling, thunderous. The flashes of lightning threatened to tear the sky asunder as they ran through the rain, deeper and deeper into the forest. The sound of the search dogs' wet gallops in the mud fading the farther they ran, the rain muddling their scent with damp earth and decaying leaves.

Though Mina's boots were dry, she could feel the heavy, suffocating wool of wet socks rubbing their feet raw. Feel the back of their knees burning, threatening to give out underneath them.

Feel the warmth of their hands holding on to each other tightly, urging one another to take just one step more, to keep running.

Mina paused, lifted her hand away from the book, and studied it. It didn't look any different, but it definitely felt warmer. She placed it against her cheek and the feeling vanished.

Rather than dwell on the disappointment, she resumed reading.

They took refuge in the hollow of a great felled redwood.

Thomas let go of Cassandra's hand and leaned against the hollow's wall before sliding down it onto the ground.

"Take off your clothes," Cassandra ordered as she stripped off her boots.

"What?" Thomas wheezed, still winded.

"We can't build a fire right now. Any wood we could find would be too wet, and even if we did find any that would work, the smoke would lead them right to us." She worked off her pants, struggling to peel the wet fabric down her thighs. "Keep the clothes on, and you're signing your own death sentence. I've worked too hard on keeping you alive to let that happen."

Thomas unlaced his boots. "What about hypothermia, then? It's freezing out here."

"I've got a bedroll in my pack we can climb into once we air dry a bit."

Cassandra began to unwrap the bindings around her breasts, and Thomas turned away, keeping his focus locked on the wall behind him as he continued to undress.

"What's the bashfulness for?" she teased. "It's nothing that you haven't seen before."

"I know, but—" Thomas stripped off his shirt. "Now doesn't seem the most appropriate time to—"

"To what?" Cassandra said, stepping closer to him, running her hands down the sculpted muscles of his back before resting them on his belt. "Look?"

Thomas shuddered as her breath brushed against his ear, raising goosebumps across the back of his neck.

"Cass—"

"I said we have to air dry, didn't I?" She kissed the raised flesh, pulling a slight whimper from him. "And you're awfully worried about keeping warm. Why not kill two birds with one stone?"

Mina shifted her breastplate, tugging at the leather to ease some of the tightness in her chest and the warmth that had left her hand to bloom across her clavicle. She placed the book down for a moment and took it off the leather, exhaling briefly in relief as the air cooled her down and filled her lungs.

She barely registered Wera and Enoch's curious glances her way as she snatched the book back up.

Thomas cleared his throat. "You know we've been running for two hours straight, right?"

"Oh, I'm painfully aware." Cassandra snaked her arms around his waist, placing a hand on his belt buckle as she pressed her bare breasts against his back, nipples perked from the cold, night air; skin smooth and slick. She chuckled, inhaling the smell of his sweat, sweetened by the rain but still carrying the enticingly bitter sting of yeast. "Our feet are going to be blistered for weeks. And—"

"And?"

The sea of dread Cassandra was avoiding drowning under, lapped against her ankles.

"There's more pain to come for us." She pressed her forehead between his shoulder blades and moved her hand away from his buckle to hug him tightly. "Which is why we should take pleasure when we can."

Thomas grabbed one of her hands in his and brought it to his lips, kissing the long-formed calluses that marred her knuckles, before placing it back against his belt buckle.

"Help me with my pants?"

Cassandra smiled and trailed kisses down his spine as she freed him, fingers well-versed from practice. Just as she guided his pants down to the ground, Thomas turned around and cupped his hand against her cheek, tilting her head back as he wrapped his arm around her waist and pulled her close.

His kiss—

Mina's throat went dry — not the burning, all-consuming fire that threatened to turn her throat to ash the other night. She coughed a little, working some saliva up to soothe it, and continued reading.

It was just words on a page. There was nothing for her body to get... whatever reaction it was getting over them.

—much like his hands, much like his entire body pressed against hers, banished the cold settling into her bones in one fell swoop. Cassandra met his hunger head-on, dragging long slow kisses out of him, growing lightheaded from the taste of his tongue between her lips. Between the few breaks they took for air, she nipped playfully at his bottom lip—

Mina's bottom lip slipped between her teeth.

—dragging a delicious, spine-tingling groan out of him that made her ache for more.

Cassandra slipped a hand in between them and slowly traced her fingers up the soft inner flesh of his thighs. Thomas let go of her waist and grabbed her wrist just as she started to snake up underneath the hem of his undergarments. Without words, he flipped the two of them around and pinned her against the wall.

"After you," he murmured as he brought her fingers to his lips and let his gaze linger over her, casting any remnants of bashfulness to the wayside and replacing them with desire. Thomas trailed slow, soft kisses from her knuckles, across her palm, all the way down the smooth, soft skin on the underside of her arm.

He draped it over his shoulder to let both of his hands travel up her waist, taking his sweet time as his kisses danced across her clavicle. Cassandra whimpered as the tips of his hair, still cold and wet, brushed against the heat of her body as his kneading hands and hungry lips completed their long pilgrimage to her breasts.

A flash of orange light burst next to Mina, and she jumped out of her chair, snapping the book shut and holding it aloft; ready to strike.

"It's just a candle!" Sebastian shouted from his seat across the room. Mina's eyes darted from the candle to him. "It looked like you needed a little extra light."

"I—" Mina swallowed to catch her breath and focus her too-warm mind. "I can see in the dark."

Sebastian's eyes widened, and he tucked his bottom lip firmly beneath his top lip. "That's right... you can..."

They stared at each other for a moment.

"How's the book?" "I'm heading to bed." Their voices clashed against each other.

Mina snapped the book shut and shoved it back onto the shelf. She couldn't talk to him like this, not with her brain, *her body*, feeling like she was slowly boiling alive.

"Is everything alright? You seem—"

"Headache," she answered, racing out the door.

The warmth of the tap water or her brief brushes against Sebastian's hand was one thing, but this was... too much. She wasn't dying or anything. Her heart beat just fine, though a little fast. She could breathe, though it was a little shallow. But no matter how fast she ran, no matter how much the air whipped past her face as she raced down the hall, nothing cooled her.

It only made her warmer, in fact.

Mina rifled through the infirmary's medicine cabinets, trying to decipher Tanir's tight, slanted cursive for anything labeled as a soporific. The best thing for a fever was sleep. Not that she had ever had a fever, but considering that's what Mrs. Harlowe said every time her husband's temperature ran high, Mina figured it was worth a shot.

A thick, glass vial, labeled **Moespamire** with three bolded 'z's beneath, caught her eye and, without a second thought, she uncorked it and took a giant swig. It was tasteless, went down easy, and with a quick listen to make sure the halls were clear upstairs, she dashed up to her room.

Sleep. Sleep the fever off. She climbed into bed and closed her eyes, wondering how long it would take for the potion to—

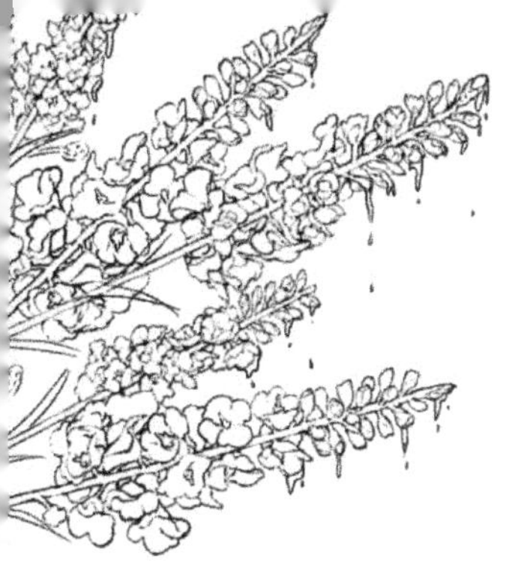

XV
Revelation

It was raining.

Thunder rolled off in the distance. Flashes of lightning painted veins of amber across the night sky as they took partial shelter under the willow that hung low over the lake near her cabin.

Scattered raindrops splashed cool against her too-warm body, the cause of which was not unknown, but standing right in front of her.

Sebastian stared back at her, lips parted in awe. The lightning's reflection filled the umber of his eyes with flickering sparks. His arms rested on either side of her: strong, glistening with raindrops that slipped slowly down the curves of his muscles. One in particular caught her eye as it rolled down his clavicle, through the wet tufts of hair that adorned his chest, and dropped into the obsidian water lapping against his bare stomach.

"Mina."

She looked back up at him, eyes locking on his parted lips. She didn't hesitate this time. The warmth within her was too much. She had to give it back to him.

Sebastian's mouth met hers halfway, out-matching her need tenfold.

Every pass of his lips between hers, the lingering taste of bergamot on his tongue, his breath raggedly brushing across her cheeks, created an ebb and flow of heat between them. Mina threaded her fingers through his still-damp hair, pulling him closer to let the rain rolling down between them douse the flames.

But Sebastian wanted them to burn.

His hands left the rock behind her, one moving to firmly grip the back of her neck, deepening his kiss while the other slipped up her back, igniting her spine with molten lava. Mina was all too happy to melt against his touch. The warmth now only uncomfortable because she needed more.

Her heartbeat screamed in her ears as Sebastian trailed his eager, hungry mouth down her jaw onto the sensitive, soft skin of her neck. A whimper bubbled up her throat. She'd never been touched there, let alone kissed. Every inch he touched sparked and cindered, their roles reversed. She was but a small, smoldering flame, and Sebastian was oxygen, working her into a wildfire.

He ran his fingertips over the back of her bindings, burning the fabric and exposing her breasts as the linen fell free into the dark water. Sebastian stepped into her, placing a firm, but sorely needed pressure between her thighs, soothing the throbbing ache for just a moment as he pulled away from her neck to look at her.

Hunger, desire, lust, joy, culminated in a playful smile upon his lips as he ran one hand up the curve of her side, taking his time, studying her like she wasn't about to combust at any moment. The hand she watched so many times, holding a pen, molding flame, intertwining with hers— caressed her breast with a reverence often saved for sacred objects.

She could not run from the shudder of pure delight that rippled through her body as his thumb circled her peaked nipple, hitching her breath with a shaky gasp.

Sebastian leaned down and pressed his forehead against hers. "That's my girl."

A wave of need rushed through her, overtaking her as she kissed him greedily and rolled her hips forward, sparking a whole new fire as she dragged her core across his thigh. He urged her to continue, to let the heat consume her, to relish in the sensation of the cool water soothing the sensitive bundle of nerves she'd just discovered, making it even more irresistible to grind against him.

Mina bit into his bottom lip, desperate for something to hold on to as his nimble fingers stoked the flames, kneading at her breast, and his other hand wandered lower, down her ribs.

"Mina."

Over her hip.

"Mina."

Across her stomach.

"M-mina?"

Her heart was pounding, no, knocking against her chest as his hand dipped under the water.

"Mina?!"

Her heart burst.

🜁

Mina awoke with a jolt, heart beating as hard as the fist pounding against the door.

"Mina?! If you don't answer me, I'm coming in!" Sebastian called from outside, voice wavering with worry.

She spat out the corner of the pillow that had somehow worked its way into her mouth and untangled herself from the bunched-up bedsheets between her legs, making it in time to stop the doorknob from turning.

"I'm up," she panted, opening the door just a crack and blinding herself briefly with the bright hall light.

"Thank The Gods," Sebastian sighed in relief. The worry tightening his face and shoulders disappeared. His gaze darted over her body, bouncing from top to bottom, making her squirm as she recalled them doing the same thing in her dream, only indulging instead of analyzing.

"What?" she snapped.

"You look... flustered? Is something wrong?"

"What would be wrong?"

"Normally, you answer in two knocks, not twenty. And you went to bed early last night with a headache—"

"I took a sleeping potion," she interjected, much more forcefully than she intended. "For the headache."

Sebastian furrowed his brow in confusion. "And it worked?"

"It's the same magic as sleep spells, is it not?"

"Depends on the potion."

"Moespamire?"

Sebastian let out a low whistle. "Then twenty knocks makes sense. Must have been one hell of a headache for you to have left your breastplate behind." He pulled out her breastplate from behind his back, and she ripped it from his hand before he could offer it to her.

"It was," she grumbled.

"Do you know what caused it?"

"Reading," Mina answered without thinking, too distracted by the strong smell of lavender wafting off the leather. Sebastian must have had it cleaned during the night.

"I knew you were having trouble with it. Straining your eyes like that is known to cause a headache. Next time, take a seat closer to the fire so you can have more light to read by, alright?"

"I'll make a note. Is this all?" Mina held up her breastplate.

"No. I'm afraid I'll need some assistance in my study this morning."

"The jewelry box?" she asked.

"The jewelry box," he confirmed. "I'll give you a few minutes to get ready?"

"No need." Mina stepped around the door and locked it behind her as she threw on her breastplate.

"Okay then. Mina, come assist me in my study," he commanded and waited for her to fasten her armor. "You know, you could pull a set of pajamas out of the Junk Room. Might be more comfortable than sleeping in armor."

"I don't sleep in pajamas."

"You sleep in your armor back at your cabin?" he asked.

"No. I sleep nude." Mina froze as she adjusted the final buckle, the memory of their naked bodies pressed against each other, slick with rain and sweat, passed over her skin like a phantom.

"O-oh! Well, that—" Sebastian cleared the accent from his throat and turned his focus to the ceiling, finding the crown molding quite interesting as faint splotches of red spread across his cheeks. "—certainly sounds comfortable. I um— tend to prefer boxers. I'm a mess when I wake up, and I don't think my crew would appreciate seeing all of my ass if there was some late-night emergency."

I'd appreciate it, Mina thought, earning her a brilliant spike of pain too quick for her to hide her grimace.

"Come along," he said, curtly, catching her wince. "We can chat as we work. Don't want to interrupt Tanir's sleep more than I might have knocking on your door." Sebastian headed off, leading her down the hall and up the stairs to his study.

In the few days since she last entered Sebastian's cluttered workshop, the place had changed dramatically. Still crowded, still a labyrinth of curios from acology to zoology, but even more vibrant. The bowed shelves and stuffed cabinets bore wood of various shades of brown, some covered with red and blue paint, the odds and ends they housed boasting some of the same shades. Despite all the new colors, new discoveries she could make about plants and products she had only thought of in grayscale, Mina still found herself drawn to the drawer filled with amber stones.

"Open the seventh drawer to your left," Sebastian said, pausing to gather whatever he needed for that morning's work.

Mina's hand drifted over against her will, peeling her away from the glistening amber. Sebastian's handwriting looked more like a child's scribbles than words on the drawer's label, making it impossible to tell what was inside until she opened it up.

The slight smile on her face was instant.

She grabbed one of the stones and twisted it back and forth in the light, illuminating shifting swirls of red, orange, blue, and a handful of other colors she couldn't see deep inside its smooth, bulbous form.

"Is it magic?" she asked.

"Not yet," Sebastian said. "Those stones are fire agate. Now that you can see red and blue, I figured the color shift would be interesting. Once you can see all the colors, though, a new pendant might be in order."

There was a flutter in her stomach, and her smile tried in vain to spread wider, "No."

"No?"

"Another one." She twisted the agate a final time and put it back in the drawer. "Not new." She turned around and dared to sneak a glance at the wizard, prepared to accept the pain of whatever kind look was sure to linger on his face.

"Duly noted," he said with a soft smile on his lips, eyes tracing down her neck to where the pendant he had made lay hidden under her breastplate. Mina had expected to be stung, not burnt.

She shifted her focus to the wooden crate on his desk, hoping to stop the searing pain blistering over her skin before the warmth it left in its wake could spread anywhere other than her face. Things had finally started to cool down after her fever-fueled hallucinations, the last thing she needed was to get all distraught in front of Sebastian like she did last night.

"That the box?" she asked, gesturing to the crate.

"Yes and no." Sebastian pulled on a pair of thick workman's gloves. "I've been keeping the jewelry box inside here to keep anyone from touching the actual thing by accident."

Mina walked over to his desk and peered across it, watching intently as he removed the crate's lid and carefully pulled out the jewelry box.

"That's poisoned?" She leaned in close as he placed it down on a metal tray. The box itself was barely a box at all. It more resembled just a solid block of wood, pulled straight from a carpenter's workbench and stained in some deep color Mina couldn't recognize. "And it's a box?"

"Yes and yes. It's a clever fucking thing. The only way to start to work out how to solve it is to touch it, but as soon as you touch it, the thousands of microscopic nettles coating it inject their poison. Unfortunately, a very brave raccoon thought he could find a bit of food in that crate the night after we pulled it out of Dormina's Tomb. If it wasn't for the ringed tail, I wouldn't have been able to identify what the hell the creature was after the poison took its toll."

"What kind of poison?"

"Gympiewhirl nettle. They must have made it out of cut a gympiewhirl bough, then had a druid manipulate its growth pattern to have the nettles spring out of the bare wood instead of the leaves."

Mina picked up the box and Sebastian gave a warbled yipe out of fear. Her diaphragm spasmed at the sound, and she let out a slight wheeze as the corners of her mouth flitted upwards. She turned the jewelry box over and over in her hands, feeling for some sort of seam or hint for how to open it.

"So gympiewhirl nettle is one of the poisons you're immune to then?" he asked.

"Clearly."

"If you have to put it down for some reason, set it on the metal tray. We're not sure if those nettles come out easily, and I'd rather not find out by having my throat close up while I'm trying to work on my guild forms."

"Eh. Breathing's overrated." Mina bit her tongue as she rubbed her thumb against the corners of the box, failing to find an opening.

"Try turning that knot on the underside," Sebastian suggested.

Mina flipped the box over and ran her thumb in a circle around the knot, barely a third of an inch in diameter. Clockwise didn't budge, but counterclockwise gave way, turning the pitched patch of wood. Three times around she swirled it and then — click.

Faster than she'd ever seen him move, Sebastian rounded his desk to stand behind her. He grabbed her by the shoulders and pushed her forward, pressing her thighs against the wooden desktop, and swung a large magnifying glass, hung on a stand, over her hands.

Mina struggled to breathe, not out of pain, but out of an overwhelming awareness of how much of him was pressed up against her back. Sebastian, consumed by his love of puzzles, was too engrossed to notice.

"Turn it over slowly. Long sides first, then short," he instructed.

She did as he commanded, angling the box towards the light and near the magnifying glass to help him see without leaning so close to her neck. The warmth of his chest against her spine was spreading and pulling her focus to bodies and lakes and things she shouldn't be thinking about.

"Anything?" Sebastian asked.

"Anything?" Mina repeated.

"Have you noticed any movement? Heard any soft clicks or shifting plates?"

"Besides that knot, no movement. For sound, I'd have to close my eyes to focus. There's too much whirring and bubbling and ticking going on."

"Close your eyes then."

His command drew her eyelids shut like window curtains.

"How am I supposed to know what pieces to move?"

"It's simple. Mina, let me use your hands."

Her breathing hitched as Sebastian placed his hands on top of hers, somehow pressing more of his body against her.

"What— that— you—" Mina stammered for the right words, fumbling of her own accord and against the magical blocks tying up her tongue. "Poison!" she managed to choke out.

"I'll be careful and go slow, alright?" The rumble of his voice hummed across her back.

Mina resisted the urge to lean into it.

"You really do have a fucking death wish," she grumbled.

Sebastian huffed a laugh. "You're one to talk, Little Miss 'Let me just run head first into battle and severely injure myself'."

"It's not like I have any choice," she defended, trying to untangle the sudden guilt twisting her stomach.

"I've told you before, you always have a choice. Now," Sebastian's words brushed across her ear as he leaned in to get a closer look at the box, "tell me if you hear anything or feel anything shift in the box as I guide your hands."

Mina was quick to pick up his hand movements, little presses and pulls. He was so sure of the gestures that it granted her a sense of ease.

The cacophony of Sebastian's study was loud, but not as loud as their heartbeats, syncopated in rhythm but matching in speed. It must have been the combination of his natural excitement for puzzle-solving and the fear of his grip accidentally slipping. A good sign. Perhaps if he was able to feel how hard her heart was hammering at her chest, he'd think she was scared too.

Gently, he guided her fingers over the wood grain, pressing lightly from time to time, looking for some type of button, dragging them across in search of movement.

"There," Mina said as the faintest click caught her attention. "Whatever you just did made a click."

"Oh. That is goddamn genius," Sebastian marveled. "Open your eyes, Mina."

Her eyes snapped open. The overhead lamp briefly blinded her with its shine.

"Look at the figure of the wood."

Mina blinked her eyes to clear the blotches of white obscuring her vision and looked down at the box through the magnifying glass.

"You see where I've got your thumb? It's right on this little strip of veining. Was the click when I pressed down on your thumb or dragged it?"

"It was when you started to drag, but you were pressing down pretty firmly."

He pressed down. "Like this?"

"A little harder," Mina said. "There you go."

The pressure correct, he stroked her thumb along the wood and the strip shifted along with it. It moved about a quarter of an inch, exposing a pale sliver of the box's inner wall, before stopping.

Sebastian chuckled. "Amazing. The madman who made this took a hunk of wood and ripped it along the grain, so the pieces were made of the wood's natural figure. That way, it just looked like a solid block."

"Sounds like a lot of work for a jewelry box."

"Which means that there must be one hell of a prize." He shook her hands excitedly. "Close your eyes again. Tell me when you hear a click and what caused it."

Sebastian's movements were methodical, purposeful. As much as she was listening to the box, he was listening to her: stopping when she told him, adjusting his grip under her guidance, taking care in how he touched her.

They moved as one. Breathing together, low and even, synced by a singular focus. The warmth from his hands spread throughout her body, a different kind of consumption than in her dream. Gradual, gentle. Not combustion, not the brilliant, desperate burn of wildfire racing to fuel itself. A stable flame. The well-tended hearth of a home.

They turned the knot again and the box broke apart.

"Look at that," Sebastian whispered.

Mina opened her eyes.

She held a box of ebony in her hands, the slivers of gympiewhirl now scattered on the metal tray below. Sebastian pulled his hands away from hers, but still stood against her back.

"You can open it."

"What if it's trapped?"

Sebastian shifted to grab something out of his pocket. He held his hand over the box, a soft, amber glow coating his fingertips, and sprinkled a pinch of dried white flower petals on top of it.

"And that is?"

"Eyebright petals. If the box is enchanted, they'll burn away as soon as they touch it."

The petals settled on the lid, and after a moment, Sebastian blew them off.

"All clear."

Mina's fingers fumbled as she opened it, weightless and shaky in the absence of Sebastian's guidance. The lid lifted easily, revealing a velvet lining just as dark as the box's wood, and a bare velvet cushion.

"It's empty."

"Probably not," Sebastian pulled away from her. "The necklace might be cloaked by an illusion. Let me grab my all-seeing eyeglass."

Her body followed after him for just a moment, a subtle sway that would have given away how much her foolish mind missed his warmth if he'd been paying attention.

Mina bridled herself and tilted the box back and forth as Sebastian rummaged around his study, listening for the sound of something shifting inside, looking for a slight ripple of light over the cushion denoting an enchantment. Under the light of the work lamp, she caught a thin dent in the finish on the lid's side, an odd defect considering how much detail and care was given to the box's creation. Perhaps it had been dropped prior to its sealing. Perhaps someone who'd grown too frustrated with its outer puzzle had tried to smash the box open and was only able to make a small dent.

Or perhaps it was there on purpose.

Mina pressed her fingernail into it and the lid's bottom popped out, revealing a necklace. A fat oval pendant, beset with pearls and smaller gemstones in its setting and attached to a thick wheat-patterned chain, had been crammed into the small velvet-lined compartment; keeping it still and silent, no matter how much the box was turned or tilted.

She called over her shoulder. "Found it."

"Really?"

Mina turned around to face him and lifted the pendant out of the box.

The world blurred just as Sebastian smiled, his voice muffled, and Mina's knees folded underneath her — too fatigued to stand any longer — into darkness.

"Rub that salve on her hand," Tanir's voice, clouded, echoed in the darkness.

Her arm ignited.

Mina jolted awake, tearing her arm away from the heat as she blinked the heavy swirls of sleep from her eyes.

"Thank The Gods," Sebastian exhaled for the second time that morning, a heavier sigh than the last time; more pained, more relieved.

Mina tried to sit up, her body feeling as though it had been dipped in lead.

"Did Tanir cast a slow spell on me?" she groaned, her throat just as stiff as her spine.

"It's a side effect of a rather nasty sleep spell," Tanir answered from somewhere in the room. "Sebastian, did you rub that salve on her hand?"

"I started too, but it hurt her enough to wake her up."

Mina looked down at her hand, numb and covered in a dark brown slave, patches of raw, red skin showing through it on her fingertips.

"I started to wake before the pain," she said, and lugged her hand over to rub the ointment in. She looked around the study for any signs of damage — any signs of her transforming and wreaking havoc — but only found piles of books and papers scattered across the floor, thrown off the chests she was lying on in a hurry.

She looked at Sebastian's clavicle. "No monster?"

"No monster," he confirmed. "You just collapsed."

Tanir placed a hand on his shoulder and he stood. She crouched down in his place, still dressed in her nightgown, gray hair tucked neatly into a bonnet, holding a brightly glowing crystal in her hand.

"Mina, look at me," she said, drawing Mina's attention as she shone the crystal across her eyes. "Are you nauseous?"

"No."

"What's your name?"

"Mina."

"Where are you right now?"

"The wizard's study."

"What did you eat for dinner last night?"

"Fried chicken with cranberry dressing, mashed potatoes, collard greens, and cornbread."

"And what's the last thing you remember doing?"

"Holding up that necklace, everything going blurry and muffled, then getting so tired my knees gave out."

Tanir put the crystal down and turned over her shoulder towards Sebastian. "There's no concussion and no memory-altering effects from the necklace."

"A concussion would have healed by now," Mina noted.

"I know that, dear," Tanir whispered to her. "But he needed to hear it."

Mina lifted her heavy head to look at the wizard pacing back and forth. A neurotic mess.

"I should have told you to put the box down the minute I stepped away," he muttered, hands tugging at the roots of his hair. "I checked it for the traps but the necklace? It was a rookie mistake and I could have given you a whole other curse on top of that... or worse! Gods, I could have killed you! For a second there I thought that I had!"

"But you didn't," Mina reminded him.

He threw his arms in the air. "But I could have! I have to be more careful. Not be so goddamn self-absorbed. Too focused on my own goddamn interests to care abo—"

Tanir's hands shot up to cover her ears as Mina placed her fingers between her lips and cut off his tirade with an ear-splitting whistle.

Sebastian jumped and whirled on his heels to face her, eyes wide with shock.

"Partnership," she spat, folding her arms across her chest. "I shouldn't have touched the necklace. I should have put the box down. I should have thought just as much as you. We'll remember for next time. No more fretting about it."

Sebastian blinked rapidly in disbelief, then pouted. "You have every right to be furious with me."

"I'm not," Mina moved to stand, pushing against the lingering stiffness in her knees. "But I will be if you keep talking that way." She looked at Tanir. "Breakfast?"

Tanir looked between her and Sebastian. "Uh... I was hoping to get changed first."

"Change then." Mina walked to the door. "Come on, Wizard."

"Come on, what?" he balked.

"Your stomach's too empty. It's filling your head with stupid thoughts."

🜁

As the day wore on, Sebastian's demeanor returned to his standard state of overthinking, rather than sinking into the mire of regret and self-deprecation he'd worked up for himself.

Mina's mind, however, kept getting stuck in the muck.

Or more accurately, the lake.

The wind as they climbed was brutal, lashing. The troop's usual banter was cut to a minimum as they were too focused on keeping their teeth from chattering and their tongue from freezing to the roofs of their mouths. Mina tried to focus on the wind as they went, hoping that maybe she could harness it, calm it down a bit, but it was far too wild, lacking rhythm or reason, just like her unruly heartbeat.

If she could just get them talking again, maybe she could distract herself enough to where the wind was the only thing she felt, not Sebastian's hands igniting sparks across her breast as he teased at her nipples.

She had never thought about anyone doing that, ever. Not even herself. Sure, she had read plenty of books filled with sex, but usually, she just glazed over the words. They were just steps, movements the characters took. Warriors drew their blades, detectives inspected dead bodies for evidence, and if two characters meet and the main focus of the book is them learning about each other, seven times out of ten they fornicated.

Mina usually steered away from the stories where it was only about them getting closer to each other because of that. Adventure, action, an end goal other than marriage, if she was picking up a romance novel there needed to be a plot other than seeing how many ways and in how many places a creature could copulate. What was the point otherwise?

Thomas trailed, slow, soft kisses from her knuckles—

Sebastian's warm fingers, gentle and methodical, gliding up her arms.

Sebastian's stubble raising goosebumps across the wanton bite marks he left on her neck.

Mina grabbed a pointy pebble off the trail and stuck it in her boot.

Another affliction, more thoughts of Sebastian she had to understand in order to flush the infection out.

"Wera," Mina said as they ate a too-quiet lunch.

Wera peered over the rim of her soup bowl, opting to drink straight from it, so the residual heat could warm her hands. "Mina?"

"Drawing lessons after dinner," she stated.

"After dinner?" Sebastian interjected before Wera could speak. "Like right after dinner?"

"Right after dinner."

"Could drawing lessons wait until a little bit after that?" he pushed. "Like maybe an hour or..."

"No."

Wera sat the bowl down. "Look Meens, it's colder than a witch's tit out there, alright? After dinner, I'm gonna a take a long, hot bath—"

"There's a bathtub in my room," Mina interrupted.

Wera's mouth hung open for a moment, while the others all choked and sputtered. Mina glared daggers at her, kicking her under the table, prodding her to speak.

Her eyes darted back and forth between her and Sebastian. "I-it'll be hard to give you drawing lessons from the bathtub. Paper and water don't exactly mix."

"I have ears. You can talk," Mina pressed.

"Okay but—"

"We have a deal."

Mina's stomach turned as she said it, the ribbon of their pact tightening around her wrist as it bent Wera's will.

There was just the briefest flash of frost ferns swirling over Wera's irises before her shoulders slouched in defeat.

"You're right," she sighed, as if her resignation was her own idea. "We have a deal."

"Okay then," Sebastian snipped slightly. He picked up his silverware to eat and sat them right back down again with a clatter. "What if we skip your magic lesson today, so you and Wera can have your drawing lesson now? That way you can draw, Wera will be able to take a nice bath alone in her room, and I get to— do what I have to do."

"What you have to do?" Mina questioned, tilting her head towards the wizard in doubt.

Sebastian's expression was tense, but did not give away the cause of it. "Yes."

"Progress stops if you don't keep moving," she argued. "Magic lessons keep things moving."

A million thoughts, scattered in a light panic, flitted in the shadows of Sebastian's eyes.

The shadows disappeared at the flash of an idea and the snap of his fingers. "Then the magic lessons will be right after dinner! How does that sound? Wera?"

"Sounds good to me," she spat out quickly.

"Mina?" Sebastian asked, voice higher, hinging on her answer.

The broken, needy way he whined her name at the lake echoed in her ears.

She turned away from him, back to her own bowl of soup, finding her face warmer than the food itself. "Whatever."

Enoch changed the subject, thankfully, to the weather; spurring idle conversation as Mina grew cold once again, warring with herself for forcing Wera's hand. Her tongue would tear itself out before she could confess to it, before she could let the cartographer know exactly what it meant to make a deal with a fae creature. Let her know just how far Mina could take their little pact if she were more sadistic.

After they cleared their bowls, a silence hung between the pair until they got into the safety of the guest room.

"Look, I don't mind helping you, but it's hard to keep things a secret when you make a scene in front of everyone like that!" Wera chided.

"You should have gone along with it from the start then," Mina countered.

"Or you could have just agreed to wait for me to take my bath. It would have taken an hour at the most. Now everyone's gonna think that our 'drawing lessons' are more than drawing lessons!"

"They'll think we're talking about the wizard?"

Wera shook her head and gave an exasperated chuckle. "They'll think we'll be talking about anything *but* the wizard."

"Then there is no issue." Mina crossed her arms. "Let them think what they think."

"Alright then." Wera made herself comfortable on Mina's bed. "What Sebastian-ism do you need me to break down for you so urgently?"

"It's no 'ism'." Mina locked eyes with her. "I dreamt he was going to have sex with me."

Wera froze. Her eyes glazed over for a moment.

"You... dreamt that he was... going to have sex with you?" She restrung the sentence together. "You had a sex dream about Sebastian?"

"There was no sex. Just the start of sex."

"So y'all were foolin' around?"

"Is foolin' around what leads to sex?" Mina asked. "I thought it meant adultery."

Wera's eyes narrowed. "I feel like you're dodging my question."

"I might be."

"Well then, semantics aside," Wera tucked her legs underneath her and leaned forward onto her elbows in anticipation. "How was it?"

The heat of his palm ghosted down her side. "Hot."

A wicked smile slashed across Wera's face.

"Yeah, it was," she drawled out as she nodded. "What did he do?" She gasped sharply, “What did you do?”

“I— uh — he— um—” She was warming up again as she recalled the dream in detail, the same uneasiness the book gave her coursing through her veins. “I touched him.”

“Where?”

“On the mouth.”

“With your?”

“Mouth.”

“So you kissed him?”

“We met halfway.”

“Was there tongue?”

“And biting.”

“That’s not surprising,” Wera noted. “You seem like you’d be into biting. Where were y’all?” She wriggled her eyebrows suggestively. “His study? The hot spring?”

“A lake by my cabin.” Mina looked towards the wall, but when confronted by her Sebastian mural, dropped her gaze to the ground. She pulled at the collar of her breastplate, hoping to get some cool air beneath it. “I don’t see how that is relevant.”

“It’s all relevant, Mina! Dreams have meaning, you know. Dreaming your teeth are falling out means you’re about to lose something important to you. Dreaming you’re smooching a wizard all the way back at your place means...” Wera paused for a moment as something held her back from speaking. “... other things.”

“Other things?”

“Did your dream hurt?”

“No.”

“Then I’m gonna keep my mouth shut when it comes to ‘other things’. So was it just a little make-out session that made you all hot and bothered?”

“Hot and bothered... fits. But it was more. There were hands and grabbing—”

“Where?”

“Fucking everywhere,” Mina hissed in exasperation.

“But no sex?”

“I woke up just as his hand,” her hand snaked down her body, demonstrating of its own accord, “dipped below the water.”

“So when you woke up, you dipped your hand down below, right?”

“No. I got up and answered the door.” Mina looked up from the floor at her. “What would my hand have done?”

Wera scoffed. “Gotten you off? Released some of the pent-up tension your dream built up? Well, the dream and that book of yours.”

“Is that what books like that are supposed to do? Curse you with fever?”

“No. They’re supposed to turn you on,” Wera emphasized. “Which clearly it did.”

Mina stared at Wera, blankly.

“You do know what I mean when I say—”

"I know what you mean," Mina snipped. "I just— for what—" She kicked the bed frame, attempting to release the frustration of her failing speech and feverish thoughts. "This is Hell."

"Is it?" Wera stood. "Or is it just different?"

She tapped the toe of her boot against the wooden frame in contemplation. "Can it be both?"

"It can be. But sooner rather than later — at this rate especially — different is gonna turn into familiar. Which is why I, your Sebastian expert and amazing female confidante, am gonna give you two questions to mull over as a homework assignment."

"I didn't know that homework assignments were a part of this," Mina grumbled.

"They are now," Wera snickered.

"Just ask whatever fucking questions you're going to ask."

"One. Would it..." Wera pondered the right word, "*annoy* you if you had that dream again? And two. Would it annoy you if what happened in your dream happened in reality? Not that the whole being in a lake thing could happen — we're a little far away for that — but the other things..."

Wera patted her on the shoulder. Mina's thoughts spiraled into a whirlwind around her questions, too much to notice the sting. "Consider it while we hike. Gods know this wind is too fucking cold for us to distract you with talk."

🜁

Consider Sebastian's lips pressed against hers.

Consider him turning his head as he guided her hands across the jewelry box to softly nip at her neck.

Consider it as a reality, not just a dream, not misinterpreted as a hallucination. As real as the frigid wind shearing across their cheeks, slowing their ascent. As real as the billowing clouds shrouded the sky, weighing the air with the thick, damp promise of snow.

Perhaps for the first time in her life, Mina was thankful for the cold. It kept the growing heat within her from consuming her completely, from melting her into something unknown.

The worsening weather, the errant sweeps of snow picked up from the rocky mountain face adding a level of uncertainty to their footsteps, served not as a means to occupy her mind — to pull her from these considerations — but to distract the part of her that would fight against it. There were more dangerous things to look out for than risqué thoughts.

A tap on her shoulder pulled her mind out of its mire.

"I think it best we set up camp early!" Sebastian tried to shout through the thick woolen scarf wrapped twice over his mouth.

"There's an alcove up ahead." With his face masked behind his goggles and scarf, amber hair tucked away beneath a knit hat, Mina found the voice to shout back.

She led them to a sheltered overhang, worn over time into a massive cliff face. Her knees shook with every step closer to it, her stomach cramping as the danger faded away, allowing her thoughts to cave in on themselves.

She stayed outside the commorancy as long as possible, "keeping watch" as Wera and Sir Gargic struggled to set the ring up against the wind. The knight swore and spat as globs of Wera's paint flew off her brush and splattered against his armor, but even watching him suffer was only a brief relief from the inevitable.

Mina kept her eyes to the ground as she walked into the foyer, taking her time kicking the snow off her boots, aiming to stall long enough for Sebastian to finish unraveling himself from his cold weather gear and head off to busy himself with something other than her.

"Fish curry with some fresh naan for dinner, everyone?" he asked with an extra-chipper lilt to his tone that made her heart spasm.

The others all groaned in agreement, too spent from the freeze to open their mouths to speak.

"Don't forget that your magic lesson is right after, Mina."

She missed the corner of the shoe rack and slammed her boot on the ground.

"Do you need me to chaperone again, young man?" Enoch teased.

Sebastian huffed a brief, but bitter laugh. "No, but I would like you to all join us in the garden if you have the time. It'll be good to have an extra set of eyes just to see if there's anything I'm missing."

"I get to watch you trip over your own feet?" Wera joked. "Sign me up."

"Oh, he doesn't dance with Mina," Enoch corrected.

"Why not?" Tanir and Wera asked in tandem.

"Well, I— uh—" Sebastian stammered.

"He's training her to fight, not make her debut!" Sir Gargic scoffed.

"E-exactly!"

"Sure, but that combo move they did was lethal!" Wera countered, thrusting her hands forward in a mimic of their combined cast. "You can't tell me that honing those attacks wouldn't be worthwhile."

"I mean, that attack was intense," Enoch said. "But how often would we really need to use something like that?"

"There could be finesse attacks to discover through practice," Tanir offered. "Maybe something like an advanced defensive maneuver?"

"Now, you sound like a general," Sir Gargic said.

"I'd prefer a tactician, if anything."

Sebastian reached into his pocket and pulled out his pocket watch. "Let's talk this over as we eat, shall we? We should be mindful of the time."

"Fine by me. I'm starving," Wera said as she led them down the hall.

"Come along, Mina," Sebastian called over his shoulder, clearly catching her attempt to linger behind. "Let's eat."

She let his command puppet her legs for her as the idea of dancing with Sebastian whittled away at what little clear thought she had left.

The brilliant crimson of the curry should have been enough to bring her back into reality, but instead, it only reminded her of the red that flushed across Sebastian's face at the notion of her naked earlier that morning. Was that a good thing or a bad thing? And why did she care if it was?

Damn Wera. Her considerations were spreading.

"Are you finished?"

Sebastian's voice, closer to her than before, pulled her out of her head. Mina looked down to find her bowl empty, and the others around the table long gone.

"What?" Mina asked, looking at his figure in the doorway, but keeping her focus pointedly at the well-worn knees of his plaid, brown slacks.

"Are you finished dinner?" Sebastian clicked his pocket watch open yet again, its metallic chime goading her like birdsong to a cat. "If so, let's head to the garden."

Mina inhaled deeply as she stood, hoping the rush of air in her lungs would press against her heart and suffocate it until it beat at a reasonable rate.

She followed him out the door and down the hall, still unable to manage lifting her head and looking directly at him. Seeing the back of his head would be too much to bear. She wouldn't be able to help but *consider* what it would feel like to run her fingers through his hair.

"Dammit," Sebastian stopped in the middle of the hall, looking at his watch. "Mina?"

"That's my name," she grumbled.

"I need you to check on something for me. Head up to the third floor and enter the room to the left of my study."

The threads of his command tugged at her feet insistently.

"What am I checking specifically?"

"Umm... it's hard to describe. You'll know it when you see it. Just go quickly. But not too quickly! Go whatever pace will get you there in exactly..." Sebastian glanced at the pocket watch again, "...three minutes and twenty-five seconds from now."

The strings pulled taut, spinning her around on her heels and setting her off on a brisk pace down the hall. Perhaps she should have been more cautious, more wary about whatever lay waiting for her in this room based on Sebastian's uncertainty, but the relief she felt from leaving his presence eclipsed the notion entirely.

She passed the other study rooms in the hall that held Sebastian's, their doors bearing distinct placards: the crest of Lanholde on Sir Gargic's, a needle and spool of thread on Tanir's, and on the door to the left of Sebastian's interlocking cogs... nothing.

Well, nothing for that moment at least, for as she reached for the door handle the placard began to change. A bright orange spark appeared with a pop and traveled across it with a searing hiss, leaving a thin trail of burnt wood in its wake.

Mina glanced down on either side of the hall for any sign of Sebastian, even listened briefly for another heartbeat or his familiar footsteps, but came up empty.

The hissing rose in pitch, bringing Mina's attention back to the door in time to see the spark leap off it and burst into a million pieces. She raced forward to stomp the embers out as they fell, only for them to vanish before they even touched the floor.

She looked up to assess the damage:

A wood-burnt violin.

Sebastian's command tugged her arm up towards the door handle, but it didn't have to. She was more than willing to enter it.

Mina froze in the doorway, mouth agape at the amber-dipped music shop in front of her. Half of her expected a sunset-colored clerk to come up and greet her, ask her if she was looking to purchase anything in particular, or try to upsell her on a new fiddle.

But as she stepped deeper into the room — weaving around the string instruments that hung from the ceiling, running her fingers across the keys on an upright piano against the wall — and came across a luthier's workbench, a desk settled beneath an endless rotating bookshelf filled with sheet music, and a full-length mirror the perfect height to check one's posture, she realized it was not a shop but a study.

Why hadn't Sebastian mentioned this? He knew better than anyone that she—

"...and the third is for areas of individual study."

All hope of slowing her heart rate flew out the window. He hadn't mentioned the study because it hadn't existed before that moment. It didn't need to. There was no individual who studied music in his troop.

Not until she came along.

What other need was there to build a music study that made a point to have veins of amber running through the wood furnishings, polished to perfection to burn beautifully in the light?

Legs shaking, fearful of her realization, she approached the piano and touched its keys once more.

No pain.

She braced herself, and began to play the opening notes to "'Til the Dawn". The piano's clear and well-turned chords hummed through the air and her chest.

No pain.

The hum lingered in her bones long after the notes faded. Her newfound smile spread a bit wider, gaining a small amount of ground against the curse that stilled her face.

She raced downstairs, overcome with the sudden need to see him, to confirm that this wasn't some trick of the mind, that she hadn't fallen asleep at the dinner table and landed into another dream.

She found him in the garden, the others — even Wera who was supposed to be bathing — were all scattered about alongside him, overtly busying themselves.

"A music study?!" she shrieked, drawing everyone but Sebastian's attention as he continued to peruse the collection of boulders leading down to the garden's stream.

"Yes. It's new." He reached down and pulled some flowers from between the stones. "I command you to use it and its contents freely. Just as you do the rest of this commorancy." He held the flowers out to her. "Is this the soapwort you were telling me about the other day?"

"For what purpose?" Mina pressed.

Sebastian kept his head down, hiding his face from her view.

"For the laundry. You said that they—"

"Not the soapwort, dammit!" she snapped, her smile washing from her face in annoyance. "The music study!"

"Oh. Well," he continued to pick the flowers, hands trembling lightly. "No purpose really. The Northern Practitioner's Music Club is always looking for new members."

"I didn't apply to any club."

"I know. Unfortunately, the Guild requires all apprentices to join at least one club. You can switch, though. I bounced around a few myself before I found my fit with the Tinkerer's Collective." Sebastian stood, yet still kept his face turned away as he fell into a ramble. "I figured the music club wouldn't irk you too much. They needed proof of musical talent, however, so I will admit I had to record you playing your violin from outside your room the other day. I did not enjoy doing so, but commanding you to play for me felt... wrong. Not to mention, if you had known what was going on, there could have been unplanned for—"

"What do you mean by *apprentice?*" she interrupted before he could slip deeper into one of his thought spirals.

That turned his head. Sebastian turned to face her, complexion entirely flushed red.

"Don't take it as if I'm your superior or anything!" he blurted, voice rising in pitch and speed. "It was just easier for paperwork's sake, and I am teaching you magic so it is a legitimate title. B-but I don't think that I know more than you or that I'm responsible for you! It was just a formality!"

"Since when?"

"Uh, w-well," Sebastian fumbled for his pocket watch. "Since about fifteen minutes and forty-two seconds ago? Unless you're asking about the official application. That was submitted about f-four days ago." He swallowed nervously as his gaze darted across her face, trying to gauge her reaction.

Four days ago. Right after she had shown him how horrible she could truly be. He had seen her slaughter hundreds without so much as batting an eye, seen her rage get the best of her, and still decided to tie their fates even tighter together. He kept talking with her, kept offering to hone her skills, make her world a little better, despite the frustrations she clearly caused him.

Mina could sense her mind closing in on the true reason behind his actions as snippets of old stories, poems, and lyrics telling tales of good people and their deeds attached themselves to her memories of Sebastian.

The Baker closing his beloved shop to travel by The Butcher's side.

A monk who traveled across the continent, selling books of poetry penned by her deceased sister so that her name would not be forgotten.

Songs of hope and sunshine, sung by a woman well past the point of having children of her own, to a scared little girl she could not hold to comfort.

Mina stopped herself before she dove too deep, fearing that if she jumped in the waves she made, they would wash it all away... or that as soon as she touched it, it would freeze and cloud its surface with thick permafrost. Instead, she let herself study it, revealing not her eyes of gray and slate hair but gentle eyes of brown and hair of blazing amber studying her back.

Considering her, for much longer than she could have ever imagined.

Mina smiled softly, smaller than the one she'd been trying to expand, but somehow stronger in conviction, and met Sebastian's worried gaze.

"This is unnecessary," she said.

She gladly bore the sting of watching Sebastian's face soften, worry fading away to fondness, as a delicate smile, one even The God of Art themselves couldn't capture, bloomed across his lips.

"Not to me," he replied.

A cool breeze brushed across her cheek, a cruel reminder of the warmth she missed. Her heartbeat pounded in her ears as her skin hummed electric, just like that first dream; that wonderful misremembrance.

What's one more burn from him? she thought as the breeze drove her one step forward...

... and her curse sundered her mind apart.

Mina stumbled backwards, clutching at her skull as a force, more powerful than a thousand barrels of gunpowder, ruptured inside of her. Her vision went white, ears ringing so sharply she wanted to tear their drums out.

Then it was gone.

"Mina?" Sebastian called from a few dozen yards away, the others now standing beside him, watching her cautiously from across the garden.

That hadn't been a stumble. Her body had fled from him on its own. She ran her hand across her face to remove the blood she was sure ran down her cheeks, but found her hands clean. Her stomach turned. This wasn't like the inflictions she was used to. This was a wholly new punishment.

"Did I say something wrong or?"

"No," she hollered back, surprisingly even despite how badly her body trembled.

"Well, ya sure did bolt like he did!" Sir Gargic added.

"I don't know what happened!" she admitted.

"Well..." Sebastian carded a hand through his hair and tugged at his roots. "Can you come back?"

"If I'm told to."

He nodded absentmindedly, "Alright. Come back here."

Mina conjured the wind at her heels and returned to him in three long leaps.

"Tell me what you just experienced," he said with a sigh.

Mina's teeth cemented together, and she looked at Sebastian as helplessly as she could manage. He closed his eyes in acknowledgment, inhaling deeply as he frowned.

Her heart ached at the sight.

"Mina, dear," Tanir spoke. "Did something frighten you?"

She tore her eyes away from Sebastian. "Frighten me?"

"You went from smiling to terrified," Enoch said.

"Do you even know how badly you're shaking right now?" Wera asked.

"I know I am!" Mina snapped at her, frustrated with herself, with the things she could not control. "But it's not because I'm scared!"

"It's alright." Sebastian exhaled. "It's all alright." He opened his eyes and his frown curved into a sad smile that pained her heart even more. "I believe you. I know I've thrown a lot of information and a lot of new things at you in a very short amount of time. How about we take an hour to unwind, then you and I can meet back here for your lessons?"

"I can handle it now," she insisted, not wanting to disappoint him any more than she clearly had.

"I was going to suggest an hour delay anyway. Take the time to explore the music study."

Her heels were turned for her, and she stomped towards the garden door.

"I'm not upset with you either!" he shouted after her. "I really was planning—"

The door slammed shut behind her, cutting him off.

Mina stomped through the halls and up the stairs in brooding silence until Sebastian's command carried her into the music study.

Then she screamed.

She didn't care if they heard her. She wanted them to hear. Wanted her scream to pierce through the planes and shred the ears of the bitch who cursed her.

Hadn't enough been ruined? Hadn't her punishment been served twice-fold by now?

Her hands shook with rage, with the need to tear the world apart, gut the cancers that had the gall to taint joyous things, and remake it in her image. The walls of instruments and compositions, of an endless potential for beauty, now mocked her. Sebastian had worked so hard to give her such beautiful things — such beautiful things just for her hands to wield — only to have it thrown back in his face.

His frustration, disappointment, sadness fueled her madness.

How dare She?

The dark parts of her roiled as her hands blackened.

How dare She?

Mina stepped further into the room, placing a hand on her iron necklace.

Her fingers curled around its band.

How dare—

Twang!

The violins' strings snapped from her freezing aura as she walked past them, drawing her focus not only to them but to the mirror behind them.

A stranger stared back at her.

A creature that the naive would call ethereal when the right term would be eldritch. Skin the dark blue of a long winter's night, hair spun from snow, and pupilless eyes of blue ice; if it were not for silver chain-print scars that marred the near-perfect flesh, Mina would have thought it was Her.

She yanked her hand away from her necklace and brought it to her cheek.

So this is what She had sought to make her into.

How dare She?

So this had been what Sebastian had seen. This terrible, horrible creature.

Yet, he still approached it.

Still approached her.

Despite everything.

Mina blinked and found herself in the mirror.

Despite everything.

Her anger morphed into something different. Perhaps right now she could not turn dreams into reality, could not shape the world how she wished, but just two weeks ago she could not smile. Staying alongside Sebastian carried the promise of someday. Of loosened chains, and a whole new life.

And until that someday, Mina wasn't going to let Her take away what little she did have.

She took the damaged violins and sat them on the workbench, making note to repair them after her lesson with Sebastian finished, then took a seat at the piano. It had been a while since she played, but her hands still knew the keys and had a thousand new songs to try.

Bright, cheery ones that sounded of bird song and spring.

Songs that were never sung in the palace of ice Mina had been forced to call home.

Songs that She could never take away.

🜁

"Where are the others?"

Mina returned to an empty garden, a gramophone, and a Sebastian weaving springs of lavender into a wreath.

"They were really only here to see how you reacted to the study. They helped me with the idea. I hope you're not too cross with them over it."

"Who said I was cross?" Mina sat next to him and plucked a few stems for herself. "My posture is quite straight."

Sebastian snorted back a laugh.

Silence hung heavy between them. Even the babbling stream was quieted by it.

"You'd tell me if you were, wouldn't you?" he asked, a lilting waver behind it.

"If I'm told to," she replied, then added. "Unfortunately."

"Unfortunately?"

"Things that are forced don't often read as true," she said. "Words can be forced, reactions can be forced."

"I've seen it," he said. "Sometimes something says 'no' for you." He threaded another stem into the chain. "I'm trying not to be like that."

Mina looked around the ground beside her and, spotting a patch of newly sprouted stinging nettle, plucked a couple of sprigs. She rolled them up into a little ball and packed it inside her cheek.

"I've noticed," she said. The sharp pain as the admittance pinched her throat subsided quickly against the nettle's anti-inflammatories.

Sebastian's hand slipped, dropping a stem. "Oh."

"I played the piano. It's in tune." She swallowed the nettle as she changed the subject.

"The music club does take care of their instruments." He picked up the dropped flower and tried weaving it in again.

"Their instruments?"

"All of those instruments are on loan from the club and some of them are actively in rotation. The instruments on the hooks and shelves will change out as other members of the club use them. They'll only leave if they're back in their original place, so if there's an instrument you think you'll use a lot, just don't put it back where you found it."

"Then I'll need to fix those violins quickly," Mina mumbled.

"What happened to them?"

She took a deep breath, bolstering herself. He wasn't afraid of what she was. She shouldn't be, either.

"A change in temperature."

"Ah."

"The strings were the only things that snapped, so..." She tied the final two lavender stems together around her wrist, and shook her arm to test the bracelet she fashioned's hold. "... an easy fix."

"Best that we get started on our lesson, then." Sebastian stood and tossed the wreath of lavender on top of her head.

Mina closed her eyes and smiled as its smell rained over her.

"Enoch found this encyclopedia of dance styles in one of his libraries for you to use." He magically pulled a thick textbook out of the small back pocket of his pants. "Come take a look and tell me which one you think you could focus your magic through."

She stood and walked over to join him by the gramophone, picking up the book after he set it down. She leafed through the pages idly, watching Sebastian reach into the inside pocket of his jacket and pull out a small stack of records.

"Are the pants for books and pocket watches, while the jacket is for records and teapots?" she asked.

Sebastian stilled, "Are the pants for...", and turned to her with that cartoonish expression of confusion that tickled her diaphragm.

"The pockets," she wiggled her finger in the air, pointing it at his jacket and slacks, "hold different things?"

Sebastian blinked away his confusion. "In a sense. It's more like they store things differently."

"Explain."

"Well, with Tanir's help, I've altered my pants' pockets with this fabric that'll shrink down a decently impressive number of objects. The jackets' inner pockets are just a smaller entrance to the Junk Room's pocket dimension. I got it as a gift from the Guild for my 10th membership anniversary."

"What about the outside pockets?"

"Those are just regular pockets."

"Tanir couldn't make them shrinking pockets?"

"She could, but then I'd have nowhere to place the commorancy," he said. "the Junk Room works the same as the library and the music study. It's just a giant storehouse for the Northern Practitioners to leave what they don't need and take what they do. If there's a 'free commorancy' available, then someone's definitely gonna take it, so the inner pockets are a no-go. And you can't put a shrinking thing in a shrinking thing. The magics cancel out and make everything pop back to their normal size."

"That might be useful as a surprise attack," Mina remarked. "Ambush. Boom. Exploding pants."

Sebastian's mouth puckered in a wrinkled smile, nostrils flaring as he held back a laugh. "Pick a damn dance routine, will you?" he said, chuckling between each word.

Content with his reaction, Mina turned her attention to the textbook. She ran a finger down its table of contents, purposefully skipping over the section labeled "Partner Dances", until she settled on something she knew the wizard wouldn't have expected of her.

"Ribbon dancing?" he questioned as she held the page out to him.

"But the wind is the ribbon," she replied.

Sebastian arched an eyebrow and tapped his fingers against his lips in contemplation. "It's an interesting notion. I can see some of the combat applications. What song?"

"Vivari em di Dara Tolmi," she said. "Nataly Amanecer's rendition."

He inhaled deeply and reached into his jacket. "You are full of surprises this evening. That's an unexpectedly modern choice for you."

"She was performing at the Autumn Equinox Festival the last time I went to sell in town. I purchased the sheets to learn the song, but I was contracted to lead a band of hooligans up to Lanholde before I could play it."

Sebastian snickered. "Hooligans, huh?"

He pulled the record out of his pocket and twirled it by the points of its cardstock cover between his fingers. "I haven't heard her take on this song, but I've always liked her work." He placed the record on the turntable and held the needle aloft as it began to spin.

"Ready?" he asked.

Mina sat the textbook down and walked over to a patch of lawn with plenty of room for her to move. "Start the music."

She closed her eyes and rolled her shoulders out as the accordion and guitar greeted each other. She recalled the last time she heard those opening chords, how dull the world around her was back then, how the driving melody poured from the town square's stage and flooded every street, and how as much as she enjoyed the sound she could not express it any more than buying the sheets.

She'd let herself enjoy it now as much as she could, even if that enjoyment felt like it was captured in one of her drawings rather than felt. The wind pooled around her ankles without needing to be prodded. As she raised her arm to the sound of the cello and second guitar layering in, it willingly snaked up her body to swirl in the palm of her hand; just as eager to begin as she was.

Though the training had been grueling, torturous — with every correction of her form delivered with the crack of a cane or jab of a frozen livestock prod — ribbon dancing had been her favorite to learn. There were no grand ballets or choreography standards she was forced to perfect. The only rule was that the movement had to make sense, had to be a proper conduit to elevate the music beyond auditory sense.

As the alto's crooning stretched out of the gramophone, the wind outstretched from her fingertips, turning it into a spiraling ribbon of air as she circled her wrist. Her control was contingent, fragile, one errant thought and she'd lose it. This wind was a spiteful thing, not unlike herself at times, so she bowed to its whims as she took her first step forward, letting it guide her as they both got lost in the music.

Despite all of her agility and athleticism, Mina had never felt lighter on her feet. Perhaps it was because the curse of chains around her had lost some of its hold. Perhaps it was the wind guiding her figures, allowing her mind to not think for once in a very long time. She did not care for the cause, for she was simply living in the symptom: twirling, flipping, tumbling as weightless as the ribbon of air she wielded.

The music picked up pace. The singer praised the painted skies of sunset as a symbol of liberation, the promise of freedom granted by the dark shelter of night. Pivoting penchés into arabesques, aerial cartwheels into side saltos, Mina spun faster and faster to match the tempo.

To praise the sunset, that beautiful, beautiful sunset dripping liquid copper to bathe the world in its amber light. Just as much a promise of freedom to her as flames, and embers, and sparks. The wind turned heavy in her grasp, pulling her into tight chassé turns as the song reached its end.

Her final pose was stopped short by a sudden warble of surprise. Mina jolted to a stop, eyes shooting open just in time to see Sebastian spinning towards her. Her control slipped in her panic, prompting the wild wind to wrap around them and send them tumbling to the ground.

Mina gasped in pain as billows of steam clouded the last ribbons of dissipating wind. Sebastian, as dizzy as he was, lifted as much of himself off of her as possible.

"Sorry," he panted, eyes struggling to focus. "Are you still steaming?"

"No," she said, making the mistake of looking down to see his legs bent on either side of hers, rather than his arms. His legs were long, but she hadn't expected his thighs to have so much muscle to them. Next time they were in the hot spring, she'd have to pay closer attention.

"Okay good. Do you have any herbs on you?"

"No, but—" Mina tore her gaze away from him to search the grass beside her. She ripped up a handful of a wood sorrel's false shamrocks and shoved it into her mouth. "Now I do," she mumbled.

Sebastian blinked the last of his dizzy spell away. "Close your eyes."

She did, stomach fluttering. The warmth of his body so close to hers, the sound of his ragged breath and rapid heartbeat, filled the gap in her senses.

"That was fantastic!" he praised.

Mina winced from the burst of pain at the base of her brain, but her small smile remained on her face.

"It was wild. I could only catch glimpses of the wind from time to time when you picked up some brush, but the shift in the air was massive. When you did those tight, circle twirls, objects were drawn towards you. Those big loops pushed things back. A couple of the flicks even nicked some blades of grass! And that last move!" Sebastian laughed. "I didn't even see that lasso coming!"

"Neither did I," Mina said. "The wind did that on its own."

"Oh?"

"All of that 'control'? I wasn't really controlling any of it besides the dancing part, but even then, I let the wind's pull guide what moves I made next."

"Open your eyes."

She did, and found Sebastian staring back at her with intense scrutiny.

"Are you being sarcastic?" he asked.

"No."

The scrutiny held firm, but his brows folded in confusion. "By control, do you mean you listened to it? Like how your 'tuning fork' works?"

"Not in the tuning fork way, but listening, touching."

"Touching?"

"It brushes against my right ankle, instinct says to use that as the planted foot for the next turn. It circles around my wrist, I know to circle it myself."

Sebastian stared at her.

"It's a new thing," she explained, needing to clear his confusion. "The arrows don't work that way. I tell it what to do, in that case, subconsciously. Fire doesn't do that?"

He pursed his lips and turned his scrutiny inward.

"I mean... there are urges," he said. "They're not as bad as they used to be, but when I was younger and trying to control my magic by suppressing it, it would feel like the heat would burn me alive if I didn't let some flames out."

Mina steadied her breathing as she tried to keep her focus from drifting away from his face to his arms on either side of her head: an image that would surely drive her back into that lake. Back into the heat of his hands trailing down her body, the embers of his tongue dancing across her own. Burning alive? He couldn't have picked a worse choice of words at that moment.

"Perhaps it's because you're channeling your magic from an external source, while mine is internal." His fingers tapped against the grass as his pursed lips wiggled back and forth in thought. He groaned and hung his head down, amber hair less than an inch away from tickling her nose. "If only someone in the Guild would get back to me!"

"Back to you about what?" she asked.

"I said I'd submit a query to the Northern Practitioners, remember? I still have yet to hear anything back."

"But you've heard back on other things?"

Sebastian lifted his head to look up at her. "I got your music room in order, didn't I?"

Her chest tightened, heart slamming against it trying to escape her encroaching fever... or trying to leap to him. Mina closed her eyes, remembering the pain, the trembling. She did not want the chains to pull her from him. She did not want Sebastian to think she feared him. Not in this moment.

"I know," she said, though it made her teeth ache. "As we climb higher, teleportation magics find no purchase. The magic's too wild for the leylines to connect properly. It's unexpected that you've been able to use the Junk Room for this long, let alone any means of outside contact."

"That's because we're in a pocket realm," he explained. "Leylines bolster magics that help you cross between the realms, but not across the same one. So this baby," Sebastian knocked on the ground. "Is more stable than she's ever been."

"Clementine?" she asked. "Is that what you named her?"

"How did you—"

"After Bormir and Eirlys attacked. That's the word you told Tanir to use to expand the commorancy," she said. "Unless that's a fruit you... eat a lot of?"

Sebastian chuckled. "It's a nickname a childhood friend of mine called me once. After my hair."

"Your hair?" she asked, though she could already guess the answer.

"It's orange. Close to the color of clementines, but mine's a little less bright, a little more warm. I'd say it's closer to the color oak trees' leaves turn in autumn. Some people will call me a redhead, which might confuse you a bit."

"It's not red," she stated.

"Exactly," he agreed. "You'd be able to see it now if it was."

I can see it now. It was the first one.

Her heart yearned to tell him, but her mind thought better of it, terrified of the consequences. She'd tell him eventually, make up some lie one day that she could see it. But not now.

It wasn't right to now.

"Mina?" he said as she remained quiet.

"That's my name," she said.

"Tell me why your eyes are closed," he commanded.

A hundred answers came to mind, but there was only one she could speak. "You're too close."

"I'm—" Sebastian paused, finally realizing what position they had been speaking to each other so casually in. Mina both missed the shade his body gave and relished in its retreat as he jumped back. She opened her eyes at the thud of his ass hitting the ground in front of her and propped herself up on her elbows.

She expected to find him staring at her, wide-eyed and worried, but seeing his face completely flushed scarlet was new.

"I didn't realize," he said gravely.

Mina's diaphragm seized sharply, drawing a snort out of her as a smile crossed her lips. "I noticed."

The red on his face burned even brighter, and two plumes of smoke billowed out from between his fingers as his palms singed the grass beneath them. The smoke wafted up into his face, breaking him out of whatever trance she had put him in, and he hopped to his feet.

"We should get back to your lesson!" he blurted, accent slipping in as he turned on his heels and headed back to the still-playing gramophone. "Try it with your eyes open this time. Do you have a different song in mind?"

"No." She grabbed another handful of wood sorrel and shoved it in her mouth. "Dealer's choice."

🜁

Mina couldn't sleep.

It had been hours since her magic lesson ended. Hours since she came to understand that her considerations, that her growing yearning for her dreams to become reality, were for naught. Yet, her body and subconscious mind fought against it, slowly building her fever back up again as the clock ticked.

She tried her best to soothe it. Stripped herself of her clothes, stuck her head under the tap turned cold, and now she laid on top of her sheets, staring at the ceiling and counting every tick of the clock in a futile attempt to keep her mind from wandering.

And when it did wander, she couldn't decide whether she wanted to touch him or be touched by him. She ran her fingers in circles on top of her sheets, wishing they were running up his arms, tingling his skin just like he had done to her while they worked in his study — anything she could do to see how flustered she could make him, how bright the scarlet in his face could shine. But then her fingers twisted in the bedsheets, wanting to be entwined in his hair as his hands and lips explored every inch of her skin.

Mina pulled her pillow over her face and screamed into it in frustration.

If this is what being turned on was, being aroused as so many of the stories she read had described, it was no wonder why people went to such great lengths to relieve it. That relief usually came from someone else, however, but the echoes of Wera's teasing prompted another solution.

Mina slipped her hand between her thighs, something she had tried before after a story had described the act of masturbation in detail to no avail, and flinched in surprise to feel how wet she was. Slick, juices, dripping, damp; now she understood all those descriptors. She glided her palm over her folds, sending a shiver through her body, just like rolling her hips forward on Sebastian's thigh had done in her dream.

She bucked against her hand, palm picking up its pace as she chased the feeling, picturing him above her in the garden.

Instead of just hovering above her, taunting her unintentionally as he rambled on and on about her magic, he took advantage of their position. Mina ran her free hand in between her breasts, imagining Sebastian dropping kisses up her sternum, amber hair tickling her nose as he climbed higher and higher, slotting his thigh between her legs as her lips slotted between his.

She pressed the heel of her hand against her clit on instinct, sending a bolt of pleasure so fast and ferocious through her body that her thighs snapped shut, crushing her palm. Mina growled in frustration; she needed something sturdier. She snatched the pillow covering her face and placed it between her legs. A lilted, breathy moan escaped her lips as she thrust her hips forward to test it.

Mina flipped herself over, burying her face into the blankets beneath. Tanir overhearing her playing the violin was one thing, but this? She'd read how people moaned, whimpered, screamed during, but she never realized how little control they had over it.

Her hips writhed against the pillow, finding a more satisfying rhythm with the mattress putting weight against each thrust. She dove back into her fantasy, her mouth full of the taste of bergamot, a burning palm slowly turning her nipple into a glowing ember, a hand pressed against her back urging her to use his body to her content.

A sensation, not unlike the threads of Sebastian's commands, built, winding tighter and tighter, wringing wanton moans and shuddering gasps out of her throat. It was terrifying, but she didn't want to stop — couldn't stop — not until the fever subsided. Not until she had her fill of him.

Sebastian panted in her ear, just as shaky as she was, as he broke away from her lips and whispered, "That's my girl."

The lightning strike raced through her body once more at his praise, bringing not pain and deafness as it had before, but a trembling release. The tension snapped, rippling across her flesh, shaking one last desperate cry out of her. Mina stilled, breathing deeply as the fever subsided and left her eyelids heavy in its wake.

Relief, tenfold to floating on warm water but just as fleeting, coaxed sleep to wrap its arms around her, claiming her before her mind could stoke the embers once again.

XVI
Bastion of Flame

Mina took a hot bath when she awoke, finding that with as much torture as it put her through, she missed the lingering warmth of her "fever". Thoughts of Sebastian still flitted through her mind at random moments: while brushing her teeth, retying her chest bindings, stretching out the odd crick in her neck. Granted, the dozens of portraits of him that hung above her desk — watching her with a dozen different expressions — didn't help matters, but Mina had grown used to it. The room would feel off without them now.

She slung her pack over her shoulders, lighter now that she decided to leave her violin and beddown gear behind, and inspected the crown of lavender she'd hung on the back of her door to dry. It would take until they reached Lanholde for it to dry completely, but perhaps she'd mention something to Sebastian. Asking if she could use the oven for it would do the trick.

"Morning, Mina," Tanir greeted as she walked into the kitchen.

"Beastie," Sir Gargic grunted.

She looked at the clock on the wall, it was ten minutes past their usual breakfast start. One of the others being late was expected but three?

"Where are the others?" Mina asked as she sat down beside Tanir, adding to the table's imbalance.

"Damn kids were up late as hell last night working on their damn atlas." Sir Gargic crossed his arms over his chest. "As for Windenhofer, he's probably caught up in his study again."

"He shouldn't be. The jewelry box has been solved."

"He's got more work to do besides that damn box," he snipped. "He's got a contract to fulfill, just like you do."

"Perhaps we should eat without them," Tanir said. "Your hunger's making you sound like a jealous girlfriend, Sir Gargic."

"Well, perhaps if your employer focused his attention on his work rather than *extracurricular* pursuits, we wouldn't have to make that choice."

The kitchen door opened and Mina turned towards it, hoping that Sir Gargic's grievances had summoned Sebastian, but instead found the deep, dark eye-bags of Enoch and Wera.

They froze mid-step, tired eyes squinting slightly as they looked at Sebastian's empty chair.

"Did he eat and leave already?" Enoch asked, voice husky and creaking on every syllable.

"No, unfortunately," Tanir answered with a sigh of annoyance.

"There's no way we beat him here," Wera droned, voice nearly as deep as Enoch's. "He went to bed hours ago."

"And when did you two head to bed?" Sir Gargic pressed.

"We didn't," Wera answered and gave Enoch a slight shove to coax him into the room.

"We have a mountain to climb," Mina stated.

"And Tanir's got a tincture of invigoration," she retorted, crawling onto the bench.

"And I've told you both time and time again, that's only for emergencies," Tanir scolded.

Enoch slid his arms and chest onto the table. "But this is an emergency, Tani. We have a mountain to climb."

Mina stood and headed towards the door.

"Where are you going?" Sir Gargic asked.

"We're fifteen minutes behind. I'm going to get the wizard."

"Then I'm coming with ya. Let him have a piece of my mind about—"

"It'll only take a minute. Order breakfast, jealous girlfriend." Mina summoned the wind to her heels and raced out of the room.

The picture frames hummed as she skidded to a stop in front of Sebastian's study.

She knocked.

No answer.

She knocked again.

No answer.

Mina closed her eyes and placed her ear to the door. The whirring, bubbling, ticking, standard tinkerings of his workshop sang behind it, but Sebastian's footsteps and heartbeat were distinctly missing from their chorus.

"Still sleeping?" Mina asked herself before taking off again, racing to Sebastian's bedroom at the end of the second-floor hall.

She knocked.

And a stilted groan, as if someone had been startled, answered back.

She knocked again.

"Hold on," Sebastian choked out, so muffled and strained that if it weren't for her superb hearing, she would have missed it.

"Wizard?" Mina called. "Are you coming?"

A strangled, clipped moan replied, much louder than his murmurs. She must have just woken him up...

Or he was injured.

"Wizard?" she asked again.

Silence.

Mina tugged on the door handle and found it locked.

"What are you doing?!" Sebastian squealed.

"You sound injured!" she said.

"I-I'm fine!" he stammered, too unsure to put her mind at ease.

"Then open the door!"

"I— hoo— I really can't right now." His tone was all over the place, the rhythm off, accent much thicker. "B-but I assure you I am," he inhaled shakily, "fine."

"I don't believe you." She shook the handle some more, listening for any weaknesses in the frame and hinges she could exploit with her strength.

"Mina!"

There was the frantic rustle of thrown bedsheets, the squeak of mattress springs, but Mina was too focused on the soft click of a loosened leaf of the upper right hinge to pay it any mind until the handle was pulled taut.

"The hell are you doing?!" Sebastian shouted, a shrill sound halfway between a shriek and a hiss. She could hear his ragged breathing through the door as if it were in her ear. His heart was racing too fast for her comfort.

Something was wrong with him.

"Breaking the door down!"

"I told you I'm fine!"

"You don't sound it!" she snapped. "If you were, you wouldn't have been late to breakfast!"

She tugged the handle, hard, lurching it against Sebastian's hold.

"Fuckin—" he swore.

Mina yelped in pain as the door handle turned bright orange in her grasp. She yanked her hands away before burns could mar them.

"What the hell?!"

"Mina! Go and eat breakfast!" he yipped.

The threads of his commands seized her, turned her feet against her, and pulled her down the hall.

"I swear to The Gods if you're dying in there right now, I'll fucking kill you!" Mina screamed, shaking the frames that hung on the walls just as hard as her wind would.

The others jumped as she threw the kitchen door open. Mina snapped her head towards the utensils, and they shook under her icy glare.

"Fix me a damn plate."

A platter piled high with eggs and pancakes appeared at her place at the table before she sat.

"S-so," Wera chattered. "T-the c-c-cold s-s-shoulder'sss s-still a thing, h-huh?"

"He's a stubborn fucking idiot," Mina snipped as she shoveled a huge forkful of flapjacks into her mouth.

Sir Gargic shifted in his seat and trilled his lips.

"I'm the jealous girlfriend?" he mumbled.

"Got something to say, Knight?" Mina turned her fury his way.

Tanir clamped a hand over his mouth before he could answer. "No, he doesn't."

"So— uh—" Enoch interjected. "I hate to ask, but... is Sebastian coming?"

“I don’t fucking know. Fucking asshole sounds as if he’s goddamn dying, I try to see if he’s dying, and he fucking burns my fucking hands and commands me to ‘go and eat breakfast’,” she imitated his voice poorly and stabbed the yolk of one of her eggs, taking small satisfaction in watching it ooze. “So here I am, eating my goddamn breakfast.”

“He burned your hands?” Tanir asked. “That’s not like him.”

“I know that!” The bladed hand of worry wrapped around her heart, making it harder for it to fuel her anger. “But he’s too fucking bullheaded to put two and two together himself.”

The kitchen door creaked open. Mina kept her eyes trained on the slowly widening crack until the daggers she was staring found purchase in brown eyes.

“See?” Sebastian swallowed nervously, opening the door a little wider to show his full body. “Told you I’m fine.”

Mina took her fork and threw it, burying it into the door, further in towards the center than she planned, as Sebastian pulled it towards him as a shield. The kitchen replaced her fork immediately.

Sebastian peered around the door. “Oh. You aimed wide.”

Mina turned her attention to her pancakes.

“You burnt her hands?” Tanir asked, her tone sharp and judging.

“It was that hot?!” He swung the door open and rushed into the room, footsteps still their familiar rhythm even with their rising tempo and crescendo. “Mina.”

“I’m eating.”

“Show me your hands.” She was forced to drop her fork onto the table with a clatter and raise her hands back over her head.

“You really are commanding today, aren’t you, Wizard?” she bristled.

She could feel the heat off his hands from where they hovered just around hers, stopping just before he grabbed them at her remark.

“You’re right.” He pulled his hands away. “I’m sorry for hurting you. I didn't realize it was that hot.”

Mina lowered her hands, colder than she cared for them to be at the moment, and went to grab her fork when the side of her face lit aflame.

Sebastian leaned down, face barely an inch away from her cheek. “But next time when I tell you I’m fine, don’t try to tear my bedroom door off its hinges.” Whether it was sleep adding gravel to his voice or a purposeful change in timbre did not matter, goosebumps still crawled up her arms from it. “Deal?”

“No deal.” Mina suppressed a shudder and took a defiant bite of her pancakes.

“Mina.”

“Didn’t you almost break into my room the other day?” she said. “Seems a bit hypocritical to ask me not to do the same.”

“That was different. You weren’t answering, and you never not answer.”

“And you were making strange noises,” Mina leaned away a bit so she could turn and look at him clearly, “and you’ve never made noises like that.”

Mina was new to noticing people blushing, but she was damn certain no human in the entire mortal realm had ever turned such a brilliant shade of red so quickly as Sebastian did.

"Strange noises, huh?" Wera remarked.

Enoch groaned, "I'm too tired for this. Sebastian, I respect you immensely, but could you please stop making an ass of yourself and eat breakfast so we can go? The sooner you're done, the sooner we can start climbing, and the sooner we start climbing, the sooner I can go to sleep."

🜁

The wind threw the front door back in Mina's face.

She stared at it for a moment, blinking as she tried to compute what had happened, then went to open it once again.

The wind shrieked in defiance, grabbed the door in its icy grip, and tried to tear it apart for daring to stand in its way. Mina held her footing, digging her heels in, and yanked the door back before it could be swept into the swirling gray vortex outside.

"Climbing will have to wait," she stated.

"How long?" Sir Gargic asked impatiently.

"I'm not certain. A day at the very least," she replied, pulling her hands away slowly after she locked the door, just to make sure it wouldn't shoot open. "Maybe more. Worst I've been through out here was a week."

Sir Gargic closed his eyes like he was in pain and rubbed at his wrinkled forehead. "A week?"

"That's what I said."

"It can't be a fucking week, Windenhofer," he sang his annoyance.

"Sometimes nature has other plans, Sir Gargic," Sebastian replied. "But I'm sure that was a rare case, right, Mina?"

"It's only happened twice," she said. "You don't have anything that can change the weather, do you, Wizard?"

He pursed his lips, thinking for a moment, then shrugged his shoulders. "Nope. Looks like we'll just need to hunker down and keep an eye out for when it clears."

"So I took that tincture for nothing?" Enoch asked, looking more tired than he had been slouched over the kitchen table despite how jittery his body was.

"Not for nothing!" Wera cheered, much more chipper than Mina had ever seen her. She threw her arm behind his neck and brought him down to her level. "Now, we can finish the addendum on parallel sinkholes!"

"A day off would be nice," Tanir mused. "Good for our bodies to take a break, and for me to get some good, solid hours in on the quilt I'm making."

"A new quilt?" Sebastian asked excitedly.

"Mhmm," Tanir smiled. "I'm doing another landscape. Got the inspiration for the design a few days back."

"Guess I'll go and send word to the Capitol that there might be a delay," Sir Gargic huffed and started to walk away.

"Sir Gargic?" Sebastian called after him.

The knight stopped and looked back.

"How about a game of chess later tonight? Best out of three?"

Sir Gargic's beard bristled back and forth, it was looking a little less push broom as it started to grow out.

"Alright. You better have some drink in ya though," he said. "I'd like to have a fair shot this time."

Sebastian chuckled. "Duly noted." He turned his attention to Mina. "What about you, Mina?"

"I'll be keeping an eye on the storm," she said.

"The whole day?"

"Until it clears."

"You said it could be up to a week," Tanir said. "You're gonna just wait here for a whole week?"

"I'll eat and sleep and use the facilities. So not a whole week."

"Or you could practice your magic, use the hot spring, read a book..." Wera listed. "There's a lot of not boring options."

"I don't know. She might have the right idea. Sitting down, doing nothing, sounds awful nice right now."

"You're projecting your wants and desires onto someone else again, Enoch."

"Well, if I can't fulfill them, someone has to."

"Why don't you spend your time in the music study? Learn a new instrument perhaps, maybe compose something?" Sebastian suggested.

"Compose something?" she repeated, the idea sparking her interest.

"If you can compose something," Sebastian corrected himself unnecessarily. "I didn't mean to assume."

"I can compose."

"If you don't want to, you don't have to. It's just a suggestion."

"I can compose."

"Alright then," Sebastian nodded as a soft smile crawled up on his face. "Compose something." His gaze lingered on her for a moment before a slight blush colored his cheeks.

Enoch cleared his throat, snapping Sebastian out of whatever thought he was stuck on.

He inhaled sharply and turned on his heels to head up the stairs. "If any of you need me, I should be in my study."

"You got it, boss," Wera saluted as they watched Sebastian walk away. Mina couldn't help but let her gaze linger on his thighs.

Tanir gave a sympathetic sigh. "I think he's forgotten that we're all heading the same way."

"It's hard to keep your bearings straight when you keep falling head over heels," Enoch explained.

"Does he have a concussion or something?" Mina asked.

Wera's lips curved into a wry smile, its cause indiscernible. "Or something."

They headed upstairs and parted ways: Tanir to her sewing room, Wera and Enoch to the library, and Mina to the music study. She paused before she entered, closing her eyes to listen to the bubbling and ticking inside the study next door. The floorboards creaked beneath Sebastian's feet as he rocked back and forth, setting the beat as he hummed through his work.

"...oh ho... what a way to go..." the lyrics slipped out in a half-voiced baritone before devolving back into a hum.

Mina smiled at another flutter in her diaphragm. While the feeling was odd, it wasn't entirely unpleasant. She'd have to remember to ask Tanir about it later.

The instruments had changed, just as Sebastian said. The standards still remained, stings, a piano, some woodwinds and drums, but among them sat more exotic tools. Mina was drawn to a long talharpa, its wood dark and ornate but, as she picked up its bow and ran it across the strings, the deep bass of it felt harsh. It was too low, she needed a baritone, not a bass; something to match the wizardly hum still lingering in her ears.

She scoured the violins, picking up each and studying them intently, searching for one with heavier strings. Ebony wood, so well-worn that patches of varnish had been stripped off by the bow over time; a baritone-tuned violin sported a lion's head carved into the scroll, jaws open mid-roar.

She grabbed its bow, ran it over the strings, and ground her teeth at the out-of-tune shriek it gave.

No wonder such a beautiful instrument had been tossed into a hand-me-down rotation; its original owner had no idea how to care for it. Mina studied it closely and found that its disharmony was not caused by just a few poorly wound strings, but a chin rest pressing unpadded against the body and over-worn pegs that no longer fit snugly in their holes.

She sat down at the workbench and set to fixing, unscrewing the chin rest to place a pad of fresh leather underneath, sanding down and staining a new set of pegs, remembering as much as she could from the hours she'd spent lingering in the luthier's shop as he worked — finding it much easier to wait among the hanging herbs and instruments of the family business than to wander aimlessly around the town drawing unwanted attention.

She ran her bow against the strings and the tension in her shoulders melted at its warm hum. The hum drew her fingers across the fretboard to play the rising half of an f-major arpeggio, conjuring sparks of inspiration that had her running for pen and paper.

Violin for the melody, plucked triplets interwoven across an upright bass, a brush ran across a bodhrán before striking it with the handle like rolling footsteps. Mina bounced back and forth around the study in her attempt to become a one-woman orchestra. A bandura to summon embers, a euphonium to conjure flames, and a hulusi for smoke. The dark ink from the quill looked as if it had burned the unheard concerto onto the parchment as she wrote.

There was an off-beat knock at the door.

"Mina?" Tanir called from outside. "Did you hear the bell? It's lunchtime."

Mina huffed in displeasure as she set her quill down and stomped to the door. She walked right past Tanir as she exited.

"Is something the matter?" she asked as she jogged to catch up with her.

"No."

"You seem disgruntled."

"I was in the middle of composing."

Tanir sighed. "That's what Sebastian was worried about. I'll tell him to rescind the command."

Mina stopped so abruptly, Tanir ran into her back.

"Don't," she wheeled around and snapped.

"Really? You've been working for six hours straight now. Have you even stopped to use the restroom?"

"I'll use it after I eat then go back to work," she said. "I know my limits."

"I understand that, but these commands often supersede those limits, which is what worries us," Tanir explained. "Sebastian wants to allow you to do more, but not at the risk of harming you. What happened yesterday was—"

"My fault."

Tanir's brows furrowed. "Your fault?"

"Commands had nothing to do with it." Mina turned around and resumed walking. "Rescind nothing. Let's eat."

The others were halfway finished eating by the time they arrived. Mina sat down at the table, mind already back in composition mode, running the stanzas she'd written over and over again in her head to make sure the melodies and harmonies were interwoven correctly.

Sebastian's gaze flickered over her before looking to Tanir. "Is everything alright?"

"Just fine. Mina was just deep in her work and didn't hear the bell," she answered as she sat.

Mina glared at the kitchen. The utensils jolted to work on making her meal, and jolted an idea.

Sebastian sighed. "That's what I thought. Mina, if it's my fault you're overworking yourself—"

"Can the utensils leave the kitchen?" she interrupted.

"What?" he asked.

"The utensils. Can they leave the kitchen? Are they trainable?"

"Umm. Sort of? Depends on what you're asking them to do."

"Explain."

"Well, you can't train a spoon to bend in half. Or a rolling pin to bounce on its handle like it's a pogo stick."

"But I can train it to hit something?"

"What? Are you trying to turn our pots and pans against us?" Sir Gargic scoffed.

"If you keep making stupid comments I just might," Mina snipped. "Well, Wizard?"

"Yes, I suppose. What are you—"

"I'm taking them."

"Mina, I'm sure whatever you're working on, we can help—"

"No," she cut Tanir off. "For many reasons."

Mina's meal slid in front of her, and she dug in without looking, too busy studying the utensils and working out how she would use them to care what she was shoveling in her mouth. She couldn't taste it anyways.

"Just give her the utensils, please?" Wera groaned. The heel of her hand pressed firmly against her forehead, keeping her head aloft as she ate. Enoch looked no better with his chin rested on the table, eyes half-lidded and glazed over. The tincture must have worn off, exasperating their exhaustion. "Hearing you argue back and forth is giving me a headache."

"This isn't an argument. They're just looking for answers," Mina explained.

"Then just answer them."

"I am."

"Not really, you just keep asking questions back."

"I'm looking for answers too," she said. "I thought you said you're getting a headache from arguing?"

Wera groaned loudly and dropped her forehead against the table.

"Serves you right," Enoch croaked out.

"Alright, let's focus back in," Sebastian interjected. "What utensils are you asking for?"

"Tongs, tweezers, whisks, ladles, butter knives, and a few forks just in case."

"What the hell will there be left to cook dinner with?!" Sir Gargic squawked.

Sebastian nodded in thought. "Alright. Feel free to take them."

Sir Gargic opened his mouth to protest. Sebastian raised a hand to silence him. "It's been a while since I've cooked. I'll handle dinner tonight."

Mina lifted her plate up to her lips and titled it back, swallowing the rice-based dish in a few gulps before standing.

"Utensils. You heard the wizard. If I named you, follow me."

🜁

"Again."

Mina closed her eyes, listening intently as her makeshift orchestra followed her lead. They'd picked up on her teaching quickly, were remarkably good at keeping rhythm, tune, and tempo, but there was something still off about their performance. Even her playing was lackluster despite her perfect execution. It was as if she were hearing just the surface of the piece, not the depths below it.

Depths she wasn't quite sure how to explore.

"Stop," she commanded, and the utensils froze.

Mina sat down on the floor to think. She closed her eyes again and listened next door, hoping to hear the same hum that inspired the piece, but was only met with lifeless ticking and bubbling.

"He's downstairs cooking, Mina," she muttered to herself. "He has to because you stole half his kitchen supplies."

A baritone hum, measured footsteps, contemplative triplets. Sparks, embers, flame, smoke. Each stave captured the elements perfectly, but the score itself rang just as empty as the wizard's vacant study, untouched and cold.

Mina opened her eyes. It was cold. She was composing a concerto inspired by fire, and yet she played it as if she were handling ice. She stood and picked up her violin, holding out a hand to still the utensils.

Warmth. The amber glow of a fireplace. Hand brushing against hand.

The f-major arpeggio conjured a flutter in her chest, just like the laugh that inspired it.

The rush of warm wind, white-hot immolation, rising steam, her bow became a tool to mold the music to her memories. The utensils, unprovoked by her, fell instep. Perhaps it reminded them of the heat of their kitchen, a signal that it was time for them to work. They played with the same warmth, fueling the bonfires of her crescendos, simmering low on the notes she sustained: kindling to her fire, just as she intended.

She held the final note as long as she could, basking in the goosebumps it raised across her skin, the satisfied buzz it left in its wake.

And when at last it faded, and the utensils laid down their handles, the dinner bell rang.

Mina picked up a quill and scrawled the title at the top of her score, feeling more clever than ever.

"Come along," she said as she tucked the score under her arm. "Bring the instruments. We'll eat dinner and then we'll—"

She barely heard the pang of her violin bouncing off the ground as her vision went white from an explosive surge of pain. Mina reached forward as she fell to her knees, grabbing onto the door handle for dear life, as every nerve in her body screamed in agony.

The pain subsided as quickly as it came, swept away by the sound of a single sheet of paper drifting to the floor.

She blinked rapidly, trying to clear the blur and white from her eyes. The blur faded, but the white...

Mina's stomach dropped as she took in the thick frost that spread across the wooden door up to the ceiling above and onto the floor below, sprouting from the doorknob in her grip. She removed her hand slowly, cautious not to shatter it, and set her sights on gathering her violin and the sheet music that had slipped from beneath her arm.

The utensils clattered in confusion as she set the reassembled score back on her music stand. She took a chisel off her workbench and began to break the ice around the frame.

So the curse didn't make her run away back then, her subconscious had. If she had touched Sebastian then—

Mina exhaled her fears.

I won't let Her win.

This wasn't touching Sebastian, this was something different. She needed to do this, she wanted to do this, she just had to find a way to work around this minor frostbitten setback.

"Come along," she repeated as she pried the door open carefully. "Leave the instruments."

🜂

"You're on time!" Sebastian cheered as she entered the kitchen. "And you brought back our kitchen friends."

Mina stared at Sebastian as the utensils wove through her legs to enter the room.

"Were you," she swallowed to clear the anxiety clogging up her throat, "outside?"

Sebastian cocked his head to the side in question from behind the kitchen counter, sending a small clump of white powder sliding off his bangs and onto his nose. He went crossed-eyed and jerked his head back for a second before chuckling.

"No, it's just flour." He gestured to the kitchen table. "I made pizza!"

"Oh." Mina looked at the large round flatbreads scattered across the table, some with large triangle slices missing as the group helped themselves. "I've never had pizza."

"Well, I'm honored that mine will be your first."

"Even if I can't taste it?"

"Even if you can't taste it."

Mina took her place next to Tanir and looked over the different options.

"This one's plain cheese," Wera said through a mouthful of sauce and dough. "The middle left is sausage. The middle right is vegetable, and the one on the end is spicy salami."

"There's malbec in your one cup," Enoch said. "Didn't want to surprise you like last time."

"You two look less dead," Mina remarked as she grabbed a plain slice.

"I forced them to take a nap because they're children, apparently," Tanir said. "They'll still need a full night's rest, but at least they're less miserable now."

Mina's hum of understanding shifted to a much louder hum of pleasant surprise as she took her first bite.

"Holy shit," she swore as she tried to wrap her head around the onslaught of complex flavors perking her taste buds.

A manic laugh burst out of Sebastian, unlike anything she'd ever heard from him.

"You can taste it?!" he shouted in joyous disbelief.

"I don't know what I'm tasting," she said as she took another, bigger bite. "But I really, really don't hate it." The back of her throat stung from the compliment, but she washed it down with the wine, which was much more palatable when paired with the pizza's sauce and cheese.

She held the glass up towards Enoch and pointed to it. "I get this now."

"You'd really get if you could get drunk off of it," he said.

"How's that go?"

"It's like you're half asleep? Everything slows, your head gets light while your limbs get heavy."

"Sounds terrible."

"Sometimes," he shrugged. "Sometimes you need to just be a little unmoored."

"When you're finished with your slice, try some of the other three," Sebastian said as he walked over and took his seat at the head of the table. He grabbed three slices of the spicy salami, tore one off, put it on his plate, then slid it down her. He folded the two in his hand on top of each other like a sandwich before taking a bite. "That way we can see if it's just the basic elements you can taste or if it extends to other flavors."

Mina scarfed down her slice crust and all, relishing in how the flavors shifted with each bite, then grabbed one of the other slices. The vegetable had a unique crunch to it, a cooler taste compared to the cheese, closer to the sauce's flavor. The sausage bolstered the cheese and added in another flavor that buzzed against her tongue. The spicy salami lit her mouth on fire.

Between coughs, she chugged down as much water as possible while considering sticking her mouth under the faucet.

"I warned you that he likes things spicy," Wera tutted. "Yet you went ahead and scarfed down that slice with reckless abandon."

Sebastian sighed dramatically. "And here I was hoping to have someone to bond with over hot pepper varieties."

"You'll need to travel to the Realm of Devils for that," Mina choked out as the lava eroding her throat and tongue finally started to cool.

"What do you think, Sir Gargic?" Sebastian asked. "Think we can make a stop on the way?"

"That depends." He brushed some crumbs out of his beard. "Are you planning to bring the head of one of the Lords of Ruin to King Fritz?"

"Hmm. Not me, but I'm sure Mina could manage it," he said. "By the way, Mina, how's the composition coming along?"

Mina's stomach flipped in excitement.

"It's done."

"It's done? Already?" Enoch squawked. "What did you write?"

"A concerto."

"In ten hours?"

"It was nearly done at lunch. I stole the utensils to iron out the kinks and rehearse it," she said as she kicked Wera under the table.

"Ow! What the—" she locked eyes with Mina's pressing glare. "Oh— uh—. You rehearsed it, huh? Can you play it for us?"

Mina smiled lightly. "If I'm told to."

"Alright then. An hour after we're finished eating, play your concerto for us in the library," Sebastian commanded. "After which it's our chess match, Sir Gargic. I haven't forgotten."

"Good."

"What's the title of your concerto, Mina?" Tanir asked.

"Ask me after," she replied, turning to face the medic while looking pointedly at Sebastian.

He gulped down his bite harshly as his cheeks flushed red.

Mina was starting to like the shade just as much as she adored his hair color.

🜁

Mina's hands were shaking, not out of fear or overwork, but from nerves.

The woman who faced beasts and monsters, charged after evil fae, had suffered through unimaginable torments, was nervous to play a song in front of a small crowd. Especially when that crowd contained a certain amber-haired wizard.

The last of the utensils glided into position, standing at attention near their assigned instrument. Mina grabbed a sprig of herbs out of her pocket and stuffed it into her lip, just in case things went awry.

"Fastening a few bellows to breathe into the brass and woodwinds is brilliant," Sebastian remarked as he sat down in his chair. "Perhaps next magic lesson, we try to see if you can direct the wind to blow against them instead."

Mina hummed in acknowledgment, looking over the instruments one final time to make sure everything was properly aligned.

"Ready?" she asked.

"One moment," he said. "Enoch? Do you mind coming up with a catchy introduction?"

Enoch cleared his throat as he stood from his seat, chest puffed and posture grandiose. "Distinguished members of Windenhofer Procurements. I am proud to present to you the virtuoso vixen, Mina!"

The group clapped, and she turned to face them, closing her eyes to help ease her nerves and lifting her violin to her chin.

Warmth.

The opening notes resonated off of the books and wood of the library, nesting on the shelves as if they were settling in after a long journey home. The orchestra settled in with them, a family reunion, a place for her song to blossom and grow, to ignite and blaze.

She lost herself in the music, allowing the heat, the burn, the sizzle, the sear, the comfort, the yearning, the lingering, to roll through her without obstacle. Mina could not put into words how she was feeling, she could not touch him to truly figure those feelings out, but she could still feel them as muted and foreign as they were, and she'd be damned if she'd let Her take that away again.

Smoke billowed from the hulusi. Embers sparked from the bandora's strings. The concerto built and built — his trilling fingers from the xylophone, footsteps rolling from the drums, his laugh, his smile guiding her bow — echoing her own consumption until it burned through the kindling, the air, and fell to rest among a bed of coals lit by the flickering low-g note; held suspended until its warmth settled to stillness in the violin's body.

Mina expected applause, but was met with sniffles and silence.

She inhaled sharply as her heart dropped into her stomach, preparing for the worst.

"Fucking hell, Meens," Wera was the first to speak, voice broken and warbling. "That was beautiful."

Mina angled her face towards her and opened her eyes. Wera stared at her slack-jawed in awe while Tanir and Enoch wiped away tears.

Enoch blew his nose on his handkerchief. "I'd offer to write lyrics to it, but I don't know if I could do it justice."

"Another time, perhaps," Mina said.

"Mina."

Her heart shot back up to slam against her chest as Sebastian called her name.

"Tell me the title."

She grabbed another sprig of herbs and popped it in her mouth as she turned to face him.

"'Bastion of Flame'," she answered.

He inhaled sharply, a thousand, no, a million emotions swirling in his eyes.

"The title fits?" she asked.

A slight smile lifted the corner of his lips. "Yes, I think it's a great song ti—"

"No," she interjected. "You."

Sebastian swallowed. "What?"

She took another cheek-full of herbs, preparing for the sting that was sure to come.

"You uphold your fire. You defend others. That defines a bastion, does it not, *Bastion?*"

He had long past earned the right to be called by his proper name, yet no matter how many chains loosened the words would not come. They'd probably never come, not until her curse was broken, or she no longer cared about him. The latter would never be a possibility, not anymore. Not when he had given her so much.

Giving him a name, close to his proper one, was the closest thing to a 'thank you' Mina could give.

Disbelief fell away under realization's rising dawn in his eyes, bringing in its brilliance an expression she had read a million lines of prose about but never saw in practice: adoration. The healing herbs could not keep up with the surge of pain rushing to drown her mind and butcher her nerves, but they allowed her to bask in the glow of his adoration for a moment. A moment she could hold on to for lifetimes to come.

"Why yes," he said, voice hoarse. The bow of his lips drew back in a soft smile that struck truer than all the wide-spread grins he'd ever given her. "It does."

She closed her eyes as the pain became too much to bear, but still smiled despite it.

A slightly bigger one this time.

INTERLUDE

THE EQUAL AND OPPOSITE REACTION

Sebastian worked on a pendant; a beautiful, intricate thing that he had traveled across the world for. Silver mined from the abyssal caves of Ortria and fire opals plucked from the foothills of an undersea volcano formed a setting resembling sheet music around a beautiful amber stone fetched from the river just outside their home. Sebastian passed a polishing cloth over it one last time, muttering a well-practiced incantation, and held it up to the light to watch it ripple across the image of a woman, sitting on the moon, playing her violin for an audience of stars.

She was going to love it.

Three steps from his workshop and he was already walking out the backdoor into the garden, down the flagstone path they had laid together. He found her where she always spent sunny afternoons: asleep in a lavender patch.

"Lila doar," he sang softly. "Lila doar."

Mina's brows knit together, inhaling sharply as she stretched. Her eyes fluttered open, gray as the overcast skies of Autumn that often had him yearning for harvest pies.

"'Bastian? Is something wrong?" she asked, squinting as her eyes adjusted to the light.

"No." Sebastian joined her in the lavender, slotting into the matted-down bed that had formed. She sat up slightly as she shifted over to make room. "I just have a present for you, and couldn't be patient."

"A present for me?" She tilted her head to the side. "What for?"

"I said I'd make you a fire opal pendant, didn't I?" He held it out to her, and she took it, without hesitation.

Without any sign of pain.

She balanced it between her slender fingertips, twisting it back and forth to make the light dance across it, just like she'd done in the commorancy's study so long ago. Her soft pink lips curled into a smile that unwound what little tension nested in his shoulders.

"That you did." She handed it back to him and turned around. "Put it on?"

He unhooked the clasp holding the iron collar around her neck and slipped the pendant onto it carefully. He placed a kiss against her nape as he closed it, her soft skin cool against his lips. She hummed contently as she leaned back against him.

Sebastian wrapped his arms around her, and she slotted herself perfectly against his chest.

He chuckled lightly. "You still sleepy?"

She yawned. "You're not? We were both up early." Mina let her full weight fall back against him, coaxing him further and further to lie back on the lavender. He followed her willingly, letting out a yawn himself, eyes growing heavy.

"That's true," he mumbled and pulled her closer. "Thank you for your help this morning."

She interlaced her fingers with his. "I could have done more if I was told to."

He hummed in disapproval. "No more of that. You've done more than enough. You always do."

Mina squeezed his hands tightly, and Sebastian buried his nose into her hair, inhaling deeply.

△

He awoke, coughing and gasping for breath as he nearly suffocated himself with his pillowcase.

His coughing turned into a fit of laughter. No wonder he'd been able to smell the lavender in her hair so clearly! He was practically choking on it!

Sebastian flopped onto his back and stared at the canopy over his bed, wishing it were the sky above his home in Yosorick. Wishing that Mina was sleeping soundly beside him, wrapped up in his arms, just like the way she had been only once before.

The smile that often plagued love-struck fools claimed another victim.

Maybe he would get his wish. He already had one fulfilled last night, more so than he ever intended.

Mina played a song for him — composed a masterpiece for him — and to top it all off, made an effort to try and speak his name despite all the headache it must have caused her. He knew better than to assume her actions reflected any deeper emotion. Too many gifts and grand gestures, promises of summer vacations and big, happy families, only to be deposited at the peeling yellow door of Saint Turpan's Orphanage once again, had taught him that.

But it had to mean something, didn't it? Something good?

The consistent deterioration of her curse seemed to suggest as much.

Sebastian looked at the clock on the wall and hopped to his feet. He'd woken up half an hour before his alarm and intended to make the most of it by making breakfast.

It wasn't often that the cooking bug bit Sebastian, but after seeing everyone's reaction to his pizza — with one person's in particular reaction truly bolstering his pride — he hoped to capture that feeling once again.

And test a small, cockamamie hypothesis he had. Another foolish wish, really.

The kitchen spurred to life as he walked into it.

"At ease," he said. "I'll be doing most of the cooking again this morning. I will need a loaf of brioche, though, if you could work your magic."

The utensils set to work, gathering the flour and yeast, while he pulled out the eggs and milk. Vanilla, white sugar, brown sugar, and cinnamon. A whisk jumped into his hand as he reached for it and the bread — fresh out of the oven, baked at a speed only possibly by magical means — slid across the counter to rest next to his sweetened egg and milk mixture. He carried both over to the stove, snapping his fingers to light the flame beneath the iron griddle top.

As the griddle heated, he grabbed another dish to fill with cinnamon and the twin sugars. It was a bit over the top and Enoch was sure to grumble about how sweet it was, but it was a favorite of Sebastian's. Bread, then egg mixture, then cinnamon mixture, then griddle.

"Kitchen, would you mind putting some breakfast sausage on?" he asked as he flipped over the first few pieces he placed down. His stomach gurgled as the smell of cinnamon and caramelized sugar filled the air. He scraped the top of his spatula across the toast and smiled at the crunchy ring it gave.

"You're cooking?" Mina asked behind him, a slight lilt to her voice. Incredibly slight, but still another sign of the progress they had made. He didn't jump as much as he used to at her quiet entrances, but his heart still raced all the same.

"I am." He glanced over his shoulder at her. "How do you usually eat your eggs?"

"Yolk up," she said as she walked towards him, curiosity locked onto the griddle. "Those aren't eggs."

"No, this is cinnamon toast. Or as my one temporary grandmother called it: 'Better Than Sin-namon Toast'," he replied. "The eggs and the sausage go with it. In fact. Could you get started cooking the eggs for me?"

"No," she said.

He dropped the wet piece of toast in his hand onto the griddle with a splat.

"No?" he arched an eyebrow as he studied her expression carefully. Had he offended her in some way? She seemed interested in cooking, so he thought that—

"I'm a terrible cook," she said. "Seasonings, proper temperatures, proper consistencies. Never needed them. Never learned them."

"I see." He went to tap his lips as he thought, but pursed them instead to keep from covering his face in egg. "*Could* you learn?"

Mina paused for a moment, looking between him and the griddle.

"Breakfast could be ruined."

"The kitchen can always make more eggs."

"You'd lose focus on the toast."

"What? You don't think I can do two things at once?" Sebastian teased and placed his non-eggy hand over his heart dramatically, "You wound me, lila doar."

She sneered without any menace behind it.

"You teach me eggs. At lunch, I'll show you how to use soapwort for laundry," Mina insisted.

He smiled. "Sounds more than fair to me. Grab a carton of eggs and a pad of butter. We'll do Wera and Sir Gargic's eggs first, then Tanir and Enoch's. Yours and mine won't take long to cook, so they're best saved for last."

She snaked behind him and grabbed the ingredients.

"You eat yours yolk up too?" she asked.

"No, mine I do over easy. But they're essentially the same. Both have a runny yolk." He laid the last of the slices onto the griddle and went to wash his hands in the sink.

A long beat of silence hung over the sizzle of the griddle and the rush of the tap.

"The yolk is supposed to be runny?" Mina asked.

Sebastian swallowed his laughter. "Guess we've got our work cut out for us, then."

Hands clean, he rejoined her at the stove, scooping up a spatula as he went to flip the toast over.

"Alright, you'll need a bowl," Sebastian pointed to the empty counter space beside her and a bowl slid onto it, "and a fork." A fork leapt out of the cutlery drawer and skittered over to join them. "Then take your egg and crack it open into the bowl.

Mina picked up an egg out of the carton and smashed it against the bowl's lip, sending a few bits of shell into it along with the raw yolk and whites as she cracked the rest of it open with two hands.

"Okay now, dump it into the sink, and we'll start again."

She glared at him. "I cracked the egg into the bowl like you said."

"Yes, but you got a bunch of shell in it. We don't want that," he explained.

"Oh." She looked down at the bowl. "I thought that having a little bit of shell was part of it. Sort of how sometimes you get a bone in your fish or a pin feather in your chicken?"

"Those shouldn't be in your food either."

A subtle sadness crossed her face. She hummed morosely, then took the bowl and dumped the yolk out.

"My first time making scrambled eggs, I just smashed the whole egg into a bowl and mixed it up," he told her. "Mrs. Solana thought I was trying to pull a prank on her when I served it to her for her Mother's Day breakfast in bed." He chuckled to sweeten the bitter taste the memory left on his tongue. "My knuckles were sore for a full week."

"She sounds monster-esque," Mina remarked as she grabbed another egg and attempted to crack it. There was a slight edge to her voice, a building anger.

"No. Just a woman forced by her husband to try and be a mother when she really shouldn't have been."

"So she was your mother?"

"For three months. Then it was back to the orphanage." He scooped the finished toast onto a platter, and peered down into Mina's bowl. There were no bits of shell this time. "You'll need to crack five more."

She grabbed another egg. "How long were you there?"

"I was in and out until I was sixteen."

"What happened then?"

"I accidentally burnt part of the orphanage down," he admitted. He'd long gotten over the shame. "The benefactors were pissed, wanted me arrested even, but some of the nuns knew I was innocent and insisted they'd finally find me a wizard to apprentice under."

"They should have gotten you one earlier, Bastion," she said.

The growing heaviness in his chest lightened a little hearing her say his almost name.

"They tried. They'd been writing to the benefactors about it since my magic manifested, but they said no every time." He grabbed the final egg and cracked it for her, tapping it against the counter then splitting it with one hand. "Serves them right, I suppose. All the non-refundable application, processing, and match assessment fees they made off me over the years went to fixing the west boys' hall rather than their pockets."

The fork hopped into the bowl for Mina, and jiggled itself along the side until she picked it up and started stirring.

"What are their names?"

"Who?" Sebastian asked. "The benefactors?"

"Clearly."

"Why?"

"To collect the interest they owe you from getting all those application fees," she said. "Factoring inflation, and if interest is accrued until payout, it would be a hefty sum."

Sebastian couldn't help but stare at her in puzzled awe.

Mina looked up from her bowl once the whites and yolks had been turned into a pale yellow soup and stared right back at him, tilting her head to the side. "What?"

"You surprise me every day," he said.

Mina winced but did not look away. Instead, she reached into her pocket, pulled out a sprig of verbena, and popped it into her mouth. "I know a lot of things."

"Besides cooking," he teased. "Pour that mixture onto the griddle and run your spatula through it until it starts to clump."

Mina gave a taunting sneer, then poured the eggs onto the flat top. "That's because cooking's not important to me. Money is."

"Because money can buy you books and music?" he asked.

Her small, close-lipped smile, growing less and less rare to see as the days passed by, crawled up her face. "Clearly."

Besides his occasional instruction, they cooked silently alongside each other. A comfortable silence left undisturbed for the most part as the others made their way into the kitchen until—

"Didn't know you had a domesticated side to you, beastie."

Mina cracked the egg in her hand against the counter too hard, oozing yolk and shell all over it.

A flicker of anger burned against the back of Sebastian's neck, and he inhaled deeply to tamper it from growing any larger. So long as he could keep his and Mina's tempers in check, Sir Gargic would be out of their lives in just ten short days. Or, at the very least, Sebastian's contract would be fulfilled and his services paid for. After which he would have no qualms with giving the man a piece of his mind.

"Good morning, Sir Gargic," he turned around to address the knight. "You might want to start eating. I wouldn't want your food to get cold."

I'd much rather it burn your tongue.

Sir Gargic glared at Sebastian like a disappointed parent before sniffing sharply and waddling off towards the table.

His anger burned a little hotter, fueled by an older memory, and he exhaled to blow it out.

"Keep breathing that way, and you'll pass out," Mina muttered under her breath as she passed by him to wash her hands in the sink.

Unease crawled up his spine and roiled in his stomach. She'd noticed he was angry, and since she'd noticed he was angry she'd think he was upset, and that would only lead to upsetting her, and Sebastian would not let that happen. No unnecessary upsets.

Today was going to be a good day.

"Right." He clapped his hands together. "How about I make my own eggs, Mina, while you make your own? That way we can—"

"No," she cut him off as she finished drying off her hands and returned to the stove. "I've got it."

She grabbed another egg and cracked it again, perfectly this time.

"I just flip them over once?" she asked as she picked up another.

"Yes. When most of the whites are cooked at the bottom, but there's still some runny at the top. When you do, do it gently. It's more like tipping the yolk over rather than flipping it with force."

"Go sit then."

"What?"

"Go sit. I'll finish."

"Mina—"

"Your food will get cold." She worked the spatula under one of the eggs and flipped it over gently. She faced him and jerked her head towards the table as she chewed on another sprig of herbs. She must have popped it into her mouth when he wasn't looking. "Go."

Sebastian pouted for a moment, dismayed that he had to swallow his 'thank you', then gave a soft smile.

Today was going to be a good day.

△

A sea of brilliant white and blue surrounded them. The sun burned bright as it rose high in the clear sky. If it weren't for his noxulars, Sebastian would have been climbing this mountain blind.

Though blind or not, he certainly wouldn't have missed the giant wall of rock the fifteen-hundred-foot mountain they were scaling fed into.

"I could smell the cinnamon, too." Mina's voice snapped him out of his transfixion. "I forgot to mention that."

Sebastian's neck ached from staring up at The Lithe for so long, but he still managed to chuckle as he recalled Mina's chin covered in syrup.

"Well, you were a little bit preoccupied with trying to see how many pieces of toast you could fit into your mouth at once."

"You try going from bland to super sweet and see if you can control yourself."

"I don't know," he teased. "Even when I had my first piece of candy as a kid, I wasn't that bad. I might have to start calling you something other than lila doar."

Mina didn't look back at him like he hoped she would. "Like what?"

"Hmm. Hummingbird?"

She spat in disgust. "No."

"Sticky Fingers Joe?"

"Joe?" Mina questioned. "Where'd you get 'Joe' from?"

"It's a thing. Mobsters always have funny names like that. Sticky Fingers Joe. Two Stroke Willy. Patches McGillicuddy."

"So you're saying that because I ate a lot of sweet things, I'm a criminal."

"Yup. You're Mina the Syrup Swindler, wanted across the continent for stealing sweets and hustling honey across county lines."

Mina snorted that little snort that had started to follow their clever quips and goofier expressions. The beginnings of a laugh, like a motor struggling to start, but it still carried the promise that it would run again. That a true, full laugh was bound to break through at any moment, so long as the conditions were right.

Today was a good day. The sun was high in the sky, there was nothing but mountains and snow around them: the perfect conditions for an experiment.

"I heard tale that they're thinking of changing the reward from money to marshmallows, just to see if you'll turn yourself in for it."

Another snort. "So you're telling me they sweetened the pot?"

He chuckled. "Yeah, but all those marshmallows got them in a pretty sticky situation."

"How sticky?"

"Uh oh, I've said too much. I can hear you getting hungry again."

"No, I—" her words cut out for a moment as another snort stole her breath and broke loose. "No, I'm not."

"I can't believe you!" he feigned disapproval. "A dozen constables are covered in caramel because you can't keep your mitts free of molasses, and your stomachs' rumbling at the thought!"

Her steps staggered a bit, and she began to double over.

"You're... being... ridiculous," she choked out between snorts and stunted breaths.

Sebastian used her slowing steps to his advantage and bounded in front of her.

"I am not being ridiculous! This is a serious situation! Your confection obsession has gotten out of hand! Kingdoms are crumbling like cookies! Peasants are panhandling for pastries! The sovereigns are scrambling to solve this saccharin shortage, and it's all your fault! Overall, Mina—" Sebastian grabbed her by her shoulders to shake her, hoping that the sting it might cause would be minimal and well worth the end it would bring. "We're in a real jam."

He plastered on his most exaggerated expression of panic despite the smile tugging at the corners of his lips, and watched as Mina's trembling lips parted and her shaking, snorting breaths broke apart into boisterous, bubbling, barks of laughter.

Mina broke away from him and stumbled back, falling on her ass and covering her eyes to shield herself from his smile as her body shook with laughter. It was broken, rough, and raucous, wheezing and discordant, and absolutely beautiful. Sebastian found himself swept up in it, laughing right along with her.

Just as the world seemed to do, rumbling with laughter so loud, he barely heard Wera shout his name.

But he definitely felt the wave of surging snowfall smack against his back.

The brilliant white swallowed him whole, plunging him into dark depths of deep green that if it weren't for the weight and cold, he would have thought he'd suddenly been tossed into the sea. He tried in vain to right himself against the unrelenting rush of snow, only to have his legs thrown over his head, his shoulders knocked against the rocks they just climbed. He couldn't hear his group. Mina's laughter was barely a memory. There was nothing but the roar of the avalanche and the sound of his frantic heartbeat hammering in his ears.

Something hard smacked against his stomach, knocking out the small amount of breath he had left in his lungs as it got caught in his wake. It followed him until the surge finally buried him and its rampage passed overhead.

Sebastian would have screamed if he had the breath to when the something started to move. Maybe he would have even thought to reach down and grab it if the world wasn't spinning around him, growing darker and darker as the little air left in the pocket of snow he was wedged in slowly drained away.

The something crawled across his stomach, then swiped a pattern across it. It felt nice, oddly enough, like it was trying to calm him down as death claimed him. Until it smacked against his stomach, stinging him despite the thick layers of his wool coat. It resumed its pattern once it regained his attention, and Sebastian summoned the last dredges of his intelligence to try and figure out what pattern it was forming.

An "M".

It was spelling something.

"E" "L" "T".

Melt.

It wanted him to melt something. The snow, probably. Lighting himself and his clothes on fire would probably be a bad idea, but raising his body temperature, heating just the surface of his skin, should do the trick. His magic rushed to the surface of his body. Whether it was eager to follow his last dying cast or to escape his dying body, he wasn't quite sure.

The snow around his body shifted as it melted, dripping cool water on his face, and the something pulled on his coat.

Pulling him down? No. Pulling itself up.

"Bastion."

With a little more wiggle room, he looked down and through the dark caught a flash of green refracted off from what normally would be gray eyes.

"Melt it as slow as you can or else it will collapse in," Mina rasped. "Just enough so I can get to you without brute forcing it."

Sebastian said nothing, not with so little air, but determination fueled him. Mina was stuck. She needed his help. If he was going to die, at the very least, he would try dying to get her out.

A steady warmth. He could manage that.

Glowing eyes emerged, bringing a pale button nose and tightly drawn pink lips along with them. Mina's face connected to Mina's head. Her shoulders revealed themselves to be connected to the something — her hand — gripping onto his coat.

"Stop," she commanded as the snow grave a deep, squealing groan. Sebastian snuffed his flame out immediately, and his body trembled from the sudden shock of cold. It was a little easier to breathe now, with his lungs able to expand a bit in the pocket of snow he'd been able to carve out, but it wouldn't last long, not with two people splitting the limited amount of air.

Mina ripped off the sleeves of her undershirt and placed her bare arms against the thawing snow. Pops and cracks echoed around them. The melting slush refroze to form a barrier of ice.

She wriggled herself free from the snow entombing her legs, eyes closed and face twisted in a wince as she used his body like a ladder.

"I'm hurting you," he grumbled, voice weaker and more strained than he liked. Perhaps it was expressing the pain he did not feel. It felt impossible to move his limbs any more than an inch, and he was grateful for the darkness hiding the damage.

Wait a moment. It was dark.

He must have lost his noxulars at some point.

"It's necessary," she grunted as she finally got to her feet, body completely pressed against his, the top of her hair brushing against his lips. He could barely feel any of it. Her eyes were still shut tightly, her bottom lip now sunk between her teeth, seconds away from drawing blood.

"I can melt more—"

"Do that and this becomes our grave," she cut him off. She contorted her body as much as she could and, with a high-pitched whimper of pain, finally managed to wrench her bow free. "Close your eyes and turn your head away."

The bow could barely fit between them, its wood angled and odd as she tried to level it.

"What are you doing?"

"I'm seeing how deep we are and getting some more air in here without causing a cave-in. Now turn your fucking head so I can look where I'm aiming."

Sebastian closed his eyes and turned away from her. A shuddered breath of relief left her lips. Was it that awful for her to be so close to him?

No. It was the curse. She couldn't get too close to anybody. The shock and lack of oxygen took a toll on his common sense.

A slight whistle of wind, the squeal of water condensing to form an arrow of ice, Sebastian held his breath at the twangs of her bowstring drawing back and flinched on reflex at the snap of her firing.

"Shit," Mina whispered.

"Did it not go through?" he asked.

"No, it did." She paused for a moment. "I cut your cheek."

"Did you?" He went to reach for his face to check, but it was too tight and his arms were too heavy to move carefully enough to avoid touching her anymore. "I didn't feel it."

"We need to get out of here." There was a slight wobble to her voice that he wouldn't have picked up if it wasn't for his lack of feeling and lack of sight. "It sounds as if there's about two yards of snow above us. If I'm told to, I can jump both of us out of here, but you'll need to clear the path as we do. Your arms are dislocated, though."

Sebastian gave an uneasy chuckle. "That explains why they're so hard to move, then."

"Your hands are your conduit. Maybe if—"

"I don't need to use my hands. It's been a minute since I've done it, but I taught myself how to breathe fire as a fun little parlor trick."

"A parlor trick will evaporate six feet of thickly packed snow?"

Sebastian smiled despite the reality of their situation. "Well, I won't be able to talk for a while afterwards, but that beats slowly suffocating to death."

"The others. You'll be looking for them when we get out?"

It was a leading question. The kind she always asked when she was trying to steer him towards some request or conclusion she couldn't state outright. The kind of question his blossoming concussion didn't care for at the moment. Was she really doubting he would go searching for the others? Didn't she want to go search for them too? After what happened with Enoch back at Rabbet's Pass, he would have sworn she'd—

She still couldn't go after them, even after all the big strides she'd made.

Just because he made her laugh didn't mean things would magically get better. He should have thought of some solution to this problem after how terribly she was shaking back then, fighting against her want to save Enoch, and the awful curse that bound her.

Making her laugh, play violin, take magic lessons, was that really what she wanted? Or was that all just him? And why, when the people closest to him were potentially suffocating to death, was he thinking about anything other than them?

If he was going to roast his vocal cords to shreds, he better get his commands out now.

"Don't hate me too much if I mess the wording up, alright? My head got knocked around quite a bit," he said. "Mina, get me out of this snow and assist me in rescuing the others."

There was a shuffling, the scrape of her bow against the ice as she sheathed it, and then a pressure, tight and reassuring, wrapped around him.

"You can open your eyes now," Mina said, her voice more muffled than before.

Sebastian opened his eyes and went to turn his head, but stopped when his chin bumped against something hard.

"Just tilt your head back and aim the fire upward," Mina instructed, her words partially swallowed by his coat as he held on to him. "We'll go on the count of three. Ready?"

He caught the faint scent of lavender in her hair.

Damn his arms.

Sebastian inhaled deep and slow, diverting his magic from his hands to his lungs. They burned as the heat pooled where it wasn't supposed to be, feeding off the limited air inside, until he could barely hold it.

"Three. Two." Mina bent her legs, her grip around his waist tightening, urging the fire up against the back of his throat. "One."

Tears streamed down Sebastian's cheeks from the wind tearing across his face and the flames searing the inside of his mouth. The bright amber glow gave way to the brilliant blue sky and blinding white seas of snow quicker than he thought, but the damage was done. Hopefully, Tanir had a cure in the commorancy.

Hopefully, Tanir was still alive.

The reality of their situation fell upon Sebastian as they fell back into the snow. Mina placed him down as gently as she could. The blazing sunlight turned her into a blurred shadow, the only source of shade in an ocean of icy nothing, and Sebastian had to close his eyes to keep his stomach from upturning and rubbing stinging bile into the fresh burns marring his mouth.

He whimpered as she grabbed the corner of his jaw and forced it open to place a small chunk of soft snow on his tongue. The snow melted, sending cool water trickling down his throat, a momentary bout of relief before a burst of pain ripped through the right side of his body as she reset his shoulder.

"One more," Mina said, though he could barely hear her over the thrumming in his ears. She opened his mouth again and placed another chunk of snow on his tongue before snapping his other shoulder back into its socket.

"Done," she said. "You can open your eyes."

Sebastian shook his head no.

"Headache?"

He nodded.

"Can you chew?"

He shook his head.

Mina shifted, the leather of her breastplate squeaking as she pulled something out of it. Her hand was on his jaw again, holding it open as she scooped up another handful of snow. This time, however, she tilted his head back for him so that the unusual chunks that peppered the melting show slid down his throat without him needing to swallow.

"I had to chew it so it's lost some of its initial potency, but the headache should fade a bit. Should reduce the inflammation in your throat and shoulders too," she said.

She tied a piece of fabric around his head, covering his eyes and dampening the light. "I kept my sleeves to reattach later. You should be able to see through it a bit."

Sebastian opened his eyes, and while Mina was still a bit blurred, she was less of a shade now, more of a mirage with her white armor and pale skin nearly indistinguishable against the frozen mountainside. The herbs unwound some of the pressure in his skull and the stiffness in his shoulders, enough for him to make his hands meet. He tapped against his iron ring, and through the tiny windows of the fabric's weave caught four beams of bright red light shooting across the snow.

"I'll carry you to them. You melt the snow a bit, then I'll pull them out," she said.

Sebastian nodded.

"Can you stand?"

He could, but he didn't want to. He made his way to his feet, muscles screaming as he did. Guess the lack of pain in his shoulders opened the floodgates for the rest of his body to suffer.

Mina scooped him up before he could get fully upright, draping him over her shoulder and gripping the back of his knees with her hands. He wrapped his arms around her middle as tightly as he could, and she took off, dropping him back on the ground faster than he could blink.

She placed her ear against the snow, then guided his palms against it.

"Enoch. About five feet under."

He launched a flash of fire forward, evaporating the snow beneath his hands in a clean five-foot-long tube. The rest of his faculties were wounded, but his magic surged with power. He would not allow himself to be useless. Not when he was the one who got them into this mess.

A sharp gasp of air rang out, the first sign of life.

"Th-th-th—"

Mina leaped into the hole and yanked Enoch out before he could finish his sentence.

"Stay," she commanded as she deposited him on the surface. "We need to get the others."

Sir Gargic was close by, Tanir about fifty feet from him, and Wera...

"I can't hear her breathing," Mina said, a slight shake in her voice. "But she's down there. Twenty feet."

Twenty feet evaporated exactly, his raw and battered palms be damned.

He waved his arms as much as he could to get Tanir's attention.

"You'll need to bring her to me," Tanir cried behind him. "My femur's broken."

"Bastion," Mina panted as she leapt back out of the snow. A cold body was rested against his chest, curly hair tickling his nose. "Hold on to her. Keep her warm. Her heart's still beating."

Sebastian wrapped his arms around Wera as Mina scooped the pair of them up, pushing his magic further against its limits.

Mina hissed in pain, but held strong, rushing them to Tanir.

"What happened to her clothes?" Tanir asked. "Enoch, Gargic, huddle against her if you can!"

"They're in the bottom of the hole," Mina answered. "She took them off before she passed out."

"And why the hell would she do that?" Sir Gargic snapped.

"We need them, even if they're wet," Tanir ignored him. "Without them, she won't be able to retain any of our body heat."

Mina ran off, crunching snow fading away the farther she got.

"She'll be alright, Sebastian." Pale golden light flickered through his blindfold from Tanir's hands as she placed them over Wera's heart and muttered an incantation. "She's better off than Enoch was in the caves. I've strengthened her heart, so as we get her temperature up she should come to soon, alright?"

Sebastian forced his body temperature higher.

"Alright?"

"He can't speak," Mina said as she returned, throwing Wera's clothes on top of them.

"What did you do to him?" Sir Gargic snarled.

Sebastian fought the urge to grab the knight's arm and burn a hole through it.

"He breathed fire to get us out."

"S-so that's soot around his m-mouth," Enoch shivered against him. "G-good."

"Let me see," Tanir demanded.

Sebastian opened his mouth carefully. The herbs helped the burns scab over a bit, but the flesh was so sensitive that if he moved too quickly, he was afraid he'd tear them open.

"And what about his eyes?"

"He's concussed and the sun glare off the snow was too much without his noxulars," Mina answered.

"Even your lungs are burnt, aren't they? There's an inhalant for you once we get into the commorancy. Let's get Wera up and moving, then I'll cast a minor rejuvenation spell on you so you can speak enough to open it."

"What about your damn leg?" Sir Gargic asked.

"I cast a pain inhibitor incantation on myself. I won't feel anything for at least another two hours. I'll take care of you all first, then we'll address my leg."

A shiver and a whimper shook against Sebastian's chest.

"There's our girl," Tanir cooed. "Wera, can you hear me? Can you open your eyes?"

"It hurts," Wera sobbed, a quiet, strained sob that threatened to rip Sebastian's heart out of his chest.

"I know, dearie. I know. It'll get better as you warm up, alright?" she consoled. "Enoch's gonna grab your hand, can you feel it?"

"Mhmm."

"That's good. Can you try and squeeze it?"

"She can," Enoch said.

"Alright then. Enoch, Sir Gargic, huddle close to her so I can attend to Sebastian."

Tanir placed one hand against Sebastian's throat and one over his mouth. She chanted lowly, and the numbing, searing healed, then stiffened, swollen skin and sinew tingled. Breathing came easier, his lungs expanding a little more. His throat still felt as if he had swallowed a rock and kept it stuck there, but the rock could at least move. Her hands moved to the side of his head, and she pressed her thumbs into his temples, rubbing small circles into them as she continued her casting. The pressure in his head faded, unclouding his thoughts.

She untied the blindfold as she pulled her hands away from him. "There. Don't start reciting soliloquies, but you should be cleared up enough to say a few words."

"Thank... you..." he choked out as his eyes adjusted to the light.

Tanir smiled back at him, but the smile was lopsided, her pupils too wide. Side effects of the spell that kept her from feeling the pain of her leg, twisted at an ungodly angle behind her.

Wera's coat lay on top of her trembling body, her skin bright red and lips bright blue, frost slowly melting off the tips of her hair that touched him.

Sir Gargic and Enoch laid on either side of them, huddling against his legs and wrapping their arms over her to try and hold in the heat he conjured, perhaps even trying to warm themselves.

Enoch's face was just as red as Wera's, the tip of his nose as bright as a circus clown's. His hand lying across her body was twice the size it should have been, stretching out his glove with its swelling. Thank The Gods it wasn't the one he wrote with.

Sir Gargic's padded armor was dented and pierced — scored so severely that if he hadn't been wearing it, he surely would have severed his arm or had his skull split in two. His left eye was swelling shut, dark red blood pooling beneath the skin, and he kept shifting, wincing as Wera brushed up against some pain plaguing his right side.

His gaze drifted up to Mina, standing off to the side watching them, expression blank.

"Mmmina," he forced out. Her focus snapped to him immediately. "C-camp... h-here?"

"There's no other choice," she said. "I'll stay and keep watch while you all take care of yourselves. If another avalanche comes, I can divert it from swallowing the commorancy."

Sebastian nodded and groaned in effort as he reached into the outside pocket of his coat.

It was empty.

Quickly, pushing past the pain as his heart raced, he checked his other pocket.

Nothing.

"No," he sputtered. "No, no, no."

"Easy now! You shouldn't move that much," Tanir said.

"T-t-t-" The words lodged against the rock in his throat as his panic built. "N-no c-camp—"

"What do you mean no camp?" Sebastian was ripped out from underneath Wera, yanked up by his lapels. Mina shoved her hands into the outside pocket of his coat. "The outside pocket! That's where you keep it, right?"

"Oi! Beastie! Drop the wizard, or I'll cut you down where you stand!" Sir Gargic threatened.

Mina turned his pockets inside out, even stuck her hand in the inner pockets, hitting a bottom that wasn't supposed to be there.

"Bastion, where—" she looked up at him, granting him the heartbreaking pleasure of watching the gray of her eyes darken from a pale overcast to the deep slate of a building cyclone.

"L-lost," he croaked. "I'm—"

Mina dropped him back on the ground.

Her expression was unreadable, gaze distant and dulled.

"You can't just toss people around you—"

"Shut your fucking mouth before I shut it for you," Mina cut Sir Gargic off — voice even, and monotone, and dangerous — without bothering to turn towards him.

"Don't you dare tell me wha—"

Sebastian blinked and Mina's knee was pressed against Sir Gargic's spine as one hand wrenched his head back, and the other, fingertips blackened with frostbite, gripped his jaw.

"I will not hesitate to shatter the jaw of an imbecile who never learned when to hold his tongue. So keep your fucking mouth shut so I can have some quiet while I figure out a way to un*fuck* us." She dug her fingernails in. "Understand?"

Sir Gargic's lips curled into a sneer, parting to deliver another ill-advised comment, before falling slack under the effects of Tanir's hastily muttered sleep spell. Mina released his head and left it face down in the snow.

"He should stay like that for at least an hour," Tanir's words went unacknowledged as Mina's icy gaze fell on Sebastian.

"The only shelter around is at the base of The Lithe," she stated. "It's a ten-hour hike, which none of you can manage. I can make it there by myself in twenty minutes and can carry up to six hundred pounds across my arms."

"Carry us..." The words gargled out of his throat like bubbling tar, "to the base... of The Lithe."

"Wizard and Cartographer, Medic, Archivist and Knight," she said. "The medic's leg should be set first before she's carried."

"Can... you... set... it?"

"If I'm told to."

Sebastian swallowed in vain, hoping to ease some of the pain spreading down his throat from overuse. "Set... Tanir's... leg... before you... carry her."

Another blink and he was up in Mina's arms once more, with a shivering and whimpering Wera sprawled over top of him.

"Hold her. Close your eyes. Keep your head against me." Were the only words of warning he had before the wind roared around him, clawing at his face. Wera's trembling against his chest was the only sense of ground he had as they fell sideways through the air, tossed about by nature's fury once again in Mina's gale-force. The heat he conjured to keep Wera from falling back into the depths of hypothermia fled quickly against the frozen winds. His ears stiffened, aching as if they were about to snap off at any moment, the tip of his nose threatening to splinter and crack.

Then with a jolt, it all stopped. And everything was dark.

Mina's arms slipped out from under him, and his back fell against stone.

"Now the medic," Mina said, and a gust of wind lashed against his wind-burnt cheeks.

He opened his eyes and found himself tucked into a small alcove deep in the shadow of the massive cliff.

"'B-b-bastian?" Wera shivered, voice weaker than he liked. "Are we d-d-dead?"

"No," he croaked.

"T-t-then w-w-why d-d-do you s-s-sound like it?"

"Shhh." Sebastian smoothed his hand across her hair as much as he could, and she settled into him more, trembling muscles unlocking as his body's warm aura made progress loosening the cold's tight grip.

He studied the walls of the alcove, the little scratches and pits marring the dark slate. Some of them taking shape into words: Tai Arlowa, Chi B. Bea, E.V. Lily. Kat Drex. Dozens of names of those who had followed Mina on this expedition, who had survived the frosts and beasts and storms, and were far better off than they were now.

Mina's glare, stoic and damning, haunted him. He focused on recounting the supplies they still had on hand instead. Most of the others still had their packs from what he could recall. His pants pocket held his pocket watch, some rope, a canteen, some spell components, a notebook and pencil, a compass, a pocket knife, no food.

Not a single scrap of food.

The shrill whistle of wind broke his focus as Tanir appeared beside him, pale and dizzy-eyed, her leg now straightened and braced between two bows — one for arrows and one for a violin — held together on either side of her thigh by scraps of linen.

"Her violin broke," Tanir panted, dropping her arms to let splintered chunks of wood fall into her lap. "She said to use it to start a fire."

A wave of nausea washed over him.

She looked down at Wera. "How's her heart rate?"

Sebastian placed two fingers against the pulse point in her neck. "Stronger."

"I think my ribs are broken," Wera said, a slight wheeze behind her words.

"Then we should flip you onto your back, dear," Tanir said.

"But I can finally feel my nose again."

"Yes, but you might also be driving part of your ribs into your lungs, and fixing a punctured lung is gonna be tricky right now."

With a whine of protest, Wera tried to turn herself over, limbs still shaking. Sebastian helped her over as best as he could, which earned him an eyeful of shooting stars when she landed with a thud back against him and knocked the air out of his sore lungs.

"Your... leg..." he rasped out with a cough and pointed to Tanir's brace.

"It'll be fine, I think. I won't know for sure until the pain block wears off," she said, then gestured to the rock her injured leg rested on. "I am surprised she propped it up."

"Her... violin... how..."

"You should really rest your voice, dear," she interjected. "I don't know what components in my pack survived, and while I can do small casts to help boost the healing process, straining your vocal cords might scar them for good." She studied him for a moment. "The one on your face is bad enough. Hopefully, my sewing kit's still in there so I can stitch it up and minimize the damage."

Another gust smacked them in the face.

Mina dropped the still sleeping Sir Gargic off her shoulder onto the ground, and placed Enoch down as well, minding his ill-twisted ankle.

Wordlessly, she opened up his coat and rummaged around his belt.

"W-what are you d-doing?" Enoch said, blinking rapidly to clear something out of his eyes.

"Taking a dagger."

"W-why?"

"To hunt with."

"B-but your s-sword—"

She pulled a dagger out and tucked it into her own belt, next to a scrap of fabric; her other sleeve.

"Build the fire," she addressed everyone and no one. "I'll be back."

She turned her back to them and the wind pooled around her ankles.

"Mina..." Sebastian croaked.

"I'll be back," she repeated and took off.

Sebastian stared at the empty space she left behind, hoping that if he blinked enough, she'd reappear.

"Sebastian," Tanir called. "Do as she says." She tapped the back of his hand with the snapped neck of Mina's violin. "Build the fire."

△

Click. Click.

The scratched cover of his pocket watch flashed amber in the firelight as he flipped it open and closed, hoping the hour hand would jump back an hour, or several. That maybe the intersecting leylines affected the watch's gears just as much as they affected his coat pockets.

Mina's violin burned away hours ago, save for the pegs he selfishly stuffed in his pocket before throwing the scroll on the meager flame. Enoch bravely volunteered the books of poetry and short stories that remained in his pack to fuel it. Now, they sat around a small pile of burning parchment and leather, watching love sonnets turn to cinder.

The contract kept her from abandoning us before, Sebastian reminded himself. *Unless...*

Just as Sebastian turned to Sir Gargic, a whistle of wind — louder than all the others that had gotten his hopes up as they rushed past the alcove — shrieked. Everyone's attention locked to the entrance, watching, waiting, hoping.

A bush filled with dead rodents of various species appeared and collapsed against the wall. Its wielder stood behind it, a multi-headed beast.

Mina sloughed her kills off her shoulders onto the floor, but still retained the hunch from their weight against her shoulders. She hobbled over to the bush and began to snap off its branches.

"We've eaten already, Meens," Wera said, breaking the tense silence.

"How much?" she asked.

"A half portion of rations each? Between the five of us, we probably only had three meals worth of dry goods left in our packs after the fall."

"This is to dry the wood quicker." She dropped the brush near the fire after picking the carcasses from it. "Once I gut and clean these, I'll mix the bones with the branches. They'll make the wood last longer."

Sebastian opened his mouth to speak, but a shooting pain in the back of his throat discouraged the action. He picked up his notebook and charcoal and jotted his thoughts down quickly, then nudged Wera.

She squinted at the notebook, struggling to read his writing without her glasses. He turned to Enoch instead, pulling his forlorn expression away from his smoldering books.

"Sebastian wants to know if you ate," Enoch read.

"I ate," she replied without looking his way. "Tanir's asleep?"

"She used the last of her energy for the day to put herself under. Pain blocker enchantments really take a lot out of her and—"

Mina cut Wera off. "I don't need to hear anymore. Just needed to know if I had to bury someone."

Sir Gargic scoffed in the corner, and Mina stilled.

The fire popped, the wind howled, and Sir Gargic held his tongue.

She resumed breaking the branches apart until she was left with a gnarled, sickly-angled trunk. Sebastian finished writing out the final details of his plan and held it out for Enoch to read.

"Sebastian has a plan. He—"

Crack.

"Unless that plan involves me traveling back in time and telling him to shove that fucking commorancy up his ass, then it doesn't matter." She snapped the trunk apart with her bare hands and threw the pieces onto the ground. "No more mistakes."

Sebastian wanted to throw up.

"Mmmina—"

Her gray eyes glowed red through the shadows as they fell upon him.

"Save your breath," she snapped. Her eyes darted down to the fire.

As she limped towards the dwindling flames her figure took form: the soles of her boots were torn and held in place by tied entrails, her pants were tattered, and a strip of bloodied fabric hung from her forearm as she unwound it, revealing dozens of slow healing cuts. She dropped it into the flame, filling the alcove with an acrid, metallic stench that reignited the fire and illuminated her face.

Gaunt and haggard, streaks of darkened blood poured from every spot they could, some patches drier. Some hauntingly fresh.

"There," she rasped as a fresh stream of blood trickled out of the corner of her mouth. "Now, I can see what I'm carving."

"There are still some herbs in Tanir's pouch," Wera blurted out.

Mina took Enoch's dagger out of her belt and turned her back to them. "Is your iron paint gone?"

"No."

"Paint the circle, raise that eight-hour dome, and sleep. I'll keep watch outside of it."

Sebastian scribbled furiously and shoved the notebook at Enoch.

"Sebastian says he won't cast it unless you're sleeping in the dome too."

"The darker the night gets, the lower the temperature will drop. Having a body that freezes everything it touches among you will only make the hypothermia you all have barely escaped succumbing to set in quicker." The sick pop of dislocated bones rang out of the darkness. "Paint the circle, raise the dome, and sleep."

Her words were final, a door slamming shut. Disappointment. Tired, bitter disappointment in him that made him feel so much younger, so much smaller than he was.

And just like then, to ease the guilt that could not be uneased, Sebastian did as he was told.

XVIII

Once Upon a Time

On the first day,

In the dim morning light, Mina stared up at The Lithe.

In a few minutes, Sebastian's dome would break, the bubble of warmth he radiated would disperse, and they all would awake dazed, starving, and sensitive; like hatchlings still too fragile for the world they'd been born into.

Mina hadn't slept. There had been too much to do. The meat had to be butchered and smoked, new harnesses had to be fashioned to replace the few that had fallen out of her pack during the slide, and their heart rates had to be monitored, lest one of them stilled while she closed her eyes. Tonight she would sleep. She could last until tonight.

The Lithe loomed above her.

She had no other choice but to.

Sir Gargic's snoring hiked in volume, signaling the spell's end, just seconds before a chorus of shocked gasps rang out. Mina scanned the frozen expanse behind them, watching for the worst and hoping to find no signs of it, and inhaled deeply: preparing herself to face them.

"There's smoked hare kept warm beneath the coals," she announced as she entered the alcove. "Eat, relieve yourselves, then I'll harness you, and we'll start to climb."

They looked terrible, but she doubted she looked any better. The cuts along her arm had healed, but the flesh still ached. Her eyes, her lips, her nose, dry and tender to the touch; every muscle in her body wound too tight, and her joints throbbed. Her body had fought against her every kill after the first, but she could still stand, still climb. She bore no broken bones, still had her voice and mind, so the pains she felt were nothing compared to theirs. She could bear more.

She had no other choice but to.

She turned her attention to her smoking tent, removing the now-dried goat skins instead of watching the others struggle. Instead of staring at the cut that marred Sebastian's cheek.

"Do I have permission to speak now?" Sir Gargic asked.

"So long as you don't say anything stupid," Mina replied.

"How do you expect us to climb this thing with Tanir's femur busted and Enoch's ankle swelling up bigger than a grapefruit? Not to mention I can barely see out of my eye and my clavicle's too fractured for me to hold a rope."

"It'll be just like Rabbet's Pass. I'll bear most of your weight. Those who have the tools to — and can — will scale the face with me, while those who are too injured to do so will just be carried. We need to cover twenty-five hundred feet today. There's a ledge to make camp at near that height."

"Twenty-five hundred," Enoch fretted. "Why not just a thousand? I'm sure the king would understand if we took a little more time."

"There's nowhere to rest at a thousand feet," she replied. "And I was only able to scrounge up enough food to last close to four days. Bastion, you'll need to stuff as much jerky as you can into your pants pockets. These goat pelts need to be wrapped around Tanir from torso to foot to make sure she is stabilized as we climb. The order will be me, Enoch, Wera, Tanir, Bastion, and Sir Gargic; lightest to heaviest to combat the winds from taking us with them."

"What if we need to relieve ourselves as we climb?" Wera asked.

"If you all had the means to hold on to the mountain as you went, I would say to just drop your trousers and go. I tore up my spare clothes to use as bandages and fire starter if we need it. I'd take those and some of these woolhare hides and fashion yourselves diapers." Mina wrapped the last batch of jerky up in a scrap from her linen undershirt. "Smaller batches of jerky and kindling have been divided among your packs."

"Sebastian wants to know if you slept," Enoch said.

"I did," she lied without missing a beat.

They ate. Tanir treated their wounds as best as she could, then sedated herself once again as Mina, under Sebastian's command, swaddled her in the goat skins and rigged her body to a harness.

"Did you... really sleep?" Sebastian asked as she tightened his harness around his hips. Sleep and Tanir's healing touch had helped his voice sound a little less ghoulish, but the strain and pain behind each syllable pierced through her ears straight to her heart. The incessant wheeze underscoring his every breath reminding her just how much she failed him.

"I told you I did," she grumbled, tightening one of the knots with a snap. "Don't waste your words asking questions you already know the answer to."

"How?" he croaked.

"What do you mean 'how'? I closed my eyes."

A swallowed, frustrated groan rumbled in his chest as he lifted his notebook and scribbled inside it. He thrust it in her face, glowering at her in the background as her tired eyes adjusted focus to read his chicken scratch handwriting.

I find it hard to believe that you butchered and smoked about 100 pounds of meat, prepped their hides, made bundles of kindling and harness rigs, and still slept last night.

Mina shoved his notebook out of her face.

"You don't know what I can do," she sneered, the words coming out harsher than she meant them to. Sebastian's face fell, eyes dulling as he turned away from her and shoved his notebook back in his pocket. Too low on herbs to afford an apology, she moved on to the final harness: Sir Gargic's.

"Beastie. Level with me here. Soldier to soldier. Is this really the smartest plan?"

"I'm no soldier," she grunted as she threaded the harness between his legs, "and since when did you care about my opinion?"

"Since I spent the entire night, sitting in silence, trying to figure out any goddamn way we could survive this without you, and came up with nothing."

"Oh, so it took almost certain death to think that I'm worth anything." She pulled the rope tight across his stomach, making sure it dug into the fat. "I'll keep that in mind going forward."

"Don't be like that. I'm laying my pride aside to ask you for some reassurance, alright?" he defended himself. He leaned down to whisper in her ear. "You're the one who got us in this goddamn mess with that banshee laugh of yours. The least you can fucking do is tell me how you plan to get us out of it."

A chill ran down her spine. The base of her skull pulsed. Her focus pulled into herself.

It was her fault. All her fault.

She laughed. She relied on the tent. She didn't prepare. She didn't keep her distance.

My fault. All my fault.

She pulled the rope taut and pulled herself out of the spiral. She'd done enough of that during her hunt last night, and lost most of her prey because of it.

"It's the only option. Unless resorting to cannibalism, killing Tanir and Enoch for food before we take the long way around, and adding on another two weeks of surviving this frozen wasteland is acceptable. Surviving another ice storm without shelter would be a treat, too." She fastened the rope that connected him to Sebastian through the front loops of his harness.

"And you'll be able to carry us all?" he asked, complexion much paler, voice meek with worry.

"I have no choice but to."

With Sir Gargic secured, she made her way to the front of the pack. "All secured. Bastion, cast that levitation spell on Tanir just long enough to get her up a ways." Mina wrapped the rope around her chest in an x-pattern, interweaving it with her pack to distribute their weight and making sure there was no room for it to slip. If they were going down, she was going down with them.

A stabbing pain shot through her skull at the thought.

"Ready?" she asked Enoch behind her. He shook his head nervously, one dagger held, the other bound to his mangled hand to form makeshift ice axes.

They began to ascend.

Finding the rhythm to their climb was tricky between Tanir's free weight, Enoch using just his arms and Sir Gargic using just his legs, but with some coaching and the fuel of fear, they found it, ascending foot after foot as the air whipped their backs for daring to defy it.

Hours passed. The tundra below vanished beneath the clouds. And while their breathing had gone ragged from what she could hear, there was no cause for concern yet. They were holding up quite well despite their injuries, adrenaline kicking in and keeping their breaks to a minimum.

Their heart rates were slightly elevated, but even tempoed and strong.

Mina's eyelids dipped for a moment, growing heavy, pulled in by the drumming of hearts and a softness layered beneath the wind's whistle.

She jolted awake as her ice axe struck the stone, her body finishing the movement while her consciousness failed her. The wind's siren song drew her ear once more, coaxing her eyes to close even though her heart was racing.

"Enoch!" she shouted over her shoulder.

"What?" he replied.

"Tell me a story!"

"A what?!"

"A story!"

"Why?!"

"Just..." She was tired. She was slipping. She couldn't handle this. "... because I said so!"

"Do I have to yell it?!"

"No. I'll hear it even if you whisper. Just tell me a story about something!"

"Okay... uh..." Enoch's voice dipped into a panting whisper, trapping her attention far easier than shouting would have.

"This is the tale of Queen Farica. The Heart of The Forest.

"A hundred and fifty years ago, there was a Kingdom known as Nuvaria. It once stood between what were the Kingdoms of Tovell and Rentair. Although you would know these lands by their current name, The Tovarren Empire.

"During the height of Nuvaria's prosperity, King Goredan the Golden and Queen Sahra the Gentle sat upon the throne. Their kingdom was thriving. Trade was booming after rich veins of copper and quartz had been discovered within their hills, and a grove of magic ash trees was found by the king himself underground in the forest surrounding his castle. The downtrodden from neighboring kingdoms, even from countries far away, flocked to their lands; hearing tales that not a single citizen went hungry there. A claim that archaeologists later found to be true.

"All was fruitful in Nuvaria, save for the king and queen, who had tried for years to have a child to no avail. One year, to give thanks to the gods they believed to bless their lands with such great fortune, they toured their country, paying visits to the wise sages that called it home; thanking them for their dedication to their faith and the miracles they worked. Liosa, Shepherd of Souls, was the last sage they visited. After breaking bread and accepting their gifts, she showed them the gardens surrounding her hovel, which had caught the royals' curiosity.

"'My sister tends these fields,' Liosa told them. 'For those souls I help cross over, who have no family to claim their vessels, she returns their bodies to the earth, and from them grows life anew.'

"'Though our visit is to honor you, might I ask if I may take some oranges from your garden?' Queen Sahra asked, her eyes and stomach drawn to the brilliant, ripe fruits, bigger than her husband's great fists, hanging heavy on the trees' branches. 'We'll gladly compensate you for the crop.'

"'I have no qualms, Your Majesty,' Liosa replied, 'but let me ask my sister first, out of respect for her hard work.'

"Liosa sent a crow to her sister, who was away handling other matters. It returned shortly after, granting the queen permission to take just four oranges and instructing her to eat only one per week and save the fourth for the next time the queen took ill.

"Queen Sahra, so enticed by the fruit, ate the first one on the carriage ride home, and even shared some of her slices with her darling husband.

"She did as Liosa's sister said, eating only one per week even though she was sorely tempted to take more, and still split the bounty with her husband despite his protests that she should have it all for herself. The last orange, however, she did eat wholly on her own when, a few weeks later, a terrible wave of illness washed over her, turning her stomach and leaving her quite lethargic.

"At once the nausea and fatigue faded, but the court physicians were wary, and after tests and examinations determined... that the queen was at last with child.

"Blessed by whatever magics were imbued in those oranges, Queen Sahra's pregnancy was an easy one. Excitement grew throughout the kingdom as her stomach did, and when at last the babe was born — right as the sun crested the horizon on the morning of the spring equinox — their entire country broke out in celebration.

"A tiny princess, they named her Farica for the peaceful slumber she fell into against her mother's chest after choosing to coo instead of cry when she greeted the world for the first time.

"Jubilated, King Goredan decided to hold a grand celebration in honor of his healthy firstborn and invited his own noblemen, the rulers of nearby Tovell and Rentair, and the twelve sages of Nuvaria to attend.

"Pomp and circumstance were in full swing. Parades and festivals of grand display preluded the event. Libations and well-wishes were as bountiful as the quartz in their hills. The sages, to honor their sovereigns, cast blessings on the princess. Wit, beauty, grace, strength, bravery, cunning, patience, endurance, talent, humor, insight—

"Liosa was the last to approach the child and as her lips parted to speak her gift, the torches lighting the room snuffed out, casting the dining hall in darkness.

"'How dare you scorn the one who gave you that child?' an unknown voice echoed in the darkness.

"In a flash of lightning and plume of smoke, a woman in black appeared beside Farica's crib: Liosa's sister, Caitir. A solitary sage but a sage, nonetheless, The Doyenne of Decomposition reached out her crooked finger and dug her hooked nail between the baby princess' brows.

"'The bodies of the dead fertilized the crop that gave this child life, and for your insult they shall claim it back! Upon her eighteenth year, she shall prick her finger on a splinter of ash and die!'

"Farica, for the first time in her short life, cried as Caitir scratched her nail across her flesh, drawing blood and sealing the child's fate. In another flash, the thirteenth sage vanished, leaving a party filled with sorrow in her absence.

"The queen and king rushed to comfort their wailing child, but Liosa held a hand up to still them.

"'I cannot completely undo the curse my sister placed upon her,' Liosa said, 'for the vengeance she sought is just. But I can spare the child's life if you so will it.'

"'Yes of course!' King Goredan cried. 'Save our daughter's life, and we will be forever in your debt.'

"'As you wish.' Liosa leaned into Farica's crib. 'A splinter of ash shall not be her death, but rather this child shall sleep, unharmed, for seventy years.' Liosa kissed the wound her sister left, staining the blood upon her lips. When she pulled away, only a faint scar remained.

"In the days that followed, King Goredan called his people to action; asking them to turn in every piece of ash wood they had, either destroying them or selling them in mass to whoever would take them fast enough. He had his beloved ash tree grove sealed off from the world and hidden under layers of enchantments that — even if Farica managed somehow to get close to it — would turn her right back around.

"Time passed and Farica grew up into a beautiful young woman, with long blonde hair as soft as silk, eyes greener than the purest emerald found in the Gilded Sea, skin smooth and almost flawless save for that thin scar, breast full and—"

"Enoch!" Mina interrupted. "I get it! She's hot! Move on!"

"You asked me to tell you a story!" he shouted back.

"And lusting over some eighteen-year-old ain't exactly a story!"

"She's not eighteen now!"

"Enoch!"

"Fine, fine!" he barked back. He inhaled deeply, steadying his ragged breathing as he continued:

"She turned eighteen and the entire kingdom held their breath. One month went by, then two, then six. With less than a week until her nineteenth birthday, the king and queen believed she was in the clear. That they had bested Caitir's curse. But then — while the king and queen were a county away celebrating the nuptials of one of their dukes — in the dead of night, under the light of a blue moon, Princess Farica wandered into the forest.

"She did not know what called her there, but she knew she had to follow it. The years of her father and mother's warnings were far gone from her mind. She had to go into the woods, travel deep within its arms.

"The enchantments they placed upon it were for naught. The thick wall of briar parted as she approached. She wove her way through the illusory maze. The beasts bent and bowed to drive her away, were slain. As she reached the blocked-off entrance to the underground, sealed with two-ton boulders and cement, Farica simply placed a hand upon it, and it crumbled into dust.

"Down, down, down, she wandered through the dark caverns, sure-footed as if she had trotted across the cold stone floors a thousand times, and soon found herself in the enchanted grove. Untouched by man for close to nineteen years, the ash trees were full and thriving, with younger saplings licking at their roots. But one tree towered above them all. Four times thicker and four times taller than its children, a great ash sat in the center of the grove. Its leaves whispered in the evening wind, calling her name.

"'Farica. Fair Farica.'

"The princess approached it, and in awe of its magnificence, sat against its trunk. The last thing she remembered was leaning her head back to look up at the moonlight through its leaves, and a sharp prick against the palm of her hand as she ran them along its roots absentmindedly.

"The curse took hold of the princess and the Kingdom of Nuvaria in an instant, throwing them all into a deep slumber. Their allies in Tovell tried to send aid, but the second their troops set foot on Nuvarian soil, they were put to sleep as well. Never to wake up.

"Nature reclaimed the land as time passed, those who were merely sleeping became corpses as vines took root across their backs. Mushrooms sprouted in the soft, dark recesses of snoring mouths. Lichen and mold ate their very flesh. The Kingdom of Nuvaria became The Slumbering Forest, its history and existence fading away from memory as the generations passed by, becoming little more than folklore by the time Prince Embrek was born.

"The Crown Prince of both Tovell and Rentair by his mother Queen Binti of Rentair and his father King Oxar of Tovell, the tales of a beautiful sleeping princess deep within The Slumbering Forest had been his bedtime story every night. So at the ripe age of twenty, exactly seventy years after Nuvaria had fallen, he bravely rode into the woods, and was the first man to withstand its enchantments.

"The same pull that lured Princess Farica to her slumber, guided Prince Embrek to the grove. And upon seeing her, untouched by nature, as beautiful as the day she closed her eyes, he was moved to his knees and kissed her softly upon the lips.

"The princess opened her eyes, and with just one glimpse, fell madly in love with the prince. They wed shortly after and once Embrek ascended the throne, by the union of his marriage and the birthright from his lineage, The Tovarren Empire was formed."

Mina released a long-held breath as, through the cloud cover, the first ledge emerged. She pulled herself over it, then slowly coaxed the others up by the rope. As soon as they cleared the edge, they collapsed onto the frozen hunk of rock: panting, trembling, pale-faced, but alive, and largely unharmed.

The odd whistle in the wind — the lullaby that had been tugging at her eyelids — vanished, which was both a relief and a worry. Perhaps it was just a certain pitch the wind was hitting today, much like her rhythmic chanting had lured Wera into a trance before.

A notebook slid in front of Mina as she pulled the kindling out of her bag and began to build the fire.

What were you and Enoch yelling about? Was something wrong?

She pushed the notebook back towards Sebastian without looking at him.

"Nothing was wrong," she replied.

Sebastian scratched something out in his notebook, wrote something else, and slid across the rock once more, but not towards her.

"Mina demanded that I tell her a story," Enoch said. "Then had the gall to judge my artistry."

"Going on and on about how beautiful some princess was is hardly artistry," Mina grumbled.

More scratching in his notebook.

"I tried to ask but all she said was 'because I said so'," Enoch mimicked her pitch and monotone speech. Mina let one of the wood pieces slip out of her grasp and smack his wounded ankle.

The notebook slid in front of her and Mina tried her best not to look at it, but the pull of the command written upon it was too strong.

Tell me why you asked Enoch to tell you a story. The charcoal marks dug deep into the paper, the straight lines of his 'L's' and 'T's' much sharper than usual.

"I needed something to focus on so I wouldn't fall asleep," she confessed against her will.

She didn't need to look at Sebastian to know he was giving her a disappointed glare.

"And before you scribble anything about 'how you all could have lent a hand in prepping things' or 'how we could have waited a day', the answer to both is no." Mina tore some of the lingering pages out of one of the books Enoch sacrificed, crumpled them up, and shoved them in between the gaps in the wood.

"You were all far too injured to lend a hand — still are — and needed as much rest as possible because one more day of waiting means one more day of food to scrounge for. One more day for another ice storm to form. One more day for Tanir's leg to go unhealed, and Enoch's ankle and hand, and Wera's ribs, and Gargic's clavicle, and your throat and lungs." Her worries tumbled out.

"We are surviving not just against the elements, or against the fae who may or may not be hunting us, but against *time*. One more day is the difference between life and death right now. Hell, even an hour could be."

She stood before they could protest, say kind or consoling words she couldn't bear to hear, especially when the herbs she had left to ease her pain and hold back the beast inside were so low.

"I'll sleep tonight," she stated. "Start the fire, feed yourselves, I'll keep lookout."

Mina walked away towards the far edge of the landing, and they let her, thanks to Wera's quiet whisper to Sebastian: "I think she needs some space."

Night fell quickly, and they did as she said, even going so far as to set up their dome and paint an iron circle without asking her to join them. Her heart ached when she heard Wera's snoring and realized, but it was for the best.

She watched the horizon until sleep finally claimed her, her last thought worrying about a cluster of clouds off in the distance.

🜁

Another pound of chains wrapped around her neck.

And another.

And another.

They sang out in a sharp clap against her ringing eardrums as they landed against the other fifty pounds of chain hung and twisted around her tiny body, threatening to pull her apart and crush her at the same time.

"Now children, tell teacher what Riktanya did wrong," a voice comprised of all the voices of 'teachers', 'governors', 'governesses', 'guards', 'attendants', that punished her throughout the years spoke.

"She let her guard down," a boy said.

Bormir.

"Precisely."

Hisssssssssss.

"I'm sorry! I'm sorry!" she shrieked, voice high and squeaky, tears flowing down her face without hesitation. "Please don't!"

Hissssssssss.

That metallic viper, barbed metal fangs hanging off each chain-link scale, slithered across the icy floors as the teacher readied their whip.

"Another mistake."

Mina struggled against the chains that bound her, pinching her still human flesh between their links, tearing it, bruising it.

"No! No! No!" Her child's voice was so shrill in her panic, yet the drag of chains still rang out above it. "I'm sorry! I'm sorry!"

"How many times has your Mother told you not to beg!"

The viper struck against her back, its fangs sinking into the scar-riddled flesh. The teacher dragged the chain down as they recalled it, raking it barbs down the thin skin on her spine, making sure to tear it apart.

Riktanya screamed, broken, heaving keens of apologies, as the barbed chains lashed against her over and over again. The younger children were silent, but the older ones, the ones who had been there long enough to have suffered beatings of their own, laughed each time she choked on the blood-stained slobber oozing down her chin.

Hissssssssss. Crack!

Against her thighs.

Hissssssssss. Crack!

Down her arms.

Hissssssssss. Crack!

Hissssssssss. Crack!

Hissssssssss. Crack!

Hissssssssss. Crack!

Across her face.

🜁

On the second day,

Mina woke up gasping for air as stinging sleet rained down upon her.

Immediately, she looked to her left across the ledge. The sleet bounced and rolled off the invisible force field as the pile of tired bodies underneath continued to sleep soundly.

She laid back on the cold, hard rock and stared at the coal-colored clouds above her. It wasn't another ice storm, but the sleet was less than ideal. There would be a higher chance of the others slipping, and their clothes would get soaked through, which would make staving off hypothermia even harder than it already was. There was a tarp in her pack that she could fashion ponchos out of for them since she was up, but as she moved to sit up and start, every nerve in her body seized in pain and knocked her back on the ground.

Though she wouldn't admit it, her body and subconscious knew that keeping them alive — keeping them with her — had nothing to do with her chances of survival. They hurt those chances, in fact. If it wasn't for her contract, she was sure the second she knew the commorancy was lost, her curse would have driven her from them. Just like it had when she tried to embrace Sebastian. But she was bound to them, bound to stay by their side and lead them up the mountain so long as even a single member of their party was standing.

Which is exactly what she was fighting against.

Let them die.

The thought made her skin crawl and stomach lurch. Every ache, every pain she withstood from helping them served to fuel it, feeding it and letting it fester. An unignorable rot that returned, no matter how many times she tried to carve it out.

"Fight alongside us, not for us."

"Be my partner, not my protector."

Commands from days ago that still held strong and made the pain more bearable. They were fighting the elements alongside each other. Surviving together, just as Sebastian willed. But how long would that will last? Especially when she couldn't help but disappoint him.

Hurt him.

Three sprigs of herbs left. If the pain became bad enough to transform her, she'd have three chances to stop it, and with not knowing how many days of travel they'd have left — and Bormir and Eirlys' whereabouts — she had to be careful not to push herself to that level for unnecessary reasons.

Bormir's laughter, filled with childlike wonder at the sight of her suffering, was easy for her to pull out from the crowd in her memories. In the years before she left, it had been the strongest among them, the most cruel, growing louder and louder as the older kids left the nursery. But it wasn't his true laugh, light and rapid like a hummingbird's wings. She hadn't heard that since she was chosen by the Matron.

But that look in his eye...

"We're under attack!" Sir Gargic shouted out of his sleep. He went to draw his blade out of habit and squawked in pain from jerking his arm so suddenly.

The others woke with a jolt as well.

"It's sleet," Mina stated. "It's gonna be a slick climb today. You should all try to keep dry while you eat. It'll stave off the hypothermia a bit. Bastion, how long can you keep that levitation spell of yours up?"

"Didn't you say the winds blowing against it would fuck things up?" Enoch read for him.

"It'd be on Tanir, Enoch, and Gargic, you and Wera would keep them anchored in between," she replied, gaze still locked on the cloudy sky. "Them being a little floaty is easier to control than if someone's grip slips and turns us into skydiving dominoes."

"Then he says he can keep it going for as long as needed."

"Got it."

They ate. Mina ate too. Tanir did her morning healings, then knocked herself out once more, and Mina found herself missing her comforting disposition... which only served to raise bile up her throat.

Idiot. She's still alive. Spare yourself the pain.

The notebook appeared in front of her face as she harnessed Sebastian once again.

Tell me the truth. Did you sleep?

"I did," she responded. "Not long, but enough that exhaustion shouldn't affect me. Plus, getting slowly tenderized by sleet doesn't really scream 'nap time'."

He pulled the notebook away, scribbled something on the dampening paper, and dipped it back into her field of view.

There's that clever wit :)

Barbs dug into her heart. She snapped the notebook shut, causing him to yipe in pain as she caught his fingers in it.

"Stop that," she warned and stomped away.

Mina didn't mind the sting of sleet against her face as she climbed. It was tangible, focusing. The softened shards of ice bouncing off the stone and clothes, weapons and packs, created a discordant cacophony where no lullaby could be found.

One hundred feet, two hundred, three, four, five.

The climb was going much smoother than she thought. Sure, the odd tug of the wind every now and again as it turned those floating into sails took some adjusting, but Sebastian and Wera were holding firm, barely slipping as they scaled the frozen wall.

Six hundred, seven—

Hissssssssss.

Mina stilled.

It was a trick of the mind. A chunk of rock off in the distance skittering down the cliff.

Eight hundred—

Hissssssssss.

Her ice axe bounced off the rock, but she quickly recovered and drove it into the stone.

Her heart pounded against her chest. A slight tremor took root in her limbs, trembling with the urge to run.

Hands shaking, she continued climbing.

Ni—

Hissssssssss.

She froze. *"Run"* screamed louder in her mind, nearly drowning out her common sense. They were free scaling a cliff, thousands of feet up in the air. There were no chains here, no cross tutors, no—

Hissssssssss. Crack!

Mina let go of her axes to cover her head. The crampons on her feet squealed and loosened out of the rock from the sudden shift in her weight. The sinking feeling of falling snapped her out of her cowardice just in time to clumsily grasp the end of the axes' handles. The blades shifted, waiting to give way at any moment and send her and the rest of them tumbling down to their deaths.

She needed to shift her weight forward, regain her footing, but her body wouldn't move.

Hissssssssss.

Say you're sorry! Say it! A much younger voice screamed in her mind.

"Enoch!" Mina shouted over the wind and sleet. "Tell me a story!"

"Mina! You're—" She could hear the panic in his voice as he realized how fucked she was.

Hissssssssss.

"Tell me a fucking story, Enoch!" she shrieked.

Hisssssss—

"The Prince of Nettles!" Enoch proclaimed before dropping into a whisper like the day prior. "That's the title King Ja—"

Hisssssss—

"Louder, Enoch! As loud as you can!"

"That's the title King Jadiel of Kraedia proudly bears!" he bellowed. Mina's body unlocked, and she shifted forward, driving her crampons back into The Lithe and securing herself to it once more.

"The crown upon his head was forged of solid gold and molded to form a ring of vines!"

She readjusted her grip. Her heart still raced — she kept trying to coerce her mind to focus on the story, focus on the climb instead of listening for that accursed whip — but she could move. Stiffly, albeit, but it was movement nonetheless.

"How'd he get such a title, you ask? Well, let me tell you!

"About twenty years ago, you may recall, that Kraedia was ruled by King Yeriel and Queen Valeria. Between them, they had seven children, a firstborn son, a firstborn daughter, and the others they considered nothing more than spares, with Jadiel as the youngest; the most expendable of them all.

"Their cruelty was not limited to their children, it spread throughout their land. Their citizens were kept destitute, sickly, were worked like dogs, and the streets outside their palace walls ran thick with shit and vermin. The royal guard beat all those who dared protest against them, making examples out of broken limbs and bleeding flesh. The rich merchants and dignitaries used the citizens' desperation to enslave them, wounding their bodies and their will until they were nothing left but husks.

"This is what the witch Azmera saw when she was summoned to their palace. The witch had expected that perhaps Kraedia had fallen upon hard times. That the king and queen had summoned her to use her earth-based magics to help heal their rotting lands. But when she stepped through the palace gates and found lush gardens of flowers and fruit — grown for nothing more than decoration as the fallen bounties lay rotten at their trunks — her stomach turned.

"'We wish to have eighteen topiaries grown in the shape of our eldest son Ignacio's form. His eighteenth birthday is tomorrow. Begin now.' Queen Valeria commanded.

"'Your majesties, would you not think it wiser to ask me to grow produce for a great feast instead so that you may celebrate your son's birth with your people?' Azmera asked.

"'A grand feast? A grand feast would be wonderful, don't you think, mama? I bet all the people outside wouldn't shout so much if their bellies were full!' Young Jadiel said.

"His siblings mocked him, scolded him for his ignorance and ill manners, spitting like vultures competing over a carcass.

"'Governess!' King Yeriel called. 'Bring the switch! The spare of spares needs to be reminded of his place.'

"Azmera waited with bated breath to see if any of his family would speak out against this, spare the poor boy from being humiliated in front of a guest. Instead, they all watched in anticipation and amusement, eyes lighting up as the governess grabbed the thrashing boy and ripped down his pants.

"As the switch came down, the boy's skin sprouted vines. Thick, nettled vines that wrapped around his limbs and transformed him into an unholy creature of nature's wrath. The witch disappeared, content to let her monster purge the castle of its toxins.

"Confused, frightened, enraged, thorns flew from Jadiel's body like a hail of arrows, slaughtering his cruel family in a brutal display. His mind, twisted by the transformation, felt relief at the sight. The dark parts of him that wished for the pain inflicted upon him to be returned to them tenfold, satisfied. But there was still a laundry list of those who had caused him to suffer, he could not let them go undisturbed.

"Jadiel tore through the palace, unleashing havoc on all his tormentors, the vile muck that deigned to call themselves human, until a familiar cry pierced through the chaos. Through new eyes he searched for the source and found his nursemaid, the only woman in the palace to ever treat him with kindness, pierced by thorns and slowly dying on the floor.

"His rage snuffed out as quickly as it came at the sight, and he fled, taking refuge in the nearby forest — Sharmon Woods if you know it — to hide himself away so he wouldn't hurt anyone else.

"Time passed. With the main line of succession slaughtered, a distant cousin took the throne. A man by the name of Mauro, who was even crueler and more callous than the old king and queen, and knew the truth behind their untimely demise. Knew that Jadiel, the only threat to his rule, lay in wait somewhere in the woods.

"'A lifetime of food!' The royal decrees read. 'Riches untold! A dry roof over your head! Bring the head of the thorned beast to the palace and claim a grand reward!'

"And for years, month after month, week after week, many tried — but none returned.

"Then one day a young man, a curious horticulturalist by the name of Oromo, wandered into Sharmon Woods. He did not come to slay the beast. In fact, he didn't know a beast lived in the forest at all. He was simply curious about the pollution and decay that had malformed the forest, and wished to discover some way to restore it back to health.

"The damage to the land was more than he planned for, and soon Oromo found himself without clean water to drink or berries to forage. Thirst and hunger getting the best of him, he thought to turn back, hoping he could make the return trip before starving — when a patch of green, verdant and vibrant, glistened through the browning, sallow vegetation.

"An oasis with trees bowed heavy with fruit. A pond so clear and cool and filled with thriving plants and fish. Deer and rabbits, squirrels and birds — animals that he'd yet to see a single one of during the miles and miles he had journeyed — grazed and sang, frolicked and flew. They fled as he approached, rightfully untrustworthy of humans, and Oromo fell to his knees at the edge of the pond.

"'What are you doing here?' A voice of rustling leaves and creaking branches asked.

"Oromo looked at his reflection in the water, and a writhing mass of nettled vines loomed behind him, glowing blue eyes glaring at him from the entanglement. Startled, Oromo jumped, and fell into the pond.

"'My apologies!' he shouted as he surfaced, coughing and gasping to clear the water from his nose. 'I did not mean to startle the animals away! I was just thirsty and this was the first source of clean water I found while exploring these woods!'

"The cursed Jadiel narrowed his glowing eyes. 'Then fill your canteen and leave.'

"'Might I gather some fruit and vegetation to sustain me for the rest of my journey? I promise not to be greedy, I wouldn't wish to take away from the creatures that feed here, but with the woods so polluted there isn't much that's edible for me to forage.'

"The beast skittered away, extending its vined arms to loop around some tree boughs and pull him up into the canopy. 'Fine. But I'll be watching.'

"Oromo climbed out of the pond and kept his focus on the pair of glowing eyes peering at him through the shadows.

"'Do you mind if I take my clothes off to dry as I gather?' he asked. 'I fear I'll catch an illness or an infection if I continue on drenched and shivering.'

"'Do as you must, but quickly.' Jadiel said. 'You're scaring off the wildlife.'

"Oromo left his clothing to dry on a sun-soaked rock and explored the oasis, picking enough to fill his pack and nothing more.

"'This is truly a beautiful grove you live in. Did you cultivate it yourself?' Oromo asked as he sat down and ate a handful of mulberries next to his still-drying clothes.

"'Why do you ask?' Jadiel pressed.

"'I'm a horticulturalist!' Oromo proudly proclaimed. 'I'm wandering these woods to find a means to rid it of its poison. If you have any knowledge to share, I'd love to hear it!'

"'Why?' Jadiel rasped.

"'Why?' Oromo repeated.

"Jadiel descended from the canopy and stalked towards him, vines expanding and nettles sharpening as he came to loom over him, blocking out the sun. 'What reason do you have to help this forest? Do you wish to bring the trees back to life just to chop them down? Spread fresh brush across the ground to fatten up the deer before you slaughter them in mass? Or by poison do you mean me, and wish to learn the secrets of my pitiful existence so that you might stand a chance to strike me down?'

"'No—'" Enoch's voice cut off with a cough. It had been slowly growing raspy as he continued to shout against the freezing sleet.

Hisss—

"'No!'" Enoch repeated, his voice horribly hoarse.

"'What reason would I have to harm you?' Oromo reasoned. 'You haven't hurt me in any way. You allowed me to drink from your pond, eat from your garden, dry my clothes. To be quite honest, I believe I owe you a kindness. I live in a small cottage in Patishe. I could bring you supplies to help you with your cultivation as a thank you, if you'd like.'

"Jadiel retracted his thorns and shrunk down in size. He studied Oromo for a moment.

"'A pail,' he said.

"'Just a pail?' Oromo clarified. 'Are you sure you wouldn't want some fertilizer or a spade to help transplant new vegetation?'

"'A pail,' Jadiel repeated. 'Do not tell anyone of what you've found here, and keep watch for anyone following you. If you see someone, do not come. And if I catch wind that you have told anyone about this place, I'll pierce you with my nettles and string you up as a warning to others.'"

Another rasping cough, grating and painful, tore out of Enoch's throat.

"I don't think I can keep going," he choked out.

Hisss—

"You have to!" Mina pushed.

Hisssss—

"My voice is giving out from all the shouting. If I could whisper—"

Hisss—

"It has to be loud, and it has to be right now!"

"I'm telling you, I can't—"

Hisssssssssss. Crack!

Mina's body seized in fear. Anger and desperation drowned her mind in a rush, floating a horrible notion to the surface. A life raft, as disgusting as it was.

She reached and tugged on it, feeling Enoch's frantic heartbeat pulse through the invisible ribbon binding him to her.

"Enoch Elias Dapple," she bellowed, his full name appearing in her mind as if she knew it as well as her own. "I demand you keep telling this tale as loud as you can until I tell you to cease as payment for saving your life!"

The Fae's Folly snapped.

"The next day Oromo returned," Enoch hollered, every word gritted and grating, "pail and a hammock in hand."

"'What is that for?' Jadiel asked as Oromo set up the hammock.

"'A place for you to sleep. I'm sure you prefer the canopy, but I have a feeling you tend to rest on your vines, and I can't imagine that would be comfortable.' Oromo replied.

"Once it was finished, Jadiel sat inside of it and immediately tore it to shreds with his nettles.

"Oromo stifled his laughter. 'I'll bring a stronger one tomorrow. Your nettles are sharper than I thought.'

"And so Oromo returned the next day, and the day after that, and every day that followed after. He and Jadiel grew closer. Jadiel showed him how to cleanse the earth and rear the plants to grow in abundance. Oromo brought him gifts and tales from outside the woods. One day, one of the bounty hunters came to collect Jadiel's head, thinking themselves smart for approaching in daylight, and after advancing on him, met his untimely end.

"Jadiel thought that Oromo would shun him, would flee in fear, and never return again. Instead, Oromo used the skills Jadiel had taught him to repair his broken vines, cleansing the wounds with his tears and lamenting how anyone could hurt such a kind creature as he.

"What the pair didn't know was that another hunter was watching from afar, and had stalked them back to the oasis. The hunter stayed all night, waiting for when Oromo left, then slunk back to Kraedia to tattle to King Mauro.

"Chaos and bloodshed greeted Oromo when he returned the following day. The creatures Jadiel cared for lay slain, the pond they drank from turned crimson from their blood. Before Oromo could call out Jadiel's name, he was racing towards him, form nearly unrecognizable. His vines wrapped around him, forming a shield for a brief moment before suddenly falling limp.

"'We saved the man! The beast is slain!' a soldier cheered.

"Oromo fell to his knees beside Jadiel's limp body, tears streaming down his face, in disbelief at how still he was. Such a lively, joyous creature, now motionless as his vines withered.

"'Take his head back to the king!' the soldiers hollered, and Oromo threw his body on top of Jadiel. The nettles pierced and tore his skin, but he did not care about the pain.

"'You have taken enough from me!' Oromo shouted. 'You will not touch his body! Not while I live!'

"'Easy enough. The arrow that thing stopped was meant for you anyway.' The soldiers drew back their bows and Oromo held Jadiel even tighter.

"'At least I'll be able to tell you I love you on the other side,' Oromo confessed and pressed a tear-slicked kiss between Jadiel's closed eyes.

"But his lips did not touch vine or plant of any kind. Instead, he was met with smooth copper flesh. The soldiers stilled their advance as the nettled vines that cursed the long-lost prince dried and crumbled away, revealing his true body. With a gasp, Jadiel awoke. True love's kiss had brought him back to life.

"The soldiers, recognizing the true king of Kraedia, laid down their weapons and fell to their knees, fumbling apologies for attempting to take his life. But Jadiel couldn't care less about their sorries. He was too busy holding Oromo in his arms and peppering tear-slicked kisses of his own against his lips, like he had been yearning to do for the longest time.

"As penance for their aggression, the soldiers helped to remove Mauro from his throne so that Jadiel and his love could ascend and repair the years of neglect that had befallen his people."

Mina gripped the ledge of the outcropping so hard her fingers embedded into the stone.

"The first thing they did was teach the jobless townsfolk how to cleanse the earth—"

Mina hoisted herself over it and pulled the others up.

"Mauro's self-absorbed nature had left the castle's coffers overly full, so the citizens were compensated for their efforts, which—"

"Enoch, you sound awful," Wera wheezed as she climbed onto the landing.

"And soon their economy was booming, produce and game were abundant!" Enoch kept on chattering away, voice cutting in and out painfully.

"Enoch... you're crying..." Sebastian rasped, though now his wounded vocal cords sounded like music compared to the archivist's.

"Shut up," Mina said once Sir Gargic was over the edge. Enoch fell silent.

She untied herself from them and drew her sword. Back and forth she waved it through the air, dowsing for any vibration, any sense to source the hissing chains that taunted her. They had fallen silent, but she would not let her childish fear get the better of her, not anymore. She was prepared to face it now.

After a few minutes, she sheathed it and retied the rope to her belt. "I'm going scouting."

She secured the rope to one of her own steel pitons and embedded it in the stone.

"But the fire—" Tanir mumbled, waking from her self-induced slumber.

"What about the fire?"

Mina turned to find Sebastian struggling to start the blaze, his sparks fading quickly as he conjured them, the ones that did burn turning to ash as soon as they hit the sleet-dampened wood. She held no dry tinder in her pack, but the wind weaving through her fingers reminded her of a trick Mr. Harlowe had used one unseasonably cold summer evening.

She ran her fingers through her hair as she drew her sword again. The intertwining wind wicked the moisture away as she cut off a large swatch of it with one quick swing. She matted it together, movements a blur at the thought of her tormentor thinking her a coward, then pulled a small tin of pine pitch and her flint from her pack.

A stripe of pitch smeared along a piece of kindling, matted hair stuffed underneath the stack, with a single strike of her flint against her sword, the fire ignited.

"I'm going scouting," she repeated and rappelled off the side of the landing into the storm.

Nothing. Hours of searching, and she'd gotten nothing but aching bones and a rumbling stomach. The sleet had subsided, the wind's howl now empty as it chilled the rain coating the face of The Lithe and turned it into a sheet of solid ice. The slight darkening of her vision was the only sign that the sun had set behind the thick veil of clouds as she made her way back to the campsite.

Mina paused for a moment before climbing over the lip and watched the group's shadows stretch against the wall, shifting back and forth in time with the flickers of firelight.

"He seems shaken," Tanir slurred. The cycle of pain and sleep enchantments she put herself under were taking a toll. "Are you sure nothing else happened?"

"It was hard to pick up through the sleet and the wind exactly what she was shouting at him," Wera said, every word still airy and tinted with a heavy wheeze. "But other than that, I was a little too busy trying not to slip into a five-thousand-foot free fall."

"And he didn't stop until Mina told him to? With how swollen his throat was, it had to have been a spell or something that made him continue. The pain must have been excruciating."

"I swear to The Gods if she charmed him, Windenhofer—"

What Mina assumed to be Sebastian's shadow held up a notebook.

Sir Gargic gave a cruel snort. "Yeah, and I never thought she'd be demanding fairy tales like a spoiled brat at bedtime."

She jumped up and over onto the outcropping in one smooth leap, shoulders squared and jaw tight, ready to defend her actions despite the guilt eating at her stomach.

If they were to cast her out for using her nature to keep them alive, then she'd gladly leave them to rot, save herself the suffering.

Finally face the scorn from them that had been a long time coming.

"Speak of the devil," he grumbled.

"But you're already here, Gargic," she snipped back as she untied herself. "I see you were able to keep the fire going."

"Windenhofer had to add a few locks to really get it going after your dramatic—"

"He *what?*" Mina's head snapped up to face them, honing in on Sebastian.

A hole opened in her chest. A black hole, slowly sucking in every ounce of feeling in her limbs at the sight of Sebastian's amber locks, blunt and ill-shorn.

How dare he.

"How dare you." The words slipped out, her nerves too taxed — body, mind, too ready for a fight to hold back.

The sheepish smile Sebastian wore slipped off his face.

"You're in the middle of a frozen wasteland! How stupid could you be?!" she continued, the numbness in her extremities left plenty of room for hatred to grow. It slipped beneath her sinew, puppeting her, urging her to act. To retaliate.

"That's why he did it, Mina," Tanir tried to explain. "Wera offered hers, but because of Sebastian's natural—"

"You could have commanded me back! Told me to cut more of mine! I have no need for it!" She drew her sword and cut a chunk away. "Here! For tomorrow!" She reached up and grabbed another section, "And the day after that!"

Her scalp burned as her blade scraped across it, and she welcomed the agony. It was penance for how horrible she was, how weak.

"And after that! And after that!" She shouted as she hacked away her failures, attacked the true source of her suffering. If she hadn't been so fucking pathetic, none of this would have happened. She wouldn't have to see their agony, wouldn't have an empty stomach and aching bones, wouldn't have cared about some stupid wizard's stupid fucking hair when death was looming over her, scythe at the back of her neck.

If she were stronger, none of this would have mattered.

Forget the blade, she knotted her fingers into her hair and pulled the locks out from the root, tearing skin and drawing blood along with it. Best to cull the problem from its core and—

"Stop it!" Sebastian squawked.

Mina froze, eyes locked on his horrified face. Tears rolled down his cheeks. The growing hole in her heart threatened to swallow her.

"Mina," Wera spoke up. "I really think you ought to eat something, then go to sleep."

Sebastian's command wound around Mina so tightly, she couldn't open her mouth to reply. He didn't want her to move, didn't want her to speak, it was a miracle he didn't stop her breathing. She'd understand it if he did. There was even a small part of her that wanted him to. What use was she to him anyway?

What use is he if he can't do the bare minimum to keep himself alive?

Sebastian inhaled shakily and turned his face away to dry his eyes. "Do as Wera says."

And she did.

She sheathed her sword, stuffed her hair in her pocket, finished untying herself, ate a few pieces of jerky, then fell asleep on the cold stone.

All in silence.

All wishing to be *truly* numb again.

🜁

She sat on a chair in Mother's room, gaze locked on the window, watching her siblings running drills in the snow banks below.

"Your hair is getting long," Mother said as She raked Her fingernails across her scalp. "And it's getting lighter by the day." She pulled a strand free and ran Her fingers along it as if She were evaluating the quality of silk. "Soon it'll be just as white as mine."

She let the strand drop. Her nails screeched across the marble of Her vanity as She picked up Her brush.

Riktanya gripped the bottom of the chair tightly.

The thin bristles, needles plucked from the hide of some poor fae creature, raked across her scalp. They snagged against each hair as She pulled the brush along, threatening to tear them from her scalp micrometer by micrometer.

No matter how many times She brushed her hair, the pain was still the same. But Riktanya learned better than to cry about it.

An aching scalp was one thing. An aching scalp and fifty lashes was another.

"It's such a shame you scar so easily during your adjustments," She lamented. "But I'm sure Sloin will find a remedy soon. And if they don't, another alchemist is easy to find." Her grip on her hair tightened as She worked on a knot that wasn't there. "I want you to remember that, dear one. It's a weakness to hold on to things that serve no purpose."

"Yes, Mother."

"And we are not weak."

"We are not weak," Riktanya repeated.

Mother's brush stilled. Her fingers crawled along her scalp, pointed nails prodding the sensitive flesh. She paused and circled a specific spot, something about it catching Her interest. The strands wrapped around Her finger and with a forceful yank, She tore them out.

Blood filled Riktanya's mouth as she bit the inside of her cheek to keep from screaming.

Mother sighed and held the chunk of hair She pulled in front of Riktanya's face. Specks of blood dotted the dark roots.

"Looks like you'll need another treatment."

"Perhaps it's just the blood discoloring it," Riktanya offered. "I've been washing it with the snow melt like You said and eating every single crumb of my meals!"

"Every single crumb," Mother drawled. "How interesting. Klakille!"

Mother's attendant entered the room with a platter covered by a silver cloche in hand.

"Every. Single. Crumb." Mother emphasized. Klakille removed the cloche to reveal a plate of bones, the cartilage and sinew that clung to them frozen over. "These are awfully big crumbs, don't you think?"

"But the others don't eat them!" Riktanya protested.

Mother hooked Her finger under her chin, digging Her nail into her skin as She turned Riktanya's head to face Her. "The others aren't nearly as stubborn as you are. The others were not chosen."

Riktanya's body betrayed her, jolting her forward to run as a glint flickered across Mother's bright blue eyes. Mother pulled her back, throwing her to the floor by her hair with a crack.

"Treatment first, Klakille, then Riktanya will finish her crumbs," She said as She dragged her across the floor.

Riktanya kicked and screamed, grabbed at her hair to try and pull it free from Her iron grip.

"Mina. Wake up."

△

On the third day,

Sebastian was standing above her when she awoke, frowning. Brown eyes dulled with conflicting emotions.

"You're scared," he croaked.

Mina turned away from him as she got up to stand. After last night, she didn't deserve to look at him. "It was a nightmare."

"About what?"

"About distant things," She looked out into the sea of clouds and snow. It wasn't too bright out yet. "How long was I out?"

Sebastian pulled out his notebook this time:

The dome dispelled just a few minutes ago. You were crying out about an hour before that. I'm sorry I couldn't wake you sooner.

The last sentence sent a jolt of pain down her spine.

"Right. Eat, relieve yourselves, then we climb."

More scribbling in the notebook.

Enoch's voice is gone. Tanir says it's laryngitis. Should we change the order?

"No," Mina said. "I'll stuff my ears with some wool."

Are you hearing things? Did you almost fall asleep again?

"No to the second one." Mina busied herself with preparing her pack. She paused. A tuft of her hair tumbled out as she removed her canteen. The wind quickly snatched it up and sent it soaring off the ledge.

Sebastian held his notebook in front of her face.

Are you sure you're of sound mind enough to make the climb?

Mina scoffed. "Whether or not I'm sound doesn't matter. We have to climb."

Scribble, cross out, scribble, cross out.

I'll catch you if you fall.

The words burned her eyes, pierced her mind, caught like briars in her throat, but she let herself look at them a little longer.

She was not worthy of such words.

Sebastian closed his notebook and walked away.

Mina bit off half a sprig of herbs.

Enoch didn't look at her when she strapped him into his harness. She couldn't blame him for it. He climbed along as best as he could with the others, no longer needing to float now that the sleet had ended, but his unwilled silence hung heavy around her neck.

Her heartbeat was just as heavy, amplified by the wool stuffed in her ears. It beat faster than its usual tempo, though considering the past few days, perhaps fast *was* its new tempo. But it was even, as was her breath—

—as was the voice that whispered:

"Dear one."

Mina's heart rate spiked.

"My dear one."

Her body sought to betray her again, pulled at her to race up the cliff, to let the rushing winds take her far away from Her, just like they had when she was a little girl.

But she wasn't a little girl. She wasn't little Riktanya. She was Mina.

"Dear one."

"Don't call me that," she growled, and her voice rang louder than her heartbeat, louder than the muffed rushing winds beyond her makeshift earplugs.

"Rik—"

"Once upon a time!" she shouted loud enough to drown Her out. "A little girl was lost in the woods. She did not know they were woods, though, for she had never been in one before then. She thought trees were strange pillars that, even stranger, grew clouds. Thought that the grass below her feet was hair and that she was standing on a giant's head!

"The little girl was terrified and confused as to how she got there. So as little kids tend to do when they're scared, she ran and ran and ran, deeper and deeper into the woods, and got herself even more lost.

"She wandered the woods for days, had no clue how to find food, but managed to find a stream. So she would always have water to drink, she decided to continue wandering alongside it. Being thirsty had far worse consequences than being hungry.

"Eventually, the stream led into a small lake. And just beyond that lake, a cluster of little wooden buildings surrounding a small log cabin. The little girl hid behind the trees, not yet realizing that the shift of light in her vision meant it was night, and watched the buildings warily. Until she saw a set of flapping wings through the mesh windows of one of the outer buildings.

"The little girl snuck up to the building and peered inside to find it filled with hens. Her stomach rumbled at the sight. Breaking in was easy, the lock was old and snapped off when she gave it a good solid tug. She didn't realize how noisy the chickens were being while she feasted upon one, not until the coop door opened and a brilliant light blinded her mid-meal.

"'Oh my,' a woman holding a lantern shouted. 'Lars! Come quickly!'"

Mina paused a moment. She'd never been able to say Mr. Harlowe's name before.

"My dear—"

"The woman and her husband would have been right to be cautious of the little girl after finding her covered in blood, spitting pins out of her mouth as she ate through one of their chickens, feathers and all. But instead, they brought her into their home, fed her, clothed her. The little girl had grown so used to pain that she didn't recognize that something was wrong. Not until she woke up, not in the bed the couple had laid her down in, but on the cabin floor, surrounded by the debris from her bestial rampage.

"The couple had every right to turn her away, to kill her, but they didn't. The girl would learn later in life that the couple had found each other late, too late to have children, but the thought of one padding around their cabin had always lingered in the back of their minds. They knew what she was, were willing to learn what her nature entailed, and after a night of hearing the beast tearing aimlessly about their cabin, searching for warmth, decided they could not abandon her.

"Yet they could not have their cabin destroyed every time they put her to bed either.

"The woman's husband, an alpinist and woodsman, observed the little girl carefully and noticed that it was easier on the girl when she did things on her own. He decided to teach her all that he knew, teach her how to survive.

"The little girl slept in a lean-to she built with her own hands, she ate meals caught and foraged by her own hands, and the things she gathered that she could not find use for — extra pelts, fat and bones, herbs and flowers that just happened to fall in her basket — she left for the woodsman and his wife to find.

"They spent a few years like this, until one day — while the woodsman had left to lead an expedition up the mountain — a group of bandits came to vandalize the cabin.

"When he returned, he found them strung up in the trees surrounding the cabin, hearts torn out of their chests by the jaws of a terrible beast. The little girl found a sword of iron abandoned in the woods a few weeks after.

"The next change came two years after that, when the woodsman returned from an expedition hobbling and wounded.

"'You can't keep doing this!' the woman scolded. 'Your body's older now, it can't take the stress.'

"'And we can't lose out on the money,' the woodsman countered. '*I* can't sleep at night knowing that foolish adventurers will try to climb those mountains without a guide and get themselves killed.'

"'There are other guides!'

"'Not like me, Heidi!'"

Mina paused again, the twinge of a smile pulled at the corner of her lips.

"Rik—"

"'You know that!'

"'Well then take Mina at least!'

"'What? But—'

"'Any troublemaker knows well enough by now to leave this place alone, and the girl could bury herself in a bank of snow buck-naked and not shiver once! She's stronger than ten oxen, can move faster than storm winds, and already knows nearly all the survival tricks in the world because you taught them to her! You'd be a fool not to take her!'

"And so, when the next contract came, the little girl, now a young woman, followed the woodsman and made her first trip through the Sandere Woods and up the Fallow Peaks. They led ten expeditions together over the next three years. Then things changed again."

Mina's chest ached, her eyes stung, but she continued.

"The woman had fallen ill. The woodsman and the girl had taken an expedition much later in the fall than they normally would accept, and while the woman knew how to keep things on her own quite well, age was taking its toll on her too, and she was unable to keep the cabin as warm as she needed to combat the illnesses that winter often breeds.

"The woodsman decided to stay with her and take care of her. The girl, unable to do anything of worth for the couple, continued to lead the expeditions on her own, and, having little use for the gilt they offered back then, left the pay outside the cabin. The woman lasted much longer than her illness typically allowed. Perhaps the woodsman used it to acquire medicine.

"Then, one morning, the girl woke not to the call of a rooster, but to a hollow sob.

"The girl buried the body where the woodsman told her to; on a small hill that overlooked the lake. The woodsman and his wife often had picnics there. He would tell her about all the adventurers he'd met, how his expeditions had gone, and news from Lanholde. She would tell him about the new soap and lotions she had made, how her wares had sold at market, gossip from town, and new books she had read while he was gone.

"The woodsman was not quite the same after that. He barely ate, he barely drank. He left one day to go into town and when he returned he just stood in the middle of the clearing, staring at the cabin door. The girl knew he was waiting to see if the woman would come out to greet him like she always did.

"One night while he ate his dinner and the girl ate hers, outside and apart from each other, the woodsman said, 'If I were to die, it should be during sunrise. Her smile always reminded me of it.'

"The next morning the girl awoke not to the call of a rooster and not to a sob, but to the sound of footsteps as the woodsman walked outside, to the middle of a clearing, to watch the sunrise over the lake.

"There was never much the girl could do for either of them.

"But this, due to the cruelty of her existence, came easy. Her blade never flew faster, so clean that you never would have known his head was no longer attached."

The words caught in her throat, her nose stuffed up, tears welled in her eyes.

But She never allowed time to grieve.

"My dear one."

Mina took a deep breath, a rebellious breath against the weight that threatened to collapse her chest in.

"The girl buried him with the woman. It would have been foolish to waste any more land for the dead.

"After that, it was quiet. The girl moved into the cabin, no longer needing the lean-to now that they were gone. Not knowing anything else, she made soaps and lotions, collected herbs and flowers and animal skins, and sold them at markets as the woman had. Adventurers would come along just as they always had, and she would lead them up the mountain. The sun rose and set. Leaves fell and grew.

"Then one day, while the girl was stalking through the woods, hunting a large stag whose massive antlers and hide were sure to fetch a high price at market, she found a witch woman hanging upside down in one of her snare traps.

"The witch woman babbled on and on about nonsense, about how she had been on a long journey, had been looking to atone, but the girl needed only for her snare to be free. So she cut her down and went to walk away.

"'Wait! I know what you are!' the witch cried after her. 'I know what has been done to you. My third eye sees the chains that bind you, and I can undo them!'

"The girl stopped. She went to speak but found her jaw unable to move.

"'I see them tightening, holding your tongue. Don't you grow tired of their weight? Imagine how much freedom you could have without them.'

"'For what price?' the girl asked, knowing all too well that everything in this realm had a cost.

"'No cost,' the witch said. 'I am trying to atone. The wind must have led me here for that.'

"The witch followed the girl back to her cabin, jabbering all the way about her life, while all the girl could think of was how she'd never find the stag again with all her carrying on. Every beast within a mile must have fled from her constant droning.

"'Will you get on with it?' the girl asked after having suffered through the witch's chattering as she helped herself to a cup of tea.

"'Silly me. You can't really appreciate conversation, can you?' She dusted off the crumbs of a biscuit that had to have been much too stale to eat and stood. 'Close your eyes and let's fix that first, shall we?'

"The girl did as she was told. The witch cupped her hands over her ears."

Mina could feel the chains pulling tight around her jaw.

"And when she opened her eyes, the witch was dead. Frozen solid, skin blackened with frostbite, eyes wide in terror.

"The girl picked up her body and dragged it outside to dispose of it. Then dropped it when she heard an unfamiliar sound. Bright and trilling. Bird song. Later she'd learn it was a cardinal."

Mina reached the next outcropping, yet she kept speaking. She didn't mind remembering this part of her life.

"She spent the next days roaming the woods, climbing trees to find what birds were singing in them."

Enoch climbed over the ledge.

"And then the next time she went to town, she discovered how different voices could sound. Squeaky ones, gruff ones, warm ones."

Wera climbed over the edge.

"It was daunting at first, so much noise, so the girl stuck to quiet back alleys to ease the pounding in her head."

Together, they pulled Tanir over. The bottom of her bundle bounced and scraped against the ledge.

"And as she was walking, that's when she heard it first, mu—"

The ledge broke away under Sebastian's feet. Mina jolted forward and grabbed him by the lapels of his coat.

Then everything went white.

Pain. Excruciating pain.

The kind that made her flee before, yet there was nowhere left to run.

Hot hands grabbed onto her arm, burning fingers digging into her skin.

It's a weakness to hold on to things that serve no purpose.

All she had to do was let go and this would all be over. All the pain. She could go back to her cabin, and her bird song, her music, and her memories. There'd be no rimefae to worry about, no vindictive false siblings. She could be at peace, live a simple, quiet life until death claimed her.

Her fingers twitched against his lapel. Frost spread rapidly from her dark chain-print hand, climbing to pierce his throat.

It was a weakness to hold on.

He was a weakness.

"Partnership."

Something shifted the chains, pulled against them. When had they gotten so tight?

"Remember, Mina?"

The pain faded into a dull thrum.

"We're partners."

The white cleared, and she was met with wide brown eyes searching her face in desperation. Sebastian's palms glowed a brilliant orange against the blackened, chain-scarred skin spreading up her arm as he clung to her for dear life.

She tightened her grip around his lapel, shattering the ice, and yanked him and the panicking Sir Gargic up with one sharp pull. They landed with a hard thud behind her, but her focus was glued to her hand, and to the deep sea of mist she almost made their grave.

"Mina," Sebastian croaked. She could hear him scrambling to his feet towards her.

"Don't," she warned, voice distant and frail. "Just don't."

She watched her skin turn back to normal, the darkness leaving it and spreading to the sky as night rolled in. The hole in her chest was even hungrier now, the numbness finally consumed her. She pulled the wool out of her ears to help it along. Partially because her heartbeat had been a hindrance.

Partially because she was waiting to hear Her voice again.

Wanting to hear it, even.

A thought like that would have turned her stomach, but she was too numb to be hungry, let alone sick.

Eventually, something came through the numbness. Mina turned away from the abyss, following the thread tugging at her chin to look back.

Sebastian sat with his back to the cliff face as the others slept in a pile on and around his legs. From beneath the dome, he held up his notebook to face her.

Come here.

Threads pulled her legs towards him.

"You should be asleep," she said.

He crossed out the command and wrote another: **Sit down.**

She did; back to the cliff, just a few inches from the invisible dome separating them.

Was the story that you were telling true?

"Really? That's what you called me over for?"

That, and seeing you so close to the edge was making me nervous.

The hole deepened.

"You're a fool, you know."

You didn't answer my question.

"It was true."

I'm happy to hear that you had people like that in your life.

"You shouldn't be. I almost dropped you off a cliff."

No, you didn't.

"*I* did. Just because I didn't look as I normally do, doesn't mean that it isn't me."

Mina. It's the same case as after we left Rabbet's Pass.

"Exactly. It's the same. It'll never change. I'll always be this. I'll always be capable of..." she held a fist out in front of her and opened it, "...that."

And I'm always capable of burning everyone in this dome alive in my sleep.

"You have control over that."

Not if I get a bad enough nightmare.

Mina hung her head.

"I keep hurting you. I see it in your eyes every time," she whispered. The words instantly gave her a headache, and she pulled the half sprig of herbs out of her pocket. "I only have a small amount of these, and we've got close to two weeks left. It'll only get worse."

I didn't know that.

"I know." She chewed slowly. The longer the herbs lasted, the longer she could release some of the apologies weighing on her chest. "Your hair. You shouldn't have had to do that. I should have thought ahead and wrapped some of the tinder in scraps of beeswax cloth to waterproof it. Keep your hat on as we climb to keep the heat in."

I look that bad, huh?

Mina ran a hand through her own hair and grimaced at the wiry patches and thick scabs on her scalp from her incensed hack job the night prior.

"I'm certain I look much worse."

I might have some glue in my pocket. Maybe we can take the bunches you got stored in your pack and stick them back on.

Mina smiled at the image. A small smile as she was a few days out of practice.

"Or I could sharpen my blade after we finish the climb tomorrow and shave it all off. Start from scratch."

That's not a bad idea. Can I make an appointment at Mina's Barbershop too?

"I don't know." Mina yawned, the warmth coming from his side of the dome made her eyelids heavy. "Can you?"

I think I can.

"I charge a hefty price."

How much?

"How much you got?"

I can do an amazing impression of a barn owl singing a lullaby right now.

Mina snorted, holding back the laugh that sorely wanted to come out.

"I'll take your word for it."

Her eyelids grew heavier and heavier. Her body drifting towards the warmth, she let her head rest against it and guide her to sleep.

△

On the fourth day,

Snow fell.
And they were gone.

XIX

CHOICES

It's a special kind of panic that occurs when a planned-for fear becomes reality.

The heart's beating is thrown off rhythm. Breathing becomes hard as the mind begins to race.

Mina recognized the signs, but could not stop the panic from setting in any better than she could stop her anger from rising at Sir Gargic's goads, or her head from aching when Sebastian smiled at her.

Not when she realized that she'd been the one to break the iron ring around them by leaning on the warmth of the dome. By the flecks of paint in the cracks of her knuckles, her arm must have fallen limp in slumber and placed her hand across the strip. Wera must have thinned the paints somehow to make it last longer. She barely felt the burn from it.

Most worrisome of all, however, was that it was not the sound of them leaving that woke her up, or the sudden lack of warmth, but the dome finally dispelling beneath her, dropping her body to the ground.

There were no footprints, no scuffed rocks or cracked ice to suggest that they had climbed, their packs were even missing. If it weren't for the ring of paint and the cold charcoal of the fire they had made, it would have been as if they had never existed.

Mina closed her eyes and listened for a foot brushing every third step, a gentle, spell-induced snore, high-pitched hums of a ring spun nervously, the squeak of a thick leather breastplate, fingers tapping out triplets, anything.

All there was, was silence. She couldn't even hear the snow hitting the stone beneath her.

Panic turned to fury.

Silent snow.

The flurries swirled against gravity, an updraft containing no wind pointing to the top of The Lithe.

It was a trap.

They could have been taken right to the top or ten miles away for all Mina knew. With the snow blocking her hearing, searching for them herself would be near impossible, possibly even suicidal depending on whatever Bormir was planning.

Which was good.

It meant she didn't have to stab herself this time.

Mina wore her pack backwards, summoned the wind to her heels, and leapt without trying to trick her mind about what she was doing.

She wasn't climbing to save herself, to get The Lithe over with. She was climbing to save them.

Her skull threatened to split, her vision blurred. Every nerve in her body seized and spiked; contorting her muscles, threatening to break her bones. But still, she climbed.

She could never tell them how sorry she was for treating them cruelly.

Her hearing dulled into a shrill ring.

She could never thank them for their endless kindness, for their acceptance.

Her limbs numbed, and her ice axes fell from her hands into the clouds below.

But she could try to save them. She might die, but she'd die knowing that when they saw her, hungry and wild in a body with no resemblance to her own, that she'd died trying to save them.

She leapt once more and everything went black.

🜁

Endless hunger.

Ceaseless cold.

She was falling yet again, surrounded by frigid air.

Heat. She needed heat.

Her wings unfurled and she righted herself. The waves that wrapped around the world to form her vision were too slow, too cold, save for one little stream. A remnant of warmth gone by.

The track of her prey.

Endless hunger.

Ceaseless cold.

The trail grew stronger as she flew upward, her stomach growling as the pattern turned familiar.

There it was, the heart that had escaped her. The heat it gave wasn't as strong now, didn't radiate with the warmth it once promised.

Relentless rage.

She crested the top of the cliff and surged forward, furious over the heat that she'd been denied. She would claim it now out of spite, swallow it whole in the hopes that it would give some relief, then tear its body to shreds as penance for denying her salvation.

Swirls of snow tried to hide it from her, but she could see its pulsing radiation, the heartbeat slow and close to ending. Her wings beat faster and faster, flying low to the ground, determined to get there before it stilled.

"Foithe."

🜁

Normally, it took a minute for her body to adjust to the transformation. The beast would fall asleep due to lack of feed, and she'd wake up as herself, allowing herself a few moments of dark bliss to forget about her animalistic thoughts, and for her body to right itself back to its true form without pain.

It took only a blink to become herself after that fae word was spoken, and the pain was excruciating.

Or maybe the pain was from the hand on the back of her neck plucking her out of the air and driving her into the ground.

"You see, children," Bormir proclaimed. "That is how you capture a stray who's wandered too far from The Matron's embrace."

He pressed her face against the hard, frozen rock beneath her, threatening to cave her nose in.

"I really was hoping you'd come up with a more clever solution to come claim your pets," he leaned down and whispered in her ear, "but at least it gave me the excuse to test out the magic word Mother told me."

It would be impossible to escape his hold like this, and to harness the wind when she was so wounded would require losing herself to her fae nature. Exactly what the arrogant prick wanted.

"Where are they?" she seethed into the snow.

"Your little playthings?" Bormir wrenched her head up by her hair. "Why, they're right here."

Mina's eyes adjusted to the light, and her anger turned tenfold.

Sir Gargic, Enoch, Tanir, Wera, and Sebastian all stood rigid, eyes closed and skin paled by thick patches of frost. Five rimefae draped themselves around them as if they were nothing more than statues.

It took everything in Mina not to give into the howling jealousy that demanded her to rip out the throat of the man wrapping locks of Sebastian's hair around his fingers and leaving short icy curls in his wake.

"Thank you so much, cousin, for keeping this darling one safe for me," Eirlys said as she ran her ice-formed hand along the curve of Enoch's mustache. She reached the tip of it and broke off the hairs with a sickening snap. "But it's time for you to share your toys."

With Bormir's adjusted hold, Mina hiked her leg up and swept his legs out from underneath him. His hand let go of her hair and she surged forward.

She couldn't fight them all at once, not with how wounded she was. She just needed to separate them. A second apart would be enough to grab them. It just would need to be a second with *all* of them loose.

Enoch would be first, Eirlys was sure to be frightened by her approach as she drew her sword at gale-force speed. But instead of Eirlys backing away, Tanir stepped forward. Mina pivoted in time to drive her sword strike into the ground and roll away from the swing of Tanir's axe.

"Dolcemar's really quite the talent, isn't she?" Bormir gestured to the young fae sitting on top of Wera's shoulders. "Cover someone in frost, and she can puppet them so well you'd hardly believe they weren't moving on their own."

They all stepped away from the fae beside them and raised the weapons Dolcemar forced them to wield.

"They all are quite talented really. Of course, you're familiar with Eirlys' transport abilities."

Mina caught the shimmer of Eirlys in the sheet of ice beneath her too late and got an icy fist to the chin as her punishment. The hit sent her tumbling towards Wera, who swung a frozen sword in a sweeping arc. Mina parried the blow away, but barely had a moment to breathe before she was met with a flurry of lanky-armed blows accompanied by a low hum.

Her counterstrikes were usually faster, yet each swing was knocked to the side as her eyes kept closing just before she found purchase.

"Tyoma's got a real dreamlike quality to them don't they?" Bormir taunted. "And Androniki's avalanches really pack a punch."

One heavy-lidded blink and Tyoma's bony arms transformed into a thick-knuckled fist that finished the job that Bormir had started: breaking her nose with a wet crunch.

Mina shook the stars out of her eyes and went to swing at the behemoth—

"Dear one."

She froze and earned herself another punch to the face.

Long, spindly fingers curled around her throat as Her voice purred in her ear, "My dear one."

The fingers squeezed, slowly but surely choking out what little breath she had as Bormir stepped into her narrowing field of vision.

"And Iraina is quite the impressionist."

"***Hissssssssss. Crack!***" Iraina kicked the back of her knees and dropped her to the ground.

Bormir leaned forward, and waved the commorancy's card in front of her face. "But snagging this little gem? This was all me."

Mina wanted to spit in his face, to call down the winds and have them smash them all into a bloody pulp, just like she had those poor frostlyons. But the others would still be covered in Dolcemar's frost, and her darker self might drop them off a cliff in callousness.

"Name your price," she rasped.

"Name your price?" Bormir's brows lifted as he chuckled in amusement. "Is that the best she can beg, *Bastion?*"

A blade of ice tucked under her chin as Sebastian's puppeted body threatened to slice her jugular if she swallowed a little too harshly. It was disturbing to see him hold a weapon.

Disturbing to see the ice remain solid in his palm.

"Beat me. Kill me even." The pain in her throat was paltry to all the other ails she bore. "Just let them go."

"Really? Let them go?" Bormir tutted. He grabbed her jaw and twisted her face back and forth to study it. "You really must be in pain; otherwise you wouldn't be signing their death certificate so willingly. You really think if we let them go, they'll be all right? Sister, that fop barely made it out alive after spending minutes with Eirlys." He leaned in closer. "We've had them for hours."

She stared at the frozen hilt in Sebastian's hand, pleading for just one drip to fall from it.

"Oh, don't look so dismayed, sister. I'm not that cruel. There's still hope!" He slapped her, quick and stinging, to bring her attention back to him. "We're going to let you try to save them. In exchange, The Matron asks you to make a choice. Either leave them once they're healed and come home with us, or die like dogs together in three days' time."

"You think you can kill us?" Mina seethed.

"I think that the veil between here and the Rime is very thin at this part of the Peaks, and I have plenty of students who would jump at the chance to impress Mother by lending a hand in bringing Her precious daughter home."

"And what use will I be to Her if I'm dead?"

"Well, it certainly would be easier to remake you in Her image if you're unable to fight back," Bormir said. "And you know Mother has deals and contracts with all kinds of individuals. Surely She has a few who hold some expertise in the necrotic arts. Or maybe once you're gone, She'll have the good sense to cut Her losses and choose a new successor." His smile was still sickly, but for a moment, the delight left his eyes. "As you and I both know, the reasonings behind Mother's whims are a mystery."

Sebastian and Bormir backed away, and with a nod of his head, Iraina let go of her throat. She hit Mina's temple with the heel of her hand, erupting another burst of stars in Mina's vision as she collapsed to the ground. Bormir flicked the commorancy's card into the snow in front of her.

It was a well-worn playing card: The Ace of Spades. The edges tattered and torn in some places. The ink, displaying the spade-shaped tent in the center, fading in places.

"You've got until midnight three days from now," Bormir said as his "students" lined up beside him. "I look forward to your decision."

A snow squall swept them away and left her friends behind in crumpled heaps on the ground.

Two and a half sprigs, that's all she had left to sustain her long enough to help them.

Her body shook with nerves, with pain, both most likely. Yet, her mind was clearer than it had been in days. With fumbling fingers, she ate the half sprig, picked up the card, and placed it against her lips.

"Clementine," she whispered over it. The card vibrated in her hand and she threw it to the side as it expanded.

It would be too taxing for her to carry them one by one inside, and too risky. Their heartbeats were so quiet, so slow as she moved as fast and as carefully as she could to bundle them together in a tarp, binding them with rope to pull them across the snow. The throbbing pain that seared her hands and tore at her hair kept her from fixating on just how cold they were, how much of their flesh frostbite had claimed, how at any second those low heartbeats could fall silent.

Out of mercy, the wind blew at her back, granting her some ease as she trudged forward. Fifty feet of distance between them and the tent felt like fifty miles.

She had only half a sprig left by the time she made it through the door.

"Kitchen!" she hollered so desperately the picture frames on the wall shook with lament. "Your master needs you! Light the stove, ignite the burners, make it as hot as you can!"

Her stomach turned against her, leaving her retching as she threw open the kitchen door. The cookware jumped to attention, turning to her as they stoked the coals in the wood stove and boiled empty pots.

"Cut them free of the rope and tarp, and cover them with warm, dry washcloths and towels," she heaved, barely swallowing the last bit of herbs down.

Mina ran out of the room, wind at her heels, and crashed into the infirmary dizzy and writhing. Her fingers barely closed around the botanical cabinet's handles as she threw its doors open. She stuffed her mouth with herbs, choking on the leaves as they tickled the back of her throat, but kept chewing as her body rolled between waves of pain and numbness like a ship tossed about a stormy sea.

Warming blankets, botanicals Mrs. Harlowe had used to make her thawing drought, and smelling salts. She raced back to the kitchen and threw the ingredients onto the counter. "Boil these in cider until the leaves are fully wilted. Turn off the heat, pour in two-thirds cup of cinnamon whiskey then, after five minutes, bring it over and start ladling it slowly down their throats."

She set about stripping them of their clothes, drying their cold wet skin with the dish towels the cutlery piled on top of them, then wrapped them in warming blankets. It grew harder and harder to keep her body from shaking, to keep her breathing steady, to keep her stomach from turning on itself over and over again. Blood splatters fell upon their blankets, upon their cheeks, upon her hands as her body tore itself apart in protest for defying her curse with such selfless acts.

The tongs and spatulas took over wrapping them as her hands cramped up, and the chopsticks and rolling pins helped to dry them; leaving her to face her greatest pain alone.

Mina fumbled to undress Sebastian and found his clothes were slightly drier than the others. A sign that there was still some fire burning in him, even though his heart beat shallow. Even though his skin was so sickly pale, the amber of his hair too dark, underneath his eyes and the hollows of his cheeks too sunken.

She chewed her herbs to keep the pain at bay, keep her mind focused on the steps needed to wake him. On his survival. Nothing more.

Anything more and she'd be useless to him.

Anything more and he'd be as frozen as her music study door.

Just as she covered his naked body with the warming blanket, the pot of thawing drought slid across the tile floor with a trail of ladles bouncing after it. Mina snatched one as it passed and scooped a spoonful of the cider out of the pot.

"Like this," she instructed them, her voice trembling as much as her arms were as she lifted Sebastian's head gently and slowly poured the liquid into his mouth. Her gloves shredded, she was rubbing her hand across a bed of nails as she coaxed his throat to swallow. The blue pallor faded from his lips, but his heartbeat did not strengthen.

"Come on," Mina pleaded. "Come on." She was reaching the end of her capability. She could feel the curse knocking at the door. The leather of tattered armor creaked with freeze, the ice lying in wait for the herbs to ebb, for her to act just a sliver more foolishly than she already was. She uncapped the smelling salts and waved them under his nose, her last offering.

And Sebastian awoke with a shiver, eyelids heavy as they struggled to open.

What little hold Mina had on sense crumbled away.

"You're alive," she stated. They were the only words she could say, yet each syllable carried with it every sentiment she wished she could share.

"You're alive."

Thank The Gods.

"You're alive."

I haven't lost you.

"You're alive."

I'd be lost if you were gone.

She was drowning in something she could not name. Blood gave way to tears, large heaving tears that dared to blur the image of him awake, and blinking, and breathing, and—

"I'm alive, Mina," he said. His voice was still gruff and garbled from his injury, but her heart nearly burst from her chest all the same to hear it. To hear him say her name. "I'm sorry that I worried you."

Her stomach tried to turn again at his words, sickened by how sweet they were. She stuffed more herbs inside her cheeks and swallowed it all back harshly.

"Do not move," she said, moving away from him even though she did not want to, fearing her returning to find him frozen again. "I have to try and wake the others."

"Mina." He slipped a hand out from under the blanket, palm open, reaching.

She wanted nothing more than to take it, to hold it, feel its heat, his heartbeat, and never let go.

But the tips of his fingers were dark with frostbite and all she could see was it spreading from her touch, staining him, ruining him.

Her voice broke. "I have to try and wake the others."

🜁

They all sat on the kitchen floor, drinking their thawing drought as the kitchen prepared them a proper meal. With Sebastian awoken and Tanir following shortly after, his commands and her instructions made it much more bearable for Mina to gather the proper medicines needed to heal their wounds. Tanir's leg was back in order, though she would forever bear a slight limp. The broken bones in Enoch's hand and ankle, Wera's ribs, and Sir Gargic's clavicle were reconstructed with some salves and potions, even Sebastian and Enoch's throats were healed.

Their bodies were as back to normal as possible. Save for Mina and Sebastian's choppy hairstyles, it was almost as if nothing had changed from the last time they had dinner in the commorancy. Except that they were eating on the floor, swaddled in blankets, most of them half-drunk with thousand-yard stares.

"So all of that... was Bormir and Eirlys," Wera said, breaking the silence that followed Mina's recounting of events.

"And four others. Dolcemar, Tyoma, Androniki, and Iraina." She took another sip of the drought, hoping it would ease the nausea still wreaking havoc on her stomach.

"And you went up against them, all by yourself, and made it out alive?" Sir Gargic pressed.

"Barely."

"What deal did you make?"

Mina's cup stilled before she took another sip. Bile burned the back of her throat. "What *deal*?"

"Gargic," Sebastian warned.

"Those motherfuckers hate her and couldn't give two shits less about us, Windenhofer. We all know that if they had the chance to fucking wipe us all off the map, they would have taken it."

"No, they wouldn't. If you truly hate someone, you don't just kill them," Mina corrected. Bormir's vacant stare and brilliant smile loomed over her, just waiting in the corner of her eye. "You break them first."

"So they'll keep torturing us until they get bored, then kill us?" Enoch asked.

"Not if I can help it," Sebastian said. "Tonight I'll work on something to better secure the commorancy for when we're hiking. Mina, if you could tell me all that you know about these new rimefae—"

"Tomorrow," she interrupted.

"Pardon?"

She forced herself to make eye contact. "We can talk about it tomorrow morning. Healing should be the focus tonight. Planning can wait a few hours."

Sebastian's gaze darted back and forth, studying her. She willed her face to remain as unreadable as possible, even as another wave of nausea twisted her innards.

"You're right." He gave a tight-lipped smile and nodded, "It can wait for tomorrow."

Bowls of rabbit stew and grilled cheese sandwiches slid across the floor and settled in front of each of them. Mina's stomach cramped up at the sight.

"Enoch," she said.

He flinched when she called his name. Another stabbing pain rolled through her gut. "What is it, Mina?"

"I won't make you tell stories again."

He gave a somber nod, shoulders loosening up as he accepted her non-apology. "Did you enjoy them at least?"

"They served their purpose."

"Which was?" Wera asked.

"Distraction," Mina and Sebastian answered in tandem. Indigestion seared up her stomach and settled in her chest.

"Is something wrong, Mina?" Tanir asked. "You're not eating."

"I'm not hungry," she said. "Too many herbs."

"How many did you take?"

"I don't know that many can be measured."

"You might have actually taken enough for the negative side effects to impact you." Tanir frowned. "There are some tonics in the infirmary that can soothe your stomach. If you go and look for—"

"I'll wait until after you all have finished eating," she interjected. "That way, you can show me where to look, and I'm not tearing your shelves apart any more than I already have."

That way, she could spend a little longer with them.

That way she could just sit and have one last dinner with them, even though it wasn't perfect. Even though they were on the floor. Even though they were all still shivering and struggling to smile. Even though her stomach was dangerously close to rupturing out of her throat.

She closed her eyes once their attention was off of her and on to Tanir, who was discussing all the tinctures and salves they'd have to apply to help the frostbite fade from their fingers and toes. She listened to the legato crescendos and decrescendos of their breath, underscored by the syncopated rhythms of their heartbeats. For all the ails that had befallen them because of her, for all the cruel words, swallowed sorries, and lack of compliments, for all the ways her existence in their lives had wounded them—

They're alive.

They're alive.

They're alive.

Perhaps that would be enough for atonement.

Perhaps that would be enough for them to forgive her.

⚝

All was quiet in the commorancy.

Mina tiptoed through her music study one final time to marvel at the instruments, to run her fingers along the veins of amber, to see herself in the mirror of a place made just for her. The ebony violin still hung among its stringed brothers.

Hopefully someone will pick it up again soon.

She smoothed her thumb down the slope of the lion's head on its scroll and left it behind, unplayed.

It was strange to walk without her sword on her hip as she made her way down to the garden. The false sky above had darkened and now twinkled with conjured stars. Fireflies drifted lazily in the air as she plucked a few stems of lavender to hide in her bindings. They'd only last a day in the tundra, but it felt right to take them. They were one of the few mementos she could take that wouldn't be used against her.

Or maybe they would be. The Matron was terribly clever with Her torments.

She walked down the hall to the main entrance, taking her time, letting her gaze linger on the photos and art pieces that hung on the walls as she passed them. Would they hang up the drawings she left behind after she was gone? Or would they be too scorned by her leaving that they'd rather forget her existence entirely? Picturing the latter made it easier for her to move forward, but the first option was more likely. She could hear Wera teasing Sebastian about it now. Could see his face flushing that charming shade of crimson she'd never see again.

Inhale.

Exhale.

In front of the doorway, the threads of her contract slithered across her skin in wait. She reached for the handle, thinking about his command that they'd be partners, that partners often had to save one another, how they couldn't be partners if they were both dead — anything to loosen the binds enough for her to leave.

She had to leave. No matter how much her stomach hurt. No matter how much her chest ached. That pain was nothing compared to the alternative.

Her hand turned the lock and grabbed the handle, a good sign compared to when she first tried to flee, but her wrist would not twist to turn the knob.

"Come on," she whispered to herself. "We have to do this."

"What do you have to do?" Sebastian asked behind her.

Mina stilled, the aches and pains she'd been keeping at bay rising tenfold. He must have used that silence spell of his to hide his footsteps.

"I have to go out and scout for the morning," she kept her voice steady, cold, even with another wave of tears threatening to spill. "With the storms and Bormir's meddling, I want to make sure the trail hasn't been altered before we set out."

"Then why are you struggling to open the door?"

"I don't know," she lied. "Did you improve the warding spell?"

"No. I haven't changed a thing." He dropped the silence spell purposefully so she could hear each of his steps creak across the floor as he moved closer. "But it seems, perhaps, that you have."

"I don't know what you—"

"That door would open if you were just going to scout. Because scouting means that you're coming back." He swallowed, his voice hollowing, a slight shake behind it that rippled across her skin: "I thought we were past this."

I thought so, too.

Stuck. Torn in two. Her newly found tears rolled down her cheeks. Quietly.

If she wanted to stand a chance at leaving, she could not face him.

"Bastion," her voice shook against her control. "Let me go."

A sniffle. "Tell me why." The tin of his accent squeezed her heart.

"They'll kill you if I stay."

He laughed, broken, disbelieving. Tears making every note of it flat. "Do you really think we would die so easily?"

"You almost died today."

"I've almost died many times."

"At the hands of rimefae who are only here for me?"

"After having to be handicapped by an avalanche and days of climbing and infighting!" he snapped, anger, sadness, betrayal reverberating off the walls. "If they were truly capable of slaughtering us, they would have just faced us head-on! Mina, there are other options—"

"There are other options," she cut him off, too sad to shout, too resolved to her fate. "And this is one of them. Let me go."

"No." He stepped closer, the heat radiating from him brushing against her back. If he touched her—

"How many times have you told me that I have a choice?" she pleaded, allowing her tears to break her voice, allowing her fear to color every word with warning. "I don't often get to choose what pains I am dealt in this world! So let me choose this!"

He did not take another step, but his tone was sharper, demanding. "Tell me what could possibly make you leaving the easier pain to bear."

She did not need a command to answer. "Because I won't be the cause of your end! I can take whatever torment, whatever torture, whatever hell awaits me with Her, with them, as long as I know that you all live."

"Well, I cannot bear the thought of you suffering for us. So, it appears we are at an impasse." She could hear his teeth grinding, the floorboards creaked as he grounded his weight in defiance.

"Bas—"

"I will follow after you," he stated. "Even if I tore up the contract and let you go, I would follow after you."

"You're a fool," she snapped, his promises bringing up bittersweet bile to burn her tongue.

"I never claimed that I wasn't."

Mina's shuttering breath rattled against the door, the metal knob groaned under her white-knuckled grip. "I've given you nothing but misery and suffering."

"And companionship, and laughter, and joy, and song, and so many wonderful things I cannot name without harming you."

And harm they did. Mina's head spun with a pounding headache as her heart fought to escape her rib cage. A ring of black pulsed in the corners of her vision, and the tears continued to pour.

"Foithe," she spoke in fae tongue, fearful.

"What?"

"If you're going to continue talking this way, remember that word," she strained. "Bormir used it to return me to myself."

"Good. It'll be useful when we face him together," Sebastian said, clipped, final. "If you insist on going now, that's fine. I command you to stay here while I get dressed, and then we can go *scouting* together."

As the strings of his command took hold, she abandoned the doorknob. Abandoned any hope of this being an easy exit as his footsteps started to trail away.

"You're being an idiot," she turned and seethed at the back of his head.

He faced her, doubling back her way, furious as hot tears rolled down his cheeks. "*I'm* being an idiot? You're the one going off after six rimefae without your sword!"

"I'm not going after them." She looked him in the eye, committing the anguish she caused him to memory. "I'm going to meet them."

"Meet them for what?"

Mina opened her mouth to speak. Sebastian raised a finger to pause her, voice breaking, his anger revealing heartbreaking desperation. "Do not lie to me."

The command pulled the truth out of her throat. "Either I go with them, or all of us die in three days."

"Go with them *where?*"

Bormir's laughter echoed behind the memory of barbed chains and endless walls of blue ice. She could still feel the cold, could still feel the sting; even stronger now after their fae fingers messed with her head, dredging up old memories she foolishly hoped time would forget.

"Back," the word broke with a sob.

His expression softened, brown, watering eyes widening in pity — no, something far kinder. Though it terrified her, she would spend decades, millennia, suffering to keep that kindness in his eyes. They could tear open her back, crush her spine, peel apart her scalp, and she would bear it.

"So you left your sword but not your necklace?" he asked gently, eyes flitting to the amber he gave her, still burning brightly around her neck. She hadn't even considered taking it off.

Mina smiled slightly, though she did not know why; her heart still ached and her tears still flowed. "I can't make it easy on them, can I?"

"Three days is mighty generous of them," Sebastian gave a slight smile back as his hands came to rest on either side of the door frame behind her. The warmth radiating off his body, a comfort she did not deserve.

"Generous?" Mina huffed a broken, sob-filled laugh at the notion of Bormir being anything close to giving.

"Gives us plenty of time to come up with one hell of a battle plan."

Another wave of fresh tears joined the ones already wetting her cheeks as she let her teeth ache under his kind, worried gaze. Far too kind for the mess she had made of him.

"What is it?" he asked.

"I ruined your hair," she admitted, sobs shaking her body now, "and scarred your face."

Sebastian ran his hand through the poor cut. "We're both shaving our heads, remember? As for the scar," he tilted his chin slightly to show off the thin line of scar tissue running up his cheek. "I think it makes me look quite roguish. Don't worry about it."

"Is that a command?" she asked, as the tears began to slow and her chest started to loosen.

"No." His expression relaxed into a kind smile. "I'd find it an honor if you worried about me."

He must have seen her eyes gloss over in pain from his words, for he pulled away and started making his way towards the kitchen. "Come along. You'll have a cup of chamomile tea, then head back to bed. I need you well-rested and less forgetful in the morning."

"Forgetful?" she asked as she followed him, relieved to have the threads of his command pull her away from the door.

"I told you I would never send anyone away without very good reason." He shrugged and wiped his tears off his cheeks with the back of his sleeve. "Six murderous rimefae? That's barely a reason at all, and most definitely not a good one."

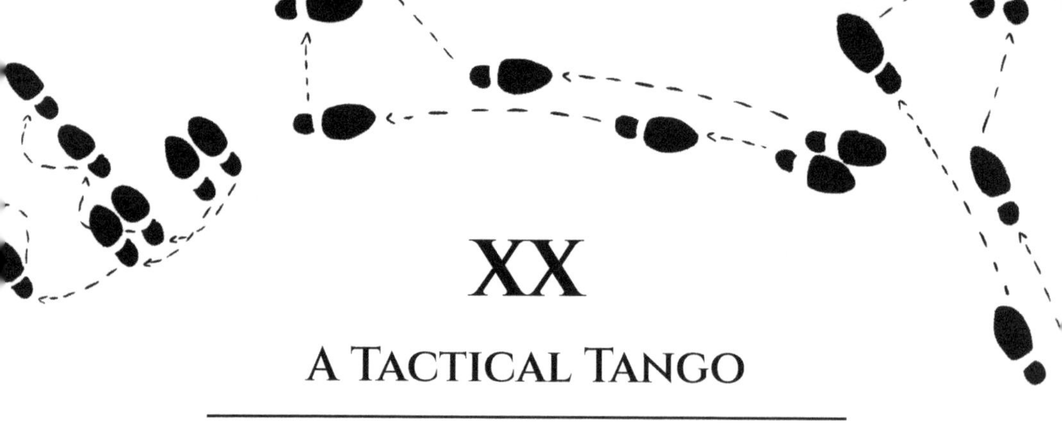

XX

A Tactical Tango

They planned their attack over cinnamon pancakes; turning the kitchen into a pseudo-war room. Which, unsurprisingly, Sir Gargic took great joy in.

"Alright. We've got six rimefuckers to deal with," he said as he laid out six hand-carved wooden tokens onto the gridded roll of parchment Wera provided.

"Maybe more," Mina noted. "No matter which course of action we take, Bormir will meet us where the veil between realms is thinnest. Did you have a map of The Glacian Plateau?"

Wera rummaged through the pile of atlases she'd brought. "Here's this one by Sir Roger Sherman. It's about two hundred years old, so be careful with the paper."

"He was the royal cartographer under the reign of King Theobald Reinhart, King Fritz's third great-grandfather, and known to be a bit of a lush," Enoch added.

"I can see that," Mina pointed to a big, sharp-edged scrawling on the upper right of the map. "This is supposed to be Reagan's Crevasse? What even is the scale?"

Wera sighed. "There's no scale. Now you see why I've been grilling you for every little detail about this place. It might help if you flip it around. Sir Sherman charted it coming from Lanholde, not heading to it."

Mina spun the book around, and recognized some more of the landmarks, well, the suggestion of landmarks. "I guess it's a little more legible. There's a few pockets I know for certain to avoid. Recet's Den, Reagan's Crevasse, and the patches of frazil ice flats somewhere around here, here, and here. Take one wrong step, take one shortcut between a snow drift, and you're on the other side."

"So, we might be facing them in Elphyne?" Tanir asked. "If it's so easy to cross over—"

"Absolutely not." Mina looked up from the map to Sebastian. "Did you find the rings you made?"

"I remembered dreaming about an aurora. It must have been easier to charm me since I lost my noxulars." Sebastian reached into his pants pocket and pulled out all the iron rings he made. "Explains how we left the dome. Eirlys must have pulled us through the ice patches below us once the rings were minimized in my pocket."

How dare they.

"Mina! Two hundred years old!" Wera exclaimed and yanked the book away from her. The upper left corners of some of the pages were missing. Mina opened the fist she didn't know she made and found them crumpled to dust in her palm.

"It's a shitty map anyways." She wiped the dust off on her pants. "That corner had a forest drawn in it!"

"Those were Cecil's Snow Drifts."

"My point exactly."

"How many exits are there to Recet's Den?" Sir Gargic asked.

"One," Mina answered. "Recet was an arctic lindwyrm that used his den to travel between planes and hold his horde."

"So it's full of treasure too?"

"No." Mina paused for a moment to work out her wording. "When he was slain, the riches that were collected were taken by his killer."

"I would have heard tale of someone killing a lindwyrm and claiming his horde," Enoch started to scoff before his eyes went wide. "Unless it was you."

"No. It wasn't me. I wouldn't have taken this contract if it were me."

"So, it was someone you knew on the other side," Tanir surmised. "Which is how you know the veil's so thin there."

Mina's mouth cemented shut.

"However the hell she knows about it doesn't matter, the outcome is the same," Sir Gargic interjected. He slid his wooden tokens across the grid onto the rudimentary sketch of the den Wera was drawing. "This is where we should ambush them."

"It only has one exit," Tanir worried.

"Two technically," Sebastian corrected. One way out through our realm, the other through Elphyne."

"Exactly. Which means they either gotta get through us or head back to where they came from. And with it being a lindwyrm's den, the roof of it will be low. Too low for them to fly out of our range of attack."

"Won't they know what we're doing?" Tanir asked. "Low ceilings, few exits. It screams 'obvious trap'."

"Which could be exactly what we want." Sebastian drummed his fingers against his lips. "Bormir has been using Mina's weaknesses against her this entire time. Her short temper, her inability to fly, her susceptibility to sleep magic."

If Mina didn't know that Sebastian was just naturally perceptive, she would have thought he was keeping a list of her shortcomings to use against her.

"His silent snow counteracts her hearing, and their shared history allows him to utilize less surface-level weaknesses that we don't know about. So," he clapped his hands together, "the game becomes 'what do we know about Mina that they don't know.'"

"They don't know that you can command her," Tanir answered.

"Correct! Now, what do they know about Mina that isn't as true anymore?"

"That she can see some colors?" Enoch offered.

"That she can fight alongside us now," Wera said. "And, by proxy, can run defense in a fight."

"Exactly."

"However, that means they'll keep going after you all, to distract me," Mina countered.

Sebastian smiled. "Which is exactly what we want."

"Alright, now you've lost me, Windenhofer." Sir Gargic gave a heavy sigh in exasperation. "What happened to 'respecting me when commanding a militia'?"

"We're not a militia," he corrected, smile turning a bit smug. "We're an independently owned contracting service specializing in procuring difficult-to-obtain artifacts and materials across the spectrum from mundane to magical."

Sir Gargic glared at him. "Do you know what I do to the soldiers who get cheeky with me?"

"I don't—"

Sir Gargic opened his mouth.

"—and I never will. Because we're not soldiers. We're an independently owned—"

"Just make your damn point!" he hollered.

Mina pinched her nose to muffle the snort of laughter she couldn't suppress.

"My point is that Bormir wouldn't have given Mina that ultimatum if both of the options wouldn't work out for him. If she chooses to have us all try to stand against him three days from now, he's got all the time in the world to build up a small fae army, lay any traps, scout us out like he clearly did before the avalanche, and can strike whenever and wherever is the most advantageous for him." Sebastian explained.

"However, on the flip side, if Mina surrenders herself to him, he barely has to lift a finger even if she does put up a fight. In fact —" he waved a hand her way, "and I mean no offense with this — to him, her attempting to fight the six of them would be the stupidest option she could take. But is, of course, the one he's the most afraid of."

"And how do you know what he's afraid of?" Sir Gargic countered.

That sadness, that look of distance in Bormir's eyes.

"Because if he wasn't, they would have tried to fight me alone already," Mina answered.

Sebastian snapped his fingers and pointed at her, not breaking his staring contest with Sir Gargic. "Bingo. They could have separated her from us during that avalanche, and they didn't. Instead, they wanted her to suffer, to weaken her body and her spirit so that she'd come willingly."

"At Rabbet's Pass they did separate her from us," realization dawned on Tanir as she turned to Mina. "When you knocked them out of the sky in your chained form, you must have come close to killing them, even while you were extremely wounded."

"So, you're saying I should fight them alone in Recet's Den while I'm—" Dread encroached, her solid blue-eyed reflection sneered back at her, delighting at the idea of finishing the job she started. "I can't do that."

"Oh, come on now, beastie! You're a one-woman army in that form!" Sir Gargic urged.

Mina looked at Sebastian. Being so close to the veil, being so close to what She wanted her to become. "Both of the options work out for Bormir. And he made sure to say that I should meet them where the veil is the thinnest." The ghost of chains slithered across her skin. "He knows that I have a short temper, and he was very thrilled to see me... changed."

"I'm not suggesting that you change," Sebastian clarified, putting together her puzzle pieces quickly. Perhaps already assembling them before she even spoke. "Fight them alone? Yes. But only for a moment." He turned to Enoch and grinned. "You're really gonna love this idea."

"Last time you said that to me, we wound up shitfaced and hanging by a rope off the side of a coal magnate's airship," he grumbled.

"Yeah. And it made for a good story, didn't it?"

"So, this'll make a good story?"

"Imagine what would have happened if Mina did go and turn herself over to Bormir last night."

"You would have woken us all up in a panic, and we would have gone after her," Wera said matter-of-factly.

"Precisely! And if we did go after Mina and caught up with her right when she got to Bormir and his crew, what would they have done?"

"Attacked us." Sir Gargic rolled his eyes. "Obviously."

"And Mina, if that happened, what would you have done?"

"Killed you myself for doing something so stupid?"

"Close enough. You'd go after us, even though you'd be completely unprepared for it." Sebastian raised his eyebrows, "But what if you were prepared for it?"

"Oh my Gods." Enoch's eyes lit up, and his jaw hung a gape. "You want us to put on an act!"

"I told you you'd love it."

He paced about the room, the spark of inspiration shimmering in his eyes as he twirled the end of his mustache. "We make Bormir think that Mina will go alone, planning to face them all by herself to keep us out of harm's way. Then we show up, Mina acts surprised that we're here, and when they go to attack us, Mina will be able to intercept it without injury because of your commands!"

Sir Gargic grumbled a hum in thought. He tugged at his beard. "Plus, if beastie does a fine enough job before we arrive, they'll be tired out, and much easier to kill."

The notion crawled up her spine and sat heavy on Mina's heart. The sadness, the distance, old echoes of laughter not yet cruel, adding weight.

"No," Mina said.

Sebastian turned to face her, the perfect depiction of confusion twisting his brows, gaping his mouth, "No?"

"No to killing them," she doubled down. "We're not killing them."

"Oh what, the fae who've been trying to kill and torture us for weeks are suddenly not monstrous enough for you to kill?" Sir Gargic taunted. "You were so ready to kill us the other day."

If they were back at Rabbet's Pass, her answer would have been different. If Bormir hadn't been involved, her answer would have been different. If those old memories, new feelings, were never drudged up.

Maybe that's what they wanted. All those mind games they played on The Lithe could have been a ploy to re-endear her to them. But as cruel as they were, they were once like her. They never asked to become so cold. They never asked to be taken into the Rime and forced to play family.

Mina inhaled deeply to rein in the anger he tried to goad out of her. "If the goal is to kill them, it'll be much harder for me to mind my temper." It was the truth, in a way. A deep, terrible part of her yearned to see Bormir lifeless at her feet.

She couldn't feed that. She wouldn't.

"Then we'll need to do some research on effective ways to detain fae creatures," Sebastian said, voice clipped with a bitter finality as he studied her intently. Mina's shoulders stiffened against his unsaid disapproval. "Enoch?"

"I'll start combing the stacks," he said as he rushed out of the room, excitement adding a spring to his step.

"And while he does that, let's get to know our enemy better." Sebastian moved on, tapping on each of Sir Gargic's wooden tokens. "Eirlys, Dolcemar, Tyoma, Androniki, Iraina, Bormir." There was an edge behind his voice as he said Bormir's name. "What have we got?"

🜁

Being scanned by Sebastian's projection terminal felt odd. A red beam of light ran up and down her body. Not something she could hold, yet she could feel it trailing up, like one long, rolling wave under her skin.

A bright, metallic chime rang out of the terminal.

"Alright," Sebastian said. The light turned off as he adjusted some dials. "Now is the movement pattern portion. The terminal's going to conjure a bunch of random enemies to fight. They'll be in ascending difficulty." Strands of bright red light projected out of the terminal, covering the walls, the floor, everything with thousands of little dots. "Just make sure you keep in the mapping field so it can capture your fight style."

"It'll capture the sword, too?" she asked.

"Yes. Make sure to use as many different techniques you know of. Sword, bow, hand-to-hand..." He stepped back from the machine and took his seat next to Tanir on the sidelines. "Even throw in the wind ribbon you've been working on. It's unique to you, but there might be some properties to it that are similar to techniques the rimefae could use."

"Understood," Mina drew her sword as she walked back to the center of the field. "When will it start?"

A small red hornet appeared out of nowhere and sped towards her. Mina caught it and crushed it in her hand just as it dived, stinger first, at her face.

"Now?" Sebastian said.

One hornet turned into a swarm.

"And you're certain it'll be able to capture me at full speed?" she shouted over the whir of her sword as she spun it round her hand like a propeller, rendering the swarm into dusty minced meat.

"There's only one way to know for sure!" he shouted back.

The buzz of hornets turned into the flap of wings as a flock of a hundred skrills, nasty birds with acid-coated talons, formed out of the ether and descended upon Mina.

Or at least they tried to. Their talons found purchase on the training mat, followed shortly by their beaks as their heads were severed from their bodies.

Mina swung around the rafter she landed on after carving through the flock and dealt with the terminal's next challenge — a mass of wriggling, flying serpents — swiftly. So swiftly, she was certain Tanir and Sebastian had no idea they had been conjured.

Whatever mechanisms powered the projection terminal buzzed and squealed from the effort of keeping up with her, churning out creature after creature only to have it dispersed within seconds. It spat out terrifying behemoths to try and buy itself time, but the bigger the beast, the easier it was for her to slay. It switched tactics to focus on smaller targets, things that would be difficult for her to take out all at once, mixed in with the larger creatures. Mina changed her approach as well, using the gale that surged from her bow to blow back the pests as she pierced the giants.

Sword, bow, Mina wasn't one to hesitate, yet she found herself reluctant to try and harness the wind for combat. It would be the least effective manner of fighting. She'd have to slow down considerably, given her novice ability at conjuring. And any mess up would be captured by the terminal, leading to inaccurate data. The rimefae wouldn't mess up their magic. Their unique skills were expertly honed, as much a part of their DNA as the blood in their veins was. If she made a mistake here, if she didn't fight to the best of her ability, then the practice drills based off of her would be inefficient, inaccurate. And inaccuracy meant death.

"Mina! Come on! Fight with the wind!"

Which was something Sebastian foolishly had no concerns about.

The threads of Sebastian's command had her sheathing her bow and closing her eyes in the middle of a raging pack of correlks' charge. Their corkscrew horns aimed for her stomach, hooves thunderous as they threatened to shatter the ground beneath her. The wind climbed up from her heels and weaved through her fingers with little coaxing. Perhaps it was the command, perhaps it was the threat of the horde, she did not know exactly what enticed it to obey. It pressed back against her hands, urging her to pull her arms to the side while twisting her palms to face outward.

"M-mina?" Tanir called out in worry.

The pack was just a few yards away now, her guts mere seconds from being hung around their horns like garland, when the wind curled around to tickle the back of her hands.

Mina swung her arms together in front of her in a grand clap.

"Oh shi—"

A wall of wind raked along the path her hands led, sending the correlks, Mina, and anything else unanchored flying across the room.

The projection terminal, however, was neither one of those things.

Mina caught herself as she landed on the wall, turning her body at just the right angle to plant her feet against it. Her first instinct was to look for Sebastian, but the wave of giant, jumping arrownids rushing towards her — fangs extended — changed her plans.

The terminal was taking her misstep to seek revenge in the form of spindly legs and compound eyes.

She ran along the wall as fast as she could, but the insects were too many in number to continue avoiding. The wind still tugged at her hands, the commanding thread still binding her to wield it. Mina swung her hands out in frustration, imagining the ribbon as a clever arrownid sprung out of the corner of her vision and descended upon her.

The wind turned heavy in her grasp as it caught the insect in midair, wrapping around it just like she had Sebastian in the garden. Mina pulled against the air current, and the monstrous insect came with it, knocking out a couple dozen of its kin as she combed it through the swarm. She released it, splattering simulated bug guts against the wall.

Mina repeated the process, keeping her focus on maintaining the ribbon, catching the bugs that were bold enough to leap at her and using them to thin the herd. As she regained her speed, she managed to channel a second ribbon of wind in her other hand, just in time for the terminal to give a bright, melodic chime causing the hundreds — knocked down from thousands by her efforts — of arrownids still chasing her to vanish.

Sebastian and Tanir crawled out from under the benches, hair windblown and wild, but otherwise unharmed.

"I'm not using that against, Bormir," Mina said, skidding down the wall to land back on the training mats. "It's too slow, and too unpredictable."

"But you were getting it towards the end there!" Sebastian said as he helped Tanir stand. "I think. It was a little hard to see through all the bugs."

Mina sneered and turned her attention to Tanir, knowing that debating with him any further wouldn't lead anywhere useful. "You see what you'll have to do, right?"

"It's gonna need to be one hell of a slow spell," Tanir said, tucking her gray flyaways back into her braids. "Six targets without any honing components is hard enough to muster, but maintaining it while fighting—"

"Then get honing components," Mina interjected. "We need every advantage to stand a chance."

"It's not that simple. It has to be part of the target's body. Some hair, some spit—"

"Blood?"

"Do you have some of their blood dried on your armor from yesterday?" Sebastian asked.

"It can't be dried blood, unfortunately," Tanir said with a heavy sigh. "If it's anything that comes out as a liquid, it's got to stay as a liquid in order to be the most potent focus."

"Then use my blood," Mina said.

Sebastian's brow furrowed. "I thought you weren't siblings."

"We're not. But there are some... similarities." A chill ran through her veins. "You don't need it to be exact, do you? If you needed to slow down some rabbits, would any old rabbit fur do?"

"It would have to be the same breed, so it is possible to use your blood if it's similar to theirs," Tanir explained. "But I'll be slowing you down as well once I cast it, and we run the risk of it only affecting you when I do it."

"I already know what it's like to be under its effects. They don't," she reasoned. "And if it's only hitting me, then just dispel it. I've got a backup plan involving Wera in that case."

Sebastian frowned. "You didn't mention a backup plan during breakfast."

"That's because I thought of it after Wera mentioned that she was going to iron-up her paints towards the end of our discussion." She gestured to the terminal. "But we need to get that thing up and running, and hear back from Enoch before I suggest anything."

"Could you at least give me a hint?" He angled himself to appear in her field of vision, trying to draw her attention to him instead of Tanir. There was an uneasy lilt to his voice. "Otherwise, I'll worry it's something dangerously stupid."

"It's not dangerously stupid," she scoffed. "Not if we're smart about it."

"Mina." His expression dropped, stern with a slight tint of worry.

She rolled her eyes, bracing for his disapproval yet again. "Remember how Wera aerosolized that poison? If she did that with her paint, it would actually work to poison them."

"And you."

"Again, I'll know what to expect."

"No." He brushed past her towards the terminal, response curt and decided, leaving no room to argue. "To both options. Tanir, I believe in your talents. I'm sure you'll be able to figure out another method to boost your concentration."

"In less than two days?" Mina pressed. "When we have to hike tomorrow in order to keep up appearances?"

Sebastian didn't respond, didn't bother to even glance over his shoulder at her request. His back was tense, posture much too stiff, and she didn't need to close her eyes to hear him grinding his teeth. He was upset, but there was no obvious reason behind it. She was still here, wasn't she? Still making the stupid choice to risk their lives rather than sacrifice her own.

"I'll figure something out, Mina," Tanir whispered to her. "It might be best to try and think of things that will keep you out of harm's way as much as possible."

"We're planning an attack. Harm is unavoidable!" Mina whisper-hissed back.

"I know, but—" she glanced over at Sebastian and pursed her lips into a tight frown. "Maybe don't *plan* to put yourself in harm's way. There's still plenty of options we can consider, alright?"

"Mina," Sebastian called. "How tall did you say Androniki was?"

"About three inches shorter than yourself," she called back.

"Could you come take a look to make sure I got it right?" An edge of annoyance carried on the question.

"I'm gonna go," Tanir said to Mina before calling towards Sebastian. "I'm going to source immobilization enchantments, dear. Do you still need me here?"

"No. Thank you, Tani. You're dismissed."

Tanir smiled and nodded at Mina, wearing an expression she couldn't quite parse, and made her way out of the training room.

So you dismiss my ideas, but expect me to come when you call? Now *she* was grinding her teeth as she joined Sebastian at the terminal.

"How's this look?" he gestured to the small projection preview of a man hovering above the dais.

"He needs more muscle. He's about two Sir Gargics wide," she answered, short, snippy.

"Good Gods," he muttered and fiddled with the dials to adjust the measurements, too absorbed in his machine to pay her change in attitude any mind.

"I thought partners listen to each other," she pressed, holding back the growl building just behind her teeth. "Both of those plans have merit, and you know it."

"You and I have very different definitions of the word 'merit'," he huffed.

She did not care for his passive-aggressive tone. He made her confess her fears last night. Why did he get to hide behind sardonic comments now?

"Oh, what? Just because I'd be a little bit slower or might breathe in a little bit of iron, suddenly all the other benefits fly out the window?"

Sebastian smacked his hands against the terminal, too big a reaction to her question. "Yes, Mina! Fucking obviously! Any plan that could cause you undue harm holds absolutely no merit."

"Then you should just null my contract then," she goaded, her cleverness getting the better of her. If he thought he could intimidate her into just doing whatever he wanted, just because they were following his little plan, he was sorely mistaken.

He glared at her, the same fear and anger from last night revealing itself to still be bubbling underneath, teeth gritting together as he hissed, "I told you that—"

"By your logic, any plan that could cause me undue harm holds no merit. This entire scheme we're concocting could cause me undue harm, will cause me undue harm in fact, especially when the alternative is me waltzing out of this place and turning myself over to Bormir."

Sparks flew in his eyes. He lifted his hands off the terminal, closing his glowing palms into fists. "I won't allow—"

"*Your* plan has me facing off against six rimefae by myself, and I can tell you with an alarming degree of certainty that Androniki's gonna cave my nose in again," she challenged, a know-it-all snicker crawling up her face. "Bet ya that wouldn't happen if I just surrendered. Instead, he'd probably just sling me over his shoulder and skip across the veil whistling. Lot less harm in that, don't you think?"

Sebastian pursed his lips, his nostrils flared like a bull's, yet he said nothing back.

She jutted her chin forward, raising on her tiptoes to sneer in his face: "Are you listening to me now?"

His right eye twitched. "I am."

"The slow spell is a bit of a nuisance, I'll admit. But think back to my fight against Tanir. If I wasn't able to figure out her casting point, I can guarantee she would have handed me my ass. Bormir will be wise enough to adapt, but the others are his apprentices. I'm almost certain they've never had to rest on their technique alone, and, slowed, all the flaws in their form will be easier for you all to spot and take advantage of," Mina explained, pointed, defiant, determined. "As for the iron. You and the others have your system for dealing with Wera's poison spray. Do you think I'm incapable of covering my nose and mouth with a cloth?"

"It could get in your eyes," he countered weakly. The sparks slowly fell into a smolder.

"You know I can fight with my eyes closed." Mina scanned his face. His jaw was still clenched, nostrils still flared. In the warm umber of his eyes, a distant dullness settled in as they cooled. "Did the wind knock out all of your common sense when I swept away those correlks?"

"Why don't you want to kill them? Bormir and his students?" he asked. He did not search her face for an answer as he asked. He looked her dead in the eye, tired of putting the pieces together.

Cold guilt formed a lump in her throat. "I didn't think you were the type to condone killing."

"I'm not, it's just..." He looked away from her, rapping his fingers atop the terminal, debating with himself. "As much as I hate to admit it, Sir Gargic has a point. You talk about how you only kill monsters. What they've done, what they're doing, is by all accounts monstrous."

"It's—" The memory of Bormir's childhood laugh, light and carefree, echoed in her ears. "—complicated."

He closed his eyes. The circles under them were much darker than usual. "Complicated in a way that you can't tell me, or complicated in a way that you won't tell me?"

That's what it was. He was afraid that she was hiding something from him.

Again.

"Would you kill a kid who bullied you back when you were in the orphanage, now?" she asked.

"Only if they were trying to kill me," he answered with a bite of bitterness, jaw tensing.

"And what if something were compelling you to do it? Against your will?" Her hand ached with the memory of holding Sebastian over the edge of the cliff, the same dark thoughts that urged her to tear Bormir and Eirlys out of the sky calling for his death.

He turned to her then, a slight flicker of surprise crossing his face to see her still looking at him, plainly, honestly. Mina didn't want to hide from him anymore. Hiding things led to her nearly losing him.

"I would try my best to fight against it." His expression softened. It hurt so much, Mina's eyes threatened to blister, but she did not look away. "Especially if my temper was easily flared."

He inhaled deeply.

Exhaled.

"The slow spell I can see working." He nodded, leaving fear behind and returning to his usual, strategic self. "The aerosolized iron I'm not too keen on. We'll need to find a safe way to test it."

Mina knocked her knuckles against the projection terminal. "That's what we have this thing for, right?"

He gave a gentle smile that made her teeth ache. "Right."

"Then let's make sure their projections are as accurate as possible." She took a closer look at the mini model meant to represent Androniki hovering over the terminal. "You'll need to adjust the force of its punch by about three times my own, but the body type is accurate."

"*Three* times?"

"I paired him up with Tanir for a reason. With your lack of close combat skills, you wouldn't stand a chance."

"I could learn close combat," he grumbled under his breath, but wisely didn't press the issue.

They had pressed each other's buttons enough for the moment.

🜂

The Mirror-Minas, as Wera so cleverly called them, were eerie to look at. The adjustments Sebastian made to make each of the copies match their rimefae counterpart were significant, but her nose still hung on their faces. Their idle stance was wide-legged like Mina's, shoulders held straighter and tauter than they needed to be. Mina was thankful he had chosen to leave their bodies detail-less. Seeing a duplicate Bormir wearing her patchwork leathers would have had her rethinking her incredibly small wardrobe.

"Are we sure we want to run this without Enoch?" Sir Gargic asked.

"We're just running the beginning of the fight," Sebastian said. "The rest of how we approach this will be based on his research, so it's best not to bother him until we've ironed out the kinks." He pulled out his pocket watch. "What do you think, Mina? Give you ten minutes, then burst in?"

"That'll do for now." Mina drew her sword and rolled out her shoulders. She grimaced as the Tyoma-Mina rolled their shoulders in the same pattern. "We'll have to test longer lengths once we have a full plan, but repeating this sequence a few times should build up my endurance."

"Alright." Sebastian waved his hand in a gesture Mina didn't quite recognize, then dipped down close to her face, cupping his hand against his cheek to cover his mouth, and whispered, "The starting phrase is kumquat."

Mina flinched as his breath tickled against her ear, shifting away from him quickly as her heart raced and chest warmed.

"G-got it." Mina kept her eyes forward on Bormir-Mina, trying to calm herself down, not wanting that white pain and lack of control to seize her once again. Sebastian straightened up and lingered for a moment, clearly considering whether he should comment on her reaction, but thankfully decided to walk away towards the faux den entrance the projection terminal had created.

"Whenever you're ready!" he shouted over his shoulder.

Mina faced her mutated mirrors.

Dolcemar, Tyoma, Androniki, Iraina, Eirlys, Bormir. In the real fight she wouldn't have as much time to size them up, to work out the best plan of attack based on their positioning, their weapons, but for now...

Bormir would most likely gloat, proud peacock that he was, taunting her and diminishing her. He'd expect her to go for him first. Tyoma she'd have to keep away from, the aura of fatigue was too strong. Dolcemar would have no effect on her. Eirlys would be ranged attacks, Androniki close combat, and Iraina—

"Kumquat," Mina said as she drew her sword and rushed the impressionist, wind at her heels and blade aimed for her throat.

The element of surprise was on Mina's side as she was able to nick Iraina's neck before the faux-rimefae sped off, dodging the brunt of her swing. The others descended upon her like locusts to wheat.

Her focus could not falter for a second, not with the adjustments Sebastian had made at her behest. Eirlys launched barrage after barrage of ice arrows instead of spikes, phasing in and out of random spots around the cave walls. Tyoma was trained to shadow Mina, always trying to get close to handicap her. Androniki's strength was set to triple her own. Dolcemar was the one Mina knew the least about tactics-wise, so she was set to fill in any gaps in their defense. And Bormir, as much as she hated it, was granted her wind and programmed to utilize every aspect of her move set without limitation.

Her sword could barely find purchase, leaving only glancing blows and slight slashes as her attack quickly turned into a game of keep-away. But at least there were cuts. In the real fight, the iron would leave them a little more weary, a little more pained, and chasing after her would tire them out enough for—

"Mina!"

Sebastian's shout broke her concentration, and earned her another caved-in nose as Androniki-Mina's right hook connected and sent her flying across the room. She hit the wall with a sickening crack, vision going starry as her skull bounced off the stone.

"Teetotaler!" Sebastian exclaimed, pausing the Mirror-Minas' mid-rush.

Mina landed limply on the floor. The others crowded around her, looks of deep concern on their faces spinning around her, as she fumbled out some herbs from her pocket.

"Let's not just shout my name, huh?" her voice sounded as if she were speaking underwater as she pinched the bridge of her nose together to help it heal straight. "In fact, don't talk, just attack."

"Just attack?" Sir Gargic scoffed. "All we're seeing is a bunch of blurs! How the hell are we supposed to aim?"

"The patches of ice." She let go at the familiar cracking of her cartilage reconstructing. "It'll grab their attention and limit the amount of entry and exit points she has to escape."

"That'll be up to me and you then, 'Bastian," Wera said. "'Til we get Enoch in here, at least. You go low, I go high?"

"That works just fine," he agreed with an absentminded mutter, too busy watching her heal to pay any real attention to the others. "Mina, are you... ready to go again?"

She sat up and twisted sharply, realigning her spine in a trickle of sharp pops. "Ready."

Sebastian inhaled sharply, trying to wrangle his discomfort. "Okay then. Back outside we go."

"See ya in ten, Meens!" Wera cheered.

"See ya in ten," she grumbled back.

The terminal reset the Mirror-Minas in different positions this time. But Mina's attack plan was still the same. Iraina's throat, then keep away.

"Kumquat."

Knowing what was waiting for her hardly made another ten minutes of combat any easier. Though she did land a few more hits than before. Before this training session ended she'd have to handicap Iraina's throat twice. That way she'd—

Brilliant flashes of amber flame shot around her. Illuminating beneath her feet as Wera's paint splattered above.

The Mirror-Minas hesitated for a moment as the terminal re-calibrated to consider the new combatants. Mina stilled herself, catching a much-needed breath for a fleeting moment before Eirlys-Mina summoned a barrage of arrows.

She knew that the projection's arrows were not piercing — that their collars would generate a shield to absorb more of the force — but she still rushed forward, body remembering the fear that drove it forward when Eirlys' spikes hurdled towards them back in Rabbet's Pass. She was fighting alongside them now, protecting them was part of that command.

The wind at her heels raced up her body freely this time, pooling with such force around her blade, with such eagerness to protect, that when she swung: it tore her arm out of its socket.

"Argh!" Mina cried out in pain, falling to the floor once again as the momentum of her attack threw her off balance. She landed in a heap at their feet, hissing in pain as she grabbed her dangling arm.

"Teetotaler," Sebastian called. "What the hell happened?"

"The arm tornado thing," she hissed in pain.

"Sebastian, could you?" Tanir asked.

"Mina. I command you to let Tanir tend to your arm," he said offhandedly. "Why did you try that?"

"To stop the arrows! How else do you think I'm gonna be able to stop all of them in one hit?"

"Some other way that doesn't put you out-of-commission immediately?" Sir Gargic suggested belittlingly.

"Some other way that doesn't put you out-of-commission immedi-AHH!" Tanir popped her arm back into its socket, cutting off her mocking.

"Take your herbs," she instructed.

"If you can't control it, don't use it," Sebastian followed up.

"Is that a command? Because the way I see it, we really don't have a choice. I just have to practice it some more." Mina sat up and glanced at her sword. "The wind was easier to summon this time, at least."

"How about we just run that part then, huh?" Wera said. "Have Eirlys-Mina fire shots at us and have you block them until you get a handle on the wind."

"Fine." Sebastian pointed a finger in Mina's face. "But if you keep getting hurt, we're coming up with another plan."

Mina swatted his finger away. "I won't keep getting hurt."

But she did.

A lot.

It was astounding how many joints Mina could dislocate with one attack, and how many positions she could wind up contorting into as she fell.

"One more time," she wheezed through her legs as she rolled to stop against the cave wall, right wrist and left hip dislocated.

"Mina," Sebastian sighed.

She dropped herself onto her left side, popping the joint back into place with a sickening snap. "If I jump when I swing it, there won't be any resistance from the ground to work against my hips."

"And your wrist?"

"I can wield left-handed."

Sebastian pinched the bridge of his nose and closed his eyes. The heel of his foot bounced in triplets rather than his fingers. "Look, I'll just use my channeled inferno technique. That should evaporate Eirlys' ice instantly."

"But the whole crux of this plan is to catch them off guard, throw them off their rhythm by showing Mina can't be hurt when protecting us," Tanir countered.

"They can still be thrown off their rhythm!" His shoulders jerked up as he chirped, tampered frustration slowly getting the best of him.

"Sure, but beastie will still be in the eye of the storm instead of with us at the entrance for a starting formation," Sir Gargic huffed. "They'll be playing keep away to keep us separated."

"What if y'all danced?"

Four confused expressions turned Wera's way.

"Have the fumes from your paints gone to your head?" Sir Gargic snipped.

Wera gave a sneering, 'fuck-you' smile. "No. I'm suggesting Meens and 'Bastian do a combo attack like the one they used to take out the learbix." She addressed the pair in question. "Dancing helps her control the wind better, right?"

"And a fire blast like that would definitely clear the ice barrage," Tanir noted. "It might even singe the rimefae a good bit as well, considering you won't be hindered by the rain like before."

"Has to be something more subtle than fire. Maybe smoke?" Sir Gargic suggested. "That'd give us some cover, create even more confusion."

Wera snapped her fingers. "Steam! Instead of fire, do you think you could make Mina's wind hot enough to turn Eirlys' ice to steam?"

Sebastian's nervous fidgeting dissipated, a dumbfounded reel taking its place. "I—uh—"

"It's worth a shot," Mina stood and turned to him. "Is tango the only dance style you know?"

"I know uh—" His cheeks and neck turned red, accent spurring forth in its full glory. "W-waltzing, and um, just normal dancing."

"Normal dancing?"

"Like you do at taverns and stuff..."

Wera snickered. "He's a really saucy dancer when he's tipsy."

Sebastian sputtered and chuffed nervously, "I don't— It's not—"

"I don't have time to learn a new dance style and waltzing is too soft for combat," Mina said, sparing him from any more discomfort. "Tango will work. It's more—"

"Passionate?" Wera suggested with a waggle of her eyebrows.

A sudden surge of heat dried the words off Mina's tongue.

"Direct," Sir Gargic corrected. "The tango has a direction to it. A fierceness."

Mina swallowed harshly, throat filled with sand. "What he said. Now. Let's run it."

"H-hold on a minute!" Sebastian grabbed Mina's hand as she went to retake her starting position. Urged by the command, she held his back.

"I'm not that good of a dancer," he whispered, wearing a wobbly, nervous half-smile while his eyes pleaded for mercy.

"We're not actually dancing a tango," she reassured him, brow knitting just a bit in confusion.

"Right, we're trying to keep everyone from being turned into human colanders, which is a lot trickier."

"Do you have an idea of how to make the wind hot enough to steam them?"

"I do—"

"Then I'll handle the dancing part. I'll lead you."

"Okay, but will it be the same move every time?"

"Probably not."

The wobble settled on a tense, tight line, the pleading look turning unnecessarily desperate. "Mina, I—"

"You'll catch me if I fall. Remember?" Mina squeezed his hand to reassure him, despite how painful it was.

Sebastian lifted his worried brows. "But you're gonna be coming at me so fast," he said meekly.

Having a bit more hope in Wera's plan, his cartoonish concern tickled her enough that she couldn't help the light laugh that escaped her. She had just had her shoulder dislocated a dozen times over, and dropping her during a practice run was his biggest worry?

"Just blade your feet and I'll handle the rest. Stepping into a tango figure is far easier than harnessing a tornado." She pulled her hand away as a minute ended and the soft, steady grip of his palm turned into a vice lined with nails.

Mina walked into position and waited.

Back at the entrance, Sebastian gave a heavy, unsure sigh, feet dragging as he returned to his starting stance as well. "Kumquat."

Mina took off running at the first flicker of an ice arrow. Sebastian's focus was intense, eyes trying their best to keep track of her as she raced towards him. He bent his knees a little more in anticipation, setting himself up perfectly, unknowingly.

The shift in the air around him was palpable. A slight shimmer that drew the wind up from around her heels to course around her body. His palms did not glow, but rather his entire body hummed with a faint amber light. Genius that he was, rather than conjuring a flame, he was heating the air her wind drew from.

She leapt around him to slow her approach slightly, ghosting her hand across his shoulders in warning. He dropped his arm, allowing her to hook around him with ease. She grabbed hold of his outstretched hand, rested her left hip against his knee for purchase, and his dropped arm gripped her waist tightly as her right leg swung through the air. An arch of wind, filled with the energy of her speed and his heat, surged forward and met the arrows: breaking the illusion in an instant.

"Teetotaler!" Wera called to stop the projection before it began the next phase of attacks. "Holy shit! That was fucking awesome!"

"That wasn't so hard, was it?" Mina couldn't help the smile on her face as she turned away from the frozen Mirror-Minas to face him. The smile faltered, however, when she realized just how close their faces were.

"N-no," he stammered, equally shocked by the proximity. "Not hard at all."

Her heart raced more than it had fighting against her copies. Despite her body's want to stay in his arms, Mina leapt out of the lift. A moment longer, and she was sure that blinding pain and cursed train of thought would take over once again.

"We should probably run that again," Tanir suggested. "Considering we don't know in what state of combat we'll find you in, Mina."

"Makes perfect sense to me!" Wera agreed cheerfully. "How about we try—"

"I got it!" The door to the training room flew open as Enoch strode into the room, chest puffed out in pride. "I know how we can get rid of them without—" He stopped in his tracks with a jolt, attention drawn to the Mirror-Minas paused mid-retaliation. "Dear Gods, those are terrifying."

"But necessary," Sebastian straightened his jacket and collected himself. A tinge of crimson still stained his cheeks. "You found something?"

"Yes," Enoch opened up the thick leather book in his hand, turning to the page he kept marked with his thumb. "Do you know any banishing spells?"

"A banishing spell?" Sir Gargic balked. "And where the hell would we be banishing them to?"

"To the Realm of the Fae," he answered.

"Enoch," Wera sighed. "The veil is so thin around here, they'll probably just pop back out."

"If a fae finds themselves far from where the leylines thin the veil, they will conjure a Circle of Recalling to call upon the despot of their domain to summon them home," Enoch turned his nose up at her dismissal and read. "The circles appear to us as fairy rings: odd circles of mushrooms, stones, wildflowers, etc. The lingering magic connecting these rings to their associated sovranfae is what causes uncareful mortals who cross into them to wander into fairyland accidentally. Lady Hitchman, Master Willock, and I have utilized this same concept as a way to send unwanted fae back to their realm for one full moon cycle."

Enoch stuck his tongue out at Wera as he handed the book over to Sebastian. "Apparently, if a fae gets summoned back by their despot, they are required by fairy law to remain in their homeland for a full month as a tithe."

Whatever warmth still lingering on Mina's skin vanished. Cold crept in from deep within her, deep within her blood. A sovranfae.

Her sovranfae.

Her.

"The circle seems to be an important component." Sebastian's index finger tapped against the leather cover as he read. He wore a light grimace, a contemplative grimace. Not the look of horror he should have been bearing at Enoch's suggestion. "There's a number we could use, but we'd have to set it up ahead, and I'd have to focus on casting the banishment rather than fight."

"Does it say how the circle is able to make contact with the sovranfae?" Tanir asked, foolishly, as if it were as harmless as writing a letter. "Maybe there's a way to appeal to them—"

"No!" Mina shouted, fear getting the best of her. They all jumped at her sudden exclamation. She inhaled deeply to regain her composure and rein in her building panic. They were just discussing their plan, nothing was final yet. There were no chains wrapped around their necks, turning them pale, stealing the light from their eyes, as sharpened fingernails sank into their chests digging for—

She locked eyes with Sebastian, her dull pleading well-earned. "No."

The tension in his jaw and stiffness in his shoulder returned. Perhaps he could feel Her cold too.

"There's no need to worry," Enoch assured. "It doesn't call on the sovranfae themselves. It hones in on the unique genetic components that link the creature to its domain, like a homing beacon."

"So we'd need to grab some hair from them while we're fighting? The damn things are already gonna be difficult enough to handle. And to be down a wizard as well?" Sir Gargic groused.

"It's a lot of moving parts, Enoch," Sebastian handed the book towards him. "We'll have to find another solution."

Enoch pushed it back. "There is no other solution! Not unless you can get me to a proper library and give me a week to scour its shelves!"

The hiss of chains slithered in the back of Mina's mind, and she ran her trembling fingers across the iron band resting against her clavicle. The faintest memory of them, whipping in the air, searching for her as she left the Rime all those years ago. Blind in their search, even though she was within their reach.

There was another solution. Another way to drag them back. As much as the idea of it terrified her, as much as she could still feel their icy barbs wrapped around her, squeezing, tearing, she knew it to be true.

If she removed it, the chains would return. She was certain of it. And if they were blind enough that a simple necklace of iron could hide their quarry, perhaps they could be tricked into believing that their quarry was more than one.

And The Matron would punish her children severely for being tricked. Much longer than a month.

"We don't need a circle. Or a spell to send them back," she said, interrupting their bickering, voice hollow as the terrified part of her begged her not to speak the thought aloud. "Just some blood and some iron. And some really, really tricky timing."

"What are you suggesting, beastie?"

She held on to the amber pendant, shifting it back and forth. She wouldn't let Her take her away. *They* wouldn't let Her take her away. "When the streetlamps come on at night, what do guardians do to their children?"

Sebastian's eyes widened, his breath catching in his chest. "Mina—"

"I'll only have to remove it completely for a second, *just a second*," she assured him as well as herself as the words flew out of her mouth, her fear desperate to rid herself of the idea. "Getting my blood on them is a lot more manageable than collecting their hair, but I don't know what'll happen if so much of my blood is away from my body. So maybe we should use something like that iron aerosol idea I had to keep them grounded until they're all coated. Is there a big enough magnet we can use to draw the iron out of them when it's time?"

"That'll be an awful lot of blood I'll have to draw," Tanir fretted.

"I'll make sure to eat a lot of steak to make up for it."

"And what if your blood doesn't work?" Sir Gargic pressed. "Then we'll have, what, a crazy sovranfae coming after us on top of the other fuckers we'll have to deal with?"

Yes!

"No." She shut the sniveling side of her down. Fear had no place here. Fear would surely lead to her failure. "The minute I grab it back, the veil will close again. I'm certain of it."

"Because if there's no beacon drawing the magic to this plane, then there will be no reason for it to linger," Enoch said.

"Exactly."

"I've got a better idea than the paint, but it'll take some practice and depends on if we can get a magnet big enough." Wera pulled the curl she was twirling and released it to bounce back to its brethren. "What do you think, 'Bastian? Is it doable?"

"Your hands are trembling," he noted. Despite the others' plotting and questioning, his focus hadn't left her for a moment. Even his breathing had stilled, still hanging on a hitch, waiting for her signal.

"I know," Mina said. "But it'll just be for a moment..." The little scared voice slipped out with a subtle shutter: "Right?"

You'll catch me if I fall?

A thousand thoughts, a thousand plans, a thousand emotions passed through his gaze, none of them happy. His palms pulsed with amber heat before settling, resigned, with a deep inhale as his breathing started up again. He closed his eyes and reopened them: determination.

"I can make a magnet powerful enough," he said with a certainty that stilled her trembling hands, soothed that fearful voice. "What else does your idea involve, Wera?"

She smiled wickedly. "Turpentine and dancing."

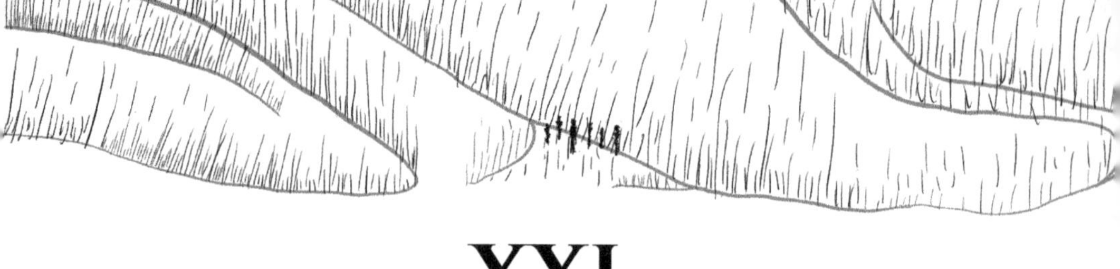

XXI

The Ties That Bind

The whistling wind, the crunch of their footsteps, and the hum of her blade were the only sounds that followed them as they continued their hike across the tundra. If the others could hear her sword, Mina did not know, and wouldn't know until they made camp for the night.

They were playing disgruntled and traumatized, hamming up their injuries as she diverted from the trail as inconspicuously as possible. Her sword's buzz taunted her. Bormir wanted her to know that he was near. That he was watching.

That he was allowing her to choose instead of killing them all outright.

At this leg of the journey the expeditions she led, joyous that the worst of their trials were over, would often have a pep in their step. They'd chatter excitedly to each other, discussing what resources of theirs they could indulge in to commemorate their journey's end. Some travelers, who heard of the unprecedented ease of this last stretch, would even plan to bring libations to toast "living through The Lithe". Those parties often wound up being the ones to lose men along the way, an unfortunate side effect of having such a blasé attitude in the face of clear danger.

Had Sebastian prepared something? Not that he was blasé about danger, but he seemed like the type to want to celebrate the end of things. If they made it to the end, of course.

She ran through their plan over and over again in her head, imaging all the possible points of failure, figuring out ways to turn those failures in their favor, or at the very least keep them from dying at Bormir's hands.

Sebastian did the same. The far-off look in his eyes, his twitching lips, and the ceaseless drumming of his fingertips as they paused to eat a quiet lunch out in the open told her that much. "They had to make up for lost time," Sir Gargic grumbled when Sebastian purposefully called for them to stop and set up the commorancy for lunch. Enoch had crafted quite the act, one that painted them as disgruntled, divided, and defeated.

And Mina, for her part in this play, had no trouble acting irritated and disheartened by it.

They should be celebrating, not worrying whether or not they'd be hearing their funeral dirge in less than two days' time.

"My Gods! If I had known you all could act so well, I would have put together some readings for my play much earlier," Enoch said once they were safely locked behind the commorancy's door.

Wera feigned a gag. "Spare me."

"Oh, really? You wouldn't want to see Mina read for Lilias?"

She paused for a moment, leaving her boot to dangle off the tip of her toe as she removed it.

"Lilias? Like The Cunning Sisters of Warwick *Lilias?*"

A devilish grin curled up Enoch's face. "You see my genius, right?"

"Tanir. Is dinner better served after or before you draw her blood?" Sebastian asked, ignoring the pair's excitement.

"After. We'll want to have some type of beef or venison, with plenty of vegetables. Spinach for sure."

"Alright then." He looked at Mina, stare still distant, contemplative. "She'll draw your blood, we'll eat, then run a few practice battles in the training room."

"That works," she replied and tapped on the hilt of her sword. "They were watching us by the way."

"Well, at least someone enjoyed my work," Enoch grumbled under his breath.

"Noted." Sebastian walked towards the staircase. "Sir Gargic, come with me to my study. I'll be finishing up the magnetic breastplate and need to see how it fits you."

The knight grunted in acknowledgment and followed him up the stairs.

"That's not good," Tanir mumbled, the fine wrinkles around her mouth deepening with her frown.

"Really not good," Wera concurred, nodding as a similar pout took place on her lips.

"What is it?" Mina asked.

Tanir sighed. "Let's go and get you set up. We'll talk as you drip. Wera, care to assist?"

"Gladly."

Mina followed the pair. An uncomfortable confusion knotted up her stomach by their lack of an answer. Sebastian wasn't upset with her again, was he?

No, he'd tell her if he was.

Wouldn't he?

"Oh, that's fine!" Enoch called after them. "Just go ahead and ignore me too!"

Wera turned around to walk backwards. "Come along, Enoch, you brilliant, culture-defining playwright in the making. How could we ever deign to forget you?"

He huffed and stomped after them. "Alright smart ass. Sue me for wanting just a little acknowledgement, why don't you?"

"Take a seat on the table," Tanir instructed as they entered the infirmary. "Wera, the drip bags are in the lime green cabinet. Enoch, grab the roll of tubing off the middle shelf by the laxatives."

"What is it?" Mina repeated, needing an answer as quickly as possible. Him being upset was not a factor in her scenarios. It wasn't allowed to be.

"A laxative?" Enoch asked.

"No. With Bastion. What is it?"

"He's thinking too much," Wera answered.

"Isn't he always thinking too much?" she countered.

"Yeah, but this is *too* too much. He's turned serious. I don't think he's ever been this serious, especially not for this long."

"Excessively contemplative is the more poetic term for it," Enoch said.

"Excessively contemplative was when he was trying to figure out what to make his Master for dinner the last time he popped over for a visit." Tanir crossed back over to the table with needles and iodine in hand. She slipped on a pair of gloves made from the same leather as Mina's, only hers had a lot less patches. "I think he's truly worried about this fight."

Tanir grabbed Mina's arm and rubbed the iodine around the inner crook. "Can't say I blame him, though. I'm nervous as hell, too."

"It will work out," Mina said. "No matter what, you all will make it to Lanholde."

Tanir pouted, wrinkles exaggerating in the action, aging her by ten years in a flash.

"What's that face?"

"What face?" she walked away from her to rummage through the drawers. "Keep your arm down until the bag is full and here—" She threw a metal grip trainer at her. "Squeeze this to make it flow faster."

Mina snatched the gripper out of the air one-handed. "You're avoiding my question."

"You said 'you all' instead of 'we'," Wera said. "Which implies that there's a chance that you won't be coming with us to Lanholde. Which is exactly what Sebastian is excessively contemplating about."

"Oh." A deep, dull ache seized Mina's heart, the knots of worry in her stomach pulling taut. He didn't need to worry about that, she was worrying about it enough for the both of them. "I keep running through it myself."

"You do?" Enoch asked.

She watched her blood flow down the tube, a much darker red than it should be. "I need to be prepared for anything to ensure the best possible outcome."

"Tell him that," Wera interjected.

"Really?"

"Really. He needs to hear it." A small, warm smile gave Mina a headache as it crawled up Wera's face. "It'll turn excessive contemplation to mild contemplation. I guarantee it."

🜁

"Again," Sebastian panted. He wiped the glaze of sweat off his forehead, leaving a trail of soot behind.

"No, Sebastian," Tanir wheezed. Despite being hunched over, leaning on her axe handle as if it were a fifth limb, her voice carried weight. "That's the last time we're running it. I'm calling it."

"Tani—"

"We have more hiking and an actual battle to fight tomorrow. We need to rest."

Sebastian glanced over the others, all of them battered and bruised, clearly exhausted. Save for Mina who, bearing the broken jaw she had to reset after Bormir-Mina got a neat right hook in before Sir Gargic activated the magnet, still stood strong.

He waved them off. "Fine then. Go rest up."

"You too," Tanir pressed.

"Mina and I will run our part of the opening sequence a few more times, then I will. The timing's a bit off with igniting the turpentine."

"Sebastian."

"It shouldn't take more than half an hour. Mina will hold me to that. Won't you?" he asked her.

"If I'm told to."

"See?"

Tanir glared at him. "Then tell her too."

Sebastian pursed his lips in discontent, nostrils flaring slightly. "Mina. In a half hour from now, bother the absolute piss out of me until I leave this training room and head to bed."

"Oooo," Wera cooed. "I think I can manage to stay up for another half an hour to witness that."

"No," Tanir snipped. "We're all going to bed. Doctor's orders."

They gave little protest to her decree and hobbled out of the room, leaving Mina, Sebastian, and the mirages of her false family behind.

"Alright." Soot stained the roots of his hair as he ran his hand through it. "Take it from Eirlys' range attack?"

"Makes sense."

He walked over to the terminal, steps stiffer than usual. The percussion of his footsteps was off rhythm, and he favored his right leg a little more than his left.

"You're limping," she noted.

"I think I've got a couple of nasty blisters forming on my left foot. I can push through it, though. We have to get this right."

"You said the timing's off with igniting the turpentine? How can we test that without Wera and her iron concoction?"

"I'll just ignite the oxygen you pull in to form the arrows," he said. "It's the technique I want to practice, not so much the full execution."

"But aren't the rate of ignitions between turpentine and oxygen different?"

Sebastian remained silent, twisting away at the dials on the terminal until he was satisfied with its programming.

"Start word is Mat. Stop word is Clock," he said as he walked past her to take his starting position. Mina inhaled sharply, his ignorance of her question not going unnoticed, and took her place as well.

"Ready?" he asked.

"Ready," she answered.

"Mat."

The projection started. Eirlys summoned her arrows. Mina ran towards Sebastian, he bent his knees to catch her, and as she whipped around him, her leg swiped through the air.

"Clock!" she called as she sat on his thigh.

The arrows hung in the air, just a foot away from piercing them.

"What is it?" Sebastian fretted, looking down at his self frantically. "I thought I did the catch alright. The position seems correct."

"You're too serious."

He looked up at her, face contorted with confusion. "What?"

"And excessively contemplative." She placed her hand against her chest. "I am too."

His brows knit together even tighter, one arching from the strain. "That... makes sense? This is a very serious situation that requires a lot of contemplation."

"But you're *too* serious."

The knot of his brows fell: frustration, anger.

"And what? I'm supposed to make jokes and smile while I'm trying to make damn fucking sure my friends don't die, and you're not trapped in Elphyne for a month?" he snapped, temper popping like hot coals for a fleeting moment, then extinguished by immediate regret. He looked away from her to the floor. "Let's just run this through a couple of times, okay? I don't want to take things out on you. It's not your fault."

"It is my fault."

He closed his eyes, face scrunching up tightly as he clenched his jaw.

"Mina," he hissed.

"You know it is."

"No, it fucking isn't!" She could feel the heat of the palm supporting her waist through her armor as he shouted. "It's whatever evil ass sovranfae that cursed you's fucking fault! And these fucking goons who think they have a goddamn right to call you family! What fucking brother would treat his goddamn sister like this? What fucking person would want their family to suffer like you are?"

Sparks danced across his fingertips as gestured towards the projections in front of them.

"Gods, I would have given fucking anything to have a goddamn family, and here they are treating you like dirt. To what end? What the hell do they get out of it?!"

"Satisfaction," she mumbled, awed by his unfiltered anger.

"How?!" He opened his eyes. "How could anyone find joy in harming you? It feels like I'm stabbing myself in the chest every time I do accidentally!"

"They have no choice but to."

"There's always a choice."

"Not when punishments are involved. Not when—" her jaw locked for a moment before she pivoted. "I understand them, and I don't blame them. I could have been the same."

"But you're not."

"I can be similar. You've seen it. Cold... cruel..."

"Similar is not the same. You chose not to be that way. To leave them all behind."

A guilt, much older and much deeper, rooted within her, crawled up and seized her heart.

"I didn't choose that," she admitted, surprised and saddened that it came out so freely. "I didn't choose to leave them behind."

Sebastian's forehead was so wrinkled in turmoil, Mina feared he'd pull a muscle, but the heat in his hands dissipated as his anger was washed away by study.

"You meant to bring them with you when you left?"

Mina stared at him blankly, mouth cemented shut. She reached up and stroked her necklace.

"No. That's not it..." His eyes locked on the band, embers building back. "You meant to get help for them, but couldn't say anything."

Mina winced. The heat returned to Sebastian's palm: immediately searing.

"Excessively contemplative," he said evenly, threatening to melt the iron around her neck with the growing burn behind his stare. "Now I'm excessively contemplating making a summoning circle so I can rend that sovranfae to ash."

"Do not do that," Mina warned, a chill surging at the thought of The Matron's spindly hands reaching out for him, toying with him to torment her. A slight breeze kicked up around them as swirls of steam trickled from where his palm met her back. Where the heat of his anger met the freeze of her fear, her fury.

A moment of tension hung in the air between them. His eyes lifted to meet her own. And for so unknowable reason, a devilish smirk curled up Sebastian's lips, rolling a bubbling laughter through him. The first true laugh she heard from him in days.

It was beautiful.

"Gods help whoever pisses the two of us off, huh?"

That ringing pain chimed in her head again, and she stood to put some distance between them.

"Right," Sebastian groaned slightly as he stood. "Let's run it one more time then. For both of our sake."

Mina gave a curt nod, fear, frustration, and joy tying up her tongue, and walked away to retake her starting position.

"Ready?" he called from behind her.

They had to nail this combination to survive. That's all this was. Survival.

"Ready."

"Mat."

The simulation reset. Eirlys conjured her arrows. Mina took off.

Her hand ghosted across his shoulder, and she wrapped around him, dropping into his hold and swiping her leg through the air effortlessly.

There wasn't any moment to pause once the arrows were dispersed and the shattered projection gave off the illusion of thick, cloaking steam. With a twist of his torso, she spun out off his knee, allowing him to stand tall beside her before pulling them back together by their connected hands.

Left hand connected with right to hold "the bow," and their other hands, as one, ran along the length of their outstretched arms. Mina kept her eyes closed to focus as she formed the arrows out of the air around them; aiming them in the direction of the projections' hums.

Their hands brushed against their cheeks as they reached the end of their draw and they released.

Six arrows of blazing amber fire soared through the air. So fast, a windstorm kicked up in their wake as they buried themselves in each of the Mirror-Minas.

"Clock," Sebastian called.

They let go of each other, but did not step apart.

"Timing seems right," Mina noted.

"It was easier to ignite them this time, too. I could sense where you were conjuring the arrows without having to look."

"Really?"

"Yeah. I noticed you've been closing your eyes when you draw so I did the same to try and hear what you were hearing. There were a bunch of soft, different-pitched whistles, and I could feel the breeze brush in different directions. So, I set the sparks to drift along them," he explained. "They carried very well, which is good to note. Perhaps there could be—"

Threads tugged not at Mina's body, but at her mind as all her thoughts fell away, suffocated by one overbearing notion: annoy.

She stuck a finger in Sebastian's face. He flinched slightly and crossed his eyes to look at the digit hovering in front of his nose.

"What? Do I have something on my face or?"

"I'm not touching you," she said.

His eyes uncrossed. "What?"

She wiggled her pointer finger and sang teasingly, "I'm not touching you!"

"I can tell?"

Taking full advantage of her supernatural speed, she rushed to his side and, with a quick swipe of her tongue across her finger, stuck the wet digit in his ear.

"Eugh!" Sebastian swatted her hand away and he jumped back. "Why?!"

"I'm bothering the piss—" she appeared in front of him and flicked his nose, "bothering the piss—" she flipped over him, tugging his hair as she passed, "bothering the piss out of you!" She kicked him sharply in the ass, not enough to hurt, but enough to have him yipe as he stumbled forward.

"Mina! Quit it!"

The command rolled off her shoulders.

"Not until you head to—" She leaped onto his back and sang in his ear in the highest pitch in her register, "—bed!"

"Gah! But I have to turn off—"

She took two fistfuls of his hair and jerked his head back and forth. "Bed! Bed! Bed! Beeeeeed!!"

"Argh! Okay! I'm going!" he shouted as he trudged over to the terminal. "Just stop shaking my head so I can see the dials!"

Mina hooked her fingers into his mouth.

"Wah. Wat wowks," he garbled.

She tugged at the corners of his mouth to move his lips as she deepened her voice. "Mina. Sit. Mina. Stay. Mina, do exactly what I say. I've got fire at my fingertips. I've got full and bow-like lips. I push and pull you with my threads. And yet, I will not go to bed!"

The terminal powered down, dissolving the Mirror-Minas.

"Awight! Wi durned wit awff."

"You're still in the training room!" she sang before sinking her teeth into his neck.

Sebastian jolted in surprise.

"Mina!" he squealed as much as her fingers would let him.

She lapped her tongue against his skin in wiggling, sloppy circles. The action sent him running to the door, and she tightened her thighs around his middle to hold on. As he crossed the threshold, her entire body seized in pain, and she let go, dropping to the ground with a hard thud.

"Oh thank Gods," Sebastian exasperated as he rested his forehead against the hallway wall.

"You asked for it," Mina grumbled.

He flipped around and gazed at her with a wide-eyed, incredulous stare. His face and neck were deeply flushed, almost resembling his hair in vibrancy.

"I did *not* ask you to do *that* to my neck."

"Well, if you *asked* me to do it, then it wouldn't be bothersome, now would it?"

He sputtered. "It— that—"

Mina stood as the threads started to pull at her again. Part of her enjoyed seeing him so flustered, and his command — yet to be truly complete — fed that notion.

"You shouldn't linger any longer," she warned. She held out her hands and twiddled her fingers in the air. "The command isn't finished until you head to bed, and I'm starting to wonder if you're ticklish."

"Wha—" Sebastian backed away from her slowly, accent shaking forth in his wavering tone. "W-what do you mean by that? I-I'm heading to bed!"

She stepped closer. "Not fast enough."

She smiled, perhaps the biggest smile she had mustered so far. "Let's see how fast you can run, Wizard."

🜁

Wine and tomatoes still lingered on her tongue as she played.

The melody of Sebastian's song poured out of the ebony violin, flooding her room and drowning out the ticking of the hour hand as it approached eleven. Mina lost herself in the music and the drawings of her friends. Done in all the colors Mina could see, she had taken their brief respite to capture them in pastels, adding a smiling Wera, Tanir, and Enoch to the hang among her wall of Sebastians. She was committing them to memory. Deep memory. The kind that no amount of magic or torment could take from her. Just in case.

The song came to an end, and the last dredges of warmth it seemed to conjure in her chest faded as the clock chimed eleven times.

She took the now-dried lavender wreath off her head and set the violin down on her desk. She carefully removed the amber pendant from around her collar and placed it in between them. She didn't want to risk losing it when she broke the clasp and unleashed hell upon herself.

In the bathroom mirror, she glanced over her reflection, wanting to commit the image to memory as well.

Just in case.

It was easy to forget yourself in the Rime. The magic that polluted the air throughout the realm left no one unchanged, no matter how long a person journeyed through it. She would not allow it to change her any more than it already had.

She could see the slight tint of blue that stained every part of her now, but the blush of her lips dared to pierce through it. There was a light behind the gray of her eyes, the dull glaze they used to carry only evident in her memory, and her hair was a mess. Longer in places, shorter in others, it resembled more of a novice's attempt at culling a field of flax than a hairstyle.

She ran a hand through it and smiled, despite the horrible memories behind it. To see the expression on her face was foreign and breathtaking, and it only served to widen her smile more.

She had no choice but to succeed. She and Sebastian had to shave their heads together after. A fresh start.

Three knocks rang out against her door.

"Mina?" Sebastian called from the other side. "Are you ready?"

He was waiting just outside of her door frame, and studied her from tip to toe as she stepped into the hall, still worrying.

"New armor?" he asked.

"My whytewing armor's too shredded. That final transformation did them in. And my other leathers would freeze and snap in the cold. the Junk Room had this at least," She ran her hands down the fur, unable to feel its softness. "It's made from caribou so it should hold up."

"You should have—"

"It weighs the same as the one I've been wearing during practice. It's more flexible, even." She lifted her leg up straight until her knee brushed against her ear. "See?"

His cheeks flushed red and he averted his gaze. "Yes, I see." He cleared his throat. "Do you have everything?"

"Sword, hidden flask of blood," she lowered her leg down and named the objects as she pointed to them on her body. "Knives, herbs, necklace. All set."

"Good." He nodded tightly. "The others are waiting downstairs."

They walked down the hall together in silence, a tension between them tightening with every step towards the staircase. Their steps seemed to grow louder, more consuming, more damning. An approaching finality behind them. Mina had the need to say something, but what was there to say? What *could* she say?

"Mina," Sebastian stopped at the top of the stairs.

She stopped alongside him. "What is it?"

"I want to make a deal with you. Another contract, if you will."

"Now?"

"It's sort of a Plan Z."

Just in case.

Without a second thought, Mina grabbed a knife out of her belt and cut a small slit in her palm. She held her bloodied hand, knife lying flat on top of it, out towards him.

"Blood contracts are nearly impossible to break."

His gaze flicked between her hand and her face, mouth slightly agape in disbelief. "I haven't even told you what I'm asking of you."

"I've already signed one contract without reading it," she said, a slight smile tugging at the corner of her lips. "What's one more?"

Sebastian grabbed the knife and cut a small nick in his palm, wincing as he did. He flexed his fingers to get the blood flowing, then took her hand in his.

"Mina." He closed his eyes as he spoke, focusing on the particulars of his wording. "I shall do everything within my power to keep you in this mortal realm unless you truly wish to leave it, and will do everything within my power to keep those that cursed you from causing you any more harm."

Something stirred in Mina's chest. Greater than any flutter. Deeper than any ache she bore. She inhaled deeply, bracing herself for the inevitable pain that was sure to strike.

"For this, I swear that I will continue to fight alongside you so long as you call upon me to do so. That I shall continue to be your partner," she added, "and as such, will keep you and those you care about from harm to the best of my ability." She squeezed his hand, despite the action feeling like squeezing a handful of needles. He opened his eyes and met hers. "By my blood, my word is binding."

The Fae's Folly wrapped beyond their hands. Sebastian flinched in surprise, gaze leaving hers to look down at his arm as the invisible bind coursed beneath their skin, weaving up through their veins, to wrap around their hearts. Together, they inhaled sharply as the organs, in tandem, skipped a beat. The Folly tied its knot.

"Have you done that often?" Sebastian asked, an unsure waiver shaking his voice.

"Not like that." She let go of his hand as the ringing pain in her head layered on top of the piercing in her palm. She pulled a sprig of herbs out of her pocket, bit off half, and handed out the other to him. "Can't go into this kind of fight with a wounded hand."

He plucked the herb out from between her fingers and stuck it in his mouth. The slight smile on his face contorted as he chewed into a grimace of disgust.

"Ugh. It's so bitter." His tongue flicked out of his mouth a bit, trying to escape the taste. Mina laughed wholeheartedly.

"You look like a lizard," she said between chuckles.

"Well, I was born under a salamander moon, remember?" Sebastian crossed his eyes as he flicked his tongue out like a snake and hissed. Mina's discordant laughter shook the picture frames.

"Oi! You two!" Sir Gargic's shout echoed up from the floor below them. "Quit clowning around! We've got a goddamn schedule to keep!"

Mina was unsurprised to see the knight glaring at them when she reached the foyer, disgruntled pout and flaring nostrils giving him the appearance of an ornery snapping turtle. Tanir and Enoch's expressions were much kinder, their grins were tight, eyes slightly clouded with worry, as was expected. While Wera...

"Fucking finally! Let's go, let's go, let's go!" She bounced on the tip of her toes, fingers twitching, body jittering.

"How much of the tincture did she take?" Sebastian asked Tanir.

"She drank half the bottle."

"If we don't get a move on it soon, I think my heart will explode!" Wera sung.

Tanir sighed, "It won't."

"Well, maybe take a couple laps around the hall while we wait our ten, alright?" he suggested.

"Right!" Wera turned to Mina. "Meens, I better see that big Androno-motherfucker's nose coming out of the back of his skull when I get there. Give them fucking hell!" She gave her a double thumbs-up, then took off down the hall in a full sprint.

"You're sure the invigoration will hold up against Tyoma's aura of fatigue?" Enoch asked.

"I already tested it with a few brief sleeping spells of my own. The moment they hit her, the magics canceled each other out and left just one normal Wera," Tanir explained.

"Everyone got their vials?" Mina asked. "Enoch, you prepared your daggers for Eirlys?"

He twirled one of the daggers between his fingers, the blade reforged to hold veins of pure, dark iron. "Payback's a bitch."

"This *Iraina* better put up a good fight," Sir Gargic grumbled. "If I did all this training just to be able to knock her out in two strikes—"

"Then it'll just go to show how skilled of a fighter you are." Sebastian clapped a hand on his shoulder. "Breastplate still fitting well?"

Sir Gargic gave a begrudging harrumph in affirmation.

"Then we're all set." Mina stared at the front door.

"We'll be right behind you, Mina," Sebastian said. "You'll be up against them alone for only ten minutes."

She inhaled sharply, "I know," and opened the door.

⚠

It had been a long while since she crossed the Fallow Peaks alone, especially so slowly. The tundra was a void beneath the moonless sky, yet still, the stars were shining. They and the wind at her back were her only companions as she wove through the snowdrifts and frozen boulders.

Were she not trying to conserve as much energy for the battle before her, she would have run and saved herself the trouble of listening for missing footsteps.

Instead of Wera and Enoch's scribbling, the crunch of her heels breaking through layers of frost met her ears. Instead of the slight snip of Tanir's embroidery scissors, her sheath belt chimed with every step. Instead of Sebastian's hums of contemplation, the wind whistled a hollow tune.

A chill ran through her, not from the cold, but from a sensation she couldn't quite place. One that had her even missing the low wheeze that rattled in Sir Gargic's lungs. The same sense of off-balance that haunted her first expedition without Mr. Harlowe, only much stronger. More of a possession than a haunting.

Just a little while longer. They'll be right behind me.

The boulders and snow drifts grew larger, dwarfing her threefold as she descended closer and closer to the den, following the trail the lindwyrm had carved into the rock decades ago. The air thickened, indistinguishable by sight but heavy as fog. It rested against her skin, pulled at the ends of her hair, filled her lungs with icy slush. Now she shivered. A true, chilled shiver.

The Barren Rime's freeze.

The wrath of Winter unbound.

How did she ever withstand it?

She inhaled deeply, remembering warmth, remembering the weightlessness of the hot spring, anything to keep the cold from dragging her down, and continued on, entering the den with the slightly seething presence Enoch scripted her to have.

In its center, an aurora illuminated the well-worn walls of the cave. Ribbons of light wove suspended in midair, signifying the crossing point. A threadbare patch in the veil.

Eirlys and Iraina came dancing through as Mina stepped further into the den. The others followed in calm, straight-shouldered strides, with Bormir, peacock that he was, strutting confidently behind them.

A tom cat too proud of the brood he produced.

"I'm glad to see that the Mortal Realm hasn't completely rotted away at your sense, sister. Though I will say I am a little disappointed. You were cutting so close to the deadline, I was already considering where I was going to mount that menacing firecrotch's head in my study. Over the fireplace mantle is a little overdone, you know?" He smirked as he looked around the den. "Interesting location, by the way. Feeling a little nostalgic for Governor Gilbran's lectures?"

"No." Mina drew her sword. "But it is a fitting place to bury snakes."

Bormir's smile grew wider. Venom glazed over his eyes.

"It appears I thought too highly of you. But I will say I'm not surprised." The ends of his hair crumbled away into snowfall and reformed into a rapier in his palm. "Low ceilings to keep us in your range of attack, only two exits — one of which you can't cross through until we rip that mongrel collar off your neck. Funny, what someone who so desperately wanted to be free chains themselves too. But then again, you always were a hypocrite."

Hypocrite.

The word tugged at Mina more than she cared for.

She sneered and charged, feigning that the comment incensed her. With the wind at her heels, she threw herself at Bormir. He thrust his rapier to parry her attack— and meet air as she pivoted at the last moment and swiped at Iraina's throat.

The rimefae's scream cut off as the tip of the iron blade pierced just below her chin, severing her vocal cords perfectly.

Never once in their simulations had Mina hit her target exactly. Iraina-Mina had always pulled away just in time, either avoiding the blow completely or adjusting to minimize the impact. Iraina-Mina was always faster.

I'm faster.

Her moment of astonishment was short-lived as the telltale whistle of Eirlys' ice spears sent her running. Androniki's arm swung into view, and Mina used it as leverage to knock the hulk off his feet and throw him into the approaching Tyoma.

Dolcemar let out a primal scream, long claws of ice jutting from each hand as she launched out of an ice patch alongside another ice spear flurry. A distraction, something loud and wild to pull her focus and keep her from noticing the swirling snow in her peripherals.

Mina jumped to her left, into the snow, disrupting Bormir's reassembly long enough to catch his blade against hers.

"What is it, Riktanya?" Bormir mocked as he unlocked his rapier and sought to drive her back with his rapid, cutthroat strikes. "Don't like being called on the carpet?"

More ice spears raced towards them, passing through Bormir easily and forcing Mina to dodge as she blocked, losing the ground she was holding against him. Frantic footsteps charged behind her, lithe with firm heel strikes: Tyoma again. She dipped low, letting one of Eirlys' spears catch her in the shoulder as she parried Bormir above her head and slipped through his legs. She ripped one of her knives out of her belt and threw it, nicking the tip off of Bormir's pointed left ear before it found purchase in Tyoma's left bicep.

"What's the matter, Bormir?" Mina mocked back as she seized hold of the polearm Iraina tried to catch her with. She yanked the weapon out of her hands forcefully, lurching her forward before sending her stumbling backwards by driving an elbow into her face. "Too afraid to fight me unhindered?"

Androniki and Dolcemar charged at her in tandem, the latter slightly faster than her counterpart. She launched herself at Mina once again, claws out. She was too hungry for it. Her form was nearly non-existent, relying on sheer force to try and catch her enemies off guard. Mina took a step back, grabbed the girl by the wrists as she leapt past her, and drove her pitchfork-claws into Androniki's chest. A flash of white caught Mina's attention, and she pivoted, dual rimefae in tow, to catch Eirlys' next barrage into Androniki's back.

"Or are you admitting you don't stand a chance at killing me without a sleep spell?"

Bormir barked a cruel laugh and surged towards her, leathery wings flapping furiously to try and match her speed. Mina released Androniki and Dolcemar in time to dodge his jab, but could not get her sword up fast enough to block the swipe that raked across her midsection.

"I'm afraid? What a fucking joke!" he snarled. "You're the one who's running away!" Mina parried his next strike and leapt backwards, propelling herself across the cave and away from him and the encroaching rimefae.

The plan was to bounce off the rock, but two arms emerged out of the wall against her back, nails digging into her shoulders. Mina stabbed her sword into the patch of ice behind her, loosing Eirlys' hold on it and pulling her forward. Bormir was on Mina the second Eirlys was thrown from her shoulders.

His rapier pierced through the shoulder of her armor and into the ice beside her, pinning her down. "But what else can I expect from a selfish turncoat?"

With the wind at her heels, she brought her knees up and drove both feet into his chest, tearing the rapier out of his grasp and launching him clear across the cavern. The rapier deconstructed and a hail of ice spears rained upon her as she slid down the wall. Mina twirled her blade in front of her as she fell, breaking as many of the projectiles as she could.

Androniki waited below for her, charging at lightning speed to connect a sweeping haymaker to her temple. Mina blocked it with her blade. He shrieked as the iron seared his knuckles, taking some velocity out of his punch.

Her eyelids grew heavy. Tyoma was close again.

She grazed her forearm with her blade, shooting searing pain through her to keep her awake just long enough to break away from Androniki and dive under Tyoma's legs as they sent a sweeping kick towards her head. The toe of their boot cracked the stone behind her.

A selfish turncoat.

The words ate away at her, stirring up that long-buried guilt.

How dare he?

The unwanted thought, thick with disdained ichor, turned her focus back outward just in time for an arm to wrap around her neck.

Bormir kicked out the back of her knee, dropping her into a kneel as he tightened his headlock.

He tutted in performative disapproval. "What is it, sister? Did I hit a nerve?"

Right on time, bright bolts of amber fire soared through the air, evaporating the ice patches that littered the cavern. Eirlys shrieked in annoyance.

"Let her go!" Sebastian shouted behind them.

Bormir chuckled, and tugged Mina along by the throat as he turned to face him.

Sebastian, Wera, Tanir, Enoch, and Sir Gargic all stood in formation. Expressions stern and stances ready to strike.

Mina knew exactly how she was getting out of his hold if he wasn't going to toy with her, but how he squeezed her windpipe as he leaned down to her whisper in her ear told her there would be no need for Plan B. Ever since they were children, Bormir loved to gloat.

The sickly smile he wore shaped his breath as it hissed across her eardrum.

"If only you had wings, you wouldn't have left any footprints," he taunted. "Mother always told us that our enemy is only as strong as their weakness. She'll be so disappointed to hear just how many you've let yourself have."

He straightened, and loosened his grip on her neck, just enough for her to break free without hassle, as Eirlys summoned her barrage of icicles once again.

Mina ran, wind to her back, lifting her heels and carrying her legs to her top speed. She was faster than all of them, Bormir knew this. He was banking on her getting there, blocking Eirlys' attack, and ruining herself.

And she did. She got there.

She swung around Sebastian, gliding into his arms as easily as the breeze glides across the ocean, but shattered the encroaching ice with the force of a hurricane.

"Their form is sloppy. And I'm faster." She whispered in his ear under the shroud of steam. She inhaled deeply and held her breath just before Wera's iron and turpentine filled the air.

Lead coated Mina's skin as Tanir's slow spell took hold, but it did not stall her movement. It did earn some confused grunts from the fae behind their shroud, however. Push, pull, left hand connected with right to hold "the bow". Together, she and Sebastian ran along the length of their outstretched arms.

Mina did not need to close her eyes to find her focus. The wind was with her, listening, wanting to bend to her will.

The steam and iron and turpentine coalesced to form six perfect arrows.

Without words, without a glance between each other, they released their hold at the same moment, setting the arrows ablaze and soaring through the air as Sebastian's fire forged them into beautiful bolts of solid iron.

A chorus of pain rang out as each arrow hit its target exactly where she wanted.

"You're right, Bormir," she called. "You should exploit all of your opponent's weaknesses. If you know them, of course." Mina smiled as big as she could muster as the steam cleared, brandished her sword once more, and tutted just like he had. "She'll be so disappointed to hear how inaccurate you were."

Iron bolt embedded in his shoulder, the threads that held his veil of aloof confidence snapped. With a roar of pure rage, Bormir began to unravel.

Mina met him in the middle, unafraid of his insane ire, as the battle broke out in earnest. Blade against blade, his halved speed and the iron slowly seeping into his veins had no effect on his technique, his anger honed.

Keeping his attention on her long enough to hear five breaks of glass was easy enough — the intensity in his eyes didn't waver at the cries of his compatriots around him — managing to do so without losing an appendage, however, was another story.

In all their training simulations, Bormir-Mina never fought like this. In all their matches as kids even, he never fought with such ferocity. His style had always been goading, irksome, aiming to supersede his enemy by making a mockery out of them. The notions of ridicule and debasement that once telegraphed his every move were gone. His blade sang in a new language now, one that tore at a part of Mina she'd long ignored.

"Do you think I care about Her disappointment?" he snarled. Mina snapped his rapier and another appeared in his opposite hand. "I've lived my entire life as a disappointment to Her!"

He kept his blade against hers, using it as a guidepost as he spun around her to try and stab her in the back.

A glass vial shattered to her left.

"I do everything perfectly. I'm the best fighter out of our siblings. The first to be made governor. I've brought Her whatever head She asked for, reared Her children in Her image. Yet still, I am *nothing* compared to you!"

Mina pivoted along with him and parried his sword up as he tried to strike. His torso wide open, she lunged forward with a jab.

A glass vial shattered behind her.

"A deformed betrayer still holds the title of *dear one* — is *still* chosen time after time, despite how cruelly you've treated Her." Her jab was too slow. Bormir's stomach scattered into flurries around it. "She talks about you as if you will reinvent the heavens, and yet you throw that love aside! Do you know what I would give for that? What I have given for that?!"

Mina jumped back and raised her blade to block his rapier as he sought to bring it down upon her head. He didn't flinch as he grabbed the strong of her sword, wrenched it out of her hands, and threw it across the room. His rapier arched, trajectory aimed for certain purchase against her throat, and was shattered to pieces as she instinctively raised her forearm to block it — instinctually summoning a brief gauntlet made of whirlwinds around it.

A glass vial shattered near the aurora.

Bormir gave no pause. He followed the momentum of his broken strike and used it to deliver a bone-snapping kick to her ribs.

"I've suffered, and scrapped, and sacrificed, while you were here frolicking through lush forests and whining about some small, stupid curse!" Mina grabbed his leg and yanked him towards her, hoping to throw him off balance and knock him to the ground. "It must have been sooo *nice* to finally be rid of us! No one to look through anymore. No one you had to feign kinship with."

Her maneuver was for naught as with a flap of his wings, Bormir kept his center of balance, and leveraged the close range he created to lift his free leg and drive his knee into her temple.

The world spun, her muscles gave out, and Mina dropped to the ground. When her ears stopped ringing, she heard a glass vial shattering to the far right. When the pins and needles faded, she felt a crushing weight on her chest.

When her vision cleared, she saw a pale hand, nails sharpened and poised for attack, rush towards her.

"She wants you back. Dead or alive." Bormir dug his fingers into her jaw and leaned close enough for his nose to press against hers. "But She never specified that you should be whole. I wonder how hard it will be to reanimate you if you're minced into a thousand pieces. Mother will be very cross with me, but whatever punishment She doles will be well worth never having to suffer through watching Her welcome you home."

She had never seen such hatred in his eyes. Such hurt. She had seen him suffer punishment after punishment, belittling after belittling, but there had always been a spark of defiance behind the sadness. Even when that defiance had turned towards her, even when he saw her as a rival more than a sister, there was never such coldness, such pain.

Was she really the cause?

Did her leaving—

The fifth vial broke, and Bormir finally noticed. He pulled his face away from hers, and held her head down by her mouth

"What is—"

There was no time for introspection. Mina sunk her teeth into his hand, ripped the vial of blood off of her belt, and broke it over Bormir's head. He tumbled off of her, clutching his face as he stumbled to his feet. Mina stood, adrenaline and muscle memory taking over while her mind roiled in turmoiled questions. She hooked her fingers underneath her iron collar as Bormir stood to his full height, wings spread wide and silhouetted by the aurora behind him.

There would be chains, but

only for a moment.

They would hiss and rattle, but

only for a moment.

She tore the band from her neck, shattering the thin clasp that held it, and whistled as she threw it up above her head and held it aloft, just above her hand, with a thin ribbon of wind.

A deep, deep shiver ran through her, chattering her teeth. It was cold enough for her to see her breath.

The hum of Sir Gargic's armor activating was drowned out by the rattling scream of the veil tearing open. Her necklace pulled against the wind but held in place. The iron arrows embedded in the rimefae, however, ripped out of them just as The Matron's Chains struck.

Surging through the veil like vipers on the attack, they wrapped around their prey, spiked chains of ice sinking their fangs into their flesh, and pulled them through the gateway. Mina released her wind just as a chain curved to wrap around Bormir's midsection.

Even if her trembling hand couldn't catch her collar, it would still fall around her arm, still granting her safety as it touched her skin.

But then,

Bormir scattered himself.

"Mina stay here!" Sebastian's desperate command was the last thing she heard before Bormir's silent snowfall swallowed her in a rush.

Childlike fear consuming her, Mina dropped her arms in front of her face, losing her iron necklace in the blizzard; a thin plea for protection from the writhing mass of chains that seized her. Their burrs tore at her flesh as they tugged, straining against unseen threads in the hundreds, maybe thousands, tugging back; the force between them threatening to rend her apart.

Hand over hand, Bormir clawed up the chains that bound her; the veil behind him tearing wider and wider with each link he climbed. The chains doubled, tripled. A writhing swarm lashing at his back, hungry to find purchase, as he scattered himself over and over again to avoid them. His wings were long gone, either filling the air or taken back in chunks to the other side. His scalp was stripped bare, his left leg crumbled below the knee, the right fading in and out of existence. The focus it took to keep regenerating his arms and torso had to be immense. And the pain?

Fury and agony fueled his vehement determination to reach her.

Had to be immense.

In shock, Mina could hardly feel the barbs and briers, her joints being pulled and pushed in and out of her sockets, her ligaments tearing in this tug-of-war between worlds. True anguish — a pain crueler and more damning than she had ever felt — came from Bormir's hand wrapping around her throat.

"What makes *them* worth this?!" he shouted, a deafening roar against the silent snow. "You're smarter than this! You could free yourself of any mortal contract. Why do you continue to let yourself be chained?" His fingers dug into her skin, but the sting of his dagger-point nails sunk into her heart. "You were so eager to leave us. The moment you saw freedom you took it, ran with it, didn't even think for a moment to unshackle us. Fannar, Vetle, Barys, Izotz, are gone because of you. I am *this* because of you. You ran away and left us to rot, yet you fight for mortals who you've known for no more than a month?!"

She opened her mouth to speak, to force through the curse and the pain, to shout that he was wrong. She hadn't just left them. She had tried for years to tell the Harlowes of her siblings, of the dozens of children suffering alongside her in the Rime, only to have her teeth cemented together and her jaw broken by The Matron's will at the very thought.

Bormir's chokehold tightened, a crushing vice, as the veil unfurled behind him, illuminating the thousands of threads that rooted her to this realm in its fae light. Pure heartbreak and madness swirled in his bloodshot eyes to see them. Threads of spun ruby and amber, glistening shades of flame richer than Mina had ever seen, revealing their true beauty in the glow of something so cold and damning.

"So that's how it is," he hissed as he squeezed black dots into her vision. "Fuck your kin and those who suffered with you, who patched your wounds and promised you their fealty. You give your love to a group of strangers. To a man who you share no history with, who you barely know, who's only suffering through your cruelty for his own gains!"

Mina clawed at his wrist desperately as she struggled for air.

"What happens when you get to Lanholde, you stupid clod? Do you think they'll put up with your heartlessness when they have no need of you? You're nothing more than a means to an end to them! She's offering you power! Family! Forgiveness! How dare you waste that on them!" Tears of deep black blood streamed down Bormir's cheeks, voice breaking, revealing the betrayed boy still grieving underneath. "How dare you leave me to rot! I've done nothing to deserve it, Riktanya! Nothing! Nothing! Nothing!"

A burning hand shot out over her shoulder and seized Bormir's wrist.

"That is quite enough," Sebastian hissed.

Arms, hands, bodies, grabbed onto her. With a jolt, the chains loosened a link, some falling away into the veil entirely. Bormir struggled to keep his hold on her throat under the heat of Sebastian's grasp, refocusing his snowfall to try and slow the melting — allowing more chains to sink their fangs into his back.

"I will respect her wishes and will spare your life, but I will not allow you to hurt her anymore."

"You bastard," Bormir spat, blood staining his lips. "We're her family!"

"I think you *vastly* misunderstand what that word means," Sebastian stated. The flames surging up his arm turned from warm amber to a blinding white. Bormir shouted, fingers unlocking from around her neck, and Sebastian released him.

Mina lunged forward and grabbed his hand before the hungry chains dragged him out of her reach.

"I tried!" she screamed. The words coarse and rough, but finally able to be free. "You have to know that I tried! I swear it!"

A thin sliver of ribbon slithered down her arm and bound their hands to confirm her truth. The anger and betrayal in Bormir's eyes flickered out, his expression relaxing into something dull and chilling.

His hand turned to flurries in her fingertips.

"I tried. Do you hear me?!" she hollered as the veil swallowed him whole. "I tried, Bormir! I tried!"

"Sir Gargic!" Sebastian called.

"I've got it!"

Meaty hands dropped a familiar weight around her neck, and a searing one melted the broken clasp closed behind it.

They all fell back onto the frozen cavern floor as the chains snapped, turning to slush, while their surviving links slithered back into their realm. With a flash of light, the veil healed itself, returning to a gently undulating aurora once more.

"I tried," Mina sobbed. The phrase, the only thought she could cling to as the pain finally took hold. Steam rose from her skin where they held her, blistering her flesh as her vision spun and blurred. "I tried. I tried."

"He knows, Mina," Sebastian consoled. "He knows."

His tight hug burned as the world went dark.

△

On the summer solstice, the River Gelu flowed—

"Come on!"

"Shhh! Keep your voice down, and stay behind the rocks!"

—just like snow only fell for the summer fae on Winter's zenith, flowers bloomed in autumn on Spring's first dawn, and the leaves fell from all the budding trees of Ostara as the harvest moon rose with dusk.

Some would say it was foolish for them to be outside on such a day.

But it would be even more foolish for them to miss out on such a rare event.

That's what Bormir said, at least, to justify going against Mother's rules.

"We're going to miss it!" he whispered as he tugged at her arm.

"We're not going to miss it," Riktanya whispered back. "Mother can't mess with the skies today. The sun will take its time."

She kept watch for any signs of guards or governors — even servants were not to be trusted — as they darted from boulder to boulder, edging closer to the river's bank.

"What do you think it tastes like?" Bormir asked.

"Tastes like?"

"The water! We've never had it this fresh before. All we ever have is snow."

A curious excitement had Riktanya dashing ahead of her brother. What if it did taste different?

"Maybe it'll taste like honey! Or maybe like salt! I read that mortals mine salt from mountains," she said.

"I think it will taste like all the seasons."

"Really?"

"The Gelu runs through all of them. If coming from the mountains would make it salty, then running through Spring should make it taste springy."

The river's babbling broke the silence that hung heavy in the winter air, a beautiful melody that had the pair nearly dancing through the last boulders to reach it. The water glistened under the endless gray sky, solstice magic granting amnesty from Winter's harsh embrace.

They both dropped to their knees beside it and stuck their hands in.

"It's almost warm!" Riktanya gasped.

Bormir scooped some up in his hands and drank.

"How does it taste?"

He swished the water around his mouth, brows knitting in consideration, and swallowed.

"Different."

"Different how?"

A wry smile crawled up Bormir's face, followed by the telltale glint of mischief that warned her to be ready for anything. "Taste it yourself."

He slapped the water with his hand, soaking Riktanya's dress before she could get out of the way. Bormir shook with laughter.

The almost warm water froze quickly in the cold air.

It was only fair that his clothes would be stiff for the trek back to the palace as well.

Riktanya kicked the river's edge and splashed him from head to toe. She laughed heartily as he sputtered and spat, then shrieked in delight when he leapt up and tackled her, sending them both into the shallow water of the river bank.

They splashed and swam, skipped rocks and blew bubbles until Mother found them back then.

But this time the light remained. An endless afternoon of play for two children, laughing and smiling for the first time in a long while.

Interlude

Just a Little Pick Me Up

Despite his tired body, Sebastian's sleep was restless. Throughout the night he would wake, startled by shapeless dreams he could not remember, but made his heart race all the same. Waking from these nightmares gave only a brief relief as his next thought was Mina screaming, shaking with pain and anguish in his arms, reaching for a hand that was long gone.

That was the right call, wasn't it? Letting him go.

From how tightly he choked her, Bormir wouldn't have let go until one of them was dead. And there was no way in Hell Sebastian was going to let that happen.

Small swirls of smoke wafted in front of him. Sebastian lifted his hands in the air and out of the sheets they were slowly scorching.

He closed his eyes and breathed in through his nose.

The battle's over. Mina's safe and sleeping soundly in the infirmary.

He counted to seven as he held his breath.

Everyone else has only minor injuries, and are resting as well.

He exhaled out of his mouth.

All that remained was the last trek to Lanholde, and to hope that Mina didn't despise him too much for damning Bormir to whatever torment awaited him in Elphyne.

He looked at the clock that hung above his door frame. Six in the morning. A more reasonable time to wake up compared to the three times his nightmares woke him prior.

His palms cooled, he rubbed his aching eyes and swung himself out of bed. A cup of tea or seven would surely help his restless body unwind a bit, and perhaps making breakfast for the group again would bolster their spirits after a long night. Maybe it would work as a peace offering for Mina too. His cinnamon toast did seem to bring a smile to her face before.

He waved a hand to put the kitchen at ease when he entered, and put on a kettle. Out of habit, he lit the burner with a snap of his fingers, earning him a slight zap of pain up his right arm. He rubbed the tender skin on his hand, still shiny and pink from burning well beyond its limit. Tanir's burn salve worked wonders to get it this healed, another treatment should do the trick.

Sebastian leaned back against the counter and stared at his palm while the kettle heated. There was nothing wrong with testing his limits, but between the white flames and the fire breathing, he'd been doing so a little too recklessly. Not that recklessness hadn't been necessary at the moment, but—

A nervous shudder crawled up the back of his neck.

—his emotions had gotten the better of him. A very dangerous thing for elemental magic.

The door behind him creaked open, pulling his focus away from his hands to the pair of gray eyes peeking through the crack.

"You're up," he stated, standing ramrod straight, breath catching in his chest a bit. His exhaustion left him immediately. "I didn't wake you, did I?"

"No," Mina said as she walked further into the kitchen. "You're making tea?" Her voice was still rough around the edges, even though the bruise Bormir had left around her neck had faded overnight.

He nodded quickly, ignoring the ache in his chest. "I'll add some water to it."

With shaking hands, he took the kettle off and filled it up a little more, grateful for something physical to keep him from drowning in the rising tide of emotions. His arms ached to scoop her up and hold her. Knees trembled, wanting to buckle and beg for her forgiveness. He peered back over his shoulder to find Mina sitting on the counter where he had been leaning, dully watching the flame with a far-off look.

She looked so small, nearly as lost as she had been after Rabbet's Pass.

"I didn't mean for it to happen like that," he confessed, opting to address the wound he caused head-on, rather than giving it room to fester. "But I—"

"I don't think it could have happened any other way," she interjected, response pouring out of her faster than he expected as her gaze stuck to the burner. "I didn't think he hated me enough to sacrifice himself that way. I thought he was just—" her voice caught as a few tears rolled down her cheeks. She brushed them off with her knuckles and cleared her throat. "Thinking doesn't really mean much if you know nothing, I guess."

Sebastian sat the kettle back on the burner and turned around to face her. Her eyes were on him now, not as distant as they just were, but still clouded. She was hurting, but she was searching for something too, searching for something in him. Answers, maybe? Forgiveness, perhaps?

"How did you find me through the snow?" she asked.

Facts would help more than feelings. Feelings would only hurt her. Hurt her even more than he already had, even if it had been all according to plan.

"The pact we made beforehand, I think." He placed his hand against his chest, the phantom pull of a thousand threads still wrapped around his heart. "Not a few seconds after he scattered, I felt this pull in my chest like my lungs were going to rip out of it. Gargic's breastplate caught your sword and necklace, so thankfully finding those were easy, but we were stumbling around blindly until those binds appeared. Those were Fae's Folly, am I right?"

The muscles in her jaw clenched and unclenched.

"Enoch's research would have the answer," she circumvented. "How much did you hear before you reached me?"

"Just the bullshit he was spewing about us abandoning you." He gently moved his hand off his chest and let both hover slightly at his side, just in case his lingering anger at the memory ignited them. "Which is absolute horseshit, by the way. We're not going to suddenly treat you poorly once your contract is fulfilled."

Mina closed her eyes and let out a long exhale, shoulders relaxing a bit.

That must have been what she was looking for. Reassurance.

A bitterness overcame him. Did that bastard really have enough sway to leave her questioning their loyalty? Hadn't everything they'd been through, everything he'd done for her, proven their ardor?

The kettle whistled and Sebastian snuffed out the flame beneath it. His emotions were too complex, he had to keep them simple. He was grateful Mina was here. Grateful she was alive.

He opened up one of the cabinets and pulled out the tin of bergamot tea.

He was pissed that Bormir said such awful things. Pissed that he hurt her.

He scooped a few teaspoons of the leaves into the pot. A pair of mugs and the honey pot danced over to him.

There was no reason for him to be pissed at her as well. Anger shouldn't be a transitive property.

"Are the others injured?" Mina asked, but did not pause for him to answer. "The most direct path to the kingdom's border is on some uneven terrain, so if they're having any trouble walking—"

"No. Not really," he interjected. "Honestly, we got more beat up by the Mirror-Minas than the real things." Which was a relief. He should feel relieved right now. Not whatever mixture of jealousy and self-loathing threatened to overtake him. "You were right. They were shockingly sloppy, especially when compared to fighting against you."

He ladled the last bit of honey between the mugs and glanced over his shoulder back at her. The tenseness in her shoulders and the distant stare were back: focus nowhere in particular, brows slightly drawn in thought.

"What is it?" he asked.

"It's..." Her jaw clenched and unclenched, brows flitting from what he assumed to be a flash of pain. "...odd."

"Their fighting?" he clarified. "Like 'Eirlys being too old' odd?"

She glanced up at him, brows lifting now. "Perhaps."

Sebastian inhaled, exhaled, poured the tea — now properly steeped — into each cup, and stirred up the honey to incorporate it. She wanted to focus on figuring out the inconsistencies with the rimefae; a problem to solve. He could do that.

"It sounds like there's some strange fae magic afoot to me," he said as he stirred. "But then again, all fae magic is quite strange. Tea here or at the table?"

She did not answer.

"Mina?" Sebastian turned back around and found her staring at the floor, tears streaming down her face. "Shit."

All the bitterness, all the complexities, left him.

He crouched down in front of her so he could look her in the eye. "Did I say something wrong?"

She shook her head no.

"Can you talk about what's going on?"

She closed her eyes and shook her head again.

"This has to stop," she said.

Sebastian's heart dropped into his stomach.

"What has to stop?" he asked.

The journey? The conversation? Making tea for you? Caring for you? Knowing me? Being near me?

You hate me now, don't you?

Mina waved her hand in front of her face. "This. I don't know how to stop it."

His heart returned to its normal position, aching, but still better than drowning in a sudden tsunami of dread. He gripped the edge of the counter to keep himself from wiping the tears off her chin.

"Tea can help a bit if talking can't," he offered, echoing an old sentiment of Tanir's.

"It can?" she sniffled, and opened her swelling eyes just a crack.

"I like to think so. Sometimes you need a bit of a distraction to help you get through something sad." He fought against his instinct to smile — to help put her at ease — fearing that the action would only serve to hurt her more in her delicate state. "Could you have a cup of tea with me, then assist me with breakfast? It could keep your mind occupied."

"If I'm told to," she answered.

"Have a cup of tea with me at the table, Mina. Then assist me with cooking breakfast after." He stood, grabbed the mugs, packed up the turmoil seeing her so downtrodden caused him. She didn't need to see that. "Gods know we could both use a bit of distraction."

△

Morale, overall, was lacking. Sebastian could admit that their victory felt hollow, but he hadn't expected everyone to be so low in spirit. Wera looked as though her very soul had been drained out of her, but whether that was from the battle or the tincture's side effects was hard to tell. Everyone else was quiet, deep in thought as they ate. It was hard for Sebastian not to slip into rumination himself.

"How much further have we got, beastie?" Sir Gargic broke the silence.

"About five more days worth of walking to reach the border. Then a sixth traveling from Kowleth Outpost to the Capitol, seven in total if you go without a cart."

"Can you make it five?"

"Five?" Mina repeated.

"Is there a reason for the rush?" Sebastian asked.

"With all the delays we've had, we're closer to our deadline than the king would appreciate," he grumbled. "Now that the bulk of our troubles have been dealt with, I think it's imperative that we make up as much time as possible."

"We'll still be under a month though as we are," Sebastian countered. "Twenty-seven days."

"And what if there's another storm? Or some great monster ambushes us, and we're laid up for a few days?"

"I'll see what can be done," Mina spoke before Sebastian could argue again. "The diversion to the den has added a bit of time as well. If you all can pick up the pace today, however, we should be able to gain a few hours back."

Wera rattled out a long exhale. "Taniiiirrrr. Is there a potion that can make me fly?"

"'Fraid not, dear," Tanir replied.

"Miiiiiiinnnaaaaaa." Wera stretched across the table towards her. "Can you carry me?"

Mina didn't look up from the sausage link she was rolling back and forth across her plate. "If I'm told to."

Wera barely swiveled her head towards Sebastian, the effort too much for her neck apparently, and looked at him with the most pathetic, pleading pout she could manage.

"No."

She dropped her head completely onto the tabletop with a thunk. "Whhhhyyyy?"

"Just have a little more tincture," Enoch remarked snidely.

Wera glared at him. "Fuck you. Next time you black out at a tavern, I'm leaving you in the street for the horses to shit on."

"I can carry her if I'm told to." Mina stabbed the link forcefully. "There's no need to whine about it."

Sebastian exhaled long and low. "Fine. So long as it does not hinder you in any way, I command you to carry Wera during today's hike."

Mina shoved the speared link in her mouth, barely chewed it, then washed it down with water before standing and heading towards the door.

"Where are you going?" Sebastian called.

"I have to grab some things," she said, and left the kitchen without looking back.

"She's holding up better than I thought," Wera remarked.

He frowned, doubt and nerves returning. "She was sobbing on the counter an hour ago."

"Can you blame her, though?" Enoch ran his finger around the lip of his mug. "I even cried over it. That was just awful."

"It was an unfair fight. If he wasn't so injured, maybe Androniki would have proven himself to be a challenge, but his form was non-existent." Tanir smoothed her hair back. "It just felt wrong."

"They've been trying to kill us for weeks now!" Sir Gargic balked. "I don't give a rat's fat ass if they were novices or not, monsters like that deserve to be slain. Soldiers much younger and much more green than they were have died for less."

"What happened, happened," Sebastian interjected before Sir Gargic could incite a fight. "They're gone and will be out of our lives for the foreseeable future. We have to move forward as best as we can. That win didn't feel good, but we kept our promise to Mina and everybody lived."

"And we made it to the top of The Lithe. Very few adventurers can claim that," Enoch said. "Perhaps we should see if the Junk Room has a couple of nice wines and celebrate. When Sir Francis Debois and his expedition made it over the cliff, they celebrated with a three-day extravaganza."

An idea sparked to life. "That's a wonderful idea, Enoch." The perfect way to perk everyone up. A much-needed distraction. "Let's throw a party!"

Sir Gargic sputtered on his drink. "Did you not hear what I just said about making our deadline?"

"This would just be for an evening. And I think it would serve as a much-needed morale boost. I can bust out the gramophone, see what new records are in the Junk Room..." With a new project to take on, Sebastian's nerves began unwinding.

"We could have it in the garden. Ask the kitchen to make some light refreshments," Tanir offered.

"And get all dressed up?" Enoch asked excitedly. "You know I'll take any excuse to suit up."

"I don't see why not," Sebastian said. "Though, Wera, you might have to loan Mina something."

"Tomorrow, right?" she whined. "Tomorrow, when it doesn't feel like my bones are jelly?"

"So we'll have an entire day and a half of you lot being distracted?" Sir Gargic grumbled.

"Come on now," Enoch said. "How many post-battle libations did you partake in during your front-line days? I think I remember reading an account of you streaking across enemy lines after The Battle of Muuleengrad."

A begrudging, proud smirk curled up the old knight's face. "Allegedly."

"Tomorrow night then. Dinner, drink, and dancing in the garden to celebrate overcoming The Lithe." Sebastian took a bite of his omelet to accentuate the point, and found it tasted much better than it had just a moment ago.

Enoch looked him over and pouted. "You are going to do something about your hair beforehand, right?"

Sebastian smiled. "Don't you worry. I've got plans for that."

△

The day's worth of hiking finished, Sebastian knocked on Mina's door with a little extra gusto. There was the slight shuffling of bedsheets, the squeak of mattress springs.

Had she gone to sleep already? It was only seven o'clock, they had finished dinner only an hour ago.

Mina opened the door barely more than a crack, which was normal. She was avoiding his gaze a little more than usual, but that was nothing too out of the ordinary. Some days her curse seemed to be more strict than others, and with the blank stares and sudden transformations out of nowhere, perhaps—

"What is it?" she asked.

Sebastian held up the shaving razor he hid behind his back.

"We've got a promise to keep," he sang, waving the razor back and forth slowly.

The small smile crawling across her lips stopped short with a wince.

"Right," she hissed. "I'll grab my sword, and we'll head to the garden."

"The garden?" he asked.

"So we can check our reflections in the creek water as we shave."

"Why don't we just use the mirrors in the first-floor restroom?"

Mina's face puckered at the idea. "I've only ever used a lake to watch myself as I cut."

He shrugged. "Well, I'm always open to trying something new. And besides, it's not like our hair could get any worse."

"Debatable." Mina closed the door for a moment then exited, sword in hand, to join him in the hall.

"Debatable?" he repeated as they walked. "What could be worse?"

Mina glanced up at him for a moment.

"It could not grow back," she said.

Sebastian laughed. "I don't think it'd be so bad being bald. This shave will be a good test to see what I'd look like if I wind up losing my hair as I age."

"I don't think you will," Mina said.

"Really?" He ran his hand through his hair and tugged on its uneven locks. "How can you tell?"

"You're in your late twenties?" she asked.

"Thirty as of four months ago, actually."

"For thirty, you don't have any thin patches. Usually, there's a few if it's going to go. Enoch's will stick around for a while as well, surprisingly."

"What's surprising about that?"

"He seems like the type to go bald, doesn't he? Bald with that mustache... if he put on some muscle, he'd be the textbook example of a sideshow strong man."

A sense of ease overcame him. That clever playfulness of hers hadn't left. "If Enoch's the strong man, Wera's the fortune-teller. Tell me you can't see her with those thick curls of hers, and even thicker glasses, sitting behind a crystal ball."

"I can't see her with those thick curls of hers, and even thicker glasses, sitting behind a crystal ball," Mina told him, her voice forced.

He glanced down at her, confused, only to find her glaring at him.

"Sorry. That wasn't meant to be literal."

"Clearly." Her glare softened. A smirk tugged at the corner of her mouth, but was once again stopped short by another wince. Another flash of pain.

Sebastian sighed. "Right. No apologizing."

Mina huffed in frustration before asking, "Who would Tanir be?"

"In a sideshow?" She still wanted to play? Even after the pain?

"Not the bearded lady. Maybe an axe thrower with Gargic strapped to the spinning wheel."

"Now that's an image." He chuckled at the thought of Sir Gargic red-faced and fuming as he spun round and round. "Who would I be then?"

"The lion tamer. Obviously."

"The lion tamer?" he asked. "Not the ring leader?"

"Aren't they the same person?"

"The lion tamer." Sebastian considered the occupation. He could see himself handling a lion quite easily, though he wouldn't use one of those whips. A tiger too, a bear even.

A devilish, playful notion possessed him. "Would it be only lions?"

"It doesn't have to be."

"So I could tame little bears then, lila doar?"

Sebastian peered at her out of the corner of his eye. Mina kept her head forward, face as blank as possible, but there was a very faint blush of pink on the tip of her ears and the apples of her cheeks she couldn't hide.

His heartbeat quickened, a warm rush of pride swelling in his chest. She didn't seem to wince at that comment.

She cleared her throat. "I guess."

"What would you be in this hypothetical sideshow, then? The bear?"

Now, with a deep bracing breath, a smile found its way to her face as they approached the garden door. A wry, no-good-smile that if her face could show it off in full, Sebastian sure it would be inspiringly menacing.

"Nope." Mina jogged ahead and stepped halfway through the door. She looked over her shoulder back at him. "I'd be the sword swallower."

The garden door shut behind her just as his heart stopped. If he didn't know any better, he would have sworn he had set himself on fire from the sudden wave of heat that washed over him. The constant stream of thought that ran like a grand river through his mind damned up, leaving him high, dry, and stupefied as his brain tried to process the influx of information just a single, simple sentence caused.

That... was a flirt. Not an accidental, meant to be innocent but could easily be misconstrued, semi-flirtatious moment. That was an actual, purposeful, flirtatious joke by Mina, directed at him. About swallowing...

His cock gave a dangerous twitch, startling him and unleashing the floodgates of racing thought.

Maybe it was just a repeated joke she overheard in town or read in one of her books. She was grieving, after all. She could have just said it to fill the air with conversation and satisfy his need to talk and make sure she was okay.

Or she could have meant it. And if she meant it, then maybe his feelings weren't one-sided.

And if they weren't one-sided then all those moments, their pacts and promises to each other...

"Sebastian?"

Sebastian jumped a good six inches in the air as Tanir called his name.

"Oh! Didn't mean to scare you!" she said, placing a gentle hand on his arm to soothe him. "Is everything alright? You were just staring off into space, and you're flushed."

She reached up towards his forehead to check his temperature.

Sebastian grabbed her before she could and gave her a reassuring smile. "I'm fine, Tani. Just got caught up in a train of thought. What are you up to?"

"I'm heading to the garden to gather some more herbs. Mina's cleared out my reserves quite thoroughly, the poor girl."

"What a coincidence! Mina and I are heading to the garden as well." Sebastian opened the garden door for her.

"Really?" Tanir asked as she walked past him and entered. "More magic lessons?"

Sebastian spotted Mina across the garden, kneeling by the creek and sharpening her sword.

"No, actually." he brandished his straight razor and pointed it towards her. "We're shaving our heads by the creek."

In all the years he'd known the medic, Sebastian had come to learn that there wasn't much that phased Tanir. So the chill that ran down his spine at her smile falling into a tight, thin line, and a twitch shaking beneath her left eye, was quite warranted.

"You're... shaving your heads... by the creek?" she said, voice strained. "Is it for some spell or ritual or?"

"N-no?" he squeaked. "Mina and I promised we'd shave our heads together after the battle, and she's used to cutting her hair by the river back at her cabin so we thought—"

"No, you're not," Tanir stated.

"We're not?"

"Mina!" she shouted. "Don't you dare cut a single hair with that sword of yours!"

"I'm not cutting a single," Mina hollered back. "I'm cutting several!"

"No, you're not! I'll cut it!"

"Tani—"

"A beautiful girl like that deserves a proper haircut for once in her life!" Tanir cut him off. "And you! I know you did the initial chop to help us out, but to throw all the years of hard work I put into taming that wild mane of yours by shaving it?"

"I know, Tani, but—"

"I refuse to let you butcher yourselves!"

"And *I* refuse to suffer through my skull splitting open just so you can turn me into your little dress-up doll," Mina snapped as she stomped back up the hill towards them.

"You won't suffer for a single second," Tanir argued.

"Really?" she scoffed. "Obvious flaws aside, it's gonna be awful difficult for you to cut hair with gloves on, ain't it?"

"Not when you're asleep." Tanir crossed her arms and lifted her chin, daring Mina to defy her.

Her brow furrowed slightly. "What do you mean?"

"You're not freezing when you're asleep. A little cool to the touch still, but no frostbite. And you don't flinch or show any signs of pain when handled, either," she explained.

Mina turned towards Sebastian with an accusatory frown. "Did you know this?"

"S-sort of?" he stammered. "You didn't steam the few times I had to carry you after you passed out. And frostbite-wise it never affected me at all, really, but I figured that was mainly because I run hot." Sebastian looked back to Tanir. "You're sure of this?"

"I didn't need to wear my gloves at all while I patched her up last night," Tanir stated. "If anything, this'll be a good test. I can put you under a half-sleep enchantment and if you're showing any signs of pain or my fingers start to freeze up, I can just put you out completely and prop you up against a tree while I finish up. Or Sebastian can help me hold you."

Mina narrowed her eyes and tapped the pommel of her sword.

Sebastian arched his brow curiously. The tapping was new.

"How will it look?" she asked.

"A brush cut will work. Shave the sides where you cut close to the scalp, and use the haystack you created up top to have some nice texture."

"You've thought about this quite a bit," Mina grumbled.

"I half thought about cutting it while you were out cold on the infirmary table." Tanir looked at Sebastian. "Luckily, you left enough on the top that I can carve a decent taper cut out of it without losing too much of that volume we built."

"Let's get on with it then," Mina said, before Sebastian could get a word in edgewise.

Tanir clapped her hands excitedly. "Great! I'll go grab my barber's kit. I'll be right back."

She hustled out of the garden with a spring in her step.

Mina snorted. "Imagine the look on her face if she came back, and we were bald." She glanced up at him with that new, mischievous smirk tugging at the corner of her lips. "I can do it if you tell me to."

"No," Sebastian sighed. "I can't break the old woman's heart like that. She has worked hard to help me wrangle my hair."

"What's there to wrangle?"

"It can get frizzy, and I've got a lot of odd cowlicks that make it unruly when not cut properly. I'm sure you've noticed."

"Not at all."

"Really?"

"Really." Her gaze passed over the top of his head and she frowned. "The only thing I noticed is that a lot of it is missing."

She was frowning because his hair was missing? She had broken down in tears saying that she had ruined it a few days ago, and her reaction to him cutting it off in the first place...

Did she *like* his hair?

"I-I could ask Tanir to whip up a potion of hair growth," he offered, and a dozen horror stories popped up from his memory at the idea, "but I don't think hair growing out of my fingertips is desirable."

"You'd figure they'd come up with something for that already," she remarked. "By the way, what took you so long to come in here? You were right behind me in the hall."

Sebastian's heart rate quickened as the train of thought Tanir had derailed reset on its tracks.

"I had to tie my shoe," he lied.

"You're wearing loafers," Mina countered without needing to glance down at his feet.

The back of his neck broke out into a sweat. "I— um— I—"

Mina started to smile, but was stopped short once again with a wave of pain. She winced and hissed and looked away from him. Then plucked a handful of dead-nettle out of the ground and ate it.

"Alright!" Tanir returned, case of barber's tools and towel in hand. "Mina?"

"What?"

"Cooratta."

Mina's head lolled down, chin to chest, as her knees buckled slightly. Sebastian caught her by the elbow, granting her some stability as Tanir's spell took hold.

"Tanir!" he scolded. "A little warning next time!"

"Can't. The spell only works if the target is surprised." Tanir tilted Mina's chin up, and her entire head dipped back to reveal her face slack, eyes half-lidded and slightly glazed over. "Mina, dear. Sebastian's gonna walk you over to the creek so I can give you a haircut, alright?"

"I... gotta... walk?" Mina asked. Her voice heavy, mumbling, and slurred in her half-slumber.

"Yes, dear."

"Waaaallllkkkk." She pulled her elbow out of Sebastian's grasp and started to stumble towards the creek.

"The enchantment essentially tricks her body and mind into entering a sleepwalking state. Some things we say can get through to her subconscious, but the instructions are bound to get bungled, and she can't really do anything too complex."

As if on cue, Mina's foot caught on a rock, sending her falling forward face-first onto the ground.

Sebastian rushed over to her and lifted her back up onto her feet. "Come on, Mina. I'll help you walk." He took her hands in his, and Mina's head raised slowly. Her heavy-lidded eyes followed up his arms to his face and widened at the sight. A dopey, slack-jawed smile lit up her face.

"Ahhhh. Bastion!" she cooed.

A thousand butterflies fluttered in his chest.

"H-hi, Mina," he half-chuckled. "I'm gonna lead you down to the creek so Tanir can cut your hair, alright?"

"Ehheh," she droned a laugh. "Oookkaayy."

"Okay?" Sebastian looked at Tanir to confirm he hadn't misheard her.

She exchanged a look of curious shock. "Okay."

Okay. Not 'right' or 'understood' or 'clearly'.

Mina's steps were clumsy, but her grip on his hands was tight as he led her down the rock path towards the creek's bank.

"Shhh," Mina hissed as she accidentally kicked a rock into a boulder, ringing out a big, bright smack. "Keep your voice down! They'll catch us."

"Don't worry, Mina. We're almost to the creek," he assured her.

She broke out into another big, wobbly smile. "Bastion's gonna taste the seasons."

He looked at Tanir. "Is she dreaming or something?"

"Partially. She's in the in-between of sleeping and waking, so her mind's probably making up odd explanations for outside stimuli." Tanir pointed to a large, flat rock that hung over the creek's edge. "Lay her down here so I can wet her hair a bit."

Mina broke out of his grasp suddenly, giggling wildly, and rushed to kneel by the creek. With a sharp inhale, she dunked her head under the water.

"Dammit!" Sebastian ran over and ripped her out of it. "Don't drown yourself!"

"Ahh! Springtime!" Mina exclaimed. With her immense strength, it was easy for her to tear herself out of his grasp to dunk her head under the water once again.

"Well. That's one way to do it, I guess," Tanir remarked as she joined them by the water.

Mina resurfaced with a gasp. "Oh, Bastion! It's Summer!" She scooped up some of the creek water in her hands and thrust it towards his face roughly. "Try it!"

She nudged his bottom lip with the back of her knuckles, and Sebastian opened his mouth and took a small sip.

It tasted like water.

"Isn't it good?" she cooed. "It tastes like your fire!"

"My... fire?"

Mina pulled her hands back to her own lips, and dumped most of it on herself as she drank it greedily.

"Alright, Mina." Tanir grabbed her by the shoulders gently. "I need you to try and stay very still while I make your hair pretty."

Her smile vanished.

"No!" Mina swatted her hands away and surged forward into Sebastian's chest. She twisted around to rest her back against him as she raised her fists in defense. "I don't need another treatment!"

"A treatment?" Tanir cocked her head in confusion. "Mina, I'm giving you a haircut, remember? Tanir's giving you a haircut. No treatment."

She didn't move. Her knuckles turned white from how tightly she gripped her fist, and a faint tremble shook her spine as it pressed against him.

Sebastian grabbed her wrists slowly, and rubbed small circles over the sensitive skin underneath the heel of her palm with his thumbs.

"Mina, that's Tanir. She's not going to hurt you."

She did not flinch, or wince, or pull away from him. No steam billowed from his touch.

"How do you know?"

"Because I made you a promise, didn't I? I said I wouldn't let them harm you. And Tanir's not one of them."

His heart skipped a beat from a familiar tug — the one that pulled at his heart when they sealed the contract, the one that urged him into Bormir's snow — and Mina relaxed. Her fists unclenched, and she leaned against him, tilting her head back to gaze up at him through heavy-lidded eyes.

"That feels nice," she hummed.

"Guess it's a good thing we tested this out with you here," Tanir said. "I have a feeling sleep-walking Mina won't hold back in a fight."

"I want to tread lightly considering she's not all there but—" he swallowed as the soft smile curling up her face dried his throat. "Gods. It's almost as if she's not cursed at all."

"I doubt she'd appreciate staying in this state for long, though. It might be some reprieve, but I don't think she'll remember any of it."

"Agreed." He looked down at her. "Mina. I need you to sit up and turn around so Tanir can cut your hair."

Mina lolled forward and turned around wobbly to face him.

Tanir brandished her sheers. "Hold her head up and keep it straight for me. We don't want her head dipping mid-snip."

"Right. Here we go." Sebastian cupped her face gently in his hands. "Tell me if it hurts, Mina."

She frowned.

"Is something wrong?" he asked.

"Lila doar," she urged.

His chest ached from how hard his heart beat against it.

He inhaled sharply to try and calm it. "Tell me if it hurts, lila doar."

Mina hummed in contentment and nuzzled softly against his palm. "So warm..."

Sebastian brushed his thumbs over the rise of her cheeks, marveling at how soft her skin was, and how much she seemed to enjoy his touch. She didn't wince or flinch, sneer or grimace. She was all smiles. Easy, effortless smiles.

She traced idle circles with her finger on his knee as Tanir snipped away, cutting quickly and cleanly. Sebastian had half the mind to tell her to slow down a bit so that he could have time to enjoy it.

The idle circles turned to tapping, which led to humming. Mina's eyes shut as she sleepily started to sing.

"Like the river to the sea. Like the stars and moon. When the money runs out, through frost and drought, I'll provide for you. All the world for you.

"Because at the end of it all. When kingdoms rise and fall. No riches will save me, from the end that will claim me. So I'll spend my time wisely, investing in you."

The Poor Pauper's Promise. It was an older tune, often sung by old men to their wives on their anniversaries. Perhaps she had heard Mr. Harlowe sing it to his wife during her youth, but what urged her to sing it now as he held her...

Mina opened her eyes again, and somehow, through her half-sleep daze, locked their hazy focus to look into his own.

"In the winter's darkest night. 'Til my fingers blister and blue. I'll scrap and scrape, til my body's all aches, knowing I'll be warmed just by lo—"

The song caught in her throat, and she winced in pain.

Sebastian's heart ached tenfold at the sight. He hummed the last line back to her, urging her to finish the song, hoping it would lead her back into her blissful state. Instead, her brow furrowed deeper, and the skin under his hands began to darken.

"There." Tanir took her final snip. "All done."

He pulled his hands away and Mina's expression softened as her head dipped forward to rest her chin against her chest.

Tanir's face puckered as she looked over her work.

"Did you get ash on her face?" she asked, and ran a finger over the fading gray handprints he left on her cheeks.

"No," he said sadly. "It's the curse."

She sighed heavily. "So, sleep isn't the cure, just an inhibitor."

Sebastian hummed in acknowledgment, too busy following the faint outline of chain-print revealed by the fading gray. Over her mouth, her nose, down her throat. The details were near impossible to make out. If he hadn't had seen them before, exposed by the slate complexion of her rimefae form, he would have thought they were just a trick of the light.

He studied the handprints closely. Had his touch started to turn her? Is that what happened back at The Lithe when she caught him? But if it were just his touch, wouldn't she have turned as soon as he held her face?

"Mina?" Tanir called out to her. "Could you lift your head for me so I can see how your haircut looks?"

She didn't move.

Tanir rubbed her throat. "Odd. She's still under the enchantment but," she leaned down to get a clear look at her face, "it looks like she actually fell *asleep* asleep."

"Maybe put her under properly until you finish my hair," he suggested. "I think I woke her up from a nap to do this. After everything she's been through, I'm not surprised that she's tired."

"Aren't we all?" Tanir said. "Ristole."

Mina fell forward gently as a true deep sleep took hold of her, and Sebastian coaxed her down. He went to slide his legs out from underneath her head after she settled, but stilled as she gave a sad whimper at the movement.

Tanir patted him on the shoulder. "It's alright. There's a rock right behind you I can sit up on to reach anyways."

"Don't you need to wet it?"

She held up a small tin cup as she moved over her tools. "Your shirt will get a little wet, but you'll need to change anyway to get the hair off you."

"Thank you, Tani."

"Of course, dear." She draped the towel over his shoulders and scooped some creek water up into her cup. "Now tilt your head back for me."

The cool water poured down his scalp, its chill a welcome relief, cold enough to clear the thick fog clouding his mind.

"You know, I'm not one to believe in the whole 'drunken words are sober thoughts' notion." Tanir ran her fingers through his hair to work the water down to his roots. "But her being able to recognize you in this state is rather telling."

Sebastian glanced down at Mina's head in his lap. Lips slightly parted, hand prints completely faded, brow relaxed. She looked peaceful.

"What does it tell?" he asked.

"That you mean a lot to her."

His aching heart lurched at the notion.

"You think so?"

"I know it."

"I think she cares for all of us."

"True. But if Wera had chopped off her hair for a fire, I doubt she would have thrown such a hissy fit. She'd be upset, sure, but to *that* level?"

The memory of that night still made his stomach uneasy. Still made him feel so very small, helpless even. "Maybe. Tensions were rather high with everything going on."

"There are more mundane ways too. She talks with you the most out of everyone.

When you're running late to meals, she always asks where you are. Sebastian, she wrote a song about you for crying out loud!"

"That was a command."

"You told her to compose *something.* She chose to construct a whole concerto inspired by you. She even managed to capture your laugh in it."

So that wasn't just him hearing things, his mind tricking him to make something more out of Mina's performance.

He threaded his fingers through her hair on instinct. It was much softer than he imagined, lighter and silky from the short cut. A light whimper left her lips, followed by a content sigh as she nuzzled her cheek against the crook of his knee.

"She means a lot to me too," he admitted quietly.

"Then you should tell her that."

"I can't tell her how much I like her haircut without causing her pain. I don't want to think about how much agony confessing that would cause." He rested the whole of his palm on her head. "After her curse breaks, I will."

"I don't think there's time for that, dear."

Sebastian jerked his head around to face her, but Tanir's firm grasp held him in place.

"Keep your head still! You don't want me to add another scar to your cheek, do you?"

"Why wouldn't there be time?" he asked with a slight edge of panic.

"Once we arrive at Lanholde, and she's collected her payment, her contract is fulfilled. There'll be no need for her to travel with us any further, and if there's no need for her to do so I doubt her curse will allow her to continue."

"I'll just draft up another contract. Hire her on as a... mountain advisor. Or an apprenticeship agreement! Enoch could help with the wording to make it—"

"Do you really want to be her boss or her master?"

"No! I just—"

Mina stirred in his lap and lifted her hand up to rest on top of his in her sleep. He inhaled deeply to calm himself and cool the heat that had built in his palm.

"—I need more time. I don't want to hurt her."

"Your commands could help with that perhaps, along with some careful wording," Tanir offered.

"Perhaps, but—" Sebastian flipped his hand over to hold hers and rubbed his thumb over her knuckles. "How can I know if she feels the same if she can't tell me? She is more expressive now, sure, but with the curse obscuring things and messing with her mind recently, and everything that happened with Bormir..."

"Come now. You know she cares about you."

"I know. But care is different than..."

The word lingered on the tip of his tongue, but too many years of getting his hopes up, of saying it to temporary parents, made him wise enough not to jinx it.

Tanir stepped around him, and tilted up his chin to get a clearer view as she trimmed the front of his hair. "She's a clever one. If she feels the same, she will find some way to tell you."

"And if she doesn't feel the same?"

She pulled her scissors away and glanced down at Mina.

"Is it better to know now while you have her, or lose her and be left wondering?"

His shapeless nightmares coalesced at the notion, revealing just what had been keeping him up throughout the night. Chasing dark-haired figures through thick snow, only for them to vanish when he was within reach. Long, thin fingers, pale and well-callused from years of survival, reaching out to him, missing his fingertips by barely an inch before being dragged into ether by chains. Gray eyes, wide, pleading, desperate, crying. Calling to him before the jaws of a great beast — a heatseeker — swallowed them whole.

He was afraid that she would hate him, but that wasn't all that it was.

He had been angry at the thought of her doubting him, but that wasn't all that it was.

He needed to celebrate, to distract himself with music and food and cheeky conversation to escape what had truly terrified him. What still terrified him.

The snow clearing. Threads cut. An empty cavern.

The part of his heart that she had claimed, that he had given her willingly, forever being lost.

Sebastian looked down at Mina and squeezed her hand.

Though deep in slumber, she gave a soft squeeze back.

"I don't want to lose her," he whispered.

Tanir gave a kind smile. "Then you have your answer."

Exposition to a Fugue in F# Major

"What are these for?"

Wera fished a note out of her pocket and thrust it into Mina's hand.

Mina,

Pick one of the dresses Wera brings you and wear it to the party tonight.

- Sebastian

Pulled by the written command, Mina stepped to the side and let Wera and the two-foot-high pile of dresses in her arms shuffle into her room.

"Most of these are from the Junk Room," Wera grunted as she dumped the pile onto the bed. "I tried my best to find things close to your size, but Tanir agreed to tailor whichever one you choose if the fit's a little off."

She untangled the ball of dresses and laid each one out flat on the bed. It was an eclectic collection. Some short, some long. Some incredibly dated, and others incredibly stained. Or maybe it was patterned that way?

Mina picked up one of the dresses out of the pile, a hideous thing in an indiscernible color, covered in matted feathers.

"Wait." Wera paused her sorting. "You have worn a dress before, haven't you?"

"I have," she said and grimaced at a chunk of gunk hanging off one of the feathers. "But it's been a while."

"Okay well," Wera yanked the feathered monstrosity out of her hands, "don't wear that one. I just put it in as a joke."

"I was gonna say. If that's what you picked as an option for me, Gods only know what you chose for yourself."

She clicked her tongue. "I have excellent fashion sense." She gestured to her outfit. "Just because you can't appreciate the detailed color matching I put into my looks doesn't mean I have no sense of style. Your jaw's gonna drop when you see my suit tonight."

"A suit, huh?" Mina continued rooting through the pile. "Thought you were a skirt person."

Wera pulled out some more dresses, shaking them out before laying them on the bed.

"Skirts for everyday. Suits for special occasions," she replied. "It's not a special occasion if you wear the same thing you always wear, you know? Which is why I grabbed you dresses instead of fancy suits of armor."

Mina looked over the dresses laid out so far. Too many resembled the overly frilly gowns she had to wear for her dance lessons as a child, and the others just seemed... lacking. A special occasion deserved something special.

Sebastian would be dressed up too, wouldn't he?

A giddy tickle, a flutter of excitement, made her heart race and a small smile crook her lips. He probably looked wonderful in a proper suit. Especially with the haircut Tanir gave him.

She wanted to look wonderful, too.

A swatch of fabric caught her eye as the pile thinned — a shade of gray, or perhaps a color she had yet to see. She pulled it out of the pile and held it up.

It was a simple dress — puffed sleeves, a full skirt — but it felt right in her hands. Without a word, she started to undress.

"That the one?" Wera asked.

"Could be." She loosened up the ties in the back and pulled it over her head. With a bit of shuffling, she settled it in place, making sure the skirt hung properly off her hips and that the bodice was straight.

"Of course you managed to find the one dress that fits you like a glove." Wera chuckled as she looked over her. "It's simple."

"Too simple?" Mina walked into the bathroom to look in the mirror.

Wera followed after her. "Not at all, actually. It suits you. Especially the color."

She ran her hand over the neckline. It fell nicely on her, felt balanced, even with her hair being so much shorter than she'd ever had it. "What color is it?"

"Green. It'll compliment Sebastian's suit, funnily enough."

She smiled. "It will, huh?"

Wera snickered. "It totally will. Are you gonna dance with him tonight?"

"Are we training?" Mina asked, confusion replacing her smile. "If so, I'll have to cut the skirt."

"No, like, non-fighting dancing. *Dancing* dancing." She shimmied her shoulders a bit to an unheard rhythm.

"*Normal* dancing?" A sudden nervousness tightened Mina's chest. "I don't know how to normal dance."

"Well, maybe I could slip in a waltz or two into the record rotation tonight," she said. "Could you dance to that?"

"If—" The nervousness spread, fluttering underneath her skin, down to her fingertips, up to warm her cheeks. "If I'm told to."

Wera stepped closer to her, a wide, wicked smile curling up her face. She tilted her head to the side as she studied Mina. "Whatcha blushing for, Meens?"

"Blushing?"

"Ya know. When your face gets all warm and your cheeks get all red." She hovered her finger in front of her body. "Not just your cheeks, though. You got blush on the tips of your ears and down the back of your neck."

"I-I do?"

"Mhmm. What about dancing with Sebastian has got you all flushed?"

Mina winced.

"Nothing," the word tumbled out of her mouth without her urging.

Wera stepped closer. Dangerously closer.

"You're lying," she teased playfully, unaware of the harm she was causing. "You're blushing because you've got a big fat cru—"

The word dissolved into a wisp of breath, a sharp inhale as the temperature between them plummeted.

"Wera," Mina hissed through gritted teeth as the ringing in her ears and the stabbing pain in her skull grew. "Drop it."

She hated how her breath plumed in the air as she spoke, flecked with snowflakes. She hated how wide-eyed and confused Wera was at the sudden reappearance of her cold aura. To her, it probably seemed random, nonsensical, a slide backwards, when Mina knew it to be anything but.

And it was all Bormir's fault.

Wera stumbled back a few steps and the chill dissipated. The searing pain lessened into a dull ache in Mina's jaw, and the ringing ceased. A notion in the back of her mind sighed in both relief and disappointment.

"W-what—" Wera shivered as she tried to rub her arms warm. "W-why?"

Mina turned the bathtub tap on as hot as it could go to heat the air a bit. "I shouldn't dance tonight."

"If you're commanded to, that might keep whatever that is from happening, right?" Wera countered. "And if anyone can take the cold, it's Sebastian."

"I froze the music room door. Started to freeze his lapel when I caught him on The Lithe."

"And the cause?"

Mina glanced at her reflection in the slowly fogging mirror as it became just a blur of grays and blacks. "Is exactly what you think it is."

"But you've danced with him just fine before! Talked with him, laughed with him. Sure, there was definitely some pain every now and then but overall..." Wera ran her hands under the tap to warm them. "Has something changed?"

Yes.

The thought washed another wave of all-consuming pain over her. The fog turned to frost, fracturing her blurred reflection with swirling frost ferns.

"Wera," she warned.

"R-right," Wera's voice shook once again from the chill. "I'll give you a minute, then w-we can d-discuss something else while we figure out accessories."

Once she slipped out of the bathroom, Mina fell forward and gripped onto the sink. Hoarfrost crawled across the room like fire through dry brush, turning the moisture and steam dampening the walls into a thick coat of ice.

Yes, something had changed. Something could no longer be denied.

"You give your love to a group of strangers. To a man who you share no history with, who you barely know, who's only suffering through your cruelty for his own gains!" Bormir's words, while flawed in some aspects, spoke aloud the wordless truth she'd been running from.

Love.

Such a simple word ruined everything.

Mina grabbed at her chest and collapsed to her knees as her heart beat hard and fast, each pound driving the muscle against an icy iron maiden. If this is what the emotion truly felt like, then she wanted no part of it.

Where the sting of Sebastian's smile was once bearable, where the slashes across her tongue were well worth seeing him blush and fluster at her banter, now the agony was insurmountable. Though she desperately wanted to rebel against her curse, just seeing Sebastian's smile had her vision spinning. It was an act of sheer luck that Tanir had stalled Sebastian after she made her sword swallowing comment; otherwise, he would have found her on the ground, desperately clawing for dead-nettle as the grass beneath her began to wither.

The pain had only gotten worse over the past day, and now the mere mention of her possibly having feelings for him had her yearning to rip her own heart out and shove it down the bathtub drain. Which was probably what She wanted.

How dare I love someone other than my darling Mother? Especially a fire mage! How dare I love hi—

Mina fell onto her side as the room spun. She fumbled for the extra herbs she'd taken to hiding in her chest bindings as her vision went white.

She turned her thoughts to ice and snow, to the journey they had left to hike, to figuring if her sled idea would work to cut some of the time spent traveling. Anything but the wizard, as the herbs alleviated some of the pain, and the spreading coal coloring her skin faded away.

The bathroom tile was back to its regular shade of warm brown now, but the details of it were still blurry. Mina blinked the tears from her eyes and breathed deeply. Crying over it would only bring the pain back tenfold.

It was frightening to think what she would do if she truly lost herself again.

She wiped her face and picked herself off the floor. Luckily, the dress was still in good condition despite her fluctuating temperature and the patches of ice that had formed on it. She kept the tap running to help melt the ice at the bottom of the tub.

"The dress will need pockets," she announced to Wera as she opened the door out to her bedroom.

"Yeah?" Wera questioned. She stared at her, doubting and unsure. "How many?"

Mina would not let Her win. Even if she had to eat herbs every second of every day, even if she needed to inject them straight into her veins.

"As many as Tanir can muster."

△

The kitchen's hors d'oeuvres looked delicious, Enoch and Wera had truly outdone themselves when it came to decorating the garden, and his tweed suit still fit well, even though it had been a while since he had an excuse to wear it. There was no reason for Sebastian to be nervous.

And yet, he burned through three ties before he finally calmed his nerves enough to finish tying a knot.

The myrtle green paired with the deep umber of the tweed was much better than the tie he first chose, so he was grateful for that. But he would have been even more grateful if he could calm his hands from heating up like he was still a teenager burning his bedsheets after a wet dream.

"Come on, 'Bastian," he encouraged himself in the bathroom mirror as he dabbed on his cologne. "You want to throw this little party. You want to have a good time with your friends. And you want to tell Mina that you love her— have feelings for her!" The admission made him fumble the bottle of cologne out of his hands and onto the ground, shattering it.

"Shit!" Sebastian ran around the bathroom, helplessly looking for a way to clean it up as the scent of marula and cedar overwhelmed the room. "Shit! Shit! Shit!"

He jinxed it. Truly jinxed it. Saying things aloud had power, and admitting his true feelings for her aloud so carelessly was biting him in the ass immediately. How could he be so careless? It was bad enough that he had even dared to think it, but to say it out loud? Nothing good ever came from saying it out loud. And now he was going to smell like a cedar skunk!

Who could love a cedar skunk?!

The rag he scooped up the glass and cologne ignited in his hand. Startled, he dropped it. Right into the puddle of highly flammable cologne on the ground.

"No!" he yelped as he jumped out of the way of the sudden combustion.

Water. He needed water.

Sebastian grabbed a towel off the rack, dunked it in the toilet bowl, then threw it onto the small bonfire slowly consuming his bathroom tile. The flames hissed in bitter defeat as they snuffed out.

There was a knock on the door.

"Windenhofer! Are you ready to start this little shindig of yours or what?"

"Yes!" he shouted back as he stared at the soot, cologne, and toilet water slurry covering his bathroom floor. "I'm coming!"

Sir Gargic stumbled back as Sebastian threw the door open and stepped out into the hall. "Good Gods man! Are you alright?"

"Yeah," he panted. "Why?"

"Because you look like you just ran a mile."

"Dammit," Sebastian went to dab his forehead with his hand but paused when he caught the patches of soot staining his fingers. "Am I sweating that badly?"

"No, but you're definitely red-faced and out of breath."

"Oh, well, that's fixable." He gave a shaky sigh. "If it was sweat, I'd have to put on another suit. Yours looks nice, by the way."

Sir Gargic puffed out his chest and smoothed a hand over his ruffled gray cravat. "It's not my finest, but it will do the trick for tonight. The real jewel in my collection is my crushed blue velvet tailcoat."

"Really?" Sebastian was glad for any distraction to help keep his nerves in check as they walked closer and closer to the garden. "What shade of blue? Aquamarine? Navy?"

"A crisp cerulean," Sir Gargic stroked his beard as he recalled it. "A beautiful thing that suit is. King Fritz had it made for me shortly after his coronation as a thank you for my service in the war against those traitorous Gelts."

"I remember reading about that. Saw a couple things in the papers back when I was apprenticing. Must have been an awful time."

"What's really awful are the turncoats who still swear that Makarov Bonsignore would have made a better ruler. No respect for divine right these days, I tell you." He scoffed. "Everyone thinks they can solve all the world's problems when they don't have the weight of The Crown on their head."

"Well, sometimes the weight of rule can overwhelm one's vision," Sebastian remarked. "But that's what advisors and parliaments are for."

"Precisely!" Sir Gargic clapped him on the back. "We need more men like you writing the papers in Lanholde, Windenhofer. An intellect who considers things totally, instead of just churning out mud-soaked rags."

Whatever clever comment Sebastian had queued up vanished, choked out by his heart leaping up into his throat, as Sir Gargic opened the garden door.

His eyes darted across the lawn — over the cat's cradle of string lights, the piles of pillows and blankets arranged on the ground — and he sighed in relief to find only Enoch and Tanir in the room, perusing the tea sandwiches.

"Tani, Enoch, the two of you look lovely," Sebastian said as he hurried past them towards the creek. He gathered bunches of the tiny pink flowers like Mina had shown him and set to work crushing them up in between his palms to wash away the soot and toilet water staining his hands.

It was a good thing he'd gotten here before Mina had. Now he could collect his thoughts, calm his nerves down even more by distracting himself with food and conversation until she arriv—

"What are you doing?" Mina's voice poured down his spine like a waterfall.

Sebastian froze.

"Wa—" he cleared his throat to bring his pitch down to its normal baritone. "Washing my hands."

"Washing your hands?"

He watched the sooty suds dripping off his hands send rippled dancing in the water. "They were dirty."

The smell of lavender and a shadow draped across his shoulder as Mina leaned over him to get a closer look.

"You're using soapwort," she noted.

"I am." Sebastian smiled and rubbed the soapy crushed flowers between his fingers to clear the final bits of grime. "Someone quite smart told me about it."

"Oh, really?"

He dipped his hands in the cool water, a welcome sensation after his palms had been running hot all day, and stood. He pulled a handkerchief out of his pocket to dry them, then took one final deep breath before turning to face her.

"Really."

Sebastian's heart nearly burst out of his chest at the sight of her. Under a crown of dried lavender, her brilliant gray eyes sparkled like the ocean beneath a cloudy winter sky. Her new haircut pulled focus to the height of her cheekbones, the button slope of her nose, the plush rosy pout of her lips that only seemed to bloom in color with every passing day. The pendant he made her rested perfectly at the base of her neck, nestled so snugly between her clavicle, it must have always been meant to be there.

And the dress...

"We match," were the only words he could say, for the rest would surely ail her.

He forced himself to meet her gaze, lest he linger too long on how well the garment highlighted her figure.

"We do?"

"We do." If the broken cologne bottle was a bad omen, their accidental coordination would surely negate it. "My tie's the same shade of green."

Mina smiled softly, gaze drifting to his tie as it roamed over him. "Wera said this might happen."

His heart skipped a beat. "And you still chose to wear it?"

She flinched, then quickly pulled a sprig of herbs out from somewhere in her bodice.

"Clearly," she said as she crushed up the herb and tucked it inside her cheek. "Plus, it was one of the few that fit me."

"It fits you quite well."

She pulled out another sprig. "Yours does too."

"Hey!" Enoch called from across the garden. "If I wanted to have the party by the creek, I would have set all this shit up by the creek!"

"We should probably do as he says," Mina said. "I heard him mumbling all of his plans for tonight while we were hiking this morning. He's put in a lot of work."

"And we wouldn't want that to go to waste." He gestured to the path back up to the garden. "After you."

🜁

Although she was eating herbs more than the hors d'oeuvres the kitchen churned out, Mina was having fun. While the others were not exactly straight-laced and rigid in their everyday, watching the wine loosen them up and the music fill them with a jovial spirit was wonderful. The records Enoch chose were delightful, bouncing tunes that had Mina tapping her toes and bearing the burden of listening to Sir Gargic's old war stories much easier. With some clever commands from Sebastian, she was able to join in on some of the group dances — following Wera and Enoch's instructions on the steps — and garnered a chorus of giggles and friendly taunts about how stiff her movements were.

A smile could not leave her face. She even let a few hardy laughs slip at how often Tanir, cheekier than ever from the booze, pulled the rug out from Sir Gargic when his grandstanding became a little too boastful. The stings and aches and sores the actions left her with were well worth it. There was nothing a few herbs and some salves couldn't heal. Moments such as these wouldn't be as constant.

She washed another mushy lump of the medicine down with water as the record changed to something slower than the jigs and polkas that had been playing.

One in three-quarter time.

A waltz.

Mina glanced over her shoulder, hoping to find a Wera she could glare at, but instead met the lapels of a very fine tweed suit and a tie she could not discern the color of, but knew to match her dress exactly.

She followed the tie up to see Sebastian looking away from her, a slight blush dusting his cheeks.

"Mina."

Just hearing him say her name made her molars ache and her chest flutter.

"Waltzing is one of the dances you know well, right?"

She pulled a bunch of herbs out of one of the many pockets Tanir had hidden in the lining of her gown and stuffed them in the side of her cheek.

"Right," she answered.

"Could you waltz with me then?"

His heart beat so loud, she could hear it racing in his chest without needing to close her eyes. Her own heart was racing all the same.

"If I'm told to."

The tension eased from his shoulders, and he pulled his focus down from the ceiling to lock eyes with her. His eyes were warm, sparking with excitement and uncertainty within their deep honey-colored umber. His bow-like lips quirked up in an endearing, nervous smile.

He held out his hand.

"Waltz with me, Mina."

She took it, without the need of threads to guide her.

He led her out to the patch of lawn Enoch had designated as the dance floor — empty of dancers as Tanir and Enoch took a break from their marathon of jigging — and with a gentle tug of her hand guided her into their starting position.

One, two, three.

They fell into the rhythm effortlessly, and Mina was glad that no pain seemed to come as his hand slowly slipped down her spine to rest on the small of her back. He switched his grip on their leading hands to intertwine their fingers, and she hummed contently as his heat slowly warmed hers.

"Is the party what you expected?" Sebastian asked after a few turns around the garden.

"I didn't know what to expect, honestly," she said. "I've never been to a party before."

"Not even The Lithe celebrations for the expeditions you led?"

She shook her head. "I kept my distance, but there was nothing interesting going on at them anyways."

"And there's something interesting here?" he asked. She looked away from him, trying to lessen the flash of pain behind her eyes as he glanced down at her, eyebrow quirked in question.

She chewed lightly on the mush of herbs tucked in the corner of her mouth.

"Clearly," she said as the medicine faded the pain.

Sebastian squeezed her hand. "Good."

A thousand needles pierced her down her arm and into her ears. She chewed the herbs frantically.

"You know, we're getting close to the end of our expedition," he said, thankfully changing the subject.

Mina lifted her gaze to meet his once again. "Even closer if my sled plan works out."

"Your sled plan?"

"To get us to the border wall quicker, I think we should grab a toboggan or sleigh maybe — whatever would be big enough to fit the five of you — from the Junk Room and have me pull it. The path's mainly flat, with a slight downhill, the rest of the way to Lanholde. If I run close to full speed, we should be able to get to the border in about two, three days' time."

"And then?"

His heart beat faster. Perhaps he was worried about the timing.

"Then we'll just need a day of rest at Kowleth Outpost, and after that, if we can get a cart and horses, we'll be in the Capitol the following afternoon."

"And your contract will be fulfilled." A deep sadness, worry, fear, bubbled up in him, drowning the sparks of excitement in a deepening well of despair.

Her heart ached as the weight of his words found purchase, and pulled the organ down into her stomach.

"That... would be the case," she said slowly, as if each word were part of a spell that would make the inevitable come true. "My contract ends once I've delivered you all and collected my compensation."

"I could extend your contract." His heart raced so fast it was almost buzzing. "If you wanted."

"No," the word forced its way out of her throat.

His brown eyes blew wide with hurt and desperation, brows raising and furrowing deeply in the center. "No?"

Her mind raced for something to say, to explain, but everything she came up with made her throat burn or her teeth cement.

"For what reason?" she finally managed, hoping it would urge him to explain the details, what her new contract would entail so she could accept it without ailment.

"For what reason?" Sebastian repeated. His grip on her hand tightened as he scanned her face. Fear and desperation faded as he searched, finding a spark of determination as he journeyed between her eyes and her lips.

His heartbeat hammered against her eardrums.

His eyes closed. "Mina."

Dread, absolute dread, crawled up her spine as his voice tore across her scalp.

"After we've fulfilled our contacts with Lanholde I want you to continue to travel with us. Travel with me."

His command kept her dancing despite the agony pulsing through her muscles with every step, with every word he spoke.

What is he doing?

"I could bring you on as a full-time employee or as a true apprentice of the Practitioner's Guild. Whatever it would take to make you comfortable, to buy us a little more time to figure out how to undo your curse, to— "

He inhaled deeply.

Mina bit into the last shreds of herbs tucked away in her cheek, willing the song to end soon so she could let go of him and grab another bundle from her hidden pocket.

"—to keep you beside me."

The herbs shattered against her frigid tongue.

"Mina. I can't imagine going a single day without seeing you, talking with you—"

The grass began to crunch beneath their feet, withering with every step she took. She opened her mouth to speak his name, to warn him to stop, but her throat was too seized with pain to make a sound.

"I know this may be hard to hear, and please forgive me if it is, but I'm afraid if I don't say this now I'll never get the chance to." He chuckled bitterly. "Time is not on our side."

Steam poured from where she touched him. Her skin bubbled and blistered as her curse turned the gentle heat of his hand into a blazing inferno. His heartbeat was a whisper compared to the all-consuming thrum of her own.

A constant, dreadful drum building in speed — in its fury — as a voice chanted beneath it.

How dare he. How dare he.

"Every day I learn more and more about you. See you change, see you fight to overcome your situation, to forge yourself a better life. I'm grateful to know that I'm a small piece of that better life, but I'm also terribly selfish, I suppose."

He squeezed her hand again. His fingers drummed triplets against the small of her back.

White seeped into the corners of her vision with each devastating gesture.

"I know feelings are hard for you, and that you may not feel the same. But Mina, I—"

The record petered out, the threads disappeared, and despite her darker parts urging her to let him finish, to keep holding on despite the pain, to punish him for ailing her, she fought against it all — and slapped him in the face.

The force had him stumbling away from her, leaving a dull, throbbing ache through her body, and a searing, stabbing pain in her chest as her heart threatened to shatter into pieces.

Sebastian grabbed his cheek, a bright red patch — the beginning of a bruise or frostbite — spreading underneath his palm. He stared up at her, hurt and confused.

"I—" the words caught against her throat like barbed wire. The room started to spin as the barbs wrapped around her lungs, stealing her breath as her heartbeat rang louder and louder in her ears.

How dare he. How dare he.

"How dare you." The words slithered across her tongue. Horrible, horrible words that angered her enough to push past the pain for just a moment and run out of the garden.

△

By the time Sebastian blinked the static out of his vision, Mina was gone. Only the cold sting on his cheek and her voice were left behind.

"How dare you."

The chill spread across his body. Was his heart breaking? If it was, he couldn't tell. Everything was too numb from the shock. He thought it was going well. Thought he'd read her expressions correctly, and, sure, perhaps the topic of them getting to Lanholde quickly had urged him to pull the trigger a little sooner than he intended, but...

"How dare you."

His stomach lurched. There was nothing but disgust in her voice.

"Oh dear!"

Tanir.

"Are you alright?"

Enoch.

A thick pair of glasses and a mass of curly hair appeared in front of him.

Wera.

"Sebastian! What the hell happened?"

His ears popped as he opened his mouth to speak, clearing the ringing and clarifying his situation.

"She rejected me."

His chest threatened to cave in. There was his breaking heart.

"She—" Wera looked at him as if he told her the sky wasn't blue. "What?"

"I don't—" He laughed in disbelief, in pain. "I don't know what else to tell you. I was telling her how much I wanted her to keep traveling with me, how much she meant to me, how I felt about her, and she slapped me." His voice broke as he mimicked her hiss, "How dare you."

"But—" Wera backed away from him and looked towards the garden door. "I just passed her as she ran down the hall. She was crying."

Sebastian hung his head and rubbed at his cheek. It was getting harder to breathe.

"Then the notion of me confessing to her must have really been awful," he remarked.

"You two were all puppy eyes and shy smiles just a moment ago!" Enoch balked.

"And you were dancing quite well together," Tanir added.

Sebastian laughed bitterly. "Yeah, because I commanded her too. She was probably humoring me when I asked her permission." His rib cage started to collapse in on itself. "Hell, she's probably been humoring me this whole time."

"No, she hasn't," Wera insisted.

"I mean, it's not like she had a fucking choice. I amended that contract against her will, using 'helping' her as an excuse." He was horrible. "I didn't even fucking ask. It's a wonder she even put up with such a self-righteous prick."

"It's not a wonder!" she exclaimed. "If Mina really thought that, she wouldn't have bothered to get close to us! To you! Even with the commands!"

"Or she was just sucking up to a man she barely knew to keep him from using his power against her."

Disgust and despair swirled in the cavern where his heart used to be, promising to absorb him totally and remove the scum he was from this earth.

Wera's hand yanking on his tie pulled him out of it.

"Or it's her curse! Did you forget that fact, dumbass?!" she shouted.

"Of course I didn't forget that!" he hollered back, voice breaking. "But she was getting better! If she had felt the same, she would have found a way. She's always found a way!" He looked to Tanir. "Right?!"

The certainty on Tanir's face just a day ago was gone.

Wera tugged at his ear harshly, turning his focus to the grass. "Look at the ground! It's withering and covered in melting frost."

The swirling trails of brown grass beneath their feet only served to gather more tears in his eyes.

"Then I must have been torturing her," he whispered. "Maybe it's best that she left."

"Or you were making a breakthrough!" She yanked his ear back so that he faced her. Sebastian could barely feel the pain of it. "Sebastian, I know Mina—"

Wera's mouth snapped shut.

"You know what?"

Her brows furrowed. "This afternoon in Mina's—" Her mouth snapped shut again, just like Mina's did when trying to speak about her past.

"Please don't mock me right now, Wera," Sebastian bemoaned.

"I'm not! I—" An angry flash of realization passed across her face. "Son of bitch."

She grabbed him and Enoch by the arm and pulled them towards the door. "You two come with me. Tanir, ask Sir Gargic to tell you about King Fritz's childhood or something to keep from poking his nose around."

"Where are you taking us?" Enoch asked.

"To Mina's room."

"Why do I have to come along?!"

"Because I need someone with a clear head who's good at putting together stories," Wera grunted as Enoch tried to wriggle out of her grasp. "Plus, there's a good chance she's going to kill me after showing him this, and I'm not dying alone!"

Sebastian let her drag him to the second floor, knowing well enough that fighting against her would be futile, and that going back to the scene of his failure felt like a fate worse than death. What he really wanted to do was grab a sleep drought from Tanir and head to bed in the hopes of waking up to find that this whole thing was just some nightmare.

"Open it," Wera demanded as she pointed to the door knob.

"Wera, I've already hurt her enough for one evening," he argued half-heartedly. "I really don't want to completely destroy what shreds of trust I have left with her."

"I will take the blame," she said. "I'll say I hypnotized you, threatened you, whatever the fuck it'll take."

"Doesn't mean she'll believe you."

Wera grabbed his face in her hands. "Sebastian, you have trusted me to lead you. Trusted me with your life more times than I can count. I *need* you to trust me on this one, and open this fucking door."

Sebastian relented with a sigh, heated his palm precisely as hot as it needed to be to boil water, and grabbed the door knob.

"Wind hopper," he grumbled, and the lock unlatched. It felt wrong for the door to swing open and for Mina not to be peering up at him behind it, felt wrong to step into the space, and felt... odd to see a wall covered with his face.

Enoch sidled up beside him and peered into the room. "What the hell?"

Wera shoved them through the threshold and shut the door behind them.

"See?!" she exclaimed, pointing to the wall emphatically.

Sebastian was still processing the images in front of them. "Her drawing skills are certainly impressive."

"They're all of you!"

"Most of them are," he said. "There's one of Enoch and Tani and you..."

"And about fifty of you!"

"And they're all orange," Enoch added.

Wera's expression lit up. "What an astute observation, Enoch! What particular shade of orange would you say it is?"

"Particular shade?" He twirled his mustache.

"Maybe look to your right."

Sebastian turned his head in time with Enoch and only saw Mina's empty dresser.

"Oh," Enoch gasped behind him. "Oh!"

Sebastian turned around. "'Oh', what?"

He pointed between Sebastian's head and the drawings. "They're the same shade as your hair!"

"Odd, isn't it?" Wera pressed, far too chipper and pointed: tense.

"She still can't see certain colors." He shrugged. "She probably thought it was gray."

Her expression hardened. "She can tell the difference between most shades. You know this."

Disgust and disappointment bubbled into frustration. He already felt like an idiot. He didn't need Wera making it worse.

"Okay, smart ass," he snipped. "I think she would have reacted a bit seeing my hair color for the first time, don't you?"

Wera smiled, a smug wide smile. "You're right. She absolutely would have."

He grabbed her by the shoulders. "Will you stop fucking around and just tell me what the fuck you're trying to get at here!"

She grabbed him by the wrists and lifted his hands off of her. Two burnt handprints marred her suit jacket, adding to his bottomless supply of self-loathing.

"If I could. I would. But I can't," she gritted through her teeth.

"Why?!"

"Why does Mina follow your commands?"

His stomach turned. "Please don't bring that up right now."

"Because they have a contract," Enoch answered. "Did you make a contract with Mina?"

Wera glared at Sebastian. "Showing's not telling."

Frustration blended with confusion. He glanced over the drawings hanging on the wall. Mina had bound Wera not to tell him about these?

She let go of his wrists. "Now, Enoch. Sebastian made a very excellent point just a little bit ago, didn't he?"

"He did. There's no way Mina wouldn't react seeing that. Especially after only seeing—" His eyes widened. "No."

"There's that archivist mind!"

Enoch's jaw dropped. "Since then?!"

"Since what?" Sebastian said.

"Since the crysteceans. That morning, when we found you two sleeping outside. She's been able to see your hair since then."

"What?" Sebastian balked. "No, she—"

"It *was* weird that she decided to change up the walking order that day. Wasn't it?" Wera said. "And she does like looking at the fire an awful lot..."

Enoch shook his head to clear and center himself. "But that would mean—"

"That my hair was the first color she saw?" Sebastian asked as realization dawned on him. The memory of Mina picking up the amber in his study and turning it in the light flooded his mind. The way she looked just above his eyes in those early days. How close she would always sit by the fire. How she always lingered for a moment on the days they hiked until sunset to gaze up at the sky.

"One could even reasonably guess that, for some reason, Sebastian was the catalyst for her curse breaking." Wera shrugged. "Which is weird because the only for sure way to naturally break a curse like this is—"

Enoch gasped again. "True love."

Sebastian's heart started to beat again, but his mind— "Come on, there are plenty of curses that are broken by other means."

"On places and objects, sure. But on people?" Enoch counted on his fingers. "Queen Farica. King Jadiel. Regent Marquis. Clever Mary and the Blacksmith. Golden Goose at the Wishing Well. The Cunning Sisters of Warrick." He clapped his hands together. "Every. Single. Cursed. One."

"But..." Sebastian's thoughts swirled at a mile a minute. "... she's getting worse."

"Or..." Wera leaned in. "You're getting closer."

Goosebumps zipped up his spine.

"Her curse keeps people away, right? Makes sense that it would make her push the person closest to breaking it away the most," she reasoned. "Like almost dropping them off a cliff. Slapping them in the middle of a waltz."

A match strike. Sparks catching kindling.

Wera smiled. "Curses don't like to be broken."

Flashes of all those winces and grimaces, those sudden switches from amicable to adversarial. Mina never had a problem looking the others in the eye. Touching them without prompt hardly hurt her anymore. But with him...

She couldn't say his name, yet she chose to find a way to say it.

She couldn't say what she truly wanted, so she came up with a phrase to help him understand.

Despite all the pains and aches he caused, she kept coming back, kept trying, not because she had to, not because of the contract, but because she wanted to.

"I won't be the cause of your end! I can take whatever torment, whatever torture, whatever hell awaits me with Her, with them, as long as I know that you all live."

She kept protecting them, protecting him, not because she thought her life was worth less than theirs, but because she—

The first notes from a violin trickled through the floorboards above them, playing a song he once wished he'd never hear again.

His nerves, his doubts, all fell away at the sound. She had never given up on him.

"How dare you."

Determination came from the recollection. She was right. How dare he? How dare he give up on her now?

Wera patted his shoulder. "Who better than a fire wizard to warm a frozen heart, huh?"

🜂

The physical pain was gone but her heart—

Her stomach—

Her entire being was tearing itself apart.

Mina could barely see the strings through her tears, but she had to keep playing. Had to keep herself distracted so that maybe for a moment she'd forget Sebastian stumbling back from her, face contorted in pain, confusion, and betrayal. That she'd forget the sting of her palm against his cheek, forget the horrid thoughts racing through her mind, urging her to harm him.

And stop wondering what the end of his kind, kind words were. They didn't matter. It was safer if she never heard them.

Her notes shifted off-key.

How long could his unspoken feelings last if she kept hurting him anyways?

The door to the music study flew open without warning, but she didn't need one. Mina knew who it was.

"Go away," she said.

"Mina."

Stupid fucking wizard.

She played louder, tearing her bow across the strings to drown him out. "I said go away!"

"Mina, look at me!"

The threads yanked her head to face him, dried the tears from her eyes so she could see him clearly.

Her frostbitten handprint had faded. A small relief. She hadn't scarred him again. Nerves, doubt, anger — none lived in his expression. For a reason she could not discern, Sebastian seemed calm and resolute, even with his heart thundering in his chest.

Her own heartbeat surged forward to match its pace.

"Put your violin down," he commanded, "and listen to me."

"What are you doing?" she said as she set the violin down against her will. In the absence of its screech, the beat of his heart, the hum of his breathing, became a rhythm she could not ignore. "I told you to go!"

"I heard you," he said as he stepped into the room, "but I'm not going anywhere."

Her lingering tears froze on her face, the instruments creaked and the mirror beside her began to fog. With her speed, she could pass him without so much as frosting a single hair on his head.

Mina moved to run, "Then I'll go."

"Stay where you are."

The wind at her heels vanished as her raised foot cemented to the ground.

How dare he.

She stared at him, as wide-eyed and panicked as she could muster. He needed to leave, needed to run. "Wizard! Don't—"

"I hope you forgive me for this." He walked closer and closer. Her muscles roiled in pain as they tried on their own to fight against the threads binding her. At her feet, ice formed, crawling across the floor to climb up the tables, cabinets, drums, pianos, walls. Their wood squealed in protest, thinner patches cracking, splintering from the cold. Strings panged as they snapped, giving one final hum, but all of it was dull — drowned — beneath their heartbeats.

"Tell me the truth," he demanded, voice low and even. There was no malice in his gaze. "What color is my hair?"

"Amber." The answer forced its way out of her throat.

Wisps of vapor rolled off of him as he took another step towards her, he was heating the air once again. All because he wanted to ask her what color his hair was?

"When did you first see it?"

It was a stab in the chest as her heart skipped a beat at the question. How did he—

"The morning after you trapped us in your dome."

His breathing hitched at her admission. The ice evaporated beneath his feet, no matter how thick or how cold it formed.

A gentle flicker of kindness sparked in his eyes. "Why didn't you tell me that you saw it?"

His expression stung, clouding her vision with tears yet again, forming icicles off her chin as they fell.

The straight answer had her jaw seizing up, so the threads coaxed it out of her in questions.

"What if I jinxed it?" she said, voice wavering in fear. "What if it went away?"

His brow furrowed slightly. He was searching for something, trying to read her true meaning through the anguish contorting her face. "Is that why you ran away while we were dancing?"

"No."

If the cold bothered him or hurt him, she couldn't tell. He stood in front of her as if they were about to waltz once more. All she had to do was lift her arms, and they could take off spinning around the study. Dread set in as she felt her hands yearning to reach out to him, to pull him close to her despite the pain. Despite knowing that it would encase him in ice, cold enough to snuff out any fire.

"Then why did you run?" he asked softly, just above a whisper.

Her throat tightened, the cold wreaking its havoc on her body in retaliation from being unable to harm him.

"I was going to hurt you," she forced out, voice raw and stilted. "I'm going to hurt you now if you don't do as I say and go away."

He shook his head. "That's alright. A little frostbite is nothing compared to the pain I've caused you." He frowned slightly as he studied her face. "Am causing you now, even."

Mina tried to look away from him, to spare herself from the compassion in his gaze, but his commands still held. Perhaps they were the only things keeping the white creeping in the corners of her vision from swallowing her completely. The only things keeping her ears from ringing, from being swallowed by agony as the darker parts of her heart took over.

"I don't want to put you through this. But I have a theory I have to test out."

He was going to get himself killed over a theory?

"Bastion—"

"What inspired you to write 'Bastion of the Flame'?" he asked.

The icy nails of an iron maiden wrapped around her heart once more.

"You," she answered.

Sebastian kept his face as neutral as possible, but could not hide the joy in his eyes at her admission.

How dare he. How dare he.

"If you could spend every day with anybody in the world, who would it be with?"

Anger superseded her fear.

"With you," she spat, enraged at how the words cut her tongue when they should have rolled off of it like sweet water. If he had just waited until her curse had broken. If time was on their side. She wanted to enjoy these admissions, have him truly smile at her when she said them, instead of holding himself back to spare her pain.

Sebastian closed his eyes and took a deep breath, nodding slightly as he collected himself. His heart rate spiked, its rhythm spurring her own faster. What was he doing? Was this theory of his worth torturing them both?

He opened his eyes. Determined, certain, excited.

"I do believe I know how to break your curse," he said. "But I don't think it will be pleasant."

How dare he! How dare he!

The darker parts of her screamed. Mina fought against the urge to grab him as it thrashed against the threads of his commands in her mind, sending wave after wave of pain down her spine. It wanted her skull to split at such a notion, wanted the pain to swallow her whole so it could wrap its hands around his throat for even suggesting such a thing.

But the threads still held strong, just as they did against the chains, against Bormir, perhaps even stronger now.

How dare he!

No. How dare she.

How dare she try to push him away when he was here, risking everything to set her free. To save her. Just as she had been so willing to do for him over and over again.

Mina inhaled sharply. He had trusted her plan with Bormir, it was only fair to trust his plan for this.

"Do it," she hissed through yet another rush of pain.

"You're sure?"

"Certain."

He stepped into her, removing what little distance remained between the two of them, and bowed his head to let his face hover just a half-inch away from hers. "Then Mina. I have one final question." Steam swirled between them, and she longed to feel its heat. "Would you allow me to kiss you?"

All she could hear was their heartbeats, racing in time with each other, creating a beautiful round. All she could see was his face: the warm longing in his eyes, the strong slope of his nose, the thin scar she had given him on his cheek, and his lips now asking her to be the archer that wielded their bow.

All she could tell him was the truth.

"If I'm told to."

Sebastian smiled softly, and Mina was glad to bear the sting of it. "Then let me kiss you, Mina."

Her eyes fell closed as he pressed his lips against hers. It was gentle, hesitating at first, but warm. So warm.

How dare he.

How dare he hold back on her.

Mina grabbed his lapels and pulled him closer, diving headfirst into the fire.

Sebastian fell along with her, desire replacing hesitation. His hands were irons as they embraced her, scalding her back and her face. He shivered, trembled, as her ice fought against his flame.

From the dueling temperatures came wind, roaring with gale-force fury, threatening to tear them, the room, even the commorancy itself asunder. Yet still, they did not part.

Nor could they if they tried, as barbed chains of ice bound them to each other, squeezing the air from their lungs, digging briars beyond their flesh into their psyches; smothering consciousness in a wash of white.

FUGUE

F# MAJOR

He followed a woman in a white dress, the same shade as the snow that blanketed the ground and bowed the evergreens, with skin as dark as the night sky above.

He went over her, around her, through long spun-snow hair, under her frost-flecked sleeves, across her taloned fingers.

He led her towards a light, towards a heartbeat, towards a baby's cry.

He brushed against the window pane, desperate to feel the warmth of the hearth beyond it, to whirl around the herbs and flowers that hung from rafters like his cousins often did, to wipe away the crying infant's tears and pretend the brilliant spark of life inside it was his own.

"Poor thing," the woman whispered behind him, voice as sharp as falling icicles.

She placed her palm through him, against the glass, and turned it into snowflakes.

He rushed over the babe's cheeks, into its nose, its lungs, becoming its breath — her breath. Her cries subsided, yet her heart still beat strong. The spark of life barely dwindled as he basked in its warmth. He knew it to be the strongest he'd felt so far, but still, the babe shivered. She could not hold him now, not yet. She would only lose herself to the cold as the others had.

Icy hands scooped the babe from her crib and tucked her into the crook of an arm. The woman placed a frozen bundle in her place. The amber glow of the firelight painted warmth onto the snowbaby's skin and melted it to life. Frost ferns replaced the missing glass as the woman ran a finger across the sill, then brought it to her lips.

"Shhh..." the woman hissed. Piercing blue eyes leered at the babe, driving him out of her chest and back into the vast winter night.

🜁

Riktanya woke up precisely an hour before dawn. No earlier. No later. And without the need for a clock.

She shook the frost from her sheet and made her bed, making sure to fold her corners as she tucked them underneath the cold, stone slab she slept on. She folded the top exactly a fifth of the length of the visible sheet, and ran a hand over it to make sure it was perfectly straight, with not a single wrinkle in sight.

She walked to the wash basin in the corner of her room, kicked the pipe beneath it to break up the layer of ice that had formed during the night, and turned on the tap. She pulled her sleep-knotted, long, white hair back, and grimaced at the lack of blue mottling her cheeks. She tilted her head to either side, lifted her hair to see if there was anything on her neck.

It felt like something should be there. Otherwise, why would it feel so empty?

She splashed her face with water to wash away the nagging sensation, to no avail. She spread the tincture Mother gave her onto her pumice stone and tried to scrub it away, but it would not cease. Her mind was convinced that something was missing from her neck.

She rinsed off the tincture once her cheeks stopped trembling from its sting, and looked in the mirror once more.

A woman stared back. Her skin tan compared to Riktanya's pallor, dark hair cut shorter than she'd ever seen on a woman, lips the same shade of pink as raw chicken. Yet, they shared the same nose, and the same eyes.

Those were her eyes.

Fear and dread set her heart racing.

She wasn't supposed to be here.

Hissssssssss. Crack!

The lash of barbed chains struck her heart.

△

Winter's night turned to Spring's night. The girl was older, and scared.

He was a part of her now, but the connection was distant. He lived on her skin instead of in her heart, and every day in this new world pushed him further away. He summoned all the strength he could muster to urge her to keep walking, to keep following the river.

As the girl's senses dulled, it seemed as though his meager brushes were one of the few things she could still feel. Her feet were blistered, bloodied, and bruised, yet she walked without a limp. Owls screeched in warning as she passed, yet she did not flinch. Her heart was beating slower, limbs growing colder, spark dwindling.

Was she dying?

She couldn't die. She had the strongest spark.

She had to live.

The girl stopped walking by the river, suddenly changing direction and ducking into the woods.

No. No!

He left her — even though every inch he pulled away from her felt as though it would tear him apart — to get a look at what had her cowering behind a bush.

A house, pumping smoke and heat out of its chimney.

Warmth.

She needed to get there. The warmth would save her spark.

He swirled around the homestead looking for something to entice her to approach, and settled on a chicken coop.

The girl was hungry, hadn't eaten in days. She couldn't hear their clucks or caws, but surely she'd recognize their feathers, their movement. He pushed as hard as he could as he passed through the chicken wire, and sent the birds into a frenzy.

He fled back to the girl and blew through her hair as she scrambled towards the coop, stomach rumbling.

Perhaps she'd be able to taste them since he touched them.

He didn't understand what made him think that.

⚹

Riktanya woke up precisely an hour before dawn. No earlier. No later. And without the need for a clock.

She shook the frost from her sheet and made her bed, making sure to fold her corners as she tucked them underneath the cold, stone slab she slept on. She folded the top exactly a fifth of the length of the visible sheet, and ran a hand over it to make sure it was perfectly straight, with not a single wrinkle in sight.

Then she ripped the sheet off and made it again, just to make sure it was perfect. The first time felt a little off. One side felt like it was longer than the other, and such avoidable mistakes were not tolerated.

Once she was finished, she walked to the wash basin in the corner of her room, kicked the pipe beneath it to break up the layer of ice that had formed during the night, and turned on the tap. She pulled her sleep-knotted, long, white hair back, and grimaced at the lack of blue mottling her cheeks. Her hands were starting to turn, at least. Her fingertips looked as though she'd run them through the night sky's ink.

She spread the tincture Mother gave her onto her pumice stone, wet her face, and set to scrubbing. One hundred circles on each cheek: fifty clockwise, fifty counterclockwise. One hundred strokes up across her forehead: fifty left to right, fifty right to left. A hundred tiny, focused circles over her nose: making sure to linger on the crooks of her nostrils. One hundred circles on her chin: fifty clockwise, fifty counterclockwise. One hundred swipes under her jaw: all in the same direction from throat to chin, fifty traveling left to right, fifty traveling right to left.

Riktanya rinsed the pumice stone clean with shaking hands as she waited for the sting to subside. The tincture needed time to absorb, Mother had told her. If she didn't scrub hard enough or washed it too soon, she'd never be beautiful. Never be finished.

And such avoidable mistakes were not tolerated.

Her cheeks stopped pulsing, thrumming, and she washed away the slushy clusters of tincture and skin cells down the drain. The icy water did well to calm the swelling and dull the pain.

Next came her hair. A terribly unruly thing. No matter how she braided it or tied it up, it always came undone and tangled itself in her sleep.

She raked her silver, spike-toothed comb through it, starting at the ends so she'd unwork most of the knots while sparing her scalp the torture of the comb's razor-sharp tines. She pulled it back into a tight braid, wetting her hands to keep everything smooth and perfectly in place.

With a quick swish and gargle of her mouthwash, she was ready to get dressed. Today was art lessons followed by history, a short break for lunch, then dancing and combat. She picked a simple frock, one loose enough that she didn't need to cinch her corset so tightly, and a pair of sturdy wood-soled boots.

Riktanya checked her appearance in the mirror one final time and — finding not a single thing out of place — headed down to breakfast.

The dining hall was empty when she entered, save for a few servants whose duty was to blend into the scenery unless they were called to attend. Riktanya sat in her usual spot at the end of the long, long table, and fought the urge to kick her feet back and forth as they dangled over the chair.

Mother hated when she did that.

But Mother would be pleased to find her waiting patiently, dressed and cleaned without mistake. Perhaps She'd even let her have a second cup of tea with breakfast as a reward.

Riktanya's knees shook as the rhythmic clicking of heels echoed down the hall, each step growing louder and sharper until the dining room doors parted.

"Good morning, Mother," Riktanya said as The Matron entered.

Her skin crawled as Her bright blue eyes fell on her. Mother smiled, bone-white teeth splitting the void of Her face.

"Good morning, dear one."

Riktanya's heart was racing as fast as it did when she did something wrong. Yet, she had done nothing wrong. Nothing was out of place. She had made no mistakes.

Why did she feel the need to run and hide?

Mother took Her seat at the head of the table, a statue-turned-servant pulling out the chair before stepping back against the wall.

"What would you like for breakfast this morning, my dear one?" Mother asked.

"Cinnamon toast." The suggestion flew out of her mouth.

Mother cocked Her head. "Cinnamon toast?"

Why had she said that? She didn't know what cinnamon toast was or if she liked it. Cinnamon was a spice she'd only ever read about in her history books.

"I read about it in one of my history books," she half-lied. Despots were confident in what they said, they didn't yield or rescind what they asked for.

"Then it shall be cinnamon toast for breakfast," She spoke to no one and everyone at once. "With tea, one cup each."

The walls shifted as the servants left to do Her bidding. Mother folded Her hands and stared at Riktanya as they waited, barely blinking. They did not speak. They never did, not unless Riktanya was spoken to first. Conversations with Mother never went well before She had Her tea. It was better just to let Her stare. It seemed that Mother liked watching her more than speaking with her.

The servants returned, teapots and covered platters in hand.

Pale, gray liquid streamed out of the spout and into her cup, but released no steam. Not that she had ever seen steam rise from a cup, but she had the feeling that it should. She lifted the mug to her lips and drank, expecting it to be the same flavor it had always been. And it was, but she had trouble swallowing.

This was not the tea that she was used to drinking. The tea that she looked forward to having every morning.

Yet, it was.

The cover was lifted off the platter, revealing two simple slices of bread. Riktanya picked a slice up cautiously. It was hard, cold, frozen. It shattered on her tongue into a bland slush.

There was no cinnamon, no sweet crunch of sugar that would stick in her teeth for a full hour after. She pulled it away from her mouth to study it, to look and see if she missed the streaks of cinnamon she somehow knew she'd find inside, and found her fingertips unstained; lightly tanned and longer. Older.

This was wrong.

She wasn't supposed to be here.

"Now, now, dear one."

Mina looked up from her hands to find the table shortened and The Matron's soulless eyes just inches from her face. "It's rude not to finish."

The Matron sunk Her claws into her jaw, forcing her mouth open, and shoved the sharp, shattered "toast" down her throat.

△

The girl was lying by the lake, watching the clouds roll lazily through the sky. She was older once more, her appearance more familiar to him now. He knew the slope of her nose, even if the jaw below it was rounder, softer. Her hair was shorter, slate colored instead of the unkempt white tresses she bore the last time he saw her.

Just like when they first met.

But they hadn't met.

Or had they?

Who was she?

"Mina!"

The girl sat up at the man's call.

Mina...

"Mina!" The man called again.

The girl stood, and he was pulled down to lap at her heels. He slipped under every step she took, answering her unspoken desire to run as fast and as free as the wind blew through the trees, and carried her to the source of the shout.

An older man, sporting a thick gray beard and a thicker head of long gray hair pulled back into a bun, held up nine fingers.

"Nine seconds," he grunted, voice gruff, expression gruffer. It was hard to tell if he was upset by the time it took her to reach him, or if his vast wrinkles just pulled his face down that way.

"Less than ten," the girl said, voice cold.

The old man hummed in acknowledgment. "Saw a patch of blueberries down by that burled oak."

"The one by Redbreast Creek or by that charred maple?" she asked.

"The charred maple." The old man looked up at the sky. "Bet the squirrels have eaten a quarter of them by now."

The girl turned around quickly, and he was yanked to her heels yet again. The forest blurred as the wind roared past them, painting the world in vibrant swirls of green, brown, blue. A much prettier picture than the blinding white before.

Before? There was a before?

The girl slowed as she approached the fallen maple, releasing him for just a moment before he was pulled away by something else. A metallic hum called to him — to both of them — but the girl, deaf to such a sound, began to wander away from it

— nose buried in a twine-bound notebook.

He brushed across her cheek to direct her attention, tickled under her nose, whirred in her ears. She ignored him, barely blinking as he weaved through her eyelashes, continuing to glance between the foliage drawn on the pages and the foliage on the ground.

A memory of a past annoyance. Of trying to read an important passage in a desert while roaring winds kept turning the pages over his hands and obscuring his view. While the question of him having hands at one point was curious, the nagging hum took precedence. The girl *had* to find it. *Needed* to find it.

He ran across the book, catching a few pages in his swipe.

The girl flipped them back.

He ran over them again, lingering a little as they turned to keep them in place.

The girl threw the pages back open, and pinched the corners to hold them firm. In her annoyance, her growing anger, he felt a surge of strength. That glimmer of a spark.

He harnessed it and railed against the book. The girl fought back, grip on the pages tightening, tightening until—

Rip.

The page she was so focused on tore free. She tried to catch it as it flew, but he was faster. He carried it through the air, the hum growing louder as he soared closer, closer.

There was no tug as the girl kept pace with him, chasing after the page. He dove into the brush, driving the paper through branches and berries to rest on a slightly vibrating piece of iron. The girl parted the leaves above it without care, thoroughly peeved with the inconvenience, then paused.

Her expression was blank, but he could feel the spark flicker brighter for a moment. The girl reached down to grab the object, but promptly dropped it. She reared back, hissing in pain and grabbing her hand. She knit her brow, an extreme emotion considering how stoic her face usually was, but the spark did not dwindle.

It flashed in her eyes for a fleeting moment. Something he knew deeply, beyond these odd fractures of memories and notions, that hadn't been seen in a long time.

The girl tore a strip of cloth off the bottom of the tunic she wore, wrapped it around her hand, and reached for the object once more. From the brush and blueberries came a sword of solid iron, enchanted sigils etched into the blade meant to warn its wielder of approaching fae. She held it to the sun, studying the sharpness of its edge, then thrust it forward in a mock jab.

The same jab she used to raise the blade to his throat the first day they met.

Mina.

Mina!

A rush of emotion washed over him.

The girl was his Mina, though he did not know her at this age. Was this a memory? An anamnesis? Where was the Mina he knew now?

He *had* had hands once, a throat too.

But where were they now?

What was he now?

Who was he?

△

Riktanya woke up precisely an hour before dawn. No earlier. No later. And without the need for a clock. She shook the frost from her sheet and made her bed, making sure to fold her corners as she tucked them underneath the cold, stone slab she slept on. She folded the top exactly a fifth of the length of the visible sheet, and ran a hand over it to make sure it was perfectly straight, with not a single wrinkle in sight.

She ripped the sheet off and made it again, and again, just to make sure it was perfect.

Once she was finished, she walked to the wash basin in the corner of her room, kicked the pipe beneath it to break up the layer of ice that had formed during the night, and turned on the tap.

She spread the tincture Mother gave her onto her pumice stone, wet her face, and set to scrubbing. One hundred circles on each cheek. One hundred strokes up across her forehead. A hundred tiny, focused circles over her nose. One hundred circles on her chin. One hundred swipes under her jaw.

Then an extra one hundred all over, just to make sure she didn't miss a spot.

Riktanya gripped the sink until her cheeks stopped throbbing and the mist left her eyes, then washed away the blood-tinted, slushy clusters of tincture and skin cells down the drain. She sighed as the ice water hit her face and numbed some of the pain.

Next came her hair. She raked her silver, spike-toothed comb through it — starting at the ends so she'd unwork most of the knots and spare her scalp the torture of the comb's razor-sharp tines — then pulled it back into a tight braid, wetting her hands to keep everything smooth and perfectly in place.

With a quick swish and gargle of her mouthwash, she was ready to get dressed. Today was art lessons followed by history, a short break for lunch, then dancing and combat. She picked a simple frock, one loose enough that she didn't need to cinch her corset so tightly, and a pair of sturdy wood-soled boots.

Riktanya checked her appearance in the mirror one final time, just to make sure she hadn't made any mistakes.

The dining hall was empty when she entered, save for a few servants whose duty was to blend into the scenery unless they were called to attend. Riktanya sat in her usual spot at the end of the long, long table. Mother would be pleased to find her waiting so patiently, properly dressed and properly cleaned.

Rhythmic heel clicks echoed down the hall, each step growing louder and sharper until the dining room doors parted.

"Good morning, Mother," Riktanya said as Mother entered.

Mother's bright blue eyes fell on her, and She smiled, a brilliant, white sliver like the crescent moon.

"Good morning, dear one." Mother took Her seat at the head of the table. A statue-turned-servant pulled out the chair before stepping back against the wall. "What would you like for breakfast this morning?"

"Whatever you would like, Mother," Riktanya said.

Mother's smile widened, pleased by her answer.

"Pine porridge with tea," She announced. "One cup each."

The walls shifted as the servants left to do Her bidding. Mother folded Her hands and stared at Riktanya as they waited, barely blinking. They did not speak. They never did, not unless Riktanya was spoken to first. Mother liked watching her more than speaking with her, and it was always in her best interest to make sure Mother was happy.

The servants returned, teapots and covered platters in hand.

Pale, gray liquid streamed out of the spout and into her cup, while another servant removed the cover over her tar-topped porridge. She stuck her spoon into the thick mush, and swirled it around the bowl slowly, blending the rye with the black goo to dilute its bitter taste. She slipped a spoonful in her mouth as gracefully as possible and swallowed it without chewing. The bland, weak menthol of the tea helped to ease the porridge's overwhelming bitterness at least, and if she sipped it carefully she'd be able to make it last through the entire bowl.

Mother's unblinking eyes did not leave her, watching every bite, every swallow, while Her meal was left untouched. Riktanya couldn't remember the last time she saw Her eat.

"Have you finished, dear one?"

Riktanya held up her bowl, turning it so She could see it was empty.

"Yes, I have, Mother."

She studied it thoroughly, making sure no morsel was left behind. "Then you are excused."

Riktanya set down her bowl, got up from her seat, and curtsied.

"Thank you for the meal, Mother."

Mother did not say a word. She just kept watching, always watching, as Riktanya left the room.

A lone easel and canvas stood in the center of an art gallery. Past portraits, landscapes, cross stitches, embroidery, statues — over a hundred art pieces created by her hands filled the space, torn, shattered, smashed in some capacity; serving as a reminder of how far she still had to go and how much she had failed.

Governess Kirsarm stood next to the easel stone-faced, scrutinizing her every movement as she sat down in front of it.

"Today you'll be drawing a portrait of Queen Sahra the Gentle from memory in pastel." The governess tapped her long, talon-tipped, pale finger against the dark wooden case resting on the easel's tray. "You studied Nuvaria in your history lesson last week, correct?"

"Yes, governess," Riktanya said. "But I don't recall there being any pictures of her."

"There was a description of the woman, was there not?"

"Yes, governess."

"Then if you're worth anything, you'll be able to depict her image accurately from the written word alone. You have thirty minutes."

Riktanya opened the pastel case and got to work picking out her color palette, knowing full well that Governess Kirsarm's clock started as soon as she finished speaking rather than when she left the room. She tried to recall the passages she'd read on Queen Sahra as her hands sketched with a mind of their own.

A diamond-shaped face of olive-brushed skin began to form, with freckles so numerous it looked as though she'd been splattered with paint. From a high forehead sprouted a crown of curls, long and fuller than the most majestic lion's mane. Thick round glasses rested on an aquiline nose, enlarging the eyes, glimmering with a hint of mischief, behind them. Full brows, lightly cleft chin, bottom lip fuller with no bow to the top.

Riktanya stepped back a bit to take in the piece fully before deciding what tiara to draw and dropped her pastel case onto the ground.

It should be a scarf on her head, not a crown.

And this was not Queen Sahra. She knew this face too well, knew how it moved, how it laughed, how its nostrils flared when it was cross over her being rude.

She scrambled to pick up the pastels and start again before her governess came back. What had come over her? To draw some random woman instead of who she'd been asked to capture was a mistake she would have made back when she was more rebellious, less wise to the lasting sting of punishments and how truly terrible they could become.

She tried to alter the nose, rearrange the hair, paint her cheeks with blush to match the rouge the late queen had been known to wear, but her hands would not follow her orders. This was not the Queen of Nuvaria. A queen would never have ink and paint strewn about her face, dried and crusted in her strands of hair.

"Who is this, Riktanya?" Governess Kirsarm's voice slithered down her spine.

"Wera," she answered, her voice one-note, textured, and much older.

"Wera," the governess hissed.

My friend.

The thought remained unspoken as a lasso of barbed iron chains pulled taut around Mina's neck.

△

The world whirled around him as he traveled not just through space, but through time. The disorientation and brief disconnects between moments plagued him no longer. He watched leaves sprout and fall, the sky cycle through a thousand hues, the forest where she resided shifting, changing.

Then stillness.

Overcast skies.

A spring day, yet all the new growth was dull. No birds sang. The young leaves did not whisper.

It felt disrespectful to move, but a force beyond his control continued to lead him. Up a small hill, overlooking a lake, sat a shovel, two plots of dug earth — one fresh, one fresher — and Mina. The air was heavy with chill around her, frosting the fledgling grass she sat upon.

She was closer to the woman he knew now in age, though her expression was too hollow, vacant, empty.

Devoid of that spark some force within him was so eager to stoke.

Her sword rested at her feet, blade still stained with the old man's blood. Mr. Harlowe's blood, he recalled. Lars and Heidi, names carried over roaring winds. The closest thing she had to parents.

He ached deeply for her, for her loss, for the stagnant grief she could not release. He reached out to her on instinct, brushing over her shoulders, against her face.

She stood and turned away.

He followed.

△

Riktanya woke up precisely an hour before dawn. No earlier. No later. And without the need for a clock. She shook the frost from her sheet and made her bed, making sure everything was perfectly tucked and straight with not a wrinkle in sight.

She ripped the sheet off and made it again, and again, and again, just to make sure it was perfect.

Once she was finished, she walked to the wash basin in the corner of her room, kicked the pipe beneath it to break up the layer of ice that had formed during the night, and turned on the tap to scrub her face.

Seven hundred brushes of the pumice stone.

Riktanya groaned in relief as the ice water hit her face, numbing the pain as bloodied sludge rinsed down the drain.

She raked her silver, spike-toothed comb through her hair — biting her lip to try and ease the pain as its razor-sharp tines clawed across her scalp — then pulled it back into a tight braid, wetting her hands to keep everything smooth and perfectly in place.

With a quick swish and gargle of her mouthwash, she dressed herself in a simple frock, cinched her corset tight, and slipped on a pair of sturdy wood-soled boots.

Riktanya checked her appearance in the mirror once, twice, just to make sure she hadn't made any mistakes.

The dining hall was empty when she entered. Riktanya sat in her usual spot at the end of the long, long table. Mother would be pleased to find her waiting so patiently, properly dressed and properly cleaned.

Rhythmic heel clicks echoed down the hall, each step growing louder and sharper until the dining room doors parted.

"Good morning, Mother," Riktanya said as Mother entered.

Mother's bright blue eyes fell on her, and She smiled, a brilliant, white sliver like the crescent moon.

"Good morning, dear one." Mother took Her seat at the head of the table. "What would you like for breakfast this morning?"

"Whatever you would like, Mother," Riktanya said.

Mother's smile widened, pleased by her answer.

"Pine porridge with tea," She announced. "One cup each."

The walls shifted as the servants left to do Her bidding. Mother folded Her hands and stared at Riktanya as they waited, barely blinking. Mother liked watching her more than speaking with her, and it was always in her best interest to make sure Mother was happy.

The servants returned, teapots and covered platters in hand.

Riktanya swirled her spoon around the bowl, blending the rye with the black goo to dilute its bitter taste, and washed each swallow down with her tea. Mother's unblinking eyes did not leave her, watching every bite, every swallow, while Her meal was left untouched.

"Have you finished, dear one?"

Riktanya held up her bowl, turning it so She could see it was empty.

"Yes, I have, Mother."

She studied it thoroughly, making sure no morsel was left behind. "Then you are excused."

Riktanya set down her bowl, got up from her seat, and curtsied.

"Thank you for the meal, Mother."

Mother did not say a word. She just kept watching, always watching, as Riktanya left the room.

A lone easel and canvas stood in the center of an art gallery. Past portraits, landscapes, cross stitches, embroidery, statues — over a hundred art pieces created by her hands filled the space, torn, shattered, smashed in some capacity; serving as a reminder of how far she still had to go and how much she had failed.

Governess Kirsarm stood next to the easel stone-faced, scrutinizing her every movement as she sat down in front of it.

"Today you'll be drawing a portrait of The Matron in charcoal," the governess said, pointing a long, talon-tipped, pale finger at the blackened sticks sitting on the easel's ledge. "You have thirty minutes."

Riktanya picked up the charcoal and set to work, knowing full well that Governess Kirsarm's clock started as soon as she finished speaking, rather than when she left the room. Mother's face was easy enough to draw. She knew every detail of it better than her own face, in fact. Jaw sharp and square, nose long and perfectly straight, rectangular and symmetrical as if it had been carved by a master sculptor. Piercing blue eyes sat atop of high, sharp cheeks, two beacons blinding against Her deep indigo skin. Riktanya's charcoal left high angular gaps against it to depict the arch of Her fine brows, pulled taut by the tension of Her pulled-back hair.

Her long white tresses were braided and arranged to sit behind the Borean Crown, highlighting its black-stained spires of ice while hiding the spikes that secured it to Her scalp.

Riktanya stepped away, portrait finished, just in time for Governess Kirsarm to open the door and reenter the gallery. The governess judged the piece in silence, stepping back and forth around it, looking at every detail from up close and afar.

"The Matron circles Her hair in a counter-clockwise pattern," Governess Kirsarm noted. "You've drawn it in a clockwise pattern."

She ran her taloned finger over the canvas, tearing it slowly, then threw it at Riktanya's head. She caught it before its corner could clip her in the temple.

"You shame Her!" The governess shouted. "Hang this on the wall, grab a new canvas, and do it again!"

And she did, over and over again, until it was time for her history lesson.

Governor Butes was waiting for her at the top of the northeast tower, expression unamused, as he smacked a ruler impatiently against the palm of his hand.

"You're late," he glanced down at her charcoal-dusted hands, "and dirty."

"Art lesson ran long. Blame Kirsarm," Riktanya said as she sat down at her desk.

"You wouldn't have been late if you had completed her assignment correctly the first time."

Riktanya stared ahead, neither confirming nor denying that was the case. Despots did not need to apologize or explain their actions. Doing so would bait her into an even greater punishment than being tardy would have.

"Since you value my time so little, let's see if you've been using the small morsels of time you do grant me to actually learn something. Give me all the correct answers and I'll forgive your tardiness." He circled around her desk. "Who was the sixth King of Tovell?"

"King Vigmar Otrason."

"What family has ruled over Kraedia since the fall of the Morricana Empire?"

"The Valverdes."

"What ways can faefolk cross between the realms?"

"Fairy circles, leyline-thinned patches in the veil, and banishment spells."

"That is incorrect," he said. "Banishment spells do not work on the fae."

"Yes, they do," Riktanya insisted. "You just need to use something of the fae's domain to hone the cast. Bodily components work best, hair, bone, blood." She whipped around in her seat to face where he had stopped behind her. "It was a method developed by Lady Hitchman, Master Willock, and—"

Riktanya froze, shocked still by the Governor's piercing stare, His beady black eyes now damning blue.

"And who told you that? It certainly wasn't Me."

"Enoch," the voice that shook out of her throat stated, even though she did not know a man by that name.

His expression shifted, flooding with rage as the ruler He carried in His hand grew into a barbed chain whip. Mina tried to summon her wind and run, but the wind did not come. Spike-lined shackles bound her to the chair.

Governor Butes raised the whip. "Wrong. Answer."

△

He followed after her, watching her change and shift as much as the forest around her, until her visage settled on short, matted hair, patchwork leather armor, and a cluster of freshly skinned beaver pelts slung over her shoulder.

"Winter Wind blows through the valley, pushes us into our homes," Mina sang. "Pleading she knocks at our windows, scorned she continues to roam."

She stilled, song dying on her lips as she placed a hand on her hilt.

"Are you sure this is the right cabin?" a familiar woman's voice asked far away.

"Of course this is the right cabin! It's the only cabin in this damned forest!" a familiar man's voice barked back.

He rushed with Mina through the forest, leaping up into the familiar canopy that circled her cabin.

He snaked over her shoulder to get a better look down at the clearing below.

Wera and Sir Gargic. Their names came immediately as he saw them, as did hundreds and thousands of half-formed memories.

What were they doing here? How did they know Mina? How did he know them?

He followed her down from the pine she perched in, guiding her footsteps silently towards the drying rack staked beside her cabin. With a loud and forceful snap, she dropped the first rung of beaver skins onto it.

The pair jumped. Sir Gargic drew his sword as Wera bladed her feet into a wide stance, arms lifted, ready to throw her acidic ink.

"Get off the porch," Mina said as she hung another rack.

Sir Gargic's jaw fell agape, easily offended as always, while Wera relaxed.

"My apologies, miss. We're looking for the alpinist that lives here," she said. "Would that be you?"

"No," Mina said. "I'm a hunter. The alpinist lives to the west."

He wanted to laugh at the obvious lie.

Sir Gargic flared his nostrils, puffed out his chest, and stomped over towards her.

"I am Sir Murmir Gargic, General-rank Knight of the Lanholde Royal Army, proud servant to King Fritz Reinhardt."

"Never heard of him."

Sir Gargic sputtered, "You never—"

"Sir Gargic," Wera whispered, chiding him for the outburst.

"Well, he's heard of you, and has specifically recommended that we seek you out to lead us up the Fallow Peaks."

"If that's the case, then I guess your king wants you both to die," Mina droned. "I'm a hunter, not an alpinist."

Wera placed a hand on Sir Gargic's shoulder, damming up the tirade clearly building in his chest.

"How much would it cost for you to be an alpinist?" she asked, bearing her trademarked 'I'm going to win' smirk.

"Seven thousand gilt one way," Mina answered. "The real alpinist to the west charges half that."

"I'm sure." Wera shrugged. "But the alpinist we're looking for fits your description exactly. Female alpinist. Rough around the edges. Lives alone in a cabin deep in the Sandere Woods, five hundred paces off of the last bend in Woodgullet Road, heading northeast." She rattled off the details from the dossier Sir Gargic had given them.

Mina blinked slowly, then repeated. "Seven-thousand gilt one way."

"Deal," Sir Gargic said.

He pulled out a scroll from one of the pouches on his belt, while Wera brandished a quill and a bottle of ink. Sir Gargic scrawled something down on it, then turned the contract towards her direction.

His thick, stubby finger pointed at the "**7,000g**" written next to the terms of payment. "Seven-thousand gilt to be delivered direct from the Capitol's treasury upon our safe arrival." His finger traveled down the page to a long signature line. "All you need to do is sign here."

She did.

"Mina," Wera read her name aloud, standing on the tips of her toes to watch as she wrote it. "I'm Wera Alrust."

Mina snapped the quill once she finished, dropped it to the ground, and headed into her cabin.

He shouldn't have found it funny, but yet another ghost of laughter tickled him.

"Where are you going?" Sir Gargic snapped behind her. "You're under contract to—"

"Packing," Mina answered. "Can't climb a ten-thousand-foot cliff face with just a bow, a sword, and a can-do attitude." She paused in the doorway. "Just two going up?"

"Five," Wera answered. "Six if you count yourself."

"I don't."

Mina headed inside. He followed after her, slipping in through the crack of the door before it shut.

The tiny cabin was filled to the brim with books and instruments. So many, they bowed the shelves they sat on and certainly threatened to bend the foundation as well. Mina maneuvered around the stacks of drums and fiddle cases with practiced grace, picking up random odds and ends as she passed before throwing them into a large pack she took off the wall. She tucked away some of her instruments in closets, lifted piles of books and sheet music off of the floor to higher shelves, closed the windows and locked the shutters. Seeing her move through the space, organized to her yet cluttered to the untrained eye, tickled him immensely.

Just like me, he thought.

Though the question of who he was, was still unanswered.

She rifled through the pack, taking stock to make sure she had everything she needed, muttering to herself, "Flint, whytewing leathers, tarp, rations, climbing axes..." then picked up a fiddle and bow leaning against a hard wooden chair. She loosened up the strings a bit and unstrung the bow to keep the horse hairs from snapping, then shoved it into the already loaded bag. The thing had to weigh at least sixty pounds, yet Mina swung it over her shoulder as if it weighed no more than a satchel of feathers. She adjusted her bow sheath to rest between it and her back, switched out her boots with a sturdier, cleated pair, then headed out the door.

"Where are the other three?" she asked as she locked up.

"Back on the road, waiting with the wagon," Wera replied.

"You can't take a wagon up a mountain."

"We don't plan to." She smiled at Mina when she turned around. "Ready to go?"

"Lead the way."

Sir Gargic headed off, impatient and frustrated, into the thick wood. They arrived at a seldom-used road. A simple covered wagon was pulled off to the side, letting the four horses that pulled it graze lazily, while two more faces he recognized sat with them, Tanir, who was sat on the ground making daisy chains out of dandelions, and Enoch, who was busy scrawling away in his notebook as he sat in the driver's seat.

Sir Gargic's spine straightened, chest puffed out a bit as he put on a noble act to cover up his annoyance. "We've returned!" he cried, waving grandly.

They looked up from their work. Tanir abandoned her daisies and rose to meet them, while Enoch looked their way and flipped to another page in his book; quill taking off in a fury.

"Ah! Are you the young lady who will be guiding us?" Tanir smiled sweetly. "My name's Tanir and the boy on the cart is Enoch." She turned over her shoulder and hollered, "Wave hello, Enoch!"

Enoch raised his hand partially, too engrossed in whatever he was writing to look away.

"Mina." Mina met Tanir's gaze, causing her brow to furrow.

"You'll have to leave the wagon and loose the horses an hour or so up the road," she continued. "They'll slow us down and will be hunted by the beasts of the Harrow."

"Oh, uh—" Tanir swallowed. "That sounds like something you should discuss with Master Windenhofer. I'll go get him for you." She flashed another smile, this one fueled by nerves, and hurried off into the back of the wagon.

He had half the mind to follow her, but the snap of Enoch's notebook drew his attention instead.

Enoch leaned over the side of the driver's seat, resting his chin on his hand dramatically, abandoning the fierce focus he held when writing to gaze at Mina with puppy dog eyes. "Did you know you are extremely beautiful for an alpinist?"

Something in him bristled. He went to muss up Enoch's precious mustache for the comment, but found himself cemented to Mina's side.

Mina stared at Enoch blankly.

"I know," she said after a moment.

Enoch choked on his spit at her response. Wera burst out into a fit of laughter, drawing Mina's attention.

"Oh," Wera wheezed through her giggles, "this is going to be fun."

"Enough of that, Enoch!" Sir Gargic snipped, hitting him on the arm. "She comes highly recommended by The Crown of Lanholde and you will address her with the respect of such a recommendation!"

"S-sorry, M-mina," Enoch stammered, still caught off guard by her curtness as he leaned back away from her, rubbing his injured arm.

"I hear we have a new face joining our motley crew!"

His annoyance with Enoch faded completely at the sound of that voice.

His voice followed by *his body* and *his face* and *his everything* stepping out and around the caravan, smiling wide in greeting.

"Hello, I am Sebastian Windenhofer. It is wonderful to meet you!" his body extended his hand out in greeting.

Sebastian was pulled towards himself, brushed through his hair, in between his fingers.

He remembered.

He remembered the cool breeze that blew between them when they first met. At first, he thought it was a draft coming down from the mountains, carrying the first chills of Autumn. But it wasn't that.

Just as it wasn't Mina's memories he was seeing, or his own.

It was the wind's.

But if this was a memory, where was his body?

Where was Mina's body?

A deep dread washed over Sebastian, and the wind picked up, carrying him through time once again. It wondered the same thing, which was all the more frightening. What did it need him for? Was this a part of breaking her curse, or was this an entirely separate phenomenon?

And if he had forgotten who *he* was, when they did find her, would she still be his Mina?

⚠

Riktanya woke up precisely an hour before dawn. She shook the frost from her sheet and made her bed, making sure everything was perfectly tucked and straight with not a wrinkle in sight.

She ripped the sheet off and made it again, and again, and again, just to make sure it was perfect.

Once she was finished, she walked to the wash basin in the corner of her room and turned on the tap to scrub her face.

Eight hundred brushes of the pumice stone.

Riktanya groaned in relief as the ice water hit her face, numbing the pain as bloodied sludge rinsed down the drain.

She raked her silver, spike-toothed comb through her hair — biting her lip to try and ease the pain as its razor-sharp tines clawed across her scalp — then pulled it back into a tight braid, wetting her hands to keep everything smooth and perfectly in place.

With a quick swish and gargle of her mouthwash, she dressed herself in a simple frock, cinched her corset tightly, — until she couldn't hold her breath anymore — and slipped on a pair of sturdy wood-soled boots.

Riktanya checked her appearance in the mirror once, twice, three times just to make sure she hadn't made any mistakes. Her dress wasn't pretty enough for a despot. So she changed it to something stiffer, frillier, more grand.

The dining hall was empty when she entered. Riktanya sat in her usual spot at the end of the table. Mother would be pleased to find her waiting so patiently, properly dressed and properly cleaned.

The dining room doors parted.

"Good morning, Mother," Riktanya said as Mother entered.

Mother's bright blue eyes fell on her, and She smiled, a brilliant, white sliver like the crescent moon.

"Good morning, dear one." Mother took Her seat at the head of the table. "What would you like for breakfast this morning?"

"Whatever you would like, Mother," Riktanya said.

Mother's smile widened, pleased by her answer.

"Pine porridge with tea," She announced. "One cup each."

The walls shifted as the servants left to do Her bidding. Mother folded Her hands and stared at Riktanya as they waited, barely blinking. Mother liked watching her more than speaking with her, and it was always in her best interest to make sure Mother was happy.

The servants returned, teapots and covered platters in hand.

Riktanya swirled her spoon around the bowl, blending the rye with the black goo to dilute its bitter taste, and washed each swallow down with her tea. Mother's unblinking eyes did not leave her, watching every bite, every swallow, while Her meal was left untouched.

"Have you finished, dear one?"

Riktanya held up her bowl, turning it so She could see it was empty.

"Yes, I have, Mother."

She studied it thoroughly, making sure no morsel was left behind. "Then you are excused."

Riktanya set down her bowl, got up from her seat, and curtsied.

"Thank you for the meal, Mother."

Mother did not say a word. She just kept watching, always watching, as Riktanya left the room.

A lone easel and canvas stood in the center of an art gallery. Her destroyed past creations filled the space, serving as a reminder of how far she still had to go and how much she had failed.

Governess Kirsarm stood next to the easel stone-faced, scrutinizing her every movement as she sat down in front of it.

"Today you'll be drawing a portrait of The Matron in charcoal," the governess said, pointing a long, talon-tipped, pale finger at the blackened sticks sitting on the easel's ledge. "You have thirty minutes."

Riktanya picked up the charcoal and set to work, knowing full well that Governess Kirsarm's clock started as soon as she finished speaking, rather than when she left the room. Mother's face was easy enough to draw. Jaw sharp and square, nose long and perfectly straight. Piercing blue eyes, high sharp cheeks, fine brows arched high by the tension of Her pulled-back hair, braided and arranged in a clockwise pattern behind the black-stained ice spires of the Borean Crown.

Riktanya stepped away, portrait finished, just in time for Governess Kirsarm to open the door and reenter the gallery. The governess judged the piece in silence, stepping back and forth around it, looking at every detail from up close and afar.

"It's... adequate," Governess Kirsarm noted. She took the portrait off the easel and replaced it with another canvas. "Now, another. This time draw The Matron in Her ceremonial Hibernal regalia."

She did, making sure to capture every detail of Mother's snowflake-strung robe until it was time for her history lesson.

Governor Butes was waiting for her at the top of the northeast tower, expression unamused, as he smacked a ruler impatiently against the palm of his hand. He glanced out the window, assessing the shadows strewn across the ground to check her arrival time as she slipped into her seat, then set the ruler down.

He walked to the chalkboard and began to write on it, each scratch of the chalk against it screaming and squealing.

"Today, you'll be learning about the Reinhardt Rebellion, their battle plans, tactics, then you'll come up with a campaign of your own to rectify the mistakes their opposition made. So make sure to pay close attention."

Riktanya gave a curt nod, signaling him to continue.

The lesson was long and boring, the flaws in the Reinhardt Rebellion glaringly obvious. It was a shame their opposition had been too stuck in their need of tradition and honor to see them. Whether or not the governor was impressed with her proposed strategy, Riktanya couldn't tell. But the lack of cuts on her knuckles from his ruler was a sign in the right direction at least.

Lunch was quick and bland, some chicken and gruel. Mother wasn't present for this meal, it was just her and the servants, but Riktanya still made sure to finish every bite, leaving only the bones behind.

She changed out her wooden boots for heels and made her way to the ballroom for her dance lessons.

Her instructor was nowhere to be found. Just her practice dummy, arms positioned at the ready, and the old phonograph. A record was already placed upon it, its name long worn off its label. Riktanya turned the crank to start it spinning, then dropped the needle, figuring it was better to be practicing when her instructor arrived than to be accused of slacking off in their absence.

Hearing an accordion and guitar warming up surprised her. Was this a new record?

No, the notes felt too familiar for that. Perhaps this was an old song she practiced to when she was smaller. A one-off song to test her versatility.

Riktanya unlocked the wheels at the base of the dummy and took her starting position, taking its hand in hers, and placing her other on its shoulder.

The cello and second guitar wrangled in their compatriots to join the singer — an alto crooning in a muddled language — to set the pace of a waltz.

She began the steps as practiced, traveling around the dance floor with the dummy — her posture perfectly straight, steps light and lifted arms lofty.

What is the singer saying?

Her words were almost words, muffled and garbled in odd ways, as if she were singing through water or deep within a cave. Was the record warped? Was that why her instructor had placed it out? To see if the record was usable?

She twisted herself into a shallow dip, holding her weight as the song slowed. She thought it a rather quick waltz in the brief moment of silence before the music picked up tempo fantastically, switching time signatures on her.

4/4, the song was in 4/4. So many dances fit a 4/4, but what made sense when coming off a waltz? Especially at this speed. A quickstep? A samba, or—

Riktanya was swept up out of her dip and spun around by two strong arms where stiff wooden ones used to be. She should have been frightened, should have screamed her head off and attacked the animated inanimate, but something about the way it held her felt right.

Safe even.

And it sure was exhilarating being whirled around the dance floor.

The world became a whirl of color as the dummy lifted its arm and spun her tightly under it. A giddy feeling overcame her, light and airy, and when the world returned to form she was taller, dressed in a simple gown she could not tell the color of, instead of the frilly ornate monstrosity she loathed to wear. The dummy found itself dressed in finery as well, a tweed suit of dark umber with a tie shaded to match her dress.

She did not know a single step of the dance he pulled her into, but for once, she did not care. She did not care if her arms were sloppy, if she tripped over her heels or brushed against his shoes. He did not care either, he was just a dummy after all.

Wasn't he?

Her ears were catching the alto's lyrics easier now. She was singing in Yosik. Singing about freedom, liberation, of copper-dipped skies and amber light, of sunset.

Mina looked up from his chest, expecting to find kind brown eyes and a beaming smile beneath a crown of amber locks, but the dummy was just a dummy. Its face a block of wood, its arms back to sticks and body just its simple barrel chest. But she was still tall, her hands still unstained. She was herself, as she should be—

—and she was terrified.

What was she doing back in the Rime? Back in the halls of Leithlis Serdtsa? Mina patted her neck and, much to her horror, her iron collar was absent. She was without her armor, without her sword.

The music stopped.

She turned around to face the record player, face whatever awful rimefae had come for her, and found nothing but walls of bright blue ice.

"Naughty, naughty, girl." The Matron's voice slithered down her spine. Eyes, hundreds of bright blue eyes opened on the walls, the floors, the ceiling. "And here I was, trying to give you a little bit of fun."

The chains seized her before she could even think to run, sinking in their icy fangs and hoisting her aloft. Mina screamed in agony as her joints were slowly pulled out of their sockets.

"Don't tell Me you've gone soft on Me, dear one." The chains wrenched tighter. "Not after everything I've done to make you strong."

△

Sebastian raced through a month's worth of memories. From the forest to the mountains' frost. Over a night spent cramped in a dome, through a labyrinth of caves, only pausing in the moments when the wind was called to her.

After spending so many hours agonizing over how he could help her harness her magic, how to help her mitigate her emotions like he had to for his flame, he now understood the severity of her constraints, the odd barrier disconnecting her from the wind, and how only one thing truly allowed her to push past them.

Fear.

Fear summoned the wind to push back the crystecean.

Fear pulled the wind into the vortex that shattered Eirlys' ice.

Fear so intense, involute, and ingrained, the wild winds answered her call, bending to her will to strike down all those who dared disturb her.

No wonder it had been so hard for her to control willingly. Her unconscious fear — to run at a moment's notice, to defend from a distance — was the only thing that could break through the blockade between her and her magic. A blockade that was beginning to look more and more like a curse formed by frozen chains—

—that was starting to thaw.

The wind's course shifted in a memory coated in manufactured rain. A rush of gratitude, almost, from the element followed as his past self's words, frustrated and tired, shouted an accidental command demanding partnership. Sebastian understood Mina's expression now. He could feel the chains shift loose, and a new catalyst, new emotions to guide the wind to aid her, emerge.

Want.

Hope. Determination. Happiness. Pride. Relief. While not as strong or compelling as fear was, the wind could still heed their call. They're what fueled his flame to slay that charging bull, what pulled them together during her air ribbon dance. As the chains loosened, as she was allowed to feel more joy and chase what she wanted, her control grew...

...forming a barrage of flaming arrows.

He was back in Recet's Den, not back in his body but leading himself through the snow. Leading him to her. His anger rolled off of him in waves of heat, hot enough to disturb the wind's course if it were not so determined to bring an end to its master's suffering.

As his body reached her, white-hot flames melting Bormir's wrist, the wind continued to pull Sebastian along, away from the scene.

And through the veil.

An odd sensation, draining almost, as if he shouldn't be there. He could feel his flames rage against the cold, keeping it from seeping in.

Funny, Sebastian thought as his vision fell away into the veil's blinding white light, *just like when she caught me on The Lithe.*

Just like her kiss.

🜁

Riktanya woke up precisely an hour before dawn. She shook the frost from her sheet and made her bed, making sure everything was perfectly tucked and straight with not a wrinkle in sight.

She ripped the sheet off and made it again, and again, and again, and again just to make sure it was perfect.

Once she was finished, she walked to the wash basin in the corner of her room and turned on the tap to scrub her face.

Nine hundred brushes of the pumice stone.

Riktanya groaned in relief as the ice water hit her face, numbing the pain as bloodied sludge rinsed down the drain.

She raked her silver, spike-toothed comb through her hair — biting her lip to try and ease the pain as its razor-sharp tines clawed across her scalp — then pulled it back into a tight braid, wetting her hands to keep everything smooth and perfectly in place.

With a quick swish and gargle of her mouthwash, she dressed herself in a stiff, frilly gown, cinched her corset tightly — until she couldn't hold her breath anymore — and slipped on a pair of sturdy wood-soled boots. Today was art lessons followed by history, followed by a short break for lunch, then combat.

Riktanya checked her appearance in the mirror once, twice, three times just to make sure she hadn't made any mistakes.

She undid her hair and re-raked her comb through it at the sight of a single strand out of place.

The dining hall was empty when she entered. Riktanya sat in her usual spot at the end of the table. Mother would be pleased to find her waiting so patiently, properly dressed and properly cleaned.

The dining room doors parted.

"Good morning, Mother," Riktanya said as Mother entered.

Mother's bright blue eyes fell on her, and She smiled, a brilliant, white sliver like the crescent moon.

"Good morning, dear one." Mother took Her seat at the head of the table. "What would you like for breakfast this morning?"

"Whatever you would like, Mother," Riktanya said.

Mother's smile widened, pleased by her answer.

"Pine porridge with tea," She announced. "One cup each."

The walls shifted as the servants left to do Her bidding. Mother folded Her hands and stared at Riktanya as they waited, barely blinking. Mother liked watching her more than speaking with her, and it was always in her best interest to make sure Mother was happy.

The servants returned, teapots and covered platters in hand.

Riktanya swirled her spoon around the bowl, blending the rye with the black goo to dilute its bitter taste, and washed each swallow down with her tea. Mother's unblinking eyes did not leave her, watching every bite, every swallow, while Her meal was left untouched.

"Have you finished, dear one?"

Riktanya held up her bowl, turning it so She could see it was empty.

"Yes, I have, Mother."

She studied it thoroughly, making sure no morsel was left behind. "Then you are excused."

Riktanya set down her bowl, got up from her seat, and curtsied.

"Thank you for the meal, Mother."

Mother did not say a word. She just kept watching, always watching, as Riktanya left the room.

A lone easel and canvas stood in the center of an art gallery. Her destroyed past creations filled the space, serving as a reminder of how far she still had to go and how much she had failed.

So many mistakes.

Governess Kirsarm stood next to the easel stone-faced, scrutinizing her every movement as she sat down in front of it.

"Today you'll be drawing a portrait of The Matron in charcoal," the governess said, pointing a long, talon-tipped, pale finger at the blackened sticks sitting on the easel's ledge. "You have thirty minutes."

Riktanya picked up the charcoal and set to work, knowing full well that Governess Kirsarm's clock started as soon as she finished speaking, rather than when she left the room. Mother's face was easy enough to draw. Jaw sharp and square, nose long and perfectly straight. Piercing blue eyes, high sharp cheeks, fine brows arched high by the tension of Her pulled-back hair, braided and arranged in a clockwise pattern behind the black-stained ice spires of the Borean Crown.

Riktanya stepped away, portrait finished, just in time for Governess Kirsarm to open the door and reenter the gallery. The governess judged the piece in silence, stepping back and forth around it, looking at every detail from up close and afar.

"It's... adequate," Governess Kirsarm noted. She took the portrait off the easel and replaced it with another canvas. "Now, another. This time draw The Matron in Her ceremonial Hibernal regalia."

She did, making sure to capture every detail of Mother's snowflake-strung robe until it was time for her history lesson.

Governor Butes was waiting for her at the top of the northeast tower, expression unamused, as he smacked a ruler impatiently against the palm of his hand. He glanced out the window, assessing the shadows strewn across the ground to check her arrival time as she slipped into her seat, then set his ruler down.

He walked to the chalkboard and began to write on it, each scratch of the chalk against it screaming and squealing.

"Today, you'll be learning about the Reinhardt Rebellion, their battle plans, tactics, then you'll come up with a campaign of your own to rectify the mistakes their opposition made. So make sure to pay close attention."

Riktanya gave a curt nod, signaling him to continue.

The lesson was long and boring.

Lunch was quick and bland, some chicken and gruel. Mother wasn't present for this meal, it was just her and the servants, but Riktanya still made sure to finish every bite, leaving only the bones behind.

She swapped her dress for a simple linen set, and bound her feet in bandages before heading to the training grounds. Her siblings were already waiting, already standing at quiet attention like good soldiers. Good children.

They kept their focus trained on the horizon, but their resentment was palpable, hanging over her as she took her place in the line-up. If Captain Ayaz was upset by her delay, he didn't show it. He never did, not outright. He let the others punish her instead.

"One on Ones," he announced, shattering the silence over the empty, frozen field. "Izotz vs. Sarma, Fannar vs. Vetle, Barys vs. Fuyure, Riktanya vs. Bormir. Close Combat. Summon your weapons."

Riktanya closed her eyes to focus, trying her hardest to form a sword of ice out of the air.

"Come on, sister." Bormir taunted, voice dripping with disgust. "Just because you can take your sweet time whenever you want, doesn't mean the rest of us have the luxury to waste it."

His disgust became her own. The others could conjure weapons without a second thought, could sculpt snow drifts into statues if they willed it. Yet, all she could manage was a thin, lumpy sword. A bastardized arrow that would make even a novice blacksmith cringe.

"Take your positions," the captain called.

She took her place across from Bormir in the center of the field, while the others spread out to its corners. She kept her brother's gaze, not yielding, even though the hate in his eyes turned her stomach.

"Begin."

Riktanya rushed forward, knowing better than to wait. Hesitation led to death, and such mistakes would not be tolerated.

Bormir's axe caught her sword and parried her strike.

"Well, that's surprising," he snickered as he swung at her head. "I figured such a weak thing would shatter."

She dipped low, avoiding the axe's edge, and jabbed at his stomach. Bormir jumped back out of her range.

"But then again," He went to cleave her wrist. "You're still alive. Guess even the weak can weasel their way out of the inevitable."

Riktanya kept her wrist in the axe's path until the last possible second, goading him to lean forward and expose his neck. She jabbed him in the throat with her free fist, sending him stumbling back before his axe could connect.

The way he grabbed his throat, the shape of his axe — the action of her punching him at all — was familiar. But not with him.

"Since when do you wield an axe?" Riktanya asked, taking advantage of his stupor to get a swipe in at his thigh.

Bormir's iris flashed blue for a moment. Not Mother's blue, but one close to it. A blue that was caring, attentive. Their true owner's name lingered on the tip of her tongue for just a moment before she swallowed it in fear.

"What axe?" Bormir snarled as he swung his rapier at her.

She caught his blade against hers, pushing up with all her might as he forced down. Bormir grew taller, older, the hatred in his eyes turning from sibling rivalry to something more vile. A deep infection. A deep wound of long-held suffering.

Suffering that she caused.

Her fragile sword of ice shattered.

Mina rolled out of the way narrowly. The ground where she had been standing broke as his blade connected, scattering a web of cracks across the icy sheet. The instructor, the other children, were gone: just an endless field of ice and rapidly darkening skies.

"Where are you going?" Bormir seethed, His voice layered with another. With Hers. "Abandoning Me again?" His wings unfurled, tattered and withering. With one flap, He was upon her and sinking His rapier through her diaphragm. Mina tried to scream, tried to speak to Him through her pain as He lifted her off the ground, but she could not find the breath to do so.

Higher and higher they flew, the sky above them turning into a deep black void as the ground below them crumpled away into nothingness.

"Do you know what you did when you left?" He hissed as His body disintegrated. "What you did to Us?"

Behind Him, four of the others appeared. Fannar, Vetle, Barys, Izotz, if Bormir hadn't named them back in the den, she wouldn't have been able to recognize them. With every beat of their wings, with every foot they flew, their bodies rotted and contorted, bones splintering, jaws splitting until they let out an unearthly shriek.

The mournful cries of a heatseeker.

"How dare you betray Us." Tears rolled down Bormir's face. "How dare you leave Us to suffer. If you had stayed, We could have grown together, gotten strong enough to rip that crown off Her fucking head!"

"I'm s-sorry," Mina found the breath to say.

Bormir smiled, a thin, too-wide smile that split His face like a crescent moon.

"Your heart's too warm now, and your siblings are so hungry." Bormir twisted His rapier. "Prove it."

He pulled out His sword and she fell.

The rush of their wings and their harrowing cries grew louder and louder.

Mina closed her eyes and let them tear her apart.

△

Endless snow. Endless ice. Endless cold.

A pristine wasteland of white. The birthplace of winter itself.

The Barren Rime.

Sebastian's being felt as heavy as lead moving through it, the cold so deep it seeped beyond the joints and bone he no longer had to find purchase on his soul.

For both an instant and eternity he wandered through it, swept along by the wind with little choice. Whatever day the wind had settled on currently, however, was not nearly as bad as the minutes or millennia before it. The river below him was actually flowing.

"Maybe it'll taste like honey! Or maybe like salt! I read that mortals mine salt from mountains," a young girl's voice echoed somewhere along its banks.

"I think it will taste like all the seasons," a young boy replied.

"Ahh! Springtime!"

The wind was already carrying him towards the children, but the memory of Mina's sleep-addled declaration urged it along faster.

"Really?" the girl asked.

"The Gelu runs through all of them," the boy explained. "If coming from the mountains would make it salty, then running through Spring should make it taste springy."

Two children burst out from a cluster of boulders along the river bank. They were almost indistinguishable from the landscape with their pale skin and grayscale clothing, but their hair, a deep brown for the girl and a lifting blond for the boy, stuck out like sore thumbs.

They fell to their knees at the river's edge, looks of awe brightening their faces as they dipped their hands into the water.

"It's almost warm!" the girl gasped.

The boy scooped some up in his hands and drank.

"How does it taste?"

He swished the water around his mouth, brows knitting in consideration, and swallowed.

"Different."

"Different how?"

A wry smile crawled up his face, "Taste it yourself."

The boy slapped the water with his hand, soaking the girl's dress before she could get out of the way. He shook with laughter.

Her skirt froze up immediately, hardening into odd wrinkles and bunches. The girl crinkled her nose and pursed her lips in distaste, before lifting her leg back and kicking the water's edge. A splash twice the size of the boy's drenched him from head to toe.

The girl laughed a brilliant, chortly laugh, melodic in tone but broken up by rattling snorts.

Snorts Sebastian knew quite well, even if they were a bit higher in pitch than the last time he heard them.

Judging by his slightly hooked nose, Sebastian deduced that the boy tackling her into the water was Bormir. A less antagonistic version, of course. Their laughter and smiles ignited a warmth within him, and within the wind as well. It was observing, swirling above her like a moth above a flame. Wondering if it dare flutter any closer.

They splashed and swam, skipped rocks and blew bubbles. After seeing her younger self suffering for so long, it was a joy to watch Mina play, to be a kid.

To have that spark.

Incensed by a particularly raucous bout of laughter, the wind rushed towards her, drawn in by how brilliantly the spark within her shone.

Like it had once done when she was a babe, the wind rushed across her cheeks, into her nose, her lungs, becoming her breath. Mina kept on laughing, her spark twinkling in delight even as the wind tickled her ears and twirled her hair.

She did not shiver. The spark did not flicker. She could hold it now.

An unspoken thought solidified the union, heard by Sebastian only through his current state of being. A wish, a want to be as free as the wind was. To soar and sail without limits, to go beyond the Rime and see the places she had only read about in books. To chase days of laughter and smiles just like this, with her siblings by her side, and leave suffering behind.

The wind's joy contradicted Sebastian's sadness in knowing what lied ahead for her. The wind bound itself to her, each breath she took coursing its magic through her veins, into her blood.

A blood contract. Nearly impossible to break. Strengthened by her will.

"Sister?" Bormir asked, finally speaking after watching the wind swirl around her in silent, unsure awe. "What is happening?"

"She has been chosen, little one." A voice bright and haunting, like the squeals and cracks of ice beneath one's feet when standing in the center of a frozen lake, swallowed the laughter, the light, the warmth out of the air. What little color was in Bormir's face drained as a pair of hands rested on Mina's shoulders. Nails as long and dangerous as sharpened icicles, flesh as dark blue as Winter's night sky.

Mina turned around slowly, trembling in fear, and faced a pair of piercing, pupilless blue eyes.

"I'm s-sorry, Mother, I—"

The woman — the same woman who had stolen Mina from her crib — a ruler of some sort judging by the horrifying crown impaled on her head, sunk her claws into Mina's shoulders. Her breath caught from the pain.

"Do not apologize. It is beneath you now," the woman said. She peeled her covetous gaze away from Mina to glare at Bormir. "You, however. If you were so willing to disobey your Mother and extend beyond the reach of My protection, then you should be so willing to travel back alone." She looked back down at Mina, expression shifting to something too overjoyed, an enraptured possession like a child staring at its beloved baby doll. "Come, dear one. Let's go home."

Sebastian blinked, and they were gone. All of them, as the wind picked up again to carry him elsewhere. The brief respite from the all-consuming cold ending as time passed by, benumbing his being with every passing second.

△

Riktanya woke up precisely an hour before dawn. She shook the frost from her sheet and made her bed again, and again, and again, and again, and again, just to make sure it was perfect.

Once she was finished, she walked to the wash basin in the corner of her room and scrubbed her face, precisely in the same practiced pattern she always had, counting to a thousand as the pumice stone tore away the layers of her ugly, pale skin.

She raked her silver, spike-toothed comb through her hair, scraping its razor-sharp tines across her scalp. She pulled her hair back into a tight braid, wetting her hands to keep everything smooth and perfectly in place, and twisted it in a clockwise pattern to form a crown pinned upon her head.

She donned an ornate gown, stiff and frilled, a favorite of Mother's, and cinched her corset tightly until she couldn't hold her breath anymore. Until curves were formed by force on her still-growing body. She slipped on a pair of sharp, pointed heels that chimed like falling icicles with every step she took.

Riktanya did not need to check her appearance. She knew there was nothing out of place.

She sat in her usual spot at the end of the table in the empty dining room and waited for Mother to arrive patiently, properly dressed and properly cleaned.

The dining room doors parted.

"Good morning, Mother," Riktanya greeted.

Mother's bright blue eyes fell on her, and She smiled, a brilliant, white sliver like the crescent moon.

"Good morning, dear one." Mother took Her seat at the head of the table. "What would you like for breakfast this morning?"

"Let's have Our favorite," Riktanya said. "Pine porridge with tea. One cup each."

Mother's smile widened, pleased by her answer.

The walls shifted as the servants left to do Her bidding. Mother folded Her hands and stared at Riktanya as they waited, barely blinking. Riktanya stared back, thoughts quiet, numb. There would be plenty to think about later during her lessons— and even if she were capable of it, why bother with it now?

The servants returned, teapots and covered platters in hand.

Riktanya swirled her spoon around the bowl, blending the rye with the black goo to dilute its bitter taste, and washed each swallow down with her tea. Mother's unblinking eyes did not leave her, watching every bite, every swallow, while Her meal was left untouched.

"Have you finished, dear one?"

Riktanya held up her bowl, turning it so She could see it was empty.

"Yes, I have, Mother."

She studied it thoroughly, making sure no morsel was left behind. "Then you are excused."

Riktanya set down her bowl, got up from her seat, and curtsied.

"Thank you for the meal, Mother."

Mother did not say a word as Riktanya left the room.

A lone easel and canvas stood in the center of an art gallery. Her destroyed past creations filled the space, serving as a much-needed reminder of how much she had failed.

Governess Kirsarm stood next to the easel, stone-faced, as Riktanya sat down in front of it.

"Today you'll be drawing a portrait of The Matron in charcoal," the governess said, pointing a long, talon-tipped, pale finger at the blackened sticks sitting on the easel's ledge. "You have thirty minutes."

Riktanya picked up the charcoal and set to work, knowing full well that Governess Kirsarm's clock started as soon as she finished speaking, rather than when she left the room. Jaw sharp and square, nose long and perfectly straight. Piercing blue eyes, high sharp cheeks, fine brows arched high by the tension of Her pulled-back hair, braided and arranged in a clockwise pattern behind the black-stained ice spires of the Borean Crown.

Riktanya stepped away, portrait finished. Governess Kirsarm opened the door and reentered. She judged the piece in silence.

"It's... adequate," she noted. She took the portrait off the easel and replaced it with another canvas. "Now, another. This time draw The Matron in Her ceremonial Hibernal regalia."

Riktanya did.

Governor Butes was waiting for her at the top of the northeast tower, smacking a ruler against the palm of his hand. He glanced out the window, assessing the shadows strewn across the ground to check her arrival time as she sat down in her seat.

He walked to the chalkboard.

"Today, you'll be learning about the Reinhardt Rebellion," he spoke as he wrote, "their battle plans, tactics, then you'll come up with a campaign of your own to rectify the mistakes their opposition made. So make sure to pay close attention."

Riktanya gave a curt nod, signaling him to continue.

Lunch was chicken and gruel. Mother wasn't present for this meal. Riktanya still made sure to finish every bite, leaving only the bones behind.

She swapped her dress for a simple linen set and bound her feet in bandages before heading to the training grounds. Her siblings were already waiting, already standing at quiet attention like good soldiers, keeping their focus trained on the horizon.

"One on Ones," Captain Ayaz announced. "Izotz vs. Sarma, Fannar vs. Vetle, Barys vs. Fuyure, Riktanya vs. Bormir. Close Combat. Summon your weapons."

Riktanya ran her hands up her forearms, encasing from her knuckles up in spiked gauntlets of ice, while her opponent wasted his time crafting an intricate rapier.

"Take your positions," the captain called.

She took her place across from Bormir in the center of the field, while the others spread out to its corners. He wore an aggravating, smug sneer, trying to intimidate her with false confidence again.

"Begin."

Riktanya rushed forward, keeping herself subtly open for him to attack her midsection, as if she were thinking of merely running at him to get the first strike in rather than defending herself.

Bormir took the bait, striking at full force, hoping to carve her in half from her stomach to her liver. She dropped her left arm, causing him to shatter his own blade as it slammed against her gauntlet. She grabbed his wrist with her right arm and pivoted, using the momentum of her turn and the angle of balance from his blundered attack to wrench him over her shoulder and throw him to the ground with a sickening crack.

Riktanya jammed her foot into the crook of his neck and with one harsh tug popped his arm out of its socket.

"That's one match for Riktanya," Captain Ayaz called. "Bormir set your arm and resummon your weapon. Something stronger this time. You'll wield with your non-dominant hand when you go up against your next opponent."

She let go of his arm as if she were dropping trash into a chute.

"Spoiled bitch." She caught him whispering under his breath as she walked away to wait for the others' fights to finish.

She won every match, leaving blood, bruises, and broken bones in her wake as she left the battlefield to go and fulfill her Life Bearer duties.

Deep within the castle's dungeon, on the bottom floor, she filled her pitcher from the Rime Spring and made her rounds. She poured the water over her younger and punished siblings' wounds as they bore their chains or recovered from lashings, and trickled it into their mouths, holding their jaws open and guiding it down the throats of those who still had yet to learn their lesson.

She wiped the tears off the cheeks of the younger ones going through their first adjustments or first punishments, acting as if she were wiping off water she accidentally dribbled on their face.

The pets were next. The sounds of torture and pleasure, sobs and laughter, filled the halls in a discordant melody. She passed from room to room, skipping those that were occupied by fae, and filled their water bowls and baths. She tended the more severe wounds of those whose fae visitors had needed a more violent release, and watched them all for a moment to look for any odd behavior.

The group of adventurers who had boldly crossed into the Rime what felt like a year or so ago tended to hold her attention longer than the others. Sent from the mortal realm on a mission to take one of her siblings back, they had been fooled into sharing a meal with Mother, thinking they could negotiate with Her or at least strike some sort of deal.

Mother seldom made deals.

And now the adventurers acted like sheep grazing in a field, plodding across their cell floor, rubbing up and baaing at people's legs if they got close. They were Riktanya's first charms, and while Mother didn't necessarily care for them to behave as sheep, She seemed pleased by how well the charm had lasted.

Riktanya was... content with the result at least.

She sat on the floor of their cell for a while, losing herself for a moment watching them. They were so simple, barely any thoughts in their heads anymore. Perfectly happy to graze on the fields of grass they imagined they were roaming. Riktanya was the one to paint such a pretty image in their minds, but she did not know what it was actually like. The only fields she'd seen were in books.

Riktanya was pulled out of her trance by one of the "sheep" — a woman with long, flaxen hair and big brown eyes — chewing on her hair.

"Get off of me!" she shouted and shoved the woman away, knocking her onto the stone floor. Riktanya stood and hurriedly checked her appearance in the reflection of their bath water. The braid was completely disheveled, resembling more of a bird's nest than a crown.

"Stupid fucking sheep," she swore under her breath as she undid the braid quickly and tried to comb out the knots with her fingers.

She locked eyes with the 'sheep' the woman often 'grazed' with, a man with thick, rust-stained gray hair. "Control your mate," she snipped before leaving the cell in a huff, back up to her room.

She needed a proper mirror, and a proper comb to fix this mess before—

"Dear one? What happened to your hair?"

She stopped as Mother's hands rested on her shoulders.

"One of the pets mussed up my hair," she explained.

"Did you punish them for daring to touch you?"

"Of course," she lied.

"I can fix your hair, dear one." She stroked Her long, sharp nails through it. "It's been so long since I brushed it."

"Of course, Mother," she said. "I'd be honored to have You brush it."

She sat on a chair in Mother's room, gaze locked on the window, watching her siblings running drills in the snow banks below, punishments for losing so miserably against her.

"Your hair is getting long," Mother said as She raked Her fingernails along her scalp. "And it's getting lighter by the day." She pulled a strand free and ran Her fingers along it as if She were evaluating the quality of silk. "Soon it'll be just as white as Mine."

She let the strand drop. Her nails screeched across the marble of Her vanity as She picked up Her brush.

Riktanya gripped the bottom of the chair tightly.

The thin bristles, needles plucked from the hide of some poor fae creature, raked across her scalp. They snagged against each hair as She pulled the brush along, threatening to rip them from her scalp micrometer by micrometer.

"It's such a shame you scar so easily during your adjustments," She lamented. "But I'm sure Sloin will find a remedy soon. And if they don't, another alchemist is easy to find." Her grip on her hair tightened as She worked on a knot that wasn't there. "I want you to remember that, dear one. It's a weakness to hold on to things that serve no purpose."

"Yes, Mother."

"And We are not weak."

"We are not weak," Riktanya repeated.

Mother's brush stilled. Her fingers crawled along her scalp, pointed nails prodding the sensitive flesh. She paused and circled a spot. The strands wrapped around Her finger, and with a forceful yank She tore them out.

Blood filled Riktanya's mouth as she bit the inside of her cheek to keep from screaming.

Mother sighed and held the chunk of hair She pulled in front of Riktanya's face. Specks of blood dotted dark roots.

"Looks like you'll need another treatment."

"Perhaps it's just the blood discoloring it," Riktanya offered, as panic rose. "I've been washing it with the snow melt like you said and eating every single crumb of my meals!"

"Every single crumb," Mother drawled. "How interesting. Klakille!"

Mother's attendant entered the room with a platter covered by a silver cloche in hand.

"Every. Single. Crumb." Mother emphasized. Klakille removed the cloche to reveal a plate of bones, the cartilage and sinew that clung to them frozen over. "These are awfully big crumbs, don't you think?"

"But the others don't eat them!" Riktanya protested in vain, grasping at straws for whatever she could to keep in Mother's good graces.

Mother hooked Her finger under her chin, digging Her nail into the skin as She turned Riktanya's head to face Her. "The others aren't nearly as stubborn as you are. The others were not chosen."

Riktanya's body betrayed her, jolting her forward to run as a terrifying glint flickered in Her eyes. Mother pulled her back by her hair, throwing her to the floor, cracking her knees against the frozen rock.

"Treatment first, Klakille, then Riktanya will finish her crumbs," She said as She dragged her across the floor.

Riktanya kicked and screamed, grabbing at her hair to try and pull it free from Her iron grip.

△

Sebastian was rushed through a window, down a hall, surging closer, *closer*, to a girl's terrified screams.

Mina's terrified screams.

She was being dragged down a hall by her hair, as long and white as when he found her in the woods so many memories ago. He raced towards her, as desperate as the wind was to try and do something, anything, to free her from that woman's — the one she called 'mother's — grip. Her appearance shifted for the briefest moment, a flash of her older self, of the Mina he knew just as terrified as the younger one was.

Kicking and screaming as if she were dragged by her hair.

Or was trapped in the memory of her younger self.

They were close, so close, before Mina was dragged into a room and a door was slammed in his face. He expected the wind to rage against it, to blow the door off its hinges as her fear screamed at it to aid her. But instead, it set off down the halls once again, searching for what, Sebastian could not fathom.

He soared through the halls of a great palace of ice, past servants, guards, children, teens — rimefae of all ilk and ages — all strangely uniform in appearance: shades of pale ranging from white to blue, tall, and thin, and supernaturally gorgeous.

Siblings.

A shudder ran down his spine. So many similar faces, so many narrowed eyes and set scowls, save for one.

Hidden in the shadows of a doorway.

A human woman with long, flaxen hair, matted and greasy, and big brown eyes sunken into her sallow face watched through a door jamb's crack intently, clearly terrified and determined.

The hall was empty, though she couldn't see it from her limited vantage. The wind pushed Sebastian closer to her, and the woman backed up, afraid of where the gust had come from.

"Gentle," Sebastian thought, *"you're scaring her."*

The wind seemed to share his idea, as it curtailed itself into a gentle breeze. Sebastian got a better look at her now, how dirty her clothes were, the knees completely worn out of her pants, bony hands lumpy with calluses, body so gaunt the iron betrothal necklace she wore around her neck hung loose—

His own words echoed through his memory, "So it was given to you before you met the Harlowes, when you were just a kid."

Operating as one, he and the wind brushed against the woman's back, urging her gently, reassuringly, to leave the room. They needed to lead her to Mina. Needed her to give her that necklace.

Where the wind blew, Sebastian lent it his heat, drawing from the dwindling source fighting to keep the deep, determined cold of the Rime from freezing him totally. It was worth it, necessary. The woman trusted the warm breeze more in this frigid nightmare — judging by the patches of frostburn mottling her skin, she hadn't felt warmth in a long time. They guided her in and out of rooms, around corners, avoiding the castle's fae inhabitants, letting Mina's fear pull them towards her until—

Mina turned a corner, appearing in the same hall as the woman, blood trickling slowly from her scalp. The hollow look in her tear-swollen eyes barely registered the terrified woman, paralyzed and shaking, in front of her.

But then the sound of voices, of footsteps echoed from one of the halls, spurred her to action.

Mina grabbed the woman by the arm with incredible force, throwing her and them into a vacant room. She shut the door behind her, and threw a chair against it to keep it shut.

"What are you doing up here? Do you want to die?" Mina hissed.

"Please," the woman begged, dropping to her knees and clinging desperately to Mina's dress, "Please don't say anything."

"Y-you can t-talk?" What little color Mina had drained from her face. "O-okay. I can re-charm you. Make this all go away. Doesn't that sound nice? Y-you can go back to grazing a-and—"

"I was never charmed to begin with," the woman placed a hand against her necklace. "I simply played along. I couldn't leave them."

The footsteps and voices grew louder, and Mina pulled the woman back into a corner, covering her mouth with a trembling, bloodied hand. The air itself stilled as well, holding its breath as they did, waiting for the voices to pass into silence.

"I-I-I d-don't know how to get you out of here," Mina whispered as much to the woman as to herself.

"You're not going to kill me? Turn me over to them?"

"No... no... I don't want you dead. If they find you, even if I give you to them... it would only..." A distant, terrified look crossed her face. "I'll be punished for my mistake, you'll be tormented for it, and the others... they..."

Mina turned to her, "Can you run? How far? There's a ring about five miles east from here. I can't take you to it, but I can lessen the guards along the way. Y-you'll need to find a weapon to fend off the glacewraithes and hunt—"

"Five miles?"

Mina nodded.

The woman swallowed nervously, rubbing her thumb back and forth over the initials etched into her collar. "Can you get the others out?"

"No," Mina pleaded. "It's going to be hard enough to try and come up with an excuse for you breaking out, but all of them? She only let them stay as sheep because it was my first charm. If they tried to escape, if She learned that I tried to free them—" Tears gathered in her eyes. "You've been awake this whole time. You hear what they do. They'd make me do it. I-I don't want to do it."

A deep, conflicted sadness washed over the woman, her eyes glazing over as the hope of escape she held on to slowly died out. Sebastian's nerves twisted. This wasn't how the memory ended, was it? Had he guessed wrong? Had Mina not gotten the necklace from her? Had she—

"What if you left?" the woman asked, the last embers of hope igniting an idea behind her tired eyes.

Mina's eyes widened. "What?"

"You know what paths to take, are more able-bodied than I am, can fight if needed. You could cross over, gather a group, an army even." The woman unhooked the clasp of her necklace. "Take this necklace. It's iron and will protect you from the fae. If you go to the Capitol city of Yosorick and show it to—"

Mina backed away from her, expression twisted in horrified confusion. "Why would I do that?"

"You're not like the others. You don't want to be like them, right? You don't want to do the horrible stuff they do." The woman held the necklace out to her, hand trembling with desperation. "You could stop it. Stop them from hurting people. Stop them from hurting and changing the other children too. You could be with your real families again—"

"Real families? What do you— This is my family!" Mina insisted.

Sebastian and the woman's heart seemed to break at the same time.

"When was the last time that Mother of yours was with child? Or any of your family?" she asked, already knowing the answer. "The babies just arrive here, skin mottled and hair in shades unnatural to this land, correct? You know why my group came here."

Mina's focus darted back and forth between the woman's necklace and her pleading gaze, processing, realizing the weight behind the woman's questions.

"You could stop it. You could bring them all home," she placed a hand on Mina's knee. "You could be free."

Mina's appearance flickered between her younger self and older self as she stared at the outstretched necklace — as if they were fighting for control at that moment.

Her form settled, back into a young, scared girl, and backed away from the woman. "I can't."

"What?" The woman and Sebastian expressed in unison.

"I can't betray my family. I can't betray Her. I—" Mina moved to stand.

Panicked, Sebastian forced his will against the woman, hoping his efforts combined with the wind's would force her to stand, to stop her. Instead, he found himself slipping into the memory's shell, imparting his consciousness into her frail, battered form.

"Mina, stop!" Sebastian insisted, grabbing her arm. His voice, his body, was not his own, but the command that he spoke was. Her body froze against her will.

"What is this? Why can't I move?" She tried to pull her arm away, but the appendage did not budge.

"Mina, you have to take the necklace."

Her hand started to reach for the necklace slowly as she tried to fight against his command. "Is this some sort of spell? Why are you calling me 'Mina'?"

"Because that's the name you gave me. The name the Harlowes' gave you when they found you and read the letters off this collar."

"I don't— What are you— I don't know you! I never gave you that name!" she shouted.

The room began to shake.

"Not this woman, but you gave it to a wizard and his traveling group, remember?"

A rattling hiss echoed through the air, just as it had back in Recet's Den — just before the chains.

"Tanir, Enoch, Wera, Sebastian!" He shouted over the roar. The icy walls splintered and cracked. "You're not supposed to be here. You're supposed to be with them. You promised to be my partner, remember? Mina, you must remember! Take the necklace! Please!"

A thousand ribbons sprang out from his chest, wrapping around her wrist, across her breast, and pulled. Pulled her hand to grab the necklace, and pulled herself, her true self, out of the memory that imprisoned her.

The hissing, the destruction, stopped; hovering in stasis.

Mina's eyes widened, tears gathering in their corners.

"Sebastian?" she whispered.

The threads between them glowed like warm firelight.

"This isn't how I imagined you saying my name for the first time, but—" He laughed, his joy, his relief bubbling out. "I am so glad to hear it."

🜁

The veil of her memory faded. The frail, desperate woman morphed into Sebastian, still dressed in his tweed suit, looking relieved and exhausted. She took the necklace from him and threw it around her neck, then surged forward to embrace him.

It didn't hurt.

But it didn't feel exactly like him either. He was too cold. And trembling.

"You're shivering," she said and moved to pull away from him. He wrapped his arms around her and kept her close.

"I know. I thought finding you would get us out of here, but," a chill ran through him, "apparently not."

He let her pull away from him, but still kept hold of her hands. "Where is 'here', anyways?" she asked. "An illusion, one of those pocket planes like the commorancy, or?"

"I think it's your psyche. Something about the curse pulled us inside your mind."

Sebastian's lips were turning blue.

"I can't figure out why, though... or how to break it. I-if it wasn't the necklace, then maybe there's another memory we have to go to? I can't feel your wind anymore, but maybe you can summon it? It's driven by your want and your fears mainly, so maybe—"

Mina's stomach sank, a nagging, terrifying notion crossing her mind of ice spreading across his lapels, his skin, down his throat. If this was her psyche, what was her body doing?

They had been separated, she had been forced to relive the same path over and over again until she did it right, until she was perfect.

Until she was—

"She's trying to break me," she realized. "Trying to crush me into—"

Sebastian's ramblings quieted.

Mina looked down at the little girl beside her, eyes wide with fear — with hope too wanted to speak aloud. Though her hair was lighter and longer, legs shorter, shoulders slim, they still shared the same eyes, same nose, same scars. In the cold, harsh light of the Rime it was easy to see them, how much room they took on her little hands, raised and new. Mina looked down at her own hands, at the work time had done. The pattern was the same, but they were so much smaller now, smooth and slight.

Just memories now. Something to carry with her, not control her.

Not anymore.

"I won't let Her." Mina stood and helped Sebastian to his feet. Beneath them sat the memory. Her younger self and the woman, frozen in time. The necklace missing from the scene.

"What do you want to do?" he asked quietly.

"I want this to be over. I want to keep you safe." Mina took the necklace off.

She locked eyes with Sebastian as she held it over the woman's outstretched hand. "I want to show that bitch just how strong I am without Her."

She dropped the necklace and the memory shattered.

Mina held Sebastian as the chains seized them and ripped them through a void of white. Flashes of memories, of nightmares, of dreams, rushed past them, enmeshed in a web of thorned chains and amber threads. She held him as tight as she could. She wouldn't lose him. She would get him out of here, and back to reality. Back to his friends, and his inventions, and his fire, whatever the cost.

But try as she might, Sebastian was ripped from her arms as a set of long sharpened fingernails pierced through her stomach, like a spear-fisherman snagging their prey from a net.

"Not so fast, dear one," The Matron cooed, baring Her villiform teeth in a menacing smile. "Don't you know it's rude to interrupt?"

The Matron raised her high in the air, giving her a clear look behind Her massive form.

A clear look at her younger self, hair long and white, skin the deep blue of Winter's midnight, standing in front of a half-frozen Sebastian. The wind swirled around them, lashing his flesh and stealing his breath. Ice grew closer and closer to his heart with every stolen exhale.

"No!" Mina screamed. "What are you doing?!"

"What she is told!" The Matron flicked Her wrist, sloughing Mina off Her nails as if she were nothing more than a gnat She'd skewered. Mina tried to get to her feet, tried to run despite the pain, but was thrust back to the ground by a sharpened heel stabbing through her spine and pinning her down. "Protecting herself!"

The Matron grabbed her by her hair and wrenched her back, snapping a few vertebrae and filling Mina's vision with dark spots.

"Soon you'll join her. Eat his fucking heart and learn your lesson. How many times do I have to tell you to trust no one? Give your heart to no one? Look how weak he's made you. A mosquito puts up more of a fight!"

Mina did not care what She said. She knew all of it was horseshit, but there was still a part of her that had its doubts.

There was still a little girl too afraid to disobey her Mother.

Too afraid to take her only chance at freedom for fear of the disappointment and punishment that would follow.

"She's lying!" Mina shouted towards her counterpart. "You know that She's lying! He'd never hurt us!"

Riktanya did not move.

"Quiet!" The Matron ground Her heel into her back. Mina's hands shifted, contorting and twisting into gnarled gray-skinned claws — heatseeker claws — as her vision started to tunnel.

"But She is! She berated us, battered us, cursed us! She robbed us of so much, so many years without music, without color, without joy. Don't let Her rob us of love!"

Riktanya glanced back over her shoulder.

"I have love. Mother loves me. Love us."

"Is this what love looks like?!"

"Is he?" Her younger self turned around fully, eyes rimmed red, a tremor to her voice. The wind picked up around them. The ice spread. Mina's vision was nearly a pinprick now. The wings tore out of her snapped spine as her legs broke back into haunches.

She was scared.

They both were.

"I don't know!" she admitted, letting herself feel her terror, her worry, instead of running from it. "But I know we hadn't smiled until him! We never laughed so hard. Wanted to sing, to dance. We never had friends to share secrets with, to joke with, to encourage, to fight alongside."

The jealous comments whispered by her siblings. Watching them train, bond from high above. Bormir's blank, broken stare.

"Whatever love is, it's not loneliness. It's not cruelty and judgment and suffering to survive."

Cold, lonely meals, watched and unwatched. Winches and chains pulling apart her joints. Nails sinking into her scalp and dragging her down the hall.

"We don't know what it is, but we don't want to lose it."

Bright, cheery chatter, warming up snow-covered wastelands. Fighting an enemy, united as one. Sparks flying in Sebastian's eyes at their laugh. Cheers around the kitchen, boisterous and bolstering, elbows rubbing as they ate. Stitched-up clothes, and healing springs. Gentle hands tickling their scalp, while others warmed their face.

Relief, acceptance, smiles, safety.

Home.

In so little time. There had to be more for them to learn.

"Don't let Her take it from us before we have the chance to know it ourselves!"

"That's enough!" The Matron roared. She slammed the ball of Her foot into her skull.

Everything went black.

△

Endless hunger.

Ceaseless cold.

Relentless rage.

The heart she'd been chasing, been so close to tasting, was nothing more than a meager ember.

She surged towards it, screeching in anger as her wings beat with equal fury.

So close. So close. She could taste it on her tongue, feel its warmth slithering down to her gullet.

She was but a yard away — one lunge and her jaws would claim their prize — when a gust of wind billowed her wings, stilling her.

She thrashed against it — trying to break free, to divert and finally fill her aching stomach — when something grabbed her face. So tiny, so gentle.

"Foithe."

The wind rushed even faster. Across her cheeks, into her nose, her open jaws, her lungs, becoming her breath. It filled her empty stomach, brushed some of the chill off her skin. Her vision cleared as her anger subsided, revealing a face: her face, though years younger.

"I want to know it too," she said and dissolved into the wind, leaving Sebastian, still breathing, ice stalled, behind.

"How dare you!" The Matron screeched behind her. Chains raced through the air, but their fangs found no purchase, lashes bounced back by the cyclone surrounding them.

Mina placed her hand over Sebastian's heart to feel it beat against her palm. It was still strong. Still warm.

She stroked her thumb across his cheek. His weary eyes opened, lids heavy and slow.

"Mina?" he groaned. "Did you break it?"

"Almost, I think," she said. "But you can't be here for the next part."

"Why not? I want to help. I promised I would." He went to move, but Mina stopped him with a soft smile.

"You promised me you'd catch me if I fell, remember?" She stood on the tips of her toes and rested her forehead against his. "You will catch me, won't you?"

"Of course I will," he said. "Where am I going though?"

"Home."

He nodded, exhaustion clouding his mind. "Okay. I'll wait for you at home."

Her smile widened. "Sebastian?"

"Hmm?"

"I love you."

Mina kissed him gently, parting his lips and breathing life back into his lungs, fueling his flame until his heart burned beneath her hand. She released the wind's hold.

Sebastian vanished, leaving her, the wind, and her memories to face the bane of her existence alone.

Mina had never felt so powerful.

"You disgust me," The Matron hissed from across the void, twisting chains between Her fingers in a horrifying cat's cradle. "Look at what you've become. What happened to My dear one? What happened to My daughter!"

It was second nature for her to tense up at the sight of those chains rearing back, barbs glistening with the promise of agony. Ingrained in her very DNA, even. But the hands on her shoulders, wrinkled, one stained from working herbs into the soaps, the other calloused from years of scaling mountains, steadied her.

She didn't flinch as they cracked against her whirlwind.

"I was never Your daughter."

She took a step forward, leaving the Harlowes behind her, but found her sword resting in her hand; humming with excitement, eager to cut.

The Matron's eyes narrowed into slits. She curled Her hands into fists, piercing Herself with Her own nails. "How ungrateful." She pulled the chains back, reformed them into one massive whip, and swung it fast and furious. "Do you know what I did for you? What I've sacrificed for you?"

Crack.

"I fed you, clothed you, gave you a roof over your head!"

Crack.

"I taught you how to speak, how to write, how to lead!"

Crack.

"I taught you how to wield that sad excuse for a sword, and you dare to scorn Me?!"

Crack.

"After all the suffering I went through for you?!"

Crack.

The swirling wind diverted every blow as she walked closer, but it was wavering, knocked askew by the massive force.

Mina needed to get past them. She would get past them.

This was her psyche, after all.

"After everything I've done to make you strong!"

There was no crack, but a sizzle, as a wash of acid, woven through the air by the memory of its curly-haired master, turned the ice into harmless vapor.

"Nothing You did made me strong." Mina hissed, embracing her long-held anger. "You tried to make me weak, just like You."

The Matron lunged at her, faster than Mina's wind could ever carry her, nails pointed towards her heart.

"*Wolni!*" Tanir's voice echoed, followed by the hermit witch's cackle.

Mina stepped out of the way as The Matron slowed, and swung her sword at Her wrist, cutting the hand clean off. The appendage sprung to life on its own as She retreated, shrieking in pain, and leapt at Mina like a tarantula on a hunt.

A flock of daggers flew out of the ether to skewer it, clearing the path to her target.

Mina summoned the wind to her heels, just as she always had, and leapt higher than ever before, faster than ever before. Soaring without need for horrid leather wings, she drove her blade into The Matron's left eye, twisted it until the blue gushed out, mixed with black and white ichor, and ran down Her cheek.

A small price to pay for the tears She made her shed.

"I am not weak!" The Matron roared, swiping at Mina once again, only to sink Her nails into Her own cheek as Mina dodged out of the way, jumping up onto Her crown. She ran across Her scalp, dragging her sword along it, then grabbed one of Her braids and dived down to the ground. The wind followed in a downburst, pulling The Matron back and off Her feet.

The ground shook as She fell.

Mina stood over Her, one foot pinning Her to the ground, sword pointed at Her throat.

"Yet here You are, bested by a malformed disappointment."

She screamed and surged Her arms at Mina for one final strike.

Threads, thousands of brilliant amber threads spun from firelight, wrapped around them, blistering Her flesh and keeping Mina from harm.

"You're pathetic! Calling Me weak when you'd be nothing without them!" She spat.

"No," Mina leaned forward. "I'd be nothing with You. And it's a weakness to hold on to things that serve no purpose." She smiled as she lifted her sword above her head. "I hope You feel this all the way back in the Rime, You heartless bitch."

Mina drove her sword into Her throat, calling the wind down with her strike, and shattered Her into a million shards of ice. The chains wrapped around her memories — embedded in the expanse of her mind — shattered along with Her, tearing down the void.

Mina let herself fall with it, basking in the relief the darkness brought. She closed her eyes, listened to the wind rushing past her ears,

and smiled when she felt a familiar tug catch her heart.

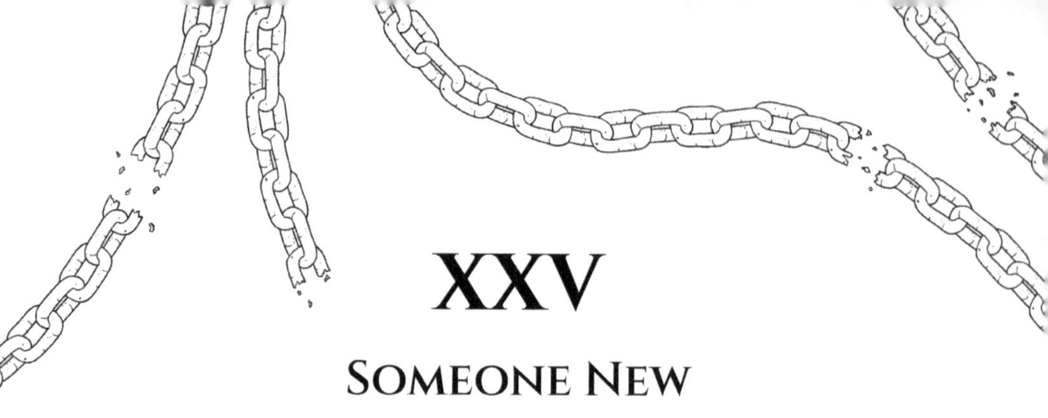

XXV

Someone New

Warmth.

A heavy warmth lay on her chest.

Mina reached a hand up to touch it, stroking its hair as she awoke.

The weight lifted immediately, just in time for her to open her eyes and see it.

"Sebastian?"

A thousand years' worth of worry lifted from his brow in an instant.

Mina had never seen a more beautiful sight.

Every shade of him. Every line. Every detail. There was such depth in his eyes, joy, relief, compassion.

And none of it hurt.

A rush of happiness washed over her, so much stronger than she had ever hoped to feel, overwhelming her and blurring her sight.

"What's wrong?" he asked, worry running back as quickly as it fled. "Are you hurt? I can go get Tani—"

"N-no," she half laughed, half sobbed. "I'm just too h-h-happy, I-I think." She tried her best to wipe her tears. "Is this what it's l-l-like all the time? I w-want to actually see the colors, not have them be all blurry."

"S-so i-it—" he stammered, accent thick, a shocked smile growing, "S-so y-you're?"

"Y-you did it, Wizard," she smiled so wide her cheeks trembled from the strain. "Another s-successful contract completed by Windenhofer Procurements."

Sebastian rushed forward and kissed her, tears of his own intermingling with hers. He stole the breath from her lungs and she was happy to give it — filled her heart with such warmth, she'd gladly let him burn it.

He pulled away from her a moment, foreheads pressing against each other, but lips too far apart for her liking.

"I love you, Mina." He whispered, giving a name to that unknown emotion that had alluded her in his gaze. "And I am sorry for every time I hurt you, for every stupidly worded command, for—"

Mina grabbed him by the collar and lifted herself up to kiss him, "I love you. I f-forgive you," she mumbled against his lips. "Now k-kiss me."

He cupped her cheek and kissed her lightly, chuckling against her lips. "There's my lila doar."

He obeyed her command eagerly, seizing her lips in his, remedying the folly of ever parting from them. Her dreams, her imaginings, paled in comparison to the real thing. To the warmth of his palm drying the tears from her cheek as he cradled it. To how the smell of him — light hints of lavender and cinnamon behind something new and intoxicating, robust and bright, blended beautifully together by a subtle bitterness — both cleansed and consumed her. His lips must have been what all those poets meant when they spoke of tenderness, of soft velvet, of devotement. She parted her own to taste him, brushing her tongue lightly across his bottom lip, and found a flavor more delicious than any she had before, tinted with sweet wine and something savory she could not uncover.

Sebastian's breath hitched at the action, and she felt his heart rate quicken against her knuckles.

His hand flexed against her cheek, tightening as his touch heated. The subtle action sparking embers through her veins and pooling warmth beyond her heart.

"Mina," he whispered, voice husky and layered with some enchanted emotion that conjured goosebumps on her arms.

"Gargic!" Wera's shout down the hall caused them both to still. "I'm sure everything is just fine!"

"Bull-fucking-shit, girlie!" the blowhard bellowed back. "It sounded like a goddamn tornado was about to tear the entire place apart!"

"But it's over now!" Enoch chimed in, "Everything's all calm and quiet—"

"Which means either both of them are dead or one of them is dead. Sorry to doubt Windenhofer, but I made sure to bring my iron falchion."

As his temperature spiked, Sebastian pulled away from her to keep from scalding her lips.

"I'm rethinking my stance on not killing him," Mina said.

"The contract didn't mention anything about breaking limbs," Sebastian noted, his frustration clipping each word. "I say we've got about fifteen seconds before they all burst in here."

Mina closed her eyes and listened to their footsteps and arguing. "More like seven. Lay down next to me," she said as she dropped her arms back on the ground beside her, twisted oddly.

"W-why?" he asked.

"So we can play dead, then scare him so hard he pisses his pants."

Sebastian's brows lifted in surprise as mischief glinted in his eyes.

"He said he has his iron sword, you know," he whispered as he laid down on his stomach and splayed out his limbs. "He could stab you."

"Good," she whispered back. "It'll give me an excuse to knock his teeth in."

They both closed their eyes and dropped their heads onto the ground at the click of the doorknob turning. The door creaked open slowly. Fabric shuffled as they all peered in.

"Maybe they left?" Tanir whispered.

Sir Gargic shushed her and stepped into the room. With her eyes closed, Mina could hear them moving through the space perfectly, picture them even. His breathing was heavy from the liquor, heartbeat fast from the fear of the unknown, as the others followed behind him. Wera and Enoch, then Tanir in the back. The sound bounced oddly off the room, though. Off untuned strings, unleveled tables, odd twists of metal, how terribly had the wind destroyed her music room?

"Shit," Sir Gargic hissed under his breath. To Mina's surprise, she heard him sheath his sword and rush over to them — no — *her.*

He was checking on her first?

Wrong move.

A rush of mischievous joy and anticipation made it hard for her to keep a smile off her face, but she channeled all her resolve, all her years of non-expression, to keep her cheeks still as his shadow crossed her face.

"Fuck," Wera swore, rushing over. "Tanir, are they?"

"I need a closer look."

As the others approached, Mina twitched her toes subtly in her shoe, conjuring the tiniest gust of wind to creep along the floor and brush against Sebastian's hand; once soft, the second with a touch more force, held the third until they all leaned over them, and then—

"Raaa!" she and Sebastian sprung to life in unison. The others jumped back and screamed, sending Sir Gargic tripping over his own feet and flipping into the belly of a broken drum.

"Sebastian Windenhofer!" Tanir scolded as the pair cackled on the floor. "What the hell has gotten into... you." Her sentence trailed off as Mina's laughter rang off the chimes and caved in cellos.

"I'll give you one guess," Sebastian said as he caught his breath.

"Holy shit," Enoch gasped from the top of the table he'd leapt onto. "You did it."

"You did it!" Wera cheered. She launched herself at Mina's back as she sat up, and pulled her into a crushing hug. "You're not cursed anymore!" She shook Mina back and forth in jubilation. "And you have such a pretty smile!"

"Th-an-ank yo-oo-ou," Mina's voice wavered as she was tossed about.

Wera stopped and gasped. "Did you hear that? She said thank you!" She looked back at Mina. "You said thank you!"

"I know." Mina pulled out of her embrace and turned around to face her. Her jaw went slack, eyes blew wide at the sight of her — the sight of them — how bright and complex they all were. Patterns in their clothing that had gone unnoticed, intricate colorings in their hair, their eyes. The blue of Tanir's eyes was quite unlike The Matron's in this new light, Enoch's hair and mustache a richer shade of black, Wera's glasses rimmed with a glistening metal Mina had never seen the shade of before.

Tears gathered in the corner of her eyes again. "You're all so colorful."

Their expressions warmed in unison, a wave of mudita driven by the tide of her own happiness.

"You're looking pretty colorful yourself, Meens," Enoch said.

She sniffled, the tears making her nose run for some reason. "I do?"

"Still as pale as fine porcelain, but there's a warmth to you now." He smiled. "Your cheeks are as just as rosy as your lips, like pink primrose blossoms breaking through the last snow of winter."

Mina touched her cheeks, and felt a little tinge of heat rise in them.

"It didn't feel like I was hugging a snowman when I grabbed you, either," Wera said. "Now it's like jumping in the ocean when it's warm out," she felt up Mina's forearm experimentally, "or grabbing a cool glass of lemonade."

"How do you lot know that isn't just some fae trick of hers, eh?" Sir Gargic grunted as he wormed his way out of the drum. "That this ain't some glamour she threw on to lure us into her trap?"

Mina's happiness vanished, turned to bitter anger and annoyance. She turned to Sir Gargic, the blotchy-skinned bastard looking even nastier in full color, and went to unleash a tirade of insults when Sebastian placed a hand on her shoulder.

"Mina," he said. "Cluck like a chicken."

She looked up at him, confused. "What?"

His focus — heated and threatening, barely holding back his temper — was solely on the knight.

"Mina, flap your arms in the air like a duck."

"What purpose does that serve?" she asked.

He looked down at her, arching an eyebrow and bending his mouth into an overdramatic, contemplative frown.

"So you're not following my commands?"

Her heart hammered in her chest at the realization. She smiled, and Sebastian smiled with her. A genuine smile that quickly turned cocky as he turned back to Sir Gargic. "We haven't made it to Lanholde quite yet, so that must mean... Could you go get her contract for me, actually? So I can make sure I've got the wording right? I believe this must mean that her curse is broken. But much to your point, Sir Gargic, we have to be sure."

Sir Gargic bristled, lips pursing and nostrils flaring in discomfort as he bitterly swallowed the reality in front of him.

"And by the way," she added with a snip, "I'm not a fucking f-fae."

"You're not?" Enoch and Wera said in unison.

Delight illuminated Tanir's face. "She's not?"

"She's not," Sebastian confirmed and moved to stand, "But we can talk about all of that downstairs. We all have a party to finish, don't we?"

He offered Mina his hand to help her stand, and she took it, happily.

Her smile faded quickly, however, at the sight of the shredded scores and mangled musical instruments decorating the room with disaster.

"And a music room to fix," Mina worried under her breath.

Sebastian squeezed her hand, sighing heavily. "Yes, but," he nodded to assure himself as much as her, "party first."

△

The halls of the commorancy were just as colorful as its inhabitants. The pictures, art, and articles that hung painted the walls with their vibrancy as much as the intricate wallpaper and their multicolored frames did. She let her eyes roam around the place freely, taking in every detail she missed, and caught a glimpse of the dress she wore as she glanced down to study the interwoven pattern of the wood floors.

"Wera?" Mina called.

"Yes?" Wera answered behind her.

"You said my dress is green?"

"Yes, it's green. Myrtle green, to be precise."

Mina ran her free hand across the bodice — Sebastian hadn't let go of her other hand after he helped her up, but she didn't mind it — admiring how smooth the fabric felt, how pretty it glistened in the light.

"What is it, lila doar?" he asked quietly.

"It's a very... The color it's..." the word danced on the tip of her tongue, clear as day in her mind, but her mouth hesitated to say it; fearful of well-known wounds.

"Pretty?" Sebastian suggested.

"More than that," she said. "B-beautiful."

He smiled, excitement bubbling in his cheeks. "You're going to love this then." Sebastian opened up the garden doors and Mina's breath abandoned her lungs, eager to frolic in the beauty in front of her.

"Now, that was the reaction I was hoping for during our tour," he remarked, "but better late than never I suppose."

Mina pulled her hand out of his and ran into the garden, collapsing onto her knees and running her hands through the grass. Had grass always been this soft and this vivid? On instinct, she kicked off her shoes, and relished in the feel of it beneath her bare heels before taking off in a sprint towards the trees. The wind pooled at her feet without needing to be asked, sensing her desire, and carried her beyond the limits of her leap to land in the boughs of an ash tree.

Its verdant leaves danced in the wind, scattering the light shining through them across its canopy like a thousand falling stars shooting across an evergreen sky.

She popped her head out of the leaves and looked at Sebastian.

"Is this because of your magic, or do all trees look l-like this?" she shouted.

"All trees look like that!" he shouted. "Well, not all. Some are different colors, different shapes..."

"And the grass? Is grass just as soft?"

He laughed. "Most of the time!"

Mina pursed her lips and kicked off the bough she stood on lightly, but the wind carried her across the garden to him with gale-force speed.

Sebastian didn't flinch at her sudden arrival, nor at the aftershock of wind that rushed against his face.

"What are you laughing at?" she asked.

"I'm imagining how you'll act when you see the woods by your cabin again," he admitted, "and the look on the squirrels' faces when they get knocked out of their nests by a wily windblown woman."

Excitement buzzed beneath her skin. "It'll be deep Autumn by then. You said the oak leaves turn the same color as your hair in Autumn."

"Nearly all the leaves change color in Autumn, save for evergreen trees," Wera commented as she approached them, carrying an overfilled plate in her hands. "Oranges, yellows, reds, browns, if you thought seeing all this for the first time," she gestured to her body and her richly patterned suit, "was a lot of color, then you're gonna lose your mind seeing those trees. Here." She handed the plate to Mina.

"What's this for?"

"I figured you'd want to try one of everything now that you can taste," she said. "Enoch's opening a couple bottles of cava. What's a party without eating and drinking while learning about just how the hell your boss broke one fucker of a curse?"

Mina's eyes roamed over the plate and her stomach rumbled in want, while her mind debated what to try first. A slice of bread, crusty and well baked, topped with cheese and a syrup of some sort drizzled on top caught her eye.

"Well," Sebastian said as they followed Wera over to the picnic blanket. "It wasn't me who broke the curse, exactly. That was Mina."

She hummed in surprise, delight, satisfaction as she bit into the toast.

"But," Enoch grunted as he wiggled the wine cork out, "true love's kiss?"

"A catalyst," Sebastian sat on the blanket, taking the plate Tanir offered him. Mina sat down in the space he left for her beside him. "It started the process but—"

"It was also exactly what She w-wanted," she said.

"She?" Sir Gargic grunted.

She swallowed down her toast. "The M-Matron."

The cork shot loose out of Enoch's hands with a loud pop.

"T-the Matron?" Enoch stammered, face blanched, as he fumbled to curtail the fizz bubbling out the top of the bottle. "Of *the Barren Rime?*" Wera took the bottle out of his trembling grasp and began to fill their glasses, mumbling under her breath about him wasting good booze.

"Ah," Mina said, through a mouthful of some sort of chewy meat wrapped in bacon. "You've heard of Her."

"Why didn't you mention her before, Enoch?" Sebastian asked. "It might have helped us figure out how to help Mina sooner."

Wera and Tanir laughed.

He looked between the both of them. "What?"

"Sebastian, dear, not even the gift of prophecy could have helped you figure it out sooner."

"I know that in the vision I was making out with Mina and her curse broke, but that doesn't necessarily mean that I'm the one to kiss her," Wera mocked as she handed Mina a glass of wine, deepening her voice in a decent imitation of Sebastian. "Or that I even have to kiss her! It could be a metaphorical kiss representing a deal being sealed or something! Prophecies are chock-full of symbolism like that."

Mina snickered at him. "That would be too obvious."

Sebastian blushed at their teasing and turned his focus to his drink.

"Let's get back on task, shall we?" Sir Gargic said, turning his disgruntled attention to Enoch. "This Matron. You know of her?"

"She is the very reason why you do not stray alone in the woods during Winter. The reason why on the Winter Solstice we throw festivals filled with fire and lights. Why it's poor luck to have a babe born in—" Enoch's eyes widened. "You're not fae. You're human."

Mina smiled sadly over her glass, pausing before she took her first sip. "Took you long enough."

Sir Gargic scoffed. "What human can catch a four-hundred-pound tree and punch through solid rock looking like that?"

"Well, Sir Gargic, there's a reason we're warned not to eat anything when crossing into the fae realm, or to stay for too long," Tanir said.

Sebastian's eyes narrowed. "You knew she was human, didn't you, Tani?"

Tanir smiled. "I didn't know for sure. It was hard to tell which symptoms were the curse and which were just Mina's nature. Plus, I've only seen the reverse of her situation once, back when I was a student."

"A changeling?" Enoch asked. "You've met an actual changeling?"

"Operated on an actual changeling, even," she added. "Poor man didn't even know he was one when he came to us after an unfortunate jousting accident. Iron didn't bother him, but his blood was black tinged with just the slightest hint of red, and his heart was on the right side of his chest instead of the left."

"So, my blood never turned," Mina said. "It was so dark, I always wondered if it had." The sweet wine that tickled her tongue turned all the more sweeter at the fact.

"Is that why she cursed ya?" Sir Gargic snapped. "'Cuz your blood wasn't dark enough?"

"Gargic," Sebastian warned.

Mina placed a hand on his knee, and locked eyes with Sir Gargic. "Because I escaped, h-hoping to get h-help and free the other children." She sneered. "Truly monstrous behavior, I know. I absolutely deserved it."

The anger and upset drained from his face for a moment, before turning back inward on himself. Sir Gargic hung his head and ran his thumb over the Royal Crest of Lanholde cast in the pommel of his iron falchion.

Mina pulled her hand away and took another sip to wash down the bitterness his witch-hunting brought to her tongue. The wine was wonderfully sweet and when paired with the bacon answered the question as to what she had tasted on Sebastian's lips.

Although, she much preferred it delivered on his kiss.

"Right, so, Mina's human. Sir Gargic's an ass. We'll unpack all of that later." Wera waved the tension off and finally sat down next to her. "How'd you break the curse?"

"I b-begged my younger self not to kill Sebastian, while an avatar of the M-Matron snapped my spine in half and turned me into a heatseeker to finish the job. B-begging worked — young me freed me of being a heatseeker, we merged — then after I freed Sebastian's life force I leveraged my psyche and wind to kick the M-matron's ass and sever the chains of Her curse," Mina answered.

The excitement on Wera's face fled it, expression going blank as she processed Mina's words.

"That's... a lot," she said after opening and closing her mouth a few times. "But hey, you can take your necklace off now, right?"

"No!" She and Sebastian exclaimed in unison.

Sebastian placed his hand on top of hers. "Someday. But not right now."

"Not until She's truly dead," Mina added.

"So, is that what's next?" Tanir asked. "After Lanholde. We've already got the cold weather clothes."

"I—" A myriad of emotions rushed through her. Her stomach twisted, skin crawled, throat went dry at the thought of them braving the Rime. At the memories of all those adventuring parties. Of her sheep. Of more children suffering as she had. "I don't know."

Sebastian intertwined his fingers with hers, the warmth of his palm pulling her away from the lingering chill of that harsh frost. "You don't have to. Not right now. Not after the intensity of the past— How long were we away?"

"Only a half an hour," Wera said.

"That was... all in half an hour," Sebastian's focus went distant. His journey into her psyche must have taken a toll on him more than she knew.

She squeezed his hand to bring him back, and smiled at him when he turned to her.

Grateful.

The spark flickered back in his eyes and he smiled back.

"A toast, then," Enoch announced and held up his wine glass. "To the new Mina. Free to do and feel as she wants, when she wants."

They all, even Sir Gargic, lifted their glasses.

"Cheers!"

🜁

Her mattress was so unbelievably soft, it had brought tears to her eyes.

Her first warm bath made her muscles so relaxed, she feared her bones would slip right out.

Even the rush of surviving the loop, of saving Sebastian, of discovering how vivid the world truly was, had faded, leaving her quiet and her eyes heavy-lidded as their party ended.

But still, Mina could not sleep.

It felt wrong to sleep alone in her room, surrounded by rich wood and plush bedding and patterned wallpaper. Foreign even. Not that she did not know the room or find comfort in it, but — the forest was her home. To spend her first night free under a ceiling instead of stars didn't sit right.

But she didn't wish to part with her comforter either.

So she wrapped herself in it and slipped out into the hall, walking gingerly across the floorboards, mind buzzing, wondering how good the soft grass of the garden would feel against her bare back.

Though, as she rounded the corner towards the staircase, she found a set of soft, rolled footsteps that could not sleep either.

They both stilled at the sight of each other, the air quiet and heavy between them as they quickly studied each other's state. Mina had never seen Sebastian in his night clothes, just a simple robe — thrown on more for modesty than warmth — and his undershorts, his hair slightly mussed from his pillow. It tickled her heart and warmed her chest...

She really needed to take Enoch up on the sense and emotion lessons he offered.

They smiled at each other in tandem, and with a slight jerk of Sebastian's head, made their way down the staircase side by side.

"What are you doing up?" he whispered. "I expected you to be deep in dreamland with how much you were yawning while we cleaned up the decorations."

"So did I but," she shrugged, "it f-felt wrong to sleep in the room."

His brow furrowed in concern. "Is there something wrong with your mattress? Too firm? Too soft? Is the room itself too warm? I can adjust some—"

"Can you make it sprout trees and a sky?" she joked.

Sebastian tapped his lips, reading her jest as an actual request. "I mean, if you give me some time, I'm sure I could."

"I'm joking. The room is perfectly f-fine," she said. "It just f-feels like I should be sleeping in the forest my first night l-like this. I'd prefer it to be my forest, of course, but the garden should do."

"Ah. I see." He smiled. "Going to sleep in the lavender again?"

"Beside it, maybe." A small flicker of sadness, of *missing*, tugged at her. "The Harlowes would often sleep under the stars on warm nights."

Sebastian hummed in acknowledgment.

"What about you?" she asked. "You seemed p-pretty tired yourself. Almost fell asleep carrying that gramophone back to the Junk Room."

"I couldn't sleep either," he said. "Body is plenty tired, but my mind keeps running laps. Figured a glass of warm milk may help calm it down."

"Warm milk calms the mind?"

"It can."

The silence returned as they reached the bottom floor. The notion of Sebastian parting ways with her as they approached the kitchen bothered her. Felt wrong, just like sleeping under a ceiling.

"Lavender does too, right?" she asked.

They stopped just outside the kitchen door.

"It does," he answered.

His gaze rested on her face, eager to hear what she had to say next, but patient enough to wait as long as she needed. Though from how still his breath was, Mina imagined she better spit it out quickly lest he ran out of air.

"There's plenty of room by the lavender for the two of us," she said.

Sebastian swallowed instead of breathing. "I don't have a blanket."

"We can s-share." Her heart hammered in her chest, beating out her breath now too.

"You're sure?"

"I wouldn't have suggested it if I wasn't."

He breathed again, and smiled.

Mina exhaled with him.

He grabbed the hand peeking out of the bottom of her comforter. "I would love that."

They made their way to the garden in silence: a comfortable, exciting silence just as warm as his palms and the comforter wrapped around her.

The garden contained just as much wonder at night as it did during its day. The false sky now dark and twinkling with stars, some constellations familiar, others not. A sky of a place she had yet to visit. Specks of amber light, paler than embers, floated in the air, flickering on and off: fireflies. The foliage and flowers were richer in color, her nocturnal vision picking up the fine details where the darkness would normally blur them.

"You said you built this based on a memory," she said, staring up at the sky as Sebastian found a level patch of grass to sit down on. "Of where?"

"A garden I played in for a summer as a child," he said, voice warm with fond remembrance. "Not terribly far from your cabin, actually. One of the families that adopted me had a summer home in Torren."

"This was their garden?"

He chuckled. "No. They lived in a townhome securely in the city. A brief walk to the beach, but far from the woods. This belonged to an apothecary's family that lived on the outskirts."

"I see," Mina slipped her comforter off her shoulders, preparing to drape it over them before she sat. "I've never seen Torren at night."

"M-mina!" Sebastian exclaimed suddenly, 'm's and 'i's humming with a Yosik edge. She whipped around to face him and found his hand covering his eyes.

"What is it?!" she asked, worried and confused.

"Where are your clothes?!"

"Oh. I um—" Mina's cheeks burned. She pulled the blanket back up to cover her. "I've told you that I sleep naked before, didn't I?"

Sebastian shifted uncomfortably, crossing his legs as a flush spread down from his face to his chest. "Y-you did. I-I-I just wasn't expecting you'd be walking around—"

"W-well, wearing a gown to bed felt stupid and— and— and— my normal clothes aren't exactly comfortable to wear to bed anymore—" She hadn't borne any mind to her being naked. She figured she'd be up before anyone else was anyway, and it would only take a few seconds to race back up to her room then. But being naked with Sebastian.

Being naked alone with Sebastian.

"I'll go grab a nightgown or something out of the Junk Room," she said, even though the rising fever in her body told her she'd be much too warm wearing it.

"N-no!" Sebastian grabbed the edge of her comforter before she could take off running. He uncovered his eyes, focusing far too intently on keeping his gaze locked on her face. "If you're more comfortable that way, I don't mind."

Mina arched an eyebrow as she studied his incredibly tense and flustered state. "It seems l-like you mind."

He inhaled sharply. "I mean, I do. But not in a bad way." He laughed awkwardly. "I swear, I'm not such a mess when it comes to seeing naked women normally."

"It's normal for you to see a lot of naked women, then?"

A cartoonish level of panic contorted his expression. "No! It's just that I'm more prepared when it does happen. The very, *very*, few times it has happened."

"You're sure?" she asked.

His panic started to subside. "I'm very sure."

"Because if you're just saying that to appease me, I'd r-rather—"

"Mina, I want to see you," he cut her off. The nerves left his voice all at once. The admission steadying him.

It calmed her as well, leaving only the fever. A warmth building under his steady watch.

She loosened the comforter around her shoulders, allowing him to pull it off and into his lap.

His gaze drifted over her, considering her, embers flickering as he trailed across the slope of her neck, the rise of her breasts, down the curve of her hips, the length of her thighs, to the tips of her toes.

She felt as though she were standing on a singular needle, waiting to see if it would pierce or snap.

She'd never been one to care what people thought of her looks. She had been raised to be pretty, suffered to be formed into something beautiful to the eyes of someone other than herself. The parts about herself she liked were those that had broken from that mold. Her dark hair kept short by her own decision. Her nose, more button and lifted than her siblings, the bridge just slightly wider from a few bad breaks that her body couldn't heal back into a more narrow shape. The calluses on her hands and feet, knees and elbows. The dips of well-worked muscles. The new warmth that colored her now, even though she was still getting used to seeing the faint kiss of tan on her skin and the inviting pink of her lips, and cheeks, and nipples.

Would he like them just as much as she did? Or would he—

"I am the luckiest person in all the realms," he said as he returned to her face, gaze filled with such warmth, such awe and love, Mina thought she would melt.

"No," Mina said, an awestruck smile on her lips. "I am."

He arched an eyebrow playfully. "Are you sure? You haven't seen me naked yet."

"Oh, I'm quite sure," she said as she lay down in the grass beside him. He spread the comforter over them both and laid back as well. "And I have seen you naked. Though you were nearly frozen and completely unconscious."

His hand stilled as he threaded his fingers through hers. "I forgot about that." He turned his focus to the stars above them. "How did I— um— measure up?"

Mina turned onto her side to face him, cupping his cheek and tilting his head to look at her. "Honestly, I was too worried about saving you to pay close attention." She ran her hand down the side of his face, over the soft skin of his neck, to tug lightly at the collar of his robe. "I'd need another look before I could judge."

Sebastian swallowed. "Well," he said breathlessly. "It's only fair." He moved to stand and Mina held him in place.

"There's no need for all that." She eased the robe off his shoulder, taking care to brush her thumb across his skin. "I'd much prefer to look up close."

"Alright then." He slid his arm out of the sleeve and laid down on his back, nodding nervously. "I have nothing to hide."

"Really?" Mina straddled him. "No tattoos or battle scars?" She pulled down his other sleeve, admiring the width of his shoulders.

"Tattoos no. Battle scars? Plenty," he said, nerves fading at the sight of her on top of him. "But I'm not ashamed of them." His hands drifted up her thighs, following a pattern only discerning eyes could see. "Are you ashamed of yours?"

"No," she answered. "But I do wish they weren't there."

Sebastian hummed sadly. "If I could take them from you, I would."

"You may have." She ran her hands down his chest, brushing her fingers through his soft patch of chest hair. "Perhaps they'll fade now that the curse is broken."

"Perhaps. Perhaps not," he said. "Either way, I'll love you just the same."

Mina's hands stilled. His heart was a bit fast, but beat strong and true.

"You will?" she asked, already knowing the answer from the way he looked at her.

The way he had always looked at her, long before either of them knew why.

"I will," he answered, even though he had no need to.

"And I'll love you as well," she said. Her hands resumed their journey down his torso. "Even though you don't have any tattoos."

He chuckled. "Were you hoping that I did?"

"No. But it seems to be a popular appearance trait in the books I've read."

"Ah."

She trailed her hands down the planes of his stomach, admiring the muscle he had built. Carved around the edges from the effort of the climb, but built up more for function. A strong core forged from his adventures, from navigating the ruins of ancient temples and taming beasts beyond his measure. She followed the path of amber hair that led beneath his cloth shorts.

His muscles rippled at her gentle touch as she untied their drawstring, goosebumps raising across his skin. She hooked her fingers under the waistband and Sebastian lifted his hips a bit, granting her permission to pull them down.

Mina kept her focus on the garment so as not to get distracted by what lay beneath it before she removed it completely. A true exercise in restraint as she passed over his well-shaped thighs and sculpted caves. She guided his feet out carefully, grabbing one ankle at a time, finding even his heels artisan-crafted.

She brought her gaze to him then, unable to resist for a moment longer as soon as the fabric left her fingertips, and found a masterpiece before her eyes.

Her hands wandered up his legs of their own volition, though her mind was not bothered by the detour. Her fingertips danced across the scars she found, some just surface level, painted in a different color of flesh. While others were deep, sewn together with glistening scar tissue. One in particular caught her eye, long and jagged and much too close to the veins that ran along the soft inside of his thigh.

She kissed it, driven by the gratitude that whatever had wounded him had not cut any deeper and stolen his life.

Sebastian shuddered, shaking a needy groan out of his throat. It stoked her fever hotter, sending her imagination reeling with what other sounds of his she could draw out.

At last, she faced the glory between his legs. His cock, a thing of beauty as it lay heavy and hard against his stomach. His balls, quite shapely and full. It was more gorgeous than any diagram she'd seen, than every adventurer she'd caught pissing in the wind during her expeditions. A fine length and fine girth, not a foot long and forearm thick like her stories often gave their leads, but a well-crafted tool. A magnificent sword, expertly forged to meet its wielder's needs and wreathed in an abundance of amber curls at the hilt.

"Well?" Sebastian said, bringing her attention to his flushed face as he propped himself up on his elbows.

She smiled. "It appears I was right." She crawled up to meet him and kissed him sweetly on the lips. "I am the l-luckiest person in all the realms."

He kissed her back, a smile on his lips. "How about we're the two luckiest people in the realms, then? Sound like a deal?"

"You should be careful who you make deals with, 'Bastian," she teased.

Sebastian chuckled as he cupped the side of her face in his hand. "I could say the same to you, lila doar." He gripped the back of her head as he kissed her deeply. A firm hold as he flipped them over, pinning her underneath him. "Made too many deals, and you wound up falling in love with the stupidest and most obnoxious man you have ever met in your entire life."

She opened her mouth to protest, but he occupied her lips instead. The hunger in his kiss fed the flames of her fever, her desire, as his hand snaked up her side. Mina's breathing hitched, a slight gasp leaving her lips at the jolt of pleasure his palm rushed through her.

"Please stop me if I hurt you," he muttered as he peppered soft kisses along her jaw. "I can usually control my fire, but with you I—"

"I can take it," the words rushed out of her. "I've waited for too long to feel the heat of your hands."

"Fuck," he hissed before he kissed her greedily, taking her bottom lip and suckling at it lightly.

A heady moan, bright and needy, left her as his hand cupped her breast, thumb brushing over her nipple tentatively to see how she'd react. She knotted her fingers in his hair and pressed her hand into the small of his back, desperate for more contact as her hips bucked against air.

Sebastian fulfilled her unspoken request, lowering himself against her more fully, placing a thigh between her legs. He pinched the sensitive bud between his molten fingertips, shooting sparks across her breast, down her spine to fuel the growing furnace at her core desperately wishing for release.

Her mouth fell open in a wanton gasp, delighting in the fraction of relief his thigh gave her as she ground against it. Sebastian seized the opportunity, stroking his tongue against hers, overwhelming her senses with his taste. Wine and honey, brie and bacon, his natural sweetness tinted with the lingering heat of peppers. A finer meal she could not ask for.

"You taste," she panted as their lips parted momentarily for air, "so good."

Sebastian chuckled. "I was about to say the same, but—" he pressed a kiss against her temple and whispered in her ear, "I haven't truly tasted you yet."

The words alone nearly set her aflame. A shudder and whimper ran through her like the hiss and pop of kindling as his lips — hot coals of their own — scalded down her neck. He journeyed down, nipping, sucking, savoring every bit of skin he passed until his mouth found respite at her breast.

Mina went to roll her hips again, but was forced to still by a smoldering palm. She looked down to Sebastian for an explanation but swallowed the whiny protest on her lips. Her stomach coiled, walls clenched at the look in his eyes. A glare of warning, which no smart soul would dare to challenge. Protective. Possessive. Promising. She'd seen him give such a look only twice before, to those who dared to try and take her away from him.

His eyes did not leave hers as his lips traveled across a valley of skin to claim her other breast — free hand snaking up her side and settling on the other so as not to leave it unattended. Unguarded.

His thigh had been but a curtsy, a test to see just how badly she wanted him. Needed him.

Her pleasure would be his to claim tonight.

She nodded shakily, acknowledging his demand of her, as every swirl of his tongue and twist of her nipple had her body trembling. He closed his eyes and gave a deep, throaty hum as she combed her nails across his shoulder blades and up his neck to nest in his hair. She scratched at his scalp, encouraging him, tugging at his roots every time his teeth grazed across the increasingly sensitive buds. He bled color into them, leaving them puffy and vibrant pink once he was satisfied.

He resumed his pilgrimage. Each kiss he placed down her stomach a test of her resolve. Her cunt wept for his attention, throbbing every time his lips met flesh. Just one more from where she needed him most, he took a detour towards her thighs.

"Sebastian," she whined.

He stifled a groan against her skin, hands gripping her tightly. She gasped at their heat, close to searing against the sensitive skin of her thighs, but did not dare pull away. The slight sting only made her want him more, need him more, knowing that it was a sign of how badly he needed her too.

At her call, he ceased his wandering, licking a long stripe up her slit. Her vision swam at the sensation, a broken moan she barely recognized as her own falling from her lips as her back arched in delight.

He slipped his tongue inside her, leaving no spot untended until he found one just at the top of her entrance that had her hands threatening to tear out his hair. Mina writhed against him as much as his hold would allow her as his relentless tongue devoured. Magma roiled beneath her skin, pooling lower, lower, pressure building as her cunt clenched around him, trying to pull him in deeper.

Her thighs quivered, muscles shaking in warning,

"B-B-Bas-t-tian," she whimpered, breath too stolen to make her plead any louder than a whisper.

Still, he heard her desperate prayer, and rubbed his thumb in circles against her aching clit.

Mina erupted.

Sparks filled her vision as she cried out. Waves of wildfire rushed through her as her body writhed in delight at its warmth. Every inch of her being was pulsing, buzzing, vibrating with life that lingered as her mind cleared, and her breath returned to her chest, leaving her only wanting more.

"Welcome back," Sebastian greeted her as her vision unblurred, meeting his gaze with newfound focus.

She untangled her fingers from his hair and caressed the side of his face. Two fingers beneath his chin was all it took to lead his lips back to hers. She relished in the taste of herself on his tongue, a savory reminder that he was hers.

He whimpered as his cock brushed against her folds. She smiled at the sound.

She wrapped her legs around his hips, pressing her heels lightly against the small of his back, and scratched nails up and down his spine in time with soft, measured thrusts, until the tip of his cock caught perfectly against her entrance.

He closed his eyes for a moment as a shudder ran through him, then steeled his focus, locking his gaze — burning with determination — with hers as he slipped inside her.

He stole her breath away yet again as her walls stretched to hold him, but her eyes did not leave his. Though his countenance was resolute — watching intently for every flutter of her eyelashes, every rise of her chest, every shift and shiver of her body as he brushed over points of pleasure she never knew she had — the shake in his quiet exhale and the small quiver in his bottom lip revealed his restraint.

And as at last he filled her, fully enveloped to his hilt, Mina pressed her lips against his and whispered, "For so long I have had so much withheld." She shifted her hips forward, angling him deeper as her walls clenched around him, pleading for him to move. "Do not hold yourself back from me now."

Sebastian kissed her, bruising, possessing, forcing her head back onto the grass as his first thrust sent her keening. He consumed her every whimper, every moan, returning a glorious chorus of his own. Each thrust the strike of a matchstick, fueling the lingering embers within her, scattering their sparks to cloud her vision and dance across her skin.

Her body demanded more of him without her urging, closing around him with every sweet withdrawal, coaxing him deeper with every plunge. The world around her fell apart as he answered it, lifting her leg on top of his shoulder to attend to parts woefully untouched. He buried his face against her neck. Panting, biting in desperation, hands clawing into the ground as she sang wordless praises and dug her nails into his back.

Her body was his body, one great being rejoicing in reunion. A wildfire, all-consuming, immolating their mortal forms and carrying their consciousness away on howling winds. They succumbed to the flames together, writhing in ecstasy, burning, burning until they were nothing more than ash.

Mina returned to herself as Sebastian spilled that last of himself inside her. A calmer, blissful warmth filling her body as if she were as light as a summer breeze. She ran her hand across the wide plains of his shoulders, summoning small, cool gusts to dance around her fingertips, unconsciously soothing the crimson scratches she had left behind.

"Feels good," Sebastian mumbled into her neck.

She hummed dreamily and nuzzled her head against his, enjoying the feel of his breath against her tender skin.

Their chests rose and fell together, heartbeats slowing in unison.

"Is it always l-like that?" she asked once she remembered how to speak.

Sebastian exhaled loudly, laughing in disbelief as he did.

"No, that was—" he wrapped his arms around her, untangling his fingers from the earth, "that was extraordinary."

He hugged her tightly, then lifted himself off her. His eyes scanned across her, a subtle pout tugging at his bottom lip. Gently he ran his fingers down the side of her neck, down to her breast.

"Shit. I marked you up pretty badly," he said with a shake in his voice. "Burned you."

Mina grabbed his hand and brought it to her lips, pressing a kiss into his palm. "They'll heal." She looked down at herself, pale flesh adorned with beautiful blooms of reds. "I love seeing your handprints on my thighs."

"My—" Sebastian looked down lower. His eyes widened, breath turning shallow as he sat back and pulled her left leg into his lap. He traced the outline of the swollen prints with his fingertips, spellbound.

Mina chuckled as his softened cock twitched.

He swallowed harshly and tore his gaze away from it.

"We have to sleep," he said to her, trying to convince himself.

"Tanir does have that tincture," she teased, wiggling her hips slightly.

His nostrils flared as he resisted the urge to look down at them.

"We have to hike miles, Mina. *Miles.* You remember what husks Wera and Enoch were, don't you?"

"We don't *have* to hike miles, remember?" She sat up, closing the distance between them, and scratched lightly at his chest hair. "I'm pulling you lot the rest of the way to meet Gargic's new deadline. I'll make sure to pick the smoothest path, too, so you can sleep on the way."

"What about you, then?"

She trailed her fingers lower. "You know I have excellent stamina."

"Mina," he warned as he grabbed her wandering hand, voice deepening in a way that made the residual warmth on her skin drift feverish yet again.

She leaned forward, brushing her nose against his, lips hovering just an inch away. "Sebastian."

He let out a frustrated groan and stood.

"Where are you going?" she called after him as he stomped away like a child denied sweets.

"I'm getting that damned comforter of yours, and we're going to bed!" he barked back. Mina sat back, admiring the marvelous view of his ass as he pulled the poor discarded comforter from a nearby tree her wind deposited it in.

"You know, the view you're giving me right now isn't making me any more tired."

"Yeah, well, you and me both," he huffed as he walked back. "Which is why you need to cover up—" Sebastian threw the blanket on top of her. Before she could throw it off her, an arm wrapped around her shoulders, yanking her down to lay against his chest. "—and settle in."

Mina popped her head out from under the blanket. "'Bastian, I—"

Sebastian pressed his thumb against her lips, caressing her jaw gently as he kissed her forehead.

"I know you can do it, but I don't want your first full day curse-free to be spent too exhausted to enjoy it." He rolled his eyes. "It's bad enough Gargic's ridiculous request has got you acting like some sort of workhorse."

"True," she mumbled against his thumb, prompting him to remove it. "But the faster I get us there, the faster we can fulfill our contracts and leave these fucking mountains."

"We, huh?" He smiled softly. "You know, you left before giving me an answer earlier."

"An answer?" Mina cocked her head in confusion. "To what?"

"To if you want to keep traveling with me or not."

A different kind of warmth filled her chest.

"Hmm," she feigned contemplation. "My answer depends on where you're going next, then."

"I was thinking a trip to the forest, perhaps to see the autumn leaves," he said. "There's one nearby that I know of that has the most darling little cabin by a lake. I could build us a fire, we could sleep under some real stars."

Mina closed her eyes and pictured it, giving way to the growing heaviness of her eyelids. The warmth of the comforter and Sebastian formed a sort of sleep spell of their own.

"I'd love that," she hummed, shifting to nestle herself deeper into the crook of his arm.

"And I love you."

"I love you too," she mumbled as his adoration sang in her ears like a lullaby. "G-good night."

"Good night, lila doar."

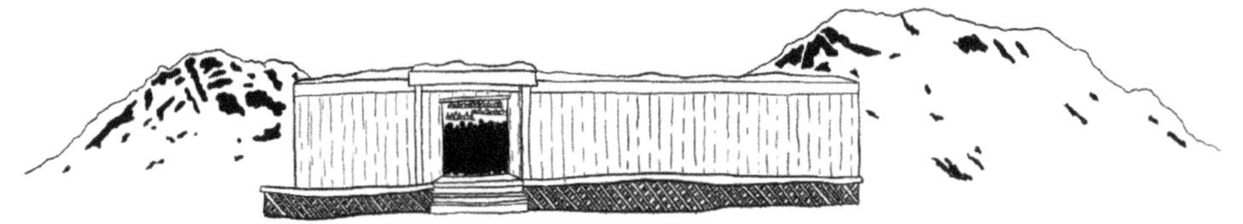

XXVI

Everyday Joys

"You're sure this is gonna work?" Sir Gargic doubted as he tightened the chinstrap on his helmet.

"That depends." Mina adjusted her harness. "Are you gonna be a good boy and do as I say?"

The old knight's nostrils flared, blowing out thick clouds of vapor in the cold air like an ornery wyrm. "I don't think doing what you say will really fucking matter if your plan is half fucking baked, lass."

Mina snickered a sneering smile at him, a new expression to her face that took no effort to conjure up in Gargic's infuriating presence. Behind the mask of her curse, she might have been making it every time he spoke, in fact. It felt as though she had had a lot of practice in it.

"The path to Recet's Den. Big ol' snake trail that it was? There's tons of them all over this place. The paths are decently defined, ice is well-worn, and there's a few that run pretty damn close to the border wall that Recet would use to pick off unsuspecting scouts and greener caravans," she explained. "On normal expeditions, I tend to steer the group to one of the paths just for ease of travel, and if they've brought skis it makes for quick work. Today though?" Mina thumped her fist against the enclosed sleigh she managed to fish out of the Junk Room. "Today's gonna be my best time yet."

"Best time yet that still lets Wera map out the place properly, please," Wera insisted.

"You mean you can't draw in seventy-five-mile-per-hour winds?" Mina quipped.

"Don't know," she shrugged. "Don't want to find out, either."

"Alright then," Mina tugged at the ropes attaching her to the sleigh's hitch as she turned around. "Sixty-five it is, then," she muttered to herself.

"What was that?" Wera asked.

"Everybody strapped in?" she called.

"All clear, Mina," Sebastian answered.

She closed her eyes and listened. To the sound of their breathing, of their lungs turning heavy cold air into life. To their heartbeats, all racing save for one calmed by trust. The wind drummed their rhythm across her skin as it lay in eager wait for her to call upon it. It pushed at her heels, urging her to run, to bask in the freedom it owed her.

Like a mighty beast awakening from its slumber, the wind roared as she took her first step, announcing its arrival in the tundra, daring anyone foolish enough to stand in its way. Mina cried out along with it, joy overflowing from the rush.

Without the weight of her companions to keep her grounded, she could become the very gale itself. A thing of unbridled beauty and drive that could reshape the world with just a simple touch. Carve monuments out of mountains, turn land into sea, recolor the sky, journey far beyond the cold to parts unknown, then run right back home again before the sun could even think to set.

The wind's rush deafened their heartbeats, but they had to be pumping just as fast as her own. She could not turn back to look at their faces but could picture them clearly, some as pale as the snowbanks blurring by, while others were as bright as the brilliant sun-soaked sky above. The trail curved and dipped, building their momentum in some parts, sending them soaring through the air in others.

They glided across a frozen lake hundreds of acres wide in mere minutes, yet she didn't tire. She could have kept running forever, kept running until the moon rose, just to see if the wind felt different in her hair beneath the night sky.

But.

A sharp whistle pierced through the triumphant roars, signaling her to slow. Had four hours truly passed already? It felt as though it had only been one.

Mina tapered her steps, zigzagging back and forth gradually to help shake off the sleigh's momentum and drag it to a natural stop.

"That went quicker than I thought it would," she said as she turned around to face them. "I could keep running right now if the rest of you are—"

Sir Gargic retched over the side of the sleigh.

"—alright."

Sebastian's breathing was ragged, but his complexion was a lot better off than his companions. He shot her a wobbly smile.

"I could have gone faster," she admitted.

"I know," he exhaled. "Appreciate you curtailing yourself. Sounded like you were h-having—" he swallowed heavily.

"F-fun?" Mina offered.

"Mhmm." He nodded.

"Are you going to vomit too?"

He inhaled sharply through his nostrils. "No. No. Just uh. Think we all need a moment of stillness before we pick up again—"

"Please not again," Enoch groaned from somewhere, hidden at the bottom of the sled.

Mina looked at Tanir as she kept an unnerving, glassy-eyed stare on the horizon.

"Perhaps a group sleep spell for the next league?" Mina suggested. "That way I can go even faster, and you all won't be so unmoored. I'll h-help you draw the maps for it later tonight, Wera?"

She shot a heavy-lidded glare at her. "I said I didn't want to find out."

"I kept it under seventy-five," she replied. "On average."

Wera tugged on Tanir's coat. "Tani... please..."

Out poured the poor medic's breakfast.

△

As Sebastian went to check on his potions, they collected themselves over a light lunch, save for Mina who, ravenous from the running, eagerly explored all the new tastes she could get her hands on.

"Good Gods," Sir Gargic admonished from across the table, beard drooping in disgust, as Mina finished her third bowl of stew. "Keep that up, and you'll be fatter than a holiday pheasant by the time we get to the Capitol."

Mina set her empty bowl on the table and picked up another roll from the basket beside it. "What's so wrong with that?"

"Well, if someone were to miraculously mistake you for a pheasant they might try to eat you up," Wera explained, voice dripping with sarcasm.

Mina barked a laugh and tore into her roll. "I'd l-like to see them try."

Sir Gargic scoffed, beard nearly melting off his face now. "Ya know, I figured you'd be a little more courteous once that curse of yours broke."

"And I figured you'd be a little less of an ass after that remorseful sourpuss of yours yesterday."

"It's not being an ass to expect someone to use a spoon while eating stew."

"Depends on the stew, and the person," Enoch interjected. "That's a Dulsten stew, right? Traditionally, the Dulsten people eat with their hands so—" He shrugged, a small smile curling his mustache up as he gave her a knowing look. "Mina's actually being quite courteous right now."

Mina gave Sir Gargic her most winning smile. "If you w-want, I can give you some world etiquette lessons. I've got about fifty mortal years worth of knowledge to impart."

"Fifty?!" Tanir squawked.

"Fifty what?" Sebastian asked as he walked into the kitchen, sweater stained a bit, remnants of his potion brewing. He stopped to lean over Mina's shoulder as he walked around the table towards his seat. "What's that?"

"Dulsten stew."

"Looks tasty." He kissed her on the cheek, turning her heart to a flutter in her chest, then took his seat. "Kitchen, I'll have a bowl, please."

"Mina's fifty years old," Tanir answered his lingering question, eyes wide and distant in disbelief.

"Closer to sixty-five, actually," she corrected. "Give or take a few years between the two realms."

If her eyebrows raised any higher, Mina feared they'd peel off her face.

"So a five-to-one, Mortal-to-Fae Year ratio," Sebastian noted with a pensive purse, eyes unfocused. "You looked about ten when I saw you find the Harlowes."

"You saw me?"

He inhaled deeply and brought his gaze back to the present, to her, with a sad smile and deep sense of knowing. Mina could feel their pact tug around her heart.

"Among other things."

Mina's appetite vanished. She dropped the rest of her roll into her empty bowl.

"Care to share with the class, 'Bastian?" Wera asked with an unsure waiver.

Sebastian collected himself. "Oh, sorry. No. It's nothing for you all to worry about, just something Mina and I will have to discuss in private."

What did She do to him?

"Well, if it ain't essential to complete our contract, then it'll have to wait," Sir Gargic harrumphed. "You and I have to go over some last-minute action items before we arrive in Kowleth tomorrow."

"Of course. I've just finished bottling the last of the Eye of Rezo elixirs The Crown requested, and I have to say they're my best batch yet." Sebastian picked up the bowl of stew that appeared on his placemat and raised it to his lips.

Sir Gargic groaned. "Not you too! Come on, man. Use a spoon!"

Sebastian paused, mid-sip, and furrowed his brow. "This is Dulsten stew. They don't use utensils in Dulsten." He looked at Enoch. "Right?"

Mina bit her tongue to hold back her laughter.

Enoch narrowed his gaze as he snickered at Sir Gargic. "Exactly right."

🜁

What did She do to him?

The question took the thrill out of running.

Mina had half the mind to just rouse Sebastian once they reached their campsite for the night and let the others slumber in the sled while she learned what 'other things' her curse had put him through. But there were contracts to be fulfilled, atlases to complete, and a music room to fix. She wasn't in the business of stealing time from others to suit her own needs.

Sir Gargic pulled Sebastian away as soon as dinner finished, and Mina expected the others to get up from the table and follow suit.

However.

"Kitchen," Enoch called. "A round of ice cream sundaes, please."

Their dirty dishes vanished and were replaced with tin serving dishes filled to the top with ice cream, covered in sauces, nuts, and candies.

"Uhh..." Mina picked up her spoon and caught a glob of hot fudge before it fell onto her placemat. "What's this?"

"Dessert," Wera hummed. She scooped a heaping amount of whipped cream into her mouth.

Mina looked to the empty chair at the head of the table. "It doesn't seem fair to have dessert without Sebastian."

Tanir patted her thigh. "Don't worry about that, dear. He's had more than his fair share of ice cream sundaes."

"Speaking of Sebastian, though." Enoch licked his spoon clean of caramel. "What are your intentions with our fiery leader?"

He pointed his spoon at her as if it were the sword of Damocles.

"My intentions," she repeated. The phrasing was familiar to her, but she could not recall the context she'd read it in.

"Once we wrap things up in Lanholde are you two gonna go back to your cabin, his place in Yosorick, part ways for a bit, or?" Wera circled her spoon in the air, stare pointed and expecting.

"I'm traveling with you all." An easy answer to give. "We'll probably have to stop by the cabin to get some of my things. Lock things up and prep it to sit for a bit. But after that," she shrugged, "wherever the next contract takes us."

"So you'll be our coworker?" Enoch asked.

"Maybe? Sebastian and I haven't really had the chance to talk it over."

Wera tutted and shook her head in disapproval. "For shame, Mina. Sleeping with the boss."

Mina bristled, dropping ice cream on her shirt. "He's not my boss!".

"Then what is he to you?" Tanir asked. "That's really what we're wondering, to be honest, dear."

"He's my partner. And I love him."

"Dammit!" Wera slammed her fist on the table as Enoch hung his head and Tanir cackled victoriously.

"I told you!" she held out her palms towards them. "Four slate each. Cough it up!"

"Hold on." Mina paused from dabbing the swirls of cream and syrup with her napkin. "This whole interrogation was just to settle a bet?"

"Sorry to put you on the spot," Tanir apologized. "But it was good to get some clarity on things. We were all hoping you'd decide to travel with us."

"And I was hoping Sebastian would've proposed," Wera grumbled as she fished four silver coins out of her skirt pocket and placed them in Tanir's awaiting hand.

"P-propose?" Mina sputtered. "I've been uncursed for less than a day!"

"Exactly, Wera," Enoch chided. "Sebastian wouldn't rush into such things, and he'd ask us to help plan it if that were the case."

"Wouldn't rush into such things?!" Wera squawked. "You bet they'd eloped!"

Enoch handed his four slate over to Tanir. "And in hindsight, I see that I may have been overzealous in my assumption. Too caught up in all the 'true love's kiss' excitement to realize that they haven't even had a proper first date yet."

"A date?" Mina asked. She mulled the word over a bit. A few of the leads in her books had gone on 'dates'. Cassandra and Thomas in *Butcher, Baker* had a picnic during one that led to them diving into a nearby river to escape some hitmen.

She could do without the hitmen part, Cassandra and Thomas were having fun before they arrived.

"I wouldn't mind going on a date with Sebastian," she said. "Maybe after we get to Lanholde, though. I know he's gonna be busy finishing up things for his end of the contract. I probably shouldn't distract him from that just to have a garden picnic."

"Oh please," Wera waved off the notion. "Knowing 'Bastian, he's already got most of his shit done. Sir Gargic's just being pedantic because he's so worried about King Fritz's ass being perfectly kissed. He'll be more than happy to make time for a date."

"Not a garden picnic, though. You can have those at any time." Enoch twirled his mustache. "How about a night on the town in Kowleth? You've been there before, haven't you? Anything fun to do?"

"I don't know about f-fun. Obvious reasons aside it's a military base, but..." There had been a few trips where she stayed the night with Mr. Harlowe after their expedition had finished, even fewer after his passing. "I know a place where there's music."

"Well, that's one thing down. I've got to look up some Kowleth guides anyway for the atlas, so I can see if there are any restaurants in the area for you two."

"And I could make you a dress! Or a couple of outfits!" Tanir added. "You didn't bring much with you save your armor, right?"

"Just the armor, but if you have better things to do, I'm sure I could find something in the Junk Room."

"Nonsense. Wera knows how much I love designing. This will be a welcome break from reorganizing my bandage cabinet."

"And a little bit later tonight, I can give you a quick make-up lesson," Wera said. "Staring too long at maps without a break makes my eyes cross."

"What can I do f-for you all in return?" Mina asked, a new warmth overcoming her, one she felt the need to spread. "On the way between the Kowleth and the Capitol, I could hunt a bit. Get you some pelts to trade. Or when we return to my cabin, I have some soaps I can g-give you."

"That's very kind of you, but all we really want is for you and Sebastian to be happy." Tanir patted her knee. "You think you can manage that, dear?"

Mina placed her hand on top of Tanir's and another ribbon tied itself. "I promise to do my best."

🜁

She stood outside the music study, listening to the room next to it.

Through the walls, Sebastian mumbled to himself instead of humming, clearly deep into preparing for their arrival in Lanholde. Nearly half a year of adventures finally coming to a head, on top of having her curse and rimefae nonsense to deal with, had to be quite stressful — and as much as they spoke to the contrary, she probably caused all of them to be behind on their work.

The least she could do was take the wrecked music room off their plates.

The study's state of destruction sank her stomach. The splintered instruments, the scattered scores — they were all on loan. The costs rang up as she sorted through it: total replacements in one pile, repairs needing supplies in another, and those she could repair immediately in the last. The things closest to the mirror — to where she and Sebastian had been standing — were in the worst shape. The mirror itself nothing more than a frame and fine sparkling dust. Most of the stringed instruments nearby had snapped necks: her ebony one included.

A deep sadness hung over her shoulders like a lead blanket as she cradled it in her hands and set it in the trash pile. The flux in temperature and the roaring winds had exasperated the cracks in the body she'd repaired, undoing her work and separating the boards even further. The lion at the scroll's tongue was long gone, snapped off and tossed about somewhere in the wreckage. She had wanted to show it to her luthier when she got back to Sandere, but now?

New hide for the drum heads, piano strings and key replacements, an orchestra's worth of violins and woodwinds — Mina sat on the floor in the middle of the categorized chaos, stomach turning. Thousands of gilt. Several thousands of gilt in damage dealt to a room she had for barely a week.

Which luckily she'd be receiving soon enough.

She patched up the legs of her desk chair — now more of a desk stool after her wind had rendered the backrest to splinters — and set to work re-rosining one of the salvageable bows.

There was a knock at the door.

"Come in."

The door creaked open, followed by a soft, "Oh, wow."

"The damage is not as extensive but," she looked up from her work and frowned at Sebastian, "it's still bad."

He ran his fingers through his hair as he looked around the room, spreading the dust that covered his hands and stained his apron through the strands. He nodded solemnly, then pointed to one of the piles. "These are?"

"Things I can repair, but I need to get supplies for," she answered. "I'll check the Junk Room to see if they have any hide thin enough to replace the drum heads, but some of the other things I'll need to find an instrument shop for. That other pile holds the ones that are completely destroyed now. I might be able to pick some parts out from there but—"

He walked towards it and picked up the severed lion's head. "The violin you used for your composition?"

Her throat went dry. "I know." She swallowed to try and clear it. "There is a lot I can fix without needing to buy anything, though. I'm working on those things now."

"Can I be of any help?" he asked, eyes wide and flitting about the room, already working out how to solve all the problems she'd created.

Mina's stomach gave another twist at the thought of burdening him further.

"Not really. The only thing I can't handle is rebinding the sheet music and scores, but I figured I'd ask Enoch to take a look at them once he and Wera finish up their atlas."

"It's an awful big 'to fix' pile, though. Surely an extra pair of hands could help."

She looked back at the pile. It easily filled a third of the room on its own.

"It would but," she turned back and smiled at him, "I know you've probably got a lot of work to catch up on now that you don't have any distractions, especially with us arriving at Kowleth tomorrow evening. You don't need to be burdened with this mess. I've got it."

He pouted, nostrils flaring slightly in the way that meant he hadn't accepted her justification.

"I caused this mess too, you know."

"I know. And I'm sure there will still be plenty of things to fix after we've fulfilled our contracts."

"Then I should start learning how to fix them now." Sebastian grabbed the less-than-sturdy piano bench and placed it down next to her. It groaned and wobbled as he sat on it, but didn't give way just yet.

"'Bastian," Mina sighed and turned back to her work.

"Do you think that I'm incapable of repairing an instrument?"

"Not at all. I've seen you work. You're m-more than capable."

"Then why can't I help?"

"Because you have better things to do, I'm sure, and I don't want to burden you with this on top of all that."

He slipped his hand gently into the crook of her arm, stilling her hand.

"Even if I did have better things to do — which I don't by the way — this wouldn't be a burden."

Mina narrowed her eyes, glaring at him without any ire. "You don't have better things to do? Really? I heard you muttering away in there." She jutted her chin towards his study.

He glanced away from her, cheeks reddening a bit in embarrassment. "I was muttering. But the potion I've been working on is currently synthesizing correctly and will be for the next hour, so—"

"And you're certain you don't have anything else you should be working on for the next hour?"

He looked back to her and smiled. "Nope. Got the Dorminian Necklace all secured and put in a less poisoned box with a note cautioning others to wear anti-magic gloves while handling it. The other artifacts we pulled from the tombs and temples I polished, restored, and arranged for presentation back when we first reclaimed them." He rubbed his hands down his apron, adding more dust to the garment. "Now I'm just brewing and distilling some of the rare ingredients The Crown requested into usable components for spell-craft. Most of them I was able to do a while ago, but some of the plant-based ones have a short shelf life, so I had to wait until we got close to arriving to make those."

"I see. Well," she fumbled around for an excuse. "I'm sure you'd much rather do something fun to relax then—"

"This is fun for me." He leaned down and picked up a lyre from the pile: its crossbar snapped and strings bouncing loose. "Look at this thing and tell me this isn't just a new kind of puzzle for me to try and solve."

She pursed her lips, feeling the tickle of a laugh coming on. "A puzzle is definitely one word for it."

"Plus, I'd get to learn from a true master of the craft who just so happens to be my favorite person."

"I don't know about a master, but your f-favorite person?" Her heart fluttered at the admission. "What about Wera?"

"Wera is one of my favorite *people*," he clarified. "You are my favorite person. But do not tell her that because she will whine about it for weeks."

"I see," she snipped, playfully. "So, 'you're my favorite person' is the line you give all the cute girls you meet."

"What?" his voice jumped up an octave. "No!"

"It's fine. It's fine." She feigned disappointment. "Wera will be more than h-happy to know that she's actually my favorite person, at least."

"She is, huh?" he doubted, eyes narrowing, lips pursing doubtfully. "Why isn't she here offering to help you clean up, then?"

"Because she and Enoch are finishing the final portion of their atlas."

A visible wave of relief washed over Sebastian. "Oh, good," he sighed. "With everything that happened, I was afraid they wouldn't make it in time."

Mina puckered her lips in a pout. "And now you know w-why I'm saying you should focus on finishing up whatever you have to do for The Crown."

"And I have an hour of free time that I would love to spend learning from you and helping you before I head back to focusing." He pulled her hand towards him and kissed her knuckles, brown eyes staring at her in plead. "Please?"

She sighed in resignation, but could not keep a smile off her lips. "Fine."

He smiled back. "Thank you, *professor*. I'll try to be a better student than you are, despite my lack of musical ability."

Mina snatched her hand back. "*I* am a f-fantastic student."

Sebastian snickered. "*You* are a sassy student. Bratty, I dare say."

"Oh! So my curse breaks and the truth comes out."

He tutted, a mischievous spark in his eye, "Guess you're a bratty professor too."

She flicked his nose lightly to distract his hands, then stuck her fingers in his sides, wiggling them quickly; tickling him.

Sebastian broke out in a fit of wild laughter as he thrashed about "S-stop i-it!!"

"Take it back!"

"N-no! Y-you're only proving my p-p-point!"

With a keening creak, the piano bench gave way, wobbly leg splitting in two and sending Sebastian crashing to the ground. He grabbed Mina's arms as he fell, pulling her down with him into a giggling pile.

"Now look what you did!" she admonished between laughs. Sebastian hugged her tightly as his laughter shook them both, pinning her arms to her sides to still her tickling fingers.

"Me?!" he squawked.

"Clearly!"

He collected himself, blinked the tears out of his eyes with a happy sigh, and kissed her. "Alright, alright," he yielded against her lips. "I'll fix the bench first, then you'll teach me to fix the lyre?"

"Only if you're on your b-best behavior."

"Oh, don't you worry about that, teach." He gave her a smile that set her heart racing and melting all at the same time. "I'll do anything to get a gold star."

She arched an eyebrow. "Anything?"

He hummed a naughty chuckle. "That seems like a discussion *after* class."

🜁

The border gate at Fort Kowleth was just as gray and dreary as Mina remembered, much to her disappointment. The high slate walls were frosted and shingled with large clusters of ice, caked on from years of blizzards and hailstorms. Two bartizans sat on either side of its gate: a simple wooden thing — fortified with iron, of course — but only tall and wide enough to let a sizable cart through the massive wall around it.

From one bartizan, a bright red flag appeared through the thin window slit signaling them to halt, while a three-note trumpet tune blared out of the bartizan on the other side.

"Proclaim yourselves and your purpose!" The left bartizan called.

"Mina the Alpinist," she called back. "Escorting Windenhofer Procurements and Sir Murmir Gargic by order of The Crown of Lanholde to the Capitol."

A long pause followed. Not the four-note tune signaling the gates to open or the two-note tune signally something was amiss. Mina rested a hand on the pommel of her sword and exchanged a warning look with Sebastian.

He stretched his arms behind his head nonchalantly, and she caught the quiet squeak of Wera uncorking one of her vials on the breeze.

There was a shuffling in both bartizans before the stone slates narrowing the outlook windows into slits snapped open on both sides.

"Mina?" The guards questioned in tandem. To the left was Adelbert, his complexion much ruddier than she was familiar with, but his long beard still twisted into twin braids. On the right held Gunda, brassy, blonde hair still worn in a too-tight bun that continued to recede her hairline. Both looked at her as if she were a talking horse performing a tap dance.

"That's my name," Mina replied.

"You look different," said Adelbert.

"I got a haircut."

"You sound different," Gunda added.

Mina rolled her eyes. She wasn't that changed, was she? "Laryngitis."

Sebastian snorted a quiet laugh.

"But—"

"Last time I checked, a game of twenty questions wasn't part of the border protocol," Sir Gargic interjected, an annoyed snip to his tone. Mina was a bit pleased to learn his impatient attitude wasn't reserved only for her.

"I swear on my forty years of service to The Crown that this is the alpinist you know. So unless there are any other concerns keeping you from permitting us entry, I highly suggest you let us through the gate so we can begin the process of getting our travel paperwork properly vetted." He shook their scrolls in the air like a child wanting their bottle refilled. "And if you are unable to do so I will be more than happy to speak with Commander Lindhagen. He is still the leader of this outpost, is he not?"

Gunda and Adelbert both jolted as they stood at attention, saluting. "Yes, sir. Sorry, sir."

They shut their slates in unison and — after some more rummaging and whispered swears — a five-note melody echoed from Gunda's bartizan while a green flag replaced the red one hanging from Adelbert's.

Mina groaned as the gate raised.

"What is it?" Sebastian asked.

"It's usually a four-note tune, not a five-note one."

"What does that signal?"

"I don't know. But I have a feeling it's going to be annoying."

He rolled his shoulders back, straightening them in preparation. "Dangerous annoying or—"

"No," she sighed. "Just *annoying* annoying."

The gate lowered and Mina found the outpost hidden behind it only a little more colorful than what she knew it to be, pigmented by the growing crowd of guards as they walked into the fort. The majority of them stood to the side, onlooking at a wide berth around those charged to inspect the expedition's paperwork and cargo.

"This is one grand reception," Sebastian commented to the guard patting him down, keeping his tone naive and cordial. "Is this how you usually greet new arrivals?"

"No," the guard, Eike, said as he ran his hands down the sides of Sebastian's coat one final time. He pulled out his pocket watch, opened it, then — satisfied to find just a clock face — placed it back in Sebastian's pocket. "Clear."

Sebastian stepped to the side and Mina went to follow him.

Eike stepped between them. "I have to check you, ma'am."

"No, you don't," Mina stated. "I don't get checked. You want to lose your hand like Hook-Nose did?"

"I know, but—"

"But what?" she snapped. Sure, he'd come out unscathed now, but he didn't need to know that. She suffered through watching a guard's hand freeze and decay back when she first arrived with Mr. Harlowe, that had been enough to earn her a pass thus far.

"Voice and look are different, but the attitude is still the same," someone from the crowd muttered under their breath.

Mina whipped around and glared daggers at them. The commenter paled. "I heard that."

"Look. I'll be quick," Eike said as he strapped on a rather thick pair of mitts. "Just don't cause any trouble, alright?"

Mina sneered at him as he approached. "I don't know how you fucking expect to feel anything on me with those things."

Eike took a deep breath to calm his nerves and reached out hesitantly to start patting down her arms. Sebastian observed, shoulders tense, just a few feet away from her. A reassuring presence that slightly dulled the feeling of being treated like a sideshow act by the guards.

Eike hummed.

"Gloves feeling a bit chilly there, Eik?" Another guard called. "It's best to get it over with quickly so that the frost doesn't seep in as deep."

"It's not that," he replied. "They're not cold at all."

"Eike, what are you doing?!" someone in the crowd shouted as the guard ripped off one of his gloves and grabbed her arm.

Nothing happened.

And a hundred blades started to glide out of their sheaths.

"What the hell are you all doing?" Sebastian moved towards them. One of the guards, a bigger brute Mina wasn't so familiar with, placed his hand against Sebastian's chest to hold him back.

"Please stand back, sir. We know this woman well. Something definitely isn't right with her."

Mina locked eyes with Sebastian, keeping her expression as calm as possible despite her growing anger. No need to start a fight and null all his hard work over a bunch of antsy idiots. "Don't worry, 'Bastian, I've got this."

"Got what? Hah?" Eike held his sword against her throat.

"I command you lot to stand down!" Sir Gargic hollered.

"Check their eyes for ice ferns or snowflakes," another guard called. "Fae charms like the last expedition reported."

"It'd be weird for a rimefae to be warm, wouldn't it?" Mina announced loud enough for all to hear. "And I'm not even that warm now, apparently. Just less cold." She scanned the crowd. "The knight asked for Commander Lindhagen to be brought, didn't he? I don't see the ol' geezer. Y'all too afraid to be made fools of in front of your daddy?"

"I bet that's just what you want, isn't it?" Eike hissed. "Want us to bring the Commander down here so you can charm him, just like you did these poor helpless travelers. What did you even do to Mina, huh? She might have been a bitch, but she didn't deserve whatever bullshit you put her through."

"What the hell is going on here?!" A deep, stern voice bellowed over the crowd.

"Oh ho ho," Mina mocked, jutting her chin a bit forwards as she smiled her biggest 'fuck you' smile. "Looks like my evil plan is working."

"Stay back, commander," Eike shouted. "It looks like we captured the fae that—"

"Dietmar!" Sir Gargic bellowed even louder. "What is the meaning of this?!"

"Soldier! Unhand that man!" Commander Lindhagen demanded, voice rumbling like the roar of a lion. The crowd parted as his massive form rushed over to Sir Gargic, crossing the clearing in a few purposeful, long-legged strides. He grabbed the guard apprehending him and yanked him off with just a one-handed pull against his shoulder. "He is a member of King Fritz's Champion Knights!"

"We're aware, sir," Eike explained through gritted teeth, frustration starting to get the better of him. "But we have to check for signs of fae magic, sir."

"Oh, please," Sir Gargic spat. "You've been staring in my eyes like a lovesick puppy dog long enough to see there ain't shit in them. Is this really how you rear your troops, Lindhagen?"

The commander's stone face wrinkled into a deep, menacing scowl. "Everyone stand down! Failure to do so will lead to your immediate dismissal!"

Swords lowered as the commander's voice echoed across the outpost. Eike's blade still pressed against Mina's throat.

She tutted. "Better be a good doggy or else master's gonna smack you on the nose with the paper."

Rage flashed in his eyes as he lowered his blade and raised his fist.

"Eike! I said to—"

Mina grabbed it, crushing his hand in her grip hard enough to break the metacarpals with a loud snap. She drove the cleated heel of her boot into his foot, pinning him in place as she wrenched his arm behind his back and dropped him to his knees.

"Good doggy," Mina patted Eike's head before addressing the commander. His hair was just as white as she remembered, but his eyes revealed themselves to be a steely shade of blue. "Lindhagen."

"Harlowe's Girl," Lindhagen grumbled unsurely, studying her closely. "What happened?"

The commander had always been respectful of her, even after the Hook-Nose incident. Even after Harlowe had passed, and his obligation had ended.

"Remember how Harlowe told ya I was wrapped up in weird magic when we first met?"

"Of course."

"Well," she couldn't help her grin as she nodded her head towards Sebastian, "the wizard unwrapped it."

Sebastian waved. “Sebastian Windenhofer, Master Level Mage of the Northern Practitioners' Guild. Owner and operator of Windenhofer Procurements.” He walked over to stand beside her and extended his hand out for a shake. “Nice to meet you. Sorry for the commotion.”

“You made her smile?” Lindhagen asked.

He shrugged. “It was a group effort, really.” He glanced at her and smiled bright enough to warm the harsh welcome they'd received. “Mina did most of the work.”

Lindhagen nodded and shook Sebastian's hand, large meaty digits enveloping his long fingers with a clap. His mouth bowed into a thoughtful frown as he looked at Mina. “Harlowe would have been glad to see it.”

He let go of Sebastian's hand and inhaled deeply, puffing out his chest and lifting his chin to address his troops. “I understand that you are all tense with the reports of fae sightings this month, but that doesn't excuse your behavior. Apologize.”

A chorus of meek sorries trickled out from the crowd.

“Sorry,” Eike hissed beneath her.

Mina released him, dropping him into the snow. He scampered to his feet and into the crowd like a dog with its tail between its legs.

“We sorted the fae problem too,” Gargic said, patting Lindhagen on the back to reclaim his attention. “Sent those beasties back where they belong myself.”

“Did you now?” Tanir remarked under her breath, and Mina bit her lip to keep from laughing.

“Right, well.” He gave Mina a passing glance of doubt before he turned to Sir Gargic. “Let's get your paperwork in order, then you and I can catch up in my office, Murmir.” Lindhagen patted him on the shoulder and addressed his troops: “Back to work!”

The crowd dispersed, and a more competent guard ushered Sir Gargic away. Lindhagen watched and waited, making sure no lingering ears were nearby.

“I'll take care of Eike,” he said, conviction in his eyes. He wasn't the sort of man to go against his word. “Harlowe's lean-to is still standing.”

“I'll be staying in town tonight,” she replied. “But, uh.” Mina cleared her throat to wrap her mouth around the words. “T-thank y-you.”

Lindhagen smiled and huffed a laugh. “Don't strain yourself, kid.”

“You were right,” Sebastian waited until the commander walked a ways away to say. He picked up the hand she used to punch Eike and ran his thumb over her knuckles. They stung a little. “Definitely *annoying* annoying.”

“Is that going to happen a lot?” Enoch asked as they reconvened.

“Not to that level, I think,” Mina replied. “News travels fast around here but, besides the soldiers stationed here at the outposts, no one in the town should know me. I normally collect my pay, give Lindhagen some coin to riffle through their rations, then start the trek back to the cabin.”

“So, you're not the best one to ask for hotel recommendations?” Wera teased.

“Wouldn't be much to recommend anyway. The Frozen Whisker is the only inn Kowleth's got.”

Enoch pouted at Mina. “And they're the only restaurant, too.”

“Then let's head on over and get out of this blasted cold,” Sir Gargic grumbled, he flashed the paperwork at Sebastian before stuffing it into the inside of his coat. "The paperwork checked out."

"Good," he nodded. "Let's celebrate with a nice inn-cooked meal and some drink." He wove his fingers through Mina's and gave her hand a reassuring squeeze. "Shall we?"

🜂

Unsurprisingly, The Frozen Whisker had plenty of vacancies. Enough for them to get a room each if they wanted, but they settled on just three despite Sir Gargic's protests. Wera and Tanir in one, Sir Gargic and Enoch in the other, and Sebastian and Mina in the last.

Mina sat on the floor as soon as they got in and set to work unstrapping her cleats from her boots. Sebastian unwound his scarf and hung it on the coat rack by the door.

"So," said Mina.

"So," said Sebastian.

"What would you say to exploring the town a bit after we eat with the crew?"

"Sounds like fun. Got someplace in particular in mind?" He ran his hands down the length of his scarf, hands glowing as he dried off the melting snow. "Wera mentioned wanting to pick up a souvenir for her nieces."

"Definitely have somewhere in mind." Mina stood, free of her cleats, and took off his hat for him. "But it'd be just the two of us going."

"Just the two of us, huh?" He smiled and shucked off his coat. "Are you asking me out on a date?"

She smiled back and stuck his hat on the top of the coat rack. "Clearly."

He snaked his arms around her waist and pulled her into a loose embrace. "Never thought *you'd* be the one asking me out on our first date."

"Enoch gave me the idea," she admitted. "There's this tavern that has music."

"A tavern that has music," his smile burned even brighter as he considered it. Mina relished that she did not have to look away; grateful to be able to bask in its glow. "Are you asking me to go dancing with you?"

Mina's face heated. She hadn't considered that there'd be dancing.

"I hadn't considered that there'd be dancing. But if you w-wanted to, I wouldn't mind it."

"*Normal* dancing?" he teased with a waggle of his eyebrows.

"I'm still rusty at it but, y-yes, normal dancing."

He laughed and kissed her on the forehead. "Yes. I would love to go normal dancing with you. Where at?"

"The Crawlspace. The few times I stayed overnight it was hard to miss the music. Some of these soldiers can play." Mina trailed her fingers over his collarbones, enjoying the soft wool of his sweater. "Tanir made me a dress for tonight, too."

His brows lifted to his hairline. "She did?"

"She did," she giggled at his excited surprise. "I'll need to pop into the commorancy to grab it, though, if that's alright?"

"Guess I'll need to go in and gussy up too." He kissed her on the forehead again and pulled away, reaching underneath his sweater and pulling out the card. "Just don't tell the others we popped in for a moment."

"Why?" Mina asked.

Sebastian knelt down and stuck it into one of the cracks between the floorboards. He kissed the card then flicked it as he spoke, "Clementine."

With each wobble back and forth, the card grew and stretched into a door. Sebastian opened it once the commorancy settled and gestured for Mina to enter.

"Out of fairness, mostly," he said as he stepped in after her. "And to expand my own horizons. It really is tempting to just stay in here all the time, ya know? But that can deprive you of some one-of-a-kind experiences."

"Wera mentioned that you have a place in Yosorick. Is it like this?" she asked as they headed upstairs.

"Elements of it are — the frames in the halls mainly — but it's not a townhome style like this. It's wider instead of tall. No infirmary, or training room. The garden's outside and not as well-kept as it could be." He chuckled at that. "I try to keep the commorancy homey but different so that being back in Yosorick doesn't feel like work." Sebastian tapped his fingers against his lips. "Which reminds me. Before we enter Reinhardt Castle tomorrow, I want to take a picture of us all in front of it. We've got to commemorate your first successful Windenhofer Procurements contract."

Mina snickered as she split off from him and started to walk towards her room.

Sebastian turned to her, amusingly confused. "What?"

"Technically, my contract isn't with Windenhofer Procurements," she said.

He rolled his eyes, "Still—"

"Still," she shrugged. "Not my first."

He grabbed her hand and led her back to him. "Then to commemorate our first adventure together. How does that sound?"

"I mean. It really depends on what your definition of adventure is." She took her turn to tease him. "The trek through the Sandere itself could be—"

"Lila doar," Sebastian warned playfully.

Mina smiled and kissed him lightly on the lips. "Our first adventure, it is."

He kissed her back, deeper this time despite the smile hanging on his lips, pulling her against him by the hem of her breastplate.

"First of many," he said before backing away. "What color are you wearing, by the way? I don't want to clash."

"Aubergine is what Tanir and Enoch called it."

"Aubergine." He repeated, nodding as if he understood the word. "What a lovely shade of..."

"Deep purple. But the redder side of purple."

"Got it." He set off towards his room, drumming his fingers on his lips as his focus fell deep into his thoughts.

Mina used her speed to her advantage, sneaking a quick wash in the tub to scrub off the grime and sweat built up from her run. She dabbed the tincture of lavender and honeysuckle she made up with Tanir's help onto her wrists and neck, before running some of the pomade Enoch gave her through her hair. The fragrances blended well together, but blending the rouge Wera loaned her into her cheeks seemed to be a much more daunting task.

"A little goes a long way," she mumbled to herself as she dipped just the tip of her pinky into the rose-colored cream. "Just a light flush."

It wasn't as noticeable as when Wera did it, but Mina would rather it be barely noticeable than wind up looking like a worked-up Sir Gargic. She was a little bolder applying it to her lips, feeling confident in her ability to follow their defined slopes.

The truly tricky bit came with putting on the dress itself. No matter how she twisted her arms, the buttons in the center of her back were impossible to reach.

"Mina?" Sebastian called outside her door.

How long have I been fucking around with these things?

"I'll be waiting out here when you're ready."

Mina paced back and forth, whipping up a mild wind in her frustration as the buttons continued to just be out of her grasp.

"Close your eyes!" she hollered.

"W-what?"

"Just—" She groaned. "Close your eyes! P-please!"

"Okay?"

"Are they closed?" she asked after a moment.

"They're closed."

Mina opened the door slowly, peeking out to make sure his eyes were truly closed before she stepped out into the hall, and turned her back towards him.

"H-help," she stammered out. "I can't reach the buttons in the back."

Sebastian laughed.

"Don't laugh!"

"I'm sorry. I can't help it," he chuckled out. "You're adorable."

"I'll be even more adorable when I get these fucking buttons buttoned," she huffed. "Are you gonna help or not?"

"I'm helping. I'm helping." His footsteps rolled across the floorboards, preluding warm, nimble fingers sorting out her buttons diligently.

"You smell nice," he noted.

"Don't smell me yet," she grumbled.

He chuckled again. "I can't really help it."

"You could hold your nose."

"I need two hands to button," he replied. "I see what you mean by the redder side of purple."

"Your eyes are supposed to be closed!"

"I can sense the redness from touch alone."

Mina groaned in frustration.

"Don't get too grumpy, lila doar," he consoled. "I'm almost done."

"I wanted to surprise you."

"I can still be surprised. Here." He finished the last button and stepped away. "My eyes are closed. If you want to head back in, then come back out, I won't see a thing."

Mina looked over her shoulder and found him standing back, hand over his eyes.

"Alright," she said to disguise a rather clever thought. She turned around to face him, opened the door behind her wide enough to make the hinges creak, then shut it.

Sebastian's brows shot up quickly as he uncovered his eyes, a shock — panic — flashing across his face for a moment before illuminating into an awestruck smile and twinkling eyes.

"There," Mina said, letting his smile echo on her lips. "Now you're surprised."

"You look beautiful." The words were said with such reverence, outside ears would have mistaken it as a prayer. "I know others have told you that so perhaps it doesn't mean much, but truly, there is no other word—"

"It means the world when you say it," she interjected, buzzing from the compliment, from the way he looked at her. "You really think so?'

"I really, really do." He studied her, mesmerized.

Mina took the moment to look him over as well. A good pair of tan slacks that accentuated the strength in his thighs and rested perfectly at his waist. He wore his shirt tucked in, a button-down in burgundy — another shade of red tinted with purple as Wera had taught her — paired with an umber, knit cardigan that was surprisingly well-structured, showcasing the breadth of his shoulders while tying together the deep browns of his belt and shoes.

"You know, even when everything was gray, I could tell you had a sense of style. But seeing it now?" She whistled. "It's bad enough that you're devastatingly handsome, but the fact that you can dress too? Thank the Gods I know how to fight."

Sebastian barked out an uncertain laugh. "Fight?! Who?!"

"All the folks who are gonna try and steal you from me."

"Please. Like anyone could hold a candle to you." He held out his hand for her to take. "Do you need to grab anything else, or are you all set?"

Mina took it, interweaving her fingers between his. "All set."

"No sword?" he asked, eyes flitting down to her hips.

Mina laughed. "No sword."

🜁

By the time they reached it, The Crawlspace truly lived up to its name. Cobbled together out of an old storage shack for the outpost's canteen, soldiers and citizens spilled out of the place as lively and loud as the music that drew them right back into its packed quarters. The building itself shook with the same rhythm as the drums, as the heart of the crowd — a swirling, beating, joyous mass of dancers — skipped and twirled in time with its tempo.

Sebastian shoved his cardigan into his shrinking pocket, mumbling about how he was grateful he didn't wear his usual coat, as they approached the boisterous beast: the heat of its dancing belly enough to keep the roof clear of snow in such a frigid place.

"I'm sure once we start dancing, the crowd will loosen a bit," he assured in her direction, though he was clearly talking to himself. He waved at his body loosely, "'Cuz of the heat and all."

"Good thing it takes a lot to make me sweat," Mina said, looping her arm around him after he finished rolling up his sleeves. "Promise you won't be too upset with me if I step on your toes?"

"You're not wearing cleats, are you?" he teased.

"Maybe I should have," Mina remarked as she looked for a crack in the cluster of people blocking the entrance. "Would certainly make it easier for us to get in."

The short set of wooden stairs leading up creaked beneath them as they stepped onto it, drawing the cluster's attention to them... and sending them scattering.

"Or we can get in like that," Sebastian noted under his breath.

The patrons watched Mina warily, patting those next to them and pulling them to the side to clear a path as she walked into The Crawlspace.

Doing everything they could to avoid touching her.

The drums fell silent, the strings and bass giving a final screech before they died with it, and the dancers gave only one utterance of protest before spotting her and shutting their mouths.

"Harlowe's Girl," the bartender, a reedy sort made up of harsh angles, called both in greeting and in warning. "What brings you in?"

"Dancing," Mina answered tersely, hackles already raising, teeth ready to bite.

A couple of short laughs bubbled around the room.

"Sorry, kid, but we can't let ya do that in here. The music should be plenty loud enough for you to hear it outside, though."

"Why can't we dance in here exactly?" Sebastian asked, his tone incredibly polite as he feigned misunderstanding.

"These folks don't get a lot of warmth around here," they replied. "Last thing any of us want is for them to lose some skin to frostbite just because they brushed up against her during a Zwiefacher."

"So none of you saw or heard about what happened when we arrived at the gate today?" he asked the crowd.

There were a few murmurs, but not a soul answered him directly.

Sebastian grabbed her hand in his and held it up for everyone to see. "Because I've been holding her hand for what has to have been a few good hours now, and I haven't got an inch of frostbite on me."

Mina looked up to see his hand holding hers; strong, warm, *defiant.* Like her hand was a prize he was proud he had chosen. Proud to call his. Mina's bite left her for a moment, bridled by a held breath and a shiver running down her spine.

"Lucky bastard," someone sitting at the bar groused.

The comment returned her to herself.

"Look Hook-Nose," Mina addressed the one-armed man. "It ain't my fault you didn't listen to Harlowe back then. He warned ya not to check me, didn't he?"

Hook-Nose rolled his eyes and took a sip of his beer, mumbling lowly to where only her ears and people next to him could possibly hear, "You could have at least said sorry."

Guilt squirmed in her stomach.

"Right, well," the bartender cleared their throat. "If there ain't no harm gonna be done, then I see no harm in letting her dance. Harlowe and the girl have gotten a lot of folks up the Peaks safely, and saved a lot of y'all's skins out there too. Letting her shuffle along with the rest of us is a small price to pay, is it not?" They nodded to the band. "Fritizi."

The joyous blare of a trumpet revived the music, but the crowd still needed a moment to find their rhythm... or exit.

"If you want to dance so badly, then do it," one of the soldiers snipped as he walked past them to leave, following the stream of patrons pouring out.

"Well, that's certainly one way to clear some room," Sebastian remarked as he turned to face her, switching his hold on her hand.

"I—," Mina sighed, a deep sadness sinking in at the disgruntled faces walking past them. "Maybe we should just go."

"Absolutely not," Sebastian scooped his arm around her waist and lifted her up into a spin. "You deserve to dance the night away." He set her down and set her twirling under his arm with a quick snap.

The motion knocked her off balance and Sebastian caught her as she fell against his chest. "And I, *very selfishly*, want to show off my girl."

A tingle buzzed up her spine, shaking the sadness out of her. "I love it when you call me that," she admitted without a second thought.

"My girl?" he asked as he helped her find her footing, leading her to sway into the beat.

"Remember when my ears popped?"

He winced. "How could I forget?"

"It was the 'that's my girl' that caused it. I l-liked it so much, the curse turned my wind back on me or something."

Sebastian hummed in consideration as something wanton flickered in his eyes. "Good to know."

Mina inhaled sharply to try and focus on dancing and calm the heat rising in her cheeks. "So, is 'normal dancing' just swaying?"

"I'm easing you into it," he teased. "Can't throw it at you all at once."

"Well, I think I've got the swaying down."

"Okay, okay," he nodded. "Next lesson then. Step out."

He slid his hands down her arms, stepping back and holding them outstretched before pulling her in again and turning them both.

"That's just a fancy fleckerl," Mina noted.

"That's the next lesson." He grinned. "Normal dancing is just using all the dance moves you know without really caring about form or what's supposed to go together. And even making some dance moves up. Look at that guy over there."

Sebastian pointed to a man to the side of them, simply jumping in place with the music, body stiff as a board while his head bobbed up and down.

"Is he possessed?" she judged.

"Sort of," he chuckled. "Not everyone is a good dancer. Luckily, between the two of us, we've got enough skills to do one hell of a two-step."

A new song began, a jaunty, driving tune that filled her with excitement.

"I know this song!"

"Do you?" he switched their grip so that they both had an equal claim in leading. "Then show me."

Instinctively, Mina pulled him into a chassé, the familiar jig calling back the quadrilles drilled into her as a child. Sebastian followed along, his long legs and loose form quickly turning their steps into more of a skip as they wove through the crowd. As they moved into a more open space, Sebastian twirled her underneath his arm. Mina giggled as she spun and stepped out of it, pulling his arm out with her before bending it so they could turn — palm to palm — in perfect time with the pre-chorus.

"And through the darkest night, though the moon may hide its light. The oceans fall and rise, so why not kings? For all the reigns and rules, I know this to be true, a tavern wench has done much more for me," she sang along with the band, voice bold and bright, overjoyed to hear the song in its full glory. To feel the beat of the drum thrum in her ribs, the fiddle buzz up her arms, the horns shake her skull.

Sebastian looped their arms together, and they spun around as the band swelled.

"So bow, bow, bow to our Lady of the Ale! Sinners, saints, and in between should bend the knee and hail! She'll lift your spirits, heal your wounds, with a pint and latest country news. More giving than a king could ever be!"

They swung through and round each other's arms, parting barely for a quick spin and twirl before coming back together again, even closer. Sebastian's voice joined hers, vibrating against her chest as he pulled her in close.

"My princess wields a shot glass with an apron as her shield. I'll follow her to any battlefield! Our Lady of The Ale! Sweet Lady of The Ale! Our faith in you shall never, ever yield!"

Sebastian dipped her in time with the final button, and raucous applause roared in their ears. They shared a look of total confusion with each other.

"That was amazing!"

"What a voice!"

"More! More!"

They straightened up and found the entire tavern's eyes on them once again, coupled with awestruck smiles instead of scared sneers.

"Harlowe's Girl!" Fritizi hollered. "Rest of the night. Whatever song you want, we'll play it as long as you sing! Deal?"

Mina looked to Sebastian in disbelief. He laughed happily and shrugged. "It's up to you. I know I could listen to you sing all night."

She turned back to Fritizi, smile beaming so brightly it felt like light poured out of her. Pride — *good* pride — swelled in her chest. "Deal!"

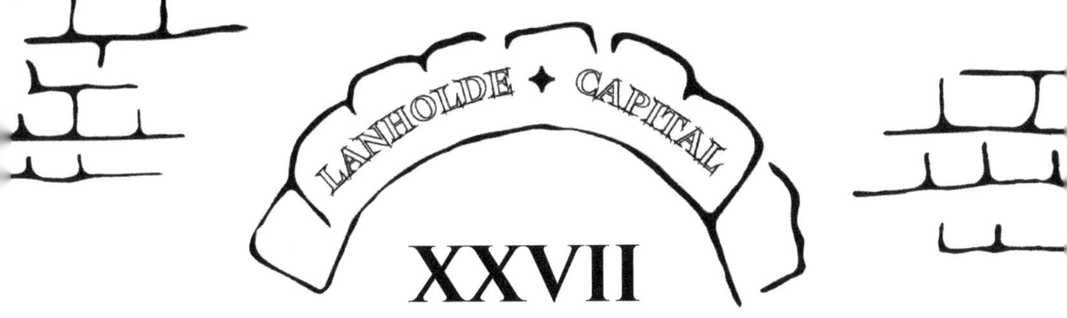

XXVII

A Royal Welcome

Mina could barely contain her laughter.

"And when Benno started jigging on the bar in that kilt of his?!"

"Shhh!" Sebastian shushed, speech slurred slightly from the rounds of drinks the patrons bought them, as they made their way down the hall to their room. "We don't want to wake the others."

"So what if we wake them up!" she whispered. "You all have been sleeping for hours on end while I've been dragging you over hill and dale!"

He unlocked the door and held it open for her. "Because if we wake them up, I'll feel too guilty to set up the commorancy."

Mina gasped cartoonishly. "What happened to having 'one-of-a-kind' experiences?"

Sebastian stuck the card in the crack, enchanted it quickly, then walked back to her.

"Simple." Mina's world flipped upside down as Sebastian bent down and threw her over his shoulder. "I want the one-of-a-kind experience of having *my girl* in my bed."

She covered her mouth to muffle her wild laughter until the commorancy door shut behind them.

"'Bastian!" She scolded, kicking her feet in the air. "I can walk just fine!"

"Nope. Sorry. Walking is not an option for you this evening."

"Oh really?" She went to raise her legs up and throw him off-balance, but was stopped by a sharp spank against her ass.

His palm wasn't burning when it struck her, but the immediate heat rushing through her sure felt like it had been.

"'Bastian!" she squeaked.

He laughed darkly. "Oh, I liked the sound of that 'Bastian." He rubbed his hand over the lingering sting before squeezing her cheek. "Perhaps I should make you say it again? You've got at least a month's worth of bratty behavior you need to make up to me, lila doar."

"Oh, please," she huffed. "If anyone's the brat here, it's—"

Sebastian spanked her again.

"—you!" Mina yiped.

"Now, now, lila doar," he teased. "Better behave, or you won't get your reward."

While she had the perfect vantage point to spank him back, a more clever form of payback came to mind.

"My reward?" she asked, playing dumb. "For doing so well with my dancing lessons, *professor?*"

Sebastian's palm warmed immediately, the arm keeping her on his shoulder flexing in response.

Mina ran her nails up and down his spine. "I really do want my reward. Is there anything I can do to earn it back, *sir?*"

Another door opened, and swiftly the world was righted as she landed on Sebastian's bed.

"Earn it, huh?" Sebastian said as he stood over her, slowly unbuttoning his shirt. "How do you intend to *earn* it?"

That wanton look that passed over him earlier now rested in his gaze, just as burning and hungry as her own desire. His erection visibly straining against his pants demanded her attention. Drool pooled in her mouth more than it had for any other meal.

He had dined upon her as if she were the finest feast in all the realm. It was only fair that she did the same.

"This can't be comfortable," she said as stroked his cock through his pants. Sebastian inhaled sharply as his body leaned into her touch. "Let me take care of you, *sir?*"

His cock twitched beneath her as she dragged her hand up to undo his belt. One button after another, she unfastened his fly and guided both his briefs and slacks down to pool at his ankles.

Her hands traveled up his thighs, admiring the scars and soft hair, before setting to appreciate the work of art in front of her. She cupped his balls first, gently, treating them delicately. They were heavy, pulled taut by desire and begging for release. His cock jumped as she caressed them, the inner muscles of his thighs rippling lightly as well, encouraging her attention, demanding more of it.

Mina traced her fingertips along the thick veins vining up his shaft, hunger growing as she watched the pre-cum dribble down his flushed tip. Sebastian placed his hand against her cheek, warm, inviting. She looked up at him — at his gorgeous mouth open slightly, breath gone ragged, his gaze filled with pure wanton awe — and dragged her tongue over it. Savory, salty, a little bit of bitter spice.

She was *starving.*

"Fuck," he whispered as she wrapped her lips around him and took him deeper into her mouth. His hand traveled from her cheek to tangle his fingers in her hair. "Good girl."

Those two words carried more power than any command or incantation ever could, drawing out a whimper as they charmed her, made her body ache to be filled, to earn more of his sweet praise.

She hollowed out her cheeks and moved, back and forth, running her tongue along his base, savoring him, taking the utmost care to notice his little tells. How his breath hitched, when he mindlessly tugged her hair...

"So good," he panted. "Feels so good." He bucked his hips forward, catching her off-guard as the tip of his cock hit the sensitive part in the back of her throat. She grunted in surprise and inhaled through her nose sharply to keep herself from gagging.

Sebastian stilled. "Shit. Sorry, I lost myself for a moment. I'll be gentle."

A new determination, a new desire, swelled in her. She wanted him to lose himself, lose himself in her, in all the ways she could please him.

In all the ways he could make her his.

She removed her hands from him, keeping his gaze as she swallowed him deeper, cushioning her lips in the soft, wild curls around his base.

"Mina, you—"

She inhaled through her nose and curled her tongue against his shaft, encouraging him, assuring him.

His expression darkened from gentle concern to pure lust.

"You," he all but growled.

Mina whimpered around him as heat pooled between her legs.

His grip on her hair tightened possessively. "So eager to please, aren't you?" He rocked his hips back slowly, dragging his cock along her tongue, testing her. "Who knew all I needed to do was promise a reward to get you to behave?"

He guided himself back in at an excruciating pace, pushing the tip of his cock past the entrance of her throat, and held it there.

"Swallow," he commanded.

She did and watched the pleasure ripple across his skin.

"That's my girl," he praised with a shudder, and she nearly fell apart from the words alone. "Stop me if it's too much, alright?"

Mina nodded as much as she could, and hummed happily as Sebastian began to move, gentle nature falling apart quickly, giving way to his lust as he fucked her throat properly.

"Fuckin' hell," his swear crumbled into satisfied grunts and moans. "You take me so fucking well. You're doing so good. So good, baby."

The praise fed her, and made her all the more hungry for it. His cock trembled on her tongue, the muscles flexing, a welcomed warning as his thrusts turned uneven. She swallowed around him, catching his thrust just in time, holding on to the back of his legs as his knees gave in. He spilled down her throat with a loud wail of surprise, music to complement the savory meal he left on her tongue. Mina sucked greedily, not wanting to waste a single drop.

She *was* good. She would be so good to him.

She released him with a parting pass of her tongue and leaned back to look at him, admiring her handiwork as he regained his footing.

"What do you think, sir?" she asked, voice hoarse. "Have I earned my rewar—"

Scooped up mid-question, warm hands parted her legs to straddle Sebastian's lap as he fell onto his bed.

"Oh yes," he praised, gazing up at her in pure awe and adoration, as his hands, nearly burning, trailed up the back of her thighs. "You have *more* than earned it."

One hand ghosted over the curve of her ass to work on those accursed buttons, while the other slipped under her dress.

Mina shuddered as he stroked the thin, damp fabric covering her.

"Poor thing," he said, peppering kisses against her neck, "You're soaked." He hooked his fingers beneath the fabric, and it fell away, leaving only the smell of smoke wafting in the air to mingle with the sweet whiskey on his breath.

"There," he said, running his fingers between her slick folds. "Much better."

His fingers slipped inside her easily and pumped at a lazy pace, blurring her thoughts with every pass of his fingertips over the tight, sensitive ring of muscle at her entrance.

"My Gods," Sebastian praised. "Do you know how perfect you are? Already so ready for me. Did you like sucking my cock that much?"

"Mmmhmm," she whimpered, gripping the bedsheets beneath him as her body trembled. "You t-taste good."

"I do, do I?" he mused. "How do I taste? Since you've been learning all those new words."

"S-savory," she panted. "Salty, and b-bitter."

"Bitter?" he asked. "That doesn't sound good."

"It's a nice b-bitter, l-like— ah!"

Sebastian's fingers slipped down to toy with her clit, sending jolts of pleasure that overloaded all sense.

"Like?" he pressed.

"L-like," she huffed, trying to focus on the taste of him still lingering on her tongue while her hips ground against his hand, demanding more attention than his light touch teased. "C-cranberries?"

He laughed lightly. The last of her buttons unfastened, he ran his hand up her bare spine, conjuring hot sparks along with it. She moaned at the sensation, and he claimed her open mouth, kissing her deeply, running his tongue along hers.

"I see what you mean," he teased. "Definitely a bit of cranberry."

"'Bastian," Mina whined. Her body pleaded to be filled, clenching around nothing with each circle of his fingers around her clit. "Please."

"I know," he said, fingers leaving her to grab at the hem of her dress. "As fantastic as this looks, we have to get you out of it. Be a good girl and sit back for me."

She did as she was told, pulling away from him to sit back, and was rewarded with the sensation of his cock pressing against her eager slit. She sank down around him, sighing in relief at the stretch, her walls pulsing in warm welcome.

He guided the hem of her dress into her hands and watched her, sparks smoldering in the honey of his eyes, as she pulled it over her head and threw it somewhere on his bedroom floor.

"You sure you don't want to fold it?" he asked wryly. "It would be a shame for such a pretty dress to get all wrinkled."

"It'll be fine," she leaned forward to kiss him. He held her back with a flat palm against her chest.

"This too," he said, tugging at her bindings.

"Just burn them like you did my knickers," she huffed in frustration.

Sebastian smirked. "Where's the fun in that?"

She glared at him. "The fun is in getting my clothes off faster."

His smirk was unwavering. "That's alright, lila doar. If you don't want to behave, I'm more than happy to let you warm my cock all night." He grabbed her hips roughly, holding them down and keeping her from riding him as she pleased.

She scolded herself slightly for how his frustrating demands turned her on; slick gliding down her walls as her cunt pulsed around him. There had to be no doubt in his mind how much of an advantage he had.

"Fine," she hissed and sat up straight. She kept her glare, wanting him to see and feel every ounce of her annoyance. To know that even though she was complying, she wouldn't allow him to have the upper hand wholly. She unwound the bindings quickly and tossed them into the ether, not caring where they landed. "Happy?"

Sebastian took his time before answering, assessing every inch of her as if he were taking in a gallery, the subtle twitches of his cock inside her giving away every silent, lustful thought.

"Very," he said. "I love you in all forms, but there is something outstanding about seeing you on top of me with nothing but the pendant I made you 'round your neck."

Mina's frustration faltered under his adoration. A slight smile curved her lips as she touched that amber stone. "What? This old thing?"

"Mmmhmm." His hands left her hips as he picked it up, pulling at it slightly for her to lean forward. "I still owe you another one."

"Another?" she asked, spellbound by the feeling of his cock dragging against her walls slowly and the affection in his eyes.

"The fire opal you admired." He released the pendant and ran his hand up her neck to grab her hair. "But only good girls get presents." He locked eyes with her, embers promising to consume her.

Mina smiled and kissed him chastely. "I can be good."

His free hand grabbed her ass, palm near burning, and he guided himself out of her: head lingering at her entrance. Mina shuttered her eyes and hummed in anticipation.

"You'll be good for me?" he asked in a husky whisper.

"So good..." she rasped. "For you..."

Sebastian buried his cock in deeply with a hard thrust, throwing her forward as he took her breast into his mouth. He fucked her properly, pace brutal, domineering. All her mind was pleasure and heat, only him and his ecstasy.

What a reward.

Her attempts to call his name, to praise him, thank him, were incoherent, broken apart by moans and whimpers as he unmade her, breaking her down to nothing more than a creature of want. Her body demanded more, and more, clenching around him, meeting his thrusts with her own until eruption.

His name found her then, shaking from her lips as she drowned in rapture, warmth filling her and unwinding her until she returned to herself.

"There you go," Sebastian sighed as she shifted, body well spent, to lie on top of him. He guided her down to lay her head against his chest, and kissed the top of her head. "You did so good, baby."

"So good," she repeated, mumbling the words as the running, the dinner, the dancing, all the efforts of the day caught up with her, taking full advantage of her fragile state.

Sebastian hugged her, his embrace warm and secure. Despite the teasing, and the hunger, his arms still felt so safe. So strong, just like when they were dancing. Just the same as when he had held her hand up, unafraid. "You are good. No matter what anybody else thinks."

"Even when I'm being a brat?" she hummed, one last tease to try and beat back exhaustion.

"Even when you're being a brat," he repeated fondly. The chesty rattle of his voice against her ear was a lullaby that made it hard to keep her eyes open. "I love you."

"I love you too," she slurred as the world went dark.

"So much," he whispered, his palms flaring a bit as his hands flexed.

"S'much," she whispered back and greeted sleep wholeheartedly.

🜁

All was gray again. The skies overcast. The world too still for a spring day. The new growth seemed withered. No birds sang. The young leaves did not whisper.

Mina sat on a small hill overlooking a lake, fresh dirt under her fingernails, fresh blood dripping from her blade. She knew exactly what day it was by the heavy sadness in her chest and the unshed tears burning behind her eyes.

The wind brushed over her shoulder, a warm hand cupped her cheek. She followed it to a being made of wind and amber, gusts shifting to curl familiar locks, but eyes solid, a somber umber, and weeping.

Her unshed tears fell at the sight.

🜁

It was no secret that Mina could perform many impressive feats. She could run faster than a train, lift as much as an elephant, punch through solid rock... But ride in a wagon? Her turning stomach angrily disagreed.

"So you can drink arsenic with your morning tea, but a little carriage ride has you on your deathbed?" Sir Gargic mocked.

"I mean you're pale, but right now, you downright look ghostly," Wera added, gold-rimmed glasses leaning forward into the edges of her vision to study her face. "Your lips even look gray."

Mina's white-knuckle grip on the wagon's back gate threatened to splinter it.

"If you two continue," she seethed through gritted teeth as she tried her best to keep her focus on the horizon, recalling the tips for conquering seasickness she read once in a naughty pirate book, "I am going to make sure I use both of your packs as my sick buckets."

"Mina, dear, if you just let me use—"

"No," she growled, cutting Tanir off. "No enchantments. My body's just being stupid, and once it realizes it's being stupid, it'll stop being stupid."

"Or it might not," she countered. "Some people experience motion sickness their entire lives. It just depends on how sensitive your inner ear—"

"Then my inner ear will just have to get unsensitive."

Tanir sighed. "Gods, you are more stubborn than a mule. Can you at least let me help you in some way? I really hate when people vomit."

"You're a medic."

"Doesn't mean I have to suddenly be okay with seeing people lose their lunch."

Mina dared to take her eyes off of the horizon to glare at her, and regretted it immediately. She swallowed back the sudden rise of bile in her throat and ignored the cold sweat beading down her spine.

"No.... Enchantments..." she forced out.

Tanir rolled her eyes and grabbed her by the arm, yanking her to her feet, "Enoch! Get in the back."

"What?" he squawked from his place on the driver's bench. "But I've got to—"

"Just sit right behind Sebastian and take your notes," she barked as she dragged Mina to the front of the wagon. "Unless you want the sounds and smells of retching to inspire your work."

Enoch opened his mouth to protest once more, but the sight of Mina's ghastly appearance had him scrambling out of his seat instead, leaving plenty of room for Tanir to throw her onto the bench beside Sebastian.

"Lila doar?" Sebastian asked. "To what do I owe the pleas—" his voice trailed off as he took his focus off the road ahead and placed it on her, "—ure..."

Mina went to respond when a firm, wrinkled hand forced open her jaw and threw a piece of hard candy into her mouth.

"There," Tanir said. "Suck on that and keep your focus on the road ahead. The ginger lozenge should help calm your stomach a bit. If you need another, just ask me for it."

"I told you, no—"

Tanir placed her palm over Mina's mouth before she could spit the candy out. "It's not enchanted."

She stomped away to the back of the wagon, shaking the damn thing so much with every step Mina wondered if she was doing it on purpose.

"Are you alright?" Sebastian asked.

Mina found the horizon line again and set her white-knuckle grip on the edge of the bench beneath her.

"I'm fine," she hissed.

"You don't look fine."

"I know. My body's being stupid. Motion sickness," she grumbled. "I can fucking do twenty-five front handsprings in a row, but one tiny fucking wagon ride makes me want to rip my entire stomach out."

"Does this usually happen when you ride in a wagon?"

"Don't know. I've never ridden in a wagon before. Couldn't really. Had to walk on the side or pull the cart myself."

"Well, I don't mind slowing the horses' pace down a bit if you'd rather walk—"

"No. I ain't lettin' no wagon get the best of me." She inhaled sharply and sat as tall as she could manage. "I'm feeling better already."

"You look *so* clammy."

"Better than ghostly."

Sebastian chuckled and shook his head. "Now, I get why Tanir's upset with you."

"What's that supposed to mean?"

He clicked his tongue in admonishment. "So stubborn, lila doar."

Mina groaned. "Please. Like you're not stubborn."

"I can be, but only for good reason. Not 'refusing to have a medic enchant me so I don't feel like vomiting every time we hit a bump in the road.'"

She scoffed. "It's not every bump."

"Really?" He arched an eyebrow and pointed at the road. "So I can ride across that cluster of potholes coming up?"

Mina snapped her head towards him and hissed, "Don't you fucking dare."

He chuckled, a cheeky smile spreading across his face, and patted her thigh. "I won't. But you should really consider having her enchant you."

Another wave of nausea began to rise. She faced the road again to curb it. "No."

"Might I ask why? It would only be for a few hours."

"Because as shitty as this feeling is, at least I feel it. I'm choosing to feel it. And I'm not gonna let it get the best of me."

"Understood." He smoothed his warm thumb back and forth over her knee. "But I will warn you that when we do get closer to the Capitol, the streets turn to cobblestone, which makes for a pretty bumpy ride. So if your stomach's not settled by then, maybe a couple of hours of nausea would be enough 'feeling'?"

Mina closed her eyes and sucked on her lozenge, letting the ginger coat and work its way down her throat. "Maybe. But I'm determined to get control of it well before then."

"Of course," he said kindly. "Just let me know how I can help."

She opened her eyes slowly as her roiling stomach soothed to a bubble, and glanced down at his hand. Warm. Flesh and bone. Not amber and windblown.

"'Bastian?"

"Need me to get a bucket?"

"No." She shook her head. "You said you saw me, among other things. What did you mean by that?"

His thumb stilled.

"What makes you ask?"

"I had a dream last night. A memory." She slipped her hand beneath his, interlacing their fingers. "The day Mr. Harlowe passed. You were there, but... not quite you."

Sebastian squeezed her hand. "Your wind was there. It just," he gave a heavy sigh, "took me along with it."

"But you said you saw me when I was ten."

"And eighteen, and thirteen, younger even, back to when you were just a babe." He turned to her, lips bowed into a small frown that hinted at a much deeper sadness. "I saw *her* take you from your crib."

Her heart lurched, a sudden pain she didn't have the time or knowledge to name stealing her breath and sending tears streaming down her face.

"O-oh."

"I'm sorry," he said, more of a whisper as his own throat dried. "We can talk about something else—"

"Did you see them?" The question, driven by a much older one, rushed out of her.

"See who?"

She looked up at him, heart leaping into her throat. "My parents?"

His eyebrows flitted in surprise for a brief moment before knitting together, drawing tears to well in his eyes. "No." He shook his head. "Just you."

She swallowed her heart and nodded, "O-okay. That's g-good. I guess." She kept nodding, trying to shake the hope, the disappointment, the longing out of her system. "If they were there, I bet they would have put up a fight to keep me."

"Oh," Sebastian smiled wobbly, "I'm sure they would have."

"*She* didn't do anything to you directly, did She?" she asked, anticipatory anger reining in her emotions a bit.

"No. No." He sniffled and turned his attention back to the road. "Honestly, the in-between from finding you to you sending me back home, I don't really remember. All of my time in there was spent as the wind, surging through decades, trying to piece it all together." He squeezed her hand again. "It feels unfair if I'm being honest."

"Unfair?"

"I know so much about you, without you giving me permission to," he said. "Honestly, I wish I kept diaries so I could just give them to you and say, 'Have at!'"

"Or. You could tell me some stories now to make up for it." Her drying tears and finished lozenge had made way for nausea to rear its head once more. "Might be a g-good distraction to keep my mind off my stomach."

He chuckled. "So you don't want to hear about the time I snuck live slugs into one of my adoptive parents' salads?"

Her stomach gurgled up a burning burp. "Not now."

"Alright, alright. Let's do one story for every memory I saw to make it even. Starting with..." He tapped his thumb against her knee in his signature triplets. "...my first day as Master Ozdemir's apprentice."

🜁

Though Sebastian's stories and Tanir's lozenges helped to soothe Mina's aching stomach, the grand outer walls of a city had never been a more welcomed sight.

The ashlar-stoned behemoth slowly blocked out the sky as they approached it. Its parapets built higher than the massive evergreens around it, granting the soldiers who patrolled across them ample vantage points. **LANHOLDE ✦ CAPITAL**, carved in stone, sat above the large wooden door that granted entrance into the Capitol city.

"Purpose and papers," a gatesman called as they approached.

Sir Gargic stomped his way to the front of the wagon and popped his head out over the driver's seat, smiling much too proudly for Mina's sensitive stomach.

"Hello boys," he practically purred as he presented their travel papers. "Did you miss me?"

The gatesmen all saluted at the sight of him.

"Sir!" They shouted in unison. "Cheers to your safe return!"

"At ease, gentlemen," he cooed as he waved the papers towards them with a flourish. One of the gatesmen grabbed them from him. "Tell me, how's the Capitol been in my absence? Sir Laakso's not working you too much, is he?"

"No, sir," the gatesman said. "It's an honor to serve The Crown in any way we can."

Sir Gargic laughed joyfully. "That's what I like to hear, son!"

The gatesman stamped the paperwork and handed it back to him. "Everything's in order, sir." He turned to Sebastian. "Driver, I'd recommend you take Marendale Way to the castle. Reinhardt Road has been real stopped up because of Harvest's Hail."

Sebastian saluted, playing along with the gatesman's assumption. "Understood, sir. A fruitful Fall to you and yours."

"And to yours." The gatesman signaled the doors to open and gave Sir Gargic one last salute.

The knight continued to linger once they passed the gate and entered the Capitol proper, hovering behind them like a parent untrusting of their child's handiwork.

"Windenhofer, let me at the reins. I want to see what's changed around town with my own eyes," he said as forced his way between them on the driver's bench.

"Uh, sure." Sebastian handed him the reins and awkwardly slipped back into the wagon. He offered out his hand. "Here, Mina."

"It might be best if the lass stays up front with me. Don't want her looking like she ate a bunch of bad clams in front of any nobles we might pass on the way to meet the Royal Consul."

Sebastian placed his hand on her shoulder. "Is that alright with you?"

"I just got my stomach wrangled so," she exhaled heavily, "it'll have to be."

He squeezed her shoulder tightly. "Alright." He leveled a stern look at Gargic. "I'll be right here if you need me."

The wagon only rocked a bit as he headed into it, letting her know he was still sitting close by. Close enough to listen in on whatever nonsense Sir Gargic was sure to say to her.

Every second they sat in silence was unnerving, especially with the way too genuine smile he wore as he gazed upon the town.

"You see that bakery right there?" he said after a moment, nodding his head in a direction Mina did not care to look at. "My great-great-grandfather helped build it."

"What are you trying to do?" Mina asked, cutting to the chase.

"Tell you a little bit of Lanholde history."

"After antagonizing me and treating me like dirt for the past month?" she doubted. "If you wanted to get chummy with me, giving me a jaunty little tour of your hometown ain't the way to do it. You want something. Out with it."

He rolled his eyes. "You may be uncursed, but you're still a beast, you know that?"

She sneered. "Then cut to the chase before this beast starts biting."

"I want to make sure you know how to behave once we get to the castle."

"How to *behave?*"

"Sure, you're a fine dancer — definitely have all the accomplishments a finished young lady should have — but you're severely lacking in decorum and etiquette. Do you even know how to properly curtsy? How to tell a noble's rank by the insignia they wear?"

Mina ran the tip of her tongue along her teeth to dull the lash it so wanted to throw his way, and smiled. "It's not by the insignia, it's by the color and type of stone they wear with their accessories. The insignias represent their family line, with a quarter-turned floreted cross of brass representing commoners awarded the status of gentry. Just like the ones you wore on the lapels of your suit during the party."

Sir Gargic puckered his lips and shifted to sit a little taller in his seat.

"I've had more etiquette classes than you've had battles, received more injuries during them too, most likely," she continued. "So you don't need to worry about this beastie. I am, unfortunately, a well-trained dog." Mina sat back in her seat, arms crossed in defense, not liking the revelation that so easily fell from her lips. "It's not like we're going to be sipping high tea with any nobles anyway. It's just drop off the goods with the Consul, sign some paperwork, get paid, and get out. I'll make sure to keep my posture straight and my mouth shut."

"Well, I'm sure some nobles will want to speak with us. We're returning from a remarkable journey that very few have finished," he countered.

"Fine. They can talk. I'm sure between the five of you, they can find plenty of wonderful conversationalists."

"Come on now. I know you and I have had our differences, but surely you'd want to share your tales of the Fallow Peaks with a captive audience."

"It's cold, there's monsters, you can die. There. End of story."

"Gods. You're such a child."

Mina's hands itched to rip out the rest of his shitty beard.

"No, Sir Gargic. I'm a beast. Remember?" She stood and headed into the wagon.

"Where are you going? You'll get sick!"

"Rather get sick than get convicted of murder." Mina stomped all the way to the back of the wagon, and stared out at the city passing by in reverse. Sebastian moved to sit beside her not a minute later.

"I'm sorry," he said.

"It's not your fault," she replied.

"I shouldn't have let him take the reins. I shouldn't let him keep talking to you like that."

She scoffed. "He'll keep talking like that whether or not you let him. Until this contract is completed, at least." Mina, despite the bitter taste Sir Gargic's questioning left on her tongue, smiled. "As soon as I get that gilt in my hand, I have many, many choice words I have to say to him. I might even challenge him to a duel."

He huffed a laugh. "A duel?"

"He cares about his pride and his accomplishments as a knight. What better way to get payback than to debase him in front of The Crown he cares so much about?" She considered the idea a little more closely. "I might even be able to make some more coin off of it too, which would help greatly."

"Help with what?" Sebastian asked.

"A project I'm working on. It's a surprise."

Sebastian smiled. "A surprise, huh? Can I get a hint?"

"Hmm. Sure." She gave a more wicked, more enticing, smile to throw him off the trail of her true intent. "I'm going to need some specialty wood and leather."

He drummed his fingers against his lips as he considered her answer, a slight blush blooming across his cheeks. "*Specialty* wood and leather?"

"That's what I said."

"There are so many things that can be."

She knocked her knee against his. "And you're thinking of all the dirty ones, aren't you?"

"Not all of them," he said. "Maybe you want to make yourself a fine leather armchair."

"A fine leather armchair, huh?"

"Or maybe you want to try your hand at specialty bookbinding." He shrugged as his blush spread to burn his ears. "Get your mind out of the gutter."

"My mind's in the gutter?" Mina leaned towards him, nose just an inch away from his, as she studied his face. "But I'm not the one blushing redder than rouge."

Sebastian went to lean in for a kiss but wound up smacking his forehead against hers when the wagon came to a sudden stop.

A pair of Royal Guards came sauntering around the back of the wagon, studying it and the occupants inside with stern expressions.

"Windenhofer?" The taller guard said as he looked over their travel and contract paperwork.

"Yes, that's me," Sebastian said, rising to meet the guards.

"It says here that you have three individuals under your employ."

"That is correct."

"Then why are there four?"

"Oh," he gestured to Mina. "As of the date of that contract's creation, Mina was not a part of Windenhofer Procurements, but she should be listed."

"Mina? I don't see no—"

"She's the alpinist, Jokinen," Sir Gargic stopped his chumming with the head guard to call.

"The alpinist?" he checked the paperwork, then looked up at Mina. "You don't look like an alpinist."

She bristled, but did her best to keep a sneer off her face to not prove Sir Gargic right."What do I look like then?"

"Like a princess or something," he said. "Hair's a little short for that, I guess. But I figured an alpinist would look, I don't know, a little rougher in the face?" He checked the paperwork again. "Mina, you said your name was?"

Another wave of nausea, driven by disgust rather than motion, passed through her. She'd rather have a sword pointed at her throat than deal with this guard's shit attempt at flattery.

"Is something the matter?" Sebastian asked.

"Jokinen, my dear lad, everything is in perfect order." Sir Gargic called again, his voice a little more perturbed. "That paperwork is as solid as redrock. I guarantee it."

"You heard the man, Jokinen," the head guard added, a gruff authority to his tone. "Best not to keep The Crown waiting."

Jokinen nodded, then folded the paperwork back up again. "Sorry about that, miss," he said to Mina. "Just trying to make sure everything's secure what with all the upper crust folks visiting for Harvest's Hail." He turned to his partner, "Sight check clear on your end, Asmo?"

A shimmer of silver magic flickered across the other guard's eyes. "All clear."

"Great." Jokinen tipped his helmet towards them. "Happy Harvest."

Sebastian nodded his head back slightly, tone that false jovial he puts on to hide his displeasure. "Happy Harvest."

Mina watched the guards walk back to the front and return the paperwork to Sir Gargic who, with a promise of grabbing a drink with the head guard later this evening, cracked the reins and led the horses towards the carriage port.

"A princess, huh?" Sebastian remarked under his breath, calling her attention to him.

"If you ever see me put on a crown, know that something is seriously wrong," she said with a shiver.

"Makes sense." He nodded wisely, a wry smile tugging at the corners of his mouth as he buried whatever was bothering him about the comment and turned towards her. "You're much more of a tiara girl."

"Absolutely not."

"No? What about a hennin?" He pulled his hand from the top of his head to hover in the air. "One of those long cone ones with ribbons running down the back?"

"I'll take that cone and shove it up your ass," she jokingly threatened as the cart stopped, swatting at his hand. Sebastian took it as an opportunity to grab her hand and bring it to his lips, kissing her knuckles lightly.

"I'm not into cones but—"

A sudden spritz of water splattered across his face.

"Flirt later," Wera snapped, "Offload now," and dropped a crate, that seemed heavier by the way she carried it, onto Mina's lap.

🜁

The palace halls were much more lively and ornate than Leithlis Serdtsa's, but that didn't help to ease the tiny voice in the back of Mina's mind straightening her spine, raising her chin just the slightest bit, urging her to leave as soon as possible. The servants standing in wait along the walls, the grand pillars holding up the grand ceilings, the echo of the maid escorting them down the hall's heels on the marble tile floors: all had her heartbeat racing much faster than she liked as they made their way to the Western Receiving Room.

"Sir Gargic has returned and wishes to present the fruits of His Majesty's request to the Consul," the maid said to the guards standing outside the door. "Are we permitted entrance?"

"You are," one guard said, stepping to the side in sync with his counterpart to grab the large door handles. "His Majesty has been waiting for you for quite some time now."

"His Majesty?" Enoch squeaked just as the doors opened in front of them, revealing an ostentatious receiving room filled with abstract stone statues, lush, plush furniture piled high with pillows beneath rug-thick curtains, gaudy Fall-themed decor, and a crowned man, lounging with his leg's spread wide on his throne.

"Welcome home!" King Fritz cheered as he stood. "Sir Gargic, my dear friend, I missed you! The entire court missed you. Didn't they, Henri?"

The plump, bald-headed man standing next to the throne gave a smile so jolly his full cheeks forced his eyes shut. "We most certainly did."

Mina dropped into a low curtsy in perfect sync with Sir Gargic's bow — muscle memory piloting her body before her forward thought could recognize it. The others followed suit, bending at the waists and casting their eyes to the ground in wait. The thick odor of autumnal spices, wafting off the length of ornately woven carpet they stood on, stung Mina's eyes.

"Your Majesty," Sir Gargic greeted evenly. If he was surprised by the king's presence, it was hidden quite well. "I am most grateful to have returned home and to be in your presence once more. I'm honored to see you so soon after my arrival as well, though, I must be honest and say that I was expecting only to meet with the Consul at this time. My apologies for any *lack of decorum* that may occur due to this misunderstanding."

Lack of decorum.

The way he dragged the phrase along incensed Mina.

As much as she loathed every facet of her upbringing, as much as the formalities and ostentatious presentation of royalty made her skin crawl, what better use were the skills she suffered to develop than to spite such a pompous ass?

"I think nothing of it. I'm just eager to see the fruits of your quest and to meet the fine adventurers who accomplished such feats. I've been hearing tales of these wondrous items and lands since I was a boy, you know?" King Fritz said as he approached them, a jovial, friendly lilt as he spoke. A different timbre to his Lanholdian accent, one well-practiced, pleasant, and polite, unlike Sir Gargic's thick-tongued gruff. "You may arise and introduce yourselves."

Mina listened for the men to straighten up before she transitioned out of her curtsy. An antiquated practice, she was sure, but one she'd practiced over and over again during her Lanholdian etiquette lessons.

"An honor to meet you, Your Majesty," Sebastian said. "I am Master Sebastian Windenhofer, Master Level Mage of the Northerner Practitioners' Guild and owner of Windenhofer Procurements." He gestured back to the group. "This is my medic, Ms. Tanir Kask."

Tanir curtsied as well as she could with her injured leg.

"My cartographer, Ms. Wera Alrust."

Wera bowed her head lightly.

"And my archivist, Mr. Enoch Dapple."

Enoch bowed deeply. "It is an honor to be in your presence, Your Majesty."

King Fritz's eyes flitted over each of them, giving them just enough recognition to be well-mannered, before his attention turned to Mina.

"And who is this lovely creature?" he asked as he approached her, smiling brightly, curiosity sparkling in his gaze.

Mina curtsied deeply again. "Good Harvest's Hail to you, Your Majesty. My name is Mina. It is my deepest honor to meet you. May your fortunes run like veins of quartz through granite."

"Mina?" he asked with a lilt of confusion in his tone, a more respectable questioning compared to the palace guard that had checked their paperwork.

She rose and smiled softly, holding back the 'eat shit' grin she wanted to boast at catching Sir Gargic's slack jaw in the corner of her vision. "Yes, Your Majesty. I am the alpinist The Crown contracted to lead Sir Gargic and Windenhofer Procurements up the Fallow Peaks."

The king was much younger than she'd expected, especially from how Sir Gargic spoke of him. He had to be no older than forty. His hair carefully coiffed to showcase his sharp widow's peak with pomade made to make its deep ebony shine. His nose was slightly upturned, face round despite how the precise cut of his beard tried to give the illusion of a sharp jawline.

Beneath his wide, golden epaulets and tailored coatee, he had the average build for a nobleman; shoulders sloped, slightly portly from the rich foods and lack of labor, and his height just barely topped her own.

An average-looking man in every sense, yet something about his presence was compelling. A sense of curiosity, an openness. 'Welcome', perhaps. His eyes were a color Mina couldn't quite place. They were striking, however, patterned like the polished green jasper Sebastian kept in his study.

"*You're* the alpinist?" he asked, an amused confusion twisting his expression slightly, breaking his kingly visage to reveal a bit of a jester beneath. Mina kept her eyes from rolling. He was one of those "fun" kings.

"Yes, Your Majesty," she assured politely, even though his doubt perturbed her. She'd mock him to Sebastian and Wera once they were in the privacy of the commorancy. "I know my appearance may not be what one typically associates with a mountain climber. But I can assure you—"

"But you're smiling," the king interjected.

Mina stared at him a moment, studying him with the same restrained confusion as he was her.

There was a heaviness in the silence.

"I beg your pardon?" she said with a smile, beat-in manners taking the reins while her mind was at a loss.

"I'm well aware that the alpinist who lives in the Sandere Woods is a woman of great skill and even greater beauty. But from the accounts of those who have traveled up the Peaks with her, she is also incredibly stoic and cold," King Fritz said. A smile, pleasantly disbelieving, curved his lips into a light laugh. "From the conviction of your greeting, your manner of speaking, and that smile of yours, I would say you're anything but that."

"Oh, well," Mina struggled to find the right words, glancing at Sebastian for some assistance. "I used to be like that, Your Majesty."

"Used to be?"

"Yes, Your Majesty," Sebastian moved to stand beside her, drawing King Fritz's curiosity his way. "When we first met Mina in Sandere Woods, her disposition was quite like your description, but we were able to discover quickly that her dour behavior was part of a rather nasty curse."

King Fritz inhaled sharply. "A curse!" He turned to Henri, smile growing even wider, eyes alighting. "I said it had to have been a curse, didn't I Henri?"

Henri nodded. "You most certainly did, Your Majesty."

"You... *said* that I was cursed?" Mina asked, respectful report slipping as the admission raised her hackles. She didn't like the idea of people talking about her without her knowing, and for royalty to be discussing her deepest pain?

He turned back around to face her, "Yes! During a state dinner a few months back, one of the guests was describing his time traveling with you, and I noted to the dinner party that it sounded like you were a Cursed One. That's partially why I suggested you for this expedition, I must admit. I wanted to see for myself if I was right."

So much for recommended for my skill. I was contracted just to settle some aristocratic bet!

His eyes glistened like a child receiving their first gold star in school. "And I was! I was right!" He chuckled. "Though I suppose I don't have to offer the aid of the Lanholde Practitioners to help break it now." He said with a slight air of sheepishness, eyes casting down a bit in apology.

Mina's internal sour sweetened a bit at that. At least he'd thought about trying to help her instead of just parading her around.

Fritz turned to Sebastian. "How did you do it? A potion or incantation of some sort?"

Sebastian cleared his throat. "We did it by more... traditional means, Your Majesty." He smiled warmly at Mina and took her hand in his.

Mina turned to him, squeezing his hand lightly, and let her gaze linger on his eyes; a familiar respite compared to the king's.

His Majesty broke out into a fit of jackal-like laughter — jester fully eclipsing the king — and smacked Sebastian's arm.

"Windenhofer, you dog!" he cheered. "You've gotten my goods and gotten the girl, haven't you?"

Sebastian blushed slightly. "It wasn't my intention, but I am quite pleased it turned out that way, Your Majesty."

King Fritz smiled, voice falling to a thoughtful hum as he took in the couple, "I bet you are." His gaze lingered a moment, an indiscernible look in his eye — close to yearning if Mina had to put a name to it — passing through as he regained his kingly composure.

He clapped his hands together, bringing them all back to reality. "Let us inspect what you've brought, get you all paid, and get you on your way then, shall we? Henri?"

"Yes, Your Majesty."

The king turned around and headed back to his throne while the Consul spoke to Sir Gargic, looking over the contract.

The servants that had followed them down the halls wheeled in large carts groaning from the weight of the quarry they carried. Sebastian left Mina's side to direct them, pointing out where to arrange the crates and chests and other bundles, while handling the more fragile objects himself. Out of a twill sack he pulled out a great claymore, so large his hands could not fit around the grip, footing stumbling a bit as he sat on the floor. Only a giant could have wielded such a thing, had Sebastian fought one for it? Tanir unfurled rare pelts, leathers and scales and furs Mina had never seen before, and placed the bones and fangs, talons and jarred specimens, of their owners beside them. Wera handled precious paintings and renderings, while Enoch dusted off ancient tomes and scrolls with practiced care.

Dozens of adventures, hundreds of stories, in just two cart fulls. An entire world she only knew through the pages of paperbacks and textbooks. An entire world she'd soon see.

Mina couldn't help but smile at the thought. She couldn't wait to see her picture hanging among theirs in the commorancy's halls.

"Alright," Henri said. "Everything looks to be in order. Hans," he called for one of the attendants, "if you could bring out the agreed upon sixty-thousand gilt for Windenhofer Procurements and the seven-thousand gilt sum for the alpinist."

Hans frowned. "Sixty-*seven* in total, my lord?"

"Yes. But I assume she would like hers in a separate pouch," he replied, gesturing to Mina offhandedly.

"My apologies, my lord, but last I heard the total was sixty-thousand not sixty-seven thousand," Hans explained. "We've only fetched sixty-thousand from the treasury."

"Boy," Sir Gargic glared at the attendant. "I sent a missive with Ms. Mina's updated—"

Henri held up a hand to ease Sir Gargic's temper, chubby cheeks wrinkled as he pursed his lips in displeasure. "Then go and fetch the other seven from the treasury."

"We can't, my lord."

"You *can't?"* he pressed, voice dripping with disapproval.

Hans swallowed nervously, but kept this posture perked and chin held high. "The treasury is currently closed and locked up for the holiday."

Henri inhaled sharply — deeply through his nose — and turned towards Mina with a tense half smile that turned her excitement into annoyance.

"I am so sorry, miss. But it seems as though we cannot pay you at this time. If you could perhaps wait a few days until Harvest's Hail is concluded? I'm sure we'd be able to find you lodging at one of the inns in town, courtesy of The Crown, of course."

"What is the issue, Henri?" King Fritz called from his throne.

Henri's shoulders seized up as he turned around and smiled widely at the king. "No issue at all, Your Majesty!"

"Really?" King Fritz said, rising from his seat once again as he pointed at Mina. "Because she's frowning. And she is far too pretty to be frowning."

"There seems to be a bit of a payment issue, Your Majesty. It seems as though we are short Mina's promised payment," Sebastian answered. Though his expression was amenable, smile welcoming, there a tinge of annoyance flexed the muscles in his neck. "But the Consul has offered to lodge us at a nearby inn until Harvest's Hail has concluded and the treasury has been reopened."

"An inn?!" King Fritz strode towards them in a huff. "You will not stay at an inn. Especially when such an egregious mistake has been made on our part." He glared at Henri. "We'll have some rooms made up for you here at the palace."

The declaration sparked an idea, and the king's stern pout returned to his playful smile. "And better yet, let's invite them all as guests to the Harvest's Hail festivities we're holding!"

He turned to them, eyes wide with excitement. If he were a puppy dog, Mina was sure his tail would be wagging, shaking his whole body even. "We're hosting some foreign dignitaries in preparation for the Barley Moon Ball. I'm sure they will all be delighted to hear your grand tales of adventure. You all can even come to the reception dinner we're having this evening! Get you all acquainted with our esteemed guests before the party." He looked at her directly. "Surely you'd want to put on a pretty dress and dance the evening away, wouldn't you, my dear? It's not often an alpinist gets to live the lavish life!"

His delivery made for an appealing pitch. The royal part of it all made her squirm a bit, but the dancing? Dressing up? She didn't mind that. Especially if Sebastian was dancing and dressing alongside her.

Especially if she would get her seven thousand by the end of it.

Mina could hear Sebastian's teeth grind a bit beneath his smile.

Maybe I should mind it.

"That is most generous, Your Majesty," he replied, his jaw tighter than it should be with his gracious tone. He turned to the group. "What do you say, all? Would you mind sticking around for a few days? I know some of you have plans, so if you need me to arrange for travel for you instead—"

"And miss getting to live like royalty for a few days?" Wera said. "My sisters can definitely wait."

A quiet inhale. Sharp. Sebastian was holding his breath.

"Tanir? Enoch?" he asked.

"I'd be more than honored to stay here, Your Majesty," Tanir said.

"It would be foolish of me to miss the chance to document this once-in-a-lifetime opportunity," Enoch added.

Sebastian turned to Mina, expression still inquisitive, lighthearted, but his eyes, behind the front: concerned. "It's really up to you. I want to make sure you get paid properly, but if you'd like to go somewhere else until after the holiday or..."

"And eighteen, and thirteen, younger even, back to when you were just a babe." Sebastian's wind-blown soul, weeping, having seen all she had been through, lingered behind in his words. He knew the halls of Leithlis Serdtsa, knew that she was standing straighter, knew that her demure demeanor went beyond proving Sir Gargic wrong.

He must be so worried for her.

Mina's heart ached at the fact. They were on the other side of their troubles now, there was no need for him to worry about her any longer.

"No. Staying here is fine for a few days," she said with a soft smile and took his hand, giving him a reassuring squeeze, just as he often did for her. "So long as you all stay with me."

"It's settled, then," King Fritz declared with another happy clap. "Henri, give them the money you do have, and I will summon Oskar to get some rooms prepared. Let us try to make the best out of this unfortunate oversight, shall we?" He turned on his heels and headed out of the throne room with a slight skip in his step, bellowing in a singsong, "Someone bring me Oskar!"

"Here is your payment, sir," Hans said, offering a rather heavy sack of coin Sebastian's way. "In fifty-gilt coins, as you requested."

"Perfect. Thank you." Sebastian grabbed the sack and minimized it as he tucked it into his pants pocket.

"I'm sure Oskar will be here shortly," Henri said, nodding his head in goodbye as he followed after the king.

"I'll come with you, my lord," Sir Gargic said, joining Henri's side and leaving them alone in the throne room — save for the servants — without so much as a passing wave goodbye.

Selfish prick.

"Are you sure you're alright with this?" Sebastian asked quietly, taking both her hands in his as the others took the abandonment as an excuse to inspect the finery and statues that filled the room.

She nodded. Doubling down. She had faced her greatest fear head-on already, stabbed the bitch straight in the heart. Some pretty dresses and pomp and circumstance were child's play by comparison. "I'll be fine."

"You were as stiff as a board and watching every corner while we were walking down the halls. Your shoulders are so square now, I could check to see if the floor is level with them. " he countered. He bowed his head, voice dropping to a whisper — big, brown eyes watching, analyzing her. "It would make absolute sense if you don't want to stay here."

"I know, but—" She watched the others, Enoch in particular. Eyes wide in wonder, mustache curled higher by his smile as he chattered excitedly at Wera and Tanir, explaining the history of one of the blob-shaped stone statues in great detail. "Everyone else seems excited," she turned back to him, and her smile bent bashfully, a giddiness fluttering in her chest, "and I'll admit I don't mind the idea of going to a proper ball with you."

"And the reception dinner tonight?"

Her expression soured. A bed of nails behind her back, lying in wait for her posture to slip as she and the other children practiced perfection around a dining table, watched by reproachful eyes.

"Well," she drawled, a mischievous glint sparkling in her eyes. "I don't know about you, but my stomach still isn't sitting right. I may have to send my condolences, but as long as a member of our troop goes, there shouldn't be any offense to His Majesty."

His lips puckered slightly, mirroring her own soured pout as he studied her face.

She lifted his hands, his palms growing warmer, and kissed his knuckles. "It'll only be a few days. You all will be here with me." She quieted her voice in reassuring reverence, "I can make it through."

He dropped his head to rest against her forehead, worry still clinging to his umber, "You're sure?"

With him by her side, there was no doubt in her mind that she could get through anything. Confidence sparked and she lifted her chin.

"I'm sure."

XXVIII

Decorum, Duty, and Diplomacy

Oskar was old, hunched, and liver-spotted. The thin wisps of hair that remained on his head were slicked across his scalp so compactly that he might as well have committed to being bald. The bags under his eyes had formed not from a poor night of sleep, but from thousands of them. Despite his incredible age, he moved quickly down the halls of the palace, speaking with purpose as clear and crisp as the ironed pleats of his pants.

"It was incredibly difficult to find five rooms for you all given the circumstances," he said as they entered one of the palace's guest wings. "So I do apologize for how scattered your lodgings are from each other."

"That's quite alright, sir," Sebastian replied. "But I can save you some trouble, we only need four rooms."

Oskar did not bother to look back at him. "Only four rooms?"

"Yes. We could even cut it down to three if you'd like. Enoch on his own. Tanir and Wera, you don't mind sharing, do you?"

"Not at all," Tanir said as Wera nodded in agreement.

"Then Mina and I in another," he finished.

Oskar's head barely bobbed in acknowledgment. "I appreciate the concern, sir, but that would be incredibly improper."

Sebastian exchanged a quick look of concern with Enoch. "Improper?"

"Only married couples or immediate family members may lodge together."

Enoch spoke up at that. "I don't mean to doubt you, Oskar, but I remember reading that that rule had been abolished recently here in Lanholde."

"In the public sense, yes, it has. If you're staying in an inn or purchasing a home you no longer have to provide a proof of marriage certificate in order to do so, but here at the palace we hold ourselves to a higher standard," he groused. "If the Empress of Dulsten and her seven concubines must all room separately from each other during their stay for Harvest's Hail, so must you."

Oskar stopped in front of one of the many doors lining the walls of the guest wing, fished out a rather cumbersome ring of keys from his pocket, and opened the door. "Mr. Enoch Dapple."

"Thank you." Enoch moved towards the room and looked back at the group. "How about we all get settled in, then meet back here in an hour to explore the town a bit?" He looked at Sebastian pointedly, speech measured, calming. "Just because we're roomed separately doesn't mean we have to do things separately, right?"

"Absolutely right," he said, taking out his pocket watch. "We'll meet back here at four."

Oskar handed Enoch a copy of his key and the party headed off.

Wera's room was next, a decent walk away from Enoch's, then even further sat Sebastian's.

He took the key from Oskar and shut the door without even looking at his room, baring a smile the entire time though his frustration was starting to slip through the happy mask. "I'd like to continue to walk along if you don't mind. I want to make sure my female compatriots arrive at their rooms safely."

"Of course, sir," Oskar said, and set off once again with little protest.

They wove through the hallways for a good ten minutes before they arrived at Tanir's room, and then went up a staircase and down two more hallways to reach Mina's chambers.

"And here you go, miss," Oskar said, opening the door for Mina and handing her the key.

"Thank you so much, Oskar," Sebastian said, clapping a hand on the man's hunched shoulder. "Mina, I'll help you unpack?"

They both went to enter the room, yet only Mina crossed the threshold.

"My apologies, sir," Oskar said as Sebastian stumbled back from hitting the invisible barrier. "It is a security measure for our high-profile guests. Only those with whom the room is attributed to can enter it." He went to put his knob-knuckled hand through the doorway, only for it to stop midway. A faint ripple wobbled in the air of the threshold. "Even I cannot enter, and I am the one who runs the booking system."

"And what if there was an emergency?" Sebastian asked, back teeth grinding, a bitter lilt turning his bright tone sarcastic. "What if a guest were to be passed out on the floor, unconscious? How would one be able to get to them?"

"Simply shout for a guard or a servant, they will ring me, and I will let down the barrier," he said, tone still droll, completely unaffected by Sebastian's clear displeasure. "Trust me, sir, we've had very few emergencies during this time, and those we did have were handled promptly. Shall I escort you back to your room?"

"No, thank you." Mina feared Sebastian's jawbone was going to break from how tightly the muscle around it tensed. "I'll be able to make my way back just fine."

Oskar nodded. "Very well, sir. If you need me, just send a servant."

Sebastian watched him walk down the hall; nostrils flared, lips pursed in thought even after Oskar had disappeared around the corner.

Mina reached out, through the doorway, and breathed a sigh of relief as her hand touched his shoulder. She wasn't trapped, but Sebastian's displeasure had her on edge.

"This isn't normal, is it?" she asked. "These barriers."

"It's not... uncommon," Sebastian said through gritted teeth.

"It's not?"

"My orphanage had something similar." He turned around and studied the door frame. "Only it was separated by age and gender rather than by person. Can't have the older kids messing with the little kids, or the teens creating more kids that'll need to be adopted, you know? And with diplomats like the Empress of Dulsten hanging around, the increased security measures make sense."

"Then what's wrong?"

Sebastian looked down at her, studying her face yet again as his fingers tapped in triplets on the door frame, thoughts racing a mile a minute trying to resolve some unspoken conflict.

"'Bastian?"

"I don't like it," he admitted in a rush, dropping his polite mask in the absence of guards and servants and royalty. "If we were sharing a room or your room wasn't practically half a mile away from the rest of ours, I'd be fine, but—" His words fell away into a strangled groan.

She placed her hand on his tapping fingers, stilling them. Just like she had always wanted to do whenever he was overthinking, ruminating to the point of upset.

"But?" she encouraged.

He looked up at their hands, closed his eyes for a moment, then let out a long exhale. He shifted his hand to intertwine his fingers with hers. His palms were hot.

"But that's not the case, and I'm being unreasonably ridiculous about it," he said. "It's only a few days, like you said." His brow furrowed, palms burning a bit hotter as a troublesome thought crossed his mind. "But if something *were* to happen. This barrier..."

"I can run half a mile in seconds, remember?" She gave his hand a gentle squeeze, unafraid of the burn. "And if anything were to happen, it would take a hell of a lot more than a silly barrier to keep me away from you." She raised her fist and jabbed the air. "Just one punch and bam! Brand new, unenchanted entrance right into your room."

He chuckled lightly and grabbed her fist, raising it to his lips to kiss her knuckles lightly. "Alright, one woman wrecking crew, let's hope it doesn't come to that."

A soft, true smile back on his lips, the warm reverence returned to his eyes as his palms went from melting to mild.

Mina's nerves eased a bit.

His gaze traced around the perimeter of the door frame, and with a heavy sigh, he grumbled, "Stupid fucking barrier."

Mina arched an eyebrow, a teasing smirk quirking her lips. "Let me guess, you were one of those teens the orphanage had to worry about?"

"No." He straightened his shoulders and raised his chin a bit. "I was very well-behaved." His thumb started to tap triplets against the back of her hand. "Which is why, as an adult, I think I've earned the right to be a little less well-behaved."

"A little less well-behaved?" She cocked her head to the side, playing naive. "You mean like bowing at the waist instead of at the hip? Using your salad fork during the fish course?"

He squinted at her in false judgement. "You know exactly what I mean, Miss 'Sword Swallower'."

Mina took her hand out of his and fanned herself dramatically, imitating the over-the-top noblewomen she'd read about. "Master Windenhofer! Whatever you're impl—"

Sebastian untwined their fingers and grabbed her wrist, pulling her forward through the doorway to silence her with a kiss. Mina flushed immediately, muscles tensing as something whispered in her ear that they shouldn't be doing this — what if someone caught them doing this — but she did not dare pull away.

"Gods. I really do love it when you say my name," he murmured as he parted to catch his breath, lips hovering just above hers, voice rumbling with a hunger that sent goosebumps down her spine.

"You do, *Master Windenhofer?*" she edged him on.

An idea sparked like embers from hot coals.

"Come along," he said, guiding her away from her guest room by her wrist, the door falling shut behind her.

"Along to where?" she asked, a giggle behind the question.

"To where all the worrisome teens went when they couldn't get past the barriers," he replied matter-of-factly, "a broom closet."

🜁

A woman with pale blonde hair fashioned into an incredibly tall pouf — adorned with a meticulously arranged assortment of faux plums and grape leaves around a small gourd hollowed out for a birdhouse — and a well-rounded bustle — in purple to match said plums — was waiting by the doors of the entrance hall near Enoch's room.

"Windenhofer Procurements, correct?" The woman asked, stepping in front of them before they could exit.

"That would be us," Sebastian answered.

"I'm Lady Dagmara Hutnik, Chancellor of Culture for Lanholde." Her voice had a purr to it, her Lanholdian accent thick and rumbling like a happy cat with a belly full of sparrow. "Oskar had mentioned that you all were looking to tour the town and participate in some of the Harvest's Hail festivities?"

"That we are."

"Wonderful!" She clapped her hands together, the sound dampened by the silk black gloves she wore. "Let's head out then, shall we?"

"We?" Sebastian asked. "We greatly appreciate the offer, my lady, but we're looking forward to exploring the Capitol on our own." He laughed. The same too-sweet laugh he used to hide his annoyance with King Fritz. "A little company outing, if you will. My archivist Enoch here is quite the culture connoisseur and has already laid out a few Lanholde staples for us to check out."

"Has he now?" Lady Dagmara's smile widened as her thick mink lashes flitted in the archivist's direction. "I'm glad to hear that someone is as invested in Lanholdian culture as I am. Did you happen to study it at university?"

Enoch's jaw hung slack. "I studied *you* at university." He bowed deeply. "Lady Dagmara it is an absolute honor to meet such a dedicated scholar of culture." Rising, he looked to Sebastian with pleading, puppy-dog eyes. "Sebastian, we have to take her up on her offer. I'm confident in my skills as a culture connoisseur and historian, but to be given a tour by the very woman who penned the definitive encyclopedia of Lanholdian cultural trends from the last thousand years?"

"Soon to be the last thousand five hundred," Lady Dagmara added, playing coy.

Enoch gasped, attention immediately engrossed in her. "You're kidding."

"While working on clearing out some of the wilds of Pinbraun, the king's men uncovered a sunken town filled with near-perfectly preserved specimens of Lanholdian life, dating at least fifteen hundred years ago. At most? Who knows."

He pouted Sebastian's way and, for a moment, Mina thought Enoch would actually transform into a begging lapdog.

Only she could hear the heavy, silent inhale Sebastian took before reapplying the plaster of his smile and saying, "Well, if Lady Dagmara wrote the book, then it would be an honor to let her lead the way."

"Then let us head off!" The lady cheered, sweeping her hand through the air. The doorman opened the doors for them in one grand motion, letting a great gust of cold wind into the foyer. Dagmara's hair did not move an inch as she stepped through the windblown threshold, barely registering the bluster that threatened to turn her bustle into a kite.

"It's a lot better on the other side," she shouted back at them. "You all climbed The Lithe, did you not? Don't tell me a little brisk breeze has you all ready to turn tail!"

Enoch stood tall and walked through the wind tunnel defiantly, leading the way for the rest of them to follow.

Sebastian arched an eyebrow Mina's way, asking wordlessly if the gust was her doing.

With a subtle shake of her head, 'no', she looped her arm around his and summoned the wind from her heels to swirl around them, diverting the wild gusts as they crossed the threshold; clothing ruffling only slightly in the breeze.

Despite the wind and despite the chill, the streets of Lanholde were filled with revelers. Red-cheeked and cheery, vendors hawked goods made from the first fruits of the fall harvest to eager tourists and townsfolk. More of the former than the latter, Mina noticed, hearing very few Lanholdian accents throughout the crowd. The locals probably knew better than to go out while the streets were packed with out-of-towners.

A tour guided by Lady Dagmara apparently meant they were stopped almost every five minutes by a shopkeeper or tourist eagerly excited to meet her... and the times they weren't stopped they were still stuck, shuffled here and there like sheep in a catching pen, herded around landmarks and festival attractions. Mina was sure Sebastian's bicep would be littered with bruises from how hard she held on to it, fingers digging into him on reflex with every brush of a stranger against her.

If it hurt him, he didn't let on.

So many bodies, different temperatures, textures, sizes. A kid ran a sticky hand over her pants as they walked by him. The slick sweat of a man bumping into her as he waddled backwards to take a photo of his family dampened her sleeve. And the smell. That stinging mix of autumn spices, said to be the favorite seasonal-scented oil of the palace by every third stand bubbling a pot of the stink, did not pair well with the ripe dung of the donkeys and horses carting wares and toting ostentatious couples on carriage rides down the streets.

Respite came floating over the cacophony from a small amphitheater and a band playing traditional songs praising the turning of the seasons. Mina peered through the crowd and — finding that the band did not have a singer, leaving the audience mercifully light in front of the stage — tugged Sebastian towards one of the open benches. She gestured for Tanir and Wera to follow with the tilt of her head, so as not to interrupt Enoch and Dagmara's intense discussion on which specific art movement inspired the design of the Capitol's lampposts.

Mina exhaled for what felt like the first time in hours as they sat, appreciating the room the amphitheater provided — appreciating Sebastian to her left, Wera to her right, people she trusted by her side instead of a sea of strangers swelling, threatening to swallow her whole.

She leaned her head against Sebastian's shoulder, loosened her grip around his arm, and rubbed her hand over the might-be bruises in time to the music. He tapped his fingers against the top of her knee, mirroring the drummer's rhythm. Wera and Tanir hummed quietly, filling in the missing melody the lyrics normally provided. Once she received her payment and finished replacing and repairing the music room's instruments, maybe she could convince the others to let her teach them how to play. Sebastian would make an excellent drummer or a piano player, even, given the length of his fingers. Considering how adept she was with fine needlework, Tanir would do well on a zither, and Enoch most certainly knew a few instruments already. The only outlier was Wera. Her humming wasn't too off-beat or off-tune... but as for what instrument would suit her, it was hard to determine what painting and drawing would translate to.

The band's song ended with a flourish, garnering moderate applause from the crowd as they reset for their next set. Some of the audience got up and left, using the short break as an excuse to move on to other things, but Mina was content to continue sitting for as long as possible, living in her happy bubble of friendship and legroom.

The pair of knobby knees that stopped in front of her face, however, seemed determined to invade it.

"Sebastian Windenhofer!" the knees cheered, prompting Sebastian to stand along with them.

"Master Kaminska!" He shook the man's hand. "Fancy meeting you here!"

"I heard you'd be wrapping up your contract with His Majesty soon. Is that what brings you to town, or are you just here for The Harvest's Hail festivities?"

"Here to close out the contract. Enjoying the festivities while we wait for payment issues to be resolved." Sebastian set his hand on Mina's shoulder. "All, this is Master Kaminska, one of the regional guild masters for the Lanholde segment of the Northern Practitioners. Master Kaminska, this is my medic Tanir, my cartographer Wera, and..."

"Mina Harlowe!" Master Kaminska finished. "There was quite a stir among the guild masters when we heard Windenhofer took on an apprentice. You possess wind magic, right?"

Mina looked up at the man, getting a lovely view of his limp mustache and thick nose hairs from her seat, and tried her best — for Sebastian's sake — to keep her annoyance at having her peace interrupted from being overtly obvious.

"So it seems," she answered.

"That's incredibly unusual, you know. I haven't heard of a wizard possessing wind magic innately, but I'm sure Master Windenhofer will do well to teach you how to wield it. Even with you being his very first apprentice!" Kaminska turned his attention back to Sebastian. "How long did you say you were in town for?"

"Seems like we'll be here until the day after the holiday ends," he replied.

"That is excellent news!" Kaminska snapped excitedly and shook a liver-spotted, knob-knuckled finger at him. "That atlas you sent along, I'm on the review board for it. I was going to write to ask if you and your team could give a presentation on it and the discoveries you've made during your trip at the Capitol's guild hall, but now that you're here for a bit, would it be too much to ask you to give a lecture on it in a day or two's time? I could even set up a commune crystal so that the rest of the review board can sit in. It would certainly help accelerate the publication timeline, maybe even get the book into the hands of a few military captains and trade merchants before the end of the year."

"The military?" Wera stood. "My maps are military-worthy?"

"I'd even say museum-worthy." His mustache quivered with a twinge of awe. "Those write-ups you've included? Ingenious. They provide the perfect glimpse into the location and its inhabitants."

"Those were my co-author Enoch's additions," she explained.

"Has he come to Lanholde with you all? For the presentation, it'd be best to have all collaborators present."

"He has," she nodded, a happy eagerness lighting her face, and looked at Sebastian, "If it has to be all collaborators then Sebastian should definitely join us. He isn't listed as an author, but his insight on the magics present in some of these locations was definitely a vital part of the project."

Kaminska's eyes lit up. "You've just given me a brilliant idea. While you and Enoch are presenting on the whole of the atlas, Windenhofer could showcase some of the magic items you brought back along with it." He looked at Sebastian. "I'm sure the king has already sent word to the guild that he wants us to appraise them. It would save us time — and you *a lot* of paperwork — if you went through them with us."

"That it would." He glanced down at Mina quickly. A passing glance, much too worrisome for her liking — especially when faced with the glow of Wera's hopeful expression — and opened his mouth to speak.

"If you work with them now, it may mean less work you'll have to do before we head back to the woods," Mina spoke before he could. "It'll probably be hard to look at the autumn leaves while writing. I'm sure Tanir and I can find something to do while you all prepare."

There was no need for her minor discomfort with palaces to interfere with his career. She'd spent years entertaining herself alone in the middle of nowhere, here she had a whole city and new senses to explore — preferably on the outskirts of the Capitol away from the festival crowds.

His worry turned to confusion. "W-well, I'm sure you could tag along with us if you wanted." Sebastian looked to Kaminska.

Kaminska frowned slightly. "I don't think they'll be able to join us as we assess the items, confidentiality agreements with The Crown and all." He looked at her and smiled. A pitying smile, like a parent telling their moping child they can only have dessert after finishing all their vegetables. "But she'll certainly be able to attend the presentation. Would scheduling it for the evening after Harvest's Hail ends work for you all? It would give us about two and half days of preparation."

"Two and a half days? Pfft." Wera trilled her lips. "Easy. We'll have a presentation that will knock your socks off."

"Fantastic! How about you three swing by the guild hall this evening to talk about the finer details? I'll have our chef whip up some dinner!"

"I'm not sure about this evening," Sebastian said with a nervous chuckle. "His Majesty invited us to dinner—"

"Master Kaminska!" Lady Dagmara's saccharine voice cut through the opening chords of the band tuning up, dashing Mina's dreams of sitting through their next set in peace once Kaminska cleared out. "I see you've found my wayward flock."

"Lady Dagmara." Kaminska bowed his head. "It is wonderful to see you. I was just working out the logistics of inviting a few of your lambs over to the guild hall to prepare a presentation on the lands and new magic objects they've discovered. But it appears His Majesty has also invited them all to dinner this evening."

"This evening's dinner?" Dagmara clarified. "Well, if it's in pursuit of knowledge and some of you do still attend, I'm sure he won't take any offense. Especially if it's to learn more about the expedition he commissioned." She pulled out a small spiral notebook and pencil out of her jacket pocket. "Who would need to be excused? I can send word to His Majesty to make him aware."

"It would be Sebastian, Wera, and Enoch," Kaminska answered.

Mina kept her face neutral as realization — an uncomfortable resignation — that her evening would be filled with seven courses and making sure she set her napkin down to her left rather than her right so she wouldn't start a war with some foreign country, settled in. She gripped the edge of the bench beneath her — wood squeaking as she squeezed, splinters popping up and sinking into her palms — as her stomach turned, nearly as nauseous as it was on the cart.

Her heart hammered against her chest.

It's just a dinner, a few hours of small talk and seeming interested, not going to war.

"Perfect," Dagmara purred as she wrote. "I'm sure His Majesty will be a little disheartened by your absences, so I'll make the suggestion that you be invited to the royal brunch tomorrow instead." She stuffed the notebook back inside her jacket. "Is that all you need? There are a few more sights I want to show these lovely folks before heading back to the palace for my late-afternoon meetings."

"No, that should be all," Kaminska said, bowing his head again. "Thank you for your assistance as always, my lady. Sebastian and all, it was a pleasure to meet you, and I look forward to the discoveries we'll make this evening."

"A pleasure, Master Kaminska," Dagmara replied.

The band's next set began as he walked away, and for a moment Mina had the hope that perhaps Lady Dagmara would be as entranced by their sound as she had been — give her a moment to calm her stupid mind and body down — but the clap of her hands, off rhythm and demanding, denied any chance for their spell to take hold.

"Let us continue on, shall we? The Bizcon Clock Tower is just about to strike the hour, and it has an outstanding cuckoo display you won't want to miss."

The others abandoned her, following after the bulbous-bustled bitch, clucking excitedly about their stupid presentation. Sebastian's hand, open, waiting — *taunting* — dropped into her field of vision.

"Mina?" he called quietly, unsure, scared almost.

She breathed, easing her hands out of their death grip, and took his, standing reluctantly. He did not start walking right away, so she pulled him along, wanting this torture over quickly to give her a few moments of freedom before she was thrust into suffering once more.

"I'm sorry," he whispered, needless worry settling back in. "But, I'm sure Tanir can more than handle—"

"Absolutely not. I'm not leaving her to the wolves," Mina snipped, keeping her voice low, frustration she refused to call panic getting the better of her. "And sending just your medic when the king *himself* invited your entire company? Do you want to be blacklisted out of work for an entire kingdom? Maybe multiple kingdoms depending on how much sway King Fritz has."

"I'm sure we can figure something out. I could still feign sick, do the paperwork from my room then—"

"Then what? Still doesn't solve the 'who's going to dinner' problem. You can't say you've got a stomach ache to Kaminska then show up at a diplomatic dinner party. Dagmara's friends with him, and rumors spread faster than worms in a kitten's stomach behind palace walls."

Sebastian's hand heated. "I'm sorry, lila doar."

The warmth pulled her out of her head, the defeat in his voice softening her ire's edge. "There's nothing to be sorry about."

"I'm letting you down," he replied. "That's more than enough to be sorry about."

Mina leaned her head against his shoulder and squeezed his hand. "You're not letting me down. I just—"

Am supposed to be fixed. Not pathetically afraid of things that are not even remotely terrifying.

"—don't want you to worry so much about me. I was raised to do this royal bullshit, ya know?"

She lifted her chin to look at him and put on her best smirk, conjuring her bravery to bolster the both of them.

He gave a tight-lipped smile back, "I know."

His palm burned a little hotter.

⚠

By the time they returned, Mina didn't have a moment to kiss Sebastian goodbye before Wera and Enoch rushed him off to head over to the guild hall. She did her best to hide her disappointment, not wanting to upset him any further, but as she put on her party dress and looked over herself in the mirror, her chest ached not seeing his matching green tie beside her.

The Barely Moon Ball wasn't too far off. She'd put on another pretty dress, and they'd dance the night away together. That's all she really wanted.

And if that limp-mustached mage tried to stop Sebastian from attending, she'd diplomatically punch his nose in.

The formal dining hall was just as ostentatious and filled with abstract stone carvings and oil-scented tapestries as the Western Receiving Room. The table was a ridiculous length and shape. Longer than the hundred-man dining table they never used in the commorancy, but curved like a snake crushed mid-slither by a wagon wheel. A few of the king's guests had already taken their seats by the time Mina and Tanir arrived, scattered about — much to Mina's chagrin — by place cards that had her and Tanir sitting just to the left of His Majesty.

Tanir turned over her shoulder and waved over one of the servants. "Sorry to bother you, but I wanted to make sure these place cards were laid out correctly."

The servant glanced at the place cards. "These are correct, madam."

She looked at the throne-like seat at the head of the table, then back to the servant. "Really? We're sitting *this* close to His Majesty?"

"Yes, madam. His Majesty wanted to make sure you were sitting next to a somewhat familiar face, considering most of your companions could not attend this evening."

Mina walked around the table to check who would be sitting in front of them, fearing the worst, but was instead met with a trio of names she did not recognize. A much better outcome than having to sit through an entire dinner watching Sir Gargic moon over his beloved king and scrutinizing every move she made.

"There are so many forks," Tanir remarked as Mina returned to her seat.

"Just follow my lead," she replied. "I can't begin to tell you how many times I practiced proper Lanholdian dinner etiquette."

"Good. At least someone knows what they're doing." She went to reach for the intricately folded napkin on her plate. Mina grabbed her wrist and gently placed it back in her lap.

"The servants will do that for you once the meal begins. Grabbing your napkin and tucking it in your collar now signifies impatience and could be considered an insult," she explained.

Tanir blanched. "Even the napkins have etiquette?"

"Everything has etiquette. We can't even speak to the other people at this table until the dinner host introduces us."

"Gods," she said and looked down at herself. "At least my gown is appropriate."

"It is. Another creation of yours?" Mina asked, admiring the slate gray satin.

"It is. I made it for the Practitioners' Gala a year ago." She snapped her head up suddenly, eyes wide. "There's not a rule against wearing an outfit twice, is there?"

Mina chuckled. "Only if you've worn the garment twice in one month or to the same event."

Tanir sighed in relief. "I don't know how you can keep all this stuff in your head on top of all the other things you know.

"Well, it was beaten into me." She shrugged, straightening her spine a bit more as the memory of cold metal nails raked along her back. "Forget which hand to hold your wine with, and you've got thirty lashes coming your way."

Mina glanced at the back of her right hand, the dim lighting of the dining hall hid the scars, but for some reason, the skin they claimed felt tighter.

"I'm so sorry," Tanir's face fell. "I didn't mean to bring up bad memories."

"Don't worry about it." Mina gave a small, sad smile, as she glanced about the dining room, flitting over the servants blending into the background; ever watching statues only to move when summoned. "This entire place brings up bad memories. I'm not a big fan of castles. Hopefully you all don't visit them too often on your adventures."

"We do," she noted, "but normally, they're centuries old, crumbling, and filled with some great monster trying to kill us."

The last of the dinner guests finally arrived, filling the empty seats in front of them with: a full-figured woman, head shaven and skin a deep shade of brown, a spindly man made of harsh angles and ashen skin beneath a curtain of long golden hair that looked unbelievably soft and unbelievably shiny, and a person with pupil-less, orange eyes, slightly pinked skin, and white hair cropped short. They only glanced Mina and Tanir's way as they sat, not wanting to break decorum by addressing them or stop the flow of their conversation.

"Were you able to make your way to the east?" the bald woman asked the spindly man. Her voice set in the back of her throat, speech rounded: Dulsten born and bred.

"I was not, but my footman was," he replied, voice deep and nasal but accent hard to place. He hissed his 's'es like a Kraedian, but his 't's were Ortria sharp and precise.

"And what was found?"

"A very stark contrast to the Capitol we're being shown. The footman was able to secure some of Emil's papers." The spindly man scratched his chin. "His cause is just from what is written."

"But is it just from what has been seen?" orange eyes asked, their voice so sonorous it raised the hair on Mina's arms. She didn't know their accent, had never seen a person who looked like them, in fact.

"Comparing the two, in some ways, yes. But most of the claims occur outside the Capitol's walls."

"You have the papers secured somewhere?" the bald woman asked.

"Of course."

"Outside of your room?"

"Naturally."

"You have concerns," orange eyes noted.

"Even the most secure fortresses have a skeleton key," the bald woman said. "If my loves were not well-trained in battle, I would have caused quite an uproar over the familial rooming policy."

"Then it seems I should continue to play dumb." Orange eyes smiled. "Innocent ignorance often reveals the truth."

Mina's stomach knotted, pulse picking up.

Wolves.

A quartet of bells ran out, signaling them to stand as King Fritz entered the dining hall.

"Good evening, everyone! Happy Harvest's Hail!" he announced, spreading his arms wide in grand welcome before making his way to his seat. "I thank you all so much for accepting my invitation. Before we eat, I would like to formally introduce you to two new guests joining us: Ms. Tanir Kask and Ms. Mina Harlowe."

All heads turned to face them. A hundred eyes.

"They were an integral part of an expedition I sponsored to procure some long-lost artifacts associated with Lanholde's illustrious history." He smiled fondly at Mina and gestured to her. "You may have heard of Mina's work, in fact. She is the female alpinist who has been leading expeditions up the Fallow Peaks and over The Lithe for the past few years."

A few eyebrows raised at that, and Mina made sure to make eye contact with each one of them, smiling politely.

We are not wolves. We are rabbits. Wolves have no reason to be wary of rabbits.

"Please welcome them warmly. Their happiness means a great deal to me." The king's kindly gaze lingered their way for a moment, and Mina sorely wished his attention would fall elsewhere. Being dear to a king was a very dangerous thing to be in a room filled with politicians.

"Let us eat!"

He sat and they all followed in unison.

"It is wonderful to meet you, Ms. Harlowe, Ms. Kask," orange eyes said, jumping at the chance to introduce themselves now that formalities were out of the way. "I'm Sovereign Coro of Molveen."

"Wonderful to meet you as well, Your Majesty. Please simply call me Mina," she replied. It felt odd in a way she did not quite understand to be called Ms. Harlowe. She hadn't given Fritz a last name, perhaps he knew Lindhagen called her "Harlowe's girl" and assumed from that.

Kaminska called me that too. But how did he—

The bald woman extended her hand across the table, knuckles facing out and fingertips pointing down towards the table. "I'm Empress Tinsae of Dulsten."

Training kicking in, Mina reached for her fingertips with her left hand and touched her forehead to the empress's knuckles. "An honor to be in your presence."

Empress Tinsae moved her hand in Tanir's direction. Tanir looked at Mina nervously. Mina nodded subtly, signaling Tanir to mimic her greeting.

Tanir placed her forehead against the empress's knuckles. "An honor to be in your presence."

The empress retracted her hand. "An honor to be perceived."

"Magistrate Strauss of Kraedia," the spindly man said, beady eyes narrowed in scrutiny at Mina. "You're the alpinist from the Sandere Woods?"

"I am, my lord," Mina replied.

"Some diplomats from Kraedia employed the Sandere alpinist to help them ascend the Fallow Peaks a few years back. The woman they described was ill-mannered, severe, stand-offish, and so cold in both appearance and behavior that simply brushing against her shoulder would give you frostbite."

The servant draping a napkin around Mina's neck paused.

"From just the few minutes I've observed you, you don't seem anything like that."

Mina took the napkin from the servant's hands and finished tucking it into her collar herself. "I will take that as a compliment then, my lord."

"Mina did use to be like that, my lord," Tanir jumped in unnecessarily. "But after traveling with us, she has most definitely warmed up."

Under the table, Mina placed a hand on Tanir's lap, hoping the medic would take the hint and hold her tongue.

"Warmed up is definitely a word for it," Strauss drolled in consideration. He studied her carefully. A predator on the hunt, looking for any sign of weakness. "The woman our diplomats described had skin so pale and lips so blue one would think a corpse had risen from beneath the snow and started walking if it wasn't for her great beauty."

"She's a Cursed One, magistrate," King Fritz interjected, chipper cadence a shock against Strauss's harrowing intonation. He smiled sympathetically at Mina. "My apologies, my dear. I'm sure you wish to keep your nature to yourself, but Magistrate Strauss is rather like a bloodhound. Once he gets a whiff of something odd, he will stop at nothing to sniff it out."

There was a glint in his eye, a glimmer of warning behind his cheerful disposition. So Fritz knew him to be a wolf too.

"A Cursed One?" Strauss leaned forward in his seat — intention turning Mina from prey to science project — much to the chagrin of the servant trying to fill his wine glass. "What manner of curse?"

"A recently broken one, thankfully," King Fritz answered for her. "You see, while I was sourcing out the best contractors to retrieve our lost artifacts, tale of Mina's accomplishments as an alpinist coupled with her unusual nature piqued my interest. I had a gut instinct that she had to be a Cursed One of some variety and wanted to see it for myself, possibly even offer the Lanholde Practitioners' Guild's assistance in finding a way to rid her of her ailment. Lucky for us both, my taste in contractors is superb." He laughed. "She arrived here mid-morning, already uncursed thanks to the fine folks at Windenhofer Procurements."

"Windenhofer," Empress Tinsae mulled over the name. "That name sounds familiar."

"Yes, Your..." Tanir glanced over to Mina.

"Excellence," Mina clarified.

"Yes, Your Excellence," she continued. "Master Sebastian Windenhofer is our employer. Before starting his procurement company in earnest, he was a guild-approved wizard for hire. About five or so years back, he helped the Dulstenix town of Varnear with a flock of alicantos that had been roosting nearby and feasting on their silver mines."

The empress's eyes lit up in recognition. "He's the wizard who trained the birds!"

Tanir smiled and nodded. "Yes. He is the wizard who trained the birds."

"Clever one that man is, feeding the birds silver in exchange for leading the Varnear miners to gold. Made me quite a lot of money."

"Perhaps I should consider hiring him for a few magic-related issues that need addressing back home," Sovereign Coro said. Their orange eyes settled on Mina. "How did he uncurse you?"

"Oh ho ho, be careful there, my dear," King Fritz teased, jester smile rising over the rim of his wine glass. "Sovereign Coro's people are known to be quite skillful in the arcane arts. Wouldn't want Master Windenhofer's trade secret to curse breaking leaked out. It might leave him stuck training birds instead of saving the suffering!"

A tease. Another warning.

What part such an innocent answer would have in the clear political chess match she found herself in between, Mina couldn't tell. But wolves fed on information, on weaknesses. Whether they were rulers or rustics, she would give them nothing. She wanted no part in their hunt.

If anything, the most this conversation with her would get them was a recommendation for a stellar set of magical contractors.

Mina gave a bright bubbly giggle, saccharine and airy, as if the king's tease was the funniest thing in the world. "I don't think Sebastian would mind if the sovereign did share his secret. It would only lead to more Cursed Ones being freed." She smiled and turned to Coro doe-eyed and cordial. "But he would know better than I exactly what did it. All I know is that it was one hell of a curse and that it took a lot of strange magic to unwind. I know he's currently busy helping the Lanholde guild assess the magical properties of the items we delivered to The Crown, but perhaps we could have you two meet to discuss it sometime before you head back to Molveen, Your Majesty."

Coro smiled, a kind smile, a *polite* smile. "I would like that."

"What gift were you left with?" Strauss asked, clearly not caring for decorum. Though he was not a ruler, something about his position must have granted him the privilege to pry.

She smothered the snip she wanted to give with sweet naïveté, "I beg your pardon?"

"Cursed Ones are left with some sort of gift after their curse has been lifted. King Jadiel has an unparalleled ability to accelerate plant growth, for example."

The wind, nestled at her heels, stirred around her ankles.

"Cold resistance and enhanced strength," she said, letting her pleasing smile fall from her face into deep, distant sadness. "But I would hardly call them gifts. Gifts are given during times of celebration. I would gladly give them up if it meant I would be spared from my past torment."

Her racing heart, the cold sweat breaking out in the small of her back, the rattle of chains whispering in her ear just from seeing the servants carrying cloche-covered platters. She looked Strauss in the eye and meant every word; not backing down under his scrutiny, making sure he would get a glimpse of all that haunted her and know how heartless his questioning truly was.

"I see." He leaned back in his chair, thin lips pursing in dissatisfaction, and picked up one of the canapés off his plate. "My apologies for bringing up such bitter memories."

"Speaking of bitter memories," Sovereign Coro said, picking up the conversation less they dare commit the social faux pas of having a second of silence. "I do apologize if this is a sensitive subject, Your Majesty, but I do sorely miss your brother's presence at the dinner table."

King Fritz sighed heavily, his slightly bemused expression wilting, as the jester faded away into a forlorn, contemplative king. "As do I." There was heaviness in the words, similar to that moment of yearning that passed over him in the receiving room.

"Is there anything I can do to resolve this conflict between you? I hate to see a family divided, and my people are known for their mediation tactics."

He shook his head. "I appreciate the offer, my friend. But I think it will take much more than clever mediation to change Emil's mind." Fritz swirled the wine in his glass, letting himself get a little lost in the way it rippled. "It pains me every day to see my people suffer at the hands of his selfishness."

"Forgive me, Your Majesty," Tanir said, too naturally kind to know it better to mind her own business. "But who is this Emil you're referring to?"

He looked up from his glass and gave her a warm, albeit sad, smile. "My younger brother," he answered. "Usually, he'd be here, delighting us with tales of his travels throughout our realm and into realms beyond." His far-off look drifted to the tablecloth, smile vanishing into a tightly drawn line, single eyebrow arching out of bitterness instead of bemusement. "But now it seems his tales have turned against me, turning me into a villain while he demands that the throne be all his own."

Mina's already upset stomach squirmed at that. She studied Fritz closely, the lines of years of wide smiles creased his soft cheeks, even with his demeanor soured. The tension he carried over the topic lived only in his face, his shoulders were in their proper royal position, his grip on his wine glass was loose. There was no clear resentment behind his disappointment, which was a relief. But for a king to admit that terrible rumors were circling about him? In front of potential alliances?

Now it was her turn to hunt.

"How?" Mina asked.

He glanced up at her, second brow raising to join the other in confusion. "How what, my dear?"

She feigned concern back. "How has he turned you into a villain?"

He pouted his lips, and cast down his gaze. A defeated air to him. "Making claims that easily incense the masses. Claiming that I tax unfairly, that I willingly ignore some great atrocities my people are suffering under, that The Crown uses its funds to support foreign causes instead of bolstering the people of Lanholde." He leaned back against his seat. "The usual things that political opponents say to swing votes in their favor or to embolden the everyman to overthrow the current regime and seat them on the throne instead," he explained.

He sat down his wine glass, his gaze glazing over in recollection — brows furrowing in the middle, searching for an answer to a question she did not know. "I've posted the tax rates publicly, shown just how much and why people get taxed as they do, had the treasurer prepare detailed breakdowns of our expenses and publish them in the papers, and asked the nobles and land-owning gentry to write me of any atrocities that were affecting my citizens, but I only received reports of small bouts of illness and missing goats."

He tapped his fingers against the foot of his wine glass. "I asked my brother to meet to discuss perhaps a joint rule of some sort, but instead he—" Fritz hung his head and rubbed at his temples with his forefinger and thumb. "It upsets me to even think about it."

"We do not fault you if you do not wish to speak about it any further, Your Majesty," Coro said, gaze flitting briefly to Mina, admonishing her for a moment. Yet another person warning her without proper cause. "I'm sure it is a difficult subject."

"It is, but I don't want my discomfort to be misconstrued." He inhaled deeply to collect himself and lifted his head. He locked eyes with Mina, striking jasper pupils rimmed by a bit of red, waterline glistening. "He decided to take the eastern half of the Capitol by force, claiming half of it was rightly his, and cut half of my people off from us just before Harvest's Hail. I've tried sending supplies over to help them, but to no avail. Every shipment that has been sent has been stopped, torn asunder, and thrown back in my face."

Mina ground her teeth as the puzzle pieces slotted together. No wonder His Majesty insisted they stay at the palace. What better way to distract the nobility from a kingdom's turmoil than by playing host to an eclectic group of adventurers? And a Cursed One to boot? Everyone loves a fairy tale, so long as they don't look too closely and see the horrors behind it.

"Really?" Mina asked, mischief and bitterness at being used spiting her molded manners, urging her to bite. "Because your face doesn't look that bad if you took an entire supply crate to it."

Mina raised her wine glass to her lips and sipped slowly as she watched King Fritz process her statement. She could return to playing dumb, lean on her isolated upbringing as an excuse to keep him from being too offended if it came to it. But his reaction would tell her all she needed to know about just what kind of man *His Majesty* truly was.

He burst out into a fit of laughter that sounded like the frantic squawks of a dying crow — drawing the attention of the entire table his way.

"Oh, thank you, my dear," he said with a joyous sigh, patting her hand in a gesture that truly seemed grateful. "With everything going on, it has been quite a while since I've had a good laugh." He picked up one of his canapés and popped it into his mouth triumphantly. The jester had once again returned. "In fact. How about we all go around and share the funniest story we know to help lighten up the evening and spark new conversations?" He pointed to a woman with ruddy brown hair and rosy cheeks. "Renet! Start us off! I know you've got quite a few saucy tales up your sleeves."

Desperate. He was a king desperate for distraction, for parties and pretty objects and adventurers and anything to keep sadness — to keep reality — from sinking in.

🜂

When her knock on Sebastian's door went unanswered, Mina placed her ear against it, closed her eyes, and listened.

The slight whistle of his breath as he slept and the even timbre of his heartbeat put her mind at ease. It was rather late. She couldn't fault him for falling asleep — they had had a long day — she only wished her body would follow suit.

She made her way back to her room and collapsed onto the much too-large and much too-soft bed. Mina never imagined a bed could be too large or too soft, or that either of those things would be bad. In the storybooks she'd read, the hero always loved a large, soft bed, yet here she was wishing the mattress was springier, that the sheets smelled slightly of lavender, and that when she stretched her arms out, her left would stop short against a warm lump, lightly whistling on every exhale.

She was being stupid. She'd slept plenty of nights alone without Sebastian, and there would probably be more in her future. It wasn't like she could go on every trip with him, and it wasn't smart to lose a night of rest over it.

Mina looked out the window that led out to a small balcony and into a sky filled with stars. She stood, grabbed the violin she had packed to restring, and finished tuning it. Playing it would be the best way to truly test if the new pegs she gave it fit — and would most definitely help to soothe her mind.

Most wolves didn't care for the violin.

The air was brisk, the breeze surprisingly calm for how high up in the mountains they were. Her room sat high enough to see beyond the walls of the Capitol, into an endless ocean of evergreens. A faint flicker of firelight within them, far to the east, caught her attention. She sat on the banister of the balcony to view it better and set her bow upon her violin. There was comfort in its familiar orange glow, no matter how far away it was.

Its ebbs and flows were her conductor, guiding her strokes. A crescendo as its glow brightened, a vibrato in perfect time with its tremble — from such a wild force a rhythm soon emerged. The shadows breaking up its light were keeping it at bay, tempering its flames to keep it from fulfilling its nature. It wanted to climb the trees, not illuminate them. Wanted to climb their bows and touch the heavens, mocking the stars and their paltry light. Or wanted to join them and help illuminate the sky for eons to come.

"Beautiful!"

Mina's bow stilled, and she looked down towards the source of the shout.

"An alpinist and a virtuoso!" King Fritz exclaimed from the courtyard below her balcony. "What can't you do?"

Of course, there were some wolves that were a little odd.

"A few things," she called back out of courtesy. "Did my playing wake you, Your Majesty?"

"No. I just find that taking a walk late in the evening helps to soothe my mind before bed," he replied. "The Barley Moon Ball tomorrow evening. You will be attending, won't you?"

She smiled tightly. "It would be rude to turn down such a gracious invitation."

"Then I shall have you play for my guests! Make sure to wear your finest dress and prepare your best song, though I doubt you have a bad one."

Then I shall have you distract from my incompetence as leader some more, fool!

"I'm very flattered, Your Majesty, but I wouldn't want to pull focus from the talented musicians you've hired for the evening."

King Fritz waved off her concern. "You'd be doing me a favor, my dear. They need to take a union break anyway and while I intend to hold a toast during it, I can only talk for so long. Having you play a song would help to fill the gap and make sure the evening stays lively." He wagged his eyebrows. "Might even get a few nobles considering sponsoring you as an artist in residence."

Mina chewed the inside of her cheek, considering his offer. It was never a bad thing for a king to owe one a favor. And a favor sealed with the Fae's Folly held a considerable amount of weight. The more mischievous part of her could have him emptying out the palace's coffers, but giving Sebastian first choice of all the magically-inclined procurement contracts in Lanholde would be much more reasonable.

"That is most thoughtful, Your Majesty," Mina smiled and bowed her head. "I will look to find a fine dress in town tomorrow."

Or from the Junk Room. If I can see Sebastian long enough to borrow one.

"Find a dress?" he scoffed. "Nonsense! I'll have the court tailor make you one, my dear."

"On such short notice? I wouldn't want to put that much pressure on them. I'm sure I can find something close to my size and have them do some quick alterations—"

"Oh, never you mind that, my dear. Izydor loves a challenge," he interjected. "I'll have a servant collect you from your chambers in the morning after breakfast and take you down to his workshop."

"Could Tanir come?" she asked. There was no way in Hell she was going to be stuck with a stuffy court tailor for hours alone. "I'm sure she would love to see him work, and I wouldn't want to leave her alone all day while the others are off with the guild."

"Of course, of course. Izydor does love to talk about his craft with anyone willing to listen. Just like I would love to listen to another gorgeous melody of yours before I head off to bed this evening." King Fritz smiled. "Would you indulge me with one more song, my dear Mina?"

If it gets you to go away.

She tucked her violin under her chin. "Of course, Your Majesty."

Usually, she had to think for a moment over what she wanted to play, but this time the song came immediately. A Lanholdian lullaby, one of the first songs she ever learned to play. Something that would turn the king's eyes heavy.

She played the song slowly, gently, until the king disappeared from her sight.

XXIX
Grand Gestures

It probably wouldn't work, but she at least had to try.

With the wind's speed behind her, Mina dropped onto Sebastian's balcony in less than fifteen seconds; too fast for any servants or guards to notice her, even if she didn't have the cover of early morning darkness.

The curtains were drawn, but a faint glow of candlelight seeped through the doors' center crack. Mina knocked a triplet beat on the wooden frame. The floorboards creaked, each squeak getting louder. The curtain parted just enough for a single, tired brown eye to peer out.

"Boo," she said, keeping her voice just barely above a whisper as she lurched forward slightly, attempting to give Sebastian a playful scare.

He threw the curtains open, and the balcony doors.

"What are you doing out here?" he squawked, a smile tugging at the corners of his lips.

"Shhh," Mina hushed. "Keep your voice down. Don't need the purity police getting all huffy over an unwed couple standing too close to each other." She went to reach through the doorway to tug at his vest but was stopped by the force field. "Dammit."

He looked down at himself. "Do I have something on my shirt?"

"I was wondering why you're wearing a shirt," she pressed her palm against the invisible barrier between them, "but apparently this stupid barrier works on all the doors."

Sebastian's hand passed through without any obstacle, and he wove his fingers in between hers. "It'd be a pretty big security issue if it wasn't, don't you think?"

"I know. I was just hoping they'd be stupid." She sighed and tugged on Sebastian's hand to lead him out onto the balcony with her. "I'm surprised you're up and dressed this early."

"I'm surprised, too," he grumbled. "This whole presentation/categorization mess is much more involved than I expected. I'm up early to get in early, then get out early, so I don't miss the ball tonight.

"You know I won't be angry if you're—"

"I will be there," he insisted, voice deepening with a conviction that made Mina's heart skip a beat.

She reached up and fiddled with the collar of his shirt. "The force field still works, you're wearing clothes, have to run off to the Guild soon..." She sighed in disappointment. "This morning surprise really isn't turning out how I hoped it would."

He slipped his arms around the small of her back, the tension in his shoulders loosening. "What were you hoping for?"

"A kiss or two. A little morning cuddle to start."

"To start, huh?"

"Mmhmm," she hummed and unbuttoned the top button of his shirt. "Don't think we'll be able to do any of that out here, though."

Sebastian fished out his pocket watch and checked the time. He looked around the balcony, peering over its edge.

"I have an idea, but it'll only give us about fifteen minutes," he said.

Mina smiled. "I'd rather have fifteen minutes with you than none."

He reached into the inner pocket of his vest and pulled out a small tin. He opened the lid, dipped two fingers into the balm inside, and smeared it along the balcony's railing. The air above it rippled as if it had been super-heated.

"There," he said as he put the tin away. "That will give us some cover."

"But I can still see out," she noted.

"Yes, but to everyone 'out', the balcony looks completely empty." He smiled and kissed her softly. "For the next fifteen minutes, at least."

Mina shelved her curiosity for another time and kissed Sebastian hungrily, letting all the want, the need, the longing, the sadness from not having him by her side for the past few hours pour out. He met her passion immediately, tugging at her hair and gripping her hip so tight that no one, not even someone with Mina's level of strength, could take her from his grasp. An emptiness she felt but did not recognize, that dogging sense of something being missing that had her clenching her jaw and restless, eased.

And she was so grateful for it.

Her lips left his not for air but to travel down the pulse point of his neck, delighting in its warmth as she willed each thankful kiss to race through his veins and deliver her appreciation throughout his entire body.

He gave a welcoming whimper as his hips rolled forward. Mina dropped a hand down to meet them, pressing her palm against the length of his hardened cock.

The clamor of armor in the courtyard beneath them caused them to pause.

"Gods, I hate dawn patrol," one of the guards whined as he yawned.

"Really?" his patrol partner replied. "I love it. You get to watch the sunrise."

The pair popped out from under the balcony's sight line and made their way through the courtyard to take their posts at the wall on the other side of it. Sebastian's hold turned bruising, his entire body tensing in defense.

Mina ran her tongue up the crook of his neck and whispered in his ear, "They can't see us, remember?"

His cock throbbed against her palm, but before she could address it, she was spun around and pressed against the railing, pinned between its stone and his hips.

"You're right," he whispered back, voice deep and ragged. "They can't see us." He pulled down the collar of Mina's nightgown, exposing her breasts. "What a shame."

He rolled her nipples between his burning fingertips. Mina's hips arched back against him in response, desperate for contact.

"Bas—"

Sebastian stole his name from her lips as she tilted her head back to moan it.

"Quiet," he commanded, mouth hot against hers. "They can still hear us." He bunched up the skirt of her nightgown around her waist and ran his hand over her damp panties.

Sebastian gave a breathy laugh as he freed his cock from his pants. "Guess I should claim you in front of an audience more often."

He pulled down her panties roughly, wasting none of the little time they had, and lined the head of his cock up to her entrance. Mina's head was swimming from the rush of everything — the thrill of disobeying, his unexpected roughness exhilaratingly demanding — but Sebastian's was remarkably clear, placing a hand over her mouth to muffle her cry as he buried his cock inside her.

He pounded into her, fast, hard. Claiming her, rearranging her, leaving no room for it to be misconstrued that she was anything but his. She watched the guards on the horizon chatting away — unable to hear them over the heavy exhales and grunts from Sebastian's mouth against her ear — completely oblivious to her unmaking. The air cloaking them rippled, the threat of its camouflage dropping growing nearer. Her walls clenched at the thought, increasing the pleasure and pushing her closer to release.

"F-fuck," Sebastian hissed, thrusting deeper and more sporadic. "My girl—" he growled. "Mine—"

He bit down on her ear lobe as he spilled inside her, jamming his tip at the perfect angle to bring her along with him. Mina shook as her vision blurred, digging her fingernails into the sweltering arm around her waist, until her mind returned to itself.

Sebastian's grip didn't loosen, if anything he held her tighter to him, releasing her earlobe to rest his head against the crook of her neck, and removing his hand from her mouth to hold her in a proper embrace.

Mina wanted nothing more than to stay like that, feeling his warmth, knowing that he was right beside her, but the air rippled once again; the waving bands undulating slower.

"'Bastian," she turned her head and kissed his temple, "I think the barrier's about to go."

He squeezed her tightly and shook his head against her shoulder. "Dammit."

"What is it?" she asked.

He inhaled deeply and released her. "It's nothing." He slipped out of her, and the first inklings of that empty feeling started to sink in once again. He kissed the crown of her head as he adjusted her nightgown. "I miss you is all. Not just the sex. All of you." He kissed her temple. "I want you to know that."

Mina turned around and gave him a soft peck on the lips as she placed his cock back in his pants.

"I know. I miss all of you too," she replied. "I kept wishing you were there at dinner last night. Those monarchs would have been so delighted by you, they would have left me alone."

"What do you mean by that?" He tensed, brows furrowing, spine pulling straight as his shoulders lifted, standing him to his full height.

"I've figured out why His Majesty was so insistent that we stay at the castle." She smoothed her hands across his chest to soothe him. "He's hoping to use us as a distraction."

"A distraction?"

"Apparently there's a tiff between him and his brother. Half of the Capitol is blocked off because of it. A Magistrate from Kraedia, the Sovereign of Molveen, and the Empress of Dulsten were curious, but their curiosity was quickly diverted when they learned who I am and who I travel with." She smiled. "Empress Tinsae was very complimentary of your work in Varnear."

"What do you mean by 'who you are'?"

Mina sighed. "Annoyingly, Strauss, the magistrate from Kraedia, had heard about me from some diplomats I led up the Peaks a few years back. He was confused about my change in personality and King Fritz told them I had been cursed, which, *annoyingly* annoyingly, led to a million questions." She rebuttoned his top shirt button. "But I put Strauss in his place, and Sovereign Coro wound up finding a way to change the subject, thankfully."

"Fritz shouldn't have told them in the first place," he grumbled.

"I know. But I think he was just trying to help or trying to get his mind off his brother. He keeps putting on that happy mask of his, but if you look closely, it seems like he's pretty heartbroken over it." She patted his chest once she finished straightening his clothes. "He's asked me to perform at the ball tonight."

"Perform what?"

"A violin piece. He heard me playing on my balcony while he was out for a stroll last night."

"Oh, how nice!" Sebastian smiled, but his eyes and the rising heat of his palms against the small of her back told another story.

Now it was Mina's turn to tense. Her slowing heart rate doubled. "What's wrong?"

"Nothing," he lied. Poorly.

"Your hands are just a few degrees away from turning this nightgown to ash." Nausea started to bubble up again. "Don't lie."

He lifted his hands off of her slightly and took a deep breath. He locked eyes with her, gaze serious and studious. "Do you want to play at the ball tonight?"

Mina shrugged. "I mean. I don't mind it. I enjoy playing, and if anything you and the others will be there, and I love playing for you all."

"But he's not forcing you to play, is he?"

"No more than him being a king, and it being unwise to say 'no' to a king, especially over something so trivial."

"And if it wasn't trivial?"

"I've spent all of my life doing things I didn't want to do," she said. "So long as the people I care about aren't at risk, there's nothing that would make me go back to a life of that. Royal title be damned." She scoffed. "Especially not someone like King Fritz. He's clearly just another emotionally repressed, entitled blue blood who's never even picked up a sword, let alone fought with one."

There was still worry in his eyes, but his posture relaxed a bit with her declaration; an easier, less forced smile warming up his face.

"Alright. I just wanted to make sure."

Mina crossed her arms over her chest and pouted. "What? Did you think I'd just roll over for some dingus with a crown and a castle?"

"No!" A cartoonish panic overtook his face. "It's just that—"

"Hey. Are you seeing that weird shimmer on that balcony?" One of the guards asked across the courtyard.

"Shit," Mina and Sebastian hissed in unison.

Sebastian kissed her quickly. "I'll swing by your room before the ball and escort you down, alright?"

"Alright." Mina shoved him back towards the balcony doors. "I love you."

"I love you too," he said, slipping back into his room as Mina leaped to the balcony above them, becoming nothing more than a blur of wind and speed.

🜁

Tanir practically skipped the entire way down to Izydor's workshop, chattering on and on about the tailor's work so much that Mina felt as though the only thing she didn't know about him was his mother's maiden name.

"I wonder if he'll have the original sketches for Lady Malwina Kor's Quincentennial Founding Festival gown," she gasped. "I saw it once on display at the cultural museum by my university back when I was a student. The attention to detail was absolutely immaculate. Somehow, he managed to sew a thousand lunar moth wings—"

"We have arrived," the servant leading them interrupted, stopping in front of a pair of tall, wooden doors.

"We've arrived," Tanir repeated. Her excitement shifted to panic as she fixed her sweater and skirt frantically.

She looked up to Mina, worried and flustered. "How do I look?"

Mina reached out and tucked a stray gray hair back behind her ear.

"Like Izydor's new muse," she answered.

Tanir flushed crimson and smacked Mina on the shoulder. "Quit that. You're gonna have me looking like a bowl of tomato soup in front of him."

She shrugged. "You don't know. Maybe he likes tomato soup. Could even be his favorite food."

"It's not," Tanir muttered under her breath as she turned towards the doors. "His favorite food is sauerkraut pierogi."

The servant opened one of the doors into a world of textile wonder. Walls upon walls of fabric bolts and trims climbed up, twenty feet, to the rafters of the room's high ceilings. Glorious garments of an unlimited variety hung from a long metal track, hovering over rows and rows of tables and sewing machines, cabinets filled with notions and accessories, all immaculately labeled and organized by color and type.

The door shut behind them quietly, removing any idea of a world outside of the woven wonderland that would have seemed uninhabited if it weren't for the terrible, off-key singing coming from the back of the workshop.

"Izydor?" Mina called.

"Yeeeeesssss?" the voice sang back in an unstable vibrato.

"My name is Mina. I'm here with my friend, Tanir. King Fritz sent us so I could get a dress made for tonight's ball?"

"Oh, yes!" Izydor chirped. "Just a moment. I don't want to lose my place." He picked up his horrid operatics once again, underscored by a very subtle wooden clinking — even in tempo and rhythm compared to his vocals — so soft Mina was sure Tanir couldn't hear it.

"He's making lace," she whispered giddily. "In his fifth memoir, 'Back to Basting', he said that he braids the bobbins with the rhythm of his favorite opera pieces in mind to give them a sense of life, and even sings along. How lucky!"

Mina eyed a sack filled with stuffing cotton nearby. "Lucky is a word for it."

Izydor's singing concluded with an unfortunate crescendo and a button clack from the bobbins, rousing applause from Tanir. He appeared from his fabric forest, bowing.

"Thank you, thank you, no encores please." Izydor straightened, then stumbled, taken aback by the sight of them through his magnifying glasses. He pushed the frames up on his forehead, restoring his eyes to their normal human size. "That's better. Now you don't look like the giant models that chase me in my nightmares, angry that I put them in heavy woolen gowns for the Summer Solstice. I am Izydor, your humble tailor for the day, it is an honor to meet you."

His posture was as perfect as his pressed purple pinstripe suit as he extended his hand out towards Mina.

"Mina," she said, shaking it, being careful not to squeeze it too harshly. "This is my dear friend, Tanir. She's quite the accomplished seamstress and has admired your work for quite some time. Thank you for allowing us into your workshop."

Tanir bowed her head. "It truly is an honor."

"This fair creature is a fan of my work?" Izydor let go of Mina's hand and approached Tanir. "And has a talent for textiles?"

"I'm a hobbyist at best."

He took her hand in his and lifted it to study the cuff of her sweater. "You made this yourself?"

Tanir didn't have to worry about Mina making her blush, Izydor was doing well enough on his own to turn her face into a bowl of tomato soup.

"Y-yes?"

"She made my entire outfit too, save for the sword belt and boots," Mina added, gesturing to herself. Aubergine dress the medic had made for her aside, apparently she had been making her outfits since her second transformation — finding it unacceptable that she'd have to wear Wera's too-short clothes whenever something happened to her armor.

Izydor shook his head. "A hobbyist." He brought Tanir's hand to his lips and kissed her knuckles. "You are more of an artisan than I am, my darling."

"Oooohhh," she cooed, barely able to keep her cool. "I'm sure you say that to all the seamstresses you meet."

"Absolutely not. If I went spewing out compliments and flattery willy-nilly, then they would hold less value. And praise should always have value!" he insisted. "Your stitches are remarkably even, so much so I'd believe it was made by machines if not for the calluses on your thumbs and forefingers. And your understanding of body and shape? You went to design school, yes?"

"Medical school, actually. I'm a field medic."

Mina swore Izydor's pupils widened, like a cat spotting a bird beneath a bush.

"Brain, beauty, and bravery!" he exclaimed. "What a woman you are!"

Tanir's knees started to tremble, threatening to give out into a faint at any moment.

Mina cleared her throat to call Izydor's attention, and give Tanir a chance to catch her breath.

"I hate to interrupt, but I don't want you to have to rush too much on the dress," she said. "Should we get to measuring?"

Izydor looked her up and down, tilted his head side to side, then pulled out the measuring tape draped around his collar and handed it to Tanir.

"Thirty-six, twenty-six, thirty-eight," he said to Tanir. "Check me."

"No!" Tanir gasped in awe.

"I can tell you her inseam and sleeve length too, but I don't want to show off."

Tanir ran over to Mina excitedly, barely giving her the chance to lift her arms before she wrapped the measuring tape around her chest.

"Thirty-six..." She moved the measuring tape down to Mina's waist. "Twenty-six..." Lastly, her hips. "Thirty-eight!"

Izydor held up his hands and shrugged. "You pick up some things along the way. Now, between the two of us, I am sure we can have the gown done just in time for Ms. Harlowe to get dressed for the evening, maybe even get something nice for you, my darling. I'll just have to set aside the veil I'm working on for later this evening."

"Between the two of us?" Tanir pointed to herself in disbelief.

"I may be a decent designer, but to not work with someone who's close with my client, has dressed them, and has a natural gift for style? I'd be a fool." He smiled so charmingly at Tanir, Mina did a quick glance to make sure the glimmers of an enchantment weren't swirling in her eyes. "So what do you say? You won't make me a fool, will you?"

Tanir looked at Mina with an odd look of hope and remorse.

"I've still got to figure out what song I'm performing tonight and practice it," she'd be heartless to suggest anything else, "so don't let me stop you."

"You sure you'll be alright?"

She patted her hilt. "I've got my sword. I've got my speed. I'll be just fine."

"Wonderful!" Izydor exclaimed. "Let us get to work then. Tanir, darling, you'll find my sketch paper in the back of my shop, to the left, on my drafting desk. And Ms. Harlowe, might I recommend the Northern Botanical Garden as a place to source inspiration? I find that all the plant life tends to rouse the muses."

Mina nodded. "I'll check it out."

Izydor and Tanir disappeared together into the fabric forest without a wave goodbye, leaving Mina questioning if this was what the others felt like when she and Sebastian were together.

She sure hoped not.

The notion of what to play dogged her all the way back to her room. Well, not so much *what* to play, but *if* she should play it.

She kept drifting back to *Bastion of Flame*, her fingers aching with the need to play it, body buzzing at the thought of the surprise on Sebastian's face if she performed it for the entire court.

Her imagining of his expression shifted. After how forlorn and distraught he seemed this morning before she parted, perhaps just playing it wouldn't be enough. It wasn't as if the crowd would immediately know who it was inspired by. They didn't know the triplet of his laugh, the drumming of his fingertips, or the thrumming of his heartbeat. And with only a violin and not her whole kitchen band, it would only be a fraction of the piece's full glory.

It needed something more. Something that made her much more nervous than it should.

Sure, she was no Enoch and was still getting the hang of saying the right things, but she had read her fair share of poetry and sheet music. Surely she could cobble together some lyrics.

Especially if the garden Izydor mentioned was as inspiring as he claimed it to be.

Mina set out with her violin, pen, paper, and a sense of determination that waned with every step through the endlessly winding rows of dull, graying green and brown foliage. Maybe the garden only provided inspiration in Spring, when everything was in bloom and filled with life, or maybe it lied deeper, a secret only the truly desperate could reach.

Either way, Mina didn't want to turn back. Being surrounded by the slow death of Autumn was much better than being stuck in the castle, trying to distract herself from the deep unease she wouldn't be rid of anytime soon.

The wind at her heels, perhaps sick of her aimless wanderings, started to steer her. Pushing right against her ankles, forward, left, closer to a circle of small, low-hanging trees, and a crackling that roused the sparks of creation within her.

A small hearth, its flame a welcome splash of color and warmth among the ashen landscape, laid burning beneath the shade of their bows. Fallen leaves and lost twigs were scattered across its basin, thinking themselves lucky enough to escape feeding the fire, until Mina scooped them up and returned them to their destiny; clearing herself a seat in the process.

It wasn't the fire she had seen the night before, that one burned beyond the Capitol to the east, a proper campfire of sorts, but this one still carried a rhythm in its flames. A melody even.

Mina hummed the main violin line alongside it, watching how it flickered, sparked, popped. Let its warmth sink into her skin, down her arms, into her pen, then onto paper. Let the amber glow it cast fill her mind with color and creation.

"Let the sunset paint your skin. Let the fire burn within. Only tinder asked for is devotion," she sang beneath her breath. "Though the sparks may sting and bite, what the fire brings to light, oh burning Bastion, such emotion."

She heard King Fritz's footsteps before he spoke. "Mina?"

Of fucking course.

"Hello, Your Majesty," she replied, bowing her head just a bit as she continued to write. "My apologies for not rising and curtsying."

He huffed a laugh. "What are you scribbling away at?"

"Lyrics."

"For tonight?" he asked with a lilt. "You wrote an original composition for my party?"

Mina rolled her eyes internally. "I figured it would be a better choice rather than picking an existing song and hoping that the band didn't have it on their setlist."

"I am deeply honored, especially after all the hardships I've put you through as of late."

She set down her pen and swallowed her sigh of annoyance as she turned her focus towards the king. "Hardships? Whatever do you mean, Your Majesty?"

He sighed as heavy as the frown on his face, rapping his fingers with a rhythmless nervousness on the ornate box in his hands. "I am just so embarrassed by the actions of my Consul and the treasury in forgetting your payment. And then Magistrate Strauss' invasive questioning last night?" He shook his head. "It's not right." He held the box out to her. "I hope these help to ease some of these offenses."

Mina took the box from him and opened the lid carefully. A pair of fine, white satin heels laid on a black velvet cushion within it.

"They're a bit enchanted so they'll fit your feet as soon as you slip them on. They're not a part of the payment owed to you in the slightest," he fretted, wringing his hands slightly, being this far from the castle allowing him to drop his royal posturing a bit. "They are simply a gift. You could even wear them to the ball tonight, my dear."

Mina looked over the pair. She wasn't a fan of the color, but it would be nice to wear a well-fitting pair of heels with her outfit, rather than the ones a size too small she had to borrow from Tanir for the dinner.

"Thank you, Your Majesty. I will wear them this evening," she said as she closed the lid to keep them from getting dirty. "And consider your offenses eased."

He smiled and exhaled in relief. "Good. I am glad. It has been such a weight on my chest to think the actions of others might make you think of me as disagreeable."

"Disagreeable?" She barely knew the guy, let alone had an opinion of him. He was just another royal looking to hide his shortcomings behind pomp and circumstance. A poor sap who would rather stay laughing away his troubles rather than face them head-on. "I do not know you very well yet, Your Majesty. But do know I do not find you disagreeable."

If anything, I pity you.

A sheepish, hopeful smile curved his lips. His hands stopped their wringing. "Then I suppose you wouldn't mind if I asked you to open up the dance floor with me this evening, my dear?"

Would you let me use you as a distraction once again?

"No, I wouldn't mind," she replied — another royal favor to call in — then added, "So long as I am allowed to dance with whoever I see fit afterwards."

"Of course. Of course. It's mainly ceremonial." He nodded then sighed, rolling his eyes and grumbling, "Tradition states that I should dance with one of the foreign guests attending but, to be frank, I think Empress Tinsae would rather bite off her own tongue than dance a waltz with me."

Mina hummed in feigned interest. "Wouldn't want that to happen."

"No, we wouldn't." He smiled, odd-colored eyes looking deep into hers, waiting for her to add to the conversation — to do the friendly thing and continue talking.

Mina gave a soft, patient smile instead. She had enough friends.

Fritz clapped his hands to end the awkwardness. "I'll let you get back to your songwriting, then. See you later this evening, my dear."

"Until this evening, Your Majesty." Mina bowed her head as he left, but she could not help but watch him go.

What an odd king.

The fire popped behind her, pulling her attention back to its heat and her work, and replacing piercing eyes with burning ones, flecked with swirling embers and filled with love.

🜂

Mina could not bring herself to go back inside the castle. In theory, she very well could go back in — had every capability to go back in — but every step she took towards it, every inch its spires grew in height as she approached, had her nervous stomach bubbling, heart racing, skin itching. Nearly the same sensation as when she first stepped into the commorancy.

Oh, how she wished Sebastian could still command her, make her stupid subconscious overcome such a silly childhood fear.

Lyrics finished, and stalling, Mina explored the palace garden further, finding more small sitting areas: some adorned with intricately carved stone statues of docile forest creatures, some with topiaries half-formed from shedding their leaves, but no other fire pits. The hedges lining the paths grew taller as she walked, reaching just about two feet over her head before they came to an end, pathway closed off by a wrought iron gate. Through the bent, curling metal, Mina could see the path continuing on, the hedges growing thicker and in greater number, with no clear end in sight. There was no lock keeping her from entering, and turning around would only lead her back to the palace.

So through the gate she went.

Mina had read about hedge mazes before, about protagonists running away from the person they desired into them, only for that person to chase after them, leading to a confrontation away from prying eyes. Or, conversely, in tales not about romance, what lay in wait for the lead was not love between the hedges but misery. Dark malignant forces hiding in the shadows, lurking in the myriad of maddening twists, lying in wait to use the seclusion lovers so pined for in mazes to corner their prey.

The click of heels deep from within the maze — sharp and metronomic like the ticking of a clock in an empty room — had her mind racing to those darker parts. She placed her hand on the hilt of her sword and closed her eyes, listening for the source. The smell of the earth, of wet leaves fallen beneath the hedges slowly decaying, drew her focus instead. She pinched her nose and tried again, listening as intently as she could to the wind, urging it to hum in her ear and paint a picture of the world as it used to do, but the seam of her woolen socks, bunched under her toes in an odd lump, muddled the mural.

"Ms. Harlowe," a not quite Kraedian, not quite Ortrian accent rumbled.

Mina jumped, snapping open her eyes and unsheathing her sword. Magistrate Strauss remained unfazed as her blade jutted his way.

"I was not expecting to find you here," he continued. He placed a long, spindly forefinger on the tip of her sword and slowly pushed it down. "My apologies for startling you."

Mina withdrew her sword immediately and dropped into a curtsy, heart racing a mile a minute from both her fear and threatening a high-ranking foreign official's life. "No. I should be the one to apologize, my lord. If I had known it was you, I never would have drawn my blade."

"Never?" he asked. "Even if I were here to harm you? Told you I was looking to gut you like a fish and hang your entrails out to dry so I could wear them as a necklace?"

Mina rose, slowly, hand back on her hilt.

"Are you saying that, my lord?"

Strauss smiled as much as a grim face such as his could smile. "No, I am not saying that. And judging by the quality of your stance, I suspect I wouldn't be long for this world if I were. It was just a joke about semantics."

Mina forced a laugh and righted herself into a more ladylike posture. "I'm afraid I missed the punchline entirely, my lord. Coming from an isolated cabin in the country, the wittiness of you city folk is still lost on me sometimes."

"Right." Strauss's smile vanished. "You came from the maze's other outlet, correct?"

"I assume so, my lord."

"What lies beyond it?"

"Some very impressive topiaries and the most darling statues of deer and rabbits," the sound of her own voice grated her ears, chipper and bright in a desperate attempt to please, to dissuade him from paying her any mind. "Oh! And a fire pit! You should really go and see it, it is a wonderful respite from the fall chill."

"Well, if that's all, then perhaps I should just turn back around. I'd much rather warm myself by the fire in my guest room." He offered his arm to her. "Let me escort you to the end, won't you? This maze is tricky, and I wouldn't want to upset His Majesty by allowing you to get lost."

"There's no need to worry about that, my lord," she replied. Her knees threatened to shake. The wind lapped at her ankles eagerly, ready and willing to run the second she called upon it. "If I get confused, I'll simply turn around and—"

"I insist."

Mina gave a curt nod. "Of course, my lord." She slipped her arm through his. Stuck her head in the wolf's maw. "Lead the way."

His hold on her arm was firm, caging, but his pace was slow, meandering almost as they wove through the hedges, twisting and turning down pathways so frequently, Mina had lost all sense of where they had started.

"You perplex me, Ms. Harlowe," he remarked.

"Perplex you, my lord?" She kept her focus ahead, trying to find some distinction in the shrubbery to help her remember where to go if she had to escape.

"I was being concise at dinner last night when relaying what I've heard about you," he placed a hand on top of hers. "I know a great deal more, in fact."

"Oh?" Mina stood a little taller, turned to him, and smiled as her stomach sunk. "From the diplomat of yours that I lead up the Peaks some time ago?"

"Magistrate Marvolo. You may remember him. Bald, beady-eyed, short-legged with a laugh like an out-of-tune horn." Strauss rolled his eyes, recalling the man. Mina remembered him immediately. He was an annoying little fuck who whined from the moment he got his first blister up until she practically punted him over the Kowleth gate. "When he got back to Kraedia he did nothing but complain about you for weeks. Still finds something to gripe about any time anyone brings up the trip to this day. 'The rudest woman he had ever met with a temper that could scare a banshee back into her grave.'"

He rapped his fingers over her knuckles over and over again, a trilling count of the second hand between his minute measuring footsteps. A cold sweat began to bead on the small of her neck. The clock was counting down.

"And yet. Last night I had dinner with this apparently horrendous woman, and she's got such poise and grace that at a glance one would think she was the most well-bred and well-finished woman on the entire continent." His tone was amused, but the cut of his 't's grew noticeably sharper. "You knew exactly how to address every nobleman you met, regardless of homeland. Could navigate the complexities of Lanholdian dinner etiquette. All without any formal training apparently because — from what I know — as of a month ago at least, you were a borderline feral hermit who barely cared about brushing her hair let alone eating with a fork. Would prefer to eat a half-cooked grouse, pin bones and all without flinching over sitting down and sharing a proper meal with the rest of your expedition."

"I didn't *prefer* it." Mina dug her heels into the ground, stopping the both of them. She inhaled deeply, holding back her anger to keep from crushing his humerus."What are you implying, magistrate?

Strauss looked up at the sky and scratched at his chin. "For a moment last night I was entertaining the idea that you were an imposter, was turning over and over again in my head as to why you'd pick some random alpinist to impersonate, but then for just the whisper of a moment that mask of yours slipped." That somewhat smile of his returned. "'Because your face doesn't look that bad if you took an entire supply crate to it.' No lady of repute would dare say such a thing to a king, but a jaded, recently uncursed alpinist might."

"So I am who I say I am," she huffed. "What's your point?"

He looked down at her as a hawk does to a fish — a wolf to a lost fawn.

"Why are *you* here?"

Mina couldn't help but bark a laugh. "Really? You're breaking me down like some great noir detective, and *that's* what you want to know?"

His severe grimace was unwavering, his fingers stopped their rapping. "Are you refusing to answer?"

Mina sneered, dropping all polite posturing and proper speech. "His Majesty's treasury shorted me my payment for the expedition so now I'm stuck here, serving as a new shiny bauble for you noble ninnies to gawk at, until the holiday's over and I can collect my coin and go."

Strauss' gaze narrowed, nostrils flaring as his lip curled up in doubt. "Then what's the act for?"

"To survive!" She pulled her arm away and threw her hands in a vague gesture around them. "To not make an ass of myself in there and ruin Sebastian's reputation! You, of all people, should know how fickle monarchs can be! I have no fucking clue what kind of ruler Fritz is! The last thing I need is to offend him and have Windenhofer Procurements blacklisted from an entire kingdom, or worst rendered defunct by mass execution!"

"That doesn't explain your urbanity."

"You didn't ask me to explain my *urbanity*, you asked me to explain why I'm here."

Strauss ground his teeth. "I see what Marvolo was talking about now."

Mina smiled, viciously. "I'm glad I meet expectations."

"Fritz doesn't know this side of you, clearly."

"*Clearly.*" Mina rolled her eyes. "I think we both can see that it's best for everyone involved in this fall-themed flaunting that we keep it that way."

"Is it, now?" Strauss straightened up to his full height and peered down at her over the long, sharp slope of his nose. "It could be quite advantageous of me to let him know that you're just humoring him."

"And it could be quite advantageous for me to inform him of your keen interest in what exactly is happening on the east side of town." Mina held her chin up, unafraid for the first time in days. "With your footman's scent, I'm sure a bloodhound fit for a king would be able to track those papers you mentioned down in no time."

Strauss frowned. "What papers?"

Mina smiled and batted her eyelashes as she placed a hand on her chest. "What act?" she cooed. "Whatever you and Coro and Tinsae have going on, I want no part of. I just want to get to tomorrow, get my payment, then leave."

"And how can I trust that you're being honest when I know you to be a liar?"

Mina's smile turned genuine, curved with a smirk. She held her hand out to him. "I swear it."

He considered her closely for a moment, hawkish gaze darting over her, sizing her up for any tricks or ill-intent. She did not waver, so he yielded, grabbing her hand and shaking it.

The ghost of the Fae's Folly glided down her arm, its presence still a part of her even without her curse, and wrapped around their hands. A chill rolled through the magistrate, causing his breath to puff out in a tiny cloud. He pulled his hand out of hers and took a step back, eyes wide and brow furrowed in confusion.

"What have you done to me?"

She shrugged. "You know what I'm saying is the truth now, right?"

"I do."

"Then you know I mean it when I say there's nothing for you to worry about." Mina curtsied. "Now I must be off, my lord. I have a ball to prepare for."

Strauss regained his footing and straightened out his coat. "Very well. First left from here, second right, then straight on until you hit the gate."

"Thank you." Mina turned on her heels and headed deeper into the maze.

"Ms. Harlowe," he called just before she reached the first left.

She stopped and turned back to face him. "Yes, my lord?"

"Do have Master Windenhofer give me his card before you all go."

"Ask him yourself. He'll be at the ball tonight," she replied. "Tall, amber hair as warm as firelight, and a brilliant smile to match." Mina couldn't help but smile as she said it. "Can't miss him."

XXX

A Truly Memorable Performance

Mina watched herself in the mirror as the clock ticked on, the minute hand steadily growing closer to turning the hour.

She pinched herself every time her mind began to slip to the tightness of her corset, the heavy frills of her gown, the hairpins poking into her scalp. She smiled at herself, frowned at herself, traced the outline of her sword hidden beneath her skirt, checked to make sure her violin was still in tune; anything to remind herself that she was still her. That this was not a nightmare. That her reflection wasn't going to change, that the walls were not going to shatter, that chains were not lying in wait for her to fuck up.

She'd manage to shoo the maid King Fritz sent to dress her away ten minutes ago. It was getting closer and closer to the start of the ball.

Where was Sebastian?

If she ran, she could make it to the guild and back, probably strip Sebastian and throw him in a suit with just enough time to be considered fashionably late. Sure, the ball gown would most certainly be ruined, but she didn't care for the white or frills or snowflake appliqués very much. If a few of them fell off, she was sure no one would notice.

She grabbed her violin case and left her room — needing to move, needing to make sure there was a hall of stone, not ice, waiting for her — and headed down it towards the stairwell.

Check Sebastian's room first, then run to the guild hall, run across the entire kingdom to find him if I have to.

"Look, if you just go to her room and ask her, she will tell you that I am her escort to the ball this evening!"

Mina's knees nearly gave out from relief hearing Sebastian's voice. She walked as fast as her heels would let her, turning the corner to find him arguing with a palace guard.

"Nice try, pal," the guard scoffed. "Minute I turn my back to go check, you could be off and up to no good. Unless your room is on this floor, I'm not allowed to let you pass until the ball is over."

"Surely, you could have sent for a servant to get me," Mina snipped, anger folding into her unease. "Or another guard. In fact, there are literally a thousand different ways for you to have consulted me without leaving your post."

The guard turned towards her, face plastered with confusion.

"Oh! And would you look at that! I thought you were worried about turning your back to him! Go ahead, Sebastian." She gestured. "Be off and up to no good!"

Sebastian smiled smugly. "Good evening, Mina. You look lovely."

Mina brushed past the guard and took the arm he offered her, holding on to it for dear life as she tugged him towards the stairwell.

"S-sorry, miss, I—"

She glared at the guard so fiercely, he blanched.

"Just be grateful I won't be late to open up the dance floor with His Majesty," she hissed and stormed down the stairs until she was certain they were out of sight.

She turned to Sebastian and hugged him tightly, needing to feel the warmth of his arms, smell his cologne, assure her spiraling mind that he was real.

"I'm sorry I kept you waiting," he whispered, squeezing her just as tightly. "Did something happen?"

She shook her head against his chest. "I just need to clear my head."

"Of what?"

"Of ice." She dug her fingers into his sides. "That this is real."

Heated palms cupped her face and tilted her head back.

"It's real," he said. "I'm here."

The kindness in his eyes, their rich chestnut, subtle embers flecking their depths, was irreplicable.

She closed her eyes and inhaled deeply. "Fuck this goddamn dress."

"Unfortunately, I'm not into fabric like that," he said, pulling a slight chuckle from her. "I was gonna say the dress looks nice, but it doesn't seem like your style."

Mina looked down at herself and frowned. "Tanir helped him design it too."

"Him?"

"Izydor, the royal tailor, and maybe Tanir's beau considering how much they were flirting with each other. I might as well have been a journalist hiding in the reeds watching two birds doing a mating dance when they met each other." She looked back up to Sebastian as she shifted the bodice back and forth, trying to loosen the laces cinching it. "We don't act like that, do we?"

"Depends on the birds, I think. Here." He motioned for her to turn around and set to work uncinching her. "Gods, you'd think your tits were a boat needing to be tied down during a hurricane with how tight this is. No wonder it's bothering you."

"It's tight, it's frilly, it's snowflaked—"

"It's white," he added with a grumble.

"Well," Mina looked down at her feet. "That's probably to match the heels. But white wouldn't have been my first choice."

The laces gave way a bit, granting her room to breathe.

"There." Sebastian drummed his fingertips on her shoulders. "A little better?"

Mina nodded, happy to fill her lungs a little more, but still a bit on edge. "A little better."

"I could make it more better. Maybe."

Mina craned her neck back to look at him. "Maybe?"

"Is Izydor going to be at the ball tonight?"

"Don't know. Barely said two words to the guy before he was off, whisking Tanir to the back of his workshop."

"So, he'd be distracted if he was there?" he asked. "Like, distracted enough to not make a scene about your dress looking vastly different from what he made?" Sebastian smiled mischievously.

Mina smiled back. "How different?"

He moved her closer to the arrowslit windows in the stairwell. "Hold your breath and keep your eyes closed."

Mina did as she was told, and Sebastian crouched down beside her, one hand pinching the hem of her gown while the other held on to the bodice.

A growing warmth rose around her, swirling, building in heat as the smell of smoke and burning tickled her nose. She couldn't help but smile in excitement from the rush of their mischief. If it looked like she had just walked out of a bonfire, perhaps she could play it off as a costume that went along with her song. That Izydor invented a new, revolutionary styling technique with fire just for it.

"There we go," Sebastian said as the heat faded. "Not too shabby, if I say so myself. Perhaps I should have gone to fashion school."

Mina opened her eyes and found the glass beads of the snowflakes melted into candle wax. Swirls of smoke formed intricate shades of black and gray that added dimension to the gradient of deep black to light-brown staining the white — breathing a much-needed warmth to the gown.

Sebastian tugged on her skirt. "So?"

Mina bent down to kiss him. "I love it."

He smiled against her lips and kissed her back before standing. "I tried to get the shoes too, but the fire wouldn't catch." He furrowed his brow and kicked the toe of her shoe lightly.

"I don't mind it," she said. "It's a nice contrast."

"Good," he said and offered her his arm. "Shall we?"

She took it. "Yes, we shall."

Everything felt steadier with Sebastian beside her, her heartbeat, her breathing, even her steps. The halls filled with more and more people as they approached the ballroom, but hardly any of them paid them notice. They were all too absorbed in showing off their outfits and accomplishments — trying to impress the people they knew held title or power — to pay any mind to some unknowns.

Enoch and Wera stood off to the side of the ballroom foyer, whispering excitedly to each other as they crowd-watched.

"Long time no see, you two," Sebastian greeted. "Cleaned up well as always."

"I don't know if we could call this cleaned up compared to Tanir over there," Wera said, gesturing towards the other side of the room with her wine glass.

Through the crowd, Tanir looked radiant in a gown seemingly poured from liquid gold. Her gray hair was down from its usual bun and styled with the utmost care, and her make-up transformed her face completely into something years younger and incredibly alluring. She hung on Izydor's arm, the perfect compliment to his intricate platinum tailcoat.

"She's with Izydor," Enoch said in shock and awe. "*The* Izydor. We've talked about his work dozens of times. She never told me she knew him!"

"She didn't. They just met today when I went to talk with him about a gown," Mina answered.

"A gown?" Enoch pulled his attention away from Tanir to look Mina up and down. "That's an Izydor original?"

"It is."

Sebastian smirked slightly.

"How did you get an Izydor original?!"

"The king asked me to play this evening," she said, holding up her violin case.

Enoch turned to Wera. "Just two days away and the world has completely changed."

"I'm never gonna be able to look at Tanir the same after this," Wera commiserated. "The woman's in her late sixties and her ass still looks like *that*?"

"Excuse me, miss." A servant approached Mina. "His Majesty has asked me to collect your instrument and sit it with the band so you're not burdened by it this evening."

"I see." Mina handed him the violin. "When will the ball actually begin?"

"The doors to the ballroom will be opening in about five minutes. His Majesty will give the guests about twenty minutes to enter, then he will ask you to accompany him for the opening dance."

"Understood. I will make sure to keep an eye out."

Sebastian's arm flexed around hers as the servant left, the wool of his suit warming slightly.

"Opening dance?" he asked with a tight smile. "I thought that was just a line you gave to the guards."

"It's tradition to open the dance floor with a dance between His Majesty and a foreign guest. He asked if I would do him the honor." She patted Sebastian's arm to soothe him. "It's only for one dance, though. I made sure of that."

"It's gonna be good for future contracting opportunities, too," Enoch added. "That and your performance will have you sticking in the minds of the upper crust — wanting to learn more about the mysterious virtuoso alpinist traveling with a band of handsome magical procurement specialists."

Mina grimaced. "Great."

"Aww," Wera teased. "Mina's gonna be popular. Gonna have to change the name to Harlowe Procurements to rake in that noble contract money."

"Empress Tinsae is already considering contracting us out again just from hearing 'Windenhofer' last night, I think the name can stay as is," Mina grumbled. "And what's with everyone calling me 'Harlowe'?"

"I believe part of it is my fault," Sebastian admitted. "I had to list a surname for you when I filed you as my apprentice with the guild. I figured you wouldn't mind 'Harlowe'. If you want to change it, though, you can. We can—"

"I don't mind it. It's just—" She mulled over the hesitation plaguing her. "I don't know if they'd want that."

"Oh please," Wera scoffed. "Who wouldn't want to give you their last name? Mina Alrust sounds pretty good if you—"

"Wera," Sebastian warned, with a little more edge than usual.

She gave him an impish smile and a wink, but was kept from delivering whatever sly retort she was planning by the ballroom doors opening and the crowd funneling inside.

The ballroom was exceedingly large and filled with more odd, ornate stonework — blobby and unnatural, as if Fritz wanted the stone to look like anything other than stone. The stunning smell of autumn spice was lesser here thanks to the lack of carpet and drapery throughout the space, but the fake fall decor was in full display: covering the ballroom in odd-shaped fabric leaves and hollowed, lacquered gourds. They were a pretty color at least, Mina noted, warm oranges and reds that made Sebastian's hair shine. A stage sat at the front of it all, hosting a small orchestra playing light instrumental music to fill the atmosphere while the partygoers perused the vast array of finger foods surrounding the dance floor.

Sebastian didn't eat a bite of it.

"What kind of dance?" he asked out of nowhere, right after Mina had popped a large piece of cheese into her mouth, her stomach finally feeling at ease from his presence.

"What?" she mumbled.

"The opening dance," he clarified. "What kind of dance is it?"

Mina swallowed. "A waltz."

He inhaled sharply, nodded, and said nothing more. Even though a thousand thoughts were running through his mind and his posture was so stiff that if something brushed against him, Mina feared he might snap in half.

She reached up and placed a finger in the middle of his forehead, pulling him from his hundred-yard stare. She tapped him. "What's going on up there?"

He smiled despite how tense he was and grabbed her finger. His hands were near scalding.

"A lot," he admitted, "I—"

"Excuse me, my dear." King Fritz interrupted, appearing beside them. "Would you do me the honor of a dance?"

Mina pulled her hand out of Sebastian's, heat spiking, leaving the skin of her finger slightly burnt and pulsing, and curtsied. "Of course, Your Majesty."

King Fritz offered his arm, and she took it, sensing every eye in the ballroom falling on her immediately; stalking them as they walked closer and closer to the dance floor.

Wolves.

The years upon years of dance lessons and etiquette took over under their gaze, lifting her chin and curling her lips into a polite smile as they took their starting position.

One. Two. Three.

One. Two. Three.

The orchestra played an old Lanholdian piece, composed by a royal conductor three hundred years ago and incredibly boring. King Fritz's posture was sloppy, but his footwork was serviceable. He wouldn't be winning any dance competitions or sweeping anyone off their feet with debonair moves, but he certainly wasn't embarrassing himself either.

"My, you are much more accomplished than I thought you would be," King Fritz remarked fondly. "I'm sure quite a few folks will be asking you for a turn about the dance floor after this."

"Perhaps," Mina said, keeping up her smile despite her disdain. "I'm sure Wera and Enoch would be happy to dance with them in my stead."

"Oh, don't say no to all of them, my dear. Dancing is a wonderful way to make important social connections."

One. Two. Three.

One. Two. Three.

"Many a business deal has been won because of a waltz," he continued. "Just remember to step on the toes of those trying to swindle you."

Mina laughed politely at his joke. "I'll make sure to take note."

The double horn closed out the song with a button, earning a round of applause as they hit their final position. Mina curtsied, King Fritz bowed slightly, and as she turned around to rejoin Sebastian, she was swarmed by partygoers.

"Hello, I'm the Duchess of Inmarn. It is wonderful to meet you, what a wonderful dress!" "Good evening, madam, would you do me the honor of your next dance?" "I have years of formal dance training, I assure you, I'd be a much better dance partner." "Wherever did you get those shoes? They must be enchanted, or are you truly that wonderful of a dancer?"

Her heartbeat thundered to the tempo of their chatter. The growing mob closed in tighter, stealing the meager amount of breath her loosened bodice had granted her. Mina tried to look through the crowd for Sebastian, but instead of amber hair, she found a set of citrine eyes.

"Ms. Harlowe," Sovereign Coro said, a buoy in a restless ocean. "Would you care to—"

"Yes, Sovereign," Mina said quickly, dropping into a curtsy and taking their hand — gripping much stronger than the fragile debutante she pretended to be would have, "I would be honored to dance with you."

"Excellent."

They made it through the crowd just in time for the next song to start and joined the other dancers in their jaunty galloping. Desperate, Mina searched through the sea of onlookers for any sign of Sebastian as they turned about the floor, certain she'd see a glimmer of his hair above the spectators considering his height. Once she found him, she'd keep track of him, and head straight in his direction the moment the dance was done.

She absolutely had to.

"Is something the matter, Ms. Harlowe?" Coro asked.

"Everything is just fine, Your Majesty," she replied, smiling as she kept searching, gritting her teeth at every bouquet of fall leaves that falsely got her hopes up. It would be too obvious for her to close her eyes and search for him. Not that she could even focus with all the smells — sweat and perfume and booze — and all the touching — thwapped by heavy skirts, feet stepped on by clumsy oafs, her hands clamming against Coro's well-manicured mitts.

"But you're looking about the room as if you're a wild bird who flew in through a window."

Mina, begrudgingly, looked at Coro so as not to seem rude. "I'm looking for Sebastian."

"What for?"

"For dancing?" she replied. "I greatly appreciate you asking me to dance, Your Majesty, especially with the onslaught of requests, but Sebastian—" A flash of amber flickered in the corner of her eye. Her focus snapped towards it. "We were looking forward to spending the evening together after he's been so busy with the guild." The flash of amber dwindled, as one of the chefs stationed at the banquet smothered their flambé with a skilled flip of their skillet. "However, despite his height and his hair giving him the distinct advantage of being easy to spot, I can't seem to find him."

"Interesting." A shimmer shuttered across Coro's pupil-less eyes. "Ah. You are unable to see him as it appears our friend Strauss has pulled him aside for a moment."

She furrowed her brow. "Where?"

"Elsewhere," they smiled, a *knowing* smile. "Looks like he's asking him for his business card."

Nausea returned, threatening to dump the contents of her stomach right in the middle of the dance floor.

"But I can have him back to you in just three more dances."

"Or you could tell me where he is, and I can go find him myself," she said, squeezing their hand a bit tighter, fighting the urge to make each metacarpal pop like fireworks.

"I wish it were that easy." Coro sighed and gave her a sad smile — a pitying smile. If they weren't in public, she'd gouge those eerie eyes out of their skull — regardless if they were a ruler or not. "Do me a favor and look at the crowd rather than through it for a moment."

"To what?' All pleasantries to her speech flew out the window. "See a bunch of people watching other people dance?"

"Watching *you* dance," they corrected. "Look at every face you pass, and you will meet their gaze directly."

She did, spitefully, eager for the chance to prove them wrong, and was instead met with eyes, dozens upon dozens, looking at her with curiosity, jealousy, excitement, intrigue, confusion, judgment.

"Shit," she hissed under her breath.

All eyes on His Majesty's distraction.

"That's definitely a word for it," Coro hummed. "I don't think you'll get very far without having to cause a scene, unfortunately. "

Mina stared at him instead of glared, smiled even wider instead of sneered. Obviously, the fucker had been talking with Strauss — knew about their little chat in the maze, probably sent Strauss after her too, looking for information.

For a weakness.

The hairs raised on the back of her neck.

"You'll get Sebastian for me in three dances' time," she hissed through her grin. "What do you want in return?"

Coro smiled, tilting their head to the side — playing dumb. "What makes you think I'd want something in return?"

"No person of power hands out favors without expecting repayment."

Their smile widened and they chuckled. "How *did* a hermit become so wise to the ways of the world?"

She tilted her head much like they had, laying on her chipper lilt thick. "Is the answer the price of collecting Sebastian, Your Majesty?"

"No. That answer is something to be earned by trust I suspect," they noted, staring deep into her eyes, glancing at the depths of her soul. "For this, I ask that you dance with three people of my choosing."

"Why?" she growled.

"Another answer to be earned by trust," they sighed in lament. "Now I owe you one, and you owe me one."

Another favor for a monarch, with far too many strings attached. Not the tenuous truce between a fox and wolf to escape a hunter's bow, but a web. Sticky and unseen, the spider offering the fly pardon so long as it brings back its friends.

"The individuals you choose must not wish me or mine harm," Mina clarified, prodding at the web's weave, grabbing on to threads in the hopes of unraveling it, "or have any sort of malignant intent directed our way."

"An interesting addendum."

"A necessary one. Especially if neither of us want to cause a scene," she insisted. "I do not care if they are a king or a commoner, if one of your dancers speaks to me or behaves in a manner I find threatening, I shall retaliate without hesitation."

"My. For a simple alpinist, you speak like a warlord."

"No. I speak as someone who knows all too well the length to which people emboldened by power will go to get what they want." She adjusted her grip around their hand to one of alliance rather than control. "You bring Sebastian to me in three dances' time. I dance with three individuals of your choosing that have no ill-intent towards me or mine. Do we have a deal?"

Coro shook her hand slightly, disguising it as part of the dance. "Deal."

The Fae's Folly threaded over her skin and twisted itself around their hands to bind it. Unlike her swear to Strauss, there was no chill that ran through the sovereign, no puff of breath or look of surprise. Granted there was no magic messing with his mind, but if Coro — as magically gifted as they were noted to be — felt it, they didn't let on.

"Dance with Countess Wioletta of Dace first. I will introduce you to her myself," they instructed. "Then Consul Ana Otero. She is the blonde woman in the mauve, long-sleeved gown wearing a circlet of rubies resembling raspberries. Then lastly, Sir Marcin Polit. The stern older gentleman, with a haircut as square as his shoulders, dressed in his military garb. He will not ask you to dance, so you must ask him. He will not refuse you, though."

Mina found the man in question immediately, a pillar of stone more than a person compared to the lively crowd around him. It was hard to tell if he was watching her or just simply looking in her direction.

"He doesn't seem to be the dancing type."

"That's because no one ever asks him."

She gave Coro a questioning glance. "I thought neither of us wanted to make a scene."

"A negative scene, Ms. Harlowe," they clarified. "Dancing with Polit will make you come off as extremely endearing and naive to the attendees. Which is precisely what you want to be at this moment."

"Innocent ignorance often reveals the truth," she replied, earning a wry smile from the monarch.

"I wonder where you heard such a clever sentiment."

Distraction for one monarch. Information for the others.

Mina's skin crawled, knees trembling, yearning to run. A hare caught in a lupine tug-of-war.

The quadrille came to a close and, true to their word, Sovereign Coro led Mina through the encroaching rush to introduce her to Countess Wioletta.

"Sovereign Coro," the countess bowed. "What a lovely display of a quadrille, and what a lovely dance partner you have."

"Thank you, Countess," Coro said, gesturing slightly with his hand for her to rise. "May I introduce you to Ms. Mina Harlowe. She was the alpinist that assisted on the artifact expedition King Fritz recently commissioned. She mentioned finding your dress rather lovely and was wondering if you'd perhaps be interested in a dance."

"What a wonderful coincidence! I was hoping to dance with this lovely creature myself, but with the mad rush, I was thinking I was going to have to use my hairpin nefariously to have a chance at getting close," Countess Wioletta said as she offered Mina her hand. "Shall we?"

"We shall," Mina replied, plastering on her widest smile and giving Coro one last glance before taking her hand and heading back onto the floor. "Would you like to lead, my lady, or shall I?"

"I think I shall lead this one. The pulka is my favorite," Wioletta said as they stepped into the pulka's starting figure. "I am curious as to how an alpinist became such a fine dancer."

"Practice, my lady," she answered, jumping in perfect time to the trumpet's opening blare. "All those years alone in a cabin leave one plenty of time to study the finer things in life."

She filled their conversation with half-truths and lies, allowing the countess to express her fascination while Mina crafted a narrative of being a simple common girl who never imagined she'd be in such a pretty dress, let alone a royal ballroom.

Innocent, ignorant, underestimated — things Mina vehemently hated being thought of as. But they would get her out of here and off the board of whatever political game she had found herself swept up in.

They had found themselves swept up in, now that Strauss the bloodhound was sniffing around Sebastian. It took all of Mina's self-control not to pierce her heel through the countess's foot and storm out of the ballroom in search of them. To fight against her stupid little deal with the orange-eyed bastard and take whatever ails it gave her to make sure Sebastian was alright.

But one meddlesome magistrate was better than a fleet of guards and a swarm of angry nobles. Sebastian could hold his own, and if he were really in trouble, she'd know it.

"...will keep you and those you care about from harm to the best of my ability."

She'd know it.

Finished with Wioletta, Consul Ana focused less on learning about Mina and more on teaching her, quizzing her on her knowledge of Lanholdian history. If Mina heard one more thing about how things 'usually' were during Harvest's Hail — had one more thing explained to her by this woman like she was an infant — she might let herself become an infant and throw a temper tantrum unlike anything they'd ever seen.

But there was still one more dance left to go, and neither Coro nor Sebastian were in sight.

So yes, it was absolutely fascinating to hear Consul Ana recount for the tenth time that this was the only instance in the Capitol's history that the eastern gates were closed outside of the Bilrant Invasion some seven hundred years ago.

Mina led their gallop around the dance floor, allotting some control as to where they landed as the dance came to an end. She curtsied to the Consul and turned her back to her before she could drone another Lanholdian fact, facing Sir Polit — doe-eyes gleaming — as she asked if he would honor her with a dance.

His all-watching stare broke at that, but his eyes were the only part of him that moved to look at her, adding to the notion that he truly was made of stone.

"From the song's introduction, I believe this will be a rather gentle waltz, sir," she said in response to his silence, giving him the sweetest smile she could muster. "With the strength of your posture, I'm sure you're the best man suited to lead me through it."

He stared at her another moment, contemplating, studying, — judging perhaps — then lifted his arm for her to take it.

She must have looked like a child compared against his massive stature. She certainly felt child-sized, especially as she constantly had to adjust her footwork to keep her toes out from underneath his boulder-sized feet. He was a stiff dancer, unsurprisingly, and frustratingly stoic. Her few attempts to be polite, asking him his name, what he did for a living, only yielded her one word answers or grunts in response.

Which she was quite fine with, all things considered. It was nice not having to talk and pretend to care and be pleasant.

"You climbed The Lithe?" Sir Polit asked out of nowhere, ruining her relief. He was staring straight at her. No pretending to look at the crowd to be polite. No adverting his gaze as she looked back up at him. Just an unbreaking stare, attentive yet apathetic.

"I invented climbing The Lithe," she corrected, forgetting to pick her pleasantries back up again.

"Why?"

"It's quicker. Less people die." Mina found her debutante smile again and gave it a more bashful tone instead of her current annoyed apathy. "Same reason I go through Rabbet's Pass instead of around it."

"Scaling straight up ten-thousand feet in roaring winds and freezing temperatures leads to less death?"

"Death comes on the Fallow Peaks not from the height, but from the cold, the storms, the beasts," she replied. "The more time you spend among them, the more certain it is that death will come."

"And you did this all for Lanholde?"

Mina's brow furrowed. She swallowed back the venom that sought to coat her tongue at the implication. "For Lanholde? I did it because I didn't want to bury another person in the snow."

Polit looked her in the eyes, emotion unreadable as he processed.

"A noble want," he said, finally blinking. "You have my gratitude."

She could have left it that, could have let silence fall between them comfortably, but some traitorous thought — maybe the relief at finally having some not mind-numbing conversation — pushed her to ask, "Why do you serve?"

His brows lifted slightly, proving that he was made of something other than rock.

"For a similar reason," he stated. "To protect the innocent."

"Regardless of kingdom?" she pressed. "A noble want loses all nobility if it only serves a selfish purpose."

His brow lowered. Not in anger but to something neutral, his all-seeing stare intensified. The waltz ended, and the oncoming crowd reminded Mina of her manners.

"My apologies, sir." She bowed her head a bit. "I intended no harm with my questions. I was just curious."

"Do not apologize," he said, eyes staring deep into her own. "You hold more wisdom than I thought."

Those wanting to dance with her lingered back, giving space to Sir Polit out of respect, possibly fear.

Sovereign Coro had neither, apparently.

"Excuse me, Sir Polit, but I was wondering if I would be able to ask Ms. Harlowe to partner with me for the Visits Quadrille."

Sir Polit regarded the sovereign with a slight bow of his head. "Of course, Your Majesty. Ms. Harlowe, it was a pleasure to dance with you."

Mina curtsied. "The pleasure was all mine, Sir Polit."

Sovereign Coro looped their arms through hers and led her towards the opposite side of the dance floor.

"You said three dances," Mina hissed through the smile she gave the crowd.

"And I've delivered," they said, waving towards the crowd just in time for it to part, and for Empress Tinsae to come through arm and arm with a flustered, but still smiling to save face, Sebastian.

Mina's frustrations — racing heartbeat, stiffened spine, clenched jaw — subsided for a moment seeing him in front of her, just as his own agitation seemed to ebb once he saw her. They gave each other a soft, apologetic smile, as their eyes told a deeper story.

Sebastian had something to tell her. She most definitely had something to tell him. And neither was good news.

"Ms. Harlowe! How wonderful it is to see you again," Empress Tinsae greeted.

"Good evening, Your Excellence," Mina replied as she curtsied. "I see you've caught yourself a wild Windenhofer."

"Snagged from a sourpuss's net, fortunately," she replied as the dance began. "Poor thing would have been stuck playing magic advisor to half of this kingdom's ruling class for the entire evening if I hadn't rescued him."

The couples interwove with each other, grabbing each other's hands in passing.

"I promise I wasn't too cross with you," Mina squeezed Sebastian's quickly as they turned, locking eyes with him, as the Fae's Folly wrapped around their hands. His brows flitted up for the briefest second, a glint of understanding flashed in his eye.

She continued, "Don't they know a ball is for dancing, not business?"

"What is dancing if not another form of a business proposition?" a man from one of the other couples in their quartet said with a chuckle. "One's own ability and choice of dance partner says more about a person than their handshake, I'd say."

"Does it now, Sir..."

"Lord Whitmyre."

"Does it now, *Lord* Whitmyre?" Mina said as she took the man's hand and turned with him. His palms were unfortunately clammy. "Now, I'm curious as to what you've deduced about me this evening."

She smiled at Sovereign Coro, raising her eyebrows slightly, challenging whatever game they were trying to play. Their smile widened, but no other reaction crossed their face.

Lord Whitmyre laughed heartily. "That you are certainly new to court life, young lady. Normally, enterprising women of your age would be dancing with those of much higher rank and note from our court than those you've chosen tonight. Save for His Majesty and the Sovereign, of course."

"Oh my," Mina said, playing up her naïveté, causing Sebastian's nostrils to flare as he held back a laugh. "I sure do hope I didn't choose people who would hurt my reputation. They all seemed quite nice."

She passed Sebastian again, hand against hand. His cordial smile pursed as his palm warmed.

"Oh, they are all well-received, but — and I mean this with absolutely no offense — they're not necessarily individuals of note. Duke Kornel of Strensborg is who I'd imagine you'd go after. Two hundred acres of a duchy all in his name and no wife or children to speak of. The other eligible women of the court have been vying for his attention this entire season to no avail, yet he has been one of the first among the slew of people coming to ask for you to accompany them after every one of your dances."

"Is he now?" she asked. "Which one is he? Being so new to this kingdom, I hardly know anyone's titles or faces."

"He's the young man standing at the edge of the dance floor to your left, Ms. Harlowe," Sovereign Coro replied. "Blond curly hair, full beard, pea soup colored velvet suit."

Mina glanced over and found the man immediately, his gaze intense and leering, focused deliberately at her chest.

"I see. While I do appreciate his attention, is there not another eligible young woman he has set his sights on?"

"Is that your way of telling us you're less than impressed with the duke?" A woman from the other couple dancing with them asked.

"No. It is that I am not currently looking for a suitor, and wouldn't want him to miss out on a wonderful match by having him covet something he cannot have."

"I told you that was an engagement necklace she wore, my lord," Lord Whitmore's partner admonished. "Who is your betrothed?"

Mina laughed giddily as she and Sebastian approached each other again.

"What, this old thing?" She gestured to her necklace. "I picked this up at a market some time ago. I *swear*, I didn't know it was an engagement necklace!" She looked at Sebastian wide-eyed and clueless, as the Fae's Folly did not bind their hands. "Master Windenhofer, did you know this?"

"I know very little about fashion, so no," he looked her in the eye and laughed.

Gods, I love how clever he is.

"Then you are unattached?" the woman asked.

"No. I am attached," Mina admitted sheepishly, giddily. "Just not betrothed."

"Well, who is the lucky dog?" Lord Whitmore teased as Mina passed him.

She kept her eyes on Whitmore as Tinsae and Coro swam in the corners of her vision in a sea of a thousand ears and eyes, watching, and waiting. They already had their assumptions, especially with how readily Coro dangled Sebastian in front of her to get their way.

They were each other's strength.

"A person," she replied cheekily.

She wouldn't let them turn their love into a weakness.

"Playing coy, are we?" Empress Tinsae remarked.

"I have to keep some secrets, don't I? Otherwise, I'm afraid you all will get bored with me."

"Bored of you, Ms. Harlowe?" Sovereign Coro said. "I think all the snow on the Fallow Peaks would melt before that happens."

They returned to their starting positions as the quadrille came to an end, and the crowd of aspiring dance partners began to close in again; Duke Shitty Suit nearly elbowing an approaching princess to keep in the front of the pack.

"Ms. Harlowe I'm afraid I've been a terrible chaperone to you this evening," Sebastian said loud enough for the encroaching mob to hear. "To maintain your honor as an attached woman, would you mind if I accompany you for the rest of this evening's dances?"

Mina curtsied. "Thank you, sir. I would happily accept such a kind offer."

She slipped her arm under Sebastian's and followed him towards the stage, away from the monarchs and crowds, and close to the cymbals and trumpets that would drown out most of their talking.

They both plastered on large, toothy smiles and started sashaying to the music, hopping around like rabbits in springtime.

"Are you alright?" he asked.

"I am," she replied. "And you? What was Strauss trying to get out of you?"

"You know about Strauss?"

"I know about Strauss," she emphasized. "Sovereign Coro told me he had cornered you. I had to strike a deal with them to get you away."

"A deal?" His grip on her hand tightened. "What kind of deal?"

"I had to dance with three people of their choosing."

"That's all?"

"That's all," she said. "I have an idea as to why, but I want to know what Strauss was asking you first."

"He was asking how I broke your curse."

A shiver ran down her spine. King Fritz's playful warning rang in her ear as her stomach churned. "Did you tell him?"

"Not in great detail, but I did cover the basics."

Mina swallowed back the bile rising in her throat. "Fuck."

The corners of his eyebrows flexed against his pleasant facade. "Should I not have?"

"I don't know." Her fingers drummed against his shoulder, hand free to disguise her growing panic as beat keeping, while the other was wrapped in the safety of his palm. "It seemed as though King Fritz didn't want Tanir and I to talk too much about it in front of him, Coro, and Tinsae last night."

Sebastian bristled, but kept his smile as his hands heated. "Why would you have to hide that?"

"Why would Strauss be so eager to learn how you broke it that he had to pull you out of the ballroom to ask?" she countered.

"He didn't pull me out. I left to get a breath of fresh air, and he found me on the balcony," he explained. "Followed shortly by a rove of enterprising noblemen curious about our procurement services."

"Keeping you away while Coro had me dancing with their chosen partners," she realized.

Perhaps they wanted more than information. But there was nothing to be gained from learning about her curse. And keeping her away from Sebastian didn't have any immediate benefits. Was it because she'd danced with the king and had been his dinner guest? Did they think that she had some sort of sway or—

"I don't like this, Mina," Sebastian said, echoing her unspoken thoughts. "I know there's some decorum that we have to follow, that the others are excited to stay here, that there's the money you're still owed, and the guild presentation, but..."

"How fast could we get the wagon?" she spat out, giving into the panic she'd been desperately trying to overcome. "With all these political games — the Capitol being split between Fritz and his brother — something bad is bound to happen, and we should be as far away from it as possible."

A great wave of relief washed over Sebastian at that, as if he'd been waiting ages for her to say it.

Her heart sank into her chest. All the tension, all the worry he'd been carrying. Was that all she had to do to ease it? Ask to leave?

"Enoch and Wera should be able to get to the stables rather quickly," he reasoned. "They'll be upset to abandon their presentation at the guild, but once we're able to regroup in the commorancy I'm sure they'll come 'round. If we're pawns in some royal chess match, I'm sure it'll be hard for any of us to slip out, though."

The music came to an end and the crowd broke out in a round of applause as King Fritz took the stage.

"Not if most of the focus is on me," she said, swallowing her nerves one last time. "Send Wera and Enoch out during my song and try to detach Tanir from Izydor's hip. I'm playing *Bastion of Flame* so I can easily ad-lib between the lyrics to give them more time."

"But—" Like the flip of a light switch, a wobbly true smile overcame him despite the urgency fueling their plan. "Lyrics?"

"Now, while our fabulous musicians take a well-earned break, another virtuoso lies among our ranks to continue our evening of merriment with a song composed just for tonight!" King Fritz bellowed. "Ms. Mina Harlowe!"

Mina curtsied, letting go of his hands with a reassuring squeeze, and headed to the stage where her violin was held in wait by two servants. She watched Sebastian shift back into the crowd — towards Wera and Enoch at the banquet table — out of the corner of her eye as she checked that the strings were in tune. The repairs she'd made had held up well, all the strings were perfect pitch, but still, she fiddled back and forth with the pegs until Sebastian was just a step away from them.

She took center stage and — at her first note — the idle chatter that had built about the room stopped, allowing pure silence to be filled by just her voice.

"Winter wind blows through the valley. Pushes us into our homes. Pleading, she knocks at our windows. Scorned, she continues to roam. Frost covers the earth, save for one burning hearth, tended to by the bastion alone."

She pulled her bow slowly across her strings, calling the crowd's attention, demanding it.

All eyes on me, she thought. *That's it. Let me delight you. Ease your mind for a few moments.*

Then her bow became a matchstick—

"Through rain and snow, its embers smolder."

—igniting the air with music.

"Though Winter tries, it cannot tame. Fire's laughter fills the valley."

The triplets of Sebastian's laughter danced from her fingertips.

"Fed by the Bastion of Flame."

Mina closed her eyes and pictured Sebastian's smile, the heat of his touch, the warmth of his kiss, the ease, excitement, emotion! All emotion his voice alone could bring her!

"Let the sunset paint your skin. Let the fire burn within. Only tinder asked for is devotion."

His warmth so easily stoked flames in others, encouraged kindness, camaraderie. His embers sparked in Tanir's gentle touch, in Enoch's kind words, in Wera's eager encouragement. Everyone was drawn to his fire and was made better from it. His hearth was the great unifier.

"Though the sparks may sting and bite, what the fire brings to light, oh burning Bastion, such emotion."

Though she had landed the killing blow — severed the chains that bound her — it was his warmth, his kindness, his love that loosened them enough for her to raise her blade. She could feel their bond still wrapped around her heart, beating in time with her own. Blissful heat blossoming in her chest she poured into her voice, into her song, blessing all those who listened to bask in a warm gentle breeze and know — for just a moment — what *home* felt like.

When she opened her eyes again, winding down from the song's apex, she found Sebastian standing in the center of the crowd, transfixed, smiling as happy tears shimmered on his cheeks.

"Winter wind blows through the valley. Spreading sparks from the fire it claimed. It beseeches their embers 'burn brighter', and stokes them into a roaring flame. The bastion can rest, knowing he's done his best, and that the wind will sing forth his name."

She lifted her bow from her strings, and the last of their hum swirled like smoke through the room into silence.

In unison, the crowd broke out into thunderous applause.

Mina smiled at Sebastian as she bowed, then set to make her way offstage as King Fritz stepped onto it to address the room.

"Stay, my dear," he said as he passed her.

And she stayed.

Sebastian's brow furrowed as she turned back around and looked out at the crowd. She locked eyes with him, then glanced at His Majesty quickly, as if to say it'll only be a moment.

He needs to peacock a bit and then we can go.

"What a performance!" Fritz announced to the crowd, stirring up another crescendo of applause. "And to think such a talent has been living away in a cabin all these years, leading good Lanholdian men through the frigid horrors of the Fallow Peaks out of the goodness of her heart."

A few gasps rushed out of the audience.

"Yes! That's right, this is the female alpinist we've been hearing so much about! Can you believe it? Not so harsh and cold-hearted as stories have told."

The crowd chuckled at that, and Sebastian grumbled something to Tanir. Tanir muttered something back, but Mina couldn't hear it.

Perhaps it was the noise of the crowd.

Mina hung her head a bit, feigning bashfulness so she could close her eyes and tune her listening, get it back under her control. If it were instructions on how to leave, it would be helpful to know. Maybe an update on Enoch and Wera's progress securing the carriage?

But all she could hear was King Fritz's pontificating, applause and laughter from the crowd, the musicians fiddling with their instruments behind her.

She went to summon the wind for assistance — focusing her senses to her heels — and found nothing.

Not a breeze. Not a draft. Not a stir.

Just stillness.

Uneasy stillness.

Stillness that had been lingering on her skin since she'd gotten dressed.

Stillness, that made it hard to breathe, had been urging her to *run.*

"When I first heard about the cruel alpinist in the Sandere Woods, I had my suspicions about how such a lovely creature could have fallen so low, and found them unfortunately true. Ms. Harlowe had been living for years cursed."

Mina lifted her head and locked eyes with Sebastian as the crowd gasped. The neck of her violin creaked under her white-knuckle grip. Every frantic beat of her heart pumped in her hands.

"Cursed by that horrid fae who's been stealing our children and tormenting our people for far too long. The Matron of the Barren Rime!"

The color drained from Sebastian's face at King Fritz's declaration.

The color drained from Mina's face at the sight of Sir Gargic's haggard beard and the slow, rolling steps of disguised guards shifting closer to Sebastian.

She tried to take a slight step forward to ready a fighting stance, but her body did not move.

"I couldn't let such an innocent soul suffer any longer, and was able to bring her here and break that awful curse, allowing for this magnificent woman to shine like the star she truly is." King Fritz said. "Smile, my dear! I know you're quite shy, but I assure you my carrying-on is almost over."

A brilliant smile came naturally to her face, spiting her anger and fear.

Trapped in her own body.

Commanded not by deals or threads, but by something deeper in her psyche. Ingrained in every fiber of her body but her mind and heart.

The crowd laughed at her misery.

Sebastian's expression fell neutral as Sir Gargic reached his side and muttered something Mina wished so desperately to hear. She'd mock him with it when she ripped his heart out through his fucking throat.

All she needed was one weakness to exploit. Needed one moment where the wording of his command faltered. Needed Sebastian or Tanir or anyone to cause a distraction, break the focus on whatever spell was being cast on her.

She looked to Coro, to Tinsae. Could they see the panic in her eyes?

Would they care to help?

Their focus was on Fritz. Baring the perfect polite smile that all politicians possessed.

Were they in on it too?

"Knowing Ms. Harlowe, though it has been brief, has changed my life completely. She's inspired me to be a better man, to stand up even taller than I have before in the face of evil, ensuring my people are safe and well taken care of. So to that end, I'd like to formally announce my intention to marry this remarkable woman, with my great aunt's necklace as a symbol of our engagement!"

Mina's stomach lurched. Bile burned at the back of her throat.

Her voice! She could still speak, couldn't she?

As the crowd applauded, she pried open her smiling mouth to protest, to refute, anything to show she did not want this, that it was a lie.

But she couldn't sense the man who had been standing behind her, gloved hands at the ready to drop a necklace — with a fat oval pendant, beset with pearls and smaller gemstones in its setting, attached to a thick wheat-patterned chain — around her neck.

Plunging her head first into darkness.

Bitter.

Thick.

Whatever was gliding down her throat was vile enough to wake her.

But barely.

Mind before body.

Bases senses. Slow sense.

Two voices.

Just as vile.

"It should work in a few moments."

Henri.

"*Should* work?"

Vile.

Fritz.

"Kaminska said it was all theoretical, but with studying the necklace firsthand and the notes from the expedition, he's confident that this will at least rouse her."

"I'll need it to do more than *rouse* her. I need a queen that's a darling, not a *dullard*."

Rage, deep and cold, billowed inside her. It screamed at her to rise, to rip out his tongue and smash his skull against the wall to show him what a dullard really was.

All it could do was open her eyes.

Mina's vision was blurry, her eyelids too slow and heavy to blink and clear them, but she could still make out King Fritz standing just a few feet from where she was lying, hands clenching Henri's lapels.

"L-look, Your Majesty," Henri squirmed, pointing to Mina's face. "Her eyes opened. That's good!"

"That's nothing." King Fritz shoved Henri away from him. "Not unless she can speak." Those piercing eyes, severe as stone, bore into her. "Leave us."

"But, Your Majesty, what if— she could—"

"Between the shoes and the necklace, she's lamer than a fucking stillborn horse," Fritz hissed, the flowery language and jovial mask he'd put on fully stripped. "Go."

Henri bowed quickly and scampered out of Mina's field of vision. A door — heavy sounding — shut.

Fritz approached, crouching down to her level, just inches away from her. If she could just lift her arm, she could tear out his fucking throat.

Her lips curled into a wobbling snarl instead.

"There's that temper I've heard so much about," he remarked. "I was worried for a moment your tryst with the firecrotch had turned you soft."

"F-f-f-uu-ck yooo—uu," Mina managed to force out through near-paralyzed vocal cords.

Fritz smiled. "No, my dear, I'll wait until you're a little less limp for that. Wouldn't be too much fun bedding a dead fish, now, would it?"

Her building anger loosened her mouth up enough for her to spit at him. He recoiled as it smacked against his cheek, knocking that shit grin off his face.

He took two fingers, swiped her loogie off, then smeared it slowly across her forehead.

"This is all your fault, you know. You can only be angry at yourself." He rubbed his fingers back and forth in a sort of caress. "I figured a fae would know better than to try and void a contract. But as the saying goes," he trailed the wet fingers down the bridge of her nose, "people do stupid things when they're in love, right?"

Mina used all her might to bite at his fingers. Fritz pulled them out of reach quickly and cracked the back of his hand across her face in retaliation.

It stung her pride more than anything else.

He seized her jaw, short, stubby digits digging into her cheeks, threatening without skill to tear her jawbone out of its sockets.

She could show him how to do it, if only her fucking arms would lift.

"I'm going to tell you how this is going to go, *my dear,*" he seethed. "I will not tolerate my property disrespecting me. Especially with how much shit my family's had to go through for you." There was a tired desperation behind his anger. "*She* promised a queen, so winsome and polished despite the odds of her cursed upbringing, that peasants and politicians would have no choice but to love her. Who could charm just as skillfully as she could slaughter. And I will have what was promised."

He moved his hand to clasp around her throat, choking her slightly, before resting it on the Dorminian necklace. "And until I have what was promised, this pretty little pendant will stay around your neck. Once Kaminska gets his potion perfected, and with a little encouragement from my *dear* pet name, I'm sure you'll make the sweetest sovereign in all the land in no time." He smoothed his thumb over the pendant. "It's a shame you changed your name. Queen Riktanya had a nice ring to it."

Mina managed to lift her hand enough to grab at his wrist.

"I-I'll k-kill y-you," she fumbled out.

"After you win me a civil war and birth me a son, at least," he mocked. "Then I'll gladly die by your hand."

A frantic knock shook the room.

"I'm busy!" Fritz shouted back.

"It's the wizard, Your Majesty. He wishes to speak with you," someone shouted from outside the door.

"Have Henri handle it. It is his job."

"He's trying, but now Magistrate Strauss is involved—"

King Fritz grit his teeth in frustration as he grumbled, "Of course he is." He smiled at Mina as he pulled his wrist out from her weak grasp. "Lucky for me, I won't need another necklace to get your wizard to behave, I imagine. He's a man with enough sense to know not to bite the hand that feeds him."

Mina forced her eyes to follow him as he left, to find whatever means of escape she could. A heavy wooden door shut behind him. It was about two yards away. She could make it.

She had no choice but to make it.

Come on, she screamed in her mind as her legs refused to answer her. *You're stronger than this!*

Are you?

She moved her arms instead, slowly, incredibly slowly. Her muscles shook with every centimeter closer to the edge of the cot she'd been laid on: jerking, falling, slipping in and out of her control regardless of the rage and determination fueling her.

Pathetic.

Her arms turned her shoulders, pulling her torso over and off-balance enough to send her tumbling to the floor. The back of her head cracked against the stone, filling her vision with spots and stars, nearly pulling her back under into sleep.

Her eyelids lulled, vision shook cross-eyed, as she forced herself to try and keep them open. She could catch full-grown trees, carry nearly a thousand pounds up The Lithe, yet she could barely lift her eyelids.

Because you're weak, that old, dark voice rang clear in her head, cruelly spliced with her own internal timbre. ***And you can only be angry at yourself for that.***

"S-s-hut up," Mina spoke aloud, desperate to hear her own voice unaltered.

The minute they didn't have the money, we should have left. Sebastian all but told us to. And we said no to what? Prove something? Make the others happy? I knew all along this place was awful. I knew I couldn't trust anybody here. Can I even trust the others? They were the ones who brought me here.

"Sssstoooppp," she whined as her chest threatened to cave in. The room spun. She had to get to the door, had to get out and find Sebastian.

He knew. He had to.

"H-he w-wanted usss t-t-to leeeaave," she groaned as she tried to turn herself over.

He wanted to absolve himself of guilt. Or keep me here. He knows how stubborn I am, how spiteful. He knew I'd double down on staying if he kept pretending to worry.

Mina could not hear the beads of her dress scraping across the floor or the desperate, fumbling slapping of her palms as she dragged herself towards the door over her thoughts.

Was she getting closer? Had she barely moved at all?

He knew about the contract. He amended it to keep me with him and fulfill his end of the bargain: a bunch of magical bullshit and a bride. Uncursed and ready to wed in order to save His Majesty some time. To fulfill Her contract.

I wondered why this entire time, haven't I? Why he kept me around, why he loved me. That was instinct, telling me something was wrong, and I ignored it. Just like ignored the crawling on my skin, every 'my dear', the fact that they stuck me in a fucking wedding dress! How pathetic, how desperate.

Mina stopped crawling. Her body would not continue. It recognized how futile this all was.

"I'm n-not—"

And now I can't even get up and save myself.

Her eyelids won their battle. The Matron's eyes awaited her in the darkness, alight with satisfaction.

Look at what you've become.

The weight of sleep dragged her under, twisting her rage to shape her dreams with visions of betrayal. Every instance of friendship, of care, of love, cast in cold, icy blue light. Of course Tanir made her gloves, it made it easier for them to ignore her boundaries. Of course Enoch got caught by Eirlys, it tested her loyalty to them. Of course Wera made a deal with her to be her confidant, that way Sebastian could know exactly how to win her over. Of course Sebastian wouldn't let her leave and face Bormir on her own, that would be bad for business.

Every smile, every kind look, every carefully crafted command morphed into malicious manipulation. A chill lingering behind every interaction, a calculation.

And then there was a pull.

A tug against her heart. Warm and pleading.

The warmth flooded her dreams with amber, melting the icy visages as the binding around her heart wound tighter and tighter until she couldn't breathe.

Until she woke up to smoke.

The ill-rooted doubts of her dreaming crumbled under one overwhelming notion, under the pulse of a racing heartbeat coursing through the invisible binds around her own.

Danger.

They were all in incredible danger.

The room was painted orange through the growing haze of thick black smoke, the stone beneath her heating steadily, threatening to turn the room into an oven.

Her body was just as unresponsive as before, but her determination was tenfold. Sebastian's fear, anger, desperation amplified her own, leaving no room for doubt to claim her.

Centimeters became inches as the tug around her heart pulled her across the floor, the door growing closer and closer as the smoke grew thicker and thicker. Her head, too heavy to lift, kept her nose pressed against the tile, dragging in the waning scraps of clean air until her knuckles rapped against the heavy, wooden door.

The knob was her next behemoth, mocking her from its high vantage point. It was as if she were trying to move the earth itself raising her arm, only managing to lift it by a few inches before she lost control and dropped to the ground.

"You're not allowed to—" a man's shout was cut off by a guttural groan outside of the room.

"Tell us which room she's in, and we'll let you go," Wera's muffled voice hissed.

"Fuck off," the man choked. "I'd rather die with honor than burn a traitor."

No other words were exchanged. Just a wet grunt and a heavy thud against the ground.

"I've got his keys," Enoch said. "You take this half of the rooms, I'll take—"

"We don't have time for that," Wera snapped.

"Then what else do you suggest we fucking do?"

Mina channeled all her strength and knocked her head against the door.

"What about the homing rings?"

"She doesn't have one."

Her lungs struggled for air. She rammed her head harder. The heartbeat through the bond grew faster and more frantic.

A shrieking squeal, a thundering boom from the other side of the hall.

"Here, take the keys we—"

Mina grit her teeth and thumped her head as fast as she could, angling to drive her forehead into it, dizzying herself with throbbing pain with each thwack.

A rushed crescendo of footsteps. The frantic jingling of keys. The door fell out from under her head.

"Wet a cloth for her face," Enoch instructed Wera. "I'll grab her." He reached down but was met with the smack of a force field.

"Fuck," Enoch slammed his fist against it. "Fuck!"

"Mina, can you move?" Wera asked, her voice lilt with panic. "You should be able to pass through. We can pull you out if we can just grab your arm."

Trembling, she lifted it barely off the ground towards them... and was stopped halfway.

"That fucking bastard only paired it to him!" Enoch snapped.

The cry that left her was instinctual, primal and mourning. She flopped her hand against the force field, willing it untrue, willing it to disappear.

Then it did.

There was a moment of stillness then — hushed swears beneath Wera and Enoch's breath while Mina basked in relief — before a wet cloth was wrapped over her nose and mouth, and she was lifted and thrown over Enoch's shoulders.

The world became a blur of smoke and stone, of sparks and heat as they ran down the hall. Screams, hundreds of screams, echoed around them, the louder ones causing them to divert down other paths, pause and hide as guards, fleeing servants, nobles, passed. They shouted about a siege, about foreign invaders, about Emil — a mass of confusion that threatened to split Mina's pounding head — until they slipped through the thinning shadows outdoors.

Enoch bucked Mina off his shoulder into darkness, where she was caught by familiar, wrinkled hands. There was a brief flash of amber light through the parting canvas as Wera hopped into the covered wagon after her, then the crack of a whip sent the world shaking as horse hooves thundered.

"Good Gods," Tanir said as she shined a glowing crystal over Mina's eyes, across her body.

The heartbeat thread-bound to her own slowed, scaring her.

"'B-bastian," Mina croaked out as best as she could. "W-where—"

"He's driving the carriage," Tanir answered. "Don't push yourself. You could have smoke inhalation. Wera, the astringent for the shoes is in that canister to your left."

Tanir's hands pried open her mouth, looked down into her throat, into her nostrils, as a spray seeped into her left shoe. Wera's fingers wedged into the sides of it, prying it free.

All sound, touch, smell, returned to her in full brilliance as the wind rushed into the wagon, blowing open the canvas curtain as it repooled around her heel, revealing the source of all the amber, all the heat, the sparks, the smoke.

The source of Sebastian's slight sniffle, the chorus of racing heartbeats from her friends, the smell of burnt hair and flesh lingering on their clothes. The anger, the fear.

Flames.

A raging inferno tore its way through the castle. Their color and pattern she knew as intimately as the hands of their master.

Sebastian's flames.

A new anger, deeper than any she had known, filled her head with one singular thought as she watched such beauty be corrupted into bane.

A familiar thought, one she once feared, but now welcomed wholeheartedly.

How da

re they.

ACKNOWLEDGMENTS

First and foremost, thank you for reading my book. Books are meant to be read and for you have to have chosen to read mine is amazing. Whenever you have read this book (or reread this book) I hope that your next few days are filled with delights, whether it be small things like the warmth of the sunshine streaming through your car window at a stoplight or big things like winning a Nobel Peace Prize.

Now onto thanking the people, places, and things that made *The Maiden of the Barren Rime* possible.

Thank you to:

- The Universe
- My editor, Kat
- My artist, Arlowa
- My Kickstarter backers
- My cats
- My friends
- My family
- My junior year English teacher, my college professors: Mote and McGee, and Jamie
- Mythology and Folklore
- Ray Bradbury
- The casts of Critical Role, Dimension 20, and The Adventure Zone
- Pomplamoose, Bring Me The Horizon, Miike Snow, MGMT, and The Oh Hellos
- Dancing
- Dean DeBlois
- The sound of leaves rustling in the wind
- This playlist:

TRANSLATIONS

CHAPTER IX

"Uneducated, huh?" Now she didn't have to pretend to be angry. "I'll show you uneducated, you bigoted piece of shit. An absolute dullard like you, who's done nothing worth note in his life except lick his king's toilet bowl clean after he shit, has no idea what the fuck I'm saying right now." Mina cleared her throat, "None of you speak Tubazi? How about Yosik, wizard?"

"You know Yosik?" Sebastian's eyes widened, a shocked smile curving up the corners of his mouth despite his best bitter acting.

"Clearly. Translate this for that know-it-all bastard. I'm shocked his eyes aren't permanently swollen shut from sniffing his king's asshole so much. At least that would explain why the halfwit couldn't be bothered to learn anything past whatever ultranationalist bullshit Landholde suckles their citizens with."

"What the hell is she saying?!" Sir Gargic snarled.

"She— uh—" Sebastian stammered.

"Don't get shy now. Tell him to uncork his tongue from between King Fuckface's ass cheeks and —" Mina placed a hand on her sword as it vibrated against her side, "— open up a fucking book —" a flicker of white flitted between patches of ice scattered around the tunnel's walls, closer and closer, "— for once!"

CHAPTER IX

"Coward," she scoffed.

"Call me that again and I'll command you to listen to the knight's Landholde history lessons."

CHAPTER XIII

"Is that face part of the lesson, professor? Or?"

CHAPTER XV

"Freedom as the Night Falls," she said. "Nataly Amanecer's rendition."

Portrait by Lou (Twitter: @asdfghjkiri)

Sweet can't remember a time where she didn't have a story in her head. Works that tell evocative, emotionally driven stories in a unique light hold a special place in her heart. She collects copies of fairytales, folklore, myths, and most any old book that sparked the imagination. The top books in this collection currently are a 126-year old copy of *Beauties of Shakespeare* and a very worn paperback copy of *Treasure Island* she stole from her grandmother's basement.

You can find her at her website (storiesbysweet.com) and on Tumblr (sweetarethediscords.tumblr.com).

DRAMATIS
The Matron
Bormír
Eírlys

Personae

King Fritz

Sir Gargic

Milton Keynes UK
Ingram Content Group UK Ltd.
UKHW010833230424
441593UK00018B/407/J